Raves for *The Stor*

"A nicely swashbucklin[g] those writers whose new

—Critical Mass

"Terrific fight scenes, excellent character development and just the right amount of political intrigue make for a great fantasy read." —Monsters & Critics

"*The Storm Witch* is an entertaining and thought-provoking novel of fantasy deeply rooted in the common experiences of humanity. Although cultures can be diverse and disparate, at heart their drives do not differ very much. I recommend this to epic fantasy readers." —Bitten by Books

"Another fine job of demonstrating the author's ability with world building, creating yet another civilization populated with believable characters and conflicts that her likeable and complex duo become involved with . . . a very entertaining read." —Night Owl Reviews

"The series is designed so that you can jump in anywhere, but, as with any series, those who read all the books will definitely get more out of them. Violette Malan's writing keeps getting better. I found this a fun, quick read." —Sci-Fi Fan Letter

"In *Path of the Sun*, Malan has provided a plot snapping with action and danger. The search for the murderer provides a dark and fascinating background to this fourth Dhulyn and Parno adventure." —Fresh Fiction

"I want *more books like these*. . . . I've a very soft spot for sword-and-sorcery, the fantasy of encounter, that features a daring team of implausibly competent, decent people against the world. The Dhulyn and Parno books aren't perfect (what product of human endeavour is?) but they scratch a good few of my narrative itches in one go." —Liz Bourke, Tor.com

VIOLETTE MALAN

THE DHULYN AND PARNO NOVELS:
VOLUME TWO

THE STORM WITCH

PATH OF THE SUN

DAW BOOKS, INC.
DONALD A. WOLLHEIM, FOUNDER
375 Hudson Street, New York, NY 10014

ELIZABETH R. WOLLHEIM
SHEILA E. GILBERT
PUBLISHERS
www.dawbooks.com

First Printing, May 2015
1 2 3 4 5 6 7 8 9

DAW TRADEMARK REGISTERED
U.S. PAT. AND TM. OFF. AND FOREIGN COUNTRIES
—MARCA REGISTRADA
HECHO EN U.S.A.

PRINTED IN THE U.S.A.

For Paul.

THE
STORM WITCH

Acknowledgments

As always, my first thanks go to the two people without whom there would be no reason to thank anyone else, my agent, Joshua Bilmes, and my editor, Sheila Gilbert. My thanks also go to my cousin José Ignacio Díaz Hellín, and Alberto Domingues Saenz, the chefs extraordinaire of Restorante Restoval in Badajoz, Spain, for the feast fit for a king. There are a whole bunch of people who are involved with helping me to promote my work, in one way or another. My first thanks go to my brother, Oscar Malan, and his wonderful wife Joanna (another chef extraordinaire) who host my book launches in his bookstore, Novel Idea, with Joanna's wonderful nibbles to help draw in the crowds. Special thanks to Melanie Babcock at Print 3 for all her help with my bookmarks and posters. Also to Chris Szabo of Bakka Phoenix Books, and from Chapters, Barbara Bell, Dan Millings, and especially Jessica Strider, who got married this year.

The right to have a character named after her was purchased at silent auction by Trudy Primeau. You'll notice I played with the spelling a bit, Trudy. Say hi to Megz for me.

One

PARNO LIONSMANE PULLED the hood of his cloak down over his forehead and hunched his shoulders against the rain. Here it was, practically high summer, what his Partner Dhulyn Wolfshead would call the Grass Moon, and the rain was coming down as though it was already well past Harvest Moon. He caught Dhulyn's eye as they sidestepped the flow of water running down the center of the narrow cobbled lane. She was frowning, and he knew that more than the weather troubled her.

"Cheer up," he told her. "A few more days at most, and the whole misunderstanding will be cleared up."

His Partner nodded, but almost as if she wasn't listening. Dhulyn was Senior to him—though she was younger, she had been longer in the Mercenary Brotherhood, having come to it as a child—and *that* was part of the problem.

"It's only the Tarkin of Hellik's court they are sending to," he added, "not all the way to Imrion."

This time Dhulyn looked at him as she nodded, and Parno smiled to himself. "I would not have thought it so difficult to find a Brother Senior to me in a city as large as Lesonika," she said. "I thought this would all be over by now."

Both looked up as thunder rumbled.

"A good thing we left the horses, after all," Dhulyn said. She dodged a fountain of water pouring from a greatly overworked overhead gutter. They'd come down from the port of Broduk on the *Catseye*, the typical wide-beamed, single-masted ship of the Midland Sea, with both their war-horses and their packhorse in makeshift stalls on the deck. Just now Dhulyn had decided that all the beasts would be happier in the warm, dry stable provided by the Mercenary House. And the crew of the *Catseye* would be happier as well. Captain Huelra didn't often ship horses—in fact, Parno was fairly certain Dhulyn Wolfshead was the only person Huelra would trust with horses aboard his ship.

"It could be worse," Parno said now.

"How?"

"It could be snowing."

Parno didn't like the way Dhulyn shook her head without even a token smile. He knew her well enough to make a good guess at her thoughts. If there could be such rain—with thunder—in the Grass Moon, why *not* snow? As it was, the hay was flattened in the fields, and oats and young barley would be washed out or stunted if the weather didn't improve soon. Which meant a poor harvest, which meant trouble. Parno brightened. Which generally meant work for the Brotherhood.

The streets inclined more sharply as they approached the harbor where the *Catseye* was moored, but even so the water was over their ankles more than once before they reached the comparatively dryer docks. Here, at least, the volume of water had somewhere to go—into the sea. Lesonika had a deep harbor, and in addition to half a score of the smaller Midland Sea vessels like the *Catseye*, one of the tall, three-masted, ocean-faring ships was also moored there.

Dhulyn slowed almost to a halt, turning her head to stare at the tall ship as they passed it, her normally bright cavalry cloak hanging in sodden folds and darkened to a dull red by the rain. Parno's own cloak, just as good a mix of inglera fleece and wool, slapped wetly around his calves as the wind took it.

"I thought so," she called out to him as he reached her side, her rough silk voice just audible over the pelting rain. "Those *were* Long Ocean Traders at the Mercenary House. Did you see them?"

"The ones in the scaly vests?" he said. "What could they want with our Brothers?"

"Delivering fressian drugs, perhaps."

Parno pursed his lips in a silent whistle, taking a longer look. If his Partner was right, and the ship was carrying even a few casks of fresa, fresnoyn, or fresnant, he was looking at more money than he'd seen in many a moon.

There were sailors out even in this weather, seeing to the mooring lines. The tide was beginning to ebb, Parno saw, and the amount of water flowing from the town into the boat basin—enormous as it was to the city dwellers—would make no difference to the sea level; lines still had to be adjusted, anchors checked. Everywhere there were bare masts, but the usual harbor sounds of creaking stays, shrouds, and halyards could not be heard over the drumming of the water and the rising noise of the wind.

"Demons and perverts," Parno cursed as a spray of water caught him fully in the face. Dhulyn's laughter did not help. They ran the final few paces to the *Catseye* and pounded up the gangplank. The usual sentry was missing, but given the rain and the wind, Parno was not surprised.

There was no glow of light from around the door of Captain Huelra's tiny cabin, and Dhulyn turned immediately toward the entrance to the hold. Their own sleeping quarters were below, their hammocks strung up along with those of the sailors, and Parno hesitated only a moment before following her. A cup of the captain's brandy would have been welcome, but the dry clothing in their packs below beckoned even more strongly. And if it came to that, Parno thought grinning, there was a newly purchased flask of Berdanan brandy hanging at his own hip.

Not that someone else's brandy didn't always taste better.

Dhulyn heaved back the hatch and dropped straight into the hold, ignoring the ladder placed to one side. She moved immediately to the right, leaving Parno a clear space to follow her. He rolled his eyes—even here, Dhulyn would follow the Brotherhood's Common Rule and enter the room as though staging an attack—but he followed her precisely, landing lightly, knees slightly bent, blinking in the lantern light, his right hand on the hilt of his sword, his left on his knife.

And froze.

"Carefully, Paledyn. No sudden moves, if you please." The thickly accented voice came from a dark-haired, heavily mustached man holding the spiked end of a *garwon* to Captain Huelra's head. Huelra sat, wrists and ankles bound, on an upturned cask of the cook's milled flour. Two candle lanterns, one on the floor and one hanging from a hook on the mast, cast double shadows over the scene. Parno gritted his teeth and resisted the urge to look at Dhulyn. He hadn't seen a *garwon* since his Schooling. Long, thin, and fiercely sharp, it was used by divers as an underwater hand weapon. The point actually rested on the skin of Huelra's temple, and could be through the comparatively thin bone and into the man's brain before either Parno or Dhulyn could move. And that did not take into account the young woman with her arbalest already cranked back and pointed at Dhulyn Wolfshead, or the half-dozen others, armed and standing farther back in the shifting shadows.

Parno noted automatically that both the mustached man and the woman were bareheaded, though both wore the oddly patterned scaly vests that he'd seen at the Mercenary House. Long Ocean Traders. He couldn't be sure about the others, though he thought at least one more also wore mail. Parno smiled. As usual, Dhulyn had been right to take precautions—better careful than cursing, that's what she always said. Anyone else would have come down the ladder the normal way, and been caught with their backs to the enemy.

He leaned against the ladder behind him and lifted his hands away from his weapons, knowing without looking that Dhulyn had already done the same. By no means were they out of options, but with that *garwon* at Huelra's temple, a straightforward attack was low on their list.

"You *are* Paledyn? What is called here the Mercenary Brotherhood?" The same man spoke again.

"We are." Without moving her hands, Dhulyn tossed her head and the hood of her wet cloak fell back to reveal her Mercenary badge, the blue and green of the tattoo across her temples and above her ears bright even in this light. Parno still was not used to seeing her with her hair so short, just a damp cloud the color of old blood around her face. Parno shook his own hood off.

"I am Dhulyn Wolfshead," his Partner said. "Called the Scholar. I was Schooled by Dorian the Black Traveler. I have fought at Sadron, Arcosa, and Bhexyllia." And Limona, thought Parno, though perhaps she was right not to mention that particular battle until the Mercenary House here in Lesonika had ruled on the consequences of it. "I fight with my Partner, Parno Lionsmane," Dhulyn concluded.

"And I am that Parno Lionsmane with whom she fights," Parno added. "Called the Chanter and Schooled by Nerysa Warhammer of Tourin."

There was a moment—just a moment—when the eyes of the arbalest woman had shifted, glancing at Dhulyn's badge, but the man holding the *garwon* on Huelra never moved.

"Come with us," the *garwon* holder said. "Now. If not, we kill your friend."

"Or," Dhulyn answered in her most reasonable tone. "We can wait until your wrist gets tired and then kill *you*."

The skeptical snort that sounded from the shadows came from the third man on the left. Parno automatically calculated distance and angle. Dhulyn did not take her eyes from the *garwon*.

"Crew of the *Catseye* are aboard our ship," the man continued in the same even tone. "You don't come, or we don't return," he shrugged. "They'll be killed."

Parno had to admit he was impressed. The mustached man spoke as though he was commenting on the weather. There weren't many who could be threatened by a Mercenary Brother and not even change color—no matter how many armed men stood in the shadows behind them.

"Huelra, is this true?"

"Wolfshead, it is. You'd been gone a few hours—and half my crew on shore leave after you—when these came on board under a trading flag, may their ship have plank worm. Why should I doubt them?" Huelra looked as though he'd like to spit, but couldn't turn his head. "They took us handily, curse their keel, and they took my crew away. That much I saw before they hauled me down here."

Parno could see that under Huelra's fear and rage was a measure of embarrassment at being so easily caught. He'd probably been flattered that the Long Ocean Traders had approached him at all.

Dhulyn smiled her wolf's smile, her lip turning back from the small scar that marked it. "If we didn't care about Huelra," she said to the trader, "we'd hardly care about his crew." This time the man blinked, and Parno stifled a smile of his own.

"It isn't necessary to hold people hostage to hire us," she added. "You might simply offer us money."

The man slowly shook his head, without moving his eyes from Dhulyn's face.

Demons and perverts, Parno thought. This was taking too long. "I'm going to take my cloak off," he said. "It's wet, and it's cold. I've brandy here in this flask, and I see no reason I shouldn't drink some. We understand that if we don't cooperate you'll kill Huelra's people. Tell us why we should stop you."

Now the man was round-eyed with surprise—though still not afraid. He turned his head, almost enough to look at the young women holding the arbalest. "You're Paledyn," he said finally. "Mercenary Brothers. People won't die when you can save them."

Interesting. Not untrue, in and of itself, just interesting the man should say so.

"Dhulyn Wolfshead is Senior Brother," Parno said. "Here and now, it is she who will decide who lives and who dies. So we might as well relax, while she's listening to your request." Parno moved his hands to the clasp of his cloak and let the sodden garment fall to the floor, where he kicked it to one side. Dhulyn was already tossing hers toward the spot where their packs were tied securely against sliding should the ship roll. This time the man did glance quickly at the woman behind him, as he lowered his *garwon*. The woman herself relaxed, but Parno noticed that she did not release the crank on the arbalest.

"Come," Dhulyn said, the merest edge of impatience in her voice. "Tell us what you require of us." Parno opened the flask of brandy, took a swallow, and tossed it to Dhulyn. She caught it neatly in her left hand, but held it without taking a drink. That made three times they had moved without anyone using a weapon. If they could keep this up, this could finish with them all drinking together.

"Malfin Cor of the Long Ocean Nomads." The man had lowered his weapon, but he had not put it down, and he still had his hand on Huelra's shoulder. "Our ship is *Wavetreader*, and this my sister-captain, Darlara Cor." The woman inclined her head.

"Offer to hire and you say no? Then what?" the woman Darlara spoke up. "Our time, and our funds, running out. You *must* cross the Long Ocean with us—"

"If not," Malfin Cor said. "We kill Captain Huelra and his crew, burn *Catseye.*"

Parno raised his eyebrows. *That* point had already been made. This did not seem like the kind of shrewd and subtle trading the Nomads had the reputation for. He waited, expecting Dhulyn to make a countersuggestion of her own, but she had fallen silent, and perfectly still. She seemed not even to notice the slight motion of the *Catseye* under her feet. Parno took the chance of looking directly at her. What he saw almost made him reach toward his sword once more. Dhulyn's face was as still as a statue, and what little natural color she had was drained away. But what shocked Parno most was the almost invisible trembling of her lower lip.

"But why must it be Mercenary Brothers you take?" When she finally spoke, even her voice seemed pale.

The two exchanged quick glances again. "Been told it must be, *will* be, it was *Seen.*"

Dhulyn's knuckles went white as her grip on the brandy flask tightened. *Blooded demons*, Parno thought. A Seer. These Nomads had been sent by a Seer. He started to relax. He and Dhulyn had been trying to find a Seer for moons now. If these Nomads had been sent by one . . .

"Paledyn we must bring," the man was saying. "Spokesmen between our people and our enemies. Spokesmen *they* will trust."

"Let me guess." Dhulyn's rough-silk voice was sour. "You need such paragons because your enemies no longer trust you to deal honorably with them?" Parno blinked. His Partner must have some reason to ignore the mention of Seers.

The two Captains Cor inclined their heads in unison, apparently unfazed by the implication. "Never been much meeting of souls between us," the woman Darlara said. "They're landsters, and we're of the Crayx."

"Even so, things looked to be getting better, with new negotiators, trade going up, but now . . ." Malfin Cor shook his head. "That's stopped. Won't even speak to us."

"You think you can force *us* to trick them for you?" Dhulyn took a swig of the brandy.

"No! Need you to deal honorably with them. Wish you to negotiate in good faith."

Dhulyn looked down at the flask in her hand, and back up at the Nomad captains. "May I suggest that kidnapping us by threatening to kill our friends may not be the best way for you to begin."

Malfin Cor took in a deep breath and released it slowly, as if he was trying to keep his temper. "Paledyn— Mercenaries, we've tried all other ways. Say we should offer money—very well, what will you take?"

Ah, he's got us there, Parno thought. He'd be having fun, if Dhulyn wasn't so pale, and so still.

Dhulyn was still hesitating. "There are other Mercenary Brothers here in Lesonika. Let me find you one of those," she finally said. "We have a matter for judgment in our House here, a matter of our Brotherhood, and we are not free to take employment until it is resolved."

Now Parno thought he understood Dhulyn's behavior. They were bound by all their oaths of Brotherhood to await the summons of their House. Kedneara, the late Queen of Tegrian, had asked for a judgment of outlawry against them—mistakenly, of course, but she'd died before being able to withdraw it. They had sworn documents from the present Queen, but if they missed this judgment, if their documents were not presented, it could very well result in outlawry for them.

And the Mercenary Brotherhood was the only home Dhulyn Wolfshead had ever known. No surprise that she was ignoring the reference to a Seer, and considering—even if only for a moment—letting Huelra and his people die rather than lose it. After all, death was what lay in store for all of them. Eventually.

But Captain Malfin Cor was shaking his head. "Must leave with this tide—now, in fact. Who knows how long it might take to find others." He lifted his hand as Dhulyn started to speak again. "It's not *we* can't wait. It's the Crayx."

"I begin to see why they have problems negotiating with these others," Parno said, under his breath.

Dhulyn nodded, but slowly. "We could agree, and then kill you all."

Parno forced his eyebrows to remain at their normal

level. *That* was a negotiating tactic he'd never heard her use before.

Another snort of laughter came out of the shadows behind Captain Darlara Cor. Before the sound died away, Parno's hand flicked out, and the hilt of his heaviest dagger bounced off the forehead of the third man to the left. There was a THUNK as the man fell to his knees and pitched forward into the flickering light of the lanterns.

"You were saying?" Dhulyn's rough voice sounded courteous and soft in the sudden silence.

Blinking, Malfin Cor cleared his throat. "You would not," he said. "You are Paledyn." This time he did not sound quite so sure. "You would swear not to."

Dhulyn sighed and Parno caught her glance, lifting his left eyebrow in answer to her look. They would be bound, no question of it. For a Mercenary Brother there was no such thing as a forced oath. They would die rather than swear one. That was their Common Rule.

"And what prevents you from killing your hostages in any case?" Parno said. "Once we've agreed and we're at sea? I only ask since you admit that you can't be trusted."

Captain Malfin Cor bit his lower lip. "Of course," he said nodding, "that would free you from *your* oaths."

A creak of rope made them all look up.

"Wolfshead." Their friend Captain Huelra's voice was tight, but there was nothing else, no plea for himself or his crew. His throat moved as he swallowed. Huelra had no say here, no control over the events around him; so, like a sensible man, he stayed quiet . . . and trusted to his gods.

Well, his gods were looking after him tonight, that was certain.

"How if I came with you myself, and my Partner remained here."

"Dhulyn!"

Even as the words left her mouth, Dhulyn knew what Parno's reaction would be. But it was too late to call them back, and whatever else happened, short of breaking the oaths of the Common Rule—short of breaking the oaths of their Partnership, to which her suggestion came perilously close—she must do whatever she could to keep Parno off the Long Ocean ship.

Without telling him why.

"Without me," she said to him now, "the Mercenary House can rule quickly, they need not wait for a Brother Senior to me. You can explain what has happened here, and I will return as quickly as I can." She turned with lifted eyebrows to Malfin Cor and his sister-captain.

"As soon as our business is finished," he said.

"No." Parno's voice startled her, she had never heard him speak so sharply before. "We are Partnered," he said. "I will not—I cannot—be left behind."

"I am Senior—" Dhulyn began.

"In Battle," Parno said, touching his forehead with the tips of his fingers.

Dhulyn held off, but there was only one answer, and her Partner knew it. "Or in Death," she answered him lifting her own hand to answer his salute. She clenched her teeth against the words she could *not* say. Another rope creaked overhead, or perhaps the same one, and she cleared her throat.

"Let Huelra and his crew go," she said, her heart tight in her chest. "Now. Free them, and we come with you." What was her alternative? Let them die? And when her Partner asked her why she'd let that happen—because he would ask her, no question—what answer could she give him? That she could not tell him why, that it was all part of the one thing she had promised never to tell him?

"Wolfshead." The tone in Huelra's voice was now completely different. Evidently, he had not been so very certain what their answer would be.

"Huelra," she said. She wondered if anyone else noticed the tightness in her voice. "You must be our advocate to our House. The documents they have already, but you must go, explain to them what has happened, and ask them to wait their judgment." She swallowed. "Ask them to look after our horses."

"It will be done, Wolfshead. Depend on me."

Dhulyn kept her attention on the last few items she was removing from their largest pack. They'd had to abandon much of their gear—not counting weapons, of course—after the battle of Limona, and even after restocking in Beolind there wasn't much. They had moved their packs only after having seen Huelra's crew restored to the *Catseye*, and the cabin they'd been given on the *Wavetreader*—Co-captain Darlara's own, as it turned out—was more than spacious. Or it would be, if Parno wasn't hovering over her like a schoolmaster looming over a student. She kept her hands busy and her eyes down. Not that it did her any good.

"*What* were you thinking?"

"Not now, my soul."

But he persisted, as she'd known he would. "How could you say you would go alone? Demons and perverts, we're Partnered, *why* would you say such a thing?"

Because you are going to die out there, she thought, her lips pressed tight. Because she'd known ever since she'd first touched him that Parno was going to die at sea. Her Vision had shown her the storm, and the deck tilting, and the wall of water that would sweep her Partner over the side. And she had promised never to tell him how he would die. Never.

"I was worried about the hearing," she said finally. "I lost my head."

Parno crouched down next to her, blocking her light, and put his hand on her shoulder. "And the Seer? You felt we must stay, and yet you wanted to go." Here he was, finding excuses for her.

"Now is not a good time to be touching me," she said from between clenched teeth.

Parno lifted his hand immediately and edged back. "Did *you* have a Vision? Is *that* what this is all about?" he said, lowering his voice.

Dhulyn froze, her hands caught flattening the pack for folding, her lower lip between her teeth. Partners did not lie to each other, as a rule. Was there any part of the truth that could serve?

"Yes," she said finally. "I've Seen that a sea voyage will prove to be unlucky for us."

Parno sat back on his heels, blowing out his cheeks. "Well, then." He rubbed at the beard stubble on his chin. "Still, what could you do? Let them kill Huelra and his people? A large price to buy our way out of some bad luck." He stood up and edged around her to where the heavy silk bag holding his pipes lay on the cabin's small table.

"Let's not worry too much, in any case," he said. "With

your Sight so chancy as it is, it may be nothing more than the sea illness. Do you want to try using the vera tiles?"

Dhulyn shook her head. She closed the latch on the locker underneath the lower bunk and sat back on her heels, delaying the moment that he would expect her to turn toward him.

"Let it wait a day or two," she said. "My woman's time is coming. And it may be best if our hosts don't know of my Mark."

Parno nodded, rubbing at his face once more. He'd have to let his beard grow again, she thought. It was hard to shave at sea unless you'd had plenty of practice. Her heart lurched again. Practice he wasn't going to get.

"It doesn't sound as though they have a problem with this Seer they've mentioned. Especially since they're doing what she asked. Still, chances are they're more familiar with the commoner ones, Menders, Finders, Healers."

"And if, unlike me, the Seer they know has been fully trained . . ."

Parno nodded. "They'll have the usual expectations."

They would, the same as any reasonable person. That she See for them, look into the future. And she would have to explain once again that her Sight was erratic, that she'd never been trained to use it properly, that her glimpses of the future were not as useful as people might think.

Very few ever believed her.

"Fine, then. Let's hide your Mark from the Nomads," Parno said. "At least until we have some idea of what they actually know about the Marked, and how they feel about them."

Dhulyn looked up at him. Parno was frowning, his eyes focused on the middle distance. Funny how he still thought of the Marked as "them," she thought. But, of course, to him she was his Partner first, and a Seer second.

"Still, it can't do any harm for us to check the tiles, just for ourselves, try to head off this bad luck you're talking about." He held up his hands as she opened her mouth. "I know what you're going to say. Unreliable. But we know much more about your Sight now than we did before. If your woman's time *is* near, *and* you use the tiles, that gives us the best possible chance of accuracy. After all, we know what to expect, it won't be the first Vision we've dealt with."

Dhulyn took a deep breath and consciously willed her hands to loosen from the fists she'd made. She was sorely tempted to tell him and be done with it, lest the short time they had left be spoiled by evasions and half-truths. But she'd sworn, hadn't she, when they'd first Partnered and she'd told Parno that she was Marked. Sworn it would be the one thing she would never tell him. The one secret that would free her to tell him everything—anything—else.

She'd done all she could to keep him off the deep seas, the Long Ocean here in the east, the larger Round Ocean in the Great King's realm far to the west. Even here, in the Midland Sea, she'd made sure they only took coastal vessels such as Captain Huelra's *Catseye*.

And she'd done what she could to keep them from this voyage as well. *Had* she done the right thing? *Could* she have left Huelra and his crew to die? Was following the honorable path of the Common Rule *really* worth Parno's life? Tradition said that one Partner did not survive the death of the other, but that hadn't even entered her thoughts until now. She looked up, but her Partner was focused on his pipes, checking the air bag for soundness. It was Parno she wanted to save, not herself. But if she acted dishonorably, if she broke the Common Rule, what kind of life was she saving for them?

Two

DHULYN WOLFSHEAD TRIED to focus her attention on the book in her hands, but not even the poems of the great Theonyn offered her any escape from her thoughts. She had hardly slept. The sound of water shushing under the hull should have been soothing, a reminder of her days of Schooling aboard the *Black Traveler*, but the sound was wrong somehow, jarring. And as for Parno's breathing, every familiar sigh filled her with reproach. Finally, as soon as there was light enough in the sky, she'd let herself out of their cabin and found a spot where she would be out of the way of the crew on watch but there'd be light enough to read.

Dhulyn wrinkled her nose. A sharp, almost spicy smell overlaid the familiar and expected odors of brine, ozone, oiled decks, and bodies too long washed in salt water. She massaged her temples with the tips of her fingers. Perhaps it was the strange smell causing her headache. And perhaps pigs would become Racha birds. She'd found a coil of rope to sit on, her back against the high rail, in a sheltered spot not far from the man at the wheel, though out of his line of sight. Her sword was hooked to her belt, and her best throwing dagger hung in its thin harness under her vest, between her shoulder blades. She badly missed the knives she would normally carry in her boot tops, but without proper deck shoes, she'd chosen to go barefoot.

The unusual rain had lasted through the night, stopping at sunrise. The wind seemed light for the speed they were making, but she'd seen no sign of oars. The watch had just changed, and Dhulyn was well aware of the looks and sideways glances of the few whose duties brought them on deck at this hour, though none of them ventured near her. She couldn't be sure what caused the interest, that she was a Mercenary Brother, or that she was reading. She had lowered her eyes once more to her book when a whisper of sound automatically made her slow her breathing and concentrate, reaching out with all her senses. A shadow fell on the page in front of her.

"You are in my light, Captain Malfin Cor," she said without lifting her eyes.

"Seem very comfortable there. Right in thinking you've been on ships before, Dhulyn?" She was getting the feel of the accent, she thought, but that unusual dropping of pronouns . . .

She closed Theonyn's book on the index finger of her right hand. "My name is pronounced 'Dillin,'" she reminded him. "But only my Brothers may call me that. You must call me Wolfshead, or Scholar. And my Partner is Lionsmane, or Chanter."

She leaned back, propping her elbow on a crosspiece of wood. This was the first opportunity she'd had to see the captain in unobstructed light. He was just a finger's width or two shorter than she was herself—and she was tall for a woman—and dressed in the same dark clothing as the rest of his crew, though his loose trousers and simple shirt looked to be of costlier fabric. Like his sister-captain, and one or two of the senior crew including the man at the wheel, Malfin Cor wore a vest—almost a cuirass—made of a peculiar thick leather that would have resembled the skin of a fish, except the scales were much too large. Dhulyn's nostrils widened. The armor also seemed to be the source of the odd smell. Rather than boots, or a town man's shoes, he wore sailor's clogs on his bare feet. The easier to kick them off if he went into the water, Dhulyn remembered from her own Schooling.

Only the captain's chin was clean-shaven. His mustache joined his sideburns, and his braid, she noticed as he turned his head away from her to watch the progress of a very young boy up the forward mast, was reinforced with leather thongs and long enough to reach all the way down his back,

and wrap around his waist to form a belt. Dhulyn resisted
the urge to touch her own hair, still barely long enough to
fall into her eyes. She looked around her. Not everyone she
could see had the same hairstyle as the captain, but certainly all who wore one of the odd leather cuirasses.

Dhulyn blew out a silent sigh. Malfin Cor was showing
no inclination to move from her side. While it was she who
drove the bargains, it was usually Parno who undertook the
job of making conversation with clients.

"Last night you called us 'Paledyn,' " she said. "I have
heard a similar word among the Berdani, but it is not much
used in general."

"More a word of the Mortaxa than ours." Malfin Cor
leaned his hip against the rail, folding his arms. "Mortaxa
tales and songs tell of warriors and sages of paramount
honor and fair dealing, the Hands, in this world, of the Slain
God." He gestured toward Dhulyn's hairline. "Known by
their shaven and tattooed heads. When we first carried tales
of the Mercenary Brotherhood back across Long Ocean,
the Mortaxa believed you must be descendants of that order."

Dhulyn nodded. It could be. It was widely held in the
Scholars' Libraries that the Mercenary Brotherhood, the
Jaldean Priesthood, and the Scholars themselves had been
formed by the last of the Caids who had the old knowledge,
before that race had died out. The Caids were supposed to
have occupied the whole world—small wonder, then, if similar tales and writings were found everywhere.

Dhulyn straightened, blinking. Perhaps there were books
there, across the Long Ocean; books that were unknown in
the continent of Boravia. They had been in such a hurry to
catch the ebbing tide the night before that there had been
no discussion of payment or fees. She wondered now if perhaps they could be paid in books. She glanced down at the
worn inseam of her linen trousers. Well, perhaps only partly
in books.

Her breath caught and she squeezed shut her eyes. For a
moment it seemed her heart stopped beating. How was it
possible that she'd forgotten? They wouldn't be paid at all.
Things wouldn't get that far.

"Something's amiss?" Malfin Cor was looking at her
with furrowed brows.

Blood. She'd need to control her face better than this. She closed her book completely and slipped it under her sword sash at the small of her back.

"You say the Mortaxa have this belief, yet it was you who were sure we would not leave Huelra and his crew to die."

Malfin Cor shrugged. "Desperation makes a man grasp at anything. There's none of us among the Crayx haven't heard the stories of the Paledyn, and many have seen the Mercenary Brotherhood. But saw last night not all feel the same way. Plus there's some begrudge having to use this voyage to come fetch you, and may try to show you how much."

"No one can grudge our presence here more than we do ourselves, Malfin Cor." Dhulyn could hear the sincerity in her own voice, and apparently the captain could, too, for he nodded and looked away.

Pain throbbed behind Dhulyn's right eye, and was answered by a sudden but familiar spasm of a muscle in her lower back, the herald of her woman's time, no doubt of it. *Sun and Moon*, just what she needed when she had to be at her sharpest.

"Tell me more about the Mortaxa," she said. Much as she would have liked to ignore the captain, his crew, and the whole blooded ship, some instinct told her to act as naturally as the circumstances would allow. If this were any other job, she would be asking questions, gathering information, formulating plans. "And all you know," she added, "of your dispute with them."

"It's a few days longer than the turning of the moon to cross Long Ocean, Dhulyn Wolfshead. Plenty of time to talk."

Nice if that were true. She shook her head, and added a roll of the eyes for effect. "You really don't know much about diplomacy and negotiation, do you?" she said. "First, *you've* asked for *my* help, so don't think to tell me how to give it to you. Second, there is no such thing as too much time to prepare."

"As you say, Paledyn." He swept her a bow with the suggestion of a smile on his lips. "But wait until your Partner joins us. As soon tell the tale but once, and my sister should be with us."

Dhulyn hesitated, this time making sure her face kept its expression of skeptical interest. Need Parno hear any of this? As she was still formulating her answer, the door to their cabin at the far end of the main deck swung open, and her Partner sauntered out, one hand tucked into his belt, and the other resting negligently on his sword hilt, head cocked as if he were strolling through some capital city's main square. Dhulyn smiled. Parno's amber colored eyes were bright and alert, and except for his bare feet—he'd been on shipboard before, and knew better than to wear his boots—he was fully dressed in trousers, shirt, and leather jerkin. In addition to his regular sword, a short sword and dagger were conspicuous on his belts. His golden hair was unusually dull in the light of the overcast sky.

Parno Lionsmane spotted Dhulyn across the stretch of deck that separated the mid and aft cabins. He smiled. He should have known she'd found the one spot where she could sit down, be in no one's way, keep her eye on most of the crew—and still be the first thing he'd see when he opened their cabin door. Still grinning, Parno made his way across the deck to where Dhulyn sat, taking care not to lurch or stagger. There weren't many of the crew up and about, but it wouldn't do to let anyone see a Mercenary Brother off-balance. He trotted up the gangway and nodded to the captain, a shortened parody of the bow his House's Scholar had taught him as a child.

"You didn't wake me," he said to his Partner when he was close enough to be heard without raising his voice. "No *Shora* this morning?"

Again, that look passed over Dhulyn's face, the paling of her skin, the parting of her lips, accompanied by a shiver as if of frozen grief. And then rapid blinking, and an even more rapid return to a normal expression, except for her lack of color. Could she be having a Vision? But Parno had never seen that look before now, and Dhulyn had been having Visions all the time he'd known her.

"What?" she said, giving him the smile she saved only for him. "I wake you up, you complain; I don't wake you up, you complain. Either way," she shrugged. "The captain's about to tell us why they need us."

"Darlara's in our cabin. Perhaps could join her," the Nomad said. "Devin, hot water?"

A small boy looked over from his post at the steersman's side, flashing a quick smile as he dashed forward toward the galley.

After giving the order, Malfin Cor stood to one side and held out his hand with a flourish, an invitation to take the gangway to the lower deck. There, under and to the right of where the wheel man stood gazing out into the far distance, was a doorway, and a cabin slightly larger than the one they had been given. Parno looked at Dhulyn. She looked back at him. Parno touched his fingertips to his forehead in the Mercenary salute.

"After you, Captain," he said. "We insist." As far as he was concerned they were here by force, job or no job, and until they found out more about the circumstances of their being here, even their client had to be treated with caution.

Parno lifted his eyebrows as they followed Cor into his cabin. He'd wager that the untidiness was not habitual, but reflected Co-captain Darlara's hasty relocation the night before. Like their own, the cabin was longer than it was wide, with bunk beds along the inner wall—the lower one with folded clothing and a jumble of land shoes on it—and two square casement windows on the outer, seaward wall more highly placed than would have been considered normal in a room built on land. What they could see of the floor showed tightly fitted tongue-and-groove planks of a dark red hardwood, though Parno suspected there would be drainage holes somewhere along the edges of the floor, or the bottom of the exterior wall, to allow any water that entered the cabin to escape.

The captains motioned them to take seats at a bench along one side of a large central table—both benches and table, Parno noticed as he slid himself in, made of seasoned pine and bolted to the floor. Dhulyn remained standing for a moment longer, looking at a set of floor-to-ceiling shelves built into the wall between the windows. Each shelf had a rail that would help keep its contents in place as the ship moved, and while most of them contained objects of daily use, metal dishes and mugs, small wooden containers and even a few glasses, there was also a small selection of rolled maps and books—which explained Dhulyn's interest.

When Dhulyn reached out her hand, however, it was not to touch the books, as Parno expected, but one of several small ceramic pots attached to the sides of the shelves, where the plants they held could take advantage of the light coming through the thick glass of the windows.

"Tansy," said Darlara Cor.

"For making tea," added her brother.

The two captains stood together on the far side of the table, the daylight full on their faces. They were the same height—a finger's width or so shorter than Dhulyn—with the same wiry build, and thick, coarse, dark hair. Malfin's mustache made it harder to see, but they also shared the same fine lips, though Darlara's were perhaps a shade fuller, the same high cheekbones and narrow noses.

Their ears were precisely the same shape, and their luminous, almost black eyes were exactly the same distance apart.

"You're twins," Parno said, leaning forward with interest. It was not so obvious with male and female siblings, but he'd seen twins once before. They were rare enough that some made a living traveling with troupes of players or musicians and putting themselves on display.

"Are," they said in unison. "Some landsters are superstitious about twins," added Darlara in her light voice.

"The Mercenary Brotherhood is Schooled to have no prejudice," Dhulyn said. "It's said that twins are often Marked. May I ask . . . ?"

The two captains looked at each other, round-eyed, clearly surprised.

"Many and many twins among Nomads," Malfin answered. "A third of us, I'd say. But never heard of anyone who's Marked."

"Marked among the Mortaxa," Darlara added when it seemed that Dhulyn was about to ask. The two Nomads exchanged so swift a glance that Parno couldn't be certain he actually saw it. "But none among us."

"Not one?" Dhulyn's voice showed surprise, not skepticism. "They're rare, I know. Fewer than three in two hundred, but to have none at all . . . Are *you* superstitious, then, about the Marked?"

"That we're not—ah here's Devin with hot water." Malfin rose at the sound of the knock, and let the boy in. Devin was balanced with unconscious ease, his two hands wrapped around the padded handle of a steaming kettle. Malfin took the kettle from the lad and shooed him out the door when he seemed inclined to stay and stare at the Mercenary Brothers. Parno smiled.

"Peppermint or ginger?" Darlara rose to her feet and went to the shelves to peer into boxes. "Though there's lemon grass here if rather have that."

"No ganje, I suppose?"

Malfin was shaking his head and his sister turned to look at them over her shoulder, a small frown creasing her forehead. "Don't use stimulants," she said.

Of course you don't. Parno kept his sour thought to himself. Just his luck. He'd slept longer than usual, and now found himself feeling groggy.

"Ginger would be fine, if there is enough of it." Dhulyn folded her hands in front of her as Malfin took a tall, round basket as wide across as a dinner plate from a drawer to one side of the bunks. Dhulyn glanced sideways at Parno. They weren't surprised when Malfin took off the lid and revealed a porcelain teapot, of a kind they'd often seen in the lands of the Great King to the West. *Of course,* Parno thought. What served the migrating nomads of the western plains would serve the seagoing nomads just as well. Not only would the basket keep the tea warm, but it would serve as padding should the pot be tossed from the table by an errant wave—or from the back of a runaway horse.

"You were saying, about the Marked," Dhulyn said, as Darlara spooned dried ginger into the pot and Malfin added hot water from the kettle.

"Wouldn't mind a few Marked among us right now, and that's a fact," Malfin said. He put the lid back on the teapot, and closed the basket once again, to allow the tea to steep. "Those skills, Mender, Finder, Healer—were part of what we traded for with the Mortaxa."

"*Were* part?"

"Yes. About a year ago—"

Dhulyn held up her hand. "Start even farther back. How long have your people been dealing with the Mortaxa? What is the history of your relationship with them?"

The two Cors, brother and sister, looked at each other, identical frowns marking each forehead. Without changing expression, Malfin retrieved a shallow box from the same drawer that had held the teapot, opened it, and offered it to

Parno. There were biscuits inside. Parno took one, but Dhulyn shook her head.

"Are shrimp flavored, very good," Darlara said with an air of abstraction, as if she were merely going through the motions of courtesy while thinking about something else. "Our mother's recipe."

"We cannot both eat at the same time," Dhulyn said. "I will wait, to see if Parno becomes ill."

Frowns disappeared as both their faces flushed. "But the tea . . ."

"Comes from the common pot," Dhulyn said. "I can assume you will not poison yourselves in order to poison us."

Now their faces showed white spots of anger. Dhulyn held up her hand, palm toward them. "We'd do this no matter where we were, or who we were eating with," she said. "Even in the court of the Great King to the West. It's our Common Rule. Better careful than cursing."

The two captains looked at each other. Finally, they both shrugged. Malfin put the box of biscuits down on the table, picked out one for himself, and began.

"Nomads have been trading with the landsters for generations—as far back as any record, story, or legend—"

"As far back as the Crayx remember," Darlara added, her formal phrasing giving the words a certain ritual feel. "Which is as far back as time." She lifted the teapot from its basket and poured out four cups, handing the first one to Dhulyn, then one each to Parno and her brother, before taking the last one for herself.

"Like all Nomads, follow the Crayx, each to our own Pod. Seven here in the Long Ocean. Thirteen in the Round, three in the Cold South, three in the Northern Bite. Each with our own trade time and trade center."

"And what is it you trade to them, if you don't mind my asking," Parno said.

Once again that lightning flash of a glance between the two captains. This time Parno knew that Dhulyn had caught it as well.

"Other oceans, other ways," Darlara said with a shrug. "*Mortaxa* had no boats or ships, none that could leave the sight of shore."

Past tense? Parno thought. They *had* no boats.

"So bring them food from the sea. Deep-water fish, seaweed, the birds and shellfish that live in the weed beds, even sponges—all the fruits of the seas and oceans."

"As well as pearls, salt, artifacts of the Caids—"

Here Parno and Dhulyn exchanged a look of their own.

"—and skins, of course." Malfin tapped his scaled vest.

"Not the scaled ones, naturally," Darlara added.

"Naturally," Dhulyn said. Under the table, her foot pressed against Parno's, silencing the question that was about to leave his lips.

"And they'd no Long Ocean vessels, no connection with the Crayx, and so no way to cross the Long Ocean and trade with Boravia," Malfin said, using the term for the land north of the Midland Sea. "Or across the Round Ocean. So those things, too," here Malfin tapped the basket that so clearly came from the Great King's realm. "Those things formed part of our trade goods as well."

"But most, we trade for them, carry their goods—fressian mostly—for a share," Darlara said. "And so we buy our own made goods, clothing, utensils."

"And land-based foods," Malfin added. "Fruits, root vegetables . . ."

"Meat," they said in unison, their tones noticeably wistful.

Dhulyn blinked, reached into the front of her multicolored, patch-worked vest, and pulled out a stick of sausage, dried and smoked for travel.

"I'm afraid it might be a bit sweaty," she said, holding it out.

Both captains had their hands halfway across the table, eyes shining, before they remembered their manners.

"Thank you, Dhulyn Wolfshead," they said.

"If you've any trade goods with you now," Parno said, "we could stop at Navra before we pass through the Straits. We know trustworthy people there."

Both Malfin and Darlara shook their heads. "Not here to trade," he said. "Just to find Paledyn."

"Would have sent someone more important," Darlara said. "But was our Pod's turn to cross, so we came." She had taken out her knife and scrupulously cut the stick of dried meat in two, giving one half to her brother before she cut a small piece off the part she'd kept for herself. The meat was dry and hard, Parno knew, and they would have to soften the bits in their mouths for a while before they could chew them, but they didn't seem to mind. He took another biscuit from the box in front of him.

"So this is the history of your trade." Dhulyn took a sip of her tea and put the small cup back down on the table in front of her. "You spoke of distrust. Has it been the cause, or the result, of war between you?"

This time the look that passed between the two captains was long, and undisguised.

"There've been disputes," Malfin said finally. "How not? But in our time all *we've* seen are fights in taverns and such."

"A blockade here, a boycott there," Darlara said, shrugging. "They're landsters, without Crayx, small surprise there's no open water between us. Times they say we hold back goods, wait until there's desperation to drive up prices, but we come and we go as the Crayx bring and take us. Tell them this, and they don't believe."

"Times they say there's been drought, or flooding, and they drive prices up," Malfin said. "And we don't always believe them."

Darlara snorted and looked quickly to one side. "Still, for generations, there's been trade and profit, even if it didn't come easy. And these past few years, when the Tarxin's son, Tar Xerwin, was spokesman for them, looked like things would get better and better."

Parno nodded, leaning forward on his elbow, and wishing the bench seats had backs. Probably the most common cause of war—as the Mercenary Brotherhood had reason to know—was dispute over trade. And even when the dispute was settled, and treaties and tariffs were formalized, that didn't mean the ones who actually did the trading would always see eye to eye.

"So what changed a year ago?"

"*Dawntreader* Pod went to their regular trade fair in Ketxan City, the capital, good to the day and all, and merchants took goods contracted for but nothing else," Malfin said.

"Nothing else?"

Darlara nodded. "No new trade. Were allowed to anchor in their usual place and put ashore. But there was no fair set up, and were told there wouldn't be. *Dawntreader* asked when next fair would be, told to wait."

"By order of the Tarxin, not the son, mind you, the Tarxin himself. Not worried at first," added Malfin. "Crayx remember, type of thing Mortaxa has done before when wanted to change old treaties, old agreements. *We* thought—"

"*We* don't go to the capital, that's not our route," Darlara interrupted. The first time, Parno realized, the twin captains hadn't spoken in turn. "Ours is Caudix, farther along the coast and a bit north. And at first our trade wasn't affected, but seven months ago, contracts were fulfilled, and our landsters turned us away as well."

"Found out *all* trade, everywhere, stopped. Told us they'd no need to be cheated by us anymore ..." Malfin's voice died away.

"*Had* you been cheating them?" Dhulyn's voice was matter-of-fact, with no judgment in it. The Mercenary Brotherhood did a great deal of negotiation and bargaining, and Parno knew there was often a very fine line between careful dealing and cheating.

"It's trade, Dhulyn Wolfshead," Malfin said, in unconscious echo of Parno's thoughts. "Each makes the best bargain they can, we and the landsters both. Times *we* feel we've caught the current ahead of them, times *they'd* feel the same."

"The captains of our oldest Pods took our protest to Xalbalil, their Tarxin, who the landsters call the Light of the Sun, and he says, will need new treaties, or maybe no treaties since now will build their own ships," Malfin said. "Breaking most ancient and treasured of agreements."

"So we think, what of it? Still cannot cross the Long Ocean without Crayx," Darlara said.

"And say they don't need us now," Malfin added. "Say have lodestone."

Dhulyn whistled. "I've read about them, but I thought they were old magic of the Caids. Has one been found?"

The two Cors gave identical shrugs. "Wouldn't know. Reminded Mortaxa that Crayx would not accept landster ships, any sent out into the Long Ocean would be destroyed. That is their right by the agreement."

"Then came a storm—"

"Winds and rain—"

"Scattering the Pods, confusing the Crayx," Malfin said. "The Mortaxa said they wouldn't even treat with us any longer," Darlara finished, "That they couldn't trust us, not now we'd threatened them."

"Many wanted to fight, but the Crayx said try talking again, that there would always be time to fight later."

Parno caught Dhulyn's eye, prepared to share a silent laugh at this familiar, and sensible, attitude, but the smile she gave him was late and stiff.

"Then the Tarxin says their Seers say Paledyn will come with a solution. We're to bring them a Paledyn, or don't come back at all."

Parno glanced again at Dhulyn, holding his breath. She was frowning, her blood-red brows drawn down in a vee. She had not missed the reference to a Seer, that was certain.

"Paledyn." Darlara reached her hand across the table between them. "Just want our rights," she said. "*They* should hold by the ancient treaties, or at least bargain to make new ones, not just toss us aside and try to wreck our ships with storms."

"Wait, wait." Dhulyn patted the air in front of her. "I don't know as much about the far side of the Long Ocean as you do, but surely even there the rain must fall."

"Think *this* weather is natural? The rains here, even here, in the Midland Sea? This is to remind us of our task, since they don't trust us to do it."

"*This* weather? You mean yesterday's rain?" Dhulyn's hand tightened on the cup she had been about to raise to her lips. Her glance met Parno's and he nodded, mindful of the storms of the day before, and the unseasonable winds that had accompanied their sailing in the *Catseye* to Lesonika.

"And more. Wait a moment."

Malfin went to the door of the cabin and opened it. "Devin," he said. "Come here a moment, lad." He turned back to the Mercenaries. "Wait until you see this, Paledyn. Then ask me again about the rain."

The young boy came in and grinned at them again. He had good teeth, Parno noticed. So did they all, now that he came to think of it.

"Show the Mercenary Brothers your ears, lad."

What Parno had taken for a scarf around the boy's head was a length of fine fishnet holding pads of linen over his ears. Both Parno and Dhulyn stood and came around the table to see. Devin tilted his head back, exposing his ears completely. Parno leaned closer. The cartilage at the top of the ears was a dull gray color, as if there was no blood circulating there.

"Can you stop in Navra for a Healer?" Dhulyn's voice was tight and Parno looked at her with surprise.

"No." Malfin shook his head. "Just enough time to get through the Straits as it is."

"*You* know what caused this," Darlara said.

Parno frowned, searching through his memory for the knowledge he felt must be there. He'd seen this type of injury before. The answer was just within his grasp when Dhulyn spoke.

"This is frostbite."

Three

"I TAKE IT YOU DON'T sail into the southernmost seas," Dhulyn said. She took the boy Devin by the chin and tilted his face to catch the light better. There were telltale marks of the killing cold on the firm curve of his left cheek as well, just below the eye, though it seemed the dead skin there would slough off without leaving more behind it than a small scar.

"Never. Frostbite—heard the word, surely—but you *know* it? You've *seen* it?"

Dhulyn nodded. "We're Mercenary Brothers, there's little we haven't seen. If there's to be no Healer, the ears will have to be trimmed of this dead flesh, or the death will spread."

While she was speaking, Dhulyn caught the attention of both captains, questioning them with raised brows, reaching her free hand up the back of her vest for her dagger. Understanding what was wanted, Parno mirrored her position on the boy's other side.

The captains hesitated, eyes narrowing as they considered. When they nodded, Dhulyn and Parno moved, their blades flashing so swiftly that it took the boy Devin a moment to even realize he'd been cut. By then, Dhulyn had taken up the pads of linen and was already pressing them to the boy's ears as Parno retied the bits of netting.

"Anyone else who was affected must be dealt with the same way," Dhulyn said. "Even fingers or toes must be cut, and quickly if the limbs are to be saved."

"Go help Jessika, boy, tell her what Dhulyn Wolfshead has said. Jessika's our Knife," Darlara said, turning to Dhulyn. "She'll see to it now she knows what needs to be done."

The boy nodded and turned to the door, his eyes as round as coins, his grin gone.

"Were crossing when this cold overtook us at the midpoint, some fifteen days from Mortaxa. Ice fell from the sky, and then a wind like a knife for three days." Darlara's eyes were still on the cabin door Devin had closed behind him.

"Knew right away it wasn't natural, any more than this rain," Malfin said.

Dhulyn shivered, and saw the same chill mirrored in Parno's eyes. Unusual for this time of year, that's what everyone had been saying about the rains. But hail? Followed by killing cold? Unnatural was the proper word.

Darlara nodded at their silence. "Not imagining things, Mercenaries. Live by the weather more than most, and can tell what's natural from what's Mage work. The Mortaxa have a Storm Witch, that's certain."

Dhulyn's hand tightened around her teacup. *Sun and Moon.* A Mage? That's all they needed.

"*Can* you be certain?"

Malfin Cor snorted. "Who else can bring ice and snow in the warm oceans?"

"Or this unnatural rain?" added his sister.

"But why would they?" Parno said. "They've sent you, you say, to find Paledyn. Why attack you on your journey?"

The two captains exchanged another look. "We've wondered," Darlara finally said. "*Did* they send us? Said Paledyn would solve all problems."

"Perhaps don't want conflict solved," Malfin said.

"Maybe just to show us what they can do. That the Witch's power extends so far . . ." Both captains shook their heads, the identical movement almost hypnotizing.

Dhulyn blinked, looked into her empty cup, and held it out as Darlara turned to the teapot. *Say there is a Mage,* she thought, or a Witch, as the Nomads called him. It did not necessarily follow that the man was doing anything more or less than defending his people. And the Nomads admitted they'd made threats.

"Say you let them build their ships," Dhulyn said. "This Storm Witch would leave you be, and you might be able to

trade for his services, as you do for the Marked. It would be
years, perhaps generations, before the Mortaxa became any
real threat to you in terms of trade. In this part of the world
there are many traders, and all find profit." Automatically,
Dhulyn's Schooled mind fell into the logical paths most useful for negotiation. "If nothing else, you'll have bought their
goodwill, and that will buy you time to learn more."

"It's not just the trade," Malfin said. "For the Mortaxa—"

"Or anyone else," interjected Darlara.

"Or anyone else," Malfin agreed, "to build ships and
travel on the oceans is an affront to the Crayx. It's *they* have
dominion over the oceans, and us their children, no one
else."

Dhulyn pursed her lips, keeping her eyes focused once
more on her refilled cup. They'd been talking long enough
that, insulated basket or no, the ginger tea was losing its
heat.

Parno cleared his throat. "Is 'Crayx' another word for
'Caid'?" he asked. Dhulyn looked up.

But both Nomads were shaking their heads.

"The Crayx knew them, in their time. Was the Caids
granted this domain," Malfin said.

"So ancient is their agreement and binding on all who
follow," Darlara agreed. "The Crayx are the guardians of
the waters of the world."

"You worship them?"

"Oh, no." Here the Nomads seemed almost to laugh
though they grew serious again at once.

"We're the same people. We belong to them," Darlara
said. "And they to us."

"As you two belong to each other."

Well, there was no disputing that. She and Parno were
Partnered, they *did* belong to each other. But as difficult as
the Partnership of Mercenary Brothers was for outsiders to
understand, at least they were sitting down together, in the
same room. Able to touch, argue, and fight side by side.

Dhulyn glanced at him and saw that Parno was wearing
his blandest look, but his left eyebrow was raised. The Mercenary Brotherhood was open-minded about the religious
beliefs of others—they had to be. But these "Crayx" were
something neither of them had ever heard of.

Malfin slid out from behind the table and stood. "Come," he said, and indicated the door. "Show you."

Dhulyn followed Darlara out of the cabin, letting Malfin and Parno bring up the rear. Darlara glanced up and over her shoulder, nodding at the woman now at the wheel, before acknowledging the mate as he moved toward them across the deck. The sun had gone behind the clouds once again, though the wind had picked up and Dhulyn's finely Schooled balance detected the slight pitch of the deck to port.

The ordinary business of the day had begun while they were in the captains' cabin, and the deck, so empty when the sun had barely risen, was almost crowded with men and women—and children, Dhulyn saw with some surprise until she remembered that these were Nomads, and like the nomads of the land, would travel with their families. All seemed busy. There was movement in and out of the cabins in the central part of the deck, where a young, fair-haired woman who was clearly the Knife was hard at work on the other frostbite victims. Much of the rest of the crew were engaged in the usual work found at all times on all ships, repairing the damage caused by salt on the metalwork, and by wear on ropes and railings. Nearest them, two white-haired men with identical laugh lines were mending a net with fingers made crooked by age, and a middle-aged woman sitting with them was putting a new end on a fraying rope.

Dhulyn slowed, looking around her. What was wrong with what she saw? Of course. There were no lines of apprentices drilling in the *Shora* as there would have been on the ship where she was Schooled. To her right, out of the wind, was a man reading to a group of small children sitting cross-legged at his feet, while a similar group of young people several years older were listening with rapt attention to a man with a *garwon* in his hands.

As if they felt her watching them, the youngest of the children turned to stare at the Mercenaries as they passed, and Dhulyn suppressed a smile as she saw Parno straighten his spine and add a slight swagger to his walk, his hand falling casually to the hilt of his sword. The others, older children and crew alike, studiously avoided looking directly at them, though Dhulyn could feel the glances that were aimed out of the corners of eyes as they followed the two captains to an unoccupied section of the rail.

Malfin leaned out, bracing both hands on the rail, his brow furrowed in concentration as he scanned the water rushing past the hull. Darlara motioned the Mercenaries forward with a gesture, inviting them to join Malfin, as she hung back. With a twitch of her left hand, Dhulyn signaled Parno to take up position at Malfin's right while she stayed back beside Darlara. It wouldn't do to have both of them turn their backs on the crew at the same time.

"Demons and perverts." Parno was using the tone he normally saved for visits to religious shrines—only with less fake courtesy and more genuine awe. "You'd better come see this, my heart." He stepped back from the rail to let her take his place, though he didn't move as far away as she had been. Dhulyn looked over the side.

As she watched, a darkness rose up from the depth of the sea, and took the form of a scaled back. A very large, very long scaled back. Finally, the tail flicked out of the water, somehow giving Dhulyn a sense of playfulness and fun.

"What is it?" She was glad to hear her own voice so steady.

"That is the Crayx."

"Ah. Now I see why your ship has no oars."

A soft "click" made Parno Lionsmane's eyes flutter open. Dhulyn was sitting at their cabin's small table with her back to him, but he had seen her in that position many times—back straight as a lance, head tilted down, fingertips resting on the edge of the table—and knew that she was looking at her vera tiles.

He blinked, just stopping himself from speaking. Looking at her tiles, seeking a Vision, was something Dhulyn hardly ever did on her own. It was always his job to nudge her, persuade her. Parno could tell the moment the Visions began by the change in Dhulyn's breathing, and the shift in the angle of her shoulders as she leaned forward. Still, he made no move to rise from his bunk. Instead, he closed his eyes again and let his own breathing slow. Whatever reason

Dhulyn had for hiding this from him, he would let her tell him in her own time.

Finally, Parno heard Dhulyn release her breath in a ragged sigh and begin putting the tiles away, almost soundlessly, into their silk-lined box. He waited until she'd slipped the box back into her pack and nudged his shoulder with her knee before he rolled over, reaching up to rub at his face.

"Bring your sword," she told him from the doorway.

Dhulyn Wolfshead raised her face to the rushing air and took a deep breath, letting it out slowly, mentally chanting the closing words of the Scholar's *Shora*. From up in the Racha's nest she could make out an edge of rosy light on the horizon as the sun began to rise. The pains from her woman's time had kept her wakeful all night, despite the valerian Parno had mixed into a cup of wine for her. Finally she'd gotten up, as quietly as she could, and used a meditation *Shora* to relax enough to try the tiles again. As usual during her woman's time, the Visions had been crisp and focused. She'd Seen a narrow path between rock and crisply trimmed hedges, an unknown Finder bending over a dark blue scrying bowl. But no matter what question she asked, what tile she used as her beginning, she could not change the Vision of Parno that appeared. Nor could she See, as she had done sometimes in the past, any Vision of Parno that might come from a different future, a future in which he did not die in the Long Ocean.

The climb up the rigging to the Racha's nest had loosened the muscles in her lower back, and helped her vent at least some of her frustration. She and Parno had always spoken of her Sight as erratic and unreliable—and so it was, since she could no more guarantee what Vision would come than she could guarantee a given cat would chase a given mouse. But the Visions themselves were clear and truthful, even if she didn't always understand them. And what she did See would come to pass, if steps were not taken to change the circumstances.

But now, if she could not See Parno in any Vision other than the one in which he died, it seemed her days of avoiding this particular future were over.

Movement drew her eyes downward. There he was now. Some instinct made him look immediately upward as he secured the cabin door behind him. His teeth flashed white in the dark gold of his beard and he lifted his fist above his right shoulder, signaling "In Battle."

Dhulyn raised her open hand, fingers spread wide, over her own right shoulder, answering the salute, "In Death."

Parno spoke, but Dhulyn shook her head at him. Between the height and the rushing air, it was impossible to hear him.

Come down, Parno signaled.

She shook her head. *You come up. It's only twenty spans.*

"If I cannot tell you," she said, knowing she was safe to speak. "Then I must never let you guess."

That had been the answer her meditation had shown her. She'd made the right choice yesterday when, talking to Malfin Cor, she'd decided to behave as though this were any normal assignment. Not waking Parno, skipping the morning *Shora*—something that all Mercenary Brothers did every day unless injured—*those* had been mistakes.

If she stepped too far from the path of her normal behavior, if she acted as if nothing—not the job, not the *Shora*, not the Common Rule—mattered anymore, Parno would notice and ask questions. As soon as he realized Dhulyn had Seen it, Parno had made her promise never to tell him how he would die. If she could not keep him alive, she could at least keep her promise.

If only it wasn't *this* death. Dhulyn gripped the narrow rail around the Racha's nest tighter and leaned out, giving Parno as encouraging a grin as she could manage. He was almost halfway up the rigging, but with luck he wouldn't notice anything unnatural about her smile.

"Don't slip and fall, my soul," she called out. Parno didn't look up, but he did make a most rude signal with his left hand. Dhulyn laughed, strangely comforted.

Mercenary Brothers expected to die, their Schooling prepared them for it. But they hoped to die in battle, and preferably at the hands of a worthy opponent. The best death—the one that they all hoped for—was at the hands of another Mercenary Brother.

Not the way Parno would die. Not drowning.

"Oh, my soul, I'm so sorry," she murmured. But not quietly enough.

"Sorry for what?"

"Sorry for this." Dhulyn swung her legs over the side of the Racha's nest, pushed Parno to one side with a foot to his sternum, and fell, catching at the rigging from time to time to slow her descent. It was a game the apprentice mercenaries had often played on the *Black Traveler*. The sound of Parno's cursing followed her all the way down until her bare feet hit the closely fitted planks of the deck.

"Crab *Shora*," she announced as Parno landed beside her, and pulled her second-best sword from its harness at her back. One of the basic twenty-seven *Shoras* that all Mercenary Brothers learned in School, the Crab was designed for right-handed sword and uneven ground. But it was just as well suited to the subtly shifting deck beneath their feet.

Parno's sword flicked out to meet hers. "Come on, then," he said, motioning her forward with beckoning fingers. "Winner gets both breakfasts."

Where are they Malfin Cor resisted the urge to crane his neck around and search out the nooks and crannies of the ship. Usually, he'd know where anyone on board was without having to look. Having landsters among them changed so many things.

Darlara motioned with her eyes to the left, toward the forward deck. *She's on upper deck, he's in my cabin*

Malfin lowered himself to the pilot's bench next to her. *Best think of it as their cabin* he said.

Darlara nodded, her eyes suddenly spreading wide open. *See their practice this morning* she asked.

Malfin shrugged, resting his elbows on his knees and leaning forward enough to look around his sister to the forward deck. He could just make out the spot of dark red that was Dhulyn Wolfshead's hair.

Seen fighters practice

Not like this, and those that did won't be forgetting it soon

Was it so strange then Without straightening, Mal turned to look at her.

Mal, it was fast Darlara leaned against his shoulder, and Malfin felt a tickle of cold run down his spine as her feelings transferred to him. *Went at each other like were crazed, on the main deck, up and down the rigging and ladders—once she ran

balancing on the rail and *he* doing his best to knock her off*
*They were all the time smiling, never a foot put wrong—so fast
couldn't always see the blades moving—any minute expected
blood to fly* Dar put her hand on his arm. *And, Mal, kept it
up until the sun was a span over the edge of the sea, and when
finished, were dripping sweat, but breathing easy like sitting in a
chair*

Malfin's eyes narrowed. *Could *hold* their breaths long, you
think*

*They're landsters, when all's said, but oh, Mal, if you'd *seen**

Mal considered his sister's thoughts carefully, but there
was none of that glow he'd sometimes felt when there was
a new man she was interested in. Not that he would have
been surprised. Both the Mercenaries were tall even for
landsters, and Dar liked them tall. And their coloring was
unusual enough to make them exotic to the Nomads. Lionsmane was brown and gold all over, like the animal he was
named for, and Wolfshead was pale as a deep-sea pearl, and
looked like she'd be just as cool to the touch—except for
her hair, red like old blood.

No, what he saw now in Darlara's thoughts wasn't lust,
but something closer to awe.

Guess I missed something then

There was only the night watch on deck, your turn tomorrow

I can't wait—look

Darlara sat up and turned to look forward. Parno Lionsmane had come out of the cabin carrying what were clearly
pipes in his hands. Dhulyn Wolfshead moved from where
she had been sitting, coming halfway down the ladder leading to the forward deck, and speaking to her Partner as she
came. He answered, she nodded, sitting down where she was
on one of the rungs, and went back to reading her book. Dar
looked at her brother and lifted her shoulders in query. He
frowned and pointed forward again. Dar looked back, and
this time she saw what Mal was drawing to her attention.
One or two of the crew were circling, closing in on Parno
Lionsmane from other parts of the ship, Goann from the
forward hatch, Mikel from the galley underneath where he
and Dar were sitting, and what looked like Conford, the new
exchange, from one of the cabins amidship. All were keeping
Pod silence, so you had to be watching to see anything. There

wouldn't be much to notice if you were down on the main deck, but from up here it was obvious.

Trouble he said to his sister.

Mercenary Brother has nothing to worry about she said.

Not even three against one Mal got to his feet and headed for the ladder. *Practice against each other is one thing, a fight with Nomads is another*

But he moved with casual deliberation. Strangers were rare aboard a Nomad ship, the crew would have been unsettled in any case, and the circumstances bringing these particular strangers made things even worse. The crew was itching for a confrontation, and the Mercenaries made as good an excuse as any. And since there was bound to be an incident, better it happened now, under his eye, and not later, perhaps when neither he nor Darlara was by.

And he had to admit he was curious. He'd seen a bit of Lionsmane's speed in the *Catseye*, but so had some of the crew, and now they'd be prepared.

Lionsmane had taken his pipes to the narrow bench, little more than a shelf, that ran along the ship's side under the main deck's rail. The instrument's air bag was partially filled, and he was looking down, attaching first the chanter and then the drones. *Chanter*. That was part of his name, and now Malfin figured he knew why. So if the Wolfshead was called Scholar . . .

Lionsmane took the chanter in his fingers and began the opening notes of a slow dance tune, his elbow squeezing out a rhythm through the drones.

"Hey, pipe-boy, do you dance nice like you play?" That was Conford's voice, heavy with anger, and Mal began to walk faster. Con had only recently come to *Wavetreader* from a Round Ocean ship. And voluntary though an exchange always was, Conford's had been particularly hard. Everything and everyone here was strange to him, and it would take him time to feel that he had a good wind and a fair current. In his mid-twenties, Conford was small and thick-muscled like most Nomads, his grin, seldom seen, showing a space where he was missing a tooth. He wore a *garwon* at his belt—which he had every right to—but was beckoning Parno forward with empty hands.

"Come on, then, show us how well you dance."

Lionsmane didn't even open his eyes, but went on playing. Malfin circled around to ship's starboard, until he was standing to the left of Dhulyn Wolfshead where she sat on the ladder, reading.

"Come on, pipe-boy. Or you gonna get your lady friend to fight for you?"

Other crew were beginning to gather, some elbowing each other, grinning. Josel looked up from the lesson he was chalking on the deck boards and shepherded the children toward the aft hatch, shaking his head as he went.

The Mercenary broke off in mid-note, the drones groaning as he released the air bag. He ignored Conford and looked toward his Partner.

"Dhulyn?"

"You go ahead." The Mercenary woman shrugged one shoulder without lifting her eyes from her book. "I did the last one," she added.

She's Senior, Mal remembered, moving forward until he was next to and below her. *Lionsmane won't act without her nod.*

"Are you sure? He seems to think you beat me this morning."

"I *did* beat you, and look again. That man's not one of the crew who watched us this morning. I think his friends are playing a trick on him."

"I like tricks."

"Well, watch out for your pipes. They won't be easy to replace out here." And she'd still never lifted her eyes from her reading.

Mal was close enough to her to speak without raising his voice. "Not even going to watch?"

"I've seen Parno kill people before."

"Kill?" Mal whirled around and took a pace toward the men. "Hoy, Mercenary, no killing."

"Don't worry, Captain," Conford said. "He won't—hrrrk!"

Malfin didn't see the Lionsmane move, but suddenly the Mercenary was standing next to Conford, who was bent over, hands clutching his stomach, eyes bulging, and the *garwon* at his belt was in the Lionsmane's hand. He tossed it to the Wolfshead, who caught it without looking up. Goann dashed forward, and the Lionsmane spun 'round, rapping her on the bridge of her nose with the chanter he held in his left hand. As Goann jerked back, hands to her face, the Mercenary hooked her feet out from under her and tipped her over into Conford, knocking them both to the deck.

Dhulyn Wolfshead turned a page.

Parno Lionsmane scratched the side of his nose with his chanter. Mikel edged backward, raising his empty hands to waist level. Lionsmane stepped back—slowly—to where his pipes lay next to the rail. He smiled as several others of the crew edged nearer to help Conford and Goann. A couple of the crew were smiling as well, Mal noticed.

"Don't worry, Captain," Dhulyn Wolfshead said, looking up from her book for the first time. "My Partner wouldn't have killed anyone. Probably." She smiled, and a small scar pulled her upper lip back in a snarl. "At least, not with his chanter. Blood's hard to clean from the sound holes."

"*Knew* Conford hadn't watched you practice this morning?" One or two from among the crew who were helping Conford and Goann back to their feet looked thoughtful, sending glances at Parno Lionsmane out of the corner of their eyes. One of the smiling ones thumped Conford on the back. Malfin was relieved to see the young crewman shaking his head with a rueful look. It seemed at least part of the anger he'd brought with him from the *Windwaver* was gone. Lionsmane had returned to his perch at the rail, reattached his chanter and was now playing a much livelier tune, somehow making the pipes sound as though they were laughing.

"Nor the other young woman either."

"Did it deliberately, to show my crew what you can do."

"You said it yourself, Captain. Your people don't know us, don't have the same beliefs in the 'Paledyn' that the Mortaxa have. It would only be a matter of time before someone decided to see just what it means to be a Mercenary Brother."

Mal leaned his left hip against the ladder, inches away from Dhulyn Wolfshead's foot. Let his crew see he was not put off. "Run into this kind of thing before?"

Wolfshead leaned back, her elbows on a rung of the ladder, the book closed on the index finger of her left hand. She looked at him with narrowed eyes, as if she was measuring him.

"There's some everywhere who have never seen a Mercenary Brother fight. The Brotherhood is very old—the Scholars say we go back to the time of the Caids, and it's said that we were once numerous. There are fewer of us now. Half of those who come to be Schooled are turned away, and half of those who are accepted leave—those whom the Schooling does not kill." She looked at him closely. "I've heard it said that one Mercenary Brother against ten ordinary soldiers is a fair fight."

Mal swallowed. "And what do you say?" he said, keeping his tone light.

She smiled her wolf's smile, lifted her shoulders and let them drop. "I say it depends on the Mercenary Brother, and on the soldiers." She looked away, and Mal relaxed. "Nevertheless, our reputation being what it is, there are always idiots who have something they need to prove, and decide that challenging a Mercenary Brother is the way to prove it."

"And do you never kill those idiots?"

"We're not assassins, and we don't kill people just because we can. Now, having said all of this to put you at your ease, Captain, let me tell you also, that not everyone on this ship is a warrior. If we decided to do it, my Partner and I could kill you all, and you would not be able to stop us."

"If you did that, the Crayx would destroy the ship."

"Good to know."

She opened her book.

A GREEN-EYED MAN, HIS DARK HAIR BRUSHED BACK FROM A RE-CEDING FOREHEAD HOLDS OUT HIS LEFT HAND. HE HAS AN EXTRA FINGER NEXT TO HIS THUMB . . .

THE STORM RAGES, PUSHING WALLS OF WATER OVER THE RAILS OF THE *WAVETREADER*, WASHING OVER DECKS, PUSHING THEM CLOSER AND CLOSER TO VERTICAL. ONE WAVE FOLLOWS AN-OTHER, THERE IS SO MUCH WATER IT IS IMPOSSIBLE TO BREATHE, ONE COULD DROWN STANDING UPRIGHT, CLINGING TO THE SHEETS. DHULYN TRIES NOT TO LOOK DOWN TO THE DECK BELOW HER, KNOWING WHAT SHE'LL SEE, HOPING THAT THIS TIME, IF SHE DOESN'T LOOK, EVERYTHING WILL CHANGE. BUT NOTHING CHANGES. HER HEAD TILTS, HER EYES NARROW. PARNO, ALMOST UNRECOGNIZABLE, HIS GOLDEN HAIR DARKENED BY THE WET. SHE

HAS NEVER BEEN ABLE TO TELL WHAT HE IS DOING, MAKING SOMETHING FAST? HELPING SOMEONE IN THE SHADOWS? THE *WAVE-TREADER* SHIVERS AS IF IT HAS STRUCK SOMETHING BELOW THE HULL, AND PARNO IS SWEPT OFF THE PITCHING SIDE OF THE DECK BY A WAVE TALLER THAN TWO MEN. SHE WAILS, HER HEART BREAKING, AND LETS GO OF THE ROPE SHE CLINGS TO . . .

A VERY SLIM, DELICATELY-BONED WOMAN WITH SANDY HAIR CROPPED SO SHORT THAT IT SHOWED HER FINELY SHAPED HEAD SITS IN THE CENTER OF A ROUND WORKTABLE. HER HAZEL EYES ARE SURROUNDED BY FAINT LINES, AND LOOK DARK AGAINST HER SKIN LIKE CREAM. SHE WEARS A HIGH-COLLARED SLEEVELESS BLOUSE IN A MUDDY ORANGE COLOR. THERE ARE FINE LINES, OF LAUGHTER AND OF CONCENTRATION, AROUND HER MOUTH AND EYES. SHE IS LOOKING DOWN AT THE LARGE, STRANGELY MARKED PARCHMENTS THAT COVER THE TABLE ALL AROUND HER. FINALLY, SHE NODS AND LEANS BACK, HER EYES CLOSED. OVER HER HEAD FORMS A MIST, AND THE DHULYN OF THE VISION STEPS CLOSER, PUTTING HER HAND ON HER SWORD HILT. THE MIST DARKENS. A TINY FLASH OF LIGHTNING SEEMS TO BOLT THROUGH IT. THE WOMAN RAISES HER BARE ARMS UNTIL HER HANDS DISAPPEAR . . .

Dhulyn scooped the vera tiles quickly into their box and shoved it out of sight just as Parno opened the cabin door.

"Come and tell a tale," he said. "They're tired of dancing and my throat is parched."

"Nothing ever changes."

Four

"THE CRAYX ARE FAR MORE visible from here," Parno Lionsmane leaned forward, his elbows resting on the light bar of wood that formed the rail of the Racha's nest on the forward mast. He glanced sideways at Malfin Cor, who was gazing out at the horizon. It was late in the afternoon watch, and while Parno hadn't expected to be alone in the lookout, he was surprised it was the co-captain who had joined him.

Parno looked down again, eyes drawn to the sinuous movements just below the water's surface. From here, you could see the whole of the beasts, not just the part that broke water. These were much larger than the *Wavetreader*, much longer than the young one they had glimpsed while they were still in the Midland Sea. Older ones, perhaps? Too large to pass through the Herculat Straits?

Malfin Cor took a deep breath, as if he'd come to some kind of decision. Parno waited, watching the man's face. Instead of speaking, however, he looked down, not at the Crayx, but at the deck of the ship to where Dhulyn sat with the teacher Josel, a small girl child practically in her lap.

Suddenly there was a great jolt, and the ship lurched sideways, as if it had struck a reef. Flung to his left, Parno reached out and caught hold of the railing, automatically looking down in time to see Dhulyn put out one hand to steady herself, the other securing the girl child. As the ship began to right itself, the mast swinging back to upright, there was another jolt, the bar in Parno's hand snapped, and he was thrown outward, plunging down. He twisted in the air, reaching for any part of the rigging that might be close enough to grab, and had just enough time to see that there was nothing beneath him when he struck the water and went under.

Dhulyn looked up when she heard the cry. One man, clinging to a broken bit of rail, was clambering back into the relative safety of the Racha's nest. But not the right man. She saw a flash of gold and brown as her Partner plunged into the water a mere arm's length from the ship's side.

Dhulyn was at the rail in a flash, discarding weapons as she went. She was already barefoot, so no boots would weigh her down. *Sun blast it!* She'd never thought she'd be sorry to have so many bits of metal hidden in her clothing.

There was no outcry, no call of "man overboard!" The crew's sudden bustle had no urgency, no fear in it. She could have sworn there was even some laughter.

Without any order given, crew members were in the rigging, spilling the wind out of the sails. As the ship slowed and began to turn, Dhulyn scanned the surface of the water for any sign of her Partner. Where was he? Had he hit his head? This was not what her Vision had always shown her. Her chest was tight, and her blood beat in her ears. This should *not* be happening.

She stopped hunting for more weapons to discard and swung herself over the rail just as Darlara Cor reached her.

"Look," the Nomad captain said.

One hand still on the rail, her bare feet braced on the outer side of the hull, Dhulyn squinted in the direction Darlara was pointing. If the woman had seen some evidence of Parno . . .

There. A black shadow in the water. Parno's head broke the surface. And then his shoulders. And then . . . he appeared to be kneeling on something.

Silence on the deck. The ship was almost completely dead in the water, floating as smooth and light as though it were docked.

Parno continued to rise until the long head of the Crayx bearing him rose out of the water.

"Sun and Moon shine on us," Dhulyn breathed. She didn't even notice when Darlara grabbed her by the wrist.

"Where is he from? Your Partner? What port?"

"No port." Dhulyn used the captain's arm to help pull herself back onto the deck. "He's from Imrion. Inland," she added, when she saw Darlara's face still blank.

By the time Dhulyn had turned around again, Parno was alongside the ship, and the Crayx was lifting him high enough to reach for the rail himself. She was not the first to the spot, but crew members cleared the way for her as she reached out for Parno, giving him a hand to help him balance as he stepped from the Crayx's head to the rail. Once there, he turned to face the beast, gave his deepest bow, touching the fingertips of his free hand to his forehead.

Dhulyn, steadying her Partner before he could topple into the water once more, raised her own hand to salute the Crayx. Any other time, she would have been fascinated by the beast itself, but now she only caught a glimpse of a long, horsey snout, pale green scales the size of her palm, and disconcertingly large, round eyes as the Crayx waggled its head in acknowledgment of the salutes before sinking once more under the waves.

"Did you see that? Demons and perverts, what a ride!" Parno was grinning, apparently none the worse for his dunking in the water—at least until he saw her face. Dhulyn was quick to force an answering smile to her lips.

"You were never worried, my heart? You know I can swim." He smoothed his wet hair back from his face with both hands.

"You might well have forgotten how," she answered, as indifferently as she could.

Malfin Cor landed on the deck and raced over to them, stepping into the small cleared area that had formed around Dhulyn, Parno, and Darlara.

"Performance over, people. Work waiting, if you please." He was smiling, as were many of the others as the crew moved to obey.

"Saw that?" Dhulyn wasn't sure to whom Malfin was speaking.

"Didn't miss a moment," Darlara said.

"Got good balance, man," Malfin said, thumping Parno on the back. "Who would have thought the Crayx could catch you up without even a braid to hook you by?"

Dhulyn raised her eyebrow in sudden comprehension. *That* was the purpose of the hairstyle worn by so many of the crew of the *Wavetreader*. It had not only cultural, but a very practical significance. If a Nomad went overboard, the Crayx could hook the person by the braid of hair that was so securely attached, to the head on one end, and around the waist at the other.

Suddenly, she felt the shortness of her own hair, carefully oiled to keep it out of her eyes.

"Do the Crayx *always* rescue anyone who falls off the ship?" She tried her best to sound merely curious, and not as though she were asking the most important question in the world.

"Need to be able to sense you," Darlara spoke with eyes narrowed, her gaze on the doorway of the cabin where Parno had gone to change his clothing.

"But if they sense you?"

The woman nodded, visibly gathered her thoughts, and turned back to Dhulyn. "Well, not during a storm, then must stay well away from the ship, in case the fury of the waves slaps them up against us." She shrugged. "Could injure themselves, or break the ship, so of course . . ."

"Not during a storm," Dhulyn said. *Of course.*

The wind had been freshening since sundown, and most of the middle watch were in the rigging, reefing the sails before it became too dangerous to go aloft.

Don't understand it *All this wind and the clouds still above us*

Mean you understand it all too well

Darlara Cor shrugged, knowing her brother could feel the movement, even if there wasn't light enough to see. Even if he weren't looking at her.

Know as well as I what brings this wind, and the rain those clouds tell of Malfin said. *But didn't come out here to look at the sky, not in the middle of my watch, you didn't*

Want to talk of the Mercenary Brothers

Thinking you don't mean both of them *It's Parno Lionsmane's caught your eye, not the woman*

He's Pod-sensed Darlara waited until Mal nodded. *Woman's not* she said. *Luckier for us if she was*

There's something, though, Mal said. *She's not an ordinary landster*

Dar shrugged, willing to concede the point.

So what about the Lionsmane

He should stay with us She looked sideways at him. *I want him*

Mal whistled, but Dar had the feeling he was not as surprised as he made out. *Nothing less* *A sworn Mercenary Brother, and Partnered*

Darlara nodded. *Partnered, well and good, but what's that mean* *Landsters, Mercenary or no, what do they know of real bonds* *There's more important things* *For one, he's Podsensed, his bloodline's useful—more use to us than to himself alone, and with us, managed well, he can have young with as many as he wants*

No way to know he wants any

Easy to find out

Said "for one"

She turned to face her brother, leaning her right elbow on the aft rail. They were standing within sight of the wheel, but Deputy Pilot Liandro Cor was notorious for his concentration, which the gusting winds only increased.

For two, he's a rare fighter, and could teach us all he knows *And for three, he'd be more on our side in the talks with the Mortaxa, couldn't help it*

Dhulyn Wolfshead would have some say there, she's Senior

Still, couldn't hurt

True. Malfin leaned both forearms on the rail next to her. *What if Lionsmane won't be parted from his Partner* *What then*

She could stay, be useful

But Malfin was already shaking his head. *Hard enough to have a senseless one on board for a short time, but for life, near impossible* And how would it be for her, left out, more and more alone* He shook his head again.

I want the Lionsmane *I'll part him from her, you'll see* *I will, or the Crayx*

They agree

The bloodline, the help, just as important to them

That wasn't a "yes," but Malfin nodded, as Darlara had known he would. He was her twin, after all, as well as her cocaptain. What she wanted for the ship and the Pod, he would also. What she wanted for herself, he would help her to get.

Parno Lionsmane stood with his back against the aft rail, where his playing would be less obtrusive for those trying to sleep in their hammocks belowdecks. The notes, carefully chosen to simulate the sounds made by the Crayx, seem to fall away into the dark silence beneath them like a leaf wafting slowly from a tree.

The sound was repeated, two octaves deeper, from the depths below them.

"Say it's easier to hear your thoughts when you play," Darlara said from his left.

"But I can't hear theirs?"

"That will come, given time. And then, if I am sharing at the same time, can also hear mine."

Parno looked at her, but from the seriousness of her face, she was stating only fact. "Interesting," he said, taking refuge in the banal from thoughts he was glad she could not hear. "Let's see what they make of this."

He began playing an old tune that the years had given many flourishes and variations, though he now played the simplest. At first, he sensed nothing else, then, a soft echoing came from the sea, and a resonance in his head as well. The crew nearest them started to tap and then stamp their feet in time to the music. Soon, it seemed that everyone on deck was joining in, and people were even coming out of the hold and the deck cabins to take part, until the *Wavetreader* itself began to shiver in time with the stamping feet, like a huge drum.

Parno concentrated on keeping the pipe's air bag filled to the maximum, and began to pace across the deck, keeping time himself. To each side Crayx surfaced, their wet scales flashing brilliant colors in the morning light.

Dhulyn sat humming in the sun, her back against the wall of the cabins on the central deck. She had a selection of weapons spread around her, like a cobbler surrounded by his tools. It was moist on shipboard, and even the air seemed to taste of salt. Like the crew working on the metal parts of the ship in rotation, Dhulyn would clean and oil some of their weapons every day, until they were on land again.

Malfin Cor approached, nodding to her and rubbing sleep from his eyes. Parno's piping, and the crew's drumming, had awakened even those below. He went to the rail across from her and looked smiling out at the Crayx.

"Did they try to kill him?" Dhulyn asked.

Captain Malfin turned, his eyes widened in shocked astonishment. "The Crayx? *Never.* Never in this world."

"But they did cause my Partner to fall. The ship did not run against rock or reef."

"No. Mean, yes."

Dhulyn took pity on the man. She would get no valuable answers if he kept tripping over his own tongue.

"Yes, they did cause him to fall. No, the ship did not run against anything."

"Well, might say that it ran against the Crayx."

"They're so clumsy, then? Or are there mean spirits among them, as there are sometimes in a herd of horses?"

His silence made her look up from her favorite wrist knife, and she paused, cleaning rag hovering in the air.

"*Horses* are individuals," he said finally. "Crayx are not . . . are not horses," he said. He took his upper lip between his teeth. Looked toward where Parno sat on the rail next to Darlara a few spans away, his feet braced against the narrow bench that ran below it. He was back to noodling on his pipes, pausing with his head at a listening angle, and noodling some more.

Dhulyn glanced back at Captain Mal, took up her wrist knife once more. "They are a flock, you herd them across the sea, they let you ride them. In what way are they not horses?" *And not individuals?*

Malfin pressed his lips into a thin line. Dhulyn waited, bent over her polishing. Either he would tell her, or he would not.

"They're a Pod," he said finally, shrugging. "Might's well say they herd us, as the other way 'round." He fixed his eyes on her face, looking for Sun and Moon only knew what reaction. Dhulyn kept her expression neutral.

"Have their migration routes," he said. "And we follow them."

"That's how you don't get lost crossing the Long Ocean," Dhulyn said, glad as always to add to her store of knowledge. "But you have sails, a rudder. You do navigate on your own."

"It can happen we get separated, and there're harbors where the Crayx can't go. There isn't always one small enough to be comfortable in the Midland Sea, for example."

"And you must sail to find them again."

"Well, yes, though they also find us."

"They see so well? Or can they track you through the water?" Dhulyn held up her hand. "Wait. They sense you. Your sister told me. Do you speak to them?"

"You believe such things are possible?" Malfin's expression was one of skepticism lightly covered with wariness.

"Do you know the Cloud People of the Antedichas Mountains?"

"Seen a few."

"Have you seen a Racha Cloud? Face tattooed with feathers." She tapped the left side of her face to show him where. "Large bird of prey on one shoulder, or flying above them?" Captain Mal nodded. "They are bonded, the Racha and the Cloud. They hear each other's thoughts, feel each other's sensations. The Cloud becomes part bird, and the Racha part human." The skepticism slowly faded from Mal's face, but the wariness had not completely disappeared.

"So," she said. "Are you all bonded, or is it only those of you who wear the scaled vests?"

The captain looked down at himself. "All of us, some more, others less. According to their potential. Those of us who wear the scales have a personal bond to the Pod, won't exchange. The scales, the skins are shed as the Crayx grows older, and larger."

"But how then . . . ?" She indicated Parno with a tilt of her head.

"Because of the music."

Dhulyn followed his glance to Parno. The Crayx were still surfacing and making sounds of their own, sounds her Partner was trying to match with his drones.

"Heard the music and knew, but wanted to be sure."

"Of course." Bumping into the ship—though granted, no one else on board seemed to be worried about that— dumping Parno into the water.

Malfin mistook the nature of her silence. "Nothing to worry you. Even if hadn't confirmed his Pod sense by touching him, could see *and* smell him. *He* wouldn't have been lost."

Dhulyn smiled, consciously stopping short of letting her lips curl back in a snarl. Even if he had a way to know of her private worry, she reminded herself, this was not a completely human person. The Crayx were citizens of a country no one else belonged to, and through their connection, the Nomads would see the world at least partly through the eyes of the Crayx, with whom they had at least as much in common as they had with any human being. Nothing they said or did—or believed—could be taken for granted.

No wonder they had trouble understanding, let alone being understood by, the landlocked Mortaxa. These negotiations would have been very interesting. Very interesting indeed. If only—She stopped that thought. No point in going down that path again.

Dhulyn put down the wrist knife. One of Parno's throwing rings had found its way into her pack and she picked it up, with a frown for the dull spot along one edge. She folded the oily cloth to expose a cleaner patch and glanced at the captain. "Now, what is it *you* want to ask *me*?" she said, smiling again at his startled look.

Malfin cleared his throat, looked toward Parno again, and back at her. "My sister has a mind to bed your man," he said finally. "If you've no objection." His tone ventured on the defiant.

Dhulyn thought she could understand that. Captain Malfin couldn't be sure just how far she accepted what he'd told her—or how far her acceptance of the outsider extended. Dhulyn had no intention of letting him know just how familiar she was with his fears. He knew nothing of what he'd call landsters' attitudes toward each other. He'd have no way of knowing how people looked sideways at her—not because she was a Mercenary Brother, but because her coloring marked her clearly as an Outlander. To say nothing of her other Mark, which couldn't be seen.

On the land, for the most part, the Marked were respected, trusted, relied upon. But there were many people who would nevertheless hesitate to welcome one into the family.

"My objections seem an odd thing for you to be worrying about," was what she said. "Considering how and why we find ourselves on your ship." He found some reassurance in *her* tone, evidently, for the tight muscles around his lips relaxed. "Why is it *you* ask me? Why not your sister?"

"To show the family agrees with her breeding plan, so *I* speak both as brother-and-twin, and as co-captain of the *Wavetreader*."

"Breeding?" Dhulyn was careful to keep her tone light, interested curiosity only, but she had to loosen her grip on the throwing ring before she cut herself.

"Have to be careful about breeding," Malfin said. "Even exchange between Pods doesn't mix the blood as much as we'd like. When find a landster with Pod sense, it's a good way to add a new bloodline."

"And if a child doesn't have 'Pod sense'?"

Malfin looked at her as though measuring something. "Have havens," he said finally. "Ashore. Different places. Where those children can be safe. Still our kin, Pod sense or no."

Light dawned as Dhulyn realized what Malfin meant. "Landed kin. Where your ships are built, and where you can make repairs that can't be done at sea."

"They are secret, the havens."

Dhulyn smiled. "I will tell no one except Parno Lionsmane."

"Have called yourselves Partners, you and the Lionsmane. Does that mean Darlara is out of luck, or that *you* would claim the child, if there is one?"

"'Partners are a sword with two edges.'" The words from the Common Rule came easily to her lips, but she knew they wouldn't satisfy the captain. How to explain it? Even Mercenary Brothers who weren't Partnered found it hard to understand. She snorted. Then again, it couldn't be harder to explain than the Crayx.

"We are life Partners, but we're not wed, or mated, or whatever you call that relationship here on the Long Ocean. It means . . . we live and fight together. We would always go into battle on the same side." She paused groping after the words. "There is a ceremony. Afterward . . . when we are in the same room, or near one another, we know it; our hearts may even beat in the same rhythm." She looked away from the captain's eyes. "Every Mercenary hopes to die in battle, on our feet, sword in hand. The best we hope for is to die at the hand of one of our own Brothers who fights for the other side. But Partners will never die at each other's hands." *Not by my hand,* she thought. *Not by my hand.* "It's something like being a twin. Impossible to explain to someone who isn't one, and no need to explain to someone who is."

"Twins don't bed with each other." It was half a question.

Dhulyn smiled and gave him half an answer. "I only said it was something like."

"I would rather give *you* a child." Parno Lionsmane had never said these words aloud, but he got the reaction he expected from his Partner.

Dhulyn smiled the smile she saved only for him and shook her head. "We've been Partnered, what, seven years? If you were likely to give me a child," she pointed out, "it would have happened already."

"You've never Seen anything?" He'd never wanted to ask, but now that they were talking about it, he had to press his advantage. He might not ever have another such excuse. She *had* been behaving oddly the last few days, but he'd put it down to nostalgia, being at sea reminding her of the childhood she'd had on the *Black Traveler* once Dorian the Schooler had rescued her from the slavers.

"Once I thought so. I Saw myself laying out a game of Tailors with a young redheaded girl. Not so dark as I, but not so golden as you."

"And you thought . . ."

"And I thought. But it turned out to be the young woman who is now Queen of Tegrian."

Parno laughed out loud. "You're right. She could have been ours, if we went by coloring alone." He frowned. "I've never fathered a child, that I know of."

"Well, I'm sure I would have noticed if I had ever quickened." She gave him such a look of wide-eyed innocence that Parno cuffed her shoulder.

"How is it you think that it never happened?"

"I was given enough potions and drugs in the years between the breaking of the Tribes and the time Dorian rescued me. I always assumed that had something to do with it."

"Shall we ask a Healer, the next time we run across one?" This time Parno thought he might have gone too far. There again was that white stiffness in Dhulyn's face that he'd seen in the hold of the *Catseye*, when they had first met the Nomads. Her eyes narrowed, and she seemed to be looking within.

"We'll still look for a Seer to train you," he assured her, more to break the silence than for any other reason. "That's still our first goal. I'm just saying, if we should happen to meet with a Healer, that's all."

"Yes," she said. Then she cleared her throat and said it again, more naturally this time. "Yes, why not? The next time we run across a Healer, we'll see what can be done."

"After all, you still have your woman's time, that must mean something."

She nodded. "But being that you cannot give me a child," she said. "What are your thoughts about giving Darlara one?"

"I have no objection, in principle." Parno cleared his own throat, half-surprised to find that he did not. "Even if you and I have a child together," he pointed out, "we wouldn't raise it ourselves."

Again, Dhulyn nodded. Most Mercenaries took steps *not* to produce children. Still, the Common Rule gave guidance even for things that rarely happened. Mercenaries who had children with other Mercenaries, not always Partners, never raised the children themselves. There was always one Schooler—at the present time it was Nerysa Warhammer, Parno's own Schooler—who kept a nursery for such children, and sometimes ordinary families were found. The life of a Mercenary Brother did not allow for the rearing of children. Tough and skilled as they were, few Mercenaries lived long enough to be certain of bringing up a child. The time was sure to come when, as Dhulyn always said, the arrow would have your name on it.

"Almost a month to cross the Long Ocean," he said.

"Usually time enough, if a man and a woman are determined."

"My soul—" Parno broke off, then reconsidered. There was one way to check, and Dhulyn would have thought of it long before he did. Her woman's time had passed, but only *just*. Her Sight would be at its clearest. "Would you See for me? Would you use the tiles?"

Parno watched her face closely, nodding to himself when the usual reluctance, the flaring of the nostrils and the twist of the lips that always followed this suggestion didn't come. She still wasn't ready to tell him why she was looking secretly at the tiles. *Goes on much longer, I'll have to ask,* he thought.

Dhulyn pushed herself upright and rounded the table, laying her hand on Parno's shoulder as she passed him. Her small pack was on the lower bunk where she'd pushed it after stowing away the weapons she had cleaned. The ancient, silk-lined olive wood box that held her personal set of vera tiles was in a pocket she'd made along one side. She rounded the table again and sat down opposite Parno, setting the box on the table between them. She searched through the tiles until she'd found Parno's own tile, the Mercenary of Spears, and gave it to him.

"Close your hand around it," she said. "Think of the question you'd like answered."

"How does that help?" he asked. "I don't bear a Mark."

"It does no harm," she said, as she sorted out the Marked tiles, the ones that did not form a part of the ordinary gambler's vera set. The straight line, representing the Finder; the Healer's rectangle, the Seer's circle with a dot in the center, the Mender's triangle, long and narrow like an Imrioni spearhead. The only unique tile, the Lens, was in its own tiny silk bag, drawstrings made from thin braids of Dhulyn's own hair. She set aside one each of the Marked tiles, then made sure all the other sets, the coins, cups, swords, and spears, along with the remaining Marks, were facedown. Placing her hands palms down on the tiles she shuffled them, all the time concentrating on Parno's question.

DHULYN IS STANDING ON THE UPPER AFT DECK, IN FRONT OF THE WHEEL. THERE IS VERY LITTLE WIND, AND IT SEEMS AS THOUGH THE SHIP DOES NOT MOVE. BUT THE CURRENT CARRIES IT, AS IT CARRIES THE CRAYX. A MOVEMENT, AND A TAIL LIFTS LAZILY OUT OF THE WATER, ONE FLUKE OF WHICH IS HOOKED THROUGH THE CHILD'S HARNESS. IN A MOMENT, DHULYN IS CLOSER TO THE RAIL, AND SHE SEES, BELOW THE CHILD, BELOW THE CRAYX, DEEPER THAN SHE SHOULD BE ABLE TO SEE WERE SHE NOT SEEING, SCHOOLS OF FISH, PLANTS FLOATING JUST AT THE EDGE OF WHERE THE LIGHT PENETRATES THE WATER. COMPARED TO THESE OBJECTS, THE SHIP MOVES SWIFTLY, INDEED.

THE CRAYX'S TAIL LIFTS THE CHILD HIGHER, OVER THE RAIL OF THE MAIN DECK, AND DEPOSITS HER, LAUGHING, ON HER STUBBY LEGS. THE CHILD CANNOT MAINTAIN HER BALANCE, AND LANDS WITH A THUD ON HER BACKSIDE. SHE DOES NOT CRY, HOWEVER,

BUT TURNS OVER ON HER KNEES AND PREPARES TO STAND UP AGAIN. HER HAIR, STILL SHORT, IS THICK, COARSE, AND A DARK GOLDEN BROWN. HER EYES, WHEN SHE TURNS TO SMILE AT DARLARA WHERE SHE STANDS BY THE RAIL, ARE A WARM AMBER.

DHULYN NODS. SO. DARLARA LIVES, AND THERE WILL BE A CHILD . . .

TWO WOMEN STAND IN A CIRCLE WITH A SHORTER, OLDER MAN. THEY ARE ALL THREE DARK-HAIRED, THOUGH THE MAN'S HAIR IS THINNING, AND ONE WOMAN HAS A PRONOUNCED WIDOW'S PEAK. THEY HOLD HANDS, AND ARE CHANTING, OR SINGING, THOUGH DHULYN CANNOT HEAR THEIR VOICES. THE MAN LIFTS HIS HANDS FREE, AND DHULYN SEES THAT HE HAS SIX FINGERS ON HIS LEFT HAND . . .

THE SLIM WOMAN AGAIN, HER DELICATE CHEEKBONES MORE HARSHLY REVEALED NOW, HER SHORT CAP OF CRISP, SANDY HAIR GRAYING. SHE PEERS INTO THE EYEPIECE OF A LONG CYLINDER ALMOST AS THICK AROUND AS THE WOMAN HERSELF IS. DHULYN CANNOT SEE THE END OF THE CYLINDER; IT PASSES THROUGH THE ROUNDED CEILING OF THE ROOM THE WOMAN STANDS IN. NEXT TO HER IS A TABLE, COVERED WITH CHARTS, AN UNROLLED PARCHMENT HELD OPEN WITH A MUG OF SOME DARK LIQUID AND A PAIR OF CARTOGRAPHER'S COMPASSES. THE WOMAN MAKES AN IMPATIENT SOUND, TURNS TO THE TABLE, SHUFFLES THE PAPERS AROUND WITH HER LONG FINGERS UNTIL SHE FINDS A SCRAP THAT HAS NO WRITING ON IT, AND MAKES A NOTE BEFORE TURNING BACK TO THE EYEPIECE. . . .

NO MORE, DHULYN THINKS, NO MORE. BUT THE VISIONS CONTINUE.

THE FLOOR TILTS AND BECOMES THE DECK OF A SHIP. A STORM RAGES—

NO!

"You're green as a grass snake, are you going to be sick?"

"Idiot! Out of the way!"

Five

"**B**UT CAN HEAR YOU *better* when you play."
Parno Lionsmane let the chanter of his pipes fall from his lips. "Which is a fine thing for them, but is doing nothing for me."

"Your mind relaxes with the music," Darlara said.

Parno rubbed the back of his neck with the hand not holding his pipes. He had an idea. "Tell them to be ready."

He set his pipes on the deck in front of him and shut his eyes, taking three deep breaths and letting them out slowly. He let his eyes fall open and fixed them on his chanter, the third sound hole down. Another three breaths. Nothing but the sound hole. A hole was nothing. Absence. No sound and no hole.

Suddenly his throat closed and his stomach dropped as a wave of fear washed over him, pimpling his skin and setting his heart hammering. He blinked, blew out his breath sharply, and looked up. The fear subsided, but his heart still hammered.

"There. Felt that."

"Anything wrong with making me feel happy?" Parno could hear the annoyance in his voice.

"Fear's the easiest to be sure of. Happy feels different for everyone."

Parno nodded. That was undoubtedly true. He leaned over to pick up his pipes, and when he glanced up, Darlara was smiling at him.

"Wouldn't have known you were afraid, if I hadn't known what was coming."

Parno stood up. "I've been afraid before," he said. "I know fear won't hurt me."

Darlara's smile changed, and he found himself smiling back.

Parno was easing the door of the cabin shut, but at a sound from behind him, he relaxed, letting the concentration of the Hunter's *Shora* dissipate. Not even he could walk into Dhulyn's room without awakening her.

"Out of curiosity," she asked, her rough silk voice coming from the dark shadow that was the lower bunk. "Where is Captain Malfin sleeping?"

"When Malfin's on watch, Darlara isn't." Parno sat down on the end of the bench nearest him, the air bag of his pipes letting out a bleat as it pushed against the table's edge.

"I heard you in the night, playing to the Crayx."

There was light enough coming through the shutters that he knew she could see him nodding. "They can hear me, that's certain. And when they answer, I can—almost—hear them. Darlara says that if I stayed here, the Pod sense would awaken fully, eventually."

"And what did you say?"

"I told her that for Mercenaries there is no 'eventually.' "

Dhulyn rolled to sit upright, swinging her legs free of her blankets. "There's that." She pulled up one leg, resting the heel of her foot on the hard wooden edge of the bunk and wrapping her arms around her knee.

Parno considered telling her about the fear, then decided against it. She would find a way to laugh at him about it. "They don't speak, exactly, but I do get glimpses," he told her instead. "They see the world differently."

"Parno, my heart, they live underwater."

Dhulyn got to her feet, pulled her sleep tunic off over her head, and reached for her linen trousers and multicolored vest, lying over the bench where she had left them.

He waved her observation away. "But think about what that means. Even in the smallest things." He frowned, searching for an example. "For us, 'down' is only a direction to fall—however carefully we might control the falling. For

the Crayx, 'down' is another right, or left, north, or south."
He shook his head. "I'm not explaining it well, but better, I
think, than it was explained to me."

"It's hard to explain what you take for granted as normal." Dhulyn frowned, reaching around to her left to tie her
first sword sash. "Do the Nomads share their thoughts with
the Crayx?"

"Just like Racha birds and their Clouds, yes. But there's
more. All adult Nomads can see through the Crayx's eyes,
and the Crayx through theirs. With the Racha, only the
bonded Cloud can hear the bird's thoughts. But while you
are with a Crayx, if it shares the thoughts of another, you
can share them, too."

"And they share your thoughts?"

"Apparently. Think of it, my soul. To be able to hear another's thoughts, even indirectly, to be able to converse,
mind to mind."

"I already know far more than I need to about what *you*
think."

Parno laughed and caught the biscuit she threw at him.
All the same, he thought, *I'd give my best sword to know
what you're thinking, right now.*

"You'd be able to do this, then, eventually?" Her brows
drew together.

"Ah well, I'll learn what I can now, and hope for more on
the trip back. These Crayx have other tasks besides teaching me."

There. There it was again. That change in her face, sub-
tler this time, but unmistakable. Ice-gray eyes suddenly
dark as she paled, the blood shifting away under her skin.
Just now, while they were talking, what he was beginning to
think of as the "old" Dhulyn had resurfaced. Animated, curious, already thinking of how to apply this new knowledge
of the Crayx to what she knew of the world, of the *Shora,* of
the Brotherhood. But now that guarded, shuttered look had
returned, her face a mask, with something hidden underneath.

Surely she couldn't believe that he would follow the
Crayx, Pod sense or no? Parno pressed his lips together,
finding himself annoyed. How many times did he have to
prove to her that he was as much a Mercenary Brother as
she was? That he wasn't going anywhere, and never would?

A good thing we're Partnered, he thought, half angry, half amused. If any other woman annoyed him this much, he'd have to kill her.

"Come, you know you'll tell me eventually," he finally said. "Whatever the problem is that's worrying you, you can't keep it to yourself forever."

A flash of consternation passed over Dhulyn's face, flecked through with surprise, and then his Partner smiled. "Did you not just tell me that for Mercenaries, there is no 'eventually'?" Almost, *almost* that was her normal tone, her normal expression.

"Not good enough. What stops you—we've changed direction," he said, coming to his feet. Mercenary Brothers could not afford to become disoriented in the heat of battle, and their sense of direction was strong and well trained. They had been traveling more or less northeast, or northeast by east with the wind steady behind them since leaving the Letanian Peninsula and the Herculat Straits—the easternmost point of the continent that was Boravia—more than half a moon before. Now they were heading almost directly north.

Dhulyn was already at the door to the cabin and Parno followed her out to the main deck where they found the crew assembling in the large open space between the afterdeck and the central cabins. Both captains were standing on the afterdeck, clearly preparing to address the crew.

By now Dhulyn Wolfshead had become accustomed to the way the Nomads reacted to Parno. The nods and small salutes—some, she saw, even touched their fingertips to their foreheads in the Mercenary manner. But what made her well-Schooled instincts uneasy was the number of people, of both sexes, who touched Parno as he passed them by.

Luckily, they didn't also touch *her*, or she would have had to do something about it. Dhulyn had quickly realized that, due to their shared Pod sense, the Nomads accepted and included Parno in a way that did not include and accept her. She was used to being excluded—even if she hadn't been a Mercenary Brother, her coloring and height marked her clearly for an Outlander. Even Darlara's increasing air of possession hadn't bothered her—she was used to women who were bedding Parno looking on him as their own. What could be more natural for the period of time the passion lasted? But this was something different. The more Parno was accepted, the more she was excluded. And not just by Darlara.

Something told Dhulyn that it was entirely due to this connection the Nomads had with Parno that space was cleared for them until they reached the front of the group, looking up to where Malfin and Darlara stood together on the aft deck. A light mist was falling, and many of the crew came pulling on rain gear, mostly short capes made from the supple discarded skins of young Crayx. But rainy and cold as it was, all of the crew were present, including children, who stood quietly with their teachers.

Now that she knew what to look for, Dhulyn could see the telltale differences in the movements and carriage of some in the crowd that showed there was already some kind of communication going on. Those on watch, for example, were clearly not being relieved, nor were they trying to move closer.

Perhaps it was this feeling of being left out that led Dhulyn, once they were near the front of the group, to touch her forehead to Ana-Paula, who stood to one side of the captains, her hand resting lightly on the big wheel. When not on watch, the chief pilot had revealed that she shared Dhulyn's interest in the games of chance that could be played with vera tiles.

"Speak aloud," Darlara said. "For Mercenaries, and for children."

Dhulyn smiled. This would be the first time she'd been put into the same category as children.

"Helm," Malfin called. "Give us the heading."

"New heading," Ana-Paula said. "North by northwest."

Any ordinary person, perhaps even the crew themselves, would have been ready to wager that no one reacted to the chief pilot's statement. But any Mercenary Brother would have sensed the sudden shifting of mood as dozens of pairs of lungs breathed in, feet were shuffled, throats cleared, and eyes flashed to meet each other.

"North by northwest, it is," Darlara said.

Now there were actual murmurs among the children.

"Most of you will have learned by now that there is another Pod to the north of us, but may not know that is *Sky-dancer Pod*."

Now the murmurs gained in substance, and even adult voices were raised in tones of excitement as crew members spoke to one another. Dhulyn caught Parno's eye. Casually, very slowly, they moved so as to stand almost back to back.

"Heard right," Darlara said, as if she were answering some remark spoken aloud. "Been seven years since we were in the same current with any of the Dancer Pods, and we'll lose less than a day by turning to share current with them now."

"Any who think our mission can't wait less than a day, speak now, you'll be heard." Malfin looked from side to side and up into the rigging, scanning the crowd for any upheld hand.

"Go ahead, Captains," someone called from the rear. A laugh rippled through the crowd.

"Mikel can't wait," someone else called out. The laughter broke out in earnest.

"Any unmarrieds from the stern watch can exchange," Darlara said, smiling. "And some from the bow watch. You know who you are. As many as three of each gender may go if there are Skydancers willing. Tell me or Malfin before the evening watch begins."

"When will we sight the *Skydancer*?" It was the teacher, Josel, who asked.

"Should see her at dawn."

The assembly broke up, some heading almost immediately belowdecks or into the upper cabins out of the cold and mist, others gathering in twos and threes to discuss the news privately.

One young man remained leaning against the starboard rail, apparently not as interested as the others. Dhulyn recognized the young man Conford, who had been tricked into challenging Parno that first morning.

"Do you disagree with the delay?" she said. "Or are you thinking of making a change?"

"That won't be me," he said, lifting his chin to point out several unmarried crew members who were putting their heads together over by the port rail. "Came only five months ago, myself. Won't exchange again. At least . . . not without leaving children." He looked back at her and Dhulyn sensed there was more to his tale than what he was telling her. "Not everyone can, or will go."

"The captains—"

"Can't," Conford said. "Nor any other who've children too young. Or who might have a relative less than two generations distant with the other Pod. The Crayx keep track, how close the bloodlines." He looked away, and then back at her from under his long, black lashes. "Captain Darlara's hoping to start a whole new line with a Mercenary babe from your Partner."

"We wish her luck," Dhulyn said.

"And you, Dhulyn Wolfshead? Like to start a line of your own?"

"I've no Pod sense," Dhulyn reminded him.

Conford's face stiffened. "Had forgotten. Meant no offense, Mercenary."

"And none taken."

"We didn't see a sign of the southerners that day," Xerwin said, pulling his travel-stained tunic over his head. His friend Naxot was unusually quiet, but it gave Xerwin a chance to practice what he would say in his report to his father the Tarxin. His officers had been left behind with the Battle Wings, manning the forts on the southeastern frontier—not that they'd contradict him, but not putting his men into embarrassing situations was what made Xerwin such a popular commander. "But the *game*, Naxot. Fattest deer I've ever seen. You should come next time, I tell you—"

"Do you think your father would be very angry if I petition to withdraw from my betrothal to your sister?"

Xerwin stiffened, turning to look at Naxot carefully for the first time since he'd arrived in his rooms. The man's face was drawn, and the worry line between his eyebrows was new. *Thank the Caids he's not looking at me,* Xerwin thought. His face was his weak spot, he knew; he still had trouble controlling his expression quickly. Nothing on Naxot's face gave him any clues, so Xerwin decided to treat his friend's words lightly.

"It won't be that much longer," he said. "Surely you can find some court woman willing to amuse you, if that's the problem?" Xerwin deliberately chose the one possibility guaranteed to make his friend blush. Naxot's family were devoted followers of the Slain God, and notoriously orthodox in their social behavior, expecting even their sons to wait for marriage. Not for Naxot the casual encounters which made Xerwin's life more tolerable. Of course, this orthodoxy made Naxot's Noble House excellent allies—the very reason Xerwin had suggested the betrothal in the first place.

But this time the little half-smile of embarrassment that usually followed any teasing along the sexual line failed to form on Naxot's face. This was serious, then.

"My father the Tarxin would be very angry," Xerwin said, judging that bluntness was called for. "Such a request would do more than damage the alliance between our families, it would be an insult he could not overlook. I would not advise your father to approach mine on this subject."

Naxot set aside the breastplate he'd been toying with, staring down at the smoothly tiled white-and-black floor between his feet. "That's why I was hoping you might speak for me."

Xerwin felt his face stiffen into what he thought of as his court mask. "I? I might speak? You wish to break off a betrothal which was made at my suggestion, and you think *I* might speak for you?" Xerwin took a deep breath. It would break Xendra's heart if he let this happen, but at the same time he had to wonder what could make Naxot back away from an alliance equally advantageous to his own family.

"When I proposed this match a year ago, you seemed pleased enough," Xerwin said, aware that a hint of steel sounded in his voice. "Come, Naxot, what's changed you?"

"I haven't changed," Naxot said finally, straightening his shoulders in a way that reminded Xerwin of one of his junior officers bringing him a bad report. "But Tara Xendra has."

Xerwin's hands balled into fists. He could see Naxot's nose smashed and bleeding on the carefully fitted tiles. The pattern began to make his eyes swim. He took a calming breath, keeping his face turned away until he had himself under control. Even if he didn't take his sister's feelings into account, he could not afford to lose the favor of such a powerful family. True, Xendra had been ill, very ill after her accident. For the longest time they feared—but the worst had not happened, thanks to the Healer and the other Marked from the Sanctuary. Xendra was still not quite herself, that was true. But to suggest that there was anything out of the ordinary . . . Xerwin turned back to his friend.

"Xendra's fine," he said. He picked up a bathing robe and pulled it on. "I haven't had a chance to visit her yet, but my advisers tell me her health has continued to improve during my absence on the frontier."

But Naxot lowered his eyes. Just like that junior officer. Xerwin's advisors had also told him the rumors.

"My sister is not Marked." Xerwin frowned, finding his sword inexplicably in his hand. He put it down, slowly. "You know as well as I that the Sanctuary has examined Xendra and declared she has no Mark. Do you suggest that my sister, daughter of Xalbalil Tarxin, the Light of the Sun, is in some way unworthy of you?"

"I would not care if she were Marked," Naxot said, so simply that Xerwin believed him. "She would still be your sister. But," he shook his head. "It is I who have become unworthy of the Tara Xendra. She is too far above me now."

Xerwin blinked at Naxot's unexpected words. "She has the same rank she's always had." A Tara could not inherit the Tarxinate, but it was not unheard of that the husband of a Tara should become Tarxin himself.

Naxot leaned toward him, eyebrows drawn down. "There may be things even your advisers were not prepared to tell you. The Tarxin, Light of the Sun, has been to see your sister many times in your absence. Each time he comes from her with some new wonder." Naxot's voice dropped to a whisper. "She has explained the magic of the lodestone, and has caused rain to fall."

Xerwin sat down heavily on the bench behind him. What was Naxot saying?

"We are living in the age of miracles." Naxot's voice was thick with awe. "First, Paledyn are reported in the lands across the Long Ocean, and now, Mages arise in our midst. The days of the Caids return."

Xerwin blinked. Naxot's orthodoxy wasn't lip service, he realized. Wasn't—like the Tarxin's—a political expediency.

"It is clear Tara Xendra has an Art," Naxot continued. "The Scholars of my House say that the Witches are Holy Women. Brides of the Slain God. They do not marry, but . . . *bless* only those whom they choose." Naxot blushed deeply.

"I cannot . . ." Naxot's voice cracked, and he lowered his eyes. "Such things—I cannot presume."

Xerwin felt the hairs on his arms rise. *Holy Woman.* It couldn't be. Little Xendra? *His* Xendra, who only a few short months ago was begging him to teach her to play *peldar*?

This time it was Xerwin who looked away, as the implication of his friend's words sank in. *Really* sank in. Holy Woman. Storm Witch. This is what had been happening in his absence, and not a word from his so-called advisers, nor from his father, the wily old jackal.

Xerwin licked his lips, drew in a deep breath through his nose, and straightened his shoulders. Naxot was right. The betrothal should be set aside, no doubt. And Xerwin should talk to his sister.

Six

WHEN THE KNOCK CAME, Carcali raised her head with a jerk. The room spun for a moment before settling down again. She gripped the edge of the table, blinking and shaking her head. This wasn't her room. Where was her desk? Why didn't her feet touch the floor? The knock sounded again, and it all came flooding back. Her room was gone, her whole world—she swallowed and pushed that thought away.

"Come," she said, and shivered at the sound of the light voice that piped from her lips. She could get the commanding tone right, but would she ever become accustomed to the voice?

She rubbed at her still unfamiliar face, looking up as the door swung open to reveal her senior lady page. The woman had likely functioned as nurse or governess, but in the months since Carcali had awakened in this body, Kendraxa had acted less and less like a nurse.

"Have the maps come?" Carcali asked. She picked up the quill pen that had fallen to one side, resting it against a smoothed chunk of marble where it would not drip on anything important. She was only now coming to terms with the tools and equipment they used here, and much valuable time had been wasted before she'd learned about the Scholars, and then still more convincing those around her that she was serious about an inquiry to them. It had finally taken an order from the Tarxin himself for her requests to be acted on.

"Well now, no, my dear. I mean Tara Xendra." Kendraxa

fiddled with the loose ends of her headdress. "The copies are being made, but it can't be done quickly."

Carcali shut her eyes. She'd forgotten the forsaken things had to be copied by hand. *That* Art had been lost along with the rest of the civilization she'd destroyed. Her nails bit into her palms as her hands formed fists. She wasn't going to think about that.

"The Tarxin is waiting for the results of my work," she said.

"The Scholars have their work as well, Tara. Your father the Tarxin, Light of the Sun, understands this."

Carcali wrinkled her nose, unconvinced. The Tarxin hadn't struck her as the kind of man who liked excuses.

"Why *are* you here, then?"

Kendraxa blinked, her eyebrows slightly raised. Carcali bit her lower lip. Again. That was blunter than anyone expected from her, since the Tara she appeared to be was only eleven years old.

"You have visitors," Kendraxa began.

Ice crawled up Carcali's spine. "Not the Healers," she said, skin crawling at the thought of the six-fingered man. "The Tarxin promised . . ." Carcali's voice faded away as her mouth dried up. The Tarxin. The father of the body she was wearing. He'd promised her no more Healers when she told him what she could do. At first, he hadn't believed her, but she'd been able, as frightened as she was, to call clouds to cover the sun. That, and what she'd told him about the lodestone had bought her his promise that the Healers wouldn't make any more attempts to push her out of Xendra's body.

But now, with all this delay—

"Please," she said, trying her hardest to push the fear out of her voice. "Please don't let them in."

"No, my dear, of course not. They can stay outside. It's a petition only, from House Fosola, south of the city. They have had two nights of cold winds, earlier than would be expected at this time of year, and now the winds have died away, they fear a killing frost in the next few days if conditions do not improve." Kendraxa waited and when Carcali didn't reply, she added, "They come with your father's permission."

Carcali's breathing was already returning to normal.

"What do they grow?"

A pause, not very long, perhaps, but long enough that Carcali knew she had done it again. This was something the girl Xendra would have known. She pressed her lips together.

"Peaches, Tara Xendra. Peaches, grapes, and other soft fruit."

"Is it only warmth they need? Not rain?"

"The petition asks for warmth only, Tara Xendra."

"Very well." Carcali was already picturing the crude map of Mortaxa she had in her possession. If she brought the winds up from the west, across the sea, was there enough coastal plain for the moisture to drop before the winds hit the higher ridges? She became aware that Kendraxa was still standing in front of her.

"Was there something else?"

Kendraxa looked at her steadily for a moment, her eyes narrowed, and her mouth in a determined line. Finally, she came closer, clasping her hands together under her bosom. "You *must* rest, my dear. You are looking very thin, and I know you are not eating enough."

Carcali stared, but the older woman did not lower her eyes. Finally, Carcali nodded.

"Once I've dealt with this frost, Kendraxa," she said. "I'll lie down. I promise."

"Shall I close the shutters?"

"I'll take care of it. Thank you, you may go."

The woman smiled stiffly, bowed, and let herself out.

Carcali sat for a few minutes, one hand hovering over the map of Mortaxa before she grabbed the map next to it. She unrolled it carefully, using the weight already on the table to hold it open. She studied it for a few minutes before she nodded. The lands belonging to House Fosola *were* close enough to appear on a map of Ketxan City. That gave her more detail and should make things easier for her.

She rubbed her face, wincing at the feel of unfamiliar cheekbones, unfamiliar lips, skin, hairline. They were asking for just a small fix, a tiny change really, in the big scheme of the climate. But it would be useful, she'd be helping people. And she should be able to do it easily, without full immersion in the weatherspheres. She'd done exactly this kind of thing plenty of times before—even apprentices could do it.

And she *had* to do it, she told herself. Her Art was her way to safety, here in this strange new world.

Carcali began to take slow, deep breaths, feeling the tingle of the Art move through her bones, dance along her muscles until she could feel the hairs lift on her arms. She closed her eyes, let her head fall back, and raised her arms, reaching literally as well as figuratively for the spheres—she brought her arms down abruptly and wrapped them around herself, biting her lip.

It was all right. No problem. She hadn't lost the connection to the body. She just had to be more careful, that was all. She couldn't risk—she *wouldn't* risk.

She refocused her attention on what she was doing.

Spoke the words.

Felt herself lighter, lifting. For a moment, floating, she looked down and saw her body, not her *real* body, but her body now, Xendra's body. *This* was the body she now wore, this dark-haired child, and *this* was the body she was anchored to, and would return to. She forced its imprint on her floating consciousness, solidifying the connection, making sure it wouldn't break.

Delicately, Carcali let herself float, keeping a firm grip on her anchor, on the body. Not the best way to perform the Art, not very accurate, but safer, so much safer, and the only way now that there were no other Weather Artists to help anchor her.

She let her eyes wander, looking for the rich reds and golden oranges that would tell her of warm air. It was farther afield than she would have expected, and full of the gray mist that meant moisture. A great soggy warmth over the sea.

She hesitated, frowning. There were two ships on the surface of the water, the sinuous movements of beasts beneath the surface. She moved closer. These had to be Nomads. No one else had ships. She looked back at the warm mass of air. Without surrendering herself to the weatherspheres, there was no way to be absolutely certain, but she was sure that the ships were far enough away. They'd be safe enough. A little rain, a little wind, nothing they couldn't handle.

Turning, careful of the anchor, like a kite on a breeze, Carcali gathered the chosen currents together, tugging the warmth free of the moisture. Suddenly, she lost control, felt the air mass twisting and spilling away from her. She refocused her attention, and reached for the warmth again, breathing it in, making it more closely a part of herself, building it into a skin around her. Turning, she looked for the place she wished the warmth to be, and found it.

Gently at first, and then with more force, she released what she had gathered, breathing out the warm air, pushing it toward the coastline where western Mortaxa met the Long Ocean, over the islands, across the coastal plain and east to the rolling hills and fruited valleys that needed protection from the frost.

They did not meet the *Skydancer* until after midday. The wind had been freshening and dying away all morning, making the topsails flap and the ropes creak. The sun that had scorched them so badly the day before was hidden behind a sky heavy with haze, making the air, if it were possible, even hotter and the sea a dull gray mass of crumpled pewter. Parno Lionsmane had taken out his pipes, but had set them aside almost at once. Dhulyn had called for a very short *Shora* that daybreak, but they both had very little energy in the breathless heat. They had been sailing northeast, and north again toward the waist of the world.

What wind there was now blew against them, and the *Wavetreader* hove to as soon as the other Pod was sighted. Parno had thought the *Wavetreader* large, but *Skydancer* was half again the smaller ship's size, four-masted, and with at least two more decks. As she bore down on them, Parno glanced around, narrowing his eyes and tightening his grip on the rail when he saw no one, most especially not Dhulyn, seemed at all concerned.

Blooded sailors, he thought. You could never tell whether to be worried or not. It did seem, however, that this was a time of "or not," as it took the other crew only a few moments to spill the winds from their sails and bring the two ships together, riding side by side—though not close enough to board in the manner of pirates. Parno could see the faces of the *Skydancer*'s crew clearly, see gold and silver glinting at wrist and throat, almost make out the color of their eyes. They were much the same physical type as the

Nomads he already knew, wiry and small, though there seemed to be more variety of skin shading and hair color than on board the *Wavetreader*.

"Can't they get us any closer?" he said to Dhulyn, thinking it must involve some deep seafaring lore he knew nothing of. "At this distance they'll have to put a boat over the side."

"Look down."

Of course. How could he have forgotten. This was more than a meeting between the two crews. Parno scanned the water between the ships and saw Crayx swimming in the open space between the two hulls. Unlike the humans, there was very little variation in color between the two Pods, but somehow Parno knew that he was looking at members of both groups.

#Welcome# #Pleasure#

Parno jerked upright and stepped back from the rail as if avoiding the point of a sword.

"What?" Dhulyn closed her hand around his wrist, her palm cool and dry against his hot skin.

Parno licked his lips. "I heard them just now, they speak to one another."

"And not just to one another, I think." Dhulyn shot a glance over her shoulder.

Parno looked around. The crew of the *Wavetreader* were gathering on deck, crowding the rail and climbing into the rigging the better to see their kin on the other ship.

"No one's saying anything." he said. "No greetings, no questions, nothing."

"The younger children are not here," Dhulyn said.

"Only those over the age of ten were allowed on deck." *And how do I know this?* he thought. There were several of the older youngsters close by them, round-eyed with anticipation. And while a few were waving, and some were wriggling and shoving each other with excitement, none of them were making a sound, neither calling across to the other ship, nor chattering to each other.

Dhulyn was right. It was not just the Crayx speaking to each other. Like a humming in his blood, only just beyond the reach of his own underdeveloped Pod sense, Parno could feel the communication taking place around him.

Movement on the other deck caught his attention as two ruddy-haired men, as alike as matched daggers, bronzed and freckled by the sun, approached the rail of the *Skydancer* just as Darlara and her brother came to the rail not far to Parno's left.

"What do you wager all the ships' captains are twins?" Dhulyn spoke in her nightwatch voice, a thread of sound audible only to him, and then only because they stood close enough to rub shoulders.

"No bet," he answered in the same voice.

Anything louder than the nightwatch whisper might well have been heard, Parno thought, for the ship around them had now fallen eerily silent. Even the children had ceased their fidgeting, and all that could be heard were the sounds of the stays creaking as the wind sang through them, a light slap as small wavelets touched against the hulls. A sail flapped once and was still. Suddenly the air seemed oppressively hot and damp, and the pressure shifted.

Dhulyn nudged him with her elbow, pointing with her chin. Darlara and Malfin stood each with one hand on the rail, their free hands linked, their eyes open and fixed on the twin captains opposite them. They and all the crew that Parno could see had similar expressions. Not, he was glad to note, the empty-eyed look he'd seen once or twice before when people shared their mental spaces with other creatures, but more like the look of thoughtful concentration that he had seen on the faces of people using their Mark to Find or Mend.

Now and again an emotion flickered across someone's expression, shown by a frown here, a lifted eyebrow there. As the communication continued, there were fewer and fewer smiles.

#Impatience# #Annoyance# #AngerFear#

Parno didn't flinch this time, though he felt himself frown in response to the momentarily glimpsed emotions.

"They communicate simultaneously, all of them at once," Dhulyn said, this time in a more normal voice, as if she felt the same need that he did to disturb the silence.

"It's certainly faster," he replied, hoping that he'd kept the longing and eagerness out of his voice.

She nodded, showing him the ghost of her smile. "Do you think there's time for us to—no, here they come."

It was most obvious in the children. Everyone around them relaxed, and took deep breaths, though they hadn't been noticeably tense. Some of the crew shrugged, and resumed whatever tasks the sighting of the *Skydancer* had interrupted, those on watch back to their posts, parents and minders hurrying to rejoin the younger children. There were looks exchanged, some frightened, some still frowning, a few speculative.

Parno waited, and when Darlara turned from the rail, she looked, as he'd expected, to him. She smiled, but with a small twist to her mouth, as if her news were mixed.

"No exchange?" he asked her, guessing what the main concern would be.

"Oh, no. That'll go as planned."

"And what won't?" Dhulyn said.

Darlara smoothed stray hairs back from her face and sighed. "*Skydancers* say the Mortaxa build their ship still, don't wait for us as agreed."

"And there have been waterspouts in the spawning grounds," Malfin added.

"Though no deaths, thank the Caids, since it's the wrong time of year." Dar gave Parno a sidelong look.

"Maybe warning us, showing us what they *could* do," Malfin said.

"Waterspouts?" Parno wasn't sure he'd heard the word before.

"Great swirling columns of water that rise up out of the ocean and then disappear again."

Parno turned to Dhulyn, watched her gray eyes go ice-cold as comprehension dawned. "Tornadoes," she said, her voice hard. "At sea, the waters would rise," she added. Her normally pale skin had whitened even further, and Parno wondered if she were actually about to faint.

"*Skydancers* say the time to negotiate has passed," Malfin said. He turned to put the sudden wind at his back. If possible, the air seemed even hotter than before.

"Cursed Mortaxa never meant to negotiate in the first place," Darlara said. "Sent us on an errand to keep us quiet and out of the way."

"Maybe so." Malfin shrugged. "But this needs more thought. We've the Paledyn now, after all. Surely the Mortaxa'll have to meet with us."

"Why? Heard what the *Skydancers* said. Cursed Mortaxa don't care what happens to any of us."

But Dhulyn had drawn a little apart, no longer listening. "You don't need us," she said, her rough silk voice gone hollow. "We don't have to be here." She had that stone look again. She looked at Parno. "They didn't need us."

"What of it? It's a bother, no doubt, but we have to be somewhere, what difference where?" Was she still worrying about that hearing back in Lesonika? Or, he wondered as another idea took form, was she now worried about the consequences of his Pod sense?

"You don't understand." She took him by the upper arms as if she were about to shake him. "We didn't have to be here. We didn't have to come!"

It took Parno a second to realize that Dhulyn was shouting, the noise of the wind had risen so high.

Then another voice was shouting, and everyone was looking up to Devin in the Racha's nest, and looking to the east in response to his signal.

There, on the horizon, a narrow band of white sky showed under the blackening cloud that stretched above it, hard-edged as a sword blade. Across that narrow band of whiteness, a thin black thread seemed to join the cloud to the sea.

A bell began to ring on deck, loud enough even to be heard over the noise of the wind.

"Get below." Dhulyn didn't wait for Parno to obey her, she took him by the arm and shoved him toward the nearest open hatch. She didn't want him in the cabin; even that was too close to the rail for comfort. If there remained any way to avoid what she'd Seen coming, this would be her only chance.

"I can help."

"You know nothing about sailing and less about storms at sea." Her skin dimpled at the sudden drop in temperature as the air pressure plummeted.

"The Crayx can help me."

"Gone," Darlara was shouting into the terrible noise.

"Can't risk staying here. Even if the spout doesn't get them, they could be smashed against the ships."

Just what Darlara had told her on that first day. The Crayx couldn't help them in a bad storm.

The main and top foresails were being hoisted, despite the force of the wind that threatened to split them, in an attempt to use that very wind to separate the two ships as quickly as possible.

"No exchange after all," Dhulyn said, though no one heard her.

The thread of dark color between the roof of cloud and the sea was thicker now. The waterspout was changing its shape with every moment, like a tremendous snake joining sky and sea. It began to widen at the top where it met the cloud, and spread out at the bottom like the base of a candlestick.

Now the same crew who had hoisted the foresails were reefing them—not tidily as they had always done before, but simply dumping them to the deck and shoving them out of the way. The ship had turned, and they would run with the sea.

Dhulyn's ears popped with the change of air pressure and suddenly she could hear the waterspout itself, a wild, shrill, rustling noise sweeping toward them, the gray waves white with foam under the twirling, swaying, monstrous pillar that came nearer and nearer, dancing across the troubled water.

Out of the corner of her eye Dhulyn saw someone miss a toehold in the rigging and go overboard—between water and wind she could not see who it was. Parno had moved over to the hatch, but was only helping to fasten it down.

A deafening CRACK to starboard, as two of the *Sky-dancer* masts broke off short, one after another. Almost in the same moment the waterspout was upon her, seeming at once to suck her up into itself as pieces fell.

As the *Wavetreader* was flung up on her beam ends, Dhulyn fell sideways, grabbing as if by instinct at the rope that caught her across the face. She wrapped her arm around it, and, turning her face into the wind, looked for another place to anchor herself—or for someone else to grab on to.

"Parno!" He could not possibly hear her, but he was looking her way, grinning like a madman. *My soul,* she mouthed.

He began to make his way up the slanting deck toward her, half walking, half climbing. Dhulyn braced her feet, and stretched out her arm until her shoulder cracked, as he reached for her hand. He turned his foot on what looked like someone's arm sticking out from under a fold of sail, and was sliding away from her as the wave hit and swept him overboard.

Dhulyn was screaming as she unwrapped her arm from the anchoring rope, screaming as she used it to swing herself over the rail and let go. Screaming as she hit the water and the breath was knocked from her lungs.

In Battle and in Death.

Seven

POUNDING. STEADY, RHYTHMIC. Not a heartbeat. The heart didn't pound so slowly. Not even with drugs. And it was softer than a heart, more distant. After a while, Dhulyn Wolfshead grew aware that movement had stopped. She tried to push that awareness away, to sink back into the black, but even that effort only helped her come more completely to herself.

She lifted her head.

Immediately, the world around her rose and fell, as if she still tossed on the waves of the Long Ocean. She turned her head to one side and was sick, the taste of salt water making her shudder as it tore itself out of her throat.

She laid her head back on her outstretched arm, blinking, her lashes stuck together with salt. Her hand shook as she raised it to her mouth, her arm weighted with fatigue. She did not have enough saliva to spit on her fingers, realized that was a good thing when she remembered she'd just vomited, and rubbed at her lashes with the back of her wrist instead. No change. Was she blind, or was it just darkness? She felt the grit of sand moving under her shoulder, brushed some off her face. She pushed, inching herself backward with arms and legs so heavy they seemed to belong to someone else. Her weakness terrified her, but then the darkness drew her down once more.

When Dhulyn woke again, the sun was just clearing the horizon, properly in the west, she noted, as her sense of direction, tortured by constant movement during the hours—

days?—in the water, reasserted itself. She raised her head, pushed herself to sit upright, and looked down, frowning, as her hand touched something damp. Her nose wrinkled, and she scrubbed the hand as vigorously as she could—which wasn't very—in a cleaner patch of sand. Apparently, she hadn't pushed herself as far from the small pool of muck and seawater she'd vomited during the night as she'd thought.

"If this is the afterlife, I'm not impressed." Dhulyn winced and put her hand up to her throat, swallowed, and winced again. As swollen and rough as that time she'd had the fever in Medwain. And no sign of lemon or honey to soothe it.

So much for calling for help. But it wasn't help she wanted. Every muscle aching as though she'd had a beating, Dhulyn rolled over until she lay on her back, closed her eyes against the slanting light and took a deep breath in through her nose, letting it out through her mouth. On the third repetition she began to repeat the words of her personal *Shora,* the triggering phrase which would enhance her concentration, her ability to focus on the *Shora* she wanted to use.

But it wouldn't matter which one she used. She already knew what any of the Hunter *Shoras* would tell her. There was nothing near her. No animal, no bird, no human. Not her Partner. Not Parno.

When the shaking stopped, the sun was already much higher in the sky. Still curled in a ball, her head still cradled in her arms. Why wasn't she dead? Tradition among the Mercenary Brotherhood had always led them to believe that no one survived the death of her Partner, and Dhulyn had gone into the water with that thought uppermost in her mind.

So why, then, was she still alive? For a moment, her heart bounded—but then she took herself in hand once more. Sense reasserted itself. She and Parno had gone into the water at almost the same moment. The Crayx were nowhere near. Had he been alive, and able to keep his head out of water, he should have washed up on the same Moon-and-Stars–cursed shore as she had. And he wasn't here.

Just as he hadn't been in any of the futures she had Seen since stepping aboard the *Wavetreader.* No future with Parno in it. Before, she'd often Seen Visions of Parno older, sometimes alone, sometimes with herself. But those futures had all stopped once their feet were on the path that led to this one.

She pushed those thoughts away, willing her mind to focus on anything rather than the yawning empty hole in the middle of her chest. How many Partnered Brothers did she know of, besides Parno and herself? There were many in the tales that made up the basis of the Common Rule. Glorious deaths. There was Dysmos Stareye and Palmond the Handless. Separated by the press of battle, they had nevertheless breathed their last breaths at the same moment. Or so the tale told.

And a fine tale it is, Dhulyn thought. *But I'm alive.*

Fanryn Bloodhand and Thionan Hawkmoon. They'd died together, if not exactly at the same moment. As the one Partner lay dying, the other stood over her, sword in hand until she was herself overrun. That was what being Partnered meant.

Dhulyn sat up, blinking, and resisted the urge to scrub at her face and eyes with her salt-and-sand–encrusted hands. She must find fresh water and soon. Three minutes without air, three days without water, three weeks without food. The trilogy of the Common Rule. And one which still applied to her, no matter what she might wish for.

"Mother Sun." Her lips moved, but Dhulyn was careful not to speak aloud. *Is it your doing that I am here?* Dhulyn rarely questioned the distant gods of her people: Sun, Moon, and Stars. As a rule, her people didn't pray much. Sun, Moon, and Stars were always with you, even when you couldn't see them, her mother once said. They answered all prayers, but not always with the answer you wanted.

"In Battle, or in Death." The Mercenary salute. Was it that simple? Partners died together because most Mercenary Brothers died in battle? Because what was enough to overwhelm one would overwhelm both? Dysmos and Palmond died in battle. As had Fanryn and Thionan. Was Parno gone and she still here because there hadn't been a battle? Must she then wait for her own death to join him once more?

"In Battle *and* in Death." The slightly modified salute between Partnered Mercenaries—and seldom used even by them. That would be where she met Parno again. *So be it.*

She looked toward the sea. That pathway to death had failed her already. Clearly, something more was expected. Something more, presumably, than lying here until dehydration finished the job the sea had not done. Dhulyn pushed herself upright and began her *Shora* ritual again. She would search for water this time, fresh water. Then she'd see what Mother Sun and Father Moon brought to her path.

The spot in the hills where the stream widened into a shallow, reed-edged pool not only provided fresh water, but a couple of the sleepier fish. They were bland eaten raw, with neither salt nor lemon to give flavor, but they were food, and something told Dhulyn that death by starvation would not serve her purpose any more than death by drowning.

Ah! In *Battle*, or in Death. Surely, if *she* died in battle, it would be enough to reunite her with Parno. And she knew just what battle would suit her best. Mercenary Brothers did not leave each other unavenged—that was part of the Common Rule as well—and Dhulyn knew where the path to her vengeance lay.

The Storm Witch.

Dhulyn nodded, whistling silently as she began to stretch out each muscle in turn. First, the long muscles of her legs, arms, and back. Then, the shorter muscles of chest, abdomen, neck, hands, feet, and face. Parno had been killed by a waterspout where no such phenomenon should be—caused by that thrice-cursed snail spawn of a Witch. And when the Storm Witch was dead, Dhulyn herself could die and join her Partner.

Dhulyn gave a sigh of contentment and stood up. Now that she was fed and watered, and had rinsed off all the sand and salt in the cool pond, she felt almost her normal self. A pang stabbed her, sharp and cold. She would never feel normal again. She pushed that thought away. *Not now.* She could not afford to indulge her grief, not now that she had plans to make, a goal to reach.

She looked at the tips of her fingers and the pads of her feet. Wrinkled, but even now smoothing out. She could not have been very long in the sea, perhaps only overnight. There was no way to be sure, however, how far that frightening force of wind and wave had carried her. She felt the seams and pockets of her clothing. Sword and long knife had been lost in the water. She felt at the back of her vest, and found the inner pocket torn open and empty. So, she drummed her fingers on her thigh. Except for the lack of shoes and weapons—other than those she was born with—she was in good condition.

Dhulyn glanced up at the sun. Almost at its midday height. She picked up her vest, pulled out the laces, squatted once more at the edge of the water, and pushed the vest under the surface. She sat back on her heels, lifting the dripping vest onto her knees, refolded the sodden garment so it could be worn as a hood, and pulled it on over her head. Better sunburn than sunstroke, she thought. The layers of stitched-in and quilted-over cloth would hold water for a long time before drying out, keeping her head cool as well as protected from the sun. She leaned forward again, pushing her hands into the soft mud along the edge of the water. Some of that would help protect her skin.

But first Dhulyn waded back into the water until she was knee-deep. She took a deep breath, felt herself relax into the Stalking Cat *Shora,* and composed herself in patience, waiting for the telltale shifting of shadows below the surface that would mean fish.

When she'd captured four more of the small fish and cleaned them with the same rock she'd used before, she wrapped them in grass she soaked in the water. Finally, she pulled her linen trousers toward her, drew the waist string completely closed, forming a bag into which she pushed the fish. She set the bag to one side, along with the stone she'd used as a knife, and another, rounder stone that fit well into the palm of her hand. She examined the rocks and scrub grass around her. She had food, weapons, and a covering for her head. No way to carry water except inside her.

Belly tight with liquid, mud liberally applied to shoulders and arms, Dhulyn rose once more to her feet and tied her trousers around her waist by the legs. She'd have to eat the fish fairly quickly as it was. They wouldn't last long in this heat, and she'd want to eat them while they would still provide some moisture.

When she reached the small ridge to the east of the pool Dhulyn stopped and looked around her. The sea was at her left, to the north and west. Should she try farther inland, or keep to the coast? Downstream was what the Common Rule usually advised, but here, downstream would only lead her back to the sea.

Dhulyn cocked her head—and her stomach dropped; her vision darkened for an instant as she realized what she was doing. Parno would not be expressing his opinion, and she would never again sort out her own decision by arguing it over with him. Never again. She pushed those bleaker thoughts away.

"Just you wait," she said aloud, not admitting even to herself whom she was addressing. First, she had to find people. Then, she could die in a civilized manner, killing someone else. But only a particular someone would do. In Battle *and* in Death.

She took a deep breath, let it out with all her force, marked a higher ridge as the edge of the next watershed, and started walking.

Carcali sat on her lesser throne next to the Tarxin and tried hard not to fidget. Part of the problem was that the body she wore was much younger than her own, and inclined to fidget, and even after several months of occupancy, her control over it wasn't what she'd like it to be. Especially here and now, where she didn't really understand what was going on, and boredom could so easily set in.

She realized she was frowning and cleared her expression. If she were being honest, she'd have to admit that anxiety rather than boredom was making her fidget. She'd sent away the servant who'd summoned her to this audience, anxious to finish her mapping of nearby weather patterns, only to find someone much more senior at her door, accompanied not so subtly by a man wearing armor and carrying a spear.

"The Tarxin Xalbalil, Light of the Sun, commands your presence immediately," the counselor had said. "You are to begin to learn the needs of the realm." In the crispness of his tone Carcali had recognized, underneath the courtesy that he had to give her as the Tara, a not very well-disguised mix of skepticism, irritable impatience, and a certain amount of resentment about having been the one sent to fetch her.

Aides had hustled her straight to the lesser throne as she entered the chamber and the Tarxin, resplendent in a tunic that seemed to be made from solid gold, hadn't even looked at her as he'd signaled to the pages at the door.

At first she'd been interested; this was the first time she had seen the man in public since she'd awakened in the body of his daughter, and she took advantage of the preliminaries to glance at him out of the corner of her eye. He was short by her own standards, but on the tall side for the Mortaxa. His hair had once been as black, and was still as thick as his daughter's, but much coarser, and very straight. Xendra must have inherited her curls from her mother. Like hers, his skin was a dark, even gold, though his showed the remains of pockmarks, and the signs of frequent shaving.

His throne was made in the shape of a sunburst, and the room was lighted in such a way that anyone not on the dais would have difficulty looking straight at him. Carcali found herself nodding. Brilliant setup, really. Someone on the Tarxin's staff should get full marks for clever promotion.

Once the audience itself began, Carcali found her attention drifting. These were minor petitions, from least nobles trying to buy their way into lesser status, to wealthy traders looking for royal favor, or hoping to have disputes settled by the Tarxin himself. Strange, really, how some things never changed. The amount of time that was spent waiting for people who thought they were more important than you to make decisions about things that weren't important to anyone.

Her mind drifted away to the last time she'd spent a morning waiting like this. The decorations in the long passage of the Artists' Hall had been more subtle, simple touches of color and abstract forms, but the bench she had waited on then was more comfortable than the lesser throne. To be fair, it wasn't that the Artists had kept her waiting, more that she'd arrived for her interview early.

Why was that, exactly? Carcali always tried to be exactly on time . . . oh, yes, *now* she remembered. She'd had a fight with her roommate, Wenora, a real fight, the kind that took you where you didn't really want to go, and she'd left their rooms before either of them said something unforgivable.

Carcali had come up with an plan to solve the crisis that had suspended all classes in the Academy and was keeping all the Artists and even the senior Mages locked away in meditation and vigil. She had expected Wenora to be pleased and excited, and she'd been hurt by her friend's lack of enthusiasm.

"Come on, Car, you're only a Crafter. What makes you think that you can come up with a solution when even the Mages and the Artists are racking their brains?"

"Master Aranwe always says that a good idea can come from anywhere," Carcali had pointed out. "That we shouldn't hold ourselves back by being afraid to say what we think."

"Oh, I see you holding yourself back—never!" There had been nothing but teasing affection in Wenora's smile. "What's your big plan, then?"

"I've written it all out, but basically, they're going about it the wrong way," she said to her friend. "The earth's warming too fast, right? Well instead of trying to patch things up down here, I say we go straight to the source. We should be trying to cool down the sun."

The look on Wenora's face was priceless. "Who could do such a thing?"

"I could do it." Carcali grinned. "It would be easier if I had help, but I'm pretty sure I could do it myself if I had to. Don't you see?" In her eagerness she'd leaned forward, but Wenora remained sitting stiffly upright. "That's why no one else has thought of this. They're used to solving problems with a nudge here and a nudge there. Pooling strengths, gathering resources. They're simply not taking into account what power like mine might be able to do."

A long silence greeted her words.

"That's right," Wenora finally said. "There's only ever been one or two as powerful as you in the whole history of the Art. What a lucky thing you're here to save us all." Carcali was surprised at the bitterness and sarcasm in the other girl's voice. She'd thought they were friends, that Wenora—they'd been roommates since their apprenticeship, for the Art's sake—surely Wenora wasn't jealous of her.

"Wenora." But her roommate was keeping her head turned aside, her lips a thin line in her stiff face.

That was when Carcali had left their rooms and gone to wait in the Artists' Hall. Wenora was scared, that was all. Everyone knew that fear made you stupid, and angry, too. Wenora would get over it, and they'd be friends again.

Finally, the summons had come and she'd followed the lay page into the Council Room. There, as she'd expected, she found the Artists, the Heads of each branch of the Weather Arts. Sue Roh of Earth, Fion Tan, of Air, Bri AnM of Fire and Mar Lene of Water. And Jenn Shan, of course, current Head Artist, and the tie-breaking vote if one should be needed. Luckily, Jenn Shan was also an Artist of Air, something Carcali felt boded well for her chances, since she was a Crafter of that Art herself. There'd be two on her side—or at least two who could follow her arguments more easily.

Carcali sat down in the candidate's chair, where she'd fully expected to be sitting for her Mage's examination in two months' time, if this crisis hadn't put all classes and all examinations on hold. She'd be the youngest qualified Mage in the history of the Academy—once she was finally examined. She crossed her ankles and laid her hands palm down on her thighs. She nodded to Jenn Shan to show that she was ready to begin.

"Your proposal is interesting." The Head Artist placed her hand on the sheaf of papers before her. "It shows your great heart, and your youthful enthusiasm. It pains me to tell you that energy and enthusiasm are not enough."

The blow was so sudden, and so unexpected that Carcali felt as if the Head Artist had borrowed the skills of the Artist of Water and frozen her solid as a lump of ice. She hadn't really expected her plan to be accepted right away—she'd figured that there would have to be some minor adjustments, and she'd been ready to welcome input and suggestions, especially from the Artists.

But to be rejected out of hand. Rejected completely.

"I don't understand," she said, shock giving her the determination to speak. "Is there a flaw in my design?"

"Your design looks feasible, on the surface," Fion Tan, Artist of Air, said. "But the amount of power required ..." The older man shook his head.

"But I could do it myself if others were unwilling, or unable, to help me—"

"No," Fion Tan shook his head. "You couldn't. That's where your own inexperience is misleading you. You're not ready. You're months away from your examinations, and you would have to pass them, and pass them with the highest distinction, before you could undertake even to help in an action as far-reaching as cooling the sun."

"I *can* do it," Carcali said, hoping she didn't sound merely stubborn. "You know I'm powerful enough."

"Powerful, yes." The Head, Jenn Shan, took back the reins of the discussion. "Disciplined, no. You could not sustain your anchors long enough, and without that, you would lose control over all the forces in your hands. Power without discipline is nothing but a danger to us all."

Fion Tan consulted a notebook he had in front of him. "Discipline has been a problem for you, hasn't it? Not unexpected in an apprentice, especially one with such a great natural ability. The Art isn't easy, and the limits, while necessary, can chafe." He turned a page. "No lesser Academy in your town, I see." He looked up. "You've resisted submitting to discipline all along, haven't you? And not just ours, but even your own."

"That's not true." Carcali's hands had formed into fists.

"Really? Then you have learned all your *Shora*? You're ready to be examined on them now?"

Carcali refused to lower her eyes, even though she felt her cheeks and ears burning.

"Your adviser has spoken to you on this point, has he not?"

Even the calmer, softer voice of the Head Artist couldn't soothe her. *That's* what this was about? She hadn't been practicing her *Shora* like a good little girl? She hadn't been following their precious stodgy old rules?

"You may not be aware that your adviser has needed to speak for you often, pleading your case, asking for more time to persuade you." This was Fion Tan again. "But even he admits that you are argumentative, that you go too much your own way in spite of others." With one hand still holding his notebook open, he tapped his own copy of her plan. "Which this proposal more than amply demonstrates. There are others among your tutors who have been pressing for more severe penalties, perhaps even expulsion from the Academy, since you show little interest in our methods, and our traditions."

"Enough." Calm as it was, Jenn Shan's voice cracked like a whip, and the Artist of Air subsided, closing his notebook. "In the face of the present crisis," Jenn Shan continued, "we lack the time to look into your candidacy, Carcali. Simply put, we cannot agree to your plan. There is no Artist powerful enough to undertake it. And while *your* power is undeniable, your skills are insufficient. The Council has decided. You may go."

Carcali had stood up and left them, turning and marching out of the Council Room with her face burning and her teeth clenched. Her skills were insufficient, were they? Sanctimonious pricks. Rather the world came to an end than try something that wasn't part of their precious traditions. She'd show them.

She'd show them right now.

She had started to run, turning down corridor after familiar corridor until she'd reached her own lab space. There she'd hoisted herself into the Weathersheres Chair and hurriedly strapped herself in, hands trembling. If even one of those stodgy old beasts who called themselves the Artists Council understood her at all, they'd be here stopping her—but no, it would never occur to them that she wouldn't just go chastened back to her room like a good little Crafter. Just showed how smart they *really* were.

Carcali lay back and closed her eyes, taking a deep breath. She felt herself lift, and relaxed into it, let herself spread thin, until she was absorbed, the air her breath, the rain and moisture her blood and fluids. At one with the heat, the cold, and the push of unbelievable pressures. She looked about herself. She was swimming in the swirl of colors that were the currents of the air, like splashes of paint on an ordinary artist's palette. All shades, all colors, every shade and tint—some without names in the human language—and each carrying its own message, its own piece of information.

And there, the hot, bright streak that was the pathway of the sun.

Pain brought Carcali back to the present. She was squeezing her hands so tightly her nails were digging into her palms.

She gradually became aware that the audience was ending, people were stepping back from the throne, and lowering their heads in respect as the Tarxin rose to his feet. At the right moment, Carcali edged forward on the lesser throne and stood up. As the Tarxin turned away, he spoke to one of his attendants.

"Bring the child."

What does he want? Carcali made a conscious effort to breathe more slowly as she stepped in front of the servant. What if he said something about her coming when she was summoned? All right, that would give her the opening she needed to explain to him why studying the maps that had finally arrived was more important than sitting through a meaningless public ceremony—no. Better if she said she'd been caught up and distracted by her work. *Don't antagonize him,* she reminded herself. He was the one keeping the Healers away.

"Daughter." The man's voice was dry and cool, the word had no feeling behind it. Carcali hesitated, unsure whether she was meant to respond. "Do you now find yourself recovered from your ordeal?"

"Yes. Yes, *Father,*" she corrected quickly.

"You are feeling well?"

"Yes, I—" The blow came so quickly Carcali did not see it, could not have ducked or moved out of the way. Her cheek felt hot. Stunned, she was raising her hand to her face when another blow landed. This time she found herself on her knees.

"You will come when I send for you. You will not daydream. You will be attentive and alert. You will not embarrass the throne again. You are showing yourself very useful, far more so than could have been expected from a girl child. Your help with the crops, your knowledge of the lodestone and your suggestions about the boat building—all to the good." Here his dry voice became even colder than before. "But do not forget yourself. Do not forget who you are."

He didn't wait to hear an answer. He was gone when she looked up.

That night the winds rose, and the rain fell. Lightning struck the Tarxin's garden house and very nearly burned it to the ground.

❧

Sweat had caused much of the mud to come off, leaving Dhulyn feeling sticky, and not a little itchy. She had eaten the fish several hours before—it had lasted even less time in this heat than she'd thought. She'd considered keeping at least part of her trousers to use as a sling, but the smell of dead fish convinced her to leave them behind. She was going to die anyway, might as well be as comfortable as possible. It wasn't until afterward she'd realized that she'd left her rocks behind as well. She'd shrugged. No Mercenary Brother was ever really unarmed. The only luck she'd had so far was to find, first another stream at which she'd drunk her fill and rewet her head covering, and then a road.

She frowned. If you could call this a road. It was flat, somewhat smooth, and showed some signs of metalwork at low points. But the few prints she could make out in the dust were puzzling. Bare feet, yes. Sandaled feet, yes. And at least one print that could have been a boot. Thin wheels about an arm's length apart, yes. An animal with four two-toed feet leaving a print something like the Berdanan camel. It took her several hours to figure out what was missing, which she blamed on the heat.

There were no hoofprints. Why were there no hoofprints? She was just too tired, and too hot to consider what this meant.

The sun had lowered enough to get in her eyes when a glint of metal down the road in front of her brought Dhulyn to a stop.

People.

Her first instinct was to find cover, buy time to assess the situation. But she thought better of it. This could be her chance to find a way to shelter, to begin gathering the information she would need to find and kill the Storm Witch.

The glint of metal disappeared into a small cloud of dust, which eventually resolved itself into two guards on foot, one armed with a crossbow, the other a sword, and two larger, huskier men carrying a sedan chair between them. The two guards, deeply tanned and wearing only leather harness above their short kilts, stopped on seeing her, and spread out to flank her. She let them. The noble in the chair tapped on the side of the chair's sunshade and the two carriers lowered their burden to the ground.

Slaves? Dhulyn thought, taking a careful breath and shaking out her hands. *Mutes?* She stood her ground as the man stepped out of the chair and approached her. He wore sandals with soles thick enough to keep his feet clear of the dirt, but even so, he was only Dhulyn's own height. His skin color was much darker than her own, but he was paler than his guards. His clothing seemed eminently suitable to the climate, a long piece of vertically creased and folded linen wrapped around his lower body, topped with a short-sleeved tunic cropped at his navel and heavily embroidered in what looked like gold thread that matched the series of tiny rings piercing the edges of his ears. His sword was slung much too low around his hips, the folds of his skirt contrived in such a way as to make the weapon seem more a piece of jewelry than a method of defense.

The noble stopped a half span in front of her, put his fists on his hips, and looked her up and down. Dhulyn knew she hardly looked the part of a Mercenary Brother, naked, unarmed, filthy with mud and sweat, scratched by thornbushes, barefoot, and smelling of old fish.

She tilted her head to one side and smiled her wolf's smile. The noble backed up half a step. The guard on the left, the swordsman, suppressed a smile. The crossbowman on the right and the two chair carriers pretended they hadn't seen anything. Somehow, they all gave the impression of having had plenty of practice at that.

"You are an escaped slave," the noble said slowly, as if he expected her to misunderstand him. He spoke the common tongue, but his accent was one Dhulyn had never heard. "Tell me quickly what House you're from and I promise I won't punish you too severely."

"You are a fool," Dhulyn said, just as slowly and clearly, aware that to him she'd be the one with the accent. "Tell me quickly you won't jump to conclusions again and I promise to stop laughing at you."

The man's face darkened to the point that Dhulyn feared for the condition of his heart. The ghost of a smile on the face of the swordsman standing behind him widened to a real grin, quickly stifled.

The noble lifted his hand and the two guards tensed. "Don't lie again," the noble said, still with great clarity.

Dhulyn raised her eyebrows. "I didn't lie," she said. "You *are* a fool."

"The scars on your back show you are a slave."

"Scars don't make me slave, just as a sword doesn't make you a warrior."

The noble dropped his hand.

Dhulyn didn't need the signal, having seen from the corner of her eye that the crossbowman was lifting his weapon. As the man's finger tightened she jumped to the left and caught the bolt in her right hand. With her left hand, she pulled off her head covering and threw it into the face of the swordsman, leaped forward, and drove the crossbow bolt into the noble's hand, pinning it to his thigh, jerked his sword to free herself—*knew it was belted too low*—as she swept the noble's feet out from under him, and turned to face the two guards.

Only to find them openmouthed, wide-eyed, and staring.

"Paledyn," the crossbowman said, his weapon hanging slack from his hand.

Dhulyn stepped backward until she had all three men clearly in her line of sight.

"What are you waiting for? Kill her!" The stupid noble was pulling at his hand, apparently unaware that was the fastest way to cripple himself.

"But, Xar, she is Paledyn." Now it was the swordsman who spoke.

Now the man turned again to face her, and the color drained from his face.

"Your p—pardon, Xara," he said. Dhulyn would have bet her second-best sword it was rage that made him stutter, not fear or awe. "I did not see—I could not have expected a woman."

"I told you not to jump to conclusions," she said.

The two guards looked from Dhulyn to the noble and back again, as if expecting something more. Finally, the noble spoke again.

"I offer you my home, roof, table, and bed. I am Loraxin, House Feld." The underlings, even the slaves by the chair, relaxed.

Again, Dhulyn was willing to bet that the House's gritted teeth spoke more of his anger than his pain.

"I am Dhulyn Wolfshead, the Scholar," she replied equally formally. "I was Schooled by Dorian the Black Traveler. I fight with my Brother—" her throat closed and she had to cough and start again. "I have fought at the sea battle of Sadron, at Arcosa for the Tarkin of Imrion, and Bhexyllia to the westward, with the Great King."

"May we tend the House's wound, Xara Paledyn?" The swordsman stepped forward.

"Lay your sword on the ground and back away from it," she said.

"I assure you, Xara—"

"Just do as I say."

The man nodded, laid his sword flat on the ground, and backed away from it. Dhulyn picked it up without taking her eyes from anyone. Just as she thought. This was a real sword, not the jeweled toy the Noble Loraxin Feld had been wearing. At her nod, the two guards bent over their employer.

"It should come out of the thigh muscle quite easily with a little cutting," she said. "Unless, of course, he's complicated matters with all this squirming about."

The crossbow bolt hadn't penetrated very deeply into the man's thigh, and they detached it quickly and cleanly using the method she had suggested. When it came to removing it from his hand, however, the two guards were clearly beyond their knowledge, though it seemed to Dhulyn that the swordsman at least was contemplating the risks involved in knocking his noble patron out.

"Allow me," she suggested. "I am not a Knife, but it appears I've had more experience with wounds than you." She nudged the crossbowman with her toe. "Bind the thigh wound, will you? And you," she said, turning to the swordsman. "Brace him against your knees and hold his hand quite still."

She'd noticed, in the brief time she'd held the thing, that the bolt itself was metal, but the fletching was the more ordinary feathers, glued to the metal shaft, and stiffened, no doubt, with the selfsame glue.

"Bring me some water."

The crossbowman had finished with the man's thigh wound, and now ran to the chair to fetch a large skin. Dhulyn accepted it with a nod, rinsed out her mouth, spat out the grit that had accumulated, rinsed again, and filled her mouth with water, swishing it through her teeth several times. Handing back the waterskin, she bent over and slipped the whole fletched section of the crossbow bolt into her mouth, losing only a few drops of water in the process.

The man's hand smelled of scent—sandalwood and rose water if she was any judge—and just a little of sweat and old leather. She worried at the fletching with her teeth until the stiffened feathers were free of their glue and she could spit them out. She eased the now clean bolt through the man's hand.

She glanced up. House Feld had fainted.

"Why not soak the fletching loose with just the water?" the swordsman said, as the other guard bound up the wound.

"It wastes water," she said. "And saliva helps to dissolve the glue faster." She picked up the skin again, rinsed out her mouth once more, and took several healthy swallows.

"I'm sure House Feld intended to offer you his chair, Paledyn," the swordsman said. "But . . ." he raised his eyebrows and indicated the unconscious man he held against his knee.

Dhulyn almost smiled. "I would not have taken it," she said. "Are we far from the table, roof, and bed that he *did* offer me?"

"We were on our way to Pont House, but we will return to Feld House at once, Paledyn."

"You will call me Dhulyn Wolfshead," she told him, walking back to the chair as the two guards lifted the unconscious noble.

She hesitated, causing both men to look over their shoulders at her. She waved them on and followed, feeling the slaves' glances flick away from her as she neared them.

Loraxin Feld became aware of the sounds of sandals slapping lightly against the road surface; light voices conversing quietly. The smell of the chair carriers. His eyes fluttered open and what he saw made him struggle to sit up. The sun was at the wrong angle, they were heading in the wrong direction. A sharp pain in his hand, and a throb in his thigh brought everything back to him with a jolt.

The Paledyn.

His heart began to pound, and he forced himself to calm down, to take a deep breath. Could this finally be the opportunity he'd been seeking for so long? He'd been looking for a way to bring himself to the attention of the Tarxin, Light of the Sun. And rumor had it that the Tarxin, Light of the Sun, was looking for a Paledyn.

And now he, Loraxin Feld, had a Paledyn.

If she *was* a Paledyn. He chewed at his lower lip. Could a *woman* be a Paledyn? He had never heard of such a thing.

What if the whole thing was a trick? His neighbors playing some dangerous joke on him? He cursed himself for a shortsighted fool. If only he hadn't been so quick to offer her roof, table, and bed. He was bound now, like it or not. Female or not. She could have been trained. And tattooed for that matter. He would need to devise some way of testing her. He closed his eyes and pretended he was still asleep. *Caids,* his hand hurt.

Eight

XERWIN HAD NOT SEEN a great deal of his sister since her accident. Once Xendra was out of danger, he'd had to rejoin his Battle Wing on the southeastern frontier almost immediately. Somewhere in those foothills were camps that—among other things—were helping escaped slaves make it through the mountains. Xerwin couldn't leave his men for very long; in the Tarxin's armies, discipline was applied from the top down.

And it didn't help that he was now Tar, and had so many more responsibilities. Xerwin had thought he was busy when all he had to worry about was the First Battle Wing and the Nomads. Though his father the Tarxin had taken the trade with the Nomads back into his own hands—and badly, Xerwin privately thought—other, more highly public duties had been added. Regular oversight of the Sanctuaries and the Libraries; inspections of the properties held directly by the Tarxinate; meetings with ambassadors—especially those from the land of his betrothed. He smiled, thinking of the headdress she had sent him, embroidered with her own hands. It would be a few years yet until she would be old enough to leave her father's house.

And now, it seemed, his own sister was not likely to leave *her* father's house. The Tarxin had agreed to break the betrothal to Naxot with very little argument. Had seemed, in fact, to be pleased with Xerwin for suggesting it.

"A very good thought, young one," he'd said, his harsh voice unusually warm. "I begin to think you may actually have the brain of a Tarxin under all that armor. It's not enough, as I've often told you, to be a good soldier."

Maybe not, Xerwin thought. Still, this latest breach with the Nomads hadn't happened on *his* watch—but his father was still speaking.

"A Storm Witch is too valuable a tool to waste in breeding."

"But she'll be sent to the temple of the Slain God." At least, that's what Naxot had told him.

"Ridiculous. Oh, they'll ask for her, of course. Let them. They've no more notion of what to do with a real Holy Woman than my dog has. Old Telxorn is trembling in his sandals at the very idea that someone with higher status than his may come to live at his temple. Besides, I'm still Tarxin here, and she is still my daughter. Let them send whatever priests or attendants she must have. But Telxorn has agreed that Xendra is better left here."

After a hefty donation to the temple. Xerwin was smart enough to keep that thought to himself. His older brother, the previous Tar, had died of expressing himself too freely. Well, probably, Xerwin thought, as he strode down the corridor toward his sister's apartments, delegated to tell her of the change in her betrothal, now that she was too valuable a tool to waste in breeding.

He wondered how his sister would like being such a valuable tool.

The guards at Xendra's door came to attention and saluted him, but did not stand aside, or open the doors to her suite to allow him to enter. He smiled and raised his eyebrows, where his father would have raised his staff.

"Gorn and Tashek, isn't it?" he said, dredging their names out of his memory. It was this kind of detail, his old general had taught him, that made men willing to follow you anywhere. "A reason I should not enter?" He nodded at the door, prepared to be given some girlish excuse.

"No one is to enter, my Tar," Swordsman Gorn said. "Orders of the Tarxin, Light of the Sun."

Xerwin's heart was suddenly in his throat. "Has something happened to her? Has her illness returned?"

The door was suddenly flung open from the inside. "Do you think you're making *enough* noise? I—Oh, I beg your pardon Tar Xerwin, I didn't see you there."

At any other time, or with any other person, the abrupt change of tone would have been funny. It wasn't Kendraxa in the doorway, but Finexa Delso, one of Xendra's newer attendants. And she was giving him the kind of smile women at court had increasingly given him since his brother had . . . died.

"The Swordsmen were just telling me that no one is to enter here, Xara Finexa. On my father's orders. But it's *on* his orders that I've come."

"Oh, Tar Xerwin, surely the Tarxin, Light of the Sun, couldn't have meant *you*." Finexa fluttered her eyelashes and extended her hand as if she was about to touch him on the arm. Xerwin wasn't averse to female companionship, but he preferred those with considerably more discretion than Finexa Delso practiced.

"I'll just see that the Tara is ready to receive you, Tar Xerwin," the woman murmured in an even more honeyed voice before turning and walking to the inner door, hips swaying.

Since her back was turned, Xerwin permitted himself a small sigh and did his best not to grimace when the door opened again and Finexa beckoned him in with smiles and demure looks.

He stood blinking at the state of the room while the woman closed the doors behind him. Much of the furniture had been pushed against the walls, and Xendra's usual pastimes—her sewing, her collection of costumed dolls, and her box of vera tiles—showed evidence of neglect. Large maps had been spread across the center of the room, where a little grouping of padded chairs and small tables had always stood. Ornaments of glass, metal, and stone had been taken down from the shelves and ledges to keep the edges of the maps from curling up.

In the center of this, on her knees, was his sister Xendra. She sat back on her heels as he came in, still frowning down at the maps in front of her.

A bruise darkened her right cheek, and Xerwin felt instant rage, clenching his hands into fists. Almost immediately, he realized that there was only one person who could have struck the Tara of Mortaxa. The one person against whom even the Tar of Mortaxa could take no vengeance.

Their father. The Tarxin.

When Xendra finally raised her eyes to his, he'd had enough time to relax his fists, take a deep breath, and smile, though he found he was still angry.

And then his anger was gone, vanished like a drop of water hitting a blade being hammered at the blacksmith's forge. In the instant that their eyes met, Xendra had looked at him as though she did not know him. And while she was now smiling, and nodding, and getting to her feet, Xerwin still had the uneasy feeling that all her recognition was on the surface.

"I expected Kendraxa," he said, grasping at any thought that might explain his sister's oddness. "Is she ill today?"

"I don't know," Xendra said. Her tone was curiously flat, and her answer definitely unexpected. Xerwin would have wagered his best short sword that Xendra had known her nurse Kendraxa's exact whereabouts ever since she was old enough to toddle after the noblewoman.

"The Tarxin sent for her yesterday morning, after the thunderstorm," his sister continued. She was standing now, but still frowning down at her maps. "I haven't seen her since."

"You didn't ask?"

At this question, Xendra looked up. "I assumed the Tarxin had other duties for her."

Xerwin swallowed, temporarily speechless. What could possibly have happened that would lead Xendra to speak of her dearest companion in that cool, matter-of-fact voice? And did it have anything to do with the bruise on Xendra's face?

Kendraxa had never had any other duties in this House but attendance on Xendra. She had come to the capital with Xendra's mother for the express purpose of looking after the children of the royal marriage. Unless Xendra herself sent the woman away, their father would probably not even remember Kendraxa existed.

And Xendra had never before called their father "the Tarxin." Never. When they were alone together she had always called him "Father."

Xendra *was* changed, he thought, and in more ways than even Naxot had suggested.

That reminded him. "I have news from our father," he said. "I don't know whether it will be welcome to you."

She looked up again, eyes narrowed, face set like stone. Whatever it was that had passed between his sister and his father, Xendra at least had not put it behind her.

"You are no longer betrothed," he said—and stopped. He could have sworn that an expression of relief had flitted over Xendra's face.

"I'm sure the Tarxin, Light of the Sun, had his reasons," she said.

Xerwin licked his lips. What was happening? A suspicion began to form in the back of his mind, one that he studiously ignored.

"It was Naxot," he said. "The Scholars of his House told him that you were a Holy Woman now, and that Brides of the Slain God didn't marry in the ordinary way."

"I see," she said. "Well." She looked around her at her maps. "I do expect to be quite busy with my other duties. You might tell the Tarxin that I'm working very hard, when you see him."

"Do you have any message for Naxot?"

"Who?"

"Naxot. Of House Lilso. Your former betrothed."

This time it was her turn to stand, blinking. "Please say whatever you think appropriate," she said finally.

The floating, hazy uneasiness that had been with him since he'd come into the room suddenly solidified. There had been that moment when it seemed Xendra hadn't recognized him. Then her total lack of concern for Kendraxa. Now she appeared not to remember a man she'd been making moon eyes at her whole life.

Who are you? Once again, hard-won caution kept him from speaking his suspicions aloud. In fact, it might be better to pretend that he had noticed nothing unusual, at least, until he had a chance to find out more.

Which begged the question. Did his father know? Xendra's accident seemed to have done more than give her the powers of a Storm Witch. But was this simply memory loss that was being concealed, or—Xerwin could hardly form the thought—was this in some way no longer his sister?

He made what excuses he could—it wasn't hard, she was already focusing on her maps—and almost ran out of his sister's rooms. When he found himself heading for the Tarxin's wing, he slowed. He needed to know more before he confronted his father—if he did so at all. Xerwin tapped his fingers on the leather-wrapped hilt of his formal sword. He needed more information. Who would be likely to have it?

He nodded slowly, lower lip between his teeth.

Kendraxa.

※

The swordsman Remm Shalyn had been assigned as her guide and servant—and her minder and jailer, Dhulyn Wolfshead suspected, though *he* at least was under no illusion that he could stop her from coming and going as she pleased. She'd been given other servants as well, among them a personal maid, a woman to bathe her, and a little page boy to run errands. They were all, as far as she could tell, terrified of her. She'd refused the voluminous skirts, constricting bodices, and teetering shoes laid out for her in her suite—fashions obviously designed to show that the wearers' husbands, fathers, brothers, or owners were rich enough that their wives, daughters, sisters, or concubines need not perform any actual labor. But as Dhulyn had learned in the courts of the Great King in the West, such dress also prevented any serious physical exercise, any running away, or even any simple walking, for Sun and Moon's sake.

Dhulyn had insisted on carrying a dagger, and wearing a version of the kilt and tunic that Remm himself was wearing, although hers was slightly longer and fuller for modesty's sake—his, not hers, Mercenary Schooling being sufficient to do away completely with body shyness. Good thing she'd had some recent practice in walking with skirts. Loraxin Feld could not actually restrict her to the women's quarters, Remm had told her, though she guessed the Noble House would certainly have liked to. According to what Remm was telling her, "roof, table, and bed" was a very specific offer, and couldn't be modified.

"So the Tarxin is your ruler." Earlier conversation had established that this land was, indeed, Mortaxa. In that, Mother Sun had smiled on her.

"Exactly, though you should say 'Light of the Sun' when you say his name or title. The Tarxina, his wife. A Tar, or Tara, son or daughter. And all of their names will begin with the most noble letter 'X.'"

Frowning, Dhulyn tried to catch the accent, the "x" sound being somewhere between a "k" and a "z."

"At present, there's Xalbalil Tarxin, Light of the Sun. His heir, son of his second Tarxina, Tar Xerwin, and Xendra the young Tara, daughter of the third Tarxina. The children of the first Tarxina have all perished."

Was it Dhulyn's imagination or did Remm's voice falter a bit when he said the Tara's name?

"The Nomads who were bringing me here spoke of a Storm Witch."

"She is part of the royal household." Again, Remm Shalyn hesitated, but said nothing further. Dhulyn nodded as though her question had no significance.

"And where does Loraxin, House Feld, fit in?"

"He's one of the least Nobility, though it wouldn't please him to hear me say so. He's entitled to be called 'Xar,' and his wife 'Xara,' but you'll notice the noble letter doesn't appear until the third syllable of his name, so that marks where he stands."

Dhulyn nodded. Remm, she'd noticed, had a proper surname of his own, not just "Feld" like the House.

"You've got some very interesting scars, if you don't mind my saying so, Dhulyn Wolfshead."

It had taken some doing to get even Remm to stop calling her "Xara Paledyn." She'd had to give up with the servants—even in her own mind, she refused to use the word "slaves."

"I was a very stubborn student, and often disciplined," she said, having learned the hard way that in some places it was best not to admit you had ever been a slave.

"And the, uh . . ." Remm Shalyn gestured at a spot on his own upper lip.

"The tip of a whip that flicked 'round and caught me on the face," she said. And so it had, though it was her then master's Steward of Keys who'd been on the other end of the whip, and not her Schooler, as she was letting Remm Shalyn believe. And a lucky thing for her it had been, for the facial scar had ruined her for her master, who'd sold her to a passing slave merchant and it was while she was in that slaver's ship that Dorian the Black had rescued her.

She'd been eleven years old, and a Mercenary ever since.

"Are you a free man, Remm Shalyn, if you don't mind my asking?"

"I don't know what things are like where you come from, Dhulyn Wolfshead, but here we don't put weapons into the hands of slaves."

"Where I come from, slavery is considered a false economy at best, and an abominable practice at worst."

"Well, for the Slain God's sake, don't mention that to House Feld, whatever you do. It would give him apoplexy, for certain."

"You never know, apoplexy may suit him."

Dhulyn took mental note that Remm Shalyn called the nobleman by his title, and not more formally as "my House." A hired guard, then, who did not consider himself a member of the Household.

They had been walking through the village that had grown up around, and indeed was mostly an extension of, Feld House. The walls of town and homes alike were whitewashed stucco, such as Dhulyn had sometimes seen in the Galanate of Navra, and covered the small prominence which some long-ago Feld had chosen as the site for his House. They were at the southern end of the village when the narrow alley they followed dead-ended in a rectangular terrace enclosed by house walls on three sides, and a low balustrade on the fourth. The terrace was featureless except for weeds growing up through the cracks between the flagstones, and what looked like two large, stone chimney tops, pierced along the sides and stoppered shut with large slabs of wood at the top like corks in a bottle.

"Ah, the cistern," Remm Shalyn said. "Would you like to see it?"

Dhulyn's shoulders were already twitching upward when she stopped the shrug and took a deep breath. "Why not?"

They retraced their steps halfway back along the alley, the ground inclining away from them as they walked, until Remm indicated an archway to their right. The entrance was recessed into the wall, and guarded by a metal grille, pocked and marked with rust, which stood open. Remm stepped back in an attitude of respect, but Dhulyn waved him in ahead of her. The temperature dropped almost immediately as they cleared the threshold and began to descend the worn stone steps. At the bottom, there was barely room for them to stand on the ledge that ran along the width of a long, narrow chamber with an arched and vaulted ceiling into which were set the stone openings they had seen from above.

"There are another seven ledges identical to this one below the surface," Remm said. He squatted down and dipped his hand into the water, shaking off the drops as he stood again. "Rain's collected from all over this quarter. They tell me the cistern's never been this full before, but we've had so much rain in the past three months . . ."

Remm went on speaking, but Dhulyn was watching the ripples of water that moved outward from where he had touched the surface as they caught and reflected the tiny slivers of light that found their way into the cistern from the terrace above them through the pierced openings of the small stone chimneys.

Ripples. Tiny waves.

Dhulyn became aware that Remm Shalyn was no longer speaking. She cleared her throat.

"So the water collects on the terrace above?"

"Mmmmm." Dhulyn glanced sideways. Remm Shalyn was studying her with his head tilted to one side. "Do they mean anything?"

"What?" She heard his voice as if from far away, and her own, equally distant, answering him.

He gestured at his own temples. "Your tattoos. Is there significance to the color or pattern?"

Dhulyn swallowed, blinking. "They show where you have been Schooled. Blue and green are the colors of Dorian the Black Traveler."

"And the black line is his mark as well?"

Something squeezed her heart and her throat closed. She took air in through her nose and released it through her mouth. Forcing her hands to relax and open. "No. The black lines show that I am Partnered. My Partner has . . . *had* an identical pattern marked on his badge. He was killed in the storm that threw me into the water."

"A great loss."

Dhulyn nodded and turned away. Remm followed her back up into the outside world.

The wind had risen in the short time they were below ground, and the sky was dark with clouds.

"It appears your cistern will be overflowing by morning."
When she glanced at him, Remm was staring at the sky,
eyebrows drawn sharply down. He tilted his head to look
sideways at her.

"You said earlier that slavery was a false economy. What
did you mean?"

Dhulyn looked up but could see nothing in the sky that
would have prompted such a question. She sighed. "Everything that I have read tells me that, though slavery has been
practiced by many since the time of the Caids, invariably
the society which depends upon it fails."

"Again, I'd keep that to myself, if I were you."

Remm started off down the alley but Dhulyn stood still,
waiting until he stopped, looked over his shoulder, and
came back to her.

"Which one of us is supposed to turn in the other?"

"Pardon, Xara?" From this angle, and in the light of the
overcast sky, it was hard to be sure, but Dhulyn thought the
man had paled under his soldier's tan.

"That's twice you've implied that you and your employer
don't see things the same way; twice you've led me to do the
same. So which of us is expected to run telling tales?"

Remm pressed his lips tight together, the muscles in his
jaw jumping. "Dhulyn Wolfshead. You are a Paledyn. Loraxin Feld has no power over you. Even now messengers
are being sent to prepare your journey to Ketxan City, to
the Tarxin himself." He glanced away and then back, his
expression grim. "Me, House Feld can destroy."

"And yet you speak so freely?"

He lifted one shoulder and let it drop. "You are a Paledyn."

And you are testing me. Though it was reckless of him to
do so. Dhulyn closed her eyes. She should feel something,
she knew, something besides this sudden exhaustion, this
hollowness. The man's danger was real. Without work as a
guard he would very likely starve, or, worse, have to sell
himself to feed whatever family he had. He was trusting her,
depending upon her as would a soldier under her command
in the field. She should care.

But before she could follow that thought, however reluctantly, she was stopped by the sound of approaching footsteps.

"Xara Paledyn, the House sends for you." In the young page's voice and eye was his awareness of what might have happened to him if he had not found her—or what might still happen if she did not come with him now.

"Is there some urgency?" she said, indicating even as she spoke that she would follow the boy.

"He has some livestock he would like your opinion on." *Horses.* She began to run. Horses to take her to the Tarxin. And where he was, the Storm Witch would be.

Dhulyn was several spans ahead of her escort by the time she reached Feld House, and was through the gate and into the large inner courtyard without stopping. She had woken up that day meaning to ask where the horses were kept, and had somehow forgotten about them. Horses would help her; she was always clear-minded with a horse under her. She was three paces into the courtyard when the gates slammed shut behind her, and she dove to one side, rolling as she hit the ground and came up crouching with her back against the baked mud wall, pulling the dagger from the back of her sash.

Quickly, she scanned the open space within the gates. It was completely deserted. No guards, no servants going about their daily chores. The sedan chair which had been standing to the right of the gate when she and Remm Shalyn had gone out for their walk was gone. As was a small handcart full of melons that had been awaiting the attention of the cooks. The gates were closed, but not, so far as she could see from this angle, barred. The main House doors were likewise shut as were the smaller gates that led to the garden and rear quarters where the animals were housed.

Pounding and shouting came from the gate and Dhulyn eased herself to her feet, though she stayed with her back to the wall. That would be Remm Shalyn, and either the gate would open to admit him, or it would not. One way or the other, this strange silent courtyard would be explained.

She smiled her wolf's smile. Her blood was running, her muscles warm, her breathing soft and easy. If something was coming to kill her, she was ready.

A sound like muffled hooves came from the inner gate leading to the animal compound and Dhulyn looked up. Was it horses after all?

But the beast that came thundering through the gate swinging its heavily horned head was no horse. It had the coloring and light hindquarters of an inglera, but was massively thick through the shoulders, and its neck supported a rack of horns as thick as her arm and as sharp as her second-best sword. Its shoulders were easily as high as her own, and the look in its red-rimmed eyes spoke of something more than normal fury.

"*Blooded* demons." Anger washed over her like a tide, setting her blood pounding in her ears and drowning her in heat. Trying to kill her, were they? Just like they'd killed her Partner, the Sun-blasted toads. Well *she* chose when she'd die, thank you very much. Not a bunch of cowards who hid behind drugged animals. What? Was her death supposed to look like an accident?

"Over here, meat pie. That's right, I'm talking to you." At the sound of her voice the beast looked in her direction, lowered its head, and began to paw the ground.

Dhulyn kicked free of the kilt wrapped around her legs and shifted her knife until she was holding it like a sword. She would much rather have had a sword, even the dainty one she'd taken from Loraxin the previous afternoon, but the dagger was all she'd found in her room when she'd awakened.

She began inching sideways toward the gate, not that she thought it would open to her hand, but in order to see if the beast would follow her. She racked her brain, trying to remember everything she could about the bull jumping she'd watched one sunny spring afternoon on the Isle of Cabrea. And the Python *Shora,* for a fighter on foot against someone armed and mounted. Surely that would help.

"Come on, stew meat, what are you waiting for?"

Much faster than she had imagined possible, given its weight and size, the beast charged and Dhulyn jumped, throwing herself up and forward, twisting and arching her body. She reached for the horn to help in her vaulting, as she'd seen bull jumpers do, but the beast hooked right, and she only brushed the horn with her fingertips as she began to fall. Twisting again, she jammed the dagger in deep, high in the animal's shoulder, and managed to control her fall long enough to avoid the worst from the flashing hooves.

She hit the ground on her own shoulder and grunted,

rolling away minus one knife and plus one blow on the left thigh. Lucky thing it *wasn't* a horse, she thought. An iron-shod hoof might have broken her leg. As it was, she'd have a bruise the size of her hand and be limping for a week, though she felt little pain now.

But the beast hooked to the right when it charged. Its right, not hers. Which told her where the horns were likely to be when it tried to gore her, and gave her a chance to be elsewhere.

She rolled to the left as the beast passed through the space she'd just occupied and crashed against the wooden doors of the gate, which shivered, but held. Dhulyn got to her feet, tested her weight on her left leg, and grinned. She'd had worse in training. As she watched the beast pace around the courtyard, she kept her weight forward on her toes, knees slightly bent, arms and hands relaxed from lowered shoulders. If she really were a bull jumper, there'd be others in the yard with her to distract the animal, tire it out for her.

She would have to do that herself. Outlast the thing.

She shrugged, aware of the wolf's smile that stretched her lips, and braided the fingers of her right hand against ill luck.

The sounds of a scuffle almost made her look up. "Pale-dyn!" came the strangled cry, and a short, businesslike sword with a worn leather grip landed point down in the dirt next to her.

Dhulyn had barely enough time to grab it up when the beast charged again. This time, trusting that the animal would hook again to the right, Dhulyn ran toward it on tip-toe, gauging her timing carefully, and when the great, horned head lowered at the last moment, she stepped up onto the beast's forehead, ran lightly down its spine, and jumped clear just as it crashed against the stuccoed wall and sank to its knees, shaking its great head.

Confused, it spun around, almost chasing its tail in rage. Dhulyn found herself back where she had started, and caught up her kilt where it lay trampled into the dirt against the courtyard wall. Dangling the fold of cloth off to her left, she approached the beast slowly.

It was breathing hoarsely, its great barrel of a chest heaving, flecks of blood showing around its nose and mouth. Whatever drug they'd given it to drive it mad was having a worse effect. Unfortunately, Dhulyn couldn't count on it dropping dead soon enough.

Sun and Stars blind you. She gritted her teeth, knowing what she had to do, and hoping that Remm Shalyn's sword was long enough to do it.

"Come on, come you." On her toes now, she twitched the trampled kilt as far to her left as she could hold it, preparing to run forward as the beast charged, hoping that it would try for the cloth rather than her. Dhulyn eyed the spot she wanted, high on the animal's left side, where the angle should let her reach through the cage of bone and find the heart.

As the animal moved, she ran toward it, calling out to it as she would to a favorite horse, arching her body and sucking in her stomach as the horns swung round. In the last possible instant she thrust in the sword, turning from her heels to put her full weight behind it. Blood gushed from the beast's mouth and she was dragged to her knees still pushing down on the hilt of Remm's sword. When she felt the great heart stop, she stood up and stepped back, pulling the sword free.

Suddenly there were people around her, a strong arm around her waist, and her knees began to buckle. Remm, blood in the corner of his mouth, and a bruise forming on the plane of his left cheek.

An inner door swung open and Loraxin Feld came running out to her side.

"I'm so sorry, Paledyn, so sorry." And he was, too, Dhulyn could tell. Sorry enough that he spoke like a child, from the heart, no formal and meaningless mouthings of apologies and forgiveness. His hands trembled, he was white as the stuccoed walls behind him, and there was sweat on his upper lip, guilt as well as remorse in his face. He had thought the beast would kill her, and would now have to deal with the fact that it had not.

"You'd have had some explanations to give the Tarxin, I think, had I died in here." Her voice sounded rough and remote through the blood that still pounded in her ears.

"Please, Tara Paledyn—" It seemed she'd been upgraded from a Xara. "I don't know how this happened—an accident in moving the inglera, I will have the slaves responsible killed. And you—" Loraxin turned on Remm Shalyn. "You are dismissed, how could you let the Paledyn come into such danger?"

"You will kill no one," Dhulyn said, blinking. "After all, this was an accident." *I should sit down, and quickly.* As if in response to her thought, Remm lifted her right arm and swung it around his shoulders, bracing her. Her knees steadied. "Remm Shalyn, you are now in my employ."

"Yes, Tara Paledyn."

Nine

A T FIRST HE COULDN'T breathe, and his lungs hurt, and his head pounded, and that part of the nightmare seemed to last forever. He knew it was a nightmare because Dhulyn was not there. He thought he saw her once, her pale face and her steel-gray eyes, the scar that made her lip curl back when she smiled in a certain way, her hair the color of old blood, held back from her face in loops of tiny braids, thick with ribbons, feathers, and hidden wires.

"My soul," she said, trailing her fingertips over his face before disappearing once again into the dark that was the whole world for him now.

An immeasurable time later he felt he was not alone.

"Dhulyn?"

#Calm# #Well-being#

Parno fell asleep.

He woke up to damp darkness. His eyes were sticky and his mouth strangely dry. Great rushing gusts of air swept around and past him; deep creakings and groanings throbbed like the skin of a drum and made his bones shiver. The skin crawled on the back of his neck. He was not alone, but he couldn't pinpoint any specific life around him. He blinked for what seemed like hours and achieved nothing but sore eyes. Parno forced himself to focus on the Lizard *Shora,* feeling the warmth of sun on rock, until he stopped twitching and even the muscles of his face relaxed.

As if it had been waiting for this, glimmers of light began

to form around him. Soft luminescence illuminated a small cavelike chamber, the size of the cheapest private room at an inn, with smaller tunnels leading away from it in several directions. The substance of the walls and floor was damp and spongy, but dark as basalt. The air smelled of fish, brine, rot, and some unidentifiable musk.

#Stay#

He recognized the mind touch of the Crayx. Were they asking him, or telling him?

"Where am I? Where is my Partner?"

Parno sensed a shift in the consciousness around him, feelings and sensations that were just short of full thoughts, and once, the fleeting image of Dhulyn preparing herself by meditation and focus to read an old book in a foreign tongue.

#You were the only Pod sense in the water# came the answer to his question. A small part of Parno felt the exhilaration of knowing that he was sharing full thoughts with the Crayx for the first time, but he pushed it away. He had more important things to consider just now.

Dhulyn had gone into the water. Parno was sure of this, though he didn't know how. He had confused memories of tumbling through raging waves until his sense of direction — even his sense of up and down — had deserted him; of great winds, and of holding his breath until it seemed his lungs would burst. Like all Mercenary Brothers, Dhulyn had superb breath control, but Parno's had been augmented by years of practice with his pipes.

He rubbed at his upper arms. He was cold and his hands felt as though they didn't belong to him. He understood with acid clarity what had happened. Dhulyn *had* gone into the water after him. But she wouldn't have been able to hold her breath as long as he could, and the Crayx wouldn't have noticed her; they wouldn't have saved her as they'd saved him. Nothing, no one, could have survived the waterspout without such help.

Dhulyn was gone.

#Calm# #Let the pain flow through and past you like a cold current# #Do not hold it within#

Parno took a deep breath of salt-and-seaweed–flavored air and felt the calmness pass through him, pushing his loss before it, sweeping it like dust from his heart and soul.

"Don't," he said. His sorrow might be the only thing he had left of her. "Leave me my grief."

#Should you not release it# #Do not allow the despair you feel to kill you#

"Why not?"

#*Wavetreader* Pod awaits you#

Parno shrugged, wondering if the gesture would translate mentally. "I'd just as soon die." *In Battle and in Death.* That was more than a mere salutation. It was a promise.

#Very well# #Resignation# #If this is what you wish, you may remain with us# #Release yourself, let your awareness float as though you were about to sleep# #We thank you for the nourishment, and we welcome you to ourselves#

Suddenly, as if his mind were a dark room and someone had thrown open a curtain, he saw, felt, knew what he was really speaking with.

The Crayx were not just the creatures that could be seen from the ship's rail, they were hundreds, perhaps thousands, of consciousnesses, all sharing, all one, a vast storehouse of memories, of . . . personalities? Of souls? Neither word seem to quite fit what he could sense. This was what Darlara had been trying to tell him. He had an impression that these beings occupied an enormous space, but not like an arena crowded with people crammed into seats, rather like a vast sky full of stars, or an endless meadow full of flowers. With a little effort, he could come upon, contact, speak with, any one individual. Or he could simply share with all. And he was being offered a place in this garden of beings.

"Wait." Parno struggled to sit upright; the material on which he was lying gave under his hands. "Am I injured? Am I dying?"

#We understood you wished to die# #If your grief is too heavy a burden, and you will not let us lift it . . .#

Was it too heavy? Parno rubbed his face with his hands. How could he live without her—easy to know how he didn't *die* with her, the Crayx had saved him, unknowingly interfering with the natural process that would have allowed them to die together.

#Sorrow# #Regret#

"You couldn't have known."

#Your soul may rest with us, if you wish it# #As long as the seas have salt and the currents flow#

What about Dhulyn's soul?
#She will go to her own place#
"Without me?"
#Should you stay with us, then without you, yes#
Parno's hands formed into fists. Partners were Partners, "in Battle and in Death." And this death wasn't going to part them, not if he had anything to say about it. He tried to stand, but found his bare feet sinking into the softness around him.
"Then I won't stay, thank you just the same."
#As you wish#

Malfin Cor was on his knees, head down over the broken foresail stay when he felt Darlara closing in on his port side.
"Can't be fixed," he said without looking up. "Not to hold any kind of strain anyway. Have to save the bits for something else. 'Least the rudder's all right." He glanced up and frowned, though he'd known she hadn't been paying attention. "What's more important than the ship?"
"Not *more* important. But, Mal, he's found."
"Not—the Lionsmane?" Mal dropped the pieces of wood to lie unnoticed on the deck and straightened, resting his hands on his thighs. That meant that one would return, at least, of the thirteen missing from the *Wavetreader* and the even more damaged *Skydancer*.
Dar nodded, barely able to speak, licking dry lips that still showed edges of salt. They had both of them been wet to the skin for the hours it had taken the winds and waters of the spout to finally pass and settle, and their clothes, hair, and skin were still coated with a fine dusting of dry salt. They would wash it off the first chance they got, but the ship came first.
"Blown so far by wind and wave that *Skydancer* Pod found him and is passing him back to us," Dar said, gripping him by the shoulder. "Mal. They offered him a chance to one with them, and he refused, wanted to come back. Told you I'd have him for my own, told you he'd stay."
"But you didn't—"
She cuffed him on the back of the head. "'Course not. How could I? They can't find to save her, so they can hardly find to drown her."

Mal blinked at the serenity in his sister's tone. " 'Course not, no. But seeing you were so set on it . . ."

"Not *that* set on it." She cuffed him again. This time he raised his arm to block it. "How could you think it?"

"Don't really."

And he didn't, not really. He didn't really think Dar would ask the Pod to kill for her.

"Wouldn't have asked for it, no," she agreed, squatting down on her heels next to him. "But not sorry for all that." She shrugged. "Without Pod sense after all."

"All thinking life's important." That was the real lesson of the Crayx, what made them all different from the landsters.

Dar nodded, but in her mind she was shrugging, and Mal knew it. Of course, all thinking life was important, it was just hard sometimes to remember that the others, those without Pod sense, *could* think.

"She wouldn't have wanted to stay," his twin said finally. "And he might not have stayed without her. Have our new bloodline, for certain. A good wind and a fair current, for us at least."

Mal nudged her with his shoulder. "He'll feel her loss, remember that."

"I'll help him."

"If he wants it."

⟨⟩

#We are ready now# #Move as we show you# #Patience#

The lambent patches in the chamber where Parno had waited as patiently as he could dimmed and died out as he got to his knees and was ready to crawl. He waited, having been warned what to expect, and when finally one of smaller passages began to glow, Parno moved into it. Following that cold luminescence, he crawled for some time in a direction he felt as "forward" before he began to go "up." The colors of the tunnel walls varied from the almost black of the place in which he had regained consciousness to a rich dark pink. The air was an even temperature, hot enough to make him sweat now that he was moving, and as humid as the jungles north of Berdana. Twice, as he crawled, his ears popped, as though he were climbing in the mountains.

Just where was he, exactly? A system of underwater caves where some magic of the Crayx kept air to breathe?

Finally, he arrived at a pale green tube in which he could stand upright.

#Are you ready#

Somehow Parno must have said he was, for the next thing he knew he was slammed by a wall of moving air and water, and propelled upward, as an arrow from a bow. He tumbled once, and before he could right himself, he shot out into daylight so bright it stabbed his eyes before he could squeeze them shut. Then he was falling, and felt water around him again, and the rough, scaled hide of the Crayx.

Parno was alone when he woke up. Really alone, no one in the room with him, no Crayx sharing the mental space in his head. The first night after his rescue, after he'd shut the door in Darlara Cor's face when she'd tried to come into the cabin with him, he'd tossed and shifted until he'd finally gotten up and gone on deck. There the *Wavetreader* Crayx had spoken with him, gently, and finally he had allowed them to smooth the sharp edge from his grief at least enough to allow him to sleep.

Last night, he hadn't even tried to sleep in his own bunk but had rolled himself in Dhulyn's bedding—and fallen asleep almost immediately. Her blankets still smelled of her, that unquantifiable essence that told the deep layers of his mind that she was still here, that he did not need to stay awake and keep watch. He had not dreamed of her again, not after surfacing from the belly of the Crayx. He wasn't sure whether or not he wished to.

He noted the amount of light that entered through the larboard shutters and briefly considered simply rolling over again and going back to sleep. But something told him that if he did, he'd find his dreams invaded by the Crayx. For all that he didn't wish to succumb to the offer made by *Sky-dancer* Pod, for all that he wasn't ready to die until he could figure out how that would allow him to join Dhulyn, he couldn't just lie here. He had to do *something*.

But when he finally rolled out of the bunk, straightened the clothing he'd somehow neglected to take off, and pushed his fingers through his hair, sweeping it back from his face, he found that his determination had deserted him. There would be people out on deck, and they would speak to him. And even if they did not, he would see that look on their faces. The look that said "We are sorry," "We are here for you," "We understand." When they couldn't possibly understand.

And not just the looks. If he went out and joined them, he could *feel* them, their compassion, and their pity echoing his own sense of loss back to him. And underneath it, a sense of puzzlement, as some in the Pod wondered why so much fuss was being made over what they saw as a temporary loss. To the Nomads, their afterlife was concrete and real—it swam beside them every day, and in some sense shared their lives. Oddly, it was only the young man Conford, the one who'd been tricked into jumping him that first day, who looked at Parno with any real understanding in his eyes.

No. Much better to stay in the cabin. His glance fell on Dhulyn's packs, neatly placed, ties tied, straps strapped. All according to the Common Rule and the dictates of her own personal neatness. Carefully not thinking too deeply about what he was doing, Parno opened the pack nearest him. Much of their heavier gear had been left behind in Lesonika with the horses—Parno grimaced. He wasn't looking forward to what he would say to Bloodbone when the mare realized he had come back without her mistress.

If he made it back. He might figure out how to join Dhulyn before that. In Battle and in Death. That's what he was counting on.

He smiled, lifting out Dhulyn's second-best sword. Its balance was off by a hair—not enough to bother anyone else, but enough that any Mercenary Brother would notice it. He laid it to one side. A short sword with a very elaborate guard. Seven throwing knives. Her spare dagger. Two wrist knives, one of Teliscan make. A dozen steel arrow shafts. Two dozen crossbow bolts. A short double-recurve bow, taken to pieces for traveling, and the tools to reassemble it. Likewise a crossbow.

And a small olive wood box in a velvet bag so old much of the nap had worn away. Typical that Dhulyn kept it in among her weapons.

"Sun, Moon, and Stars," he said, unconsciously using his

Partner's favorite expletives. He slipped off the velvet bag and stroked his fingers along the wood grain. Dhulyn's vera tiles. Not the ones she would use for gambling, but a set with extra tiles. The set she used to focus her Sight.

Parno sat back on his heels. *That* was what had been nagging at him since he'd regained consciousness in the belly of the Crayx. Dhulyn was a Seer, why hadn't she Seen what was coming? She'd even used the vera tiles several times on board without his prompting her. Usually he had to nag her.

Had she Seen this outcome? Was this the *real* reason she'd tried to stay off the *Wavetreader*? Had she Seen her own death?

But then, why hadn't she told him? Parno scratched at the beard growing in along his jaw. *Demons and perverts.* He would have let Huelra die, and his blooded crew along with him—

Why didn't she tell him?

Parno picked up the box and threw it across the cabin. It bounced against the wall with such force that it popped open, scattering tiles all over the floor.

The full horror of it swept over him in one clear wave of comprehension. What was the one thing he had made her swear, over and over, on their Brotherhood, on their Partnership, *never* to tell him? It hadn't been her own death Dhulyn had seen, but *his*. And somehow, she had *not* Seen that the Crayx would save him.

And that meant that Dhulyn had saved Huelra and his crew, had jumped into the sea herself, rather than break her oath to him. Just for that, nothing else. Parno let his head fall into his hands. This was too much. How could he live having caused her death?

But had he? Now he knew the reason for her odd behavior, her watchfulness, and her occasional abstraction. They'd seen the outcomes of Visions change before—perhaps this one, too, might not have come to pass.

Except for the Storm Witch.

Parno knew the storm that had killed Dhulyn Wolfshead was no natural occurrence—and he knew who and what to blame for his Partner's death. And what to do about it before he joined her.

He was just placing the last tile back into the box when Captain Malfin Cor knocked—and Parno grimaced when he realized he'd known who it was without asking. He didn't want this, any of this. He just wanted to be left alone to take his vengeance. But he was beginning to realize that among the Nomads—as part of the Pod—you were never alone.

"Lionsmane," came Malfin's voice. "Sit in council. Join us, please." Now Parno could hear all the missing pronouns, the "we," the "you," that the Nomads took for granted, since they could not mistake one another. He heaved another great sigh, placed Dhulyn's tiles in the center of her bunk, and opened the door, blinking at the light, though the day was still gray with cloud that hung heavy and hot overhead.

Familiar as Parno was with councils both political and military, he was unprepared for how quickly the Nomads came to order, and how thorough was the silence which fell over the crowded deck. As before, younger children were sent below, out of the way, but this time Parno could sense that their minders were linked through the Crayx with the rest of the crew.

Crews, he realized. *Skydancer Pod was also present, though he could see neither Crayx nor what was left of the damaged ship. Skydancer* itself was on its crippled way south and east, Parno picked up the thought, to be repaired in one of the havens where the landlocked Nomads lived.

His Pod sense was much stronger now, and Parno could hear and follow the buzz of thoughts much more easily than he could when the two ships had come together before the waterspout had struck. Before Dhulyn had been swept away and drowned. Parno took that thought and pushed it deep. He wasn't going to share that with anyone. Trying to focus outward instead of in, as if he was pushing notes through the chanter of his pipes, Parno found he could make out individual thoughts, as well as individual people such as Darlara and Malfin. He caught a warming glimpse of the great Crayx who had saved him. Behind these surface thoughts was a buzzing, a hum that tickled at his brain, as though he brushed up against a giant purring lion in the dark.

Darlara motioned him to a seat near her, and he nodded his thanks as he took it. It was not her fault that he was alone. She laid her fingertips lightly against his wrist, and he forced himself not to flinch away. Fortunately, at that moment, there was an unmistakable call for attention, and all the Nomads became even more focused and more silent than they had been a moment before, like an audience when the prologue stepped in front of the curtain.

#Three currents flow from this spot# came the clearest thought, giving Parno the impression of great age and size. #First, we can complete the original passage, bearing the Paledyn Parno Lionsmane# here, Parno sensed a picture of himself that was partly visual, partly the sound of piping #to the Mortaxa as we said we would#

#Second, the Treader Pods can abandon that portion of the land entirely, and attempt to establish new spawning grounds, and new trading treaties, perhaps with the landsters of the other side of the Long Ocean in Boravia or the northern continent# There was a feeling of unrest from the greater group, but no one else spoke. #This would be difficult, but it can be done# the first voice acknowledged.

#Finally, we can hold the Mortaxa to account for what they have done, and somehow carry the offensive into their currents#

The hum returned, as arguments and counterarguments crossed, as support for each of the three ideas and suggestions for the final one flowed back and forth through the shared consciousness. Parno stopped paying attention. Regardless of what the Pod decided, he knew which course of action he would follow. Finally, the tension of the buzzing changed, as the argument swelled, pulling Parno out of his own thoughts and back into the collective.

Not enough to leave the lands of the Mortaxa, we must go farther This was a human speaking; the thoughts felt younger and smaller. #We could withdraw entirely, leave the land to the landsters#

Demons and perverts, Parno thought, shaking his head, not caring who could hear him.

#What says the Paledyn Parno Lionsmane#

"Think you heard me," he said, reinforcing the uncertain power of his Pod sense by speaking the words aloud. "If you'd read any history, any politics, you'd know they're both filled with the stories of people who were exiled—or who exiled themselves. Withdrawal doesn't solve this kind of problem, it just postpones it. The Mortaxa won't leave you be, even if they agree to do it, which they haven't. They're not even abiding by the agreements you have with them now."

#Parno Lionsmane is correct# came the thought from that oldest presence. #When the landsters did not know of, or did not believe in our existence, they hunted us like animals# #We were in great danger from them, and it would be that way again# #In turning away from the land, we turn away from The First Agreement and our troubles will increase rather than decrease#

#Nor is it right and fair to our human parts to turn away entirely from the land# came another thought. #What of our kin in the havens—do we abandon them as well#

Parno felt a wave of bewildered confusion, touched through with despair.

"There's a current you haven't thought of," he said. The right thing to do was so obvious to him he was surprised that no one else had suggested it. From first meeting them in the hold of the *Catseye*, he had found the Nomads ready to fight, and they'd often spoken of their skirmishes and even their wars with the landsters over trade issues. They'd been quick enough to challenge him and Dhulyn in Lesonika, and the Crayx were ready to destroy ships that trespassed on their oceans. But then, that was all defensive thinking, wasn't it? Perhaps it took a Mercenary Brother to suggest how they could go on the offensive.

"What do you propose?" It was odd to hear Malfin's voice echo in both his ears and his mind.

"Kill the Storm Witch."

The beings around him fell silent again.

The new discussion continued well into the afternoon and evening, though most of the group had found Parno's suggestion to their liking. The general feeling seemed to be that once the Witch was removed, their relationship with the Mortaxa would return to what it had been before her coming.

Parno did his best to show them that wouldn't be true either. "They're already building ships," he pointed out. "And thinking about travel and trading on their own accounts. They claim they can produce a lodestone. These are the types of ideas that don't merely go away." The fox had been shown the henhouse, and it would be very difficult to make it forget what it knew. But his words went unheard, and eventually he stopped, keeping any further thoughts or suggestions to himself. *What does it matter what they do?* he thought, eyeing the door to his cabin and thinking of his bunk with longing. Truth was, he found it blooded hard to care what the Nomads and the Crayx decided. Or whether this would solve their present problems, or give them entirely new ones to worry about.

Parno Lionsmane had his own reasons for wanting the Storm Witch dead. Reasons that had nothing to do with the Nomads, the Crayx, the Mortaxa, or their blooded trading problems. The Storm Witch had killed his Partner, his soul, and for that, she would die.

Parno rubbed his face, massaging the crease that formed between his eyebrows while Darlara uncurled the map and adjusted the woven straps that would hold it flat on the table. The Pods had finally decided to accept his idea. And when Malfin and Darlara had suggested he lead them, the assent was close to unanimous.

"Choose someone else," he'd said, weary beyond thinking. But they had persisted, and finally he'd asked for maps. He'd said neither yes nor no, but the first thing any commander would need was information.

The shutters of the cabin's two windows were closed against the gusts of wind that threatened to put out the lamps. The parchments Mal was pulling out of the cupboard under the bunks were very old, much older than the charts kept available on the wall shelves. Their inks were faded, and many showed a dark mark along one edge, as if they had at one time been kept next to a store of oil. When Parno had declared the nautical charts useless for his purpose, it had taken Malfin a moment or two, and a nudge from the Crayx, to remember that these seldom-used maps were even on board.

Does this show the detail you need? Darlara tapped an area of shoreline marked with green dots. *This is the spawning ground—*

Parno held up one hand, still massaging his eyes with the fingertips of the other. "Can you stop that, please?"

"Don't want to exclude the Crayx."

"Not asking you to exclude them." *Blood, now* I'm *doing it.* "I'm just asking you to exclude me. My head's banging like a drum. And is there anything to drink in here?"

He felt the other two look at each other before the link connecting them all was abruptly severed. A queer emptiness echoed in his head.

"Didn't practice this morning," Darlara said with the air of someone diagnosing a problem. "Nor yesterday."

Parno gripped the edge of the table with both hands and let his breath out slowly. "My Partner's dead," he said, the words falling like lead from his mouth. "Who do you suggest I practice with?"

Darlara opened her mouth, but Parno never learned what her answer would have been. Malfin straightened from digging into the storage cupboards under his bunk and put his hand on his twin's arm.

"Who'd you practice with before Partnering? Or, say, when a Mercenary Brother's alone, who'd they practice with?"

Parno shrugged one shoulder and turned his eyes back to the faded lines of the map on the table.

Lionsmane As much as he wanted to ignore it, the touch of minds with the twins standing together so close to him was stronger than he could push away.

"Lionsmane, if you grow soft and weak, how will you lead us? How kill the Storm Witch?" Parno looked up to see the two strangely similar faces staring down at him. For a moment, he wasn't sure which of them had spoken. They were out of his mind again, now that he was paying attention.

"Your plan, isn't it? *Your* suggestion that all agreed to and follow. Will be of no use to us, or to yourself, if go on this way."

He went on looking at them, a sour feeling in his belly. He knew they were right. Whatever else had happened, he was still a Mercenary Brother; *that* he had not lost. The Common Rule still held him, still guided him. He looked down at the map again, back up at them, and unclenched his jaw. "I'll sleep now." He slid himself out from the table. "Tomorrow, first watch, you get me three fighters."

He made his way out the door, staggering across the heaving deck to his own cabin, and fell into Dhulyn's bunk like a dead man.

Ten

"N°."

"But, Dhulyn Wolfshead, this is the only proper way for someone of your status to travel." Remm Shalyn was so agitated that for an instant Dhulyn considered giving in. Then she remembered that the two sturdy bearers standing next to the sedan chair were slaves and her resolve hardened.

"What is my status, exactly?"

Remm and the Feld House Steward of Keys—it was unclear to Dhulyn whether this man was slave or free—eyed one another, each clearly hoping the other would speak.

"I would say very high, Tara Paledyn," the Steward finally said. "The Paledyns are Hands of the Slain God, and in the old chronicles sat only under the Tarxin, Light of the Sun, himself."

Like a Jaldean High Priest, Dhulyn thought. "If my status is truly as high as this," she said, "then surely I may do as I please, since you could not be expected to stop me. And I tell you for certain, I will not ride in *that*." She eyed the sedan chair and its waiting slaves with distaste. She'd already learned that there were no horses available. Not here in House Feld, nor anywhere else this side of the Long Ocean. Oh, the Mortaxa knew what horses were, but there hadn't been any in these lands since the times of the Caids. Something, some illness or some act of the Slain God had destroyed them all generations before. When attempts had been made to bring horses from Boravia, they would sicken and die within days of arrival—those that survived the trip at all. Dhulyn had let the subject drop.

Remm Shalyn and the Steward were still hovering between her and the chair.

"Remm Shalyn and I will walk," she said. "It can't take any longer than being carried."

The two men remained silent, Remm carefully looking past her and the Steward examining the ground next to her feet.

"What now?" she said. "Surely even the Tarxin—" she paused to allow them time to say "Light of the Sun," "—occasionally walks?"

"But Tara Paledyn," the Steward finally choked out. "You must take *some* servants with you. Otherwise, how will you be known for what you are?" His eyes flicked at her Mercenary badge and quickly away. "From a distance, I mean, Tara, of course."

"He's right," Remm said. "Walking you can excuse as an eccentricity, but to be otherwise unaccompanied—" he shook his head. "We'll be stopped by every guard, to say nothing of every Steward and lesser noble, between here and the city."

Dhulyn let a heavy sigh escape through her nose. It was all she could do not to roll her eyes to the Sun. "What is the minimum number I must take," she said, only to spark off another debate between Remm Shalyn and the Steward. At least, with Remm to advise her, Dhulyn was able to limit her entourage to those servants healthy enough to keep pace with her, even with her sore leg.

Finally, Remm judged that they were ready to leave. Besides Remm Shalyn himself there were the two chair men who would now function as load carriers, a young boy to use as page and runner, and two women who could serve her as maids, cook her food, and carry the shade that would protect Dhulyn from the sun.

"No," she said again. "No sunshade." They couldn't possibly carry it and keep up. When she explained to the older of the women what she wanted instead, the younger was sent off and returned with a large square of linen, rather too heavily embroidered for the purpose, but serviceable. With a silk sash Dhulyn knotted and wound, she fashioned the linen square into a draping headdress such as was worn in

he Berdanan desert. She touched the embroidery on her
unic where she'd hidden the lockpicks she'd taken from her
uined vest. She'd transfer some into her headdress as soon
as she was alone.

When she saw the size of the packs the men were ex-
ected to carry, she shook her head again.

"I understand there are no horses, but surely there are
ther beasts which can be used as pack animals? What
bout that thing in the courtyard yesterday?"

"True, the inglera are large enough," Remm said. "But
only the males are both large and strong enough, and unfor-
unately, as you saw yesterday, they lack the temperament—
hey can't be broken to household use. The females are
nore docile, but they are much smaller and weaker."

Besides, Dhulyn thought. *When you have slaves, why
hould you breed better animals?*

Finally, the Steward, after requesting permission, pre-
ented her with a small handcart. This, too, would slow them
lown, but Dhulyn agreed because most of the load the two
nen and the boy would carry was food. They would bring
ll they needed with them, since it would be unheard of for
hem to hunt on what was, after all, private property.

"All the way from here to the city," Dhulyn said. "All the
and is owned?"

"Whatever isn't part of House or Holding belongs to the
Tarxin, Light of the Sun, of course."

"Of course." Dhulyn tried to keep the sarcasm from her
oice. Technically, the whole of any country belonged to the
uler, Tarxin, or Galan, or King. But in practice, very few
ulers tried to enforce their control over vast regions of
mpty land. Apparently, the Tarxin of the Mortaxa felt dif-
erently.

Loraxin Feld came out himself to bid her a formal fare-
vell.

More likely to make sure I'm really going, she thought.
The man was still white around the eyes from the "accident"
f the day before. Dhulyn had let him know that under no
ircumstances was he to accompany her to her audience with
he Tarxin.

"Remm Shalyn tells me you are ready to leave us, Tara
'aledyn." Loraxin licked his lips.

When Dhulyn did no more than incline her head, the

man swallowed and looked ill. "Let there be shade on your journey and cool water, and may you arrive in good health." The words were barely whispered.

Dhulyn decided to take pity on the man. "I will give the Tarxin your best wishes, and tell him that you have treated me well." Her voice must have carried some sincerity at least, for Loraxin began to look less as though he would lose his breakfast. "These servants," she added, "they are mine?"

The man turned so pale as to show a tinge of green. "Of course, Tara Paledyn, of course."

Lucky I don't ask for the rest of them, she thought, smiling her wolf's smile.

Despite the delays, they still had most of the morning ahead of them when they finally set out. Their general heading was northeast, away from where Dhulyn had come out of the water, but toward, as Remm Shalyn explained it, the shoreline of another sea. It was clear, however, when she questioned him more closely, that he had very little idea of the oceans that surrounded the land, and how they connected. The land, on the other hand, he knew well.

"We'll be until midafternoon walking through the plains that surround House Feld, and then we'll see the Arxden Forest in front of us. Feld maintains a guesthouse there just as the trees begin where we should spend the night." Remm eyed the servants with them. "It'll take us most of the day tomorrow, maybe longer, to get through the forest."

"It seems a hot place to find a forest."

"Trees more than you can number, taller than buildings, what else would you call it? These are all old growth trees, preserved for the production of fressian moss, from which House Feld derives most of its income, as you may imagine."

Dhulyn nodded without saying anything more. She had more experience than many with the properties of the expensive drugs made from fressian moss.

"Tell me what I can expect at the court of the Tarxin. The ruler himself, of course . . ."

"And Tar Xerwin, the only surviving heir. The last Tarxina, the third wife, died a year ago, trying to produce a son of her own, it's been said, and the Tarxin, Light of the Sun, hasn't remarried . . . yet. But rumors have it that his health's beginning to fail. It was Tar Xerwin who was betrothed last year, not his father."

Dhulyn smiled. Wherever he got it from, Remm's irreverent attitude was a relief compared to the constant bowing and fussing of the others. He seemed even more relaxed now that he was working for her, and readier to talk.

How and what do I pay him, she wondered.

"Tara Xendra, she's the third wife's daughter. Rumor has it that, since her accident six months ago, she's become a Holy Woman, or a Weather Mage—though who knows really. Some say *she's* the one behind the discovery of the lodestone, but I don't see how *that* could be. Maybe she's Marked and they're just trying to keep her out of the Sanctuary. No official announcement's been made in any case. But you'll probably have the most to do with the Council of Houses, and the Priests of the Slain God."

Dhulyn nodded, but her thoughts had run down another path. So it was the Tarxin's own daughter, Xendra, who was the Storm Witch. That would make a hard job even harder.

"The Marked live in Sanctuaries?" she had the presence of mind to ask when she realized Remm had stopped speaking.

"How else could we be sure their talents are kept available for all and are being used wisely?" Remm gave her a wide-eyed innocent look and Dhulyn found herself smiling before she remembered she had nothing to smile about.

"And the Slain God?" she said.

Remm Shalyn became instantly serious and moved closer to her, lowering his voice. "As a Hand of the Slain God, you're obviously not a heretic yourself, Dhulyn Wolfshead. Heresy is technically legal, but unbelievers generally find themselves losing status. Most guards and the military and the Tarxin, Light of the Sun, follow the Slain One. We go to him when we die, ready to rise with him when the need comes. Some say the Nomad crisis will cause him to rise, but I say they should stop smoking fresa."

But Dhulyn had already relaxed. "We call him the Sleeping God," she said. "Soldiers and Mercenary Brothers follow him in Boravia as well. You mentioned the military—what of them?"

"The Battle Wings are stationed at outposts along the frontiers, with two training camps in the east. The Tarxin is the official Commander, but it's been Tar Xerwin's responsibility since he came to manhood. He's very popular with the men, so it's said, but they can't come closer than ten days' march of Ketxan City, so much good that would do him if he fell out with his father."

"No military in the capital itself, then?"

"The Light of the Sun's personal guard is the only official armed force in the City. The Houses have guards and escorts, naturally, but there are strict limits as to how many, and how they can be armed."

Shortly past midday, with the Arxden Forest in sight, Dhulyn called a halt for food. An outcropping of rock was tall enough to give them shade, and there were several boulders of a convenient size for sitting. Once she'd chosen the spot, however, she found she had to allow the servants to set up her own seat first, with Remm allowed—somewhat grudgingly, it seemed—to sit near her. No other seats were prepared, and at first it seemed the servants intended to stand for the whole time. When she couldn't persuade either the women or the two men to sit down with her, Dhulyn finally ordered them to sit apart in another section of shade to get at least some rest while they enjoyed their own meal. Even then there was some shuffling of feet and uncertain glances from the young page.

"If you don't rest, you won't be able to help me later on," Dhulyn pointed out finally. That did the trick, and she was able to sit down comfortably and drink her juice mixed with wine and eat smoked duck legs.

"What about a least House, like Loraxin Feld?" she said, after washing down the first of the duck. "Would he have a seat on the Council?"

Remm snorted, speaking around a mouthful of duck. "Not likely. Even though it's called the Council of Houses, it's really limited to the Great Houses, and they are very watchful over who belongs. Under them would be the lesser Houses, then least, the plain landowners, merchants, and so on—and it's not always easy to tell which is which. Loraxin Feld, for example, his family started out as merchants. They've only been a House for five or six generations, and believe me, no one forgets it. Finally, there are the tradesmen, usually family connections of a least House or landowner, or soldiers such as myself."

"And then, below everyone else, the slaves." He nodded.

"Speaking of which, what is the process for freeing them?" she asked.

Remm paused, a dried date stuffed with cheese halfway to his mouth. "Freeing them?"

"Yes, what documents do I need, what clerk do I bribe. You know, the process by which I can free these people, for example?" She gestured with her free hand to the other patch of shade.

"You want to free them?"

"Yes."

"Why?"

Dhulyn studied Remm Shalyn's face. He watched her with a measured expression. "I disapprove of the practice of slavery," she said finally.

To her surprise, Remm burst out laughing, slapping his knee with the hand that didn't have a wine cup in it. "You remind me of my great-aunt Tella. Married above herself and made up for it by having just that prim way of speaking. 'I disapprove.' " He laughed again.

Dhulyn lifted one eyebrow. No one had ever called her prim before. "You haven't answered my question."

Remm leaned forward, elbows on knees, turning the empty cup around in his fingers. Dhulyn waited. She knew a man thinking when she saw one. And she'd wager her second-best sword she knew what he was thinking about. Trust her, or not? Nothing she could say would help him decide. He'd have to come to his own conclusion, based on whatever he already knew about her.

"It's highly illegal to help a slave to his freedom. Or her freedom, for that matter." Remm stopped turning the cup, but he did not look up. "The penalty for doing so is—"

"Let me guess, slavery." At least he looked at her then, if only fleetingly. "There are no freedmen, then, in Mortaxa?"

"*Freed*men? Who would feed them? How could they live?"

"Having prepared me with this warning, what is your true answer?"

"There are those who feel as you do. They . . ." Remm looked directly at her, grinning. "They disapprove of the practice. There is a group. Runaways are helped. Some go by sea—though none of those by my hands, mine all go by land. There are lands to the south, beyond the mountains, where men can live free." He shrugged. "It's said Tar Xerwin's latest campaigns have been to the foothills, trying to find the source of the help that's been coming to the slaves."

Dhulyn eyed him carefully. "That's what *you're* doing, hiring out to these Houses, here in the outlands, helping slaves escape."

He shrugged again, grinning at her.

"My arrival, my taking you away, must be upsetting your plans."

Remm straightened, looking around at the plate of food, and offering Dhulyn the last stuffed date. "We can't free slaves everywhere we go, or it would be noticed. I don't mind going somewhere I haven't been before. I can renew old acquaintances, perhaps make some new ones."

"And you have a way to recognize one another." She waved the food away.

"We do." Remm popped the date into his mouth and chewed. Slowly.

And he obviously was not going to tell her anything more. Dhulyn began to laugh—only to stop short, her breath stopping in her throat. How could she be laughing? Only hours ago, it had seemed impossible that she would ever laugh again.

She nodded once more in the direction of the other patch of shade, where the servants—no, the slaves—waited for her to finish her lunch. "And these? How badly are they *really* needed to maintain my status?"

"We could manage," Remm said. "A Paledyn, with one sword servant—but not everyone wishes to be freed. And they *all* must agree."

Dhulyn shook her head. "Don't tell me you didn't give that careful thought when you were picking out which ones would come with us. When would it have to be done?"

"Tomorrow. There are ways out of the fressian forest. We can arrange it tonight."

~⌐

Xerwin found it harder than he'd expected to find Kendraxa. He'd been able to establish pretty quickly through his own servants that the woman was still in the House, but her exact whereabouts had not been so easy to pinpoint. It was not until the next afternoon that the Royal House Steward himself brought Xerwin the information that Kendraxa was now to be found in the Tarxina's apartments, empty since the death of the Tarxin's last wife. Xerwin had not been in his stepmother's rooms since the woman's death the year before. He found Kendraxa at a northern window, embroidering a red headdress with golden thread.

"Please, do not trouble yourself," he said as the woman hastened to rise to her feet as he entered the room. When had she become so old? He'd always thought of Kendraxa as no older than his stepmother had been, perhaps ten years older than himself. Today she looked thinner, more tired, and with more lines around her eyes than she should have. He took the seat across from her, noting that even when she was alone in the apartments, Kendraxa had taken the lesser chair.

"Are you comfortable here? You've been so long with my sister."

"I am. I thank you, Tar Xerwin. You won't remember, no reason you should, but I lived in these rooms with the Tarxina before the Tara Xendra was born, so they're familiar to me, you might say." Still, there was something subdued in her tone.

Now that it came to the moment, Xerwin hesitated. How could he ask what he'd come to ask?

"I don't think my father has ever punished Xendra this way before," he said finally, trying to keep his smile sympathetic. "Though it's hard to say which of you would feel the more deprived."

"Indeed." Kendraxa's eyes had returned to the work in her hands. The needle gleamed in the sunlight streaming in the window.

Xerwin leaned forward, his elbows on his knees. "I saw my sister yesterday," he said. "Or rather, I saw the Tara Xendra."

Kendraxa's hands stilled, the needle halfway through a stitch. *She knows,* he thought.

"How long?" he asked. "Come, you can tell me." He saw her consider it, and thought it a mark of the woman's desperate isolation that she chose to answer.

"Since the accident," she said, her fingers pulling the thread through the stitch. "Or rather, since the Marked saw to her, the Healer and Finder. When she finally came to herself . . ." Kendraxa's lips trembled.

"She was not herself."

The woman inclined her head, just once. "At first, I couldn't be sure; after such a fall, some confusion was only to be expected. So the Healer said. And I so hoped— " Kendraxa pressed her trembling lips tight for a moment before she continued. "But she only became more watchful, more cautious in what she said. Xendra was always ready to talk about herself, the Slain One knows." Kendraxa's smile was hard to see. "And her smile, so ready, so joyous. But this one," she shook her head, "this one asked too many questions, and studied the answers to things Xendra knew very well. And once or twice, in the night, she called out in a language I have never heard."

Xerwin stared at his clasped hands, saw the knuckles standing out white.

"What do you think happened?"

"Can I know? I'm a lady page, Tar Xerwin, you can guess what my education has been." She shrugged, half holding out the embroidery in her hands as evidence of what she said.

"I know you for nobody's fool, whatever your education might be," he said. "An emptyhead is not chosen as companion for a Tarxina, nor as nurse for a young Tara. Tell me what you think."

Something in his tone—or in his face—must have convinced her. She licked her lips. "How much do you remember, did you know, of your sister's illness?"

Xerwin thought. "She fell from the wall around the palace precinct, injuring her head. She was unconscious for many days. I remember you crying." He glanced up. There were tears in Kendraxa's eyes now. "The Healer came from the Sanctuary, and then she was getting better."

"You didn't know about the Finder?"

Xerwin shrugged. "I knew the Healer had come with both a Mender and a Finder. I assumed that was part of their normal practice."

"They told your father the Tarxin, Light of the Sun, that your sister's spirit was missing from her body. Your father told them to find it."

"And the Finder Found ..." Xerwin didn't really need Kendraxa's nod to answer him.

"Someone's spirit, that's certain. But Xendra's? Not so far as I can see."

Xerwin's hands formed into fists. "How can I tell my father?"

He felt Kendraxa's fingertips on his arm. "Tar Xerwin, your father already knows."

"Put up your swords!"

As the man to his right stepped back, Parno flicked out with the point of his right-hand sword and opened a cut the length of his first knuckle in the man's right pectoral muscle, where it would bleed but do no harm.

"Lionsmane, stop. You will kill someone at this rate."

No voice but Darlara's would have reached him through the concentration of the Mirror *Shora*. Parno blinked, licked away a trickle of sweat that neared his mouth. There was another voice that could have reached him, but he would never hear that one again. He stuck his left-hand sword into the wood of the deck and smoothed his oiled hair away from his face.

He glanced around at the three fighters Darlara had chosen for him. A man of his own age, Deniss showed a white swatch of hair from an old scalp cut and wore the scaled jerkin. The other two were women, Tindar and Elian, clearly twins, as alike as two grains of sand. And now even more alike as he had given each of them identical cuts, on their right collarbones. All three were pale and sweating, breathing hard.

A chink of metal to his left and Parno spun, both swords up, and took a step toward the sound before he realized it was unarmed crew who backed away from him, wide-eyed people with the money they'd been wagering in their hands.

"Can't have you killing people, Lionsmane," Darlara said.

"None of them are dead." Parno looked around, but she was alone. Her brother must be off watch. He lowered his swords again and straightened.

Dar shook her head. "Nevertheless. Teach them to move

as you do, or find some way to even the match. Five people? You unarmed?"

Parno took in a great lungful of air and let it out slowly. He was tempted to say he wouldn't bother with the sparring at all, that they should leave him alone. He couldn't face another day of staring at the maps and drawings Malfin Cor had found for him and seeing nothing more than colored lines and meaningless shapes. He rubbed the bridge of his nose between thumb and forefinger. What was so difficult about this decision? What was so important? What matter of life or death hinged on it?

His gaze dropped to the hilt of the Teliscan blade he had in his left hand. In his mind he saw Dhulyn's face when she'd given it to him. Just after Arcosa, it had been, when they'd decided to Partner. But the expression he saw her wearing now wasn't the one she'd had then. Now she was showing him her wolf's smile. His hand closed tightly enough that he could feel the steel tang under the corded grip of the sword. He had a score to settle. A reason to stay alive. He'd almost forgotten.

The Storm Witch.

Darlara and Malfin were right. To get to the Witch, to defeat her, he needed a clear head. If nothing else, a workout would help him sleep, and sleep would clear the clouds and cobwebs from his brain.

After a moment, he said, "Get me a blindfold, then."

At the edge of his senses, Parno could feel the communication going on between the crew members as those watching used their Pod sense to summon those still below.

"Captain." It was the older man. "Done for this morning. Be excused."

Darlara nodded. "Done, Deniss. You two?"

The twins grinned, showing identical gaps in their front teeth. "Like to try him blindfolded," said one, as the other nodded. Parno felt an answering grin on his own lips.

"Deniss," he called the older man to him. "Hold this for me, will you?" He handed Deniss his sword and pulled the long dagger from the back of his belt. Two swords or a blindfold he could manage. Just now he had his doubts about two swords *and* a blindfold.

The Hunter's *Shora,* one of the basic twenty-seven taught to all Mercenary Brothers, was a little *too* basic for this fight, Parno thought. It taught you to feel the direction of the wind on your skin, to move without making noise enough to frighten a mouse. But to be blindfolded he needed something more than that. He needed the Stalking Cat *Shora*. In addition to stealth, the Stalking Cat would give him heightened senses beyond what the basic Hunter's could do. If he was blindfolded, he would need to locate each opponent by their smell, feel every shift of air, hear the movement of clothing, of weapons. Dhulyn said that, properly done, the Stalking Cat would allow you to feel the beat of your opponent's heart.

And in addition to the Stalking Cat, the Crab *Shora* for the shifting of the deck, and for, Parno bared his teeth, the large claw he had in his right hand and the smaller one in his left.

A third fighter had stepped forward to replace Deniss, a tall, clean-shaven youth with the marks of frostbite on his cheeks. He carried a shorter sword than the twins did, Parno noted automatically, one with a slight curve which would be sharp along that edge.

"Conford, isn't it?" Parno said, recognizing him. "Hope you're not as angry as you were. Anger's no reliable ally in a fight."

Conford inclined his head. "Keep that in mind, Mercenary Brother."

Darlara pulled a silken sash from around her waist and approached him with it held up in her hands. Parno went down on one knee.

"Give me a moment," he said, loud enough that all could hear him. "Keep the watchers well back. I'll stand when I am ready to begin. Attack from any direction, but be so good as to come at me one at a time." He waited until his three opponents had nodded before closing his eyes and tilting his head up for the blindfold.

Darlara's fingers were cold on his skin as she wrapped the sash around his eyes twice, tying it at the back of his skull. As she moved away, Parno began to repeat to himself the trigger words of the Stalking Cat *Shora*. The first thing he felt, even before he began to breathe slowly, was the presence of the Crayx, like the hum of a crowd in the distance. Parno shut them out of his conscious thought as his heartbeat slowed, and he pricked up his ears, flared his nostrils. His skin shivered as the hairs on his arms and the back of his neck stood up.

The deck rose and fell beneath his feet. The wind came from . . . there; with it on his left cheek, he was facing aft. The twins Tindar and Elian stood to his left, their drying sweat making them easy to locate and identify. They were slightly closer together than they were to Conford, who was behind him and to his right. From the gurgle of his stomach, the man had not eaten yet this morning.

Parno rose to his feet, and in the same movement, feeling the rush of air, raised his right arm, sword in the guard position and heard/felt the jar as his blade met Conford's and the blow's weight shivered through his arm bones. He heard the man's grunt, and the drawing in of a dozen breaths. Parno pushed off with his left foot, spinning, and bringing his left hand around to where the other blade must be, to catch it with the guard of his dagger, twisting and pulling it out of his opponent's hands.

There was a gasp from the crowd of watchers as the sword fell free and clattered to the deck. From the sound, several had had to step back out of the way.

The twin sisters smelled different now, their sweat was fear sharp. They had moved apart, but thanks to the wind, and the Stalking Cat *Shora*, Parno was able to point to the right-hand one with his sword, and the left-hand one with his dagger.

"One down," he said. "Two to go."

Apparently, the twins felt that the loss of one for their side freed them to attack together, or perhaps, Parno thought, they simply could not break themselves of the habit. In either case, it worked in his favor. Even sightless, he knew that anything he struck was an enemy, and even sighted, they had to take care not to hit each other. There was no movement of air, so they ran forward with blades raised. In the last possible moment Parno ducked, rolled forward, and heard with satisfaction the sound of their bodies colliding.

An unexpected calm fell over Parno as he rolled to his feet and spun around to face in the direction of the twins. Even as he trusted to his timing, lunging forward and kicking out, knocking one of them over and apparently — judging from the sound — into the other one as they tried to get up, he could feel the *Shora* working through him, calming him with its familiar touch. A tightness he had not been aware of loosened, and he felt freer, more alive, and somehow more himself than he had done since the storm.

A shift of air, a rasp as a foot slid along the wood of the deck before being lifted clear. Conford had found his weapon again. Parno spun toward the noise, his own sword at high guard, dagger at low. Conford's sword was a slashing weapon, and the chances were he'd bring it down, or across from ... there! Parno parried, stepped quickly within the man's reach and elbowed him in the face. He felt the contact, and smelled the blood as it burst from Conford's nose. A shuffle behind him, he ducked, bringing Conford down with him as the swords of the twins sliced through the air where he'd been standing.

"Enough," Darlara said.

Parno pulled off the blindfold and wiped his face with it. He touched his forehead to each of his opponents, just as if they had been Mercenary Brothers, and set off across the deck.

Parno looked up as the door of the cabin swung open, letting in cool sunlight filtered through streaky clouds. Darlara Cor came in and closed the door behind her, leaning against it and folding her arms across his chest. Parno almost smiled, reminded of one of his sisters. He was wiping the swords he'd used with an oiled cloth.

"Was a good workout," he said. "Thank you for suggesting it. Ready whenever you are to examine those maps."

Darlara stayed silent and, except for the tapping of her left index finger against her right elbow, she didn't move. Parno stowed the extra sword and turned to meet her eyes. They seemed darker than usual in her heart-shaped face, her full mouth set in a thin, firm line.

"Promised me a child."

Parno felt the muscles in his jaw tighten as he gritted his teeth. *Demons!* The woman couldn't be serious. In the face of his loss—his Partner and, in a very real way, his future, since he could not imagine surviving his vengeance. No. Some of the calm that the *Shora* had brought him melted away. It was too much that he should be asked to consider the future of others. But he could tell from the set planes of her face that Darlara was very serious indeed.

"Can't," was all he could finally bring himself to say.

"Say you can't. Mean you won't."

"At the moment it's the same thing."

But she was already shaking her head. She let her arms fall to her sides and stepped forward enough to lean against the table. "Not so. Gave your word, to me, to the Pod. Is it worth nothing? That's not what we've come to believe."

Demons and perverts. Parno slammed his open hands down on the table. Darlara blinked, but did not back away.

"Anger changes nothing."

And the worst of it was, she was right. His anger would not bring Dhulyn back, would not restore the world to rightness. In fact, much as he hated to admit it, it might even get in the way of the things he needed to do. Using the *Shora* to spar just now had shown him that he needed to regain his equilibrium, no matter how brightly his loss still burned within him.

He sat down and thrust his hands through his hair. He felt the feather touch of Darlara's fingertips on his arm.

"Promised me a child," she said. "Doesn't mean you stay, doesn't mean we wed. A child, a new bloodline for the Pod. *You* promised."

She was in her rights to ask, to remind him. And she was tactful enough, and smart enough, not to remind him that Dhulyn, as Senior Partner, had given her permission.

"Now?" The word was bitter acid as it left his mouth.

Darlara smiled, but it was a small, sad, companionable smile, not a smile of triumph.

"Lie down," she suggested. "Just lie down for now. Need warmth and a heart beating close to yours. Come, let's lie down."

It was not until hours later, when they had done much more than lie down, that he remembered they were in Dhulyn's bed.

Eleven

"IF MY SISTER HAS become a Storm Witch, well and good. But if a new being has taken over her body—how can we know it doesn't mean us harm?" Xerwin had met Naxot on the peldar court, but they hadn't yet begun their match. He'd needed to speak to someone, this was a safe place to talk—and Naxot's interests ran sufficiently close to his own, Xerwin considered, to make him a safe companion to talk to.

Naxot stopped bouncing the rubbery pelot on his racket, catching it in his hand. "She's done nothing but good so far. She's helped with some of the crops, and has explained the magic of the lodestone."

"If she has no evil intent, why has she not declared herself?"

"Perhaps she thinks to test us in some way?"

Xerwin paused in his pacing. *I wish I could believe the way Naxot believes,* he thought, and not for the first time. But it was hard to grow up as he had and believe that his father really was the Light of the Sun.

"I suppose that's possible," he said to his friend. "But this feels more like a plot of my father's than the suggestion of the Slain God."

Naxot waved this away. "Not even your father, Light of the Sun, acts completely alone." He spun the racket in his hand and looked up. "The Priests of the Slain God have authority over the Mages and Holy Women. When Telxorn comes to invest your . . . I mean the Storm Witch, surely he will know whether there is cause for concern? And, Xerwin, let's not forget. Whether this is your sister or not, she is a Storm Witch, a Holy Woman. Whatever her purpose here, should we be questioning it?"

Xerwin picked up his racket and put his hand out for the pelot. Naxot was such a good man, straightforward and orthodox. Perhaps, after all, he was a little too orthodox for this particular problem.

Naxot Lilso took the long way back to his own House when his peldar game with Xerwin finally ended. He needed time to think. He wasn't happy with the Tar's attitude. Xerwin had always been his friend, but there were higher issues at stake here—and more than one way to favor and power at court, if it came to that. However upset Xerwin might be about his sister, and he'd always had a soft spot for the girl, a Holy Woman was a Holy Woman. Xerwin might be willing to set the religious questions aside, but Naxot could not.

Naxot's route would take him past the Tarxin's audience chamber.

RAIN HISSES DOWN ON SLICK DECKS AND DHULYN CURSES AND TRIES TO LOOK AWAY. NOT THIS VISION, PLEASE GODS, NOT *THIS* ONE. IF SHE MUST SEE THE PAST, LET IT AT LEAST BE SOMETHING USEFUL. SURELY THERE COULD BE NO REASON TO SHOW HER *THIS* PAST. BUT EVEN AS SHE TURNS HER HEAD, TWO GIGGLING FORMS RUN TOWARD HER. TWO STURDY CHILDREN, NAKED AND CLEARLY ESCAPED FROM THEIR BEDS TO PLAY IN THE RAIN. THEY ARE ABOUT THREE YEARS OLD, TODDLERS REALLY, BUT AS FIRM AND STEADY ON THEIR BARE FEET AS THOUGH THEY'D LEARNED TO WALK AT SEA. AS THEY WOULD HAVE, SHE REALIZES WHEN THEY GET CLOSE ENOUGH FOR HER TO SEE THEM CLEARLY.

GIRLS THEY ARE, TWINS, SQUARE-BUILT, WITH A MOST FAMILIAR CHIN BELOW AMBER EYES. LUCKILY, THEY HAVE THEIR MOTHER'S NOSE. BECAUSE, IN ALL ELSE, THEY APPEAR TO BE THEIR FATHER'S CHILDREN. EVEN THE COLOR OF THEIR HAIR, WET AS IT IS, IS UNMISTAKABLE. THESE ARE PARNO'S CHILDREN.

"BACK HERE, YOU TWO TERRORS," THE VOICE SOUNDS ODD TO DHULYN, BUT IT'S CLEAR. "BACK IN BED THIS MINUTE, OR THERE'LL BE NO GREAT GATHERING FOR YOU! NO PONY RIDES!"

A future for them is possible. Dhulyn's heart leaps with joy as her tears fall. . . .

The slim woman, her sandy hair still touched with gray, is back at her circular desk. Her hazel eyes are closed, the pattern of lines that surround them smooth. The woman murmurs, chanting under her breath. Over her head the mist forms, swirling and bright with sun. She thrusts her arms into it and disappears . . .

Twins again, but older, and very obviously not the same girls. These are pale as milk, even their long hair colorless as new cheese. They are bone-thin, clinging to one another as if they lacked the strength to sit up alone. They sit in a double chair, almost a throne, whose cushions and well-padded, red velvet seat only serve to make them seem paler by comparison.

They concentrate on something off to their left. They turn their heads at precisely the same moment, with precisely the same movement, to look at Dhulyn with their red eyes.

"Sister," they say. . . .

She knows this woman very well, her long face, her stone-colored eyes, and her blood-red hair. "Go now," she says. "Up into the trees," she says. "Remember what I told you, my soul?" "Keep my eyes tight shut," Dhulyn answers her mother. "Don't look no matter what I hear." "That's right, my heart. Off you go now."

And the woman who is her mother watches as the child who was Dhulyn runs away to the trees, to the place in which she was told to hide. Her mother then turns to the Dhulyn who Sees all this, and smiles.

"Mother," Dhulyn says, taking a step toward the woman of her Vision, thinking now only of the question she has longed to ask. "How, Mother?" she asks. "Why? How did you not See and prevent the breaking of the Tribes?" But even as her mother parts her lips to answer, her head tilts as she listens to other sounds, and turns away. She has one hand lifted, one finger extended as if to say "Wait."

But the Vision is gone.

Dhulyn sat down on the wide lip of the courtyard fountain and rubbed at her eyes, moving her fingers up and out, to massage her forehead and temples as well. Thank Father Moon there'd been no Vision of Parno. That would have been more than she could stand. *I cannot do this again,* she thought. She had never deliberately avoided Visions in the past, but she would from now on. The possibility of having to live through Parno's loss again and again—Dhulyn took a deep breath, and tried to slow the beating of her heart.

The night air was markedly cooler than the day, a phenomenon Dhulyn had always associated with deserts rather than cultivated land. When she'd first come out of her room, there had been thunder and lightning off in the distance, but that had stopped now. Whatever its source, the coolness was welcome. Not that she had a headache; it merely felt as though she *should* have. Experience was making her better able to recognize Visions of the past, and that same experience had taught her that such Visions always gave useful information. But she'd Seen the episode with her mother before, why would she need to See it again? Why her mother, and why that particular moment, the last time she'd seen her mother alive? Dhulyn shivered, suddenly cold. *I'm the only one left. Again.* She had escaped alive that time, when the Bascani had come and the Tribes were broken. And she'd escaped alive this time as well. She braided the fingers of her right hand in the old sign against ill luck.

"Are you trying to tell me something, my mother?" All the women of the Espadryni, what the rest of the world called the Red Horsemen, were Marked with the Sight. Which did not explain to Dhulyn's satisfaction how and why they had allowed the Tribes to be broken, leaving only Dhulyn alive.

Was she somehow *supposed* to survive Parno? As she had so evidently been meant to survive the breaking of the Tribes? Was this yet another plan to which she did not have the key? She blew out her breath through her nose. This would be the second time that she'd lost the people most important to her, her family—

Except that the Mercenary Brotherhood was her family. Parno was her Partner, certain sure. But his death did not leave her entirely alone in the world. She touched her Mercenary badge with the tips of her fingers. She still had her Brotherhood, and the Common Rule.

"Pasillon," she said, invoking the part of the Common Rule that called all Mercenary Brothers to come to the aid of—and to avenge—any other Brother. Vengeance for Parno was her first goal, she reminded herself. If she survived the killing of the Storm Witch—by no means a certainty since she was the child of the Tarxin and therefore well-guarded—then she could think about what came next.

Footsteps along the gallery on the far side of the courtyard brought her head up and her hand reaching for the knife in her belt. But it was Remm Shalyn, returning from his scouting trip into the forest.

"Dhulyn Wolfshead, are you well?" Remm saw her and stepped out from under the gallery. "The Holding Steward will be concerned that your bed is not to your liking."

Dhulyn shrugged. "I take it your expedition has been successful?"

"It has. We'll hardly have to go off our own trail."

Remm came closer, and as he passed through a shaft of moonlight, his kilt sparkled white. Dhulyn sat up straight, remembering another part of her Vision.

"Tell me, Remm Shalyn. Are there Seers in Ketxan City's Sanctuary?"

Parno shifted the straps on Malfin's table and let the yellowed parchment roll closed. With his fingertips, he massaged the skin and muscles around his eyes and along his temples. He leaned forward, his elbows on the table, his head in his hands. Strategy, that was the problem. They were limited in their tactics. Couldn't swarm, for example; there simply weren't enough of them. Hard to lay siege to a place from the sea—not that they had the numbers for that either. For a moment, while studying the map, he'd had a glimmering of an idea. If the map was still accurate—and both the captains assured him that it was—he had seen the shadow of the answer, and then it had gone, before he could put his finger on its tail. He put his hands to the edge of the table and started to push himself away before he remembered that the furniture was bolted to the floor.

The cabin door creaked open, and Malfin stuck his head into the opening.

"Lionsmane, Crayx ask for music, would you . . . ?"

Parno had to allow that the Crayx had been scrupulous about staying out of his head, and for that, if nothing else, he should honor their request and play for them. Besides, music had been known to clear his head in the past.

He slid sideways off the bench and started to the door.

But once he'd fetched his pipes from the cabin—the heavy drones, the war pipes, better for the Crayx to hear directly—he found himself leaning on the rail as he filled the air bag, unsure what to play. He attached the chanter and began to noodle, just letting his fingers float over the sound holes. He let his eyes close, shutting out the deck, the crew, the now-blazing sun, and the fitful wind that made what sail there was flap, and the rigging creak. This is what Dhulyn used to call his pipe Shora, the tuning up that prepared him to play.

With that thought, he found his fingers playing once again the children's song that had such special meaning to Dhulyn. As he coaxed the skipping notes from the chanter, he began to complicate them with the music of the drones, adding seconds and thirds, intricacies that built upon the basic notes until the children's chant became once again the hymn to the Sleeping God it had originally been.

Slowly, note by woven note, the hymn began to change, to take on specific imagery. A run of higher notes, with a sharp drone behind them, became Dhulyn's swordplay, masterful and sure, deadly and bright. Chords were her throaty laugh. The lament became more sure, more steady, as Parno realized what he was doing. He played Dhulyn, the way horses seemed to speak to her, the way weapons sang in her hands. The wolf's smile she showed to others, the smile she saved for him alone. The way she smelled after she had not bathed for many days.

Finally, not really sure how much time had passed, he lowered the pipes, and, blinking, looked around him. The watch was the same, the same faces looked back at him, though some had tears in their eyes.

#We see her now# #The music shows her to us# #Sorrow# #Compassion#

"Have not seen one tenth part of her." Even though he

muttered under his breath, Parno was all too aware of the others on deck, now studiously ignoring him.

#You are unjust to your talent and your skill# #Your song of her will live with us always now# #Is this not she#

In his mind an image he hadn't called there. Dhulyn with her right hand on the neck of a horse, the animal shadowy and unclear, turning to look over her shoulder at him, smiling, her gray eyes alight with laughter.

Parno coughed, clearing his throat, wiping away his tears with the back of his hand. "Yes," he said. "That is she."

#The image is yours, you will be able to call it whenever you wish, it will be clear and crisp# #A small thing, but strengthening your memory is a part of what we can do#

#Do not fear# This was another voice. #No other will share this image without your consent# #It is not our way, but we know that humans have private things#

#Darlara did not share you with us, for example#

Parno felt a hot flush rise up through his cheeks and dropped his eyes to his pipes. He hadn't even thought of that. Hastily, he changed the subject.

"Are those images how you keep the souls of those who go to you when they die? Like portraits?"

#Not at all# #The soul itself joins us, becoming part of the Great Pod#

"What about new Crayx? Where do their souls come from?" One by one, Parno removed the drones and began to bleed the remaining air out of the bag.

#There are no new Crayx# #We are the same, always#

"But the spawning grounds?"

#We grow always, larger and larger# #We would grow too large for the oceans, so as that time approaches, we prepare smaller bodies# #In the spawning grounds we emerge in our new bodies, leaving the old behind, as we leave behind each old layer of skin and scales#

"Then you don't produce young?" Parno restored the last piece of his disassembled pipes into their bag and looked over the side. There were several Crayx within sight. *Which of these speaks to me?* he wondered. *And how old is it?*

#We do not#

"But the Nomads . . ." Parno looked toward the cabin where Darlara was sleeping.

#Have young, though not so many as land-based humans#

Parno caught an undercurrent of thought that substituted "no Pod sense" for the phrase "land-based."

"And you have room for all of them when they die?"

#Amusement# #Souls do not occupy space#

Parno blinked. That had never occurred to him. Of course, he'd never had reason to think about souls in this way before. Which reminded him of his other question.

"How old are you? How far back do you remember?"

For the first time, the answer was not immediate. #Time is not the same for us# #We know what it is for you, we have seen the effects of its passage# #Watch#

#This is Ketxan City when we made our first treaties with humans, in the before that you humans call the time of the Caids# #Before the Great Chaos# #Before the first coming of the Green Shadow#

Before Parno could interrupt, another image came into his mind. This time he was looking across a large bay of water toward a city built up on the islands of a flat sprawling delta. A city like Tenezia, without roads, but rather canals and bridges. Unlike Tenezia, however, this long ago Ketxan boasted airy towers.

#This is Ketxan City as we see it now#

Where the broad delta had been was a massive cliff face, taller than the tallest tower Parno had ever seen. There were openings, windows, balconies, and even doors cut into the living rock, with ladders connecting some of the lower levels. At the foot of the cliff, like a ruffle on a skirt, wharfs, jetties, and piers were built out into the sea.

#This is time, yes# #There is duration, change#

"But surely you also change? You're not the same beings that you were then?"

#There is no then# #For the Great Pod, there is only now# #We thank you for the music, Parno Lionsmane#

And suddenly, he was alone.

At first he stayed where he was, enjoying the quiet sounds of the ship around him, the sun on his face. He hadn't realized he was so curious about the Crayx. Dhulyn would have been interested by what he'd learned, as she was—had been—interested in everything. He hugged his bag of pipes closer. He missed her, Caids knew how much. But somehow, whether it was the steady familiarity of the

Shora, or of his music, Parno realized that the sharpest edge of his grief had been blunted.

He pressed his lips together in a tight smile. In order to do what he wanted to do, in order to find and kill the Storm Witch, he needed to be at his very best. If the patterns and discipline of the *Shora,* and his music, restored him to his best self, it was a thing to be welcomed.

He stood, and was halfway back to the cabin to put away his pipes when a thought slowed his steps. He was almost certain that Malfin had mentioned attacking Ketxan City. But, given the cliffs he had seen in the Crayx's image of the place . . . Parno turned and made his way back to Malfin's cabin. When he entered, he found Darlara sitting across from her brother at the cleared table, a bowl of cooked grains in front of her.

"Tell me," Parno said. "These attacks on Ketxan City, how did you manage them?" So far as he could see from the image the Crayx had shown him, there was no landing place at Ketxan. He had not seen siege weapons on the *Wavetreader,* nor could he see any way to equip even much larger ships with such things. How could the Nomads, armed only with swords, garwons, and crossbows, mount a serious attack on the cliff city?

Darlara was swallowing, so it was Malfin who answered. "The Crayx push them back, enough so that we can land."

"But Mortaxa have no Pod sense, how do the Crayx push them?"

"With their water bolts," Darlara said. "May we?" She tapped her forehead. When Parno nodded, he felt the Crayx again, and the image that appeared in his mind made him laugh aloud.

"I think I see our plan," he told them.

~

Carcali was on her knees by the toy shelves. She didn't know who had last put these dolls away, but she could tell it had not been the little girl who loved them. They'd been shoved in any which way, back to front, facedown, even piled on top of one another. The dolls varied considerably in their dress, Carcali noted, as she straightened and rearranged them. There were elaborately dressed nobles and more simply dressed servants, and more than one soldier doll, all with tiny weapons. The favorites appeared to be one soldier in particular—an officer judging from his armor—and a little girl doll whose painted face was quite worn, and whose hair had been frequently rebraided. It wasn't until she heard the lock engage that Carcali looked up, this last doll still in her hands. Her stomach rumbled, and she pressed her lips together as saliva began to flow. Were they bringing food this time, or only water again? She cursed her caution now for keeping her from saying something to Tar Xerwin when he came, but he hadn't sounded all that friendly. For all she knew, the man was just another spy for the Tarxin.

When the two guards entered and stood one to each side of the door, Carcali rose, unwilling to be caught on her knees. In the last moment, she realized she was still holding the doll, and thrust it hastily behind her. She wasn't going to look any more childlike and vulnerable than she could help. Not to the man who had first struck her, and was now keeping her prisoner. Though she would have felt more confident if she wasn't sure that the Tarxin had seen her quick movement, and had correctly interpreted it.

What happened next did nothing to boost her confidence. At a signal from the Tarxin, the Honor Guard accompanying him stepped back out of the room and closed the door. Carcali waited, unsure what she should do, but determined not to be the first to speak. The Tarxin looked around the room, taking in the daybed with its gaily colored cushions, and the closed and barred door of the sheltered balcony that looked out on the sea. Finally, he turned away and appeared to study the maps on her table.

Automatically, Carcali went to stand on the other side of her worktable, though she made no move to cover the designs she'd made on the maps. The Tarxin had no Art, and wouldn't understand the meaning of the symbols she'd drawn, but she felt stronger there, close to her work.

When she glanced up, he was looking directly into her eyes. He indicated her chair, and waited until she was seated before he took the chair across from her, lifted off his gold-chased headdress, and placed it to one side. With his eyes still fixed on hers, he leaned back, patting the arms of the chair with the palms of his hands.

"I think we have seen that we each can hurt the other," he said, his voice rough as the gravel paths in the upper gardens. His eyes were large, but dark and cold. "We have each tried our strengths, and we are well matched. You have the weather Art, and can use it against me, but I am the Tarxin, and have the power to starve you or put you to death if I so choose."

Carcali's hands formed fists on the arms of her own chair.

"I can leave this body, and still control the weather."

The man across from her spread out his hands. "Then why have you not done so?"

The pain in her hands reminded Carcali to loosen her grip. Oh, how badly she would have liked to call his bluff. But he wasn't the one bluffing.

She hadn't fully disconnected since she'd reawakened in this body, it made her shiver just to think about it. What if she lost the connection again, to spend who knew how long before she somehow reconnected? If she ever did. There were so many things about this life, this world—this body— she didn't like, didn't know, and didn't understand. But it was better by far than the impersonal emptiness of the weather-spheres. She wouldn't go back there. She wouldn't. . . . But.

"If you kill me," she said, in her light child's voice. "I'd have no reason *not* to leave the body."

He just nodded and leaned back again, raising his hands and looking at her over the tent he'd made of his fingers.

"We can each of us harm the other," he repeated. "Shall we see if there is any way we can help each other?"

"I am ready to hear your proposal." Carcali leaned back herself, consciously trying to imitate his air of relaxation. But it was pretense, and she doubted he was fooled.

He might be sincere about his offer—he'd agreed to keep the Healers away once she'd shown him what she could do, and he'd kept his bargains so far. But she had to be careful. He was the one with all the power here, and he wouldn't hesitate to use it. She raised her hand to her bruised cheek.

"I will undertake never to strike you again," he said, as if in response to her gesture. "But in return you must in public treat me in all ways as your Tarxin and your father."

"Agreed," she said. "If by 'strike' you include any and all

physical discipline, including imprisoning me and withholding food."

This time he did smile, but it was, she thought, a smile of admiration.

"Agreed." He leaned forward. "You have satisfied me that to allow the Healers to treat you will destroy your Art, as you call it. There are two ways in which this Art can be useful to me. As a weapon against my enemies, and as a tool for the benefit of my people. That is what you can give me. What can I give you in return?"

Carcali tried to keep her face as impassive as the Tarxin's, fighting not to show the surge of triumph and excitement that flowed through her at his words. She had to be very careful; he was experienced and tricky. She had to be sure to ask for *exactly* what she wanted.

"I will help you in the ways you've outlined." She was pleased that her voice sounded so calm, so reasonable. "But I must be able to practice and develop my Art without interference. I need more authority as myself," she said. "As the Tara Xendra."

The Tarxin frowned, but not as though he meant to disagree with her. "That is difficult," he said. "Women do not rule here, as they do across the Long Ocean, and many will find it hard to have a woman in authority over them." He pulled at his lower lip. "It has been many generations since there was last a practitioner of the Art among our people, and the Scholars tell us that such Mages and Witches were wards of the Slain God, going to serve at his temple. In fact, Telxorn, the Chief Priest, has already asked for you."

He's trying to scare me, Carcali thought. "Perhaps I should be having this discussion with him."

"Perhaps." The Tarxin didn't look nearly worried enough. "But I remind you that whatever the common people may think about your holiness, Telxorn is a man grown old in the service of the Slain One, and to him you are still the Tara Xendra, a young girl he has known since she was born. He will expect you to be biddable and you will have to force him to give you what I offer you freely. Meanwhile, I, and the rest of my people, would suffer at the weather along with him until he finally sees what I have already seen." The man frowned, and then his face lightened as he snapped his fingers. "Of course. There has never been a practitioner of the Art with Royal Blood. We can refuse him on that basis. If you do not serve in the temple, then you will have both your status as Tara, and your status as a Holy Weather Witch. We can base your authority on that."

There was something in his tone, or the crinkle of his eyes, that told Carcali the man was being tricky, but she still found herself nodding in agreement. He wasn't being strictly truthful about the temple, but she was grateful to be kept out of the hands of the priesthood with their superstitious nonsense about the Slain God. Interesting what he'd said, though, about others seeing her only as the Tara Xendra.

"Tell me, Tarxin Xalbalil, how do you see me? Who do *you* think I am?"

He looked at her a long time, his eyebrows raised over his coal-dark eyes. "My dear child, what does it matter?"

Twelve

THE CLOUDS HAD BROKEN up sometime before dawn, making the last leg of the journey from the final guesthouse somewhat hotter and sunnier than Dhulyn would have liked. The forest was far behind them now, and for some time their road had been taking them past cultivated fields.

"This close to the capital, these are all market gardens," Remm Shalyn said, seeing her interest.

"I recognize some of the plants," Dhulyn said. "Those are artichokes, and those potatoes. They are cultivated in Boravia as well. But here, I see, harvesting has already begun. Back there, most of these crops won't be ripe enough to harvest for a moon at least."

"Why would that be?"

Dhulyn looked across at him, but Remm seemed to be perfectly serious. "You are much farther north here," she said, keeping her tone as neutral as she could. "The farther north you travel, the warmer it is, the longer the growing seasons, the earlier the sowing, and therefore the earlier the harvests."

"And are the harvests very late, then, in your homeland?" Remm was interested, Dhulyn could see, but only just enough to be polite. He had a soldier's practical grasp of things, and *that* she found familiar. A little irritating, but familiar and, in a strange way, comforting.

"In my homeland there is only grass for the horses, and then snow, and ice. It is civilized people who plant crops."

"Ice, I've heard of, packed in straw and brought by river-boat from the mountains to the south to cool the drinks of the rich, but snow?"

They had walked several spans by the time Dhulyn gave up trying to describe snow.

The fields they passed now were changing. Up ahead were what looked like grapevines. Recent rains meant the fields were well watered, but it also meant there had been a growth of weeds, and that some of the new plants needed restaking. Dhulyn noticed that for the most part the field hands did not look toward them as they passed. Slaves, of course. Each field was being supervised by an attendant who stood at one end, under a planted sunshade, watching the progress of the others.

"Are the watchers slaves as well?" Dhulyn asked following the nearest one with her eyes.

"Usually," Remm Shalyn said. "Only the very rich can afford to pay for this kind of work. In the free lands on the other side of the mountains, the farms and fields are worked by groups of free men who hold everything in common." Remm looked sideways at her, one eyebrow raised in puzzlement. "Tell me," he said. "How did you know that there would be runaway slaves?"

"Loraxin thought I was a runaway," she said. "It followed. And it also follows that there must be some place to run to."

Remm shook his head, his mouth twisted in a smile. "Are all Paledyn such deep thinkers as you?"

What answer can I give him? she thought. There were Mercenary Brothers who did not think beyond the *Shora*, for certain. She knew many such. But Dorian the Black had told her many times, "The more you know, the more likely you are to stay alive," and she'd believed him.

"So the servants I meet now will all be slaves?"

Remm Shalyn rubbed at his chin. He'd been careful to shave every morning. "Well, no. Especially not in the palace. Oh, I don't mean there won't be slaves in the kitchens, or among the cleaners, but some of the very rich live in the City, the Noble Houses—"

"The very ones who are rich enough to pay for service, and who use that method to show off their wealth."

"Exactly." Remm focused his attention on the vines they

were passing. Dhulyn looked in the same direction but saw nothing unusual. Then Remm looked down at his feet. And cleared his throat.

Dhulyn decided to wait him out.

"I am thinking, Dhulyn Wolfshead." Dhulyn raised her eyebrows, but Remm was not looking at her, so the effect was lost. "Perhaps it would be best if you uncovered your head," he said finally. "Now that we have no servants with us, it would be best if the people we will now encounter see your," he gestured at his own temple, "your Paledyn's tattoo."

"Have we much farther?"

"By midmorning, we will be at the walls."

Dhulyn squinted upward, judging the strength of the sun. Parno had often teased her that the sun did not brown her, and it was true that next to the rich gold of his own coloring she never looked darker than old ivory. But pale as she might seem, she did brown, nevertheless. She pulled off her headdress, turning it back into a linen scarf and a knotted sash, and tying both around her hips.

"Will there be a problem since we have no runner to send ahead to tell the guards we are coming?" she asked Remm Shalyn.

"The palace guards are already expecting us," he said.

Dhulyn pressed her lips together and barely stopped herself from rolling her eyes to Mother Sun. This would by no means be the first time that knowledge at the palace didn't find its way to the ordinary soldier. "And the gate guards will have been told as well?"

"The gate is not guarded."

No guards? Dhulyn pursed her lips in a silent whistle. She'd understood from what Remm had told her that the country of the Mortaxa was large, larger than any of the realms in Boravia, with the capital, Ketxan City, on the coast. But Battle Wings or no, were their enemies so far distant that the walls of the capital did not need guards? These were remarkably complacent people, and history had often told her what usually rewarded such complacency. Dhulyn knew how she would attack the city, if she were ever given the task.

The walls, when they finally arrived at them, impressed her even less. They were built of the same white-washed, stucco-covered mud bricks that she had seen used for build-ing material in Berdana, but these walls were no taller than she was herself, and only just wide enough to allow some-one to walk comfortably on the top.

And just as Remm Shalyn had said, the gates stood wide and empty.

Dhulyn looked at the gardens, walkways, and pavilions to be seen within the gates, and back at the cultivated fields without. "It seems that the primary purpose of these walls is to keep the fields separate, rather than to enclose and protect the city."

Remm frowned. "Certainly, it's considered a sign of sta-tus among the Noble Houses to have winter places in the Upper City. I think it was the present Light of the Sun's father who declared there could be no more building here."

"Naturally. It would be in the interest of those same No-ble Houses to make sure the precinct was as small and ex-clusive as possible." She looked around her, but there was nothing but gardens and the single-story pavilions as far as she could see. "And the palace?"

"There's no direct entrance from the Upper City, but do you see those pillars?"

Dhulyn looked where he was pointing and saw that there were indeed a set of five pillars to be seen to the north and east.

"That marks the official entrance to Ketxan City itself."

"The entrance?"

Remm gestured with his hands. "To the Lower City, of course. Ketxan City is built into the rock cliffs that face the Coral Sea."

As they approached the entrance to the Lower City, the buildings became more impressive, many of them built of stone. The same stone, Dhulyn guessed, which had been carved out and removed to form the rooms and corridors of the city below them. The entrance itself consisted of the five pillars they had seen from a distance, which flanked a de-scending ramp of polished terrazzo leading down to enor-mous open-worked double doors made from metal bars, like a portcullis. Dhulyn stopped, fists on her hips, and looked upward to examine the gates more carefully, disbe-lief making her shake her head.

As if to confirm her worst fears, the guard was actually a

porter, an elegantly robed man whose round eyes and widened nostrils showed exactly what he thought of a Paledyn who turned up on foot, bareheaded, wearing a short kilt, and with only one attendant. He looked as though he wished to turn them away, so Dhulyn gave him her wolf's smile. As he backed away from her, she stepped forward.

"The Tarxin, Light of the Sun, has sent for me."

Dhulyn kept her attention on the man on the throne, without in any way losing sight of the pikemen stationed along the walls, and in particular the two who stood one to each side of the Tarxin. Was he another Loraxin Feld? Would he feel the need to test her? But the guards did not move, did not even, as far as she could tell, shift their eyes to follow her as she approached the throne. She could not be sure, never having met the man before, but she would wager her second-best sword that something about her pleased the Tarxin Xalbalil very much indeed. How best to keep him that way? She had been given a chance to bathe—in fact, the Steward of Keys who had met them at the entrance to the palace itself had insisted on it—and once again she had turned down women's garments in favor of what Remm assured her was appropriate clothing for a young man of a high Noble House. Only the absence of jewelry and perfume distinguished her from many in the audience room.

Now Dhulyn ignored everyone else, took a stride forward, and, bending from the hips, placed her palms flat on the floor in front of her. Such was the bow one gave to the Great King in the West, though she suspected no one here would recognize it. It was very impressive, however, to anyone who hadn't seen it done routinely. She straightened.

"I greet you, Tarxin Xalbalil, Light of the Sun. I am Dhulyn Wolfshead, called the Scholar. I was schooled by Dorian of the River, the Black Traveler, and I have fought with my Brothers at Sadron, Arcosa, and at Bhexyllia with the Great King to the West. I have come to serve." She inclined her head again.

"I had not thought to see a female Paledyn." Though, from the evenness of his tone, the Tarxin had been warned what to expect. His voice was cold and rough, like a knife dulled by hard use drawn across a stone.

"The Slain God chooses whom he wills." Dhulyn touched

her fingers to her forehead in salute. Nothing a great ruler liked more than plenty of respect.

"That he does." The Tarxin touched his own forehead, as did everyone else in the room.

Interesting. Dhulyn kept her own face from showing any reaction, seeing the Mercenary salute used here as an acknowledgment of the Slain God.

"I have heard tales of your prowess in my land, Paledyn," the Tarxin said. "You have already fought and defeated many with your bare hands."

Did the man's eyes flick toward Remm Shalyn, still down on one knee behind her? She inclined her head. "You are too kind, Light of the Sun."

"Go now, and rest from your journey." The Tarxin flicked his hand and another Steward, not the one who had met them at the entrance, stepped forward. There was a vertical frown line between this man's gray brows, but Dhulyn had the feeling it was permanent, and had little to do with her.

"There will be feasting tonight," the Tarxin continued. "It would please me that you join us, if you are rested."

"I will attend." Dhulyn bent forward once more to touch her palms to the floor and turned to follow the Steward.

A feast? Just the place one could meet with the Storm Witch.

"But, Lionsmane, we know nothing about attacking on land."

"These maps are accurate? These bluffs here no higher than is shown?"

"Believe so." Malfin caught his sister's eye even as he nodded.

#Yes#

"Then should be able to land small forces here—" Parno tapped a spot on the coast to the west of Ketxan City that showed where the mouth of a large creek cut into the coastal bluffs. "And here." He tapped another spot to the east where there was a rocky beach. "Reading the symbols correctly? There's depth enough there and the ships can get close enough?"

"At high tide, in those two areas, yes," Malfin said. "But still don't see . . ." His voice trailed off as his sister wrapped her hand around his upper arm, her eyes fixed on Parno's face.

"Let him explain, Mal," she said. Parno wasn't sure that he was entirely comfortable at the confidence in her voice— nor at the glow in her face. He turned his eyes back to the map.

"If land here, and here," he said, once again laying his index fingers on the maps. "Should be able to make our way overland to the walls of the city here, and here." He moved his fingers. "Avoiding the cliff face of the city entirely. From what you tell me of your usual tactics, no one will be expecting an assault from the land, and there will be minimal guards along the walls. To make doubly sure of that, after dropping off the assault teams, the ship will return to sea, enter the harbor in the usual way, and bombard the city front with water bolts." He looked up at them. "See now? Will concentrate their soldiers against what they believe to be your usual frontal assault."

Mal was nodding. "But how will we coordinate the attacks?"

Parno smiled. Amazing how people couldn't see a tactical use for something they'd had their whole lives. "Pod sense." He saw the light dawn over both their faces.

#Amusement# Parno felt not only the amusement of the Crayx, but of Mal and Dar as well. #Pod sense or no# the Crayx continued #You cannot lead both expeditions and no one on board the *Wavetreader* has sufficient knowledge to maneuver on land, to tell directions for example# #You must have only one landing party, or do you wish us to summon other Pods#

Darlara nodded. "True, won't take the city with just our crew, no matter how well you train them."

Parno looked from one captain to the other. It was lucky they had him. "Don't want to take the city," he reminded them. "What would we do with it? Want to kill the Storm Witch."

With a sinking in his stomach, Parno wondered if either of *them* had noticed he'd said "we."

It was not the first time Dhulyn had attended a feast of this exalted kind. It was not even the first time she had been seated at the high table. But it was the first time she had been alone, without Parno. She forced herself to push those memories away, not to wish for his familiar grin and his ingrained knowledge of the manners of Noble Houses.

Not that even Parno's knowledge would have been of much use here, since the court of the Tarxin bore little resemblance to that of any other court Dhulyn had ever seen. It was the first time that Dhulyn had ever seen the seating order determined not merely by rank, but by gender. Here the women were seated at a separate table, set centrally and perpendicular to the high table, and presided over by a young girl who could not have seen her birth moon more than ten or eleven times.

The Stewards must have received special orders to treat Dhulyn as though she were a man, since she had been seated at the same table as the Tarxin. There was an empty chair on either side of him, something Dhulyn had never seen done in any court in Boravia, but she had been given what amounted to the place of honor, the next seat at his left hand. On her other side was his son, Tar Xerwin, the heir.

The Tar had inclined his head, a little grimly, when the Hall Steward introduced them in the anteroom, and Dhulyn had given him exactly the same degree of bow in response. She'd had the sense that his grimness had nothing to do with her, however—or at least not directly. She wondered whether she should try the Two Hearts *Shora*. The Tar would make a useful ally.

Once at table, Dhulyn was careful to observe the manners of the others, and to copy them insofar as it was possible. Everyone at the high table had their own attendant standing behind them, and though Remm Shalyn stood behind her chair, he had very little to do besides signal to the servers when he saw her plate or glass empty. The service at their table was done by young girls, their hair covered with veils and much bedecked with bangles and pendants. The ladies' table, Dhulyn was amused to see, was served by young boys, severely dressed in a manner that mimicked the uniform of the guards.

A nervous reflex caused Dhulyn to smile at the first girl who approached the table in front of her. The girl's hand shook, almost dropping the small tidbit she was placing on

Dhulyn's plate with a long pair of silver tongs. Dhulyn glanced sideways and saw the Tar lifting the morsel to his mouth with his right hand. She did the same.

A slice of cured ham so thin it was like the finest parchment, wrapped around a sugared date. Her mouth watered and she wondered whether there were any more. But what the girls were bringing now were tiny cups of clear glass, filled with a bright green liquid. Wiping her hand on the napkin to the right of her plate, as she saw both the Tarxin and Tar Xerwin do, Dhulyn lifted the glass and tossed the contents down her throat. She covered her mouth politely and coughed.

"It's unexpected, isn't it?" Tar Xerwin said. Though his tone was just as cool, his voice was a warmer, more musical version of his father's. "Pureed apple, olive oil, vinegar, and garlic."

"We are allowed to speak, then?" The man was slim, and well-muscled, not at all the type to be so precise about his food. Then again, the Tarxin himself was also slim which, given his years, meant that great attention and care were being paid to his diet.

"Indeed, though most women are more likely to faint than to talk to me."

Dhulyn cut short her laugh. "Oh. Your pardon, Tar Xerwin, I assumed you were joking."

"And yet, you are not afraid." He did not look at her when he spoke, however. His gaze appeared directed toward the ladies' table.

"Why would I be?"

"Because you see now that I was not joking."

Dhulyn shrugged. "What is the worst you can do to me?"

Now he turned to look at her. He lifted one shoulder and let it fall. "I could have you killed, or worse."

"Possibly." She looked him directly in the eyes, and smiled her wolf's smile. He did not move, only blinked, but for a moment Dhulyn thought she saw something more in his face than a bored and offended noble. "Possibly you *could* have me killed. But I'll tell you what you cannot do, Tar Xerwin. You cannot frighten me to death."

The Tar didn't exactly smile, but his eyes brightened, and his countenance seemed warmer. "To answer your question, then, yes, we are allowed to speak, but my father prefers to eat his meal in peace. If and when he wishes to discuss something with someone, he will call them up to sit next to him."

"A great honor." Dhulyn eyed the platter of thinly sliced cold meats that had been placed between her and the Tar. Evidently they were to be shared.

"It is. Don't be surprised if you're called over yourself. My father is very pleased with you."

"I saw that at my audience with him." Following Xerwin's lead, Dhulyn rolled up a slice of meat and popped it into her mouth. A cured sausage, spicy and piquant in its flavors. "Tell me, Tar Xerwin, is your father, the Light of the Sun, pleased with me as a man is pleased with a woman?"

Tar Xerwin looked startled and, for a flashing instant, younger than his polished manners and self-assured air had made him seem.

"You are direct," he said finally, with his first genuine smile. "I forgot that you are a Paledyn. To be equally direct, my father's tastes in women run differently. You would be too tall, too thin and," here his smile widened, "too dangerous for him." He waited while the platter was removed, and individual dishes set down in front of them bearing toasted slices of bread no bigger than the palm of Dhulyn's hand, covered with thin slices of something pale, and decorated with loose berries.

"Don't tell me," Dhulyn said, lifting one to her mouth and taking a bite. "Mmmm. Goose liver. I've never seen it so pale."

"Try some with the berries." When her mouth was full, Xerwin continued. "No, I would say my father thinks of you as a Paledyn, not as a woman. Note that you are seated here, and not at the women's table with my sister."

"He *is* pleased that I am female, however," Dhulyn pointed out. It seemed that the Tar, at any rate, was excused from the constant repetition of "Light of the Sun." Without turning to study the women's table more carefully, it was impossible to know which woman was the Tara Xendra.

"He is, but I think that is because the Storm Witch is also female." He glanced toward the women's table, and Dhulyn thought his lips might have hardened a little.

She nodded. It was difficult to be sure; all the seated women had their hair covered in the same type of veils worn by the serving girls, though of much richer fabrics and more expensive colors. There were several of the right age, but Dhulyn was fairly certain she had not seen the fair-haired woman of her Visions. Caution and Schooling told her it might be best, for the moment, not to ask after her. Better that she not show too much interest just at first.

"And what of you, Tar Xerwin?" she asked, careful not to let her lip curl again as she smiled. "How do you think of me?"

As she had been talking to him, Dhulyn had been careful to control her respiration, until the breaths came slower, and deeper. Slowly, her skin had grown warmer. Now she looked directly into Xerwin's eyes, parting her lips, and his breathing also slowed. The color came up into his face, and then he paled again.

"In whatever manner you would wish me to think, Dhulyn Wolfshead."

It was the first time he had said her name, and Dhulyn thought she could let it rest there, for now. The Two Hearts *Shora* had done its work.

They kept up their dance of words through the rest of the feast. Through the fish, grilled with melon sauce and mushrooms, through the inglera tenderloin topped with more goose liver and pureed apple, through the tiny individual legs of lamb, whose creamy sauce had still more apple and garlic in it. Each dish had come accompanied with a decorative edible, potatoes cut to resemble lace and deep fried, or miniature tarts of a pale yellow color and buttery taste that Xerwin told her were made from corn.

Xerwin slowly became a different person from the one who had sat down, and Dhulyn found his attitude strange altogether. Unlike the behavior she had seen in the court of the Great King to the West, Xerwin now appeared to treat her as in every way his equal. She had gathered from the Long Ocean Nomads that the Mortaxa revered Paledyns, but she had not understood that the reverence was sufficient to outweigh the ingrained prejudices of the culture. At the same time, the Two Hearts *Shora* had made her certain that Xerwin was aware of her as a woman. His heart rate had remained faster than normal, and he had managed to brush against her several times.

Dhulyn eyed the latest platter as it was set down be-

tween them. It appeared they had at last arrived at the
sweet course, and the end of the meal was in sight. There
were two small bowls of almonds, chocolate, and ganje
beaten into egg whites, a torte of chocolate layered with a
green nut, and another made of quince jelly layered with
fine slices of a sharp sheep's milk cheese.

As the young servers came around with tiny cups of
ganje, black and hot, Xerwin, and others at the head table,
were taking out small jeweled boxes. Xerwin used the point
of his dagger, equally jeweled, to add a tiny amount of powder from the box to his ganje. Others were doing the same,
though the young man on Xerwin's left side was sniffing the
powder off the back of his hand.

Fresa, Dhulyn thought. Or some other form of the fressian moss, powdered for easy consumption. In Boravia, fressian drugs were so expensive and rare no one ever used
them recreationally. There was no way of knowing what
such use might bring. Dhulyn had just raised her hand, palm
out, to Xerwin's offer of his jeweled box when the closer of
the two young men who had stood behind the Tarxin's chair
for the entire meal approached them and bent to speak quietly into Xerwin's ear.

Xerwin nodded, waited for the guard to return to his
station before standing up and offering Dhulyn his hand.
She stood, and let him lead her over one seat to sit down
again next to the Tarxin. His ganje was untouched, and
there was no sign of any type of fressian on the table in
front of him. Quiet fell over the room as people stopped
their conversations and looked toward the high table.

"My people." Rough as it was, the Tarxin's voice was
pitched to be clearly heard throughout the dining chamber.
"I have the pleasure to present the Paledyn, Dhulyn Wolfshead, escaped from the ships of the Nomads. We are greatly
favored by the appearance of another who has been
touched by the Slain God." He gestured toward the wom-
en's table.

"We know that the Paledyn is here to help us in our dispute with the Nomads of the Long Ocean. Like the Paledyns of old, Dhulyn Wolfshead will see fair dealing, and our
rights confirmed."

Will I now, Dhulyn thought. *That's confident of you.*

"I would like to ask the Paledyn, here in front of you all,

for an additional boon. I would ask her that she extend her protection over my other child, the Tara Xendra, in whom has recently manifested the Art of a Weather Mage. Come, my dear, meet the Paledyn."

It was the child, Dhulyn saw with a cold shock, who stood and crossed the short distance of floor to stand in front of her father on the far side of the table.

This wasn't possible. Dhulyn had Seen the Storm Witch several times, a tall, slim, fair-haired woman. Not a small, stocky girl with the same jet-black eyebrows as her father and her brother. She would not become tall and slim no matter how much time passed. The child raised coal-black eyes to meet Dhulyn's, and Dhulyn shivered, steeling herself to touch her forehead in salute, in recognition of the Slain God's servant.

Those eyes did not belong to a child. Those eyes were a good deal older than eleven years.

Dhulyn bowed, and smiled, and at one point touched her forehead again, all without consciously hearing anything more that was said. She found herself back in her seat next to the Tar Xerwin. His eyes were turned toward where his sister was sitting down once more at her own table. His face showed no emotion whatsoever, but Dhulyn saw that his hand gripped his cup of ganje so tightly that his knuckles stood out white.

He knows, she thought. *Whatever is happening here, he knows what it is.* And he wasn't happy about it.

Looked like she was right to use the Two Hearts *Shora.*

Thirteen

"WILL YOU COME IN?"

Tar Xerwin had escorted her to the door of the rooms Dhulyn had been given. They were only one level down from the apartments of the royal family, no doubt kept set aside for important guests and visitors. Remm Shalyn, carrying a lamp, was already at the door, waiting to open it for her. Xerwin's attendants stopped a span down the corridor, and waited for him there. This would not have been the first time, Dhulyn thought, that they had accompanied their master to some lady's door.

Though it might have been, judging from the frown on Xerwin's face.

"Dhulyn Wolfshead, I thank you for the honor, but I fear I must decline. Business of my father's will have me rise early tomorrow."

Dhulyn tilted her head toward his ear. They were almost exactly the same height. "I did not invite you to my bed, Tar Xerwin," she said, so softly that she knew only he could hear her. "I know what I saw when I looked at Tara Xendra, and from the look on your face, you are not happy with it. I ask you again, will you come in?"

The frown was startled away, to be replaced almost as rapidly with a perfect imitation of a warm smile.

So, he can control his features when he wishes to.

"As you wish, Dhulyn Wolfshead." He signaled to his attendants and, faces carefully impassive, they took up stations along the corridor.

"Remm Shalyn, I thank you for your service today. I hope that you will rest well."

His left eyelid quivered, as if he longed to wink at her, but all he said before he bowed and turned away to his own rooms was, "An honor and a pleasure, Tara Paledyn."

Upon entering her sitting room, Dhulyn smiled at Xerwin and indicated the best chair before she checked that there were no attendants waiting for her in one of the other rooms. As Remm Shalyn had told her, it was minor nobles rather than slaves who acted as body servants in the Tarxin's palace, and she had taken full advantage of this to limit her own attendants as far as she could. When she returned to the sitting room, Xerwin was still standing next to the large armchair, staring down at it as if there was something fascinating on the seat. Dhulyn checked the minuscule balcony that was the only other exit to the suite of rooms and turned back to him.

"How do I know I can trust you?" he said without looking up.

Dhulyn sat cross-legged on the divan, tucking her kilt and her feet under her. She shrugged. "You must trust someone. Why should it not be me? The chief advantage of a Paledyn, so far as I can see, is that I belong to no one, am of no faction, and can judge with clear eyes."

"The Tarxin takes it for granted that you will argue on our side."

"He's an intelligent man. As such, he would be sure to at least pretend to believe his cause is just. And you, Xerwin?"

He sighed, pulling out his little box of fresa, and placing it on the table, his eyes straying to the wooden tray on the low table to his right. Dhulyn pulled off the linen cloth to reveal a jug of water, and one of wine, along with cups of different sizes, a plate of pastries, and a bowl of fruit. "I have learned to take nothing for granted," he said.

Dhulyn smiled her wolf's smile. Spoken like the true son of a shrewd father.

"How long has the Tara Xendra been . . . not herself?"

Xerwin lowered himself into the chair and rubbed at his eyes. "Thank you for not calling her my sister."

Dhulyn poured out a cup of wine and handed it to him.

"What I saw is real, then? Whatever it may be, that child is not, or is no longer, your sister?"

Xerwin paused in the act of adding a tiny portion of fresa to his wine, hesitated, and returned it to the little box, snapping it shut. "How were you so certain? So quickly? You have never even met my sister."

Dhulyn drummed the fingers of her left hand on her knee. "I have seen such things before." She tried to keep her tone matter-of-fact, as if she were merely describing a horse she'd once seen, or a dog. The man's situation was a horrible one. She would prefer not to make it worse. "I'm sure that possession by spirits, even by gods, is not unknown even here."

He nodded. "There are tales. But, if it is a god, do they not usually make themselves known?"

Dhulyn decided there was no good end to that line of questioning. "Do you know how this occurred?"

She listened as he told of the Tara's fall, how she had hit her head and not regained consciousness.

"A Healer was not sent for immediately?"

"You understand, there seemed no need at first. Her attendants were not anxious to explain how they had allowed the accident to occur in the first place. Her head ached, and she had been frightened by the fall, but it was thought that rest alone was needed. When they could not rouse her, then they grew frightened and sent word to the Tarxin."

Dhulyn noticed that he did not call the man "my father."

"Even then," Xerwin continued, "it took time for the Tarxin to come, and he thought it best to wait another day before calling in the Marked."

"For blood's sake, *why*?" The words were out before she could stop them.

"The Tarxinate must not seem weak." Now Xerwin sounded as though he were quoting someone else's words. "I was told none of this until long after," he added.

"And when the Healer finally came?"

Dhulyn let Xerwin finish his tale uninterrupted. How the Marked never ventured out of their Sanctuary except in groups, what the Tarxin had told them to do when they informed him that the girl's spirit was lost.

"Clearly, the soul Found and Healed to the body was not that of your sister." Dhulyn poured out another glass of wine, waited until Xerwin had taken a sip, shaking her head at his offer of fresa. "When did you first suspect?"

"Only a few days ago. She was too ill at first for me to be much with her." He shrugged. "I had to return to my Battle Wing. And my duties have been increasing as well . . ." His voice trailed away, but his face grew thoughtful, so his distraction did not seem a likely result of the drug. "Do you think that was purposefully done?"

Dhulyn tilted her head, lifting one shoulder. "What told you then, when you finally saw your sister?"

"She did not know who Naxot was."

"I fear I can say the same."

"You saw the man sitting to my left? He's the heir to House Lilso, once next in importance to the Royal House, and hoping to be as important again." He'd been the one who sniffed his fresa, Dhulyn recalled. "He is—or was—Xendra's betrothed."

"She wouldn't be the first woman to forget she was betrothed," Dhulyn said with a smile.

But Xerwin saw no humor in it. "This is not some foreign prince, whose name might be knocked out of her head. Naxot is my closest ally at court, and Xendra has known him her whole life. She used to follow us around when she was a toddler, climbing into his lap and begging for sweets and kisses. She adored him."

Dhulyn noticed Xerwin's use of the past tense.

"And he was always kind to her, never brushed her off, as another of his age might have done. As I frequently did." Xerwin blinked and looked away.

Suddenly, sharp as a knife, Dhulyn felt an almost overwhelming desire for her Partner. Parno was so much better at dealing with people and their feelings, their regrets and their guilt. With a hand that trembled, just a little, Dhulyn poured out a cup of wine for herself, and took a swallow.

"What will you do, then? Destroy her?" she asked when she knew her voice would be steady. Xerwin, eyes still fixed on the wine jug, nodded, but very slowly. "Whoever it is that now occupies your sister's body is obviously a Storm Witch. She can do much good for your people."

"Naxot says the same thing, and I'm sure that's how my father thinks, though not for the same reasons. He thinks only of the power a Storm Witch brings him—principally over the Nomads at the moment, though he won't stop there. She's no more than a tool to him, as my sword is to me." He looked up, frowning. "But she isn't a tool, any more than my officers or my soldiers. She must have her own thoughts, her own plans. She is wearing Xendra's body like a glove, pretending to be my sister. If she is innocent, why the pretense? If she is evil, what can she bring to us but evil? Can I take such a chance?" He sat up straight, rested his hands on his thighs. "But you are a Paledyn, you will have your own view of these matters."

Dhulyn almost laughed aloud. "As it happens," she said, "my view is not so different from yours. It was the Witch who caused the storm which almost killed me, and did kill my Partner, another Paledyn." For a moment Dhulyn's throat closed. This was the first time she had spoken the words aloud. "If we are to destroy this spirit, we must first learn as much as possible. Will destroying the body kill it, for example? We must speak to the Marked who were there when Tara Xendra was Healed."

"Will they tell us the truth?"

"Only one way to find out. And, Xerwin," Dhulyn paused, but he did not correct her form of address. "You must remember that if we are successful in destroying the Storm Witch, it does not follow that we will be able to restore your sister."

The bleak look in his eyes told her that Xerwin had already thought of this.

"Come," she said, getting to her feet. "Sunrise comes quickly, and you must be ready to meet with the Tarxin."

Xerwin turned back at the door.

"These are strange and complicated times, Dhulyn Wolfshead. My friend Naxot says we are in the age of miracles. Mages, Paledyns." His smile was bittersweet. "And who knows what might be next. Some say the Slain God will rise."

"Oh, I think that is most unlikely."

Long after Xerwin had gone, Dhulyn was still awake, sorting through the weapons that Remm Shalyn had found for her. The swords were all of the shorter, heavier variety she had already seen, best used to slash and cut. That told her much about the style of fighting she might have to face.

She sat back in the chair. She was stalling and she knew it. It would be a simple matter to kill the girl. Nothing simpler, given that the Tarxin had put the child under her protection. All Dhulyn had to do was ask to meet with her, kill her—using bare hands if necessary—and then die fighting her way out. That had been her plan all along, sketchy though it might seem.

But would killing the body kill the Storm Witch? Or would the spirit merely be freed to inhabit some other helpless person? Because that was not part of Dhulyn's plan at all. Before she could act, she had to know. She wanted to be sure that the thing was destroyed.

Darlara usually enjoyed her time on watch. Through the Crayx she could see the whole ship, feel/taste the waters around it, sense the presence of the whole Pod, touch them lightly as they slept, performed their duties, ate, played with their children, hummed a soft lullaby, made love. And for the last few days, she put her hand on her lower belly, there had been a new life she could not yet sense directly. Or so the Crayx had told her.

But tonight, instead of joyful, Darlara felt edgy, distracted, unable to follow any one path of thought or feeling. She left her position by Ana-Paula at the wheel, and went down to the main deck, hoping that activity would clear her head, but finding her feet leading her toward the door of her own cabin, where she had left Parno Lionsmane asleep when she came on watch.

As soon as she realized where her feet were leading her, she went to the rail and leaned her elbows on it, letting her head fall into her hands.

#He still grieves# #You must have more patience#

How long

#Even now, his grief is less sharp# #There is something, a patterning, that he uses when he fights, and when he makes music, that helps him# #It restores him to himself# #Yes#

Should I tell him about the child *Would his current then flow more closely with ours*

#His current now carries him toward his revenge# #He believes he will die in taking his vengeance#

But would the child not show him that there is another current *It may be, that if knows there will be a child, might make a greater effort to live*

#It may be#

This time Darlara had her hand on the latch of the cabin door before she turned aside and went to the rail again.

Some time later, Mal, yawning and rubbing the sleep from his eyes, came and nudged her with his shoulder.

Your watch already

Jesting *How can I sleep with all this turmoil* *Will, won't, might, shouldn't, what if* *Think I can't feel that, even if don't have your thoughts*

Darlara rested her cheek against her brother's shoulder. *Sorry* *Don't know what to do*

Guessed that

Darlara butted him with her head, somehow eased by his chuckle. *Serious*

Know *But tell me what it's about* *This way, losing sleep for nothing*

It's the child

He slipped an arm around her shoulders and pulled her close. *Know for sure then*

Crayx say so *Certain*

Wonderful *The best news*

Darlara knew she should feel that way, too. And the greater part of her did. Would feel that way for the rest of her life, regardless of what Parno Lionsmane might do. But now that she had part of what she wanted, why should she not try to get all of it?

Crayx say Lionsmane might not be seeking hard to live, now that his Partner's gone *He'll get his revenge, but not carefully, thinking he might as well die*

But if he knows about the child, won't he want to stay *Won't he want to see it grow*

Darlara nodded. Of course Malfin thought the same as she did herself. They were twins, after all.

But see, what if, knowing that his promise is filled, what if that's what lets him decide to die Malfin began to frown and Darlara rushed to finish her thought. *If don't tell him, he'll still have his promise to fulfill, perhaps take better care*

Don't tell him *Are you crazed* *When you show, he'll know*

But by then he'll be with us for moons, he'll be better, he won't want to die anymore He'll stay with me, she hadn't quite the courage to form the thought clearly, though she knew Mal picked it up.

Mal, openmouthed, shook his head slowly from side to side. *He'll know you lied, and that's if Crayx don't tell him* Mal's anger could not have been plainer if he was shouting from the Racha's nest.

But he'll be alive, he'd forgive

Mal turned to look her squarely in the face. He took a step back from her, and Darlara swallowed hard. Mal had actually taken a step away from her.

"What are you thinking?" he said aloud, as if he didn't want to share her thoughts anymore. "Isn't some landster, we don't care if the shell knife we sell him falls apart in six moons. Lionsmane is Pod-sensed. Crayx know him, saved him. He's part of us." Mal tapped his chest with his closed fist. "Lie to him, lie to *all* of us." He pointed his finger at her in a way that suddenly reminded Darlara of their mother. "Tell him, or I will."

#Or we will#

"There. See?"

Darlara felt the tears spring into her eyes. Mal was right, could she *really* have been thinking about lying? The Pod did not lie to each other—could not lie, really, since the Crayx always knew the truth. And yet, she'd been thinking . . . her face fell forward into her hands and she felt her brother's strong arm once more around her shoulders.

Sorry she wept. *So sorry*

#Forgiveness# #Understanding#

Darlara straightened, wiping off her tears with the sleeve of her shirt. She patted Mal in response to his worried look and turned away.

This time she went all the way to the cabin and went in, closing the door behind her.

⟡

Carcali sat on her little balcony, the stone cold beneath her, her arms wrapped around her knees. Watching the clouds through the balusters. Something about the way that woman looked at her at the feast had taken her aback, just a little. Carcali had shrugged off the idea of these Paledyn— this Artless culture had so many superstitions. Like their Slain God and the animal worship of the Nomads, and the creepy *otherness* of the Marked. Carcali shuddered, skin crawling, remembering the six-fingered touch of the so-called Healer. Why didn't he fix his hand if he was so good?

Carcali stood up and went inside, rubbing the outside of her arms with her hands. That woman. That Paledyn, had looked at her as if she could see right through her, as if she already knew everything there was to know about her, and didn't like what she knew.

Carcali felt the warmth of rising anger. What right had that woman to look at her like that? Tattooed like a Master Artist, and no more Art about her than there was about this chair. Carcali kicked it away from the table enough to sit down.

There was no reason for her to second-guess her arrangement with the Tarxin just because some painted barbarian—*scarred,* no less—looked at her like all her aunts, her mother, and both grandmothers rolled into one. After all, making an alliance with the Tarxin was the smart thing to do. He was the most powerful person around here. If her own people had only sided with her, backed her, she wouldn't be in this mess, she—

Carcali stopped, breathing hard, tears threatening. The Tarxin was the most powerful, but that didn't make him *right*. She'd learned that lesson the hard way.

Maybe she needed other allies. Better allies. What about the brother, Xerwin? He at least made you feel you were talking to a real person when he looked at you.

Xerwin had dreamed of the Paledyn in the night. What little sleep he managed in the few hours before dawn brought the sun to his window had been broken up with images of what they had talked about the night before. Storm clouds turning into people he had not seen in years, his old guard sergeant, his mother. Images of his sister showing him the dances she had learned. Images of Dhulyn Wolfshead's smile. He dreamed that she took his face in her hands and kissed him with her cool lips.

Xerwin pushed the empty cup of ganje away, snapped his box of fresa shut, and rubbed his hand across his mouth. Well, *that* could complicate things considerably, couldn't it? It wouldn't mean the end of his betrothal—that was a purely political alliance, the girl was still a child, and he had in fact never met her. A private bonding with a Paledyn, known to all but never spoken of . . . it could be acceptable to even the most orthodox and conservative, even Naxot's House couldn't find fault. It would be the same as a bond with a Holy Woman, something only she could choose.

Such a bond as Naxot might have hoped for, if Xendra were really a Storm Witch. Or if the Storm Witch was really Xendra . . . or . . . Xerwin shook his head. No good thinking about that. It was almost time to meet with his father.

As Xerwin navigated the corridors between his own suite and his father's morning room, he found that he felt better than he had for days. Even if what he fantasized about her was not likely to come to pass, the fact that Dhulyn Wolfshead, a Paledyn, saw the situation the same way he did, gave him confidence. Before speaking with her, he'd been unsure whether to confront his father on the subject of the spirit that had usurped his sister's body. Now he knew it would be the correct thing to do.

A small gathering of people in the Tarxin's anteroom made him slow his pace. He did not immediately recognize the child emerging with her escort of two lady pages and an armsman as the Storm Witch. Instead of her usual child's white clothing, she was dressed in a robe of sky blue, embroidered over with gold. Not unlike the colors he wore himself, Xerwin realized.

"Xerwin." The Storm Witch made an abortive gesture, lifting her arms awkwardly as if she meant to embrace him, but didn't know how. A hand squeezed his heart. His sister would have known, would have run to him, regardless of protocol.

"Tara Xendra," he said, formally inclining his head to her.

"Tar Xerwin." She inclined her head also. Did he imagine it, or was there something different about her voice?

Xerwin waited until the Storm Witch and her attendants had turned into the corridor before presenting himself at the Tarxin's door. When he was admitted, he found his father standing at one of the two tables in the room set at right angles to the windows. Where the Tarxin stood were large scrolls, some held open with weights, some curled and waiting. The other table held only the plates of a solitary breakfast.

"Well done, my boy," the Tarxin said, lifting his eyes from the maps he was studying and gesturing to a chair.

"My lord?"

"You spent most of the night in the Paledyn's rooms. Well done, indeed. I've reason to congratulate you on your good thinking yet again, it seems. And it appears that women will always succumb to a pretty face, even such women as that."

Xerwin's lips parted, but something made him hold his tongue before he could explain to his father just how wrong he was. He hesitated, lowering himself into the chair slowly. It seemed wrong somehow to let his father say such things—think such things—but whether he was defending the Paledyn or himself, Xerwin didn't know.

"F–father," he said, stumbling over the word. "The Storm Witch that inhabits Xendra's body." Xerwin glanced up and found his father looking at him. The man's eyes were bright, but his face was a stone mask. Xerwin tried to remember how confident he'd felt in the corridor only moments ago.

"The Storm Witch," he said again. "Should we not find some way to rid ourselves of her?"

The Tarxin pushed the charts and scrolls on the table to one side and took the seat across from Xerwin. He leaned back in the chair, resting his elbows on the arms. Xerwin tried to keep his gaze from faltering.

"Is this the advice of the Paledyn?"

Again Xerwin hesitated, trying to see all the consequences of his answer. There was something in the way the man had said the word "Paledyn," coupled with the way he'd just spoken of her that told Xerwin his father did not think as highly of the Paledyns as he would have people believe. Caution made Xerwin change his answer.

"No, sir," he said finally.

"I should think not. What brings this thought to you, then?"

Xerwin hoped he didn't look as relieved as he felt. He made himself shrug. "If it should turn on us, it might be as well to know how to kill it."

"That is a good thought, my son. A good thought, but a

poor ploy." The Tarxin shook his head. "You have much left to learn, I see. You do not destroy a useful tool because it is dangerous. You use its strength against it. This one is such a tool. A sword to the hand, nothing more. She can be dealt with, bargained with, and used."

Xerwin blinked at the Tarxin's use of his own metaphor. "What of Xendra?" he asked.

"She is gone." The Tarxin's voice had a note of finality Xerwin had heard many times before. "There is nothing we can do for her which will justify losing the services of the Storm Witch. Do you understand?"

"Yes, sir. Of course." *He'd do the same if it was me,* Xerwin thought. *We're all just tools to him.* To use and discard. He was right to be careful, and he should try to be more careful still.

"When do you go next to the Sanctuary?"

Xerwin blinked, glad to think of something else. "Not for some days yet, seven or eight I would say."

Tarxin pulled the nearest scroll closer to him and began to unroll it. "Go today. They foretold the coming of the Paledyn—though the Caids know they might have warned us she was female—now she is here, we must see what more they can tell us."

It took Xerwin a moment to realize that he had been dismissed. Careful to take his leave in the correct manner, whether the Tarxin appeared to notice or not, Xerwin let himself out of the room and nodded at the servants waiting outside. He turned toward the stairwell as he reached the main corridor, and started walking faster as he realized he was heading toward Dhulyn Wolfshead's rooms on the lower level. They should visit the Marked, she had said. And this made as good an opportunity as any.

⟜

Parno climbed high into the rigging. He needed time, and privacy, to think. The Crayx would stay out of his thoughts— or at least pretend to, which amounted to the same thing— but even though they could not read his mind without the help of the Crayx, it was more than he could stand to see Dar's and Mal's faces hovering at his elbow.

Parno had not expected it, but the knowledge that a child was coming did change things. Everything that he had been taught, both in his Noble House and later, in the Mercenary Schools, told him that you stood by your word, that you did not walk away from your commitments and your obligations. It was always possible that he would not live to fulfill his obligation to his child—that might happen to anyone and Mercenary Brothers, in particular, were always prepared to die—but if he survived his attempt to destroy the Storm Witch, would his obligation to the child outweigh the demands of his Partnership?

He grinned, squinting his eyes into the rising wind. If Dhulyn were here, she would have an opinion, but if she were, her opinion wouldn't be necessary. He knew what the Common Rule required, and what it said about Mercenary Brothers who abandoned or did not provide for their children.

"Demons and perverts," he said.

#Do you require us# He could sense a warm humor in the question.

"Just debating with myself."

#Debate with others may be more fruitful#

"Perhaps, but I'd like to sort out my own thoughts first, if you don't mind."

#Acknowledgment#

Parno sighed. When Darlara had approached him to remind him of his promise, he hadn't been thinking clearly—hadn't been thinking at all, he saw now. The reality of a child, what that would mean, simply had not occurred to him. Almost as if, without realizing it, he had simply assumed no child would come. And now? Dhulyn had agreed to this, knowing, as she'd thought, that he would die. What would she wish him to do now? Now that she was the one gone?

"Death doesn't part us." As he said the words, he found he felt stronger, more confident. "We are still Partners, in Battle, and in Death." Dhulyn, if she *were* here, would be bringing her Scholar's training to bear on the argument.

"The child will live, or it will not live," he said, trying to remember how the lines of logic worked. "It will be Pod-sensed, or it will not." That was a very logical approach, and not something that Dar would want to consider.

If the child is Pod-sensed, he thought, *no better place for it than here on the* Wavetreader. But if it was not . . . He trusted what he had been told, that those children went to the Nomad havens, carefully hidden and safe. But in his case that was not the only option. Mercenary Brother or no, he had a family in Imrion who acknowledged him, and the child could be sent to them.

Fourteen

"THIS IS WHERE we part company."

Dhulyn brought her gaze down from the lofty ceiling of the Sanctuary Hall bright with torches and reflected daylight, and turned back to Xerwin. He shifted his eyes away from her, almost as though he were embarrassed.

"It's likely that they will answer your questions more easily than they will mine," he said. "You *are* a Paledyn, and they would trust in your fair dealing and discretion. Me, they will see as the representative of the Tarxin, and I already know what answers they gave him."

Dhulyn nodded. That made sense. "And you?"

"An errand for the Tarxin that I must perform alone."

That wasn't strictly true, Dhulyn thought as she watched Xerwin cross the hall toward the far end. An errand for the Tarxin, now that she'd believe. But whether he had to perform it alone, or whether he merely wished to—she shook her head. Xerwin did not give the appearance of regretting their alliance of the evening before, the Two Hearts *Shora* had done its work, charming him enough to listen to her, and to value what she had said. But something was troubling the young man, making him shift his eyes, and until she knew what it was, she had to treat it as a possible danger. Better cautious than cursing.

As Dhulyn waited for Remm Shalyn to return with a Sanctuary Guide, other petitioners began to trickle into the Hall. Gradually, Dhulyn became aware that many of these others were circling closer to her as they waited. Several caught her eye and smiled, inclining their heads and murmuring, "Paledyn," when they saw she was looking. Finally, an older woman in the veils and bangles of an upper servant came close enough to stretch out a hand holding a dark purple flower. Dhulyn took the blossom in her left hand, touching her forehead with the fingers of her right. As if the woman had somehow opened a door, others now came closer, two more with flowers, and a little boy with a carved wooden warrior—clearly a favorite toy from the wear— that Dhulyn held to her forehead and then returned, to the child's evident delight. As she did this, two other women came close enough to touch her outstretched arm. Dhulyn tensed, but they both backed away, touching their own foreheads.

"Tara Paledyn?"

Dhulyn had already been aware that those crowding around her to her left had parted to allow the young woman's halting approach, so she was not surprised to be addressed. And since she'd known the approach was halting, she wasn't surprised to find the girl leaning on a staff. The shoe on the left foot had been built up, and there was clearly something wrong in the way that foot was attached to the ankle. The young woman's only other distinguishing feature was that she wore no veils, her dark brown hair, pulled back and braided, was uncovered.

"If you would come with me, Tara Paledyn, the Marks you have asked to see are ready for you." There was some whispering among those watching, but though they stayed back, none seemed inclined to leave.

The Sanctuary Guide turned and led the way across the cold tiled floor toward the plain wooden doors at the closer end of the hall. Glancing sideways, Dhulyn could see the crowd following at a discreet distance as Remm Shalyn fell in at her left side.

"I am Dhulyn Wolfshead," she said to her guide. "What are you called?"

"I am Mender Fourteen," the young woman said.

Dhulyn slowed to a halt. "Your pardon if I am ignorant and offend. But do you not have names?"

The girl smiled, clearly not offended. "We do, but they

are generally used only within the Sanctuary, among ourselves."

"I would prefer to use a name, if it is allowed."

"Then I am Medolyn."

Medolyn led Dhulyn and Remm Shalyn out of the vast public entry hall through a set of double doors into what was clearly an anteroom. Another bareheaded young woman stood pressing her hands together behind a large table on which were scrolls, pens, and bottles of ink. Dhulyn smiled to herself. Clerks were clerks, it seemed, wherever one might go.

"This is the Paledyn Dhulyn Wolfshead," Medolyn said. The other girl scrambled to her feet. "This is Coria, a Finder."

"All of us clerks are," the other girl said with a grin. "Only a Finder could figure out where all the records are. You're to see the First Healer, aren't you, Tara Paledyn? And the First Mender and Finder as well, I think? They're waiting in the Blue Chamber, Medolyn. Your sword servant may remain here," Coria said to Dhulyn. "Or return to the main hall."

"I didn't think to see women being used as Stewards or clerks," Dhulyn said, as they left the anteroom and started down a long corridor lit by tall glass lamps standing in front of polished metal squares.

"There aren't so many of us that we can be particular about these things. Is it different, then, across the Long Ocean?"

Was there something more than mere curiosity in the girl's voice? Something wistful? Parno would have known, Dhulyn thought.

"It is. Men and women share all tasks and all things equally. Nor do the Marked live in Sanctuaries."

Medolyn stopped in front of a broad wooden door, inlaid with blue tiles.

"But where do they live, and how?"

"Where they choose, and by selling their services."

"But our service belongs to the Tarxin."

They're slaves, Dhulyn thought, a chill creeping up her back. *Well-treated, carefully looked after, but slaves nonetheless. He sells their services to others, I'll wager.* Thank Sun and Moon she'd told no one, not even the Nomads, of her own Mark.

"And if they don't live together, how is it ensured that the children are Marked?"

The chill spread across Dhulyn's shoulders and up the back of her neck. Were the Marked here being bred for their talent? And not as carefully as the Nomads handled their breeding. That would explain Medolyn's deformed foot. "It is not. The Marked marry whom they choose, and sometimes the children are Marked, and sometimes not. There are Guildhalls, for training—" And this was probably one of those, once upon a time. "But the Marked don't live there beyond the time they're trained."

Medolyn shook her head, her lower lip between her teeth. "It sounds . . . but perhaps I would be afraid, living on my own."

Dhulyn was spared an answer by the opening of the door. Medolyn led the way through, bowed to the three people sitting around a cold central fire bowl, and left.

"We welcome you, Tara Paledyn." The man who spoke was clearly the oldest of the trio, hawk-nosed, with pale green eyes and dark hair receding from his forehead. "I am Ellis, First Healer. This is First Finder Javen and First Mender Rascon." The Finder was a middle-aged woman whose graying hair was pulled tightly off her lined face. The Mender was the youngest of the three, a pretty woman with a heart-shaped face surrounded by dark curly hair escaping from its combs.

Dhulyn touched her forehead. "I am Dhulyn Wolfshead, called the Scholar. I was Schooled by Dorian of the River, the Black Traveler."

"If you would sit?" He indicated the fourth chair. Clearly, Dhulyn thought, the best chair in the room.

When they were all seated, and ganje had been offered and poured, the Healer spoke again.

"In what way can we serve you, Tara Paledyn?"

Dhulyn had thought of several ways to open the discussion she wanted to have, but the girl Medolyn had given her an opening she could not ignore. "Tell me," she said. "Why do you not Heal that young woman's foot?"

From the tightening of lips and the narrowing of eyes, all

three of the Marked were at least somewhat offended by her question. *Good. Get them off-balance.*

"For the same reason I don't Heal this." Ellis Healer held up his left hand. There was an extra finger between the thumb and first finger. Ah, Dhulyn thought, *this* was the Healer she'd been seeing in her Visions.

"Medolyn's foot is not the result of injury. She was born with it. As I was born with my extra finger. There is no Healer living who has enough life energy to Heal a defect of birth, at least not on this side of the Long Ocean." His tone was not quite sharp enough to be disrespectful, but the intention was there.

"I have not heard that Healers could not heal birth defects," Dhulyn said evenly. Her words surprised them, that much she could see. "But I have never seen a Mark with such a defect—though I admit, I have not seen more than a few dozen in my lifetime."

The Mender, Rascon, threw her hands into the air. "We've been telling the cursed Tarxins for generations that we can't be bred like cattle without harm being done, to our Marks as well as to ourselves, but they've never listened."

"Have you tried refusing your services?" Dhulyn was sure she knew the answer, but was curious as to how they would phrase it.

"There's a limit to how much we can defy the Tarxin," Ellis said bluntly. "According to our agreement with the Tarxinate, we are given the privileges of home, roof, table, and bed. In return we owe our services. Theoretically, we have neutrality and privacy, self-government within the shelter of the Tarxinate. However . . ." The three Marked exchanged a glance. "In recent months, the present Tarxin has been . . . encroaching on our privileges."

"Perhaps you could help us?" Rascon Mender sat forward in her eagerness, hope in her eyes.

Dhulyn did not know what to answer. Her task here was to kill the Storm Witch and avenge the death of her Partner. The Common Rule, and her own heart, demanded it. She couldn't let the plight of these people deflect her from her goal. But the Marked were, in some measure, her people as well. If they were in need, could she turn her back on them? Normally, the Common Rule kept the Mercenary

Brotherhood politically neutral, but surely she could speak to Remm Shalyn. Perhaps some of his contacts . . . ?

Dhulyn gave herself a mental shake. "I have come, as you know, with my own tasks to accomplish." Their faces, which had begun to relax, tightened once more. "If I am successful," she continued. "It may be that I can advise you as well." That would have to satisfy them, and herself, for now. Further than that she could not go.

"Tell us, then, how may we serve you?"

But even now, Dhulyn found she was unwilling to let the question of their abilities lie.

"You'll forgive my pursuing this question," she said. "But it may touch on my primary task. How is it that you would have life force enough to restore a spirit to its body, but insufficient to Heal yourself?"

"If I may answer." The others nodded and let Javen Finder continue. "Each Mark uses the life force of the Marked one," she said. "The harder the task, the greater the amount of life force used."

Dhulyn stifled her impatience. She'd asked, and now she had to listen.

"Life force is restored in the Marked one by eating, by sleep, and in some cases by singing, or playing music. But to Heal, for example, a defect of birth, that would require an amount of life force equivalent to the birth itself."

Dhulyn leaned forward, a thought having occurred to her. "I have seen Finders use scrying bowls, and Menders as well, use some tool symbolic of what they do, to focus their concentration. Would this not help you use less life force?"

Javen Finder leaned forward as well, eagerness plain on her face. "Do you know where we could find these things, Paledyn? Scholars have told us that such items were once used, but even working together, none of us Finders have been able to locate such a thing."

"The Nomads aren't able to trade for them, no matter what we offer in exchange—or so they say," Rascon Mender said, nodding.

"They say truly. The ones I have seen were the property of the Marked ones who used them," Dhulyn said. "In all my travels I have never seen them for sale, or trade." Though she had seen, in a Scholars' Library, an ancient text describing how a Finder's bowl was made—but best to say nothing of that now. No point in giving false hopes; this would be something else for Remm Shalyn to investigate for her.

Ellis Healer stared off into the middle distance. "If we were able, if we could increase our powers, we'd be able to save the pregnancies that do not come to term, and Heal the babies that do not live. There'd be more of us, more Healers, more Seers for that matter. It's all we can do right now to keep the White Twins healthy, the Slain One knows, and when they die, we'll have no more Seers." Ellis blinked, drawing in a deep breath and looking around at his colleagues.

Rascon Mender tossed back her ganje and frowned down at her empty cup.

"Are they barren, then?" Dhulyn was asking as much for herself as for them.

"As good as. You know that only women are Seers?" Dhulyn nodded. "With Seers, the Mark itself consumes the life force that they would use to produce a child. They can either See or bear children, not both. In order to produce a child, there must be enough Seers that the others get all the Visions, while each in turn produces a child."

Well, so many of her questions answered, Dhulyn thought. Here was why the Visions seemed to be linked to her woman's cycle, stronger and weaker as the blood came and went. And here was the reason she had never borne any children of her own.

"How many must there be?"

Javen Finder spread her hands. "Who can know? The White Twins were born of two Healers, maybe twenty years after the last Seer died. So far as our records go, there have never been more than three Seers at one time."

"And no Marked appear in the outside population?"

Here the three Marked exchanged a look among themselves. "Sometimes, among the slaves, yes," Ellis Healer said. "It's our right to inspect any child when they reach the correct age, but we rarely obtain such a child from a Noble House."

"Unless the child is female." All three lowered their eyes, and Rascon Mender fussed with the jug of ganje, refilling cups.

Dhulyn was not surprised. A handy way to rid yourself

of an unwanted child, and the female children would be the most unwanted.

"You have given me much to think about," she said finally, setting her cup of ganje down on the table to her right hand. "Now tell me, how did the Storm Witch come to inhabit the body of the Tarxin's daughter?"

Shock, and something like awe rippled across their faces before the Marked ones regained control of their features. *Good,* Dhulyn thought. *They'll be more likely to tell me the truth if they think I already know.* Still, at first it seemed they wouldn't say anything at all; each looked at the others, as if no one wanted to begin.

"Oh, for Sun and Moon," Dhulyn said, rubbing her forehead with the fingers of her left hand. "Speak freely, I beg you. I give you my oath as a — as a Paledyn that you will not suffer because you have told me the truth."

Rascon Mender looked at Javen Finder, and both turned to Ellis Healer. Finally, clearing his throat, he began.

"You must consider, Tara Paledyn, that we were not summoned for some two or three days after the Tara Xendra fell."

"How did she fall, exactly?" Dhulyn realized she had been thinking along the lines of a fall from a horse, but of course, without horses . . .

"She had been playing in the gardens above, and slipped while running along the top of a wall," Javen said.

"There is no doubt that she hit her head, the swelling and discoloration were still quite noticeable when we viewed her," Ellis continued. "We were told that she lost consciousness for only a very short period at that time, and while she complained of headache, she did eat her supper that evening, and fell asleep normally."

"You understand," cut in Rascon. "All this is what we were told at the time; we've no way to know whether any of it's true. The lady pages wouldn't have wanted the Tarxin, Light of the Sun, to know that they'd let his child hurt herself, so they might not have told soon enough, you see? They might have said she was fine at first just to save themselves."

"In any case, when we examined her, we found that while the body lived, it was empty, the soul was gone, and we so informed the Tarxin, Light of the Sun."

"Then I made the mistake of saying the soul was 'lost,' you see, meaning to speak it softly like, and the Tarxin, Light of the Sun, told Javen here to Find it." Rascon shook her head, and still another curl fell loose from her combs.

"And the thing was, I did Find a soul almost right away." Javen gestured with her hands. "And it was so eager to get into the body that I took it for the Tara's own soul, else why so eager?"

"So you Found, Healed, and Mended," Dhulyn said. "You have placed this soul into the Tara's body. Can you take it out? Will taking it out destroy it?"

Again, the exchange of looks between the Marked ones. Finally, Javen spoke up. "Tara Paledyn. What we tell you now no one else knows, not even others here in the Sanctuary."

"We trust in your goodness, and in your word, you see." Rascon evidently felt she needed to make things clear.

"You may do so," Dhulyn said.

"Four days after the events we tell you of, we came again to the Tara Xendra's apartments, to make sure she was feeling no further ill effects," Javen said. "It was obvious to us that she was no longer the Tara Xendra. We feared then what the Tarxin, Light of the Sun, might do."

"It's one thing not to heal his daughter, you see. It's another entirely to set some foreign spirit masquerading about in his daughter's body." Rascon's brisk tone was thinly spread over a very real fear.

"What did you do?" For it was obvious from their shifting and throat clearing that they had done something.

"We expelled the spirit from the body." Ellis Healer's voice was low.

"What?"

"We were trying—we thought we might Find the real Xendra after all, you see, since we knew this one wasn't her. But it didn't stay expelled, that was the problem. We could push it out, but we couldn't keep it out."

"So even if the real child's spirit is out there to be Found . . ."

"It can't get back into its own body, no, because the body's occupied, isn't it?" Rascon slapped her hands on her knees.

"Tara Paledyn, there is more." The Healer laced his

fingers together. "Three times we tried to expel the strange spirit, and each time there were great storms, with winds and lightnings. Once, even ice fell from the sky. It was clear to us that the spirit possessing the child's body was a Weather Mage, such as the old books speak of. We made no further attempts."

"But you *can* expel the Storm Witch, you *can* put the real child's soul back?"

"Very likely, the true soul would be easy to Heal and Mend quickly, but Paledyn, we do not have the real child's soul."

Dhulyn tapped her fingers on the arm of her chair. "Find it," she said. "Perhaps now that the stronger soul of the Storm Witch is no longer," Dhulyn waved her hands, "distracting you, you can Find the real soul more easily."

Javen Finder frowned, looking inward before she spoke. "Well, if you say so, Tara Paledyn. I'll try."

Had she made the right decision, Dhulyn wondered? Would the Storm Witch be easier, or harder to destroy outside of the body? Instinct told her that if the spirit wanted so desperately to stay in the body, expelling it was the right thing to do. Would that be the same as destroying it?

Dhulyn sighed. At the very least, she would know more. And knowledge was always like a good sword in the hand of someone who knew how to use it.

The Seers' section of the Sanctuary was well apart from the areas of the other Marked, and unlike them, the White Twins never came out of their rooms. Petitioners, even the Tarxin himself, had to go or send to them. Xerwin felt his skin crawl and forced his shoulders to stop creeping up around his ears. This was the real reason he hadn't wanted Dhulyn Wolfshead to accompany him on his errand. How could he let her see his reaction to the Seers?

As usual, he was met beyond the Seers' door by one of the elderly women who served as the White Twins' attendants. He had sent ahead to let them know he was coming. Early on, he'd learned that when he didn't, he wasn't likely to get a useful Vision, if he got one at all.

"Right this way, Tar Xerwin, if you please," the woman said the same way she always did. She kept her hands folded at her waist and toddled in front of him on her short legs like a self-important hen.

The White Twins had one of the innermost rooms of the Sanctuary, where no sunlight could find them, even by accident. Nor were their personal rooms lit by use of the mirrored panels that brought true sunlight into the inner rooms of many of the Noble Houses. This did not mean the Twins had no light in their rooms, however. The sisters were said to be afraid of the dark, and so there were always lamps lit and candles burning, dozens of them, set into cloudy glass bowls or covered with colored glass shades.

The two women were playing a game with chalks and vera tiles on the floor when he was ushered into their day room. Drawing contorted stick figures and images of the Slain God knew what strange things. As always when they saw him, they ran squealing to touch his clothes and his hair with their long white fingers, exclaiming over its color and darkness, and holding up the ends of their own white braids to compare.

"Now then, now then," he said, as he always did, sounding in his own ears like some wise old uncle from a play. "If you sit down and behave yourselves, I've got chocolate for you."

"We know you, don't we," said one, while the other nodded, and nodded and kept on nodding. They had names, but since they never answered to them, no one used them, calling them only "girls" or "my dears."

Sometimes it was hard to remember that these women were older than he was, and that though their faces were unlined, there should perhaps be some gray starting to show in the hair that had always been whiter than the sands of the beach.

"Of course you know me, I'm Xerwin," he said. They wouldn't remember his rank, or anyone else's for that matter, which Xerwin had always suspected was one of the reasons the Tarxin did not like to come. They nodded, only twice thank the Slain God, but their pink eyes were empty.

"Xerwin, Xerwin, Xerwin," sang one, sinking back to the floor.

"That's right, and now you're going to answer some questions for me, aren't you?"

"You said you had chocolate," the first one said, and the other nodded again.

"Are you sitting in your big chair? Are you behaving yourselves?" He arched his eyebrows and put his hands on his hips, as they giggled and ran for their chairs. He'd learned that if he treated the Twins as he'd treated Xendra when she was five or six, he'd get the best response.

"Now, can you sing your song for me?"

"We know lots of songs," the twin on the left said.

"But for chocolate you'll sing your special song, you know the one I like?" Xerwin began to hum a simple, repetitive tune. The twin on the left clapped her hands and begun to hum as well, while the twin on the right began to sing. Soon, her sister had joined her.

The words were nonsense as far as Xerwin could tell, though when he came for a Vision they always sang the same words, and as they sang, their voices grew stronger, deepened. They sat very still, clasping hands, breathing in unison. They reached the point in the song where they always stopped, and sat, quietly, their faces relaxed, older, their eyes focused to some great distance, true, but *focused* in a way they had not been moments before.

Recognizing his moment, Xerwin had his question ready. "What does the coming of the Paledyn mean for the Mortaxa?"

"We see a tall woman, a warrior, hair like old blood, scarred of face, but clean of soul and vision. She leads a small, dark child by the hand. They are singing." Both white women smiled, identical smiles, and Xerwin's breath caught in his throat.

"They sing a song we all know, though you never sing it with us," the twin on the right said.

Xerwin shuddered. This woman, the woman who was speaking now, and her sister—assured, confident, smiling at some secret humor—why did they appear only when the twins were Seeing? Where were they when the Visions were gone?

"When the Paledyn comes, rain will fall in the desert; the hind chase the lion; the creatures of the sea will walk the beaches."

"What does this mean?"

"Who is simple now? Who the child?" The twin on the left looked directly at him and smiled. "Should we speak more plain? The Paledyn changes all. Nothing will be as it was. The world as you know it will be gone, forever."

"For better or for worse?" But now they no longer listened.

"Trees will flower in winter; the sea will rise, the land ripple and flow."

Their voices slowly faded, and the twin on the right began singing once more. Their faces slackened and their pink eyes unfocused.

The Vision was gone, the Sight finished, and the Seers were children again. Xerwin chewed on his lower lip as he left the White Twins to the care of their attendants. He knew poetry when he heard it, and the extremity of what they'd said didn't frighten him. Change was what they meant, great change. That was what Dhulyn Wolfshead was bringing. He stepped out into the main hall and checked the people waiting there, but he saw no sign of her.

There was one change he definitely wanted, and that was to get that Storm Witch out of his sister's body. Dhulyn Wolfshead had said she would help with that, and the White Twins had definitely seen her leading a dark-haired child by the hand. But if he told his father what he'd learned here today ... Xerwin let out the breath he hadn't realized he was holding.

"What weighty Vision brings about such a sigh, Tar Xerwin?"

Xerwin looked round to find Naxot at his elbow.

"Naxot, thank the Slain God." Xerwin took his friend by the arm and led him to an uninhabited bench near the door through which the Paledyn would have passed earlier into the inner Sanctuary. Xerwin's own attendants would keep any others out of hearing distance.

"The White Twins say that the Paledyn will bring changes, great changes." He closed his hand around Naxot's wrist. "I think she may bring Xendra back."

"Can she do this?"

"Who knows? Perhaps she will persuade the Storm Witch to return to her own place."

"But the Storm Witch is a Holy Woman."

Xerwin bit down on his impatience. Naxot's orthodoxy was becoming irritating. "And Paledyns are the Hands of the Slain God."

"What will you tell the Tarxin, Light of the Sun?" Naxot said.

That is a very good question, Xerwin thought. "What if I don't tell him anything at all?" He looked at Naxot from the corner of his eye.

"Leave everything to the Slain God, Xerwin," Naxot said, patting him on the shoulder. "Do nothing rash before prayer."

"Perhaps you're right," Xerwin said, standing up as he saw the door to the inner Sanctuary opening.

Fifteen

THE SANCTUARY HALL WAS NOTICEABLY darker now that the sun had set, and the great mirrors of polished silver and glass no longer had daylight to reflect. Remm Shalyn escorted Dhulyn across the wide expanse of floor, impossibly huge now that it was empty except for them.

"I stop out here," he said, twisting up his lips and looking around him with bright eyes. "It was you they sent for, not me," he added to her raised eyebrow.

"And you'll give some thought to what we discussed?"

"I could do more than think about it, if I ask to see the First Marks, while you're with the Seers." He smiled and looked over her shoulder as a middle-aged woman appeared in the Seers' doorway. She touched her forehead to Dhulyn as they neared her, and nodded to Remm Shalyn. Remm stepped to one side, leaned his shoulder against the wall next to the door, and grinned.

"I'll be here when you come out, Dhulyn Wolfshead."

The Seers' portion of the Sanctuary was darker than even the almost deserted main hall. This was the section of the Sanctuary farthest from the cliff face, deep into the rock that formed the city. As Dhulyn followed her guide, her Mercenary-Schooled senses automatically noted the direction of each turning. If for some reason the lighting failed, Dhulyn would have no trouble finding her way back to the entrance—or to any other spot in the city she had already been.

"Are you Marked yourself, lady?" she asked the attendant who was guiding her.

"Well, I am, then," the woman said, looking back over her shoulder. "But it doesn't go deep, my Mark. I can Heal small things—scratches, sore throats, and such. I mostly look after the little ones, and for the last while I've been helping with the White Twins. They don't like change, you see, it upsets them and throws off their Visions. If they see me around them more and more, little by little, I can help with them more."

"Is their present attendant getting older?"

"You're a sharp one, then. Though, seeing as you're a Paledyn, I suppose I shouldn't be surprised. Right this way, please, Tara."

They turned yet another corner and the light dimmed even more. The single door in front of them had raised panels, but was otherwise unadorned. The attendant noticed Dhulyn's interest.

"The old Seer, the one before the Twins, she was blind, they say, so you don't see the kind of decoration we have elsewhere."

"And the White Twins, they do not care for decoration?"

"Ah well, they're children, aren't they? Their tastes are going to run a different way. You'll see, Tara."

The woman hesitated with her hand on the door latch. "You've been told what to expect, then, Tara? It's not just what they look like, you see, it's that they're really like children, and if they've a Sight for you alone, well, then I have to leave you with them, you see."

"I have been told, yes."

Nodding, the woman opened the door and stepped through, saying "Here she is, then, my dear ones, the Tara Paledyn come to see you." Dhulyn stepped forward, and heard the door shut behind her.

The room was full of soft light, candles in glass jars and lamps with colored shades. Two women, skin so white it almost glowed, sat at the farthest of three tables, spoons in their hands, bowls of porridge in front of them.

Even though Remm Shalyn had warned Dhulyn what to expect, her breath still faltered in her throat when she saw them. An Outlander, and a Red Horseman, Dhulyn was well used to being the palest person in any gathering, but these women made her look like a Berdanan. She had seen a horse once with the White Disease, and she knew that it happened occasionally with other animals, but to see these women, white as the finest parchment, their eyes red as coals—at first her mind simply rejected the image. She remembered what Parno had said about twins, that some could make their livings traveling with players. But these women could not have done such a thing. Like the horse Dhulyn had seen, their skin would not tan, and exposure to the sun would eventually kill them.

They had leaped to their feet as soon as Dhulyn cleared the doorway, flinging down their spoons and rushing to her with their arms outstretched. They ran without heed across chalk drawings of stick figures and round, four-legged beasts on the floor. One had a smear of jam on her cheek. And a fleck of gold in the pink iris of her left eye. Dhulyn braced herself as they flung themselves on her, wrapping their arms around her tightly enough to make her uncomfortable.

"Careful, careful of the blades, my hearts," she said, working her arms free as gently as she could. The hilts of sword and daggers were digging into her hipbones, and undoubtedly into the rib cages of the women hugging her.

"We Saw you coming," the one said. "We Saw you. You don't know us, but we know you, Sister. Welcome, welcome, welcome."

"Come, come." They dragged her forward, not to the table that held their suppers, but to one closer to the long row of candles. "Come see our things."

These were the toys of princesses. Wooden dolls with articulated joints, finely dressed and with little veils covering their hair. Small wooden animals populated a farmyard made with a miniature fence and stacks of vera tiles. Dhulyn pressed her lips together and looked away from the chanter that lay to one side with other musical instruments. It was altogether too much like the one Parno attached to his pipes.

"Very beautiful," Dhulyn said as one of the women held up what was obviously her favorite doll. It was hard for Dhulyn to show more than courteous interest; her own childhood had been short, and she'd had little experience with children in her Mercenary's life. She found herself hoping, as they continued to present her with their toys and precious possessions, that her smiles and exclamations were satisfying to the Twins. Oddly, she found the contrast between their behavior and their apparent age less distracting than their illness.

"We have a secret," said the golden-eyed one in a whisper. "You need to See," she said. "Come, we can all See together."

Dhulyn's heart froze in her chest. Would they understand what it might cost her, if they told anyone else what they knew? Almost as if they had read her mind, the other Twin put her finger up to her lips. "Secret," she mouthed, nodding her head over and over.

Another thought struck Dhulyn, even more dreadful than the first. "Wait, wait now." She tried to be gentle pulling back from them. "What if I don't want to See?"

"But why?" "But you must." They spoke simultaneously and then looked at each other with brows drawn down.

"I'm afraid."

The Twin on the left snickered and the one on the right elbowed her. "What of?"

"I might See my Partner's death again," Dhulyn said simply. "And I don't want to."

"But we're together." The girl seemed to be puzzled. "Together, we can choose."

"We can choose what we See, because we See together," the other explained. The other one rolled her eyes in a manner so reminiscent of a child beginning to be impatient with an adult's dimness that Dhulyn almost laughed.

"Come, come." This time they led her over to a smaller, round table which had been cleared of a great deal of chalks, pens, tiny paint brushes—and more loose vera tiles Dhulyn saw with a shiver—now lying scattered on the floor. Three chairs had been set around the table, and the Twins made her sit in one, taking the others for themselves.

"Hands now." Dhulyn took their hands, still sticky with the jam from their suppers.

"Clear your mind," said the one with the golden fleck in her eye. "Clear, clear. Clear as sky."

"What's your question? Make your question clear."

They began to sing, a tune familiar to Dhulyn, but with words she had never heard. Not nonsense sounds, she realized, with a shiver, she *had* heard words like them. This was the language of the Caids. How close to the original, she wondered, could this be?

"No, silly," the Twin on her right tugged at her hand. "That's not your question."

Dhulyn felt herself blushing. Here, all alone, was not the time for her attention to slip so easily from her task. She began by humming along with the Twins, finally singing the words she knew, the words to a children's song, to the tune.

How could she destroy the Storm Witch? That was the question she needed answered.

SUDDENLY, SHE IS STANDING IN A TINY CLEARING IN THE WOODS, WHERE SNOW LINGERS IN THE HOLLOWS, AND IN THE DEEPER BRANCHES OF THE PINES. WHERE SHE STANDS, WITH THE TWINS BESIDE HER, THE GROUND IS CLEAR.

"NEVER FEAR, DEAR ONE," SAYS THE TWIN ON HER LEFT. "WE WILL NEVER TELL ANYONE YOU ARE MARKED."

"THERE IS LITTLE WE CAN DO FOR OURSELVES," THE OTHER ADDS. "BUT WE CAN CERTAINLY DO THIS MUCH FOR YOU. YOU MUST KNOW THAT WE HAVE BEEN WAITING ALL OUR LIVES FOR YOU TO COME."

"YOU DON'T KNOW US, BUT WE KNOW YOU, AND LOVE YOU LIKE A TRUE SISTER. I AM AMAIA," THIS IS THE TWIN WITH THE GOLD-MARKED EYE. "AND THIS KERIA."

"BUT YOU ARE . . ." DHULYN FALTERS, NOT KNOWING HOW TO FINISH HER THOUGHT WITHOUT GIVING OFFENSE.

"NOT WITLESS?" THE TWO SISTERS SMILE AT EACH OTHER. "NOT NOW, NO. SO YOU SEE WHY WE SPEND AS MUCH TIME IN VISION AS WE CAN."

DHULYN LOOKS AROUND HER. SHE CAN FEEL THEIR TOUCH, THE HARDNESS OF THE COLD GROUND UNDER HER BOOTS, THE CHILL OF THE AIR, THINGS SHE DOES NOT ALWAYS FEEL IN VISIONS.

"THIS IS WHAT IT MEANS TO SEE WHILE IN COMPANY?"

"PRECISELY," AMAIA SAYS, NODDING. "IT'S NOT ONLY TO HAVE CHILDREN, AS THE HEALER TOLD YOU, THAT SEERS BAND TO-GETHER, IT IS FOR THE STRENGTH OF THE VISIONS, THE CONTROL WE HAVE OVER THE SIGHT, WHEN WE ARE TOGETHER."

"AND SO WE ARE STRONGER IN VISION," KERIA ADDS. "CLEANER, MORE OURSELVES, AS YOU ARE MORE YOURSELF, SIS-TER."

DHULYN REALIZES FOR THE FIRST TIME THAT SHE IS DRESSED IN HER OLD QUILTED, MULTICOLORED VEST, HER SOFTEST LEATHER TROUSERS, AND THE SEMLORIAN BOOTS SHE'D LEFT IN HER CABIN ON THE *WAVETREADER*. AND HER HAIR IS LONG AGAIN, ITS FINE BRAIDS KNOTTED AND TIED BACK OFF HER FACE.

"THIS IS YOUR VISION," KERIA SAYS. "WE ARE HERE ONLY TO HELP YOU, TO MAKE IT STRONGER."

"DO YOU KNOW THIS PLACE AT ALL? HAVE YOU SEEN THIS BEFORE?"

"NO, I DON'T THINK . . ." DHULYN PAUSES, SURELY THAT SMELL IS ONE SHE KNOWS. SHE TURNS TOWARD IT, AND A PATH OPENS IN THE FOREST. ALL THREE STEP INTO IT, AND AS THEY FOLLOW IT, THE FOREST CLOSES ONCE MORE BEHIND THEM AND THE PATH DISAPPEARS. VERY QUICKLY, THE PATH AHEAD OF THEM OPENS UP INTO A CLEARING, AND THERE DHULYN SEES A REDHEADED WOMAN, WIPING THE HAIR OUT OF A SMALL CHILD'S FACE.

"MY MOTHER," SHE SAYS TO THE TWINS. "AND MYSELF."

DHULYN SHAKES HER HEAD A LITTLE, THE SMALLEST OF MOVEMENTS SIDE TO SIDE. WHY THIS VISION AGAIN? HOW WILL THIS HELP HER DESTROY THE STORM WITCH? SHE HAS ALWAYS SEEN THIS VISION FROM A DIFFERENT ANGLE, AND FROM MUCH CLOSER, TOO. SHE LOOKS TOWARD THE SPOT WHICH WOULD GIVE HER THE FAMILIAR POINT OF VIEW, HALF EXPECTING TO SEE A SHADOW OF HER SEEING SELF, BUT THE PLACE IS EMPTY. FROM WHERE SHE STANDS NOW, THE TWINS TO EITHER SIDE OF HER, DHULYN CAN SEE MORE OF THE CAMP BEHIND HER MOTHER, THE OTHER FIRES, FIGURES RUNNING, HORSES LOOSE, AND THE UNMISTAKABLE RISE AND FALL OF WEAPONS IN THE NEAR DISTANCE.

"USUALLY, I CAN HEAR MY MOTHER SPEAKING," DHULYN SAYS WHEN SHE REALIZES THEY COULD HEAR NO NOISE OTHER THAN THE WIND IN THE TREES.

KERIA PUT HER HAND ON DHULYN'S ARM. "THIS IS CLEARLY ANOTHER PART OF THE STORY." AS THEY WATCH, THE CHILD KISSES HER MOTHER AND WALKS TOWARD THEM. EVEN THOUGH THEY KNOW THEY DON'T HAVE TO, ALL THREE OF THEM STEP BACK OUT OF THE CHILD'S WAY AS SHE PUSHES THROUGH UNDERBRUSH AND LOW BRANCHES. THE PATH THAT EXISTED FOR DHULYN AND THE TWINS DOES NOT EXIST FOR HER.

"DO YOU REMEMBER THIS NIGHT?" AMAIA LOOKS BACK OVER HER SHOULDER AT DHULYN'S MOTHER, WHO IS REMOVING THE LAST TRACES OF THE CHILD FROM HER CAMPSITE.

DHULYN SHAKES HER HEAD. "UNTIL I FIRST HAD THIS VISION,

NOT SO LONG AGO, I HAD NO MEMORIES OF MY MOTHER AT ALL. I COULD NOT EVEN PICTURE HER FACE. I HAVE SEEN HER IN SEVERAL VISIONS SINCE, SOMETIMES WITH FRESNOYN, SOMETIMES USING THE VERA TILES."

"BEST WE TELL NO ONE OF THE FRESNOYN," AMAIA SAYS. "THINGS ARE BAD ENOUGH WITHOUT THAT, AND WE WOULDN'T BE ABLE TO STOP THEM."

"ANOTHER SECRET," KERIA AGREES.

A PART OF DHULYN WISHES TO STAY AND WATCH WHAT HAPPENS TO THE HORSEMEN'S CAMP. SHE KNOWS THAT THIS WAS THE NIGHT IN WHICH THE TRIBES ARE BROKEN BY TREACHERY AND DECEIT, BUT SHE HAS ONLY MET ONE OTHER SURVIVOR, AND KNOWS VERY LITTLE OF WHAT OCCURS ON THIS NIGHT. STILL SHE FINDS HERSELF TURNING TO FOLLOW THE CHILD SHE WAS INTO THE HIDING PLACE HER MOTHER HAD PREPARED FOR HER.

IT IS CLOSER THAN DHULYN WOULD HAVE THOUGHT, BUT THE CHILD IS CAREFUL, PLACING HER FEET ONLY ON CLEAR SPOTS WHERE SHE WILL LEAVE NO PRINT, DUCKING UNDER SNOW-LADEN BRANCHES THAT A GROWN PERSON WOULD HAVE TO AVOID ENTIRELY. FINALLY, THE CHILD GOES TO HER KNEES AND CRAWLS INTO THE SMALLEST GAP BETWEEN THE BOUGHS OF A PINE THICKET. AS BEFORE, A PATH CLEARS FOR DHULYN AND THE WHITE SEERS. HERE IN THE THICKET THERE IS ALREADY A SMALL WATERSKIN, A POUCH WITH TRAVEL BREAD, A CLOAK, AND A PILE OF SOFT INGLERA HIDES.

BUT THE CHILD THEY FIND ASLEEP ON THE SKINS IS NOT THE YOUNG DHULYN, BUT AN OLDER, DARKER CHILD, HER THICK BLACK HAIR BRAIDED INTO A CROWN AROUND HER HEAD, HER VEILS SET TO ONE SIDE.

AMAIA BLINKS HER GOLD-FLECKED EYE AND CROUCHES DOWN ON HER HEELS, HOLDING HER HAND OUT OVER THE SLEEPING CHILD.

"THIS IS THE TARA XENDRA," SHE SAYS. "WE KNOW HER. HER BROTHER BROUGHT HER ONCE TO PLAY WITH OUR OTHER SELVES."

Parno clapped his hands and the six members of the crew he was watching held up their swords and stood back from each other. Two of them, he noted, acted with some degree of sharpness and precision. He didn't have time to School them in the Mercenary manner, but he and Dhulyn had twice taken untrained civilians and turned them into reasonable fighting units. He was confident he could do the same here, with half-trained Nomads, even without her.

"What do you think?" Malfin had come up on his left side, and Parno was certain he'd *felt* the man's approach seconds before he'd heard him.

"The second on the left, and the first on the right. They'll do. The two farthest from me fight as though the sword has only a point." Parno looked across his folded arms at the captain. "Been trained only with the *garwon,* I expect?"

Mal nodded. "Would it be better if gave you only those with some sword training?"

Parno grinned before patting Mal on the shoulder. "Would seem logical, wouldn't it? The fact is some are suited to fast training and some aren't. Those who are . . ." he shrugged. "It doesn't seem to matter whether they're already swordsmen or not."

Mal nodded. "Sar and Chels, you're on the list," he called out. "The rest of you are excused." He turned back to Parno. "Gives you seven. Be enough?"

"It will. Remember, not trying to take the city, or even to breach the walls, just to get in. The fewer the better, so long as they're the right ones."

"Still wish could come with you myself."

Parno knew the sentiment was a real one, the man was sincere. But captains had special duties, and were bound in a way that other Nomads were not. Even with a twin to share the captaincy, Malfin could no more leave his ship for this than the Crayx could leave the ocean.

Parno had spent the better part of two days drilling the weapons handlers aboard the *Wavetreader.* Almost every adult had some experience with sword, arbalest, or *garwon*—Nomad life required that all had at least a basic training—but he had found only these seven showing the aptitude that would respond to accelerated training. He wasn't surprised that the group included the twins Tindar and Elian who had sparred with him that day, as well as Conford and Mikel the bosun. But he was a little surprised at how good Conford was, all things considered. And how ready he was to listen, and learn.

Parno set his squad up in pairs, directing Conford to take his turn with the winner in each pair. "Remember what I've shown you," he said. "The first seven movements, only, until one of you is touched. Then Conford will step in. I'll be watching, so stay sharp."

"Dar told me about your family in Imrion." Mal found a place to sit on the rail. "Would really accept a connection with Nomads? Know you're a Mercenary and all, but . . ."

Parno kept his eyes on the pairs sparring in front of him as he answered. "According to the Common Rule, a Mercenary Brother has no family but the Brotherhood itself," he said. "But my family chooses to acknowledge me, regardless of the Common Rule, and what I might think." And they'd acknowledged Dhulyn as well, though that wasn't something Parno wanted to say aloud. "And at that, I'm not the one who's had the strangest time in my family, just the one who's managed to stay alive." He glanced at Mal. "And my cousin, the House now, is a very practical man. Will see this as an alliance worth cultivating."

Parno stepped across to where the fighters had begun to spread apart, within the confines of the section of deck they'd been given for their workout. He touched the elbow of the twin Tindar and waited until the swords stopped. "Don't look just at the tip of her sword," he told Tindar's opponent. "Try to see the sword, her shoulders, even her eyes, all at once. Each movement will give you a clue to the next one." He turned back to Tindar. "Vary your strokes more, if use only third and fourth, will be very easy to stop you."

"Is that how *you* got me?" But she was grinning as she said it, blinking the sweat out of her eyes. The day was warm, but windy.

"Not going to tell you *all* my secrets." When they'd resumed fighting, Parno turned back to Mal, and found Dar standing beside her brother. Parno glanced at the sun, judging from its distance above the yardarm that Mal's watch was almost over.

Dar's eyes were shining, and her smile was at once brilliant and gentle. Parno thought she had never looked so beautiful.

"Good news for us," she said. "And for your cousins." She placed the palm of her hand against her belly, in a gesture Parno had seen many a pregnant woman use before her. "Crayx say twins."

Parno blew out his breath. "Can you . . . ?" he gestured

awkwardly, not knowing exactly how to word what he wanted to ask.

"No," she said. "Too early. But Crayx can, through me. So Pod-sensed for certain, the little ones."

Parno nodded. "But will keep in mind what I said about my family, won't you? They'll acknowledge the connection. And there might be others," he added, when he sensed what he knew was a shade of doubt pass through them. "If I'm Pod-sensed, there might be others in my family as well."

At that, their faces brightened, and the tiny shadow of doubt passed from their eyes.

"Off to rest." Dar cuffed her brother on the shoulder with the back of her hand. "My watch now."

Grinning, Mal slapped Parno on the back and walked off to his cabin. Darlara slipped her arm through Parno's and he did not pull away, telling himself there was no need. There was only crew around them, only Nomads. There was no reason to keep watch, and besides, since Dar was on his left side, his best sword hand was free.

By this time most of the matches were over, and the recruits were standing in a rough circle, watching Conford spar with his latest opponent. The young man had taken his shirt off, and while there was a red stroke across his upper left arm, he seemed otherwise untouched.

"That one, Conford? Seems to stand apart," Parno said. "More skilled than the others, but there's something else."

"He's an exchange, thought you knew." Dar's face changed. "No, it was your Partner he spoke to most, remember now."

"So came from another Pod?"

The two fighters were clearly slowing down, their blades still moving, but falling lower and lower as inexperienced wrists and forearms tired.

"*Windwaver* Pod. Comes once a year from the Round Ocean, far to the east of here."

"Or far to the west, depending on where you start." It was odd to think that from the land of the Mortaxa, the Round Ocean was to the east, when children in Boravia grew up thinking of it as to the west.

Dar grinned, tucked loose hair back into the scarf she was wearing. "The Round Ocean is always where it is. It's only the Pods that move."

A shout declared the bout over, and the two fighters stood in identical postures of exhaustion, bent over, chests heaving, hands braced on thighs.

"Well done, all of you," Parno said. He drew Dar with him as he inserted himself into the group, looking at a bad bruise here, and giving an encouraging slap there.

"All are excused watches until your training finishes," Dar said. "Go clean up now, and get ready to eat."

"Conford." The younger man turned to Parno and smiled, wiping his face off with his shirt. "Come see me when you've cleaned up."

Parno waited until the man had gone to join the others before turning back to Dar. "So Conford comes from another Pod entirely?"

Dar nodded. "Good to exchange with Nomads from the other oceans, keeps the bloodlines clean, but usually happens at our Great Gatherings every five years. Conford's a special case."

"How so?"

"Usually must have four generations of unconnected blood for an exchange to be made. But Conford needed to leave his ship, and *Wavetreader* was the only Pod close enough."

Halfway up the gangway to the aft upper deck Parno stopped, and looked back along the lower deck to where his recruits were sloshing each other with water pulled up from over the side.

"He doesn't have the look of a troublemaker," he said, before following Dar the last few steps to the top.

"Oh, no. His twin had died, and he couldn't stay where she no longer was."

"Died? Some kind of accident?" Except for the frostbite they'd seen when he and Dhulyn had first come on board, Parno had observed no signs of illness among the crew. Even without the assistance of the Marked, the Nomads seemed to enjoy good health.

"She was lost overboard." Dar frowned and sat down on the pilot's bench behind and to port of the wheel. "When the moment came, wouldn't let the Crayx swallow her, as you were swallowed, and so wasn't saved." Dar waved her hand toward the sea where the Crayx were. "Doesn't live still."

Parno stayed upright, leaning his elbow against the rail, remembering his own experience inside the Crayx, and the offer they had made him. "Why wouldn't she?"

"Don't know. Some say she had the enclosure sickness, and couldn't bring herself to enter such a small space. Don't know, though, never knew someone with it. Have you heard of such things?"

"Yes," he said. "Yes, I've heard of it." It had been on the tip of his tongue to tell her that he had a mild form of the horizon sickness himself, but habit, and the Common Rule, held it back. "It must have been difficult for her in any case. So much of a ship is enclosed and small."

Dar shrugged. "Slept on deck, I imagine."

"And the Crayx could not have forced her to be saved?"

"Of course. But how could we live that way? Knowing they would force us against our will?" She turned her face toward him, her dark eyes shining though her face was somber. What she said confirmed Parno's own experience. The Crayx would not force their human partners—not even to save them.

"Too hard for Conford to stay." Dar had gone on with her story. "So took first chance of exchange that offered. Fits in well enough, but hard, very hard to be one where were always two." She rested her fingertips on his wrist. "Hard for you, too?"

Parno's jaw clenched against the wave of grief that washed through him, and it was all he could do not to clench his fists as well. From the clouding of her eyes, Darlara clearly saw this in his face, but she did not turn away, or remove her hand. At least his child—children, he corrected—had a brave mother.

"Was not Partnered my whole life," he said when he thought his voice was steady enough.

"No, but best part, most important part."

Somehow, it was easier, knowing that Dar understood.

Before he needed to say anything, Conford came up the gangway and presented himself, hair wet, clothing brushed and shaken out.

"Asked for me, Paledyn."

"Conford." Now that he knew what to look for, Parno could see the marks of strain around the younger man's eyes. The telltale signs of sleepless nights and loss of appetite. "Know what I intend to do?"

"Aye, sir. Kill the Storm Witch."

Carefully, not giving so much detail as to overwhelm, Parno explained his strategy, the landing party, the coordinated attack on the frontage of Ketxan City. At first, Conford followed him with brow furrowed and frown, but as Parno finished, the young Nomad was smiling.

"So I'm for the land?" His eyes sparkled.

"Fight well, and have good instincts, and this is the more dangerous part."

If anything, Conford seemed happier. "Aye, sir."

"Conford, I need a second. Both the captains would like to go, but you know why they can't." Conford nodded. "A second isn't someone who's there for glory, or even someone who's there to give his life for his fellows. He's someone I can count on to get the job done if I fall. And if possible, be there to bring his comrades back. Understand?"

Now he had stopped smiling, his lips pressed together in a line, but Parno felt optimistic when the younger man did not answer immediately, and without thought. It seemed that Parno had judged his man correctly. In a manner of speaking, Conford was the closest person on board to another Mercenary, in that he understood death in the depth of his soul and, in his way, was ready to die. He shared that understanding, and that readiness with Parno. Could he also share the understanding of duty and obligation?

Conford gave a short nod. "Aye, Paledyn. Understood. I can do that."

Sixteen

"YOUR FATHER THE TARXIN, Light of the Sun, has sent the Paledyn to see you, Tara Xendra."

Carcali put down the tiny finger harp but didn't turn from the toy shelves. She often found herself, instead of studying her maps and making calculations, rearranging the small wooden animals, wondering if the jewels in their harnesses could possibly be real. She sighed and turned to face the other woman. She'd already learned there wasn't much point in arguing with Finexa. Supposedly, she was only a new lady page, now that the Tara Xendra was acknowledged as a Storm Witch, and no longer a mere child whose old attendant Kendraxa was more nurse than page. In fact, Carcali suspected that Finexa reported to the Tarxin every day—or at least when there was anything to report. And refusing to meet with the painted barbarian woman would probably come under that heading. Things had been going well since her last meeting with the Tarxin. He'd seen to it that she had the supplies she needed, and had sent for one of the globes in the Scholars' Library, where they were on notice to assist her when she sent for them. She had to be careful not to do anything that would jeopardize that.

"Just taking a short break," she said, hoping she didn't sound as defensive as she felt. "Why is the Paledyn here?"

"The Light of the Sun did not say, Tara Xendra. But he has asked her to watch over you. Perhaps that explains it."

"Very well, I will see her."

Finexa's eyes narrowed, but all she did was give a shallow curtsy and turn back to the door.

Somehow, the Paledyn, when she entered, looked taller, rougher, and more dangerous standing in what was still, for all intents and purposes, the day room of an eleven-year-old girl. She had managed to find, or have made for her, a pair of pale gold linen trousers and over them she wore a green sleeveless jerkin trimmed with satin ties, and with a bright red patch sewn on one shoulder. Her blood-red hair had been knotted into several tiny braids, short enough to stand up around her face, but somehow, there was nothing remotely funny about the style. Her granite-gray eyes looked at Carcali as though she were measuring her.

The woman wasn't very old, Carcali realized, maybe only four or five years older than she was herself—her real age, not the age of this body. Something in the Paledyn's face reminded Carcali of her Wind Instructor in her first year at the Academy. The same mixture of patience, knowledge, and focus.

Carcali swallowed and stood up, coming out from behind her table. She wasn't going to be intimidated by a woman so close to her own age—a woman with tattoos and a scar on her face. The Academy, the Artists who were her superiors, all were long gone, and the Tarxin was the only one here she needed to be afraid of.

"What shall I call you?" The woman's voice was like raw silk, rough and smooth at the same time.

"I am the Tara Xendra," Carcali said as sharply as she could manage. The woman's raised eyebrows did nothing to help her keep her composure. On the contrary, the Paledyn's gesture seemed calculated to rattle her, perhaps even goad her into losing her temper. Well, she wasn't going to fall for that.

"Have you no other name that you might prefer me to use?"

For a second, Carcali's lips actually parted, as the sudden temptation to tell the Paledyn the truth was almost irresistible. Part of her wanted to see the shock and awe shake the composure of that scarred face, but a part of her simply wanted to tell someone, even this woman, everything. She let the moment pass, saying nothing at all, and the Paledyn inclined her head, all the while keeping her eyes fixed on Carcali's face.

"I am Dhulyn Wolfshead, called the Scholar. I was Schooled by Dorian of the River, the Black Traveler. You may call me Wolfshead."

Carcali gritted her teeth. She certainly wasn't going to call the woman "Scholar," no matter who else might. She turned away, crossing behind the table again to resume her seat. She froze, one hand on the arm of her chair. The Paledyn was already sitting down in the guest chair. How had she moved so quickly, so quietly, in the few seconds Carcali's back was turned? Deliberately, as if she hadn't been shaken by the Wolfshead, Carcali sat down, moving the pen and inkwell to one side, squaring them up with the edge of the worktable.

"My father the Tarxin, Light of the Sun, sent you to meet with me." Let that remind the woman who she was dealing with.

The Paledyn tilted her head to one side. "He has asked me to extend my protection over you."

"What protection can you give me, that he cannot provide?"

The woman spread her hands, palms up. For the first time she smiled, her lip curling back from her teeth in a snarl. Carcali blinked and sat up straighter, then blushed as she realized the woman had seen—and correctly judged—her reaction.

"Could he stop me from killing you myself?" the Paledyn said.

The horrible thing was the Paledyn asked this question in the same even tone that she had used all along—not in a manner intended to frighten or threaten, but as if Carcali's every answer was being weighed in a balance.

"You would never leave the city alive." Carcali's lips were almost too stiff to speak.

The woman shrugged, and her disinterest was somehow more frightening than anything else she might have done. "There are larger things," she said in her rough silk voice, "than my life, or yours."

There *were* larger things. Carcali swallowed. There were whole worlds, civilizations like the one she had destroyed with her arrogance and her pride. Carcali waited, frozen, but the Paledyn continued to sit, perfectly composed, elbows on the arms of her chair, fingertips placed together. Carcali managed to loosen the grip of her own hands.

"I have work the Tarxin has given me," she said, reaching for her stylus with a hand that trembled only slightly. "So if you're not going to kill me just at the moment . . ."

The woman's eyes brightened, and Carcali had the crazy feeling that she had almost smiled.

"Why do you not return to your own place?"

Carcali froze again, her fingers on the stylus. The Paledyn couldn't possibly know. "What do you mean? This is my place." She glanced up, but the Paledyn's face was impassive once more, the hint of brightness gone. She moved her head to the left and back again, just once.

The nape of Carcali's neck prickled as the hair stood up. For the last few days, since news of the Paledyn had arrived in the Tarxin's court, Carcali's servants and attendants had been telling her all kinds of strange tales of them—their invincibility, their honor, how it was impossible to trick or lie to them. She'd dismissed it as primitive superstition, but— *Don't be so silly,* she told herself. *What else could it be?*

"I watched you walk up to the Tarxin's table, and you do not walk like a girl who has seen her birth moon only eleven times," the woman said now. "You are developing a line here," she indicated her forehead between her brows, "when you frown, that a child of that age would not have. You do not school your expressions as carefully as a child brought up in the Tarxin of Mortaxa's court would know how to do. Even now, you look at me with a face that says you have been caught sneaking sweets. In other words, with the face of guilt. And I know," she said finally, leaning forward enough to place her hand on the edge of Carcali's table. "That the natural powers of Marked or Mage come with the maturing of the body, and I doubt very much that the body of the Tara Xendra has yet reached the beginnings of her woman's time. So, where do you come from, and why do you not return?"

"You couldn't possibly understand." The words were out before she could stop them.

"Perhaps you're right. Full understanding comes with full knowledge, something one person cannot give to another. But you could give me enough knowledge to understand how to help and protect you." The Paledyn leaned back again and Carcali took a deep breath for the first time in what felt like hours. "Come. I have told you what I know, what I see with my own eyes. Let me tell you also what I suspect. I believe you are a Caid, though how you find yourself here is more than I can know, I admit."

"What could *you* know about the Caids?" Too late, Carcali realized she hadn't denied the suggestion.

"I have spent more than a year in a Scholars' Library. I know things that the common sword-wearer does not know, even across the Long Ocean, where I think such things are better understood than they are here. I know that the Caids were not gods, as some people think of them, but people like ourselves. And I know that among them were many powerful Mages, some powerful enough to manipulate even the fabric of space and time. And some who were foolish enough to do it. So if you are, as I suspect, one of these, why do you not go back?"

"I can't." The words were out before Carcali could stop them, pushed by the guilt that was always hovering in the back of her mind, no matter how much she tried to ignore it. She would have given anything for the words to be unsaid—even she could hear the longing and despair that informed them.

"Can't or won't?"

"Can't. It's not possible." Carcali spoke through clenched teeth. Did the woman think she hadn't *tried*? Would she have suffered all that time trapped in the weatherspheres if there had been a way home?

The Paledyn's eyes narrowed. "What did you do there, that you can't go back?"

Carcali's heart stopped in her chest, her breath in her throat. She closed her mouth tight against the desire to tell her, to blurt it out. *I destroyed the world. Tell her, say it.* But then reason reasserted itself. The Paledyn *couldn't* know. That would be impossible. This was just good intuition, nothing more. She could tell that Carcali felt guilty about *something,* and was using that knowledge like a sharp knife to probe deeper. Maybe there was something to this Schooling of hers after all, if it led to such perception.

"It is a reasonable question," the woman said, when Carcali did not answer. "Considering the evil you have done here. Do you not, even now, occupy the body that belongs to another, forcing a child's spirit to wander alone and afraid? There is cold in summer, rain in the desert. Lightning cracking the sky. Hailstorms, hurricanes, and tempests. Grain dies flooded in the field, snow and ice fall on the ocean. There will be famine and there has been—" Here the Paledyn's voice caught. "Shipwreck."

Carcali grasped the edge of the table to help her stay in her seat as the room around her swayed. "I didn't do any of those things!" She looked down at her maps, at the lines she'd drawn between mountain range, shoreline, and valley. "My changes have all been local. You're lying."

The Paledyn seemed genuinely surprised, even to the extent of turning pale enough for her eyebrows to stand out like bloodstains. "Are you not a Storm Witch—*the* Storm Witch? Even I, in my Schooling aboard a fast ship, learned that where weather is involved, there is no such thing as 'local.' If you did not do these things, who did? If you believe I lie about the ravages of your storms, why do you not go, find out?" She lifted her arms in an unmistakable way, in the way a Weather Mage did to enter the spheres, and Carcali's stomach dropped. How could the woman know these things?

"I can't. I can't." Carcali put her face down on the backs of her clenched hands. How could this be happening? But she knew how, even if no one else did. Without leaving her body and entering completely into the weatherspheres, she had less control, and with less control, even the small changes she'd been making could cause damage elsewhere.

"You speak—and you act—like the child you are in appearance, rather than the woman I know you to be," the Paledyn said. "You have power, but you have no discipline. Power without discipline is dangerous."

Carcali stared at the woman on the other side of the table. How could she *know* these things? Those were almost the very words that the Artists had said to her.

"Help me." Only a few minutes ago, Carcali could never have imagined asking this woman—tattooed and scarred barbarian, she'd called her—for help. But somehow the Paledyn knew and understood things no one else here seemed to know. "Please, can you help me," she repeated. "It's the Tarxin, he's threatening me. If I don't do what he says . . ." Carcali let her words die away. The Paledyn was sitting rigid in her chair, her eyes icy, her face a mask of stone.

Carcali pulled herself up straight, hardening her own face. This woman wasn't going to help her, Carcali thought, shocked at the depth of her disappointment. "Please leave," she said. Inside she was screaming *GET OUT*, but she managed to control herself. "I don't know what you want. I can't help you." She heard the bitterness in her voice. Just for a moment she'd allowed herself to hope.

There was an odd look on the Paledyn's face as she stood and looked down at Carcali. Her eyes were narrowed, a muscle bunched at the side of her jaw. She was very pale, but somehow her eyes were not so cold. As soon as the door was closed behind her, Carcali ran over and threw the latch, leaned with her hand against the door, breathing hard.

She wasn't going to let the Paledyn Dhulyn Wolfshead make her feel guilty—at least, no more guilty than she already felt. She wrapped her arms around herself. The weather changes—they were the Tarxin's fault. If he'd left her alone, or at least given her more time . . . She was doing the best she could, but after so long without a body—she'd been so confused at first—her Art was still just barely up to apprentice standards. And as for the child, well, Carcali couldn't be responsible for what had happened to her. She never knew the child, never encountered her at all. As for the idea that she might be lost, trapped in the weatherspheres the same way Carcali had been—

Carcali suddenly bent over at the waist, unable to stop the spew of vomit that gushed out onto the tiled floor. *No,* she thought, gasping for air against the spasming of her diaphragm. She scrubbed at her mouth with a corner of her head veil before pulling the garment off and dropping it over the vomit. She forced her mind back to that immeasurable time just before she was pushed into the young Tara's body.

Her idea had worked so beautifully at first. She'd launched herself alone—and why not, she'd thought. Everyone soloed eventually, and she was so much more powerful than any of the other Crafters and Apprentices, she'd been sure that she could do it. And she'd seen right away that her solution would work. It hadn't been easy, but finally her patience and concentration put all the colors and temperatures right. She'd finished, or so she'd thought. It was only then that she'd realized she'd lost the connection with her body—and, with it, any chance to check and revise errors.

Then she'd panicked. And by the time her panic was over, it was too late, the thread connecting her to her body was well and truly gone.

Carcali did not know how long she'd been lost, floating in the spheres—time, space, even her own awareness of such things, became twisted and uncertain when the connection to the body was severed. When she'd felt a tugging at her formless self, she almost hadn't responded, almost hadn't recognized it for what it was. The feeling was so unfamiliar. Recognition had finally come, and she'd thought the Artists had found her at last, had come to save her, and she'd rushed forward, ready to admit she'd been wrong, she'd been arrogant—anything to be restored. Anything to leave behind this formless despair. A sense of great urgency had swept over her, bringing joy and relief with it.

Even when the body didn't feel perfect, Carcali hadn't worried. Of course it would feel strange after so long in the weatherspheres. By the time she realized what had happened, by the time she knew that she didn't wear her own body, that it and her friends and teachers—her whole world—were gone, mere legend to these people . . . by that time she knew she would do anything, tolerate anything, rather than to return to the nothingness of the spheres.

But there hadn't been another soul. Carcali swore there hadn't been. Whatever she may have done to her own people, and her own time, with her arrogance and haste, she was sure she had not condemned an innocent child to the torment she had experienced. The child was not a Mage, her soul could not have survived leaving her body.

Carcali was sure.

Dhulyn leaned against the wall next to the Storm Witch's door and rubbed her face with her hands. Thank Sun and Moon the lady page was nowhere to be seen. Never, never since Dorian the Black had found her standing over the body of the dead slaver, had she come so close to simply killing someone out of hand.

To think it was all an *accident*. That selfish coward—that *parasite* of a stone-souled WITCH, had killed Parno, had destroyed their lives *by accident*. She hadn't even *known*.

But that didn't make her innocent of Parno's death. That wouldn't save her, the very next time the Witch—

"Did it work? Does she trust you?"

Dhulyn had Xerwin by the throat before she registered who it was and let him go. "Sorry," she said. "You startled me."

The Tar rubbed his throat and tried to smile. "I promise not to do it again." Still rubbing his neck, he peered into her face. "You're very white. What happened in there?"

"How much has the Storm Witch been told about recent events? About the Nomads and their claims?"

Xerwin shrugged, drawing her to follow him with a tilt of his head. He glanced around him, and Dhulyn realized he had somehow freed himself of his usual attendants. "Since the Tarxin replaced me as liaison to the Nomads, I've had no say in our contacts with them. So *I* certainly haven't discussed anything with the Storm Witch. And I wouldn't think any of her maids have much head for politics."

Dhulyn refrained from correcting him. In her experience, the higher up the ladder of nobility, the less people understood that the people below them knew far more about what was happening in their lives than they ever let on. As they turned into a wider corridor, she stayed silent, fairly sure she knew where they were heading. Sure enough, Xerwin led her up a flight of stone steps, down a corridor whose latticed walls opened into a tiny courtyard, and finally up another staircase and out into the sunlit and walled garden that was the precinct of the Tarxin in the Upper City. Dhulyn let her lip curl up. In any other place there would have been a guard at the steps, but here in Ketxan City, things were done differently.

"We can talk here," Xerwin said, indicating a stone bench covered in densely woven cloths in the royal colors of gold and green. The bench sat in the shade of a trimmed willow, next to a pool where water tinkled over rocks. "This is the Tarxin's private precinct. No one is allowed up here without either the Tarxin or myself."

"What about Tara Xendra?"

Xerwin looked at her sideways, as if thinking of something for the first time. "No," he said. "Now that you men-

tion it, even she has to come with either me or the Tarxin."
He shrugged. "Of course, women aren't supposed to wander
about without escorts anyway."

"No, I suppose not." If Dhulyn's tone was a little dry,
Xerwin did not notice.

Obviously, rock and earth had been moved here to create the pond, and with it a small elevation from which almost the whole garden could be seen, and the low wall
which surrounded it. Beyond she could see the Upper City
itself, and some of the more prominent landmarks. She
drew up her feet to sit cross-legged. One of the maps she
had seen on the Storm Witch's table had been of the Upper
City.

"I saw this enclosure when I entered the City," she said.
"I was surprised that the Upper City itself had no guards or
gates."

"Why would we need guards here? The Battle Wings patrol our borders, and the only trouble we've been having is
from the south." Xerwin paused, his face thoughtful. "I
wouldn't be surprised if trouble comes from the Nomads, with
the Tarxin's new policies, but they attack only from the water."

"So you have no defensible walls, and keep no guards
here?"

"There are Stewards at the City entrance, of course, you
saw them." He turned to lean his back against the side of
the bench, placing himself farther into the shade. "And I
suppose some of the Houses might keep Stewards in their
pavilions. But you were telling me why it would matter if
anyone had been talking to the Storm Witch about our current situation with the Nomads."

Dhulyn studied Xerwin's face with some care. Like anyone who had trained others, and led soldiers in battle, she'd
had every trick tried on her, and seen hundreds who were
trying to lie. Xerwin showed none of the signs she was familiar with. Which either meant he was very good, or he was
being truthful.

"The Witch seemed to be unaware that there had been
storms at sea, that the Nomads are claiming they've been
attacked through the medium of her magic."

Xerwin shook his head. "So far as I know, she's only
been asked to adjust the weather here in Mortaxa. Little
things, rain for the fields, a warm wind when frost threat-

ened the wine grapes. Perhaps a few things farther afield, but nothing more that I'm aware of. Do you mean the Nomads have been lying all along?"

Dhulyn drummed her fingers on her knee. "You forget, Xerwin, I was myself shipwrecked. The Nomads on that vessel were sure they were attacked specifically to prevent our—*my* arrival." How much did Xerwin, or any of the Mortaxa, understand about the laws of Sun and Moon, Wind and Rain? Anyone who lived, or had been Schooled on a ship understood firsthand the connections between wind in one place and rain in another. "I mean that the Storm Witch *is* responsible for the weather the Nomads complain of, but she seems to be unaware of it herself. Is it possible that she was not told of the Nomads' complaints?"

Xerwin turned up his palms. "Who would tell a young girl of such things? And if such things are possible, how could the Storm Witch not know?"

"I assure you such things are possible. Heavy snow and rain in the mountains cause flooding in the valley; hurricanes in one place can mean days of high winds and rain even a moon's march away. As for how the Witch did not know . . ." Dhulyn shrugged. "It has always been true that a little learning is a dangerous thing."

Xerwin closed his hand around her wrist. Dhulyn froze, looked at his hand, and looked up, meeting his eyes. He swallowed, kept his eyes on hers, but took his hand away. "What do you mean?"

"The Marked can do damage, especially Healers or Menders, if they are not well trained. Even Finders may Find every horse in a town, and not the precise animal sought. So it is possible that the Storm Witch has talent and power, but insufficient training. It is also possible that in order to perform her magic well, she needs to be given information that has been withheld from her."

"How were we to have known?"

Dhulyn refrained from shrugging again. Two things had worked against the Storm Witch. First, she had wanted everyone to think she was the Tara Xendra, so she hadn't asked many questions. And second, as Xerwin had said himself, who in this place would have thought to tell a young girl—Tara or not—anything of importance?

"But if she is not guilty of the acts of malice the Nomads

accuse her of—" Xerwin was frowning, not, as Dhulyn could see, because he could not follow the thought through to its logical conclusion, but because he could not see use in the conclusion he found.

"Will that make a difference to your father? He already sees his dominion spreading over the Nomads and their oceans." Dhulyn decided to keep silent, for the moment at least, about the Crayx. "You've said yourself the Storm Witch is a sword to his hand. Will he stop himself from using it?"

Xerwin's face had settled into the impassive mask that in itself was a sign he was hiding his thoughts. Not for the first time Dhulyn thanked the Mercenary Brotherhood from keeping her out of this kind of life. If she hid things from people, it was because they were strangers, not because she was afraid.

"We might reach the Storm Witch, if she is really just unpracticed and not evil," Xerwin finally said. "But the Tarxin will never be persuaded to give up an advantage he's long sought, that's certain."

"Then we must stick to our original plan," Dhulyn agreed. Though whether she was trying to convince herself or Xerwin was something she did not want to examine too closely. "The Storm Witch is a danger to anyone who might cross her—still more so if she cannot control her magics. She is like a mad dog, or a child in a temper who sets fire to the house and kills his whole family. And if we speak of children," she added. "There is the child your sister to consider."

At this Xerwin looked up, and quickly looked away again, as if embarrassed. "I did not tell you. The White Twins, the Seers, told me they had had a Vision of you leading a young child by the hand. Could it be that you will restore my sister?"

"It could be." Dhulyn nodded slowly. "It's hard to be sure of the meanings of isolated Visions—or so I have read," she added. "It certainly appears the possibility exists." If nothing else, she thought, her own Vision showed her that the child Xendra was still alive, that her soul still existed, somehow, somewhere, in hiding. "And your sister deserves what chance she can have to be restored. That the Storm Witch refuses to consider the harm she does to your sister tells us much of her natural temperament—to say nothing of her honor. But it also points us to the way to overcome her."

"How is that?"

"She is in a terror of leaving your sister's body," Dhulyn said, remembering the adult horror and desperation in the childish face. "Such terror leads me to think that she will be destroyed if we expel her from the body."

"How can we do such a thing?"

"Can the Marked ones be brought secretly into the palace?"

#Lionsmane#

Parno set the bow he was oiling down on the tabletop, wiping his fingers clean on the scrap of rag. "Hear you," he said. He still spoke aloud when talking with the Crayx, even though he knew he didn't have to. Somehow, it kept things feeling normal for him. He supposed that one day, he would simply forget, and speak to them only with his Pod sense, as everyone else did.

#We have found someone who can tell you of the City#
#We know you do not like to listen to another's thoughts#
#But Oskarn is of the *Sunwaver Pod*, their current is now in the Round Ocean, and he cannot be brought to face you#
#He has been through the City of the Mortaxa more than once#

Parno winced. They were right, he didn't like receiving someone else's thoughts, or knowing that his were being sent. But that, too, was something he would have to get used to. He hadn't known that the Crayx could convey the thoughts of someone as far away as this Oskarn was. Did this mean that any Crayx could talk to any Crayx, anywhere in the world?

#Yes#

"Let me get out parchment and pens," Parno said, shaking his head and getting to his feet. The other cabin was still being used by whichever captain was not on watch, so Parno had had all maps and documents transferred to the one he increasingly shared with Darlara. The Crayx waited until he had fetched clean scraps to make notes on, and was seated once again.

"I'm ready."

This is many years ago Somehow, the man's thoughts, his voice, sounded differently in Parno's mind than that of any Crayx. He could tell that he was conversing with another human, that the human was male, and even that he was very old. *When the Mortaxa were better disposed toward us* *The Crayx had told us of a Pod-sensed one to the south, inland, and our Pod was the only one near* *You know that they keep slaves*

"I know," Parno said, wondering if the face he made was somehow transmitted to Oskarn along with his words.

The slaves are many, especially away from the City, and the one we sensed was a slave child *I volunteered to fetch her* *There was no other who would go so far from the sea, not even for a Pod-sensed child, but I was young, and felt myself invincible, and as it is, I was not harmed* *I hired guides who helped me find and buy the child, and I returned to my Pod with her*

"But you passed through the City to do so?"

Twice *And waited there while the sale was registered and sealed, lest there be some difficulty after*

"And you can describe the City to me? Particularly the land side?" Parno took up his pen in preparation.

I can *You have seen great palaces and buildings, such as might be seen in the vast cities of the Great King*

"I have."

From the sea, the City seems to be a palace, carved from the living rock of the cliff face, span after span, layer upon layer, showing windows and balconies, and here and there a staircase *Docks, wharfs, and piers are built, floating upon the sea, and it is here that we dock, and hold markets* *There are four entrances, two at the dock level, and two others in the third level* *But the City itself extends past this facade, deep into the bluff behind it* *Wells and shafts, cut vertically into the heart of the rock from the summit far above, carry air and light into the lower levels*

What Oskarn described as Parno took notes and made drawings, did indeed sound like a huge, many-storied palace, with innumerable corridors that functioned as streets and alleys, and large open spaces that served the purpose of public squares and buildings. Parno learned that the seaward part of the rock held the homes of Noble Houses, with the Tarxin's palace at the very top. The poorer or less important people lived lower down, and deeper into the rock—some might never see true daylight for weeks at a time, if ever.

"And the land approach? The entrances from the top?"

The Upper City is laid out like a formal garden within a decorative wall, but instead of plots of flowers and trees, the High Nobles have winter houses out in the air *At this time of year, there would be too much heat for these to be much occupied* *Few have permission to build* *The largest precinct is that of the Tarxin's palace, and is truly a garden, with its own wall for the privacy of the ruler and his family*

Parno continued to draw as Oskarn described the Upper City. Particularly the parts around the public entrance to the Lower City, and the Tarxin's walled garden. It soon became apparent that, extensive as the man's knowledge was, and as detailed his memory, he had only seen limited parts of the city. Two items stood out. First, the Upper City was like an unfortified town, with low walls and no guards. Second, the wall of the Tarxin's precinct was not high by Boravian standards. Nor was it ditched or moated. Nor, he was surprised to learn, was it usually guarded.

The guards are all the Tarxin's men, and keep to the inner City Oskarn said.

"What can you tell me of the rooms in the palace itself?"

Alas, nothing *There was no reason for me, a common Nomad, neither captain nor chief trader, to be received by the Tarxin*

No help for it, Parno thought shrugging. Once he was in the palace precincts, it would be a question of capturing someone and persuading them to tell him where the Storm Witch might be found.

Amusement

Seventeen

D HULYN KEPT ONE EYE on the movement of shadows across the jewel-bright patterns of the tiled floor in her sitting room, and the other on the pocket of thin leather she was sewing into the back of her new vest. The pocket would hold one of the daggers she'd picked out and had sharpened to her specifications. She'd asked the palace seamstresses for scraps of cloth and leather, waving aside as politely as she could their offers to do any sewing she might require with the declaration that Paledyns were required to do certain ceremonial things themselves. People would think that she had used these scraps to create, on the back of her vest, a larger version of her Mercenary badge. And so she had. What they wouldn't see was how much she'd thickened the material, and what she had hidden there.

Dhulyn bit off the thread, slipped the vest on, and reached over her shoulder, first with the left hand, then with the right, to make sure she could reach the pocket. She then repeated the whole business with the dagger in place.

Satisfied, she took the vest off once more and began to work on four shorter, wider straps that she would attach lower down on the vest, closer to her waist. These would hold the small hatchet she'd liberated on her tour of the kitchens and honed herself on the edge of the stone window ledge. Unlike the dagger, the hatchet would be sewn into the vest, and be ready to hand when it was needed. Experience had taught her that unlike a hidden dagger, once a hatchet was out, you rarely had a chance to put it back.

As the last stitch went into place, Dhulyn looked up and, her head tilted, slowed her breathing, letting herself fall into the Stalking Cat *Shora*, the better to listen. Quickly, she stood, pulled on the vest, and did up the ties. The scraps of cloth, needles, and other sewing tools, along with the old vest she'd been using as a pattern she gathered up and thrust into the inner chamber. She was leaning against the worktable, sword in hand, when the expected tap came at the door.

"Come," she said.

She'd expected Xerwin to be first through the door, but it seemed the Tar had some sense after all. Instead, it was Remm Shalyn, a wide grin on his pleasant features, who led the three Marked ones in, and Xerwin who waited in the outer corridor in case questions had to be answered. Not that there were many errands being run at this time of day, when most people were preparing for the midday meal.

"The Tar's plan worked like a throw of loaded dice, Dhulyn Wolfshead," Remm said. Though it didn't seem possible, his grin grew even wider.

"No one above, then?" She looked at Xerwin.

"Exactly as I thought," he said, unable to keep the satisfaction out of his voice. "Much too hot up there at this time of day for anyone, even the servants." By which he meant, Dhulyn knew, the garden slaves who kept the pavilions of the High Noble Houses clean and their flowers blooming. They would have gone up early in the morning to cover over valuable plants against the glare of the sun, but by this time Xerwin had expected the place to be deserted—and it seemed he had been right.

"Your pardon, Tar Xerwin," Remm said, though he had, in fact, waited until the Tar had finished speaking. "But if there is water available, the Marked ones are in need of it."

Dhulyn gestured her permission at a tray on the table to her left, which held cups and a water jug beautifully glazed in black and red, and turned back to Xerwin.

"Is this heat natural?" She could tell by the way he raised his eyebrows that he hadn't even considered it. A Storm Witch could cause a great deal of mischief if she went about it carefully.

But the Tar was shaking his head. "I'll be looking askance at the morning sea breezes next," he said. "And they've been constant my whole life. For the season and time of day, this heat is normal. Though," he added, "only last evening I overheard my attendants gossiping. Apparently one of the High Noble Houses—I didn't quite catch which—has been wondering whether perhaps the Tara Xendra could be persuaded to create cooler air for some party they're planning." It was Dhulyn's turn to raise her eyebrows, and Xerwin grinned. "I hope I'm there to see the look on the Tarxin's face if the House actually asks him."

"Don't be too sure of his answer," Dhulyn said. "If the House is important enough, the Tarxin might very well allow it."

As Xerwin pursed his lips in a silent whistle, shaking his head, Dhulyn once more checked the angle of light on the floor.

"Tar Xerwin," she said. "I believe you are eating with the Tarxin today?"

"Surely you're not trying to be rid of me?"

Dhulyn rolled her eyes and waved him toward the door. "Of course I am. I don't want anyone to come looking for you."

"With your leave, Dhulyn Wolfshead," Remm said as soon as Xerwin was gone. "Speaking of food, I should go order us some."

"Fetch it yourself," Dhulyn said. "That way no one will see how much you bring." She glanced at the Marked ones and looked back at Remm, who was nodding.

"Back shortly." He touched his forehead to her and left, pulling the door shut behind him. Dhulyn followed him to the door and listened as his footsteps and his light whistle died away. She threw the bolt, and turned back to face the Marked.

All three had put aside their veils, and except that she was seeing them in daylight, they looked much the same. Ellis Healer, a linen bag hanging over his shoulder, was still leaning on a staff, but the two women were recuperating from their journey more quickly.

"You have spoken with the White Twins," Ellis said. Rascon Mender still had her cup of water to her lips, and Javen

Finder was mopping the sweat off her face with a clean corner of her veil.

Dhulyn sheathed her sword and strode back to the table, propping one hip up on the edge. Closer together, they would be less likely to be overheard. "Who else knows?"

"No one *we've* told, that's certain," Rascon Mender said.

Ellis Healer frowned at her and she blushed, turning away to refill her cup. "Not many within the Sanctuary besides the three of us even know you were sent for. Kalinda, of course, the one who showed you in, the White Twins themselves, but . . ." he fixed Dhulyn with a watchful eye. "You will have noticed that they are fully aware only when they are Seeing."

Dhulyn nodded.

"So you will realize that they could tell no one, and as for the rest of us." He shrugged. "We make it a practice not to talk about our own affairs to the unMarked."

"And as for them—and there're some—who don't think as we do on these subjects, why, we don't tell them anything." Rascon seemed to have recovered her cheery equilibrium. "What about your man, that Remm Shalyn," she continued. "Is *he* to be trusted?"

"So far as I trust anyone, yes." Dhulyn ran her fingertips along her sword hilt. She didn't know whether it was the company of the Marked—or the number of weapons she now had hidden in her clothing—but she was beginning to feel relaxed for the first time since the storm at sea. "And do you know what the White Twins told me?"

There was a general shaking of heads, but this time the two younger Marked waited for Ellis Healer to speak. "Likewise, who would tell us? The Twins?"

Dhulyn relaxed even more. It seemed that the secret of her own Mark was safe. Now the trick would be how to tell these three what they needed to know to Find the Tara Xendra without giving away that she'd had the Vision herself.

"The White Twins have Seen the Tara Xendra, that much is clear from what they told me," she said. The others looked at one another and nodded. "The child's spirit is safe, but it is in hiding."

The Finder was shaking her head, frowning. "But that shouldn't make any difference. It's things that are lost or hidden that I Find."

"But if she were nowhere near, Javen," Rascon said. "And if the Storm Witch's soul was in the way . . ."

"Did the White Twins say anything else? Was any clue given?" Javen Finder asked.

This was the dangerous part of the path. "They spoke of a grove of trees," Dhulyn said. "A thicket in which the child lay concealed."

"A spirit child hiding in a spirit wood?" Javen Finder's face, so eager a moment ago, had fallen, and she was chewing at her lower lip. "It's not like I can Find a Vision, you know. Otherwise we'd *all* be Seers."

"I have something here that may help you." Dhulyn went to the end of the table nearest the window and folded back a piece of silk cloth to expose a small bowl, sturdy and perfectly round, glazed a deep blue on the outside and a pure white on the inside. All three Marked gathered close, looking down at it.

"Remm Shalyn had it made to my order—by a master, as you can see. The glaze both inside and out is perfect, without mar, flaw, or shadow. No hand but the maker's has touched it, neither Remm's nor mine. The water it holds is brought from a spring, and passed three times through a piece of pure undyed silk."

"How did you know what's needed?" Javen said, her voice trembling.

Dhulyn shrugged. "The two I've seen were old, passed from generation to generation. But once, many years ago, I read a fragment of an ancient book which described the making of a Finder's bowl. Much of it would make no sense unless you'd actually seen one." Dhulyn indicated the chair she'd had placed near the bowl. "Will you try?"

Javen sat down, wiping the palms of her hands dry against her skirt. She pressed her palms together, fingers against her lips, eyes closed. She took a deep breath, opened her eyes, and looked into the bowl.

"Oh, what beautiful colors," she exclaimed.

Dhulyn exchanged glances with the other Marked. Rascon was just giving a small nod, confirming that the rest of them saw only the white interior, when a knock came at the door.

"The food?"

Dhulyn drew down her brows in a frown. Would Remm

knock? Or was he too burdened by food to manage the door. She jerked her head toward the doorway to the inner room and waited until the Marked had gone through it. She shut the door on them, tossed the loose piece of silk back over the bowl, and threw open the door as if she was in a great temper.

But she swallowed the tart words she would have used to greet Remm Shalyn. A young girl, correctly veiled, stood in the open door, her eyes as round as the bangles on her wrists.

"Your pardon, T–tara P–paledyn," the girl stammered. "But the Tarxin, Light of the Sun, has asked for your presence."

For a moment Dhulyn stayed where she was, right hand gripping the edge of the door. Was the girl frightened at meeting the Paledyn? Or was it the errand itself that frightened her?

"Wait for me, young one," she said in as soft a voice as she could manage. "I will accompany you in a moment." Dhulyn shut the door in the girl's face and stood leaning against it. If this summons was Xerwin's doing, he'd have something to answer for when she caught up with him. She pushed away from the door, turning toward the inner room, and the Marked. They should be safe enough here when Remm Shalyn returned.

She wished she could say the same for herself.

Everyone who could find a clear space on deck was out taking advantage of the warm rain to refill every water cask, bag, and bottle, and to rinse off whatever clothing, skin, and hair had last been washed in salt water.

Parno Lionsmane was in the forward section of the deck that under more regular circumstances would be the designated bathing area. He'd found that while he had become used to the smell and taste of salt on his skin—and on the skin of others—he was just as pleased to be able to rinse it off. The Nomads, living together so closely, had no great feelings of body modesty, and almost his entire squad, both male and female, were in the bathing area with him. In a way, it was like being back in his Mercenary School.

More and more, except for the presence of so many children, Parno found himself reminded of his own Schooling, especially since the intensive training of his strike force so closely resembled the constant drilling and practice that Schooling required. He'd found that he was even teaching his squad versions of some basic Shoras, modified only to take into account the shortness of the time they had for training.

Once or twice, watching the squad practice, he'd looked around, unconsciously expecting to see Dhulyn off to one side, getting a different angle on the recruits. Grief still came when he thought of her, but it no longer stabbed him to the heart, or took his breath away. She had always wanted to start her own School, to do for others what Dorian the Black had done for her. It wasn't impossible, Parno thought now as Conford passed him a towel, for a School to be started on a Nomad ship. After all, the Nomads had taken him in, just as the Brotherhood had done, all those years ago, when he had been cast out by his House.

#You have a place here, should you want it# #As you did in your Brotherhood#

As I still have in my Brotherhood For the first time Parno spoke directly mind to mind with the Crayx, without speaking his thoughts aloud. But this was something he wasn't ready to share with the Nomads around him. Not even with Darlara.

#Does no one ever leave the Brotherhood then#

Parno stopped his fast answer. Of course, there were other ways to leave the Brotherhood than death. There was that Cloudwoman who'd gone back to her tribe when a Racha bird had needed her. He had himself been asked to return to his own place, for that matter, by the new head of his House. But he'd refused. Even if he'd wished to—and he hadn't—he was Partnered, and the decision was as much Dhulyn's as his own.

Partners never leave was the thought he sent the Crayx. #Of course#

Were they aware of his unexpressed thought, he wondered. I'm not Partnered any longer.

He shrugged the thought away as he pulled his shirt on over his head. "Off to your meals now," he told his squad. "Left-hand drill afterward, and don't be late."

He turned back toward the rear cabin, combing his wet

hair with his fingers. For the last few days he'd been taking the midday meal with his squad, but today Dar had asked that he share the meal with her. He entered the cabin to find her seated with her back to the window, plates of grilled fish, stewed beans, and flatbreads already on the table. Dar glanced up and smiled as he came in, and Parno found it easy to smile back.

"Have been giving thought to the naming of the children," Darlara said, passing him the platter holding the flatbread.

Parno froze with the platter in midair. "Early, isn't it?"

"Not really. It's a hard life on ship, and must give them every advantage. Are there family names you would prefer to use?"

Parno thought at once of his own father. But the form of names in Imrion—he shook his head. Too complicated, and too loaded with meaning for someone who didn't actually live in that society. He could easily imagine the explanations that would be required if the children became chief traders or captains of a ship—as they well might—and were asked why their names came from a Noble House. Besides, he knew what he really wanted.

"Could one of them be called Dhulyn?"

Darlara took so long to answer that Parno was ready to be disappointed. But she was only waiting until she had chewed and swallowed the piece of honeyed bread she had in her mouth before answering. "A beautiful name," she said. Suddenly she smiled, and rested her hand on his forearm. "Have a wonderful idea. Should name them Dhulyn and Parno."

Now it was his turn not to answer right away.

Darlara tightened her grip on his arm. *It's all right, isn't it?* *Would be brothers, or sisters.*

Somehow, speaking mind to mind made it easier.

Yes

The door of the cabin swung open and Malfin leaned in. "Told him yet?"

"Just getting to it." Darlara gave his arm a final squeeze before shifting in her seat, swinging her legs out until she was turned toward the door.

Parno looked from brother to sister, marveling once

more how alike they looked when they were both smiling. A smile began to form on his own lips. *What are you up to*

Hold your breath a bit Malfin turned to look over his shoulder and made a beckoning gesture with his hand.

"We've something for you, Lionsmane," he said aloud. "Just ready now."

Conford came in with a cloth-wrapped bundle in his hands. Parno helped Dar clear off a space on the table so Conford could put his burden down. He backed off a step, touched his forehead to Parno, looked sheepishly at his captains, and shrugged, smiling.

Captain Mal laughed and touched the crewman on the shoulder with his fist.

"Go on."

Still smiling, Conford unwrapped the cloth, exposing a Crayx-skin cuirass, identical to the ones both Mal and Dar were wearing, except that this one was a pale green with a curious coppery sheen.

"Yours, Lionsmane," Mal said.

"Try it on," Dar said. "See if it fits."

Parno knew what the skin felt like from helping Darlara take hers off. To the touch, it was like well-tanned leather, soft and giving. To a sharp blow, it was as hard as good steel, and would turn away a blade.

"Why?" he said, looking up at the three smiling faces.

"Heard from *Dawntreader* Pod," Mal said. "May be in sight of Ketxan City tomorrow."

"Thought you could use it," Dar added.

Parno nodded. "What does it mean if I wear it?" he said, bluntly. "I know it's more than just armor."

"Are bound to the *Wavetreader*," Mal said.

"As we," Dar added.

"And what does *that* mean?" Parno's voice was harsher than he'd intended. The two captains exchanged worried looks, and the smile faded from Conford's face.

#You are part of this Pod# came the answer from the Crayx. #You cannot be exchanged to another Pod# #No matter what happens, where you are, you are part of us, of *Wavetreader*#

It was like the Mercenary Brotherhood, Parno realized. You didn't need to live in a Mercenary House, or even with other Mercenaries—you could even retire, though not many lived so long. Once a Brother, always a Brother.

#Acknowledgment# #Agreement#

Mal, Dar, and even Conford were nodding.

Parno picked up the cuirass and slipped it on.

#Satisfaction#

❧

There was a guard at the door the young woman led her to, and Dhulyn handed him the sword on her hip and the knife on her belt before he could ask. After all, she still had the dagger and hatchet hidden in her vest. She saw as soon as she entered the room that those, and her hands, would be all she needed, since there was no one else there but Xerwin and the Tarxin Xalbalil. As Dhulyn entered, Xerwin was on his feet, his hand on the back of his chair. Xerwin's face was calm, there was even a slight smile on his lips. Dhulyn felt herself relax ever so slightly.

"Ah, Dhulyn Wolfshead." The Tarxin indicated the chair to his left. "Please, join us. Xerwin told me that he had left you just as you sent your servant for food, so I know you have not yet dined. This would be an excellent chance for us to confer informally."

"I thank you, Light of the Sun. It is an honor." Dhulyn touched her forehead and pulled back her chair, taking her seat. No servants, the Tarxin's manner of addressing her, his calling even Xerwin by name rather than by title, all emphasized the informality of the meal. Still, Dhulyn had some experience dealing with Noble Houses. So long as she kept to the minor formality of never using the Tarxin's name, she should be fine.

As she sat, she rapidly scanned the table, taking in the platters of fruit, fish in simple sauces, and small rolls of bread. This was the diet of a person in shaky health, she thought, perhaps with a bad heart. Was the Tarxin, then, at the point where even Healers could do little for him?

"Tell me, my dear, what do you think of my city?"

So that was how the horse was supposed to jump. Dhulyn offered the Tarxin a basket of warm bread before taking a piece for herself. If the man really expected small talk, he'd chosen the wrong Mercenary Brother.

"It's not unusual for cities of this size, located as this one is on a natural cliff face, to have no walls. But I am surprised that there is no patrol of guards at the outskirts of the Upper City."

"Guards?" From the look of his rounded eyes, the Tarxin was genuinely surprised. "Guards have not been needed since my great grandfather's day. It was he who pacified the lands from the Long Ocean in the west, to the Crescent and Coral Seas to the north, and to the Eastern River."

For pacified, substitute conquered. Dhulyn kept her thought away from her face.

The Tarxin spread a smoked fish paste on a thinly-sliced, twice-baked piece of bread and presented it to Dhulyn. "There are bands of so-called free slaves roving in the southern mountains, but the Battle Wings are there to deal with them." The Tarxin smiled at Xerwin. "The Nomads have attacked us, naturally, but only from the sea," he said while she chewed. "It seems very unlikely that *their* strategies would change now."

"When I was Schooled, I learned that 'unlikely' is a highly dangerous word. One should always prepare for what can happen, not for what *might* happen."

Tarxin Xalbalil paused in the spreading of another morsel of fish paste and looked with a frown at Xerwin. "Excellent reasoning, do you not think my son? See to it."

Xerwin put down the leg of fowl he had in his left hand and began to stand up. His father let him get all the way out of his chair before speaking.

"Oh, not now, Xerwin, please, we have a guest. After the meal will do."

"Of course, Father." When the younger man glanced across the table at her, Dhulyn gave him her best smile, careful not to let the scar turn back her lip. He lowered his eyes very quickly back to his plate.

"And how did you find the Marked in their Sanctuary, well-cared for?" At least the old man had waited until she'd served herself a slice of meat and filled her wineglass before he continued.

Dhulyn drew down her eyebrows and sat straighter in her chair, as if giving the Tarxin's question serious thought. Sun and Moon, but she hoped he didn't think to unnerve her by demonstrating that her movements were being reported. He didn't strike her as a fool, and only a fool

would have let her—Paledyn or no—wander around unwatched.

And since he wasn't a fool, she had better see to it that
she didn't relax *too* much.

"It was an unusual experience for me," she said finally.
"To see so many Marked in one place. It is done differently
in Boravia, and in the lands of the Great King as well."

The corners of the Tarxin's mouth crimped just a fraction, as if he did not care to be reminded that there was
somewhere a king greater than himself, even if so far away.
He was irritated enough, Dhulyn saw, that he did not notice
his question hadn't really been answered.

"And your visit to my daughter, that was satisfactory?"

"Indeed, my lord. She will need a great deal of support,
as I'm sure you have already realized. A child so young,
with such powers." Dhulyn shrugged and took a sip of wine.
"She might be easily manipulated, and you must choose the
people around her with great care. The Tara Xendra might
do a great deal of damage if she is left in the wrong hands."

The Tarxin nodded vigorously, as if he was pleased to
find that they were both in such accord. *Talk of being manipulated*, Dhulyn thought. She glanced at Xerwin, he
blinked at her, face straight. His father appeared to accept
that she believed the Storm Witch was a child, but did she
really trick him? It was hard to judge. Blood, what she
wouldn't give for Parno's opinion. She did not fool herself,
sharp as she was; the only advantage she had in this contest
was the old man's habit of power. He was so used to holding
all the good tiles, it might well have caused him, over the
years, to stop looking closely at other people's hands.

And he could be reasoning that he need not fool her for
long. Once she supported his side in the argument with the
Nomads—as she was clearly expected to do—he might well
decide that he had no further use for her.

Mouth full, she inclined her head toward the Tarxin, as if
to concentrate better on his words.

"I'm gratified that you both understand the problem so
clearly, and that you feel free to advise me. Like the Paledyns of old, your presence will guide us back to the balance
we have so sorely missed."

"What has caused the conflict between you and the Nomads? In Boravia, it is understood that your arrangement was well considered, and of long standing."

The Tarxin leaned back in his chair, dipping his fingers into a bowl of water to his left, and drying them on a small napkin. "We are not the same peoples," he said in a measured tone. "We are the children of the Caids, followers of the Slain God. The Nomads are animal worshipers, following—literally—those sea creatures they call the Crayx, using them as living pathways across the ocean." He shrugged. "I have seen them, they are magnificent creatures, supremely useful to navigation as any can realize, but they *are* animals. It would be as though a herdsman began to worship his cows, or the wild inglera. Diplomacy between our two peoples has always been difficult, no treaties can be solidified with marriages, for example." He spread his hands. "Enough. I am no priest or farmer, for that matter, to let myself be distracted by this. Their women have too much power, but for traders and animal worshipers they are honest enough."

Once again, Dhulyn thought he was being sincere. "What has changed, then?"

"A year ago—or was it more, Xerwin?"

Xerwin paused to finish chewing, and swallowed. "It was more . . . Father. Almost two years, I'd say."

"A pair of Scholars came to us with documents, newly translated, which you can see for yourself, Dhulyn Wolfshead—*can* you read?"

"I can."

"Excellent. Well, as I say, this was almost two years ago."

Dhulyn listened as the Tarxin, with the occasional help of Xerwin with details, told her the story she had already heard from the Nomads, but from the Mortaxan point of view. What a shame, she thought, that she was not actually here to arbitrate between them. Mediators were rarely given such full information to help them form their decisions.

She learned that over the centuries, the land-based Mortaxa had tried several times to redress what they saw as their subordinate position in world trade. Attempts at formal partnerships, up to and including marriage into Nomad trading families had always been refused. As had the purchase of ships with which to follow the Crayx—and for no good reasons, from the Mortaxan point of view. Their histories told of attempts to build their own ships and to find their own herds of Crayx, but both times the ships had left Mortaxa never to be heard from again.

And it was very clear, from what the Tarxin was saying, that they simply did not believe in the Nomads' explanation of Pod sense.

Since the consolidation of Mortaxa under the present Tarxin's great grandfather, the land had been enjoying a long period of peace and stability. *Stagnation*, Dhulyn thought, the typical outcome of entrenched slavery. And Tarxin Xalbalil began to think that now was the time to try again.

To make his own mark before he dies, she thought. He wanted to be remembered in the same way his great grandfather was.

"Xerwin, as Battle Wing Commander, had been acting as liaison with the Nomads, but for what I had in mind, a greater authority was needed." Meaning, Dhulyn guessed, that Xerwin had not agreed with his father's ideas. "I began by putting a stop to all trade," the Tarxin continued. "But even as that tactic was beginning to make itself felt, I was distracted by the terrible accident to my dear child Xendra."

Dhulyn put a solemn look on her face and nodded her sympathy. Distraction, the man called it.

"But the Slain God and the Caids have both shown me their favor, not only in restoring my daughter to health, but by making her their instrument in my dealings with the Nomads. Not only have they blessed her with the Weather Art, but they have given her other knowledge, the knowledge of the lodestone. Do you know what this is?"

"I have read of it," Dhulyn said. "A device, whether magical or not I cannot say, that can be used as a guide when there are no other signs, stars, or landmarks."

"Or when you are at sea."

"The Tara Xendra awoke with this learning?" Dhulyn said.

"This and other knowledge, yes. We saw immediately that this gave us a stronger position in our talks with the Nomads."

You would, Dhulyn thought.

"We had now something to offer them, something that would free them from their dependence on the Crayx. But when we spoke to the Nomads of this, the Nomads threatened us, saying that they would destroy any ship that attempted to cross the Long Ocean, or any other oceans or seas. That these places belonged by ancient treaty to the Crayx, as if animals can have treaties with humans."

Dhulyn fought not to let her distaste and skepticism show on her face. Of course, the Mortaxa would think the Nomads were lying, she thought. Lacking Pod sense—or the ability to see even their own slaves or the Marked as human beings—it would be inconceivable for these people to believe that the Crayx were sentient. "And did you, in your turn, threaten the Nomads with the wrath of the Storm Witch?"

The Tarxin's expression set like stone, and Dhulyn was careful to keep her eyes wide open with innocent curiosity. After a few moments the Tarxin relaxed.

"That would have been to answer their bad faith with bad faith of our own," he said.

Which doesn't mean no, she thought. "Of course," she said aloud. She leaned back in her chair, picked up her own napkin to wipe her hands. "So what, precisely, would you wish these negotiations to bring you?"

"At the least, they should allow us to build our own ships, to begin our own trade routes. We are not asking them to starve. There is trade enough for all. It would be better still for us to become partners. Using the lodestones, we could extend trade to those areas where the Crayx herds do not go."

Partners. Mentally, Dhulyn snorted, even as she nodded in apparent agreement with the Tarxin. "Would you be willing, as an opening to the bargaining, and to show good faith, to limit your preliminary trading ventures to those areas where the Nomads do not go?"

Just for a moment, Dhulyn saw again that telltale crimping of the corners of the Tarxin's mouth. "We do not know what might be found there, whether there would be any profit going to new places."

"That might be something you could learn from the Nomads. If you show yourselves to be willing to make concessions now, you might gain all the more in the future, as the Nomads learn to work with you."

"Of course. I see now why the Paledyns of old had such reputations for sagacity."

Dhulyn was spared any need to respond by the entry of a flustered noble servant.

"Your pardon, Tarxin, Light of the Sun, but Nomad ships have been sighted from the north watchtower."

Ships? Dhulyn thought.

Eighteen

"TAR XERWIN, PLEASE ESCORT the Paledyn Dhulyn Wolfshead to the north watchtower."

Xerwin got immediately to his feet, relieved to observe that Dhulyn Wolfshead had also noted the change back to formal titles, now that they were no longer alone in the room. The Paledyn bowed deeply, not quite touching the floor, before turning to follow old Harxin Slan out the door.

Xerwin had to walk around the long end of the table, so as not to pass behind the Tarxin's chair, but as he turned to take his formal leave, his father beckoned him closer. He approached his father's chair and went down on one knee.

"Do I need to tell you not to bother with the patrols she wants?" His father's voice was well-modulated and would not carry into the outer room.

"Of course, my lord Tarxin, Light of the Sun."

The Tarxin patted him on the shoulder, and made shooing motions with his hands.

Even though no one could have seen it, Xerwin's ears still burned hot with embarrassment. His father, the Tarxin, shooing him away as a farm slave might shoo away chickens. As if he would not be Tarxin one day. As if the old man thought he would never die.

"Your pardon, Paledyn," he said when he found Dhulyn Wolfshead and Harxin Slan waiting for him in the outer room. She was rearming herself with the blades she'd left there, while Harxin watched, smiling. "My father had last minute instructions."

She nodded briskly. "He is your superior officer, and his orders must be obeyed," she said.

"And you must obey them as well, my dear." It was clear from his tone that Harxin Slan's words were kindly meant, even flirtatious. The tone, Xerwin realized, that he himself might have used to a noble lady full of her own importance.

And from the look on Harxin's face, the man was just discovering what kind of mistake he'd made.

"I am a Paledyn," Dhulyn Wolfshead said, her rough silk voice somehow sharp and cutting as a knife. "I obey the Common Rule of my Brotherhood. It is for that reason I am here."

Harxin's white face flushed red, and his lips parted, but before he could dig his grave any deeper, Xerwin decided to take pity on him.

"Since the Tarxin, Light of the Sun, has asked me to escort the Tara Paledyn—" There, let the old fool be reminded that she outranked him as well. "You may return to your interrupted duties, Harxin."

"Yes, my lord Tar."

There, Harxin's color was subsiding, and he was able to speak. His short bow was carefully aimed at the space between Xerwin and the Paledyn, thereby insulting no one, before Harxin turned and left the room. Xerwin grinned. There'd be no need to call for the Healer, or for any of the lower servants to clean up the old man's blood.

"The north watchtower's not far," he said to Dhulyn Wolfshead as he led the way out of the room. As soon as they were out of earshot of the guards at the doors to the Tarxin's personal suite, he lowered his voice and spoke. "You must be quite used to that type of treatment, but I apologize for it, nevertheless."

"Are you apologizing for yourself, or for House Slan?"

Xerwin stopped in mid stride, then moved quickly to catch up. "Your meaning?"

She glanced at him sideways. "You just reminded that poor idiot that you and I have the same rank, and yet you walked out of the room before me. If I were another Tar, instead of a Tara, would you not at least have offered to let me go first?"

He couldn't tell whether she was smiling. He opened his mouth several times before finding the words he wanted.

"In your land, in Boravia, would the heir to a Tarxinate allow you to precede them out of a room?"

This time it was Dhulyn Wolfshead who stopped dead in the middle of the corridor, and waited for him to turn back to her. Her left hand was tucked into her sword belt, her right hand rested on the hilt of her sword.

"If I were guarding him, I would insist upon it," she said. Her head was tilted to one side, and Xerwin felt as though her cloud-gray eyes were measuring him. "And in my area of expertise, I would expect to be obeyed, as your father pretends that he will obey my will as Paledyn. But that isn't what you're really asking me, is it? You're asking me whether in Boravia—in Imrion or Navra, Nisvea or any other country there—a woman and a man can be of equal rank, *really* equal rank." She stepped closer to him, close enough that he could smell the wine on her breath. "Let me tell you, *Tar* Xerwin. In Boravia, it is the oldest child who inherits, male or female, so women own businesses and farmland. They are Houses, Scholars, and, yes, even Paledyns. And what's more, they are Tarkins."

A cold wave of anger washed through him, leaving his hands tingling. How dare she, how dare she speak to him in that tone. Not even his schoolmasters had ever used that tone to him. He knew his anger must have shown in his face, but the Paledyn did not back away, did not lower even her eyes, let alone her face. In fact, she seemed to be smiling to herself, as if she had tested something, and found the result she expected.

And suddenly it was as if all his anger evaporated in an instant. She was not afraid of him. It was fear that he saw in the faces of other women, he now saw. Not admiration. Perhaps not even respect. Dhulyn Wolfshead spoke the truth. Everything about her, her tone, her attitude—her very existence, proved that she spoke the truth.

"Women are all these things in Boravia." He waited until she nodded. "And slavery is not practiced there."

"No, it is not."

"And our treatment of our women—I mean, *the* women—that would be seen as a kind of slavery."

"It would."

"And the Nomads, they think as you do in Boravia. So they look at us here in Mortaxa as people they trade with, but not people they respect. Not people they will marry with. Not people they view as they view themselves. They think as little of us as we do of them." It was an uncomfortable feeling, to see this. "I see it now. It explains much that I did not understand in my dealings with them. Why, then, do they trade with us?"

Dhulyn Wolfshead merely shrugged up one shoulder and moved away. "Diplomacy between states is always rather more complicated than less," she said. "Trade is one thing, political alliance is another."

"The Seers said you would bring change. I am beginning to understand just how much."

"I bring new ideas, perhaps. If there is to be change, it is you who will do it."

"And perhaps you will help me."

Dhulyn was happy to let Xerwin keep his own silence as he led the rest of the way to the watchtower. He appeared to be taking her words to heart, and she found she was more than a little uncomfortable with the things she had said, and the way she had said them. She had not been aware that she had so much anger in her—and that was dangerous for a Mercenary Brother. Get angry, get stupid. Get stupid, get dead. That's what the Common Rule said.

One of the other things the Common Rule said was that Mercenary Brothers stayed neutral when it came to politics. They could refuse to take an offer of employment for personal reasons—up to and including having no liking for the politics, or the mustache, of the potential employer. What they weren't to do was interfere unasked with how a given country managed their own peoples.

But they have asked me. Nor did she think she was just splitting hairs. The Tarxin had asked for Paledyns, no matter how much he had intended to use them rather than be guided by them. He had asked. He'd been told by his own Seers that Paledyns would come, and offer a solution to the conflict with the Nomads. And if the solution that was offered did more than that?

There were also the Marked to consider. Did the Common Rule tell her she had to leave them in the condition she found them? Could she not do for them what she would be expected to do for any Mercenary Brother she found in the same straits?

She was glad to get to the watchtower, and the distraction of the viewing glass, a type she'd never seen before. Xerwin dismissed the regular lookout, who seemed happy to go. The sunshine was bright enough to blind.

Xerwin motioned her to use the viewing glass first, half-shrugging and with a smile.

"It looks like two ships at least," she said. "Possibly three, if there is one behind them."

"They will not be bringing Paledyns with them, since you are already here."

"They may not even be the Nomads with whom I traveled. We cannot know where the storm might have blown them."

"Now that they are here, what do you think?" he asked her. "Are my father's suggestions for dealing with the Nomads at all reasonable?"

"They would be a reasonable place to begin," she said. "If they were not based on an entirely incorrect premise."

"My father is wrong about yet another thing? You surprise me."

The words were sarcastic, but the tone, and the look on his face showed only resignation. She gave him a long, measuring glance. Or perhaps there was more than that, perhaps there was some determination as well. She might as well see what he was made of. It seemed to be a day to tell him things.

"The Crayx are not animals," she said. "They are beings as intelligent as we are ourselves, and with a longer history."

Xerwin squeezed his eyes shut, putting both hands to his forehead. "This is too much. How is this possible?" He lowered his hands. "How do you *know*?"

"They speak mind to mind, and not everyone has the ability to hear and speak with them."

"The Nomads must be lying to you. How could such an ability be limited?"

Dhulyn shook her head. Once again, his tone did not match his words. "Is the Mark not limited? Even among the Marked, is not one Mender better talented than another? You've seen the White Twins, how they are like two different sets of people. For the Sun's sake, Xerwin, a Storm

Witch inhabits your sister's body!" Dhulyn leaned against the battlement, feeling the heat of the stone through her clothes. "You, yourself, have seen stranger things than sea creatures who can speak to humans. Your deciding that they are nothing more than animals does not make them so. Any more than your confining and breeding the Marked makes them animals. And the people you enslave, they *are* people, and not dogs or cattle." *Shut up. Shut up,* she told herself. Sun and Moon, what was wrong with her?

Xerwin sat down heavily on the lookout's perch, as if Dhulyn Wolfshead's words were each as heavy as the block of stone he was sitting on. She was not looking at him now, he saw, somewhat relieved. She had turned away to face the ocean, and was looking into the middle distance, as if she were thinking of something else entirely. Xerwin was glad of the respite.

Animals who are people. People who are not animals. He rubbed at his face. His head spun so much he was afraid it would come off. *"The Paledyn changes all. Nothing will be as it was. The world as you know it will be gone, forever."* That's what the White Twins had said. Their eerie, adult voices echoed in his head. *"Rain will fall in the desert; the hind chase the lion; the creatures of the sea will walk the beaches. Trees will flower in winter; the sea lose its salt, the land ripple and flow."*

It was coming. An entirely different world. He looked over at Dhulyn Wolfshead. A better one?

His father would never stand for it. Never let it happen. *Well, then, I must do something about my father.*

"Dhulyn Wolfshead," he said. "As you say, the Tarxin may only pretend to heed your suggestions, but I will listen to you." And to begin, he thought, *I will set up the patrol of the Upper City.*

❧

Carcali let her woman Finexa drape her veils properly, making sure that her face and torso were not obscured, and that the cloth hung neatly and evenly down her back. The Tarxin had summoned her.

"Leave it," she said finally, her skin fairly itching with impatience.

"It cannot be left, Tara," Finexa said. "You go to your

father, Light of the Sun, but you must pass through public corridors to reach him, and you must be properly dressed."

She'd speak to the Tarxin about this, Carcali thought. If the Paledyn could go about dressed as she pleased, surely the Storm Witch could as well. The thought of trousers almost made her mouth water.

There were two guards outside the door waiting to escort her to the Tarxin's hall. They were called attendants, but they were more than that, just as Finexa was more than a lady page.

This time Carcali noticed that as she passed through one of the public squares Finexa had mentioned, even a few of the men who saw her acknowledged her, not just the women as before. So it did mean something to be the Storm Witch.

The Tarxin was waiting for her in his private room, off to one side of the audience chamber. Carcali bit at the inside of her lower lip. The last time she'd been in this room, the Tarxin had struck her.

"Good," he said, without looking up. "I thank you for coming so promptly."

Fine words, but a formality only. When he looked up, his face changed. He tilted his head to on side, actually looking at her now, seeing her.

"What would you like to be called?"

A shiver went up her spine. Those were almost the very same words the Paledyn had said to her. And even though the woman had meant to challenge and shake her, Carcali found she would rather have the Paledyn's distrust and challenge, than the Tarxin's false warmth.

"It would be better if I was always called the Tara Xendra, don't you think?"

His face hardened, but whatever his expression had been, it was gone quickly. Carcali steeled herself and went to one of the chairs near the wall and pulled it forward, placing it across the table from the Tarxin. She concentrated on straightening her skirts and veils as she seated herself, not looking up. She couldn't wait for him to ask her to sit down. If she meant to be treated like an equal partner, she needed to act like one.

Suddenly the Tarxin smiled, like a wolf showing all its teeth, and Carcali wished that he would frown at her again.

"I forget. Looking at you, I forget that it is not a little

girl, not quite marrying age, sitting before me. I forget that you are something else, something entirely different."

Carcali tilted her head to one side and raised her eyebrows slightly, in imitation of one of her professors when he wanted to show that more of a response was expected.

"You'd do well to remember that others will only see the child, and act accordingly."

"Others will see the Storm Witch, soon enough. Nothing so easily remedied as youth." One of the same professor's sayings. "May I ask why I'm here?"

The Tarxin leaned back in his chair, elbows resting on the arms. "The Nomads have been sighted, two ships at least, out beyond the arm of the western shore. I want you to send a storm that will either put them upon the rocks, or push them far out to sea."

"Why?"

The silence was so profound that Carcali thought she could actually hear the drop of sweat that trailed down the center of her back.

"They are our enemies." His voice was cold enough to drop the temperature of the room.

"When do you want it?"

"Now. Immediately."

Carcali shook her head. "Can't be done, not without more notice. I don't keep the kind of winds you're asking for in my pockets, you know. Air pressure has to be changed, temperatures, humidity . . . these aren't things that can just be conjured up out of nowhere." *Well, they could, she thought. But not by me, not anymore.*

He looked at her from under lowered lids. "What is it you fear?"

Carcali thanked the Art that she'd practiced controlling her face, otherwise she didn't know what else he might have picked up from her expression. "I'm afraid you're going to lose your temper with me, and forget what our agreement is," she said finally. "It seemed pretty obvious that I was telling you something you didn't want to hear."

Whether it was the reminder of their bargain, or whether he really was much more pragmatic than she gave him credit for, the Tarxin relaxed.

"How much time do you need?"

"All I can give you this minute is a guess. With a few

hours of calculations, I should be able to tell you more precisely."

"And your guess now?"

"At least two days."

"Then you have two days."

He looked down at the pages in front of him. Carcali frowned and kept her seat, pretending she hadn't noticed the dismissal. She had to say something. She *had* to. Her guilt already weighed her down—heavier, if anything, since the Paledyn's visit—she couldn't take any more.

"If the Nomads get too close to shore," she said, "Whatever I do to them will affect the shore as well."

"Can your storm melt rock?" he said, looking up.

"Well, no." Carcali blinked. "But it can destroy homes, crops."

He nodded. "Very well. Warnings can be given to those exposed. If that is all, I must return to my other work." Now he was also pretending he hadn't dismissed her already.

"Of course," she said as she rose to her feet.

"Let them know they may send the Scholar in."

She nodded, turned her back on him, and walked out.

Her guards were waiting for her in the outer room. She gave the Steward the message and watched him approach a blue-robed Scholar before setting off back to her own quarters.

So that's the way it was going to be, was it? He would tell her what to do and she would do it. Some partnership. What gave him the right—*don't be naïve,* she told herself. Power gives him the right. He dictates and others obey. Carcali sucked in a sharp breath, loudly enough that the guard walking ahead of her half turned his head to look at her over his shoulder. Carcali lowered her eyes and kept walking. Was she any better than the Tarxin? Hadn't she thought power was all it would take to solve the problem facing the Academy of Artists? Look how that had ended.

That was why her friend, Wenora, had been so angry with her; Carcali *had* been bullying people, in a way, since her talent was so much more powerful than anyone else's. Would she have become like the Tarxin if one day, as her ambition was, she'd become the Head Artist? Her footsteps slowed as she reached a wooden bench looking out over a balcony that let onto the sea. She sat down, pulling her veils closely around her.

She'd been using her power to help, back then, when everything had gone so horribly wrong. The Tarxin wanted her to hurt people. Hadn't she had enough of that? How much more? How far was she willing to go before she said stop, enough? She shivered. Xalbalil wouldn't be Tarxin forever, but how many people would be hurt while she waited for him to die? She needed an ally, and she needed one now. If the Paledyn wouldn't help her, then she had to go back to her original idea. Xendra's brother, Tar Xerwin.

She looked up. Would it seem peculiar to the guards if she asked them where Xendra's brother was to be found? Surely this was something she would be expected to know.

Finexa would know. There would be fewer questions raised if she asked Finexa.

⟡

Remm Shalyn was waiting for her when Dhulyn got back to her rooms. A waggle of his eyebrows indicated that the Marked were still there, hidden once more in her bedroom. The scrying bowl was no longer on the table, but there was a shoulder bag on a chair that didn't belong to her. She pointed to it.

"I am likely not the only person who has seen that bag hanging from the Healer's shoulder."

Remm blushed and pressed his lips together, nodding. "An oversight, I admit. Won't happen again."

"Was the Finder successful?"

He glanced at the door of her bedroom in such a way that she read the answer on his face. He'd been hoping someone else would be the one to tell her.

"The bowl worked beautifully," Javen Finder said once Remm had let them back into the sitting room. She was trying to be properly downcast and contrite, seeing they'd had no success. But her delight in the bowl was strong, and it showed in the sparkle of her eyes, despite her other feelings. "I saw colors, as I usually do, but much brighter, much clearer than usual. I Found you, Dhulyn Wolfshead, and a toy of the White Twins that's been missing for months." She lowered her eyes, glancing at the bag hanging on the chair.

"If I could keep the bowl, I could try again. I'm so sorry to have failed you."

Dhulyn grinned. If the bowl was already in the bag, they'd anticipated her answer. "The bowl is yours, and we haven't failed yet, Javen Finder," she said. "That was only the first of my ideas. There may be another way, but to try it we must return to the Sanctuary. We will need the White Twins."

All three Marked looked at each other, and Rascon Mender's lips actually parted, but she closed her mouth again when Ellis Healer gave a tiny shake of his head. Clearly, they wanted to ask how the Seers could help them. But Dhulyn had no intention of telling them yet—possibly never, if the Seers could re-create the Vision of the hiding child without her.

"We'll need time, and that we may not have. The Nomads have been sighted."

"From where?" Remm handed the shoulder bag to the Healer.

"The north tower."

"The earliest point at which they can be seen. That buys us some time." His brows drew down in a vee. "The Tarxin will call for his Council, and he'll want the Tar with him. And at the right moment—when they've decided what to tell you—they'll call for you, as well. That means the upper gardens will be clear. We'll go as soon as the summons comes for you."

"Should they wait here? We could go together to the Sanctuary after dark."

But Remm was already shaking his head. "No one would call to see them now, during the meal hour, and the midday rest. But as soon as the worst of the heat passes—and word of the Nomads gets around, as it will—there will be people in the Sanctuary, and many will ask for the senior Marked. I can take them back through the gardens, Dhulyn Wolfshead. I know the way now. No need to disturb the Tar Xerwin."

"And if you're found there?"

"With all due respect to the Tar, it's only he or his father can find us there. If it's he, then no problem, if it's the Tarxin, well." Remm Shalyn shrugged. "I confess I was curious as to what story the Tar was going to give his father to explain our presence earlier. Me, I'll just say you sent me, and I was afraid to disobey."

"Very well." Dhulyn rubbed the line she could feel forming between her brows. She looked up at the Marked. "At the end of the third watch, when the Moon has set. Expect me."

It was odd to see such a promising inlet so deserted, even at this time of day. But they had wanted a high tide to take them as far in as possible, and the fact that this was the hottest part of the day simply meant there would be fewer landsters about. The bluffs here were not as high as they were at Ketxan City, but they were cut by a narrow creek. The sun had just passed its highest point when Parno and his squad had taken one of the *Wavetreader*'s boats and set off. The Nomads knew this section of coast well, having put in often for fresh water, and though Parno hadn't felt much wind, they'd been able to use the sails on the small craft to get them almost to the beach.

Seems an odd place to be so familiar with *Is there a village nearby*

There's good fresh water upstream, above the tidal washes That was Conford. *Can beach the boat there as well, then it's a short climb to the top of the bluff*

*But have *you* been here before, Conford* Surely not, if his exchange had been so recent.

Amusement *No need* *Others have, and their knowledge is my knowledge*

Looks different in the day That was one of the twins. Tindar, Parno thought. *Only ever been here at night*

They doused the sail and took out oars as soon as they were far enough up the creek to lose the wind. In moments the prow of the boat grounded, and Sar and Chels jumped out to haul it as far up the tiny beach as they could. Parno jumped out also, still in his bare feet. His boots were tucked down the front of his tunic, he carried two swords, his daggers, knives, and even a throwing quoit. The others bore the weapons he thought they'd do best with. Swords for the most part, but Tindar's twin, Elian, also had a small ax, and Conford had his *garwon*.

Amusement *Nervousness* *Fear* This last very small.

Parno stayed off to one side while the Nomads pulled the boat far enough up the beach that the movement of waves would not trouble it. Sails and masts were stowed, and the boats turned over. With luck, they would make it back in time to catch the next high tide.

Ready

Agreement

Follow, and keep as quiet as you can

That was one thing that Pod sense gave you, he thought. You knew exactly where everyone else in your squad was, and if necessary, you knew what they were thinking. Instant communication—and completely silent. Better than the nightwatch whisper of the Mercenary Brotherhood, since it could be used over any distance.

#Not any distance# That was the unmistakable voice of a Crayx. Deeper, somehow, and more resonant, though the terms meant nothing when no real sound was made. #Go far enough inland, and we cannot hear you#

How far

#Distance on land is very hard for us# #We have heard the voice of a Pod-sensed one as far as two days' travel on foot# #Farther than that, we cannot be sure#

Not that far, then, as things were measured. A Pod-sensed child growing up almost anywhere in Boravia would be overlooked by the few Crayx who came into the Midland Sea.

#We will look more carefully now#

The trees grew thicker as they walked away from the beach, giving them much needed shade. Though they had covered their heads, and were wearing their lightest garments, the heat was oppressive, and the insects would have been a great deal more so, if it were not for the greasy salve that the Nomads used as protection. One of their most popular trade goods, it was made from an oil excreted by the Crayx. Still, Parno found he had to wave tiny insects away from his face every now and then to avoid breathing them in.

The thickness of the trees did expose one flaw in their plan, however. The Nomads were noisier on land than anyone he'd ever led before. Parno called a halt as one of them blundered through a bush.

Not our fault, nowhere to practice

Parno thought for a moment. Not only could they be heard by anyone near them, but the noise of their own movement would obscure the sound of anyone else's approach. Too bad he hadn't thought of teaching them even one of the simpler Hunter *Shoras*.

#Show us#

Startled, Parno thought for a moment before signaling to the others to rest. He waited until the watch was posted before he closed his eyes and took a deep breath. And another. His heart rate slowed, and his senses turned outward. The Stalking Cat *Shora* settled over him like a blanket, and suddenly the whole clearing was quiet, as Parno and the Nomads, linked by the Crayx, all breathed in the same silent rhythm, their eight hearts beating as one. At first it was disorienting to hear with so many ears, feel the shift of air or the pattern of sunlight with so many skins, but suddenly, as if the minds of the Crayx acted like a clearinghouse for all the different sensations, Parno felt everything fall into place.

Nineteen

✳ **M**ARVELOUS✳ THAT WAS one of the twins. ✳Like this all the time✳ she asked.

✳When using the right *Shora*✳ he answered.

A buzz of excitement passed through them all. *What a way to School people,* Parno thought. Unfortunately, it would only work with the Pod-sensed.

At first, even with the *Shora,* the Nomads were not as silent as Mercenary Brothers would have been, but they were so much quieter than they had been moments before that it was like leading an entirely different group of people. Parno found that they weren't able to keep up continuously the level of concentration required for the Stalking Cat *Shora,* but he kept them practicing between breaks, and even without it, the awareness of what was possible made them all take better care. Soon, instead of moving like raw recruits, the Nomads began to have the feel of a squad who had been training together for some time.

It was evening by the time Parno and the Nomads were out of the woods and making their way through cultivated fields and groves of fruit trees to within sight of Ketxan City. There was this to be said about a slave culture; in any other place, the lands around them would have been held by free men or tenant farmers, people who would have been up in the night, watching over their flocks or making their rounds. The Holdings would have been smaller, closer together, and therefore harder to pass unnoticed. In this place, the holdings were huge, the workers penned up at night, and the watching eyes turned inward, not outward. All of which helped to make it relatively easy for Parno and his seven Nomads.

Parno had been hoping for moonlight to help him match the Upper City to the description he'd had from Oskarn of the *Sunwaver* Pod, but the afternoon had slowly become cloudier, and the hoped-for moonlight would not now materialize. They could see lights in some of the pavilions of the Upper City, but certainly not enough to give general illumination.

See there Parno picked out what he thought would be the best route over the wall. *I'll go first, follow in order*

Agreement

In moments they were all over the wall, and had moved forward into a lane between two low buildings which showed no lights.

Silence everyone *Three people approach us*

Instantly, the Stalking Cat *Shora* enveloped them once again, precise and perfect.

People out late

Parno shook his head. *That's a patrol* *See the way they move*

Awareness *Agreement*

*Isn't that what *you* said* Conford thought. *You'd set up patrols if was your place to guard*

That wasn't precisely what he'd said, Parno thought. He'd said it was what any Mercenary would advise. But to come here and find it done ... Parno became aware of a creeping unease. Was it possible that there were Pod-sensed among the Mortaxa after all? Could they have listened to his thoughts?

#No# This was the Crayx. #Not without our knowledge# The Crayx had kept the others from feeling his unease.

Heading toward us *Will pass by*

No Parno wasn't sure exactly how he knew. *In the open, they might have missed us, but not here*

Three for certain *Can smell them* A sense of delight as the Nomad who'd spoken—Mikel?—felt the full usefulness of the Stalking Cat *Shora*.

One experienced man leads two recruits Parno felt the agreement as the others all compared the sounds and understood why he'd drawn that conclusion.

Twins, flank left. Conford, Mikel, right Parno felt them move into place, as Trudi, Sar, and Chels moved back, spreading out to cover them all.

The patrol continued to approach. Their manner was relaxed, more like people going for a walk than guards on patrol—so much so that Parno almost doubted what logic and the Stalking Cat *Shora* told him.

Inexperienced he told the others. *Not expecting trouble* *Move with me*

At exactly the right moment Parno stepped out of a shadow and cut the patrol leader's throat with a sharp stroke of the sword in his right hand. He caught the body as it fell, keeping sound to the minimum, and saw out of the corner of his eye Conford plunging his *garwon* into the second man's temple, and Mikel grappling with the third man, one hand at his throat to keep him from crying out.

Parno felt a grin spread over his face as Sar ran forward to help Mikel. They had all moved simultaneously.

All three guards were dressed in short patterned kilts—there was not enough light to show colors. They wore metaled sandals and leather harness over bare skin, and carried short swords. Only one had a crossbow hanging from his belt.

Take the weapons, and move the bodies into the shadows under that wall Parno instructed.

What now

There may be another patrol, or someone may come looking for this one when they don't report It was too late to change plans, but a good Mercenary Brother learned to adapt to circumstances as he found them. And this was a circumstance Parno had planned for. *Have to split up* he said. *As we discussed* *Conford, take Sar, Mikel, and Chels to the public entrance* *The rest of you, with me*

Agreement *Excitement*

Crayx, are you ready

#We await your word#

Dhulyn returned from the Council meeting to find Remm Shalyn alone in her quarters, weapons spread out on the table to be cleaned, oil and a cleaning cloth in his hand. *Her* weapons.

Before he could finish looking up, she was across the room, lifting his hand from the metalwork on her crossbow.

"Don't touch my things," she said. "Never touch my things."

His eyes went round at what he saw on her face, and he licked his lips. "But Dhulyn Wolfshead, it's my job. I'm your sword servant."

"No." She squeezed her eyes shut. How to make him understand? "Among the Mercenary Brotherhood there are no servants," she began. "We are Brothers. Each our own master, and our own servant."

"But if you spend your time cleaning weapons and harness, you don't have time to *be* a Mercenary Brother."

"If I don't clean my own weapons, how can I be sure they have no defects? How can I be sure they are *mine*?"

He seemed about to argue further and Dhulyn put up her hand, palm toward him. "You tell me you're my sword servant."

"Yes."

"You're to obey me."

"Yes."

She slammed her hand down on the table. "Then obey me."

Remm looked at her openmouthed for the time it took to breathe in twice. Then he began to laugh. "Very well, yes," he said when he had caught his breath. "I think I see."

Dhulyn shook her head at him, but smiled. She was finding it hard, very hard, to deal with this form of thinking, this settled condition of the mind. In Boravia, independence of thought and action could be found in many people, everywhere—in fact, much of it often had to be trained out of people to make them good troops. But here, where the common experience was that one set of people oppressed another, even a naturally independent type like Remm Shalyn, who was used to playing a difficult role, showed evidence of a narrow way of thinking.

"So how did the Council go?" he asked her, pushing himself away from the table and her weapons and going to the sideboard, where there were still pastries and a jug of drink from the midday meal.

She smiled her wolf's smile, and was given an answering grin in return.

"That Tarxin's up to something."

"He usually is." Remm poured her out a cup of fruit juice, still cool in its ceramic jug, and handed it to her. Dhulyn took it without tasting it, seated herself in the big chair to one end of the table, and slung a leg over the arm.

"Apparently, there is no cause for immediate alarm," she said. "The Nomad ships are at least three days away. Currents prevent them from coming directly to the docks from where they've been sighted. They shall have to come around from a different direction. The Tarxin has asked the representatives of the High Noble Houses to make up a small committee—which is to include me—to meet with the Nomads."

"So we can try the plan you have in mind?"

She looked at him. "Can we go openly to the Sanctuary? It wastes so much time otherwise."

Remm came and sat on the edge of the table near enough to touch her if he put out his hand. "What's your plan, Wolfshead? What can the White Twins do that you can't?"

For a moment Dhulyn studied Remm's face. He looked open, honest, trustworthy. But then, he could act a part if needed, and it would be often needed if he were a freer of slaves. He trusted her with this knowledge of himself. But given how the Marked were circumstanced here in Mortaxa, could she trust him with *her* secrets?

"The White Twins know where the spirit of the child Xendra hides. They have Seen her. Javen Finder cannot Find the child—neither by linking with the Healer and Mender, nor through using the bowl. She can't, as she says, Find a Vision. But if she could link with the Seers, experience their Vision firsthand, perhaps then she could Find the child, searching the world of the Vision, as she searches through this one.

"But the White Twins are . . ." Remm's voice trailed away. He waggled his right hand from side to side.

"Yes, they are. But they can See Xendra. The only question is whether they can also link with the Finder."

I can do it, she thought. She had linked with other Marked before, and thought she could do it again. But she was not ready to tell even the other Marked that she was herself a Seer. She could do nothing to help them, if she were locked inside the Sanctuary with them. She couldn't take the chance that their settled patterns of thinking might betray her, that even the Marked would no longer see her as Paledyn. Just as she couldn't take the chance to try a Vision herself, without Keria and Amaia. With them, she could control the Visions, take them where she wished them to go, something she could never do with any certainty before.

Without the Twins' help, there was no knowing what Visions she might See—anything might come, past or future. At the moment there was nothing of the future she wanted to See, and one particular Vision of the past she would give much never to See again.

⌁

A woman was talking to the guards at the entrance to his rooms when Xerwin returned to them after the Council meeting. The guards came to attention and when she turned to see why, he recognized her as the Xara Finexa, the Storm Witch's attendant.

"Forgive me, Tar Xerwin," she said, offering a curtsy which displayed her bosom to good effect. "Your sister, the Tara Xendra waits for you within."

Xerwin wrinkled up his nose, not caring if the woman saw it. His first instinct was simply to refuse. He had nothing to say to the Storm Witch, and could not imagine what she felt she needed to say to him. He started to signal the guard to enter before him, to eject her ... but Xerwin hesitated. Something had brought her here—even if it was merely some trick. Should he not try to discover what it was? And if she *had* something of consequence to tell him, and he missed hearing it out of misplaced caution ... he could just imagine what Dhulyn Wolfshead would say about that.

He could be tricky himself, if he needed to be.

Carcali was sitting in the window seat when Tar Xerwin came into his sitting room. She had her arms folded across her chest and her hands tucked into the long sleeves of her child's tunic. She'd been watching the sunset, reaching out and feeling the slow gathering of moisture, the formation of cloud. In her lap, cradled in the folds of her skirt, was a soft toy she had found fallen behind the closed shutter, half-formed, made from scraps of leather with raw inglera fleece for stuffing.

"What brings you here?" he said, his voice quite gruff. "What is so urgent?"

He was looking at her differently now, she noticed. He'd frowned before, but his mouth then had been softer, his eyes warmer. That frown had shown concern. Now his eyes were hard, his mouth a thin line. *He knows,* she thought. He might have wondered before, but now it was clear that he knew she wasn't his little sister. Carcali couldn't see the Tarxin telling him, so it must have been the Paledyn. She shut her eyes, suddenly tired, far more tired than the small Art she'd used so far should make her.

He was still waiting for his answer. What *did* she want from him, what *was* so urgent? It had seemed so simple when she decided to come here. Tell him what was going on, and he'd become an instant ally. Now it didn't seem that simple. She lifted the toy.

"This was for your sister, wasn't it? You were making it for her. You must have loved her very much, to do this with your own hands." She turned it over. "It's a horse, isn't it? The legs should be a little longer."

"You know horses? You've seen them?" His eyes were narrowed, calculating. He stood, leaning his hip against his worktable. She nodded.

"In my own time, my own place, yes." She held out the toy like a peace offering. "My name is Carcali," she said. She almost couldn't believe she was telling him. "And no, that's not so urgent, is it?" She rubbed her face with her hands. "I'm just tired of all the pretending. The Paledyn told you, I suppose."

"It was I told *her* you weren't my sister though, as it happened, I had no need." He came closer. "The Nomads approach. Can this wait?"

Carcali nodded out the window. "The Tarxin's asked me to send a storm to destroy the Nomad ships."

For a second he stood stone still, then he pulled out a chair and sat down. "Can you?"

She nodded. "It would take a few days, but, yes, I can do it."

"Why tell me?" His tone was cautious, wary, but with a good sprinkling of plain curiosity. Her eye fell once more on the toy. She'd come here looking for an ally, someone . . . a better man than the Tarxin, someone who cared about people, not power. Someone who would make a toy for his sister with his own hands.

"The storm won't just affect the Nomads. What I'd have to do, to follow the Tarxin's orders, would cause a lot more damage, far-reaching damage, inland as well as at sea. I've told your father this, and he doesn't care. He wants me to kill those people, no matter the consequences, and I don't want to."

"You've already done as bad."

"But not on purpose, not deliberately. It was an accident." She reached a hand toward him.

"And is it an accident that you occupy my sister's body?"

Carcali sat up straight, gripping the edge of the stone window seat. "I didn't do this, the Marked did." She cleared her throat and tried again. "When that Marked person found me and pulled me into this body, there was no one else there. I was alone in the spheres." Carcali swallowed, trying to get her lips to stop trembling. "Your sister wasn't there."

His eyebrows drew down in a deep vee, his lips pressed together.

"Your sister is gone," Carcali said, as gently as she could.

"And if she is found? Would you vacate her body?"

Carcali rubbed at her eyes. "Listen, you want me to be honest? I'll be honest. It's too late for her to be found. Only a Mage like me, trained in the Art, can leave the body for so long and then return to it." And sometimes not even a Mage like her, but she had no intention of telling him that. "And let me say again—" Carcali found she was pointing her index finger at him and quickly dropped her hand, tapping herself on the sternum instead. "I didn't take your sister's body. It isn't just that I don't want to be out there in the nothing again, not ever again. I'm really sorry for your sister, but she was gone before I ever came along. Ask them! Ask those Marked people. Would they have taken me if your sister had been there? No one gains by pushing me out again, not me, not you, not the people we can help if we work together."

Xerwin turned the toy over in his hands, frowning down

at it. A fluff of wool fell to the floor, and he stooped to pick it up. "Xendra always wanted to see a horse with her own eyes. Fond as she was of Naxot, I think she secretly hoped to be married to some ruler across the Long Ocean, to see the horses there." He put the half-made toy aside on the table and looked across at her. Carcali wanted to look away, but steeled herself not to lower her eyes.

"Why come to me?" he said finally. "Why don't you just refuse my father? What can he do to you?"

"You remember the bruise on my face?" His eyes widened, but Carcali saw that Xerwin wasn't really shocked. "He took away Kendraxa who at least was nice to me, and replaced her with that Finexa spy. And he locked my doors and starved me. It wouldn't take long for me to get too weak to practice the Art, and that's the only weapon I have. If I can destroy him, well, he can do the same to me." Carcali took a deep breath.

"Your father doesn't want a partnership with me, as he claims. He doesn't want to work with me, just to use me, control me, as he controls everything. He has no intention of negotiating with the Nomads—or anyone else—Paledyn or no Paledyn. *We* could have a real partnership, you and I. We could trust each other, we could create a world that would be the best for everyone."

"We could change the world." Xerwin was looking inward now, and Carcali would have given a great deal to know what it was he was looking at. She'd never seen that look on his face before.

She got down off the window seat and had taken a step toward him when one of the door guards knocked and entered. Finexa was in the hall behind him, wringing her hands.

"Your pardon, Tar Xerwin, it's the Nomads. They are storming the City."

<hr />

Dhulyn Wolfshead leaned far over the rail of the tiny balcony in her sitting room, craning her neck from side to side. The night was overcast, but the moonlight that made it through the clouds reflected back twofold from the water.

"I see no ships."

Just as she spoke, a great long-nosed head rose out of the water, and spat a jet of water at one of the lower floors. A small sailboat, moored at dockside, was blown upward by the force of the jet and smashed against the cliff face. A flight of arrows came from one of the middle floors, between Dhulyn and the sea, and a second beast directed its water jet upward.

"Sun and Moon, Wind and Stars." Dhulyn turned to Remm Shalyn. "I did not know they could do that."

Remm looked pale, but smiled. "I had heard," he said. "But I've never before seen it."

Dhulyn looked again at the archers. "Idiots," she said. "Those arrows will never pierce their hides, and if they're aiming for the eyes, they need a better angle."

"What about a crossbow?"

Dhulyn nodded, her eyes still on the incredible jets of water. "Can't do any harm." Which she meant precisely. With a good longbow, or a well-made recurve bow, she might confidently expect to do some damage. But with a crossbow, at this distance, "no harm" was exactly what she would do.

In minutes, Dhulyn was running down the corridor with Remm Shalyn at her heels, carrying her crossbow and a soft leather bag full of bolts. In the Grand Square outside the Tarxin's palace, she found the Senior Guard Commander directing soldiers to their posts on the lower floors.

"It's the Crayx," he told her, rather unnecessarily, she thought. "The Nomads' animals. They train them to shoot jets of water at the City face, to cover an attack."

"But what attack? We've already established that the ships are still days away."

"If their beasts are here, then the Nomads are here as well. They use these animal tricks to distract us, while they gain entry at the lower levels."

"Where the animals are, we'll find their masters," agreed the second-in-command.

Not true, Dhulyn thought. The Crayx had their regular migration routes, and for the most part they followed them, but they could and did deviate from them, and in any case, their movements were no more dependent on the movements of the Nomads than the rising of Mother Sun was dependent on a farmer's breakfast hour. And as far as she had seen, there was no one trying to gain entry from the water level.

Not the lower levels, no.

"The Upper City." Had Xerwin had time to assign patrols there as he'd intended? She thought she'd whispered, but she found all other voices stopped, and the commander turning to look at her.

"You are right," she said. "This is a distraction, but the attack will be made from above, in the Upper City."

"Nonsense." In the excitement, the commander seemed to have forgotten who he was speaking to. "The Nomads have never attacked from overland before. They cannot maneuver on land."

Dhulyn knew very well that just because something had never been done before, did not mean it was impossible. But she also knew when she would be listened to, and when she would be wasting her breath. The commander had already turned away from her. This was clearly an example of the latter.

"Commander." She waited until she had his attention. "You will not mind if I inspect the Upper City."

"Of course not, Paledyn." Relief at being rid of her was evident on his face, and had served to remind the man of his manners.

Catching Remm Shalyn's eye, Dhulyn trotted down the passage that would take them to the Upper City. The Nomads had never attacked overland before. Nothing more likely, she thought, seeing what a siege engine they had in the Crayx and their water jets. But an overland sortie—was that something she or Parno had ever discussed with the Nomads? Because it would be typical Mercenary planning, exactly what she would have done herself, if she had known what tactics the Mortaxa expected, and that the Crayx had this ability. She stopped dead in her tracks.

"Dhulyn Wolfshead? Are you ill?"

All those evenings of talk, of singing, of telling tales, was it possible that an overland attack could have been discussed? Or that the Nomads could have worked it out from some tale one of them had told?

It must be. Because there wasn't any other explanation. There couldn't be. Could there?

She took off running.

Appears was only the one patrol

Typical amateurs *Any Mercenary Brother would have known to have at least two patrols*

Lionsmane

Parno automatically looked in the direction Conford wanted him to look. There were another pair of lights. A second patrol.

As if his thoughts had just conjured them out of the air. What kind of trick was this?

Do the landsters have any other Mages he asked. *Anyone other than the Storm Witch*

Not that we know Everyone agreed on that. *There are Marked* pointed out a single individual Parno couldn't identify.

But the Marked can't conjure lights out of air Parno said. *Or read my thoughts.*

Lionsmane Tension and query were equally obvious in the flavor of the thought. Parno made a quick decision.

Won't cross our path if keep to their present heading he said. *Let them go* *Conford, proceed to the public entrance*

Agreement

Parno waited until Conford's group had melted away into the darkness—almost silently—before leading the twins and Trudi Primoh after him, swinging around westward to approach the wall of the palace precinct obliquely.

Briefly, Parno wondered whether they should have stalked the second patrol, taking one of them prisoner to ask where the Storm Witch could be found. But that was too risky. Better to get inside the palace and frighten it out of a servant or slave.

Once away from the Grand Square, Dhulyn let Remm lead her through the palace corridors to the staircase that would take them up into the royal precinct in the Upper City. Once outside, they could head for the nearest wall. As they neared the stairs, Dhulyn had Remm douse his torch, and handed him the crossbow.

"It will be considerably darker in the Upper City than it was even at the cliff face," she said. "There, the sea itself helped to reflect what little light there is. Carrying lights will make us a target, and dull our own night vision." She'd prefer in any case to trust her own *Shora*-aided eyesight.

The top of the staircase opened onto a square landing with an arched doorway to one side. This doorway, in turn, opened into the portico that sheltered the entrance proper, a small roofed pavilion made entirely of green marble. Dhulyn had noticed on her visit with Xerwin that it was perhaps three paces wide by five paces long, and raised three steps above the ground outside. When they reached the outer doorway, Dhulyn could just make out the long, tree-lined avenue that fronted the pavilion. The lighter blotches, evenly spaced, she knew to be the stone or marble benches which were laid out beneath the trees. Remm was about to step out into the avenue, already pointing to the direction of the nearest wall, when Dhulyn stopped him, taking him by the arm. There. Off to the right. A movement, like a shadow changing shape. A scuff, like the edge of a boot against stone. The sound of someone coming over the wall.

Dhulyn pulled Remm closer to her, using the nightwatch whisper. "Call for the patrol," she said. "They won't come for a female voice."

"Armsmen!" he obligingly roared out in a voice that startled even Dhulyn; it seemed impossible that so big a sound should come out of so small and compact a man. "To the palace wall! To the Tarxin!"

There was no immediate response, but Dhulyn thought she heard a soft sound over to the right. The patrol would not bother to be so quiet, were they being outflanked? Well, she knew better than to be drawn away from her defensible position. She took a quick look to the right, and the left. Not as much room as she'd like. She drew Remm with her back to the inner doorway. "Stay here," she said. "Kill anyone who gets past me." She refrained from saying she expected no one to pass her.

Sounded like just one man *Stay out here, engage the patrol if they come, and secure my exit* *Be as quick as I can* Parno ran down the stone path, wishing his boots were not quite so loud. If he'd had more time, he could have gone completely silently, but with the alarm already given, someone had to get inside quickly, and that someone was him.

This avenue of trees, with its stone benches, led toward an enclosed pavilion, the only completely enclosed structure he could see, and unless he was badly mistaken, the direction from which the voice came. This was likely the entrance to the palace below. He smiled to himself when he saw a darker, vertical patch that meant a doorway.

There, a man was approaching on the shadowed side of the avenue. Dhulyn considered her strategy again, and backed up. With only one opponent, better if she let him into the relatively confined space of the entryway. There, the darkness would be to her advantage, and she would be able to prevent him from escaping. She took a deep breath. A modified version of the Hunter's *Shora* would help her senses stay alert. She smiled her wolf's smile. She and Parno had once needed to practice *Shora* while blindfolded. This would be child's play compared to that.

There was someone in the pavilion. Parno wasn't sure how he knew it; there had been neither sound to be heard nor movement to be seen, but someone was definitely in the structure. He slowed, drawing his left-hand sword, but continued to advance, both blades at the ready. Better to deal with this person now, quickly, while there was only one of him. The darkness would be helpful.

Her senses enhanced by the *Shora,* the first thing Dhulyn noticed as her opponent passed the doorway into the darkness of the marble-cool entry was that his heartbeat was exactly in sync with her own. A shiver passed up her spine. And there was an odor, an odd, almost spicy scent that she had smelled somewhere before.

His opponent was nothing more than a darker shadow among all the others. But he knew that shadow, Parno thought, as the skin crawled on his back. Knew that shape, that angle of shoulder. That scent, subtly changed and yet familiar. His breath caught as a light seem to blaze in his mind. "No," he told it, not daring to hope. This must be Mage's work, meant to distract and detain him. There must be a Mage among the Mortaxa after all. He took a firmer grip on his swords and stepped forward.

* * *

At that single spoken syllable, Dhulyn froze. Shape, smell, and now sound. It was impossible. It could not be. It was a trick. Could she be having a Vision unaware?

"Are you a ghost?" The nightwatch voice seemed impossibly loud in this confined space.

"Come and try me, Mage's phantom."

The voice. Dhulyn began to tremble.

"I am no phantom." Dhulyn's heart pounded, hard and fast, as she lowered her sword. "I am Dhulyn Wolfshead, called the Scholar, and Schooled by Dorian of the River, the Black Traveler. I have fought at Sadron, and Arcosa, where I met my Partner, Parno Lionsmane. Together we fought at Bhexyllia, for the Great King in the West, and later at Limona, against the Tegriani."

"Tell me something no one else could know."

Dhulyn thought, ideas chasing each other hotly through her mind. There seemed so many things, and yet . . .

"I bear a Mark," she said at last. "I am a Seer. Others know it, but no one this side of the Long Ocean."

Suddenly she was crushed in two strong arms, arms she knew well, and she found that she could not breathe, not because of the pressure of those arms, but because her heart was too full, her throat too thick. She was crying. She could not remember ever crying like that before.

"Dhulyn. Dhulyn, my heart. It can't be. You're alive."

"Enemy behind," she croaked out.

Parno released her and whirled, swords raised. "Where?"

"Well, there could have been," she said, taking what felt like the first deep breath she'd had in weeks.

"But how—the Crayx could not find you anywhere."

"But they clearly found you." Dhulyn's raw silk voice sounded rougher, as if she were trying not to cry. She kept touching him, his face, his hands, running her callused fingers along the edges of his beard and lips as if to assure herself that it was really him. "Do we have time for this? I take it those are your people out there."

"Come to kill the Storm Witch." Parno blinked. He hadn't noticed before how much he'd fallen into the Nomads' form of speech.

"My thinking precisely, but there are complications."

Parno took hold of her wrists. "Don't care. I—I'm not even sure I care whether the Witch lives or dies, not now."

Dhulyn butted him in the shoulder with her head, just like a cat. "I think the matter can be resolved to our satisfaction, but we need time. Can you call off the attack?"

Her words warmed him. It was gratifying that she assumed he was in charge. Though in a way, he supposed he was.

Fall back he said to the Nomads. *Fall back, everyone* *My Partner lives* *Dhulyn Wolfshead lives* *She can take me to the Storm Witch with safety for all*

#Rejoicing# came the deeper notes of the Crayx

Are you certain

Certain *Fall back now, before there is further loss of life on either side*

Confusion *Disagreement*

#Parno Lionsmane, our people need further assurance you are well and secure#

And not insane, he thought. *Look in my thoughts* he told the Crayx. *Can you tell that I am not under any magic, that I have found my Partner, alive and well*

#We see this, and will show the others# #We will fall back, as you suggest, and await your instructions# #We remind everyone, this has all along been Lionsmane's plan# #We are at his orders#

Reluctance *Concern* *Agreement*

#We will stay linked, Lionsmane# #Call upon us as needed#

"You were talking to them, weren't you?"

He swept her up in his arms and swung her around as if they were dancing. "I tell you, it's the greatest way to coordinate a two-pronged attack that's ever been heard of." When he put her down, Dhulyn's smile had faded, and her left eyebrow was raised. Parno grinned all the harder. What an Outlander she was, after all, to be embarrassed by his show of emotion.

"Come on, my soul, my heart! We're alive! We're together again."

"Together again," she murmured.

"Dhulyn Wolfshead?"

They'd been talking throughout in the nightwatch voice, as loud as shouts to them, but virtually silent for anyone more than a pace or two away. At this tentative whisper, Parno swung away from his Partner—his Partner!—and faced the inner doorway, swords raised.

"Show a light, Remm Shalyn," Dhulyn said. "There is no enemy here, but the best of allies."

Twenty

"PART OF ME JUST WANTS to walk out of here and go home." Parno stretched his hand across the table and touched Dhulyn on the back of hers. They had started out sitting side by side on the settee in her sitting room, but when Remm Shalyn had returned from a raid to the kitchens they had taken seats at the table across from one another. Dhulyn found herself stealing glances at her Partner, as if she expected at any moment to find he had disappeared. She was afraid to look at him, and afraid to look away.

"We won't get home without the Nomads," she said. "And their quarrel with the Mortaxa is a real one."

"But this Xerwin is the one they've dealt with before, they speak well of him. If *he* can be made to see reason . . ." Parno's voice trailed off as he thought through his idea. Dhulyn tried to concentrate on the food in front of her, but she was tasting nothing. This *was* Parno—she knew it in her blood and bones—but she was still having trouble believing it. It had taken her the whole of the walk back to her rooms, all three of them being careful not to be seen by anyone else, to realize that under her joy was a thin layer of an emotion she could only define as anger, much as it shocked and shamed her. How could she be *angry* with her Partner? Why?

"Xerwin may well see reason," she said aloud. "But he is not Tarxin here, his father is. And Xalbalil has his own firm plans, which include using the Storm Witch—and myself for that matter—to subjugate the Nomads."

Remm cleared his throat. He was sitting to Dhulyn's right, Parno's left, and had been watching them as they talked, turning his attention from one to the other. "So we remove the Storm Witch, as the best and fastest method of ruining his plans."

Parno raised his index finger, swallowed, and spoke. "Do we? No, listen," he said as Dhulyn opened her mouth. "You tell me the storm was an accident. Well, I've no reason to exact any vengeance on the woman for an act of carelessness or ignorance, not now that you're alive. The Tarxin," he shrugged. "There's more than one way to deal with him. As for the Witch, well, a Weather Mage is a very useful thing."

"What you say is true." Dhulyn spoke slowly, a strange reluctance coming over her. "And there's more to consider than just her magics. There's the knowledge she has of the time of the Caids."

"The lodestone," Remm Shalyn said.

"Exactly. What else might she be able to tell us, what might she know firsthand of their knowledge?"

Parno drummed his fingers on the tabletop. "Still, something is bothering you, my heart."

"What of the child?" Dhulyn spoke as evenly as she could. "The Tara Xendra, the real child."

Parno leaned forward. "You've found her? You're sure?"

"As sure as I am that you're sitting across from me." Dhulyn made sure that Parno was looking straight at her, flicked her eyes sideways at Remm Shalyn, and tapped the table with the third finger of her left hand.

Parno sat back in his seat, brow furrowed in contemplation. "If she's safe where she is," he began. But then he shook his head. "Nothing changes the fact that the Storm Witch has taken over someone else's body—can such a being be trusted, however useful she might be?" He looked up. "We must see what can be done."

"It's too late now to go to the Sanctuary," Remm Shalyn said.

"We'd be stopped?"

Remm was already shaking his head. "The Paledyn Dhulyn Wolfshead may certainly wander about at her will. But the gates to the Sanctuary will be closed. We should wait until tomorrow night."

Dhulyn leaned forward. "But will the gates not be closed then as well?"

Remm grinned at her. "Not if arrangements have been made, ahead of time. We won't be the only people who have ever wished to consult the Marked quietly, in private. Now, it's too late, but tomorrow I can make such arrangements."

"It's late in any case, and we must get some sleep. Even if the alarms of the day are over, we'll be expected to put in an appearance in the morning."

"Not Parno Lionsmane, I take it?"

Dhulyn caught Parno's eye. He moved his head a fraction to the left, and back again. "No," she said. "Let him be our hidden dagger, for now."

Once the Mortaxan had left to spend what remained of the night in his own quarters, Parno sat once more at the table. He'd been itching for the man to leave, but now that he had, Parno found himself unexpectedly uneasy to be left alone with his Partner. He kept wanting to touch her, to reassure himself that she was really there. But at the same time he wanted to act as normally as possible. To reestablish as quickly as might be their old standing with one another.

Dhulyn stood next to her chair, her eyes still on the door. She looked thinner, Parno thought. Her hair had grown and she had started rebraiding it.

"Can you trust him?" he said.

"I have been trusting him." Dhulyn turned finally to look at him. "Can you trust the Nomads?"

"Yes." It was the simplest answer, and the truth. "Within the mind of the Crayx, it is impossible to lie, or even to disguise the truth."

Dhulyn raised her eyebrows and pursed her lips in a silent whistle. "That would certainly make many things much easier."

Parno grinned. Only his Partner would think that the truth always made things easier. Dhulyn yawned, and Parno felt his own jaws tremble in response.

"Do we keep watch?" he said, getting to his feet again.

"There's only the one way in, well, two if you count the balcony." Dhulyn looked around, frowning, as if she'd misplaced something.

"Then I say no."

Dhulyn picked up the lamp and Parno followed her into the bedroom, sat down on the edge of the bed, and rubbed his face with his hands. Every one of his muscles, and the grittiness in his eyes, was reminding him of every hour that had passed and every step he'd marched since early that morning.

Dhulyn set the lamp into its niche by the door and stayed there, leaning against the wall. "You look different," she said.

"It's my new armor." Parno glanced up, smiling, and rapped the Crayx scales with his knuckles.

"Yes." Dhulyn nodded. "And your hair is longer, though I've seen it longer still. Your beard's grown in as well." She shook her head impatiently. "It's more than that. I think it's the Crayx. You have a faraway look in your eyes, that you didn't have before. As if you are listening to someone else."

Parno had bent over to pull off a boot, but now he sat up again, feeling the muscles in his jaw tighten. "You're saying I can't? I can't listen to someone else?"

Dhulyn brought her fists to her forehead. She shook her head and in a moment her whole body seemed to shake with it. "I'm so angry with you," she said through clenched teeth. Yet Parno could swear he heard surprise in her tone. "I'm furious."

Parno stood and went to her, hands up to take her by the wrists. "You don't get furious, my heart," he began. "Or, at least—" A sudden glint in her eyes warned him and he stopped, inches from touching her. "What is it? Not your woman's time already?"

She twisted away from him. "I thought you were dead. I've been mourning you for weeks. And all that time, you were alive—"

"You're angry with me because I'm alive?" Parno blew out his breath. This was unbelievable. "And what about me? You think you're the only one who's been grieving?" He gestured around the room. "You look pretty comfortably set up for a person in mourning, I must say."

Dhulyn's face set in hard planes. "I could just smack you."

Parno made a "come here" gesture with his hands. "What's stopping you."

The first blow came so fast that Parno didn't see it, for all that he'd invited it. She'd kicked him in the face, and while his hand was still on his nose Dhulyn swung again, this time with her fist. Part of him, he realized as he ducked and propelled his shoulder into her midsection, hadn't really expected Dhulyn to hit him at all.

He got hold of her elbow and twisted, but the leverage he thought he had disappeared when she turned her hips and almost wriggled free. She stamped on his instep, but he pulled his foot back in time, though it cost him his hold on her elbow, which she drove into his stomach. He caught it again, and this time he managed to throw her to the floor, with the help of his foot behind her heel.

The next few minutes were a concentrated struggle of elbows, knees, fists, arm twisting, and head butts. At one point, Dhulyn almost got him in a classic choke hold, and it would have worked on any one other than a Mercenary Brother, but Parno knew the countermove and used it. At another point he thought he had her trapped, but in the last moment she got her knee up between them and threw him off. Not that he went far. Finally, the wall itself became his ally, and he had her pinned in the angle where the wall met the floor.

"Dhulyn," he said, and she stopped struggling.

"You *died,* you blooded son of a twisted ox. You left me alone. I almost killed myself, and all the time you were alive and well, and making a new life with the Nomads."

Parno rolled off her, wiping his bleeding nose on his sleeve. "I wanted to die, and the Crayx would have taken me—my soul—into their consciousness." He squeezed his eyes shut. "But I would never have seen you again. In Battle." She kept her head turned away. "Dhulyn."

"Or in Death," she finally said, reaching out her hand to him without turning around. Her hand was cold, and there was a scrape along the knuckles.

"I stayed alive to avenge you, to kill the Storm Witch. After that," he shrugged, finding it a pointless business when lying on the floor. "I figured there'd be no 'after that.' "

Dhulyn used her grip on his hand to roll over and face him. There was a line of dirt smudged across her left cheek, but her face was otherwise unmarked. He must have been taking care without realizing, otherwise he might have had some explanations to give. He wondered how many bruises it had cost him.

"I began that way." She cleared her throat, but lowered her eyes, fixing her glance on their entwined hands. "Thinking I'd kill her and not worry about 'after.' Then." She licked her lips. Parno watched, fascinated. He didn't think he'd ever seen her guilty before.

"Then I met the Marked," she said, still looking down at their hands. "They needed my help. I thought perhaps I'd do that first, before I joined you in death. After all." She blinked and swallowed. "After all, you would still be there."

"You're angry with me because you decided not to die right away?"

She shrugged one shoulder and nodded. "Why was it so easy?" she said. "How could it be so easy to live?"

"You call that easy?" Parno could see from her face she'd suffered the same sleepless nights, the same hopeless dreams, the same staggering pain every time the grief hit her afresh. "It was the hardest thing I've ever done."

"How was it we could? Other Partners, they haven't survived."

"We aren't 'other Partners.' We're Dhulyn Wolfshead and Parno Lionsmane."

She managed a small smile.

"I'm not joking, think about it. The Tribes of the Red Horsemen were broken when you were just a child, younger than this Tara Xendra who's missing now. Your family, your Tribe—blood, your whole race was gone. And you survived. My death wasn't going to kill you, not after that."

"Dorian of the River saved me," she said. "The Brotherhood saved me."

Now it was his turn to shrug. "And it saved me as well. My story's different only in degree. When I was cast out of Tenebro House, I lost everything. Family, name, friends, position. If my father hadn't been a sensible man, I wouldn't even have had basic skills. I would have starved."

"So your conclusion is that Mercenaries are hard to kill."

"Well, we go down fighting, that's for certain." He stood and pulled her to her feet.

"In Battle," she said.

"And in Death."

What does he mean she's still alive Darlara wanted to thump the rail. *Has he been magicked somehow*

Didn't see her Conford admitted. He and the others had reached the creek without incident, and were pulling the boat into the water. There was no reason now to wait. Either Lionsmane would be successful in dealing with the Storm Witch, or he would not.

#We did# #We saw her# That was the unmistakable voice of the Crayx. #She lives, it is certain# #Look# And into all of their minds came the image of the Mercenary woman as she had appeared to the Lionsmane. The image was dark and full of shadows at first, and Darlara began to have hopes, but quickly it cleared to reveal the woman they all remembered, thinner perhaps, and with the marks of sun on her face, but unmistakable.

What if she's gone over to their side

#Lionsmane says it is not so# #It is Lionsmane who knows her# #He is to be trusted#

Darlara bit her lip, wanting to continue the argument, but knowing that what they said was right. Mal put his hand on her shoulder and she covered it with one of her own. The other rested on her belly. It was too soon for there to be any roundness, but she touched it nonetheless.

"Dar." That her twin spoke to her, instead of using the medium of the Crayx, showed how thoroughly he understood her need to stand apart, if only for a few minutes.

"Would have stayed," she said. "Was floating into that current. Know he would have stayed."

"Don't hate him for choosing his own life."

Darlara pressed her lips together and shook her head.

"Don't hate her either," Mal added. Trust her twin to go unerringly to the right spot. "She has her rights. We have the bloodline. That's what's important."

It took her a long while, but eventually Darlara nodded in agreement. "Just that I started to hope."

#A communication comes from Lionsmane#

"Done?"

Parno opened his eyes and nodded. "What did I look like?"

Dhulyn considered. "As if you were playing a particularly difficult piece of music, and weren't sure you remembered all the notes. You've told them everything?"

"Everything you told me. The White Seers, the Marked, the spirit of the little girl. Oh, and I told them to move the decoy ships back out of sight. Let the Mortaxa think they've been scared away. Once the Storm Witch is dealt with, it will be safe for the Nomads to come back."

Dhulyn lay back on the bed. They had slept in their clothes, and she had only taken off the sashes that held the short Mortaxan swords. She'd be able to have her own weapons back now, if they could return to the *Wavetreader*.

"Parno, my soul, do you think they tell the truth, the Crayx? Are their treaties and agreements made with the Caids of old? Do their tales go back so far?"

"Not their tales, their memories." Parno stretched out beside her, his hands underneath his head. "It isn't some Crayx of long ago who knew and came to terms with the Caids, it is these Crayx, themselves. They spawn new bodies, but they are the same entities."

"They knew the Caids? Before the coming of the Green Shadow and the rise of the Sleeping God? They knew the Caids then?"

"So they say. Though they weren't always known to each other. The Crayx had been creatures of the deep ocean, living their long lives and thinking their long thoughts. Something happened which made the Crayx seek out the Caids, find the Pod-sensed ones who had always lived among them, unnoticed by anyone, and begin communication with the landsters. Once they were aware of each other, they quickly came to accommodations and agreement."

"The Caids must have been a very different folk from what we are now, if that is what occurred. Nowadays we cannot get two groups of humans who live in neighboring valleys to agree so easily."

"And a good thing, too, or we Mercenary Brothers would have very little work. No, the Crayx say they were not so different, but they had more knowledge." He laughed as Dhulyn rolled her eyes.

"That's blooded helpful," she said. "*That* much we already knew. And so awareness of the Crayx became just another piece of the old learning that we on the land lost?"

"Not entirely," Parno said. "Apparently it became customary for those with Pod sense to live at sea for long periods of time. And when the Green Shadow rose for the first time, those who were at sea stayed there, and never returned to the land, except for the havens. Eventually they became the Nomads."

Dhulyn rolled over to face him, propping her head with an elbow. "But then they must still have some of the knowledge of the Caids?"

Parno shook his head. "The Crayx never had that knowledge—nor wanted it, so far as I can make out—eventually, the Pod-sensed Caids would have started to feel the same way." When there was no response Parno looked over at his Partner. "You've gone white," he said, sitting up. "Dhulyn?"

"SISTER." "SISTER." DHULYN IS IN A LONG AND NARROW CORRIDOR, WITH WALLS OF PANELED WOOD, AND A FLOOR TILED IN BLACK-AND-WHITE DIAMOND SHAPES. A LONG ROW OF SCONCES EACH HOLD THREE CANDLES THAT SMELL WARMLY OF BEESWAX. THIS IS A FORTUNE IN WAX, SHE THINKS, AS SHE PASSES THEM BY. SHE HEARS GIGGLING COMING FROM A ROOM AHEAD OF HER AND PICKS UP HER PACE. THE ROOM, WHEN SHE REACHES IT, IS FULL OF SUNLIGHT, AIRY DRAPERIES IN EVERY COLOR OF THE RAINBOW BLOW IN A WARM BREEZE. TWO YOUNG GIRLS, WHITE BRAIDS SWINGING, TINY BREASTS BARELY FORMED UNDER THEIR SHIFTS, SQUEAL WITH DELIGHT WHEN THEY SEE HER, AND RUN TO THROW THEIR ARMS AROUND HER.

"AM I DREAMING?" SHE ASKS THEM.

"OH, NO," AMAIA SAYS, THE GOLD FLECK IN HER RED EYE SPARKLING. "WE'RE SEEING, AND WE DECIDED TO SEE YOU. COME, SEE WITH US."

THE WINDOW LOOKS OUT ONTO A BROAD CITY STREET, WITH TALL BUILDINGS, SOME HAVING AS MANY AS TEN STORIES, TO EACH SIDE OF THE THOROUGHFARE. DHULYN KNOWS IT IS NIGHT, THOUGH THERE IS SO MUCH LIGHT IN THE STREET THEY CANNOT SEE THE STARS. A YOUNG WOMAN, SLIM, WITH HER HAIR CUT IN A SHORT CAP RUNS DOWN THE STREET TOWARD THEM. IT'S HARD TO BE SURE LOOKING DOWN, BUT DHULYN THINKS SHE IS TALL. WHEN THE WOMAN LOOKS UP AT THE SKY, DHULYN SEES THAT SHE KNOWS THE WOMAN, SHE'S SEEN HER BEFORE. BUT ALWAYS OLDER, SHE THINKS.

"THAT'S THE STORM WITCH, ISN'T IT?" KERIA LAYS HER HEAD

ON DHULYN'S SHOULDER AS SHE SPEAKS. THE TWINS ARE OLDER NOW, DHULYN SEES, NO LONGER CHILDREN.

"YES, AS A YOUNG WOMAN."

"OH, SHE'S NOT SO OLD, NOT SO OLD AT ALL." AMAIA TAPS THE WINDOWSILL WITH HER INDEX FINGERS, AS IF PLAYING A DRUM. DHULYN NOTICES THAT THE GIRL BITES HER NAILS.

THE STORM WITCH RUNS INTO THE BUILDING BELOW THEM, AND DHULYN TURNS AWAY FROM THE WINDOW, HALFWAY EXPECTING HER TO RUN INTO THE ROOM. BUT THERE IS NO ONE IN THE ROOM BUT HERSELF AND THE WHITE SISTERS.

"IS THE CHILD XENDRA STILL SAFE?

KERIA SHRUGS. "WE CAN'T GO TO THE WOODS WITHOUT YOU, YOU KNOW. THAT'S YOUR PLACE. WE CAN LOOK NOW, IF YOU WISH."

DHULYN CONSIDERS. IS IT BEST TO MAKE SURE NOW, BEFORE SHE COMES BACK WITH THE OTHER MARKED?

THEY TURN BACK TO THE WINDOW AND THIS TIME IT LOOKS OUT ON A FOREST SCENE, A GROVE OF TREES, A SLEEPING CHILD. SATISFIED, DHULYN STEPS BACK.

"WE SEE YOU HAVE FOUND THE LIONSMANE," KERIA SAYS, SLIPPING HER ARM THROUGH DHULYN'S. "WE'RE VERY PLEASED FOR YOU, SISTER. IT IS HARD TO BE ALONE WHEN YOU'RE USED TO HAVING SOMEONE WITH YOU."

"WAIT." DHULYN PULLS AWAY. "DO YOU MEAN YOU KNEW WE WOULD BE REUNITED?"

"OF COURSE, WE SAW IT."

"BUT WHY DIDN'T YOU TELL ME?"

FOR AN INSTANT THE TWO SISTERS HAVE THE FACES OF STRICKEN CHILDREN. THEN AMAIA SPEAKS. "BUT, SISTER, YOU DID NOT ASK."

"It's a little sterile."

Xerwin stood to one side, watching Naxot as his friend watched the Witch Carcali spinning slowly around, taking in as much of the garden as she could from this vantage point. "This is the dry season," he said. "In the winter it's much more lush."

"Oh, I know, I'm sorry. That didn't come out the way I meant it."

But perhaps it did, Xerwin thought.

"The plants are beautiful," Carcali said.

It was still his sister's voice, even if the intonation was completely different. How long, he wondered, until he no longer heard Xendra when Carcali spoke?

"I should have said formal, not sterile," she continued, coming back down the path toward him. "The way everything is laid out in straight lines, squares, rectangles." She gestured at a nearby edging of green hedge. "Even where things are rounded, it's as if it was laid out with compasses."

"I'm sure it was," Xerwin said. "The garden has been this way as long as I can remember."

"Perhaps the Holy One would enjoy the grotto." Naxot was turning out to be tongue-tied now that he was actually in the company of the Storm Witch.

"Ooooh, a grotto, I'd love that. I guess I'm used to something a little rougher, more natural looking. We were always careful not to mess too much with what nature intended." Her voice trailed away, as they followed Naxot, and the adult expression of frowning abstraction looked very odd on her little girl's face. "I can't do what your father wants me to do," she said quietly. "I won't. This time the Nomads went away by themselves, but next time . . ." She looked up at him, squinting her eyes against the morning sun. "Next time it may not be the Nomads."

She was right. Xerwin knew she was right. But what to do? And how to do it?

"Did you have a chance to speak to the Paledyn?" she said.

"The Tarxin wanted her this morning."

"Come, you two, it's much cooler here." Naxot's voice called to them from farther along the path.

It only took the tinkling sound of moving water to make Carcali walk faster and in a moment more they were in the coolest part of the garden. Willows overhung a large pond filled with lily pads and surrounded by mossy rocks. Rough rocks had been built up on one side to create a tiny waterfall, and behind it was a small cave that could be entered using strategically-placed stepping stones.

"How lovely." Carcali squatted down and trailed her hand into the water. "Where does it come from?"

"It recycles," Xerwin said. "I'm not sure how, to tell you the truth, the gardeners look after it. All I know is that it uses the same water, over and over."

Carcali picked out a rock bright with moss and sat down, removing her court sandals and dangling her feet in the water. There was another rock close by, and Xerwin took that seat for himself. He kept his sandals on, however, his feet dry, and his eyes on the Storm Witch. Naxot remained standing to one side. He couldn't seem to relax.

"So you think my sister is gone?" Xerwin said.

She lifted her shoulders and let them drop with a small sigh. "Look, I know what you're thinking. I'd say your sister was gone anyway, wouldn't I? 'How can I trust anything she says?' you're asking yourself. Well, I don't know what will convince you."

"Either you are lying, or the Paledyn lies."

"And you don't want it to be her, I get that. And not just because you want your sister back, am I right?" She was searching his face. "If it's any consolation to you, I don't think she is lying, the Paledyn, I mean. But ..." Carcali paused, tapping her upper lip with her tongue. "It doesn't seem likely she would make that kind of mistake."

"What if the Paledyn is neither lying herself nor mistaken, but being lied *to*?"

Both Xerwin and Carcali looked up at Naxot. "Why would the Marked not lie?" Naxot said. "If the Golden Age of Mages and Paledyns is returning, the Marked will surely lose their special status. What are they, after all, but slaves with privileges?"

"Sure." Carcali was nodding. "Think about this. Those Marked people dropped the ball, didn't they? They were supposed to heal your sister by finding her wandering mind and restoring it to her body, this body." Carcali tapped herself on the chest. "Well, how good a job did they do? And they tried to fix it you know, afterward when they figured out it wasn't her—I wasn't her—you know what I mean." She didn't wait for Xerwin's nod, she went right on speaking. "And they couldn't do it, could they? So then the Paledyn comes—she's sort of like an official investigator, right? A neutral party who can look into things, arbitrate disputes, and so on?"

"That is the tradition, yes," Naxot said. "Honor and fair dealing. There have not been Paledyn on this side of the Long Ocean for generations. But they existed still in Boravia."

"Well, I didn't believe in any of that until I met her, but you have to admit, Dhulyn Wolfshead doesn't strike me as anyone's cat's-paw." Carcali frowned. "That didn't come out right, but still, you get what I meant." She lifted her feet and watched the water drops fall back into the pond before submerging them once again.

This time both Xerwin and Naxot recognized they weren't being asked anything and simply waited for her to continue.

"All right. So the Paledyn shows up, asks the Marked to explain themselves, and suddenly they claim they can find your sister. They know where she is and can get her back. Why now and not before?"

"Dhulyn Wolfshead says she was Seen by the White Twins."

Carcali looked sideways at him, with her eyebrows raised and her lips twisted. "And who are they? More of these Marked, right? It's not as though Dhulyn Wolfshead saw your sister herself, is it? I mean, I'd be inclined to believe *her*, who wouldn't? But these White Twins . . ." She shook her head.

Naxot had found a rock to sit on. "I have never heard that Seers could be used to Find. They See Visions of the future, that is all."

Carcali was nodding again. "It's too convenient. It sounds to me as if they're just trying to get out from under. You know," she added in response to Xerwin's look of puzzlement. "Trying to make out that none of this was their fault. And maybe it wasn't, not really. I mean it was your father scared them into trying something, anything, to get him what he wanted."

"And what he 'got,' as you say, was something that he wanted much more than my sister." Xerwin took in a deep lungful of air and let it out slowly. "You both make it sound very simple," he said.

"Well, it is for me, you see. That's the point." She twisted, pulling her feet from the pond, until she was facing him directly. He was grateful that she didn't touch him. "I was there. I'm the only one who really knows. I *know* your sister was nowhere near, and she couldn't have survived long outside her body, not without the training I've had. That's why it's simple for me. I know."

Xerwin nodded. What the Storm Witch—Carcali—said made a great deal of sense. Especially since it explained how Dhulyn Wolfshead could still be in the right. He made a decision. He would tell them.

"The Paledyn goes tonight to the Sanctuary," he said. "To Find my sister, she said."

"You mean she *believes* so," Naxot said. "If she is being misled, as *we* think. But we should consider that the Marked are capable of any trickery. They could expel the Storm Witch, and this time permanently." Naxot swallowed. "And so? We would lose a Weather Mage, a useful person, and gain nothing—or worse." Naxot looked from Carcali to Xerwin and back again.

Xerwin found himself nodding. Better that some good should come from his sister's loss. For he found he was convinced, his sister *was* lost. He would go to the Sanctuary himself. He would see what kind of trick the Marked had prepared for the Paledyn, and he would put a stop to it.

And then there would be only the Tarxin to deal with.

Twenty-one

"I CAN'T REMEMBER EVER being in a palace—or castle large or small—where there was not more movement than this during the night." Parno kept his voice low, though not quite in the nightwatch whisper. Remm Shalyn, in the lead position two paces in front of Dhulyn, would have no trouble hearing him. Parno would rather have walked point himself, but he was the only one of the three of them who had never been to the Sanctuary of the Marked. So Remm walked in front, sword in his right hand, a shuttered lantern giving minimum light in his left. Dhulyn was second, her hands empty, with her sword in its sheath, her wrist resting on the hilt. Parno brought up the rear, with a bare blade and a shuttered lantern of his own.

They walked quietly, but didn't trouble to keep to the deeper shadows. Back in her rooms, Dhulyn had explained to Remm what the Common Rule had to say about situations like these.

"Attitude is the best disguise," she had said. "If we come upon anyone who has the authority to stop us—"

"Or who think they have such authority."

"Or who think so," she'd agreed, grinning. "You are merely two attendants escorting the Paledyn."

So far, as Parno had pointed out, they had encountered no one to impress with their charade.

"We left the palace as soon as we came down a level," Dhulyn said in answer to his observation. "If you think of this as a city, or of each level as a town, you'd be closer to the mark. We're away from the cliff face here, so this," she waved around them. "This is a public street in an area where the lesser Houses live. They don't have grounds, in the sense that we think of in Boravia, so all they need is porters, or door guards. And they'd have little inclination to look outside their doors once night had come."

"Isn't it always night here?"

"See those sheets of metal?" Remm Shalyn used his sword to point up at a tall wooden pole. "Shafts are cut in the rock, and when the sun rises, its light is reflected down, across, wherever those mirrors are found, lighting up the whole interior of the City."

"So all keep the same schedule of days and nights?"

"Those without windows have to wait upon and serve those with," Remm said. "It follows that they keep the same schedule."

Having been given these insights, Parno had no trouble recognizing crossroads as they came upon them, or even squares, strangely emptier of life than they would have seemed when out under the stars.

"Odd to think of people setting up their barrows and their market carts here," he said.

Remm led them around two huge air shafts. Both were lined with windows and balconies all the way down to the bottom, many levels below.

"See those large openings," Remm said, pointing at several dark areas in the walls of the shafts. "For the circulation of light and air," he said. "It is a capital offense to block them, or impede them in any way. The Tarxin uses a special squad of slaves to keep them clear and clean."

"So it would be the slaves who know these ways best," Dhulyn said.

Remm slowed, looking at her over his shoulder. "And the significance of this?"

"The shafts would be the logical way to get slaves out of the City," she added.

"You are entirely too clever, Paledyn Dhulyn Wolfshead." Remm had turned to face front, but Parno would swear the man was smiling.

They were heading across the largest square they'd yet encountered, angling toward the stairs on the far side which would let them down to the level of the Marked Sanctuary.

Parno found his eyes drawn to his Partner. Everything about her, the way she moved, the easy swing of her hips, the relaxed set of her shoulder and elbows—everything was familiar, known. And yet, he felt as if he was seeing her for the first time. For a second he thought he was dreaming, that she couldn't be walking in front of him now as if she had never been gone. He clamped down on his teeth to stop his jaw from trembling, and resisted the urge to speed up and touch her.

"Three men watch us from the shadows to the left," Dhulyn said softly.

She was speaking to Remm Shalyn, Parno realized, never thinking that she would need to tell him. But the truth was he hadn't seen or sensed them until she spoke. He shook himself and took a firmer grip on his sword, hoping that Dhulyn hadn't noticed his abstraction. That was exactly the kind of daydreaming that got people killed—and the kind of daydreaming that was supposed to be impossible for Mercenary Brothers.

#You are well# came a voice in his head. Evidently his uneasiness was sufficient to call the attention of the Crayx.

Just a little embarrassed he answered them.

#Sympathetic amusement#

"So long as all they're doing is watching us." That was Remm Shalyn, responding to Dhulyn.

"Probably think we can't see them," Parno put in.

"Probably hoping we can't," Dhulyn said. "Three men in the dark, no lantern, keeping silent? Up to no good, my heart. Up to no good."

They reached the broad staircase to the lower level without further incident, and from the foot of the steps found their way easily to the gate of the Sanctuary. The gate was shut, but torches in the Sanctuary Hall were lit, as well as the lamps hanging from the ceiling.

"Is this usual?" Parno found the sudden blaze of light unexpected, and anything unexpected had to be treated with suspicion.

"It's not *un*usual," Remm said. "I believe some light is always left burning to help anyone who comes seeking a Healer, and the Marked themselves use the Sanctuary Hall as their own Grand Square. The gate is customarily locked, however, and . . ." his voice trailed off as a human shape was silhouetted on the other side of the bars.

"Is it you, Dhulyn Wolfshead?" came a young girl's voice.

Remm Shalyn stood aside and Dhulyn stepped up to the gate. "It is, Medolyn Mender. Ellis Healer expects us."

The mechanism of the gate was complicated, but silent. Finally, the left-hand leaf of the iron gates swung open, and Parno followed Dhulyn inside.

The three Marked they'd come to meet were standing off to the right, under a grouping of three oil lamps. They waited there as Dhulyn, Parno, and Remm Shalyn approached them.

"Your companions must wait here, Dhulyn Wolfshead," the older man said.

"Ellis Healer," Dhulyn said. "Rascon Mender and Javen Finder. This is my Partner, Parno Lionsmane, called the Chanter. He was Schooled by Nerysa Warhammer. Where I go, he goes."

Parno pushed back his hood, revealing his Mercenary badge. The woman introduced as Rascon Mender grinned broadly, and nudged the Finder with her elbow. The young girl, Medolyn, lifted her fingers to her mouth.

Ellis Healer looked from one to the other of them with narrowed eyes. "Can this be? There is another Paledyn?"

"I thought he was lost," Dhulyn said. "But he has been restored to me."

"We've been restored to each other," Parno corrected with a grin.

Now Ellis Healer was nodding. "The White Twins kept saying, 'Our friends are coming,' 'Our brother and sister come.' We could not understand it, and no matter how we questioned them, we would receive the same answer. Now it all makes sense, though why they should claim kinship with Paledyns is likely more than any of us will ever know. Of course your brother Paledyn is welcome to join you, but I'm afraid . . ." The Healer's glance shifted over to Remm Shalyn.

"Not to worry," the swordsman said. "It was never my intention to attend. I will stay here and help keep watch."

Parno and Dhulyn were spinning around, swords out, a heartbeat before the sounds from the gate registered on the others. Six men entered. The two in front wore their swords slung at their hip, and from the amount of jewelry they wore, and the length of their kilts, these were nobles. The other four were just as clearly guards, carrying their swords in their hands.

Parno glanced at Dhulyn, but she was watching the newcomers. Six against two, he thought. Against three if they could count on Remm Shalyn. And Dhulyn had said they could. Good odds either way.

Dhulyn did not relax when she saw that Xerwin led the intruders. Parno, she was happy to note, had moved away to her right to give her room to move her sword, but not so far that they could not work in tandem if needed. At least his time among the Nomads had not cost him his sharp edge.

"Tar Xerwin," she said, as much to inform her Partner as to greet the Tar. "I did not expect you to attend this evening." She saw Xerwin's friend's eyes narrow as he took in Parno's Mercenary badge. She was weighing the necessity of more introductions when Xerwin spoke.

"I'm not here to join you, Dhulyn Wolfshead. I'm here to stop you. I've changed my mind, I don't want this."

"*You've* changed your mind?" Dhulyn tried hard to keep the surprise out of her voice. Xerwin had been just as inclined to kill the Storm Witch as she had been herself. "And if I haven't? I have my own reasons to expel the Storm Witch." And she still did. Not as strong as they once were, perhaps, not as compelling, but the danger from the Storm Witch was still real.

"Your reason stands next to you." This was the slightly nasal voice of Xerwin's friend Naxot. "Or did I hear badly a moment ago? Is this not your lost Partner? The man you believed was killed by action of the Storm Witch? If he is restored to you, your need and right for vengeance is gone. As Paledyns, you should protect and support the other Chosen of the Slain God."

Dhulyn smiled, deliberately letting her lip curl back. "*You* would tell *me* what my responsibilities are? What of the Tara Xendra? Have you forgotten her? At the very least, we must see if she can be restored before we strike bargains with a being who would occupy the body of another."

Xerwin shook his head as though it were heavy. "My sister is gone. Some good must come from that. The Storm Witch said—"

"Well, I should think she did." Parno's tone showed that he had probably rolled his eyes. "What would you expect her to say?"

Xerwin shook his head again, his lips pressed together. "Who am I to trust?" he said in a voice rough with frustration. "The Storm Witch tells me she did not see Xendra, that my sister was not in the spheres and that my sister could not have survived there without a Mage's power. Is *that* the truth? The White Twins tell Dhulyn Wolfshead that they can See Xendra, and perhaps they can lead a Finder to her. Is that the truth? Who should I listen to? Who can I trust?"

"You must trust someone, Tar Xerwin," Ellis Healer edged forward and Dhulyn shifted to keep him out of her line of attack. "Whom shall it be?"

Xerwin blinked, and swallowed. "I would trust Dhulyn Wolfshead. I would trust you." He turned toward her. "I believe you are neutral, all the more so now that your Partner is with you. What proof can *you* offer me besides the word of the White Twins that my sister still lives?"

Dhulyn's mouth went suddenly dry. What proof indeed. She wished she had time to consult with Parno, but there was only one real answer. She must tell Xerwin she was Marked, regardless of what danger it might bring her. If she expected Xerwin to trust her, she must trust him.

"Your sister's soul lives, Xerwin. I have Seen her myself."

Xerwin's eyes grew rounder, and his mouth softened.

"What does this mean?" This was his friend, Naxot again. "Why not tell us this before?"

He trusts me, I trust him, Dhulyn reminded herself.

"You misunderstood me, Xar Naxot. I mean that I have *Seen* her myself. I do not rely on the word of the White Twins. I have Seen the Tara Xendra in a Vision of my own. I am a Seer."

The murmurs that came from the other Marked present were so soft as to be hardly more than shallow intakes of breath. Naxot's face was statue-still. Xerwin's mouth had fallen open, but he recovered very quickly.

"I am convinced," he said. "You would not say such a thing of yourself if it were not the truth. If you yourself are a Seer, and have Seen my sister's soul, I believe she lives."

"But does that mean Tara Xendra can be found and

restored?" Naxot said. He put a steadying hand on his friend the Tar's arm.

"Surely, we should at least attempt it," Dhulyn said. She'd kept her eyes on the two nobles, knowing that all the time Parno would be watching the four guards, ready for any signal, or any untoward movement.

Naxot was nodding now, a slight frown drawing down his brows. "But does it follow that we should throw away the good that can come from the Storm Witch?" His tone was reasonable, as if he merely offered an alternative idea that had no importance to him personally. As perhaps he did, Dhulyn thought. For all she knew, Naxot functioned as Xerwin's privy council, asking the questions Xerwin would not always ask himself.

"The Tara Xendra, your sister, is a sweet girl," the young man continued. "But if she is safe, if her soul is safe in her present location, should we not consider the greater good?"

Oh, no, Dhulyn thought, all but shaking her head. As soon as some noble began talking about the greater good in terms of the sacrifice of an individual—they *never,* she'd noticed, offered to sacrifice themselves. Xerwin's face had hardened, it seemed he was thinking along the same lines.

"No good can come of this evil," she said. "The Storm Witch may be of some use, may even genuinely wish to help you, but if you sacrifice an innocent child . . ." This time she did shake her head. "This is not something the Slain God would look on with pleasure." *And I should know,* she thought. "Is the Storm Witch somehow more entitled to your sister's body than Xendra is herself?"

"Here's a question I've heard no one ask," Parno said. "What's happened to the Witch's own body? How did she come to lose it? For all we know, her own people cast her out. Since she can survive in these spheres she's told you about, we do her no harm to return her there."

Naxot's parted lips indicated that he had an answer for that as well, but Xerwin forestalled him with a raised hand.

"Enough." The Tar's gesture silenced everyone, and made Dhulyn see for the first time what he would be like as Tarxin. "I have made my decision," he said, and the firmness of his voice supported his words. "Evil or not, the Storm Witch misled me for purposes of her own. My sister is alive, and deserves to be restored to her body if it is possible. Dhulyn Wolfshead, please proceed."

"No, I'm afraid that won't be possible."

This time the interruption came not from the gate, but apparently from the air, somewhere to the left of where they were standing. Parno eyed a section of wall, examining its thickly ornamented stonework with suspicion. He'd wager he and Dhulyn were the only ones not surprised when that part of the wall opened, turning as if on a pivot, and the Tarxin Xalbalil stepped out, flanked by two guards carrying pikes, and six others with swords.

"Thank you, Naxot. It appears you were correct in your estimations. You will have your reward when my son the traitor has received his."

"Naxot!" Xerwin's hand, which had gone for his sword hilt when the wall moved, hung limply at his side.

His friend still wore that stone face he'd showed them earlier. "I had to be certain," he said. "You had changed your mind about her once already. I could not side with you against the Holy Woman," he said, crossing the floor to stand near the Tarxin.

"Xerwin, I'm disappointed in you." The older man's dry voice made Parno's skin crawl. "To take the tool yourself and use it against me, that I expected, and even approved, in a way. You would not have succeeded, but at least it would show you were ready to succeed me in another sense. But to take such a weapon as the Storm Witch and to throw it away, to save a child whose only use is to warm the right man's bed—" he shook his head, but his reptilian smile never changed. "I would suspect your mother of foisting another man's child on me, if we did not look so much alike."

These words seemed to stiffen Xerwin's resolve, as his hand went once more to his sword hilt, and he looked much readier to fight than he had a moment before. Parno caught the small signal Dhulyn sent him and moved with her to flank the Tar, eyeing Xerwin's four men as he moved. One was expressionless, except for the narrowing of his eyes. He looked like he'd stand neutral if he could manage it, until he saw who would gain the upper hand. Two were shocked, and clearly unsure what they should do, but they'd likely follow Xerwin out of habit if nothing else. The fourth was positioning himself to fight—and apparently on Xerwin's side. Remm was inching himself into a better spot on Dhulyn's far side.

Seven, perhaps eight of us, ten of them. Parno eyed the two guards carrying pikes. They'd have to go first. That is, if the talking ever stopped.

"This is convenient, very convenient," the Tarxin was saying. "All the pieces on the board at the same time." He looked at Dhulyn in a way that made Parno tighten the grip on his sword—and then loosen it properly again. "Now I see how it is possible for a woman to be a Paledyn. You've had your master behind you all the while, directing your every move."

It was all Parno could do not to laugh out loud. The man was a very poor judge of character if he could look at Dhulyn and think any such thing. But now the man was addressing him, and Parno tried to hang a serious expression on his face.

"So you are my real adversary here—and I can see from your pretty tunic that you are in league with the fish lovers. Your attack was clearly a feint, allowing you to get more of your people into Ketxan City. Where have you hidden them all, I wonder?" he waved this away. "Never mind. I will be curious to see what else a search of the Sanctuary will reveal."

"My lord Tarxin, Light of the Sun, you cannot." Aghast was not too strong a word to describe the old Healer's tone. "The Sanctuary is neutral ground, ours so long as we provide our services and abide by the terms and conditions of our treaties. Our privacy is not to be violated."

"But you are in violation of your oaths and treaties," the Tarxin said in his cold raspy voice. "You are obviously in league with the enemies of the Mortaxa, so your Sanctuary is lost."

Xerwin was nodding, his expression sour, his mouth twisted to one side. "That is how we deal with everyone," he said. "They bargain away everything to keep their freedom, and then they find themselves without the freedom to say no."

"Never mind, Ellis," Dhulyn said. "If he had not found this excuse, another would have served. He won't live to hurt you."

"You're outnumbered, you silly woman. Do you think

you can fight your way through my guards, even with my foolish son on your side?"

"Odds aren't bad," Parno put in, shrugging. "Counting Xerwin and his boys, only seventeen of them against eight of us."

A soft whistling sound, a CLUNK, and one of the pikemen fell to his knees, his weapon clattering to the floor, Dhulyn's dagger sticking out of his right eye.

"Sixteen," she said.

While everyone was still standing around gawking, Dhulyn ran forward, sword in hand, Remm behind her and to her left, like a good sword servant.

Even as he was dashing forward himself to deal with the second pikeman, Parno noticed that Xerwin was not making the amateur's mistake of going for Naxot, the man who'd betrayed him. No, Xerwin was heading straight for his father. Good. It would make things easier all around if he or Dhulyn didn't have to kill him.

Then his first opponent was before him and the time for watching others was over. The Mortaxan blades were shorter, thicker, better for slashing and cutting than the longer sword Parno had. The man lifted his sword to cut down at Parno's shoulder, and Parno ran in quickly and thrust his own sword through the man's throat. As he went down, Parno slashed at the sword hand of another man, and dashed past him to where the man with the pike was holding Remm Shalyn at bay. Remm was already bleeding from a cut on his upper arm—luckily not his sword arm—when Parno came nearer.

"Leave him to me," he said. Remm grinned and moved out of the way before Parno could trample him.

Parno fell automatically into the Striking Snake *Shora*, avoiding, and occasionally parrying the pike's blade, watching the man's shoulders and neck muscles, looking for the telltale shifting that would signal a feint, or a true blow. The pike's sharp blade was clearly intended to slash as well as stab, and the man wielding it knew his job. Parno's single advantage, he knew, was that he had faced this weapon, or its cultural variation, many times before, and unlike the opponents the man was used to, was not afraid of it. In fact, it was likely that Parno had faced it in earnest, on the battlefield, more often than this man had used it. It was a tenet of the Common Rule, that drilling was one thing, and killing another.

Parno saw his opening, trusted in his Crayx armor, and stepped into the shaft, parrying and bearing down on it with the strength of his blade. He kept applying pressure, down and outward, as he slid his blade up along the shaft until he had closed to within striking range. Before the man could reverse the end of the shaft to strike him, Parno had skewered him through the heart. He had moved too quickly for the man to even think about dropping the shaft and defending himself in some other way.

The pole arm dealt with, Parno turned back to the others in time to slash at the raised sword arm of one of the Tarxin's men, just as he was swinging at Remm Shalyn, who had fallen to one knee, having slipped in someone's blood. Parno hauled Remm back to his feet and took stock. Xerwin and two of his men were engaged with three men in front of the Tarxin, who had at least drawn his knife. Dhulyn had picked up a second sword, and had maneuvered herself between everyone and the still open passage through the wall, preventing escape from that direction. One of Xerwin's men was down, as was the noble Naxot.

Eleven enemies dead, six still on their feet. Seven if you counted the Tarxin.

"Help the other guard," Parno told Remm as he headed toward Xerwin. As he reached the group around the Tarxin, the guard on Xerwin's left went down. Parno stepped over him and cut the throat of the man who'd killed him, reached under Xerwin's arm, and put his sword through the lung and heart of the Tar's opponent.

Parno looked over in time to see Dhulyn stepping over the bodies of her two opponents; Xerwin's remaining guard was bent over, hands on his knees, taking deep breaths. Remm was standing with his hand on the man's shoulder.

Parno turned back. Xerwin had stepped over the bodies around him and knocked the dagger out of his father's hand.

"The field is ours, Xerwin," Parno called. "Whatever you're planning to do, do it now."

And the Tar stood still, his blade up in the middle stance, like a man giving a demonstration of swordplay, and did not move.

"Come, boy," the Tarxin said, his voice, if possible, even colder than it had been before. "If you want the throne, this is the only way. This is what it takes to be Tarxin."

Dhulyn laid her hand on Parno's arm, and he shot a glance at her. She had her tongue pressed to her upper lip, and he knew what she was thinking, just as if the Crayx had given him her thoughts. She thought it possible that Xerwin would back away, that at the last minute he would refuse to strike the final blow, rather than admit he wanted the throne, that he was that much like his father. Just as she was thinking about stepping forward to do it herself, Xerwin, shaking his head, lifted his blade and brought it slicing down through his father's neck.

Twenty-two

"I'VE KILLED MY FATHER." Xerwin rubbed at his upper lip.

"You've killed the Tarxin, which at the moment is rather more important." Dhulyn looked around. Remm Shalyn and the other remaining guards, four of whom had come here with the dead Tarxin, were on their knees, holding their fingertips to their foreheads. The Healer was busy over one man, but even as she watched, he straightened, shaking his head. Parno, half-smiling, waggled his eyebrows at her.

"Tar Xerwin?" Dhulyn touched the younger man on the arm and he finally turned away from his father's body, blinking with some confusion at the kneeling men. Then he took a deep breath that shuddered on the way in, and touched his own forehead. The men lowered their hands and stood.

"At your service, Tarxin, Light of the Sun," Remm Shalyn said. Dhulyn saw a gleam—could it be of humor?—in the man's eyes. "Shall we take care of the slain, Light of the Sun, and see that your father's body is prepared for transport to his—to *your* private apartments?"

"Thank you, yes." Xerwin looked around him. "Try not to track blood *all* over the floor."

"Yes, Light of the Sun." That was one of the other guards, Dhulyn saw, one who had come in with Xerwin's father. None of them, she noticed, whether originally Xerwin's men or his father's, seemed particularly upset, or concerned with the death of the older man. She'd had the impression that Xalbalil Tarxin hadn't been a well-liked man, but this equanimity struck her as unusual. As unobtrusively as she could, she retrieved her throwing dagger and picked up a second sword, sliding it into her sash at the small of her back. She caught Parno's eye, flicked the third finger of her right hand, and looked at the guards. He raised his eyebrows a mere fraction, showing he understood her warning.

Dhulyn stepped back to watch as the remaining guards, aided by the Marked, dealt with the bodies. Those of the soldiers were rolled into what looked like old carpets and hangings, while those of the former Tarxin and the Xar Naxot were laid out more formally, awaiting the arrival of litters. Parno made his way around the periphery of those working until he reached her side.

"I don't think we've ever deposed a ruler so easily," Dhulyn said to him in the nightwatch voice.

"Clearly, we've been doing it wrong."

Remm, his instructions to the Marked given, came over to join them.

"Remm Shalyn," Parno said to him. "What will be the consequences from this . . . event?" Dhulyn smile her wolf's smile. Trust her Partner to be diplomatic. She would have said "assassination."

"If there were any other heirs, there might be a problem," Remm said, shrugging. "But Xerwin, Tarxin Light of the Sun, was the only remaining male child of Xalbalil Tarxin. I don't think there are even close cousins." He jerked his head toward where the old Tarxin's body lay. "Xalbalil didn't leave many relatives alive when *his* father died."

"And may we ask how that happened?" Parno asked, his left eyebrow raised.

Remm's grin was quickly quashed. "Hunting accident," he said, his tone suddenly serious. "That's what was said."

"And this one? What will be said?"

"Oh, I don't know. Cut himself shaving?" Remm blinked rapidly, but otherwise his face remained serious. "Xerwin Tarxin, Light of the Sun, will let his Council know tomorrow that his father has died in the night. There will be public announcements, days of mourning, the funeral." Remm nodded his head at Xerwin. "He'll have to be careful, certainly.

Those his father made strong will want to keep that strength. He should probably send word to the Battle Wings before he does anything else. His soldiers love him, and most of the High Noble Houses will remember that, and behave accordingly. The rest of Mortaxa?" He shrugged again. "By the time the news gets to them, it will be old, and one Tarxin's much the same as another. The transition should go relatively smoothly, all things considered."

Remm's voice died away and he backed off a few paces with a shallow bow as Xerwin himself came up to them. The new Tarxin's face was more composed now, though Dhulyn thought there was a harder line to his jaw than there had been before.

"Paledyns," he said, with a brisk nod. "I believe we came here with another purpose."

"If you would prefer to delay—" Dhulyn stopped as Xerwin shook his head.

"Things will be complicated enough in the next few weeks. If I deal with the Storm Witch now, it will be one less complication. And besides." His smile was a twisted thing. "I want my sister back. Now more than ever." He brought his hands up to his face, rubbed it, and ran his fingers back through his hair.

Dhulyn nodded, putting as much sympathy and understanding into that gesture as she could. She had noticed, however, that Xerwin had spoken of the political complications first, and his sister second.

The one guard Ellis Healer had managed to save stood off to one side, alone, with his arms wrapped around his chest. When Parno approached him and spoke, the guard shied away, then touched his forehead with his hand. He held no weapon, Dhulyn noticed, and frankly, from the look of lingering shock on his face, did not seem likely to pick one up. Most of the Marked who had come out of the inner rooms of the Sanctuary, summoned by their Seniors, were now working at cleaning the Sanctuary Hall. Young people, some still in their nightclothes, were on their knees scrubbing at the blood on the stone floor. They had brought litters for the bodies of the nobles, and women were coming with fresh hangings and rugs to cover and wrap the bodies. Xerwin left Dhulyn's side and went to them as they approached the litter that bore his father.

Dhulyn gave him a few minutes before approaching him herself. "Xerwin," she said.

Xerwin straightened, and signaled to his men. "See my father properly disposed in his own quarters. Take Naxot Lilso there as well." He looked at Dhulyn. "What should I tell his father?"

"Stay as close to the truth as you can," she said. "Tell him his son died trying to save the life of his Tarxin. Will he need to know more?"

"I'm not sure. Naxot's father has other sons. That may make a difference to him."

"Will he seek revenge?"

"He may ask for a blood price. I may have to make one of Naxot's sisters my second wife." He glanced sideways at her, seeming about to say something else on that subject, but he looked away instead. "I've time yet to think about that."

"And what of the Storm Witch? What if people ask after her?"

"What Storm Witch? That was just a trick of the old Tarxin's, to make the Nomads submit. My sister will be here, evidently nothing more than the Tara Xendra." Xerwin squared his shoulders as Ellis Healer approached. "Xalbalil Tarxin was a shrewd man, who took advantage of coincidences."

Dhulyn nodded. Who could disprove it, once the Storm Witch was gone?

"Your pardon, Light of the Sun. Tara Paledyn, the White Twins are asking for you."

Dhulyn looked back at the soldiers. Xerwin's senior guard was deploying his remaining men, and those of the old Tarxin, to carry the bodies and form a guard of honor. Remm Shalyn was shaking his head and gesturing toward her. Of course, he considered himself her sword servant, he would insist on accompanying her. That left the guardsmen, alone, with the body of a murdered Tarxin. She turned back to Xerwin. "This may not be the moment for you to leave your men leaderless and unsupervised."

He looked at her, lips parted, but did not speak.

"Better cautious, than cursing," she told him. "Go with your men, see to the old Tarxin, and even Naxot's father, if you wish. I will come to you and report."

For a moment it seemed as though he would argue with her, then abruptly he nodded. "I will await you. Come as soon as you may."

Carcali wondered if she should do something about the rain. It had started just after daybreak as a fine mist, hardly even a drizzle, and welcome, really, after the heat of the last few days. It wasn't that she hadn't expected it—after all, she had started to collect wind and storm to throw at the Nomads, though she hadn't gone very far when they'd disappeared of their own accord. The Tarxin hadn't told her to stop her efforts, but . . . *how much time is left of the deadline I gave him,* she wondered, trying to count the time backward in her head.

She shivered at a gust of cold air and pulled her shawl closer around her. Something had been bound to come of even those preliminary actions, but this rain didn't seem to be dissipating. It was definitely getting stronger, in fact, and the skies had grown darker even in the short while she'd been sitting at her balcony door.

Another gust, more violent than the first and carrying a load of rain with it, blew into the opening, soaking the side of her gown and making her cough. Carcali jumped to her feet, grabbed hold of the edge of the left door, and pushed against it with her shoulder, struggling to close it. Her large maps and sketches fluttered around the floor and the large parchment on her worktable escaped from its weight and blew over, knocking against the oil lamp and sending it crashing to the tiles.

"Tara Xendra, what are you thinking of? Thank the Slain God that lamp wasn't lit." At least Finexa's genuine fear had shaken all the simpering and archness out of her voice. Annoyance struggled with Carcali's relief. Annoyance that she couldn't shut the window herself—when would she remember that she was only eleven years old?—relief that Finexa had heard the crash and come in to help her.

"What were you doing sitting here in the dark?"

"It isn't dark," Carcali said, rubbing at the outside of her arms. "It's the middle of the afternoon."

"Too dark to work, is what I meant. Won't you come

into the other room, please, Tara. I'll get the maid to clean this up."

Carcali followed Finexa into her bedroom and threw herself onto the bed, trying her best to ignore the woman's exasperation when Finexa found the windows in there open as well.

"I'm a Storm Witch, Finexa, for the Art's sake," she said finally. "Why wouldn't I have the windows open?"

The woman subsided into a tight-lipped silence at this reminder.

Carcali sat up, her arms straight out behind her. "Has the Tarxin sent any word today?"

Finexa adjusted the mechanism that closed the slats on the shutters and pulled the curtains over them. "Not today, Tara, no. Were you expecting something?"

So she still had time left. Good. "And my brother? Has he sent me any messages?"

"No, Tara." Sound from the workroom drew Finexa to the door, and with a "tchah" of impatience she went through it to speak to the maids, throwing a perfunctory "your pardon, Tara," over her shoulder as she went.

Carcali chewed on her lower lip. She was trusting Xerwin to help her. "Leave things to me," he'd said, and she was doing just that. And she'd stopped her actions against the Nomads—partly because she wanted to, but mostly because he'd said she should. Another particularly heavy gust of wind shook the shutters.

She pulled the pillow closer and hugged it to her. *I really ought to do something about that storm,* she thought. But it couldn't do any harm to leave it a while longer. And it was good cover if the Tarxin needed to be appeased. "Just doing as ordered," she could tell him. "You think this is bad, you should see what it's like out at sea."

Carcali wondered if Xerwin even realized that they would have to kill the old man in order to be safe themselves.

Parno found that even having been warned what to expect, the White Twins were a shock. Their skin was as pale as the flesh of a fish, and their hair was not so much white as it was colorless. Their eyes were pink, as were their lips and gums, and when one of them passed close enough to a light, he could almost see the blood moving under the skin. They fell upon him, giggling, the moment he had cleared the threshold of their sitting room, following closely on Dhulyn's heels. They had touched his Crayx armor, run their cool fingers over the colors of his Mercenary badge, and felt the muscles in his forearms. They were as guileless as children — they *were* children, in all things but their physical age and their Mark.

Once they had finished "making sure he was real," as they put it, the White Twins greeted the other Marked almost as enthusiastically. An older woman stood smiling to one side, and Parno realized, as they exchanged short bows, that she must be the White Twins' attendant or guardian. Remm Shalyn, who was hovering, round-eyed, at the door, they appeared not to notice.

Parno approached him. "Your first time here?"

The younger man nodded. "I have heard about them, of course, who has not? But to actually see them." Remm didn't quite shudder, but Parno thought he might have wanted to.

"Would you prefer to wait outside?" he said, expecting a quick negative, as no young soldier would want to risk being thought a coward. To his surprise, Remm nodded.

"But I must stay if Dhulyn Wolfshead wishes it," he said. "For now, I am pledged to her service."

Parno caught Dhulyn's eye and waited until she was close enough to hear the nightwatch voice. She listened, and inclined her head once.

"Remm Shalyn," she said quietly. "Better you should stand guard outside," she said. "We may want warning if someone comes, more warning than you could give us if you stay within."

He touched his forehead with a cheerful smile and let himself out.

"I find it disconcerting to be saluted in that manner by people who are not Brothers," Parno said.

"It has something to do with the Sleeping God, whom they call the Slain God here. As Paledyns, we're considered Hands of the God."

"That's convenient."

"My thoughts exactly." She gave him the smile she saved only for him, and Parno, smiling himself, lifted his right hand and touched her cheek with the backs of his fingers.

Suddenly they were surrounded by dancing white women.

"Come, Brother, come now, quickly."

"Now how can I be your brother?" Parno said, tweaking the long braid of the twin nearest him. She must be Amaia, he thought, seeing the fleck of gold in her eye that Dhulyn had told him about. Now she took his hand and brought him, skipping, to the other side of the room. A jumble of toys lay on the floor, a tiny walled enclosure with a blocky tower made of—yes, those were vera tiles. A moat had been drawn around it with blue chalk.

"Dhulyn is our sister," Amaia said.

"And you are her brother," Keria added.

"So you must be our brother, too," Amaia concluded.

The twin sisters laughed at this, and began singing the words over and over, to a tune Parno knew very well, though to hear it now made the hairs on his arms and the back of his neck stand up. This was the same children's song he often played for Dhulyn, and though not many people knew it, it had a special meaning for the Sleeping God, and for the Marked.

"They sing this song to begin their trance," Ellis Healer said. "Though, truly, they often sing it at other times as well."

"Is there an instrument here I can use? A chanter, or even a small harp?"

Ellis beckoned the attendant over and repeated Parno's request. Smiling, she did what Parno certainly had never expected her to do. She asked the White Twins.

"Girls," she said. "My darlings, can your brother see your instruments, my dear ones? He'd love to accompany your song with music of his own."

At once the twins stopped singing and ran to a table to the right of the door, in darkness now since the lamps there were not lit. Almost immediately Keria came back to him with an instrument more like a syrinx than the chanter that he would attach to his air pipes.

"It's been a while since I played one of these," he said. He raised the instrument to his lips and gave an experimental blow, satisfying himself that he had not forgotten how.

"Will the Crayx hear you?" The sisters were standing in front of him, shoulder to shoulder, staring at him with their huge red eyes.

"I don't know," he said.

"I hope they do," said the one on the left. Keria, he thought, but with the light at this angle he could not tell which one had the gold fleck in her eye.

"Parno, my heart," Dhulyn said. "The Finder and I are ready."

"Do you know what to do?"

"We know, we know, we know," the sisters sang.

"I think that means 'yes,' " Dhulyn said, smiling.

Javen Finder was standing, her lower lip between her teeth, between her fellow Marked. Parno had never seen anyone who looked less like she wanted to be where she was. But when Dhulyn nodded to her, Javen stepped forward right away, giving a wan smile to the Mender, Rascon, who squeezed her shoulder as she went. Ellis Healer held out a canvas bag and Javen took a small blue bowl out of it. It was plain white on the inside, and Parno recognized it as a Finder's tool.

"Stand right here," Keria said.

"Right here," Amaia agreed, shifting from foot to foot in her excitement. Both of them put their hands on Javen Finder and pulled and prodded until they were satisfied that she was standing in exactly the right spot. Giggling, they waved Dhulyn over to them, twirling their hands at the wrists like flags fluttering in the breeze. When Dhulyn was close enough, each of them took one of her hands, and then linked hands themselves, standing in a circle around the blinking Finder. Javen licked her lips, held the bowl at chest height and looked into it.

"Play now, Brother," Amaia said.

"You know the tune," Keria added, already humming.

Dhulyn caught his eye, and mouthed the words he would have expected from her. "And in Death," he mouthed back, before lifting the syrinx to his lips and beginning to play. He played softly at first, and then with more power, as he renewed his familiarity with the instrument. Dhulyn winked at him, and began to sing, her rough silk voice somehow serving as a fitting accompaniment to the lighter, smoother voices of the White Twins.

As they sang, the sisters' voices grew firmer, more mature, and their faces were suddenly the faces of women his own age. At that moment all three stopped, eyes closed, still with hands linked. The Finder, too, was standing perfectly still, eyes shut tight, eyebrows working as though she was in deep thought. All four of them, Parno saw, the Finder, and the three Seers, were breathing as one.

Parno let the music die away, and lowered the syrinx from his lips. This was like watching his Partner use her tiles, she had the same serene look of calm concentration on her face. He'd thought he'd never see that look again. Never see her again. He loosened his grip on the syrinx before he broke it. All was well. A good wind and a fair current, as Darlara and her brother would say. After a moment he smiled, as he noticed that he, too, was breathing in the same rhythm as the others.

#Interest# #Excitement#

Parno was almost knocked from his feet by the force of the Crayx' thoughts. *What is it, what's happening* He had stopped himself from speaking aloud just in time.

#We can feel her# #Not her thoughts# #No, not her thoughts# #But we *can* feel her# #Giddyness# #Fascination#

For the first time, Parno had the sense that there were a great many Crayx, all communicating, all participating at once. *Who* *What are you talking about*

#Through *your* link, we can feel *her*# #Never felt before# #Euphoria# #She has no Pod sense# #But she is there, we feel her#

"Demons and perverts," Parno said aloud. Quickly he held up his hand, palm out, signaling to Ellis Healer and Rascon Mender that all was well.

#How# A blooded good question, Parno thought, as he heard it echoed back and forth.

#Lionsmane is linked to her, blood to blood, bone to bone, heart to heart#

Parno gave a silent whistle. Those were the very words of the Partnership ceremony.

#Why not before, on the *Wavetreader*# #Too many with Pod sense# #Link too delicate# Parno could tell these were questions.

#Astonishment# #She is with the child# #Your Partner is with the child#

You know of the child
#We know of *this* child# #We sensed her fear#

She's Pod-sensed Parno stood openmouthed. No words did justice to how he felt. Part of him wanted to laugh out loud. The little girl Dhulyn was trying to save, to restore to her own body—the Tarxin's daughter—was Pod-sensed.

#When she became ill, and frightened# #Lost# #We cared for her soul# #Helped her find a place to feel safe#

Is she in a forest thicket

#No, a sandy beach# #Trees come down to the water# #But only where the stream is# #Ah# #Of course# #Each finds the safe harbor they seek# #For your Partner a forest glade# #For the child herself an empty beach, a stream trickling down through a screen of trees#

And you see both places

#No# #YES# #Amusement# #Through the link we know what others know, see what others see#

And you feel my Partner there, with the child

#Amused joy#

AT LEAST THEY DON'T HAVE TO GO BACK TO WHERE HER MOTHER IS, DHULYN THINKS. PERHAPS BECAUSE IT IS THE SECOND TIME, AND THE WHITE TWINS ARE HERE TO DIRECT THE VISION MORE PRECISELY, THEY ARE STANDING IN THE PATH THAT LEADS TO THE THICKET.

"WHAT IS THIS PLACE?" THE VOICE OF JAVEN FINDER IS WHISPER-QUIET, BUT DHULYN HAS NO TROUBLE HEARING HER. JAVEN LOOKS AROUND WITH EYES MADE WIDE BY FEAR.

"THIS IS OUR VISION," KERIA ANSWERS. "OURS AND OUR SISTER, DHULYN WOLFSHEAD." JAVEN STARTS, LOOKING SIDEWAYS, AND DHULYN REALIZES THAT THE FINDER HAS NEVER HEARD THE SEERS SPEAK IN THEIR OWN UNDAMAGED VOICES.

"I THINK THIS IS WHY YOU COULDN'T FIND HER BEFORE," DHULYN SAYS. "SOMEHOW, XENDRA'S SOUL EXISTS IN THE SAME PLACE OUR VISIONS EXIST, SOMEWHERE APART FROM THE WORLD WE LIVE IN. IF YOU CAN FIND HER, NOW THAT YOU ARE HERE AS WELL...?"

JAVEN NODS AND GATHERS ALL HER COURAGE TOGETHER, PRESSING HER LIPS TIGHT, AND TAKING A FIRMER GRIP ON HER BOWL. SHE LOOKS INTO IT, AND IN A MOMENT SHE IS SMILING. "THE COLORS," SHE SAYS AGAIN, AS SHE DID WHEN SHE FIRST

LOOKED INTO THE BOWL. SHE LOOKS UP, SECURES THE BOWL IN THE CROOK OF HER RIGHT ARM, AND POINTS WITH HER LEFT HAND.

AT FIRST, DHULYN SEES NOTHING, AND THEN A FAINT, COLORED LIGHT IS SPILLING OUT OF THE BOWL, AND ALONG THE PATH, A BRILLIANT JEWELLIKE GREEN WITH SPLASHES OF GOLD SWIRLED INTO IT.

"THAT IS THE TARA XENDRA," JAVEN SAYS, JOY LIFTING HER VOICE. "SHE IS THIS WAY."

AND THEN THEY ARE FOLLOWING THE FINDER AS SHE RUNS FOLLOWING THE COLORS DOWN THE PATH TOWARD THE GROVE OF TREES, PUSHES HER WAY THROUGH THE THICK UNDERBRUSH, AND THERE, ON HER KNEES WITH A WOODEN DOLL IN HER ARMS, IS THE CHILD THEY ARE LOOKING FOR. SHE IS DRESSED IN GOLD AND GREEN, THERE IS A SMUDGE OF DIRT ON HER CHEEK, AND SHE IS CLUTCHING THE DOLL FIERCELY, HER TEETH HOLDING HER LOWER LIP. SHE STANDS WHEN THEY COME IN, AND BACKS AWAY FROM THEM. SHE LOOKS AT THEM, ONE AFTER ANOTHER, THE WHITES OF HER EYES SHOWING CLEARLY. SHE IS TERRIFIED, AND DHULYN RACKS HER BRAIN TO THINK WHAT TO SAY TO HER.

"YOU KNOW US, TARA XENDRA," AMAIA SAYS. "REMEMBER, YOUR BROTHER BROUGHT YOU ONCE TO PLAY WITH US."

"YOU KNOW ME, TARA XENDRA. I'M JAVEN FINDER. YOU REMEMBER WHEN YOUR DOG, BISCUIT, WAS LOST, AND I FOUND HIM FOR YOU?" JAVEN HAS STEPPED FORWARD, HER ARMS HELD OUT TO THE CHILD. IN THE NORMAL WORLD, SHE WOULD NEVER DREAM OF OFFERING TO TOUCH THE TARA XENDRA UNINVITED, BUT HERE, IT SEEMS NATURAL.

THE CHILD IS STILL ROUND-EYED, BUT SHE NODS.

"WELL, NOW I'VE FOUND *YOU*, AND I CAN TAKE YOU BACK TO YOUR . . . TO YOUR BROTHER, THE TAR XERWIN. WOULDN'T YOU LIKE TO SEE YOUR BROTHER?"

THE CHILD NODS AGAIN. SLOWLY HER SHOULDERS LOWER. SHE LOOKS AROUND AT THEM ONCE MORE, THIS TIME ACTUALLY SEEING THEM. HER EYEBROWS LIFT WHEN HER GLANCE MOVES OVER TO DHULYN, AND HER MOUTH FALLS OPEN.

"PALEDYN," SHE SAYS, HER VOICE FULL OF WONDER.

"GOOD THING I'M SO RECOGNIZABLE," DHULYN SAYS, SMILING CAREFULLY AT THE CHILD. SHE OFFERS THE CHILD HER HAND. "ARE YOU READY TO COME HOME, LITTLE ONE?"

NODDING, THE TARA XENDRA STEPS FORWARD AND TAKES DHULYN'S HAND. KERIA AND AMAIA ARE NODDING, SMILING.

THEY'VE SEEN THIS BEFORE, DHULYN THINKS. *ME HOLDING THE CHILD BY THE HAND.*

"JAVEN, ARE YOU READY?"

BUT THE FINDER IS SHAKING HER HEAD, LOOKING FIRST INTO THE BOWL AND THEN SEARCHING THE FLOOR OF THE LITTLE SHADOWED PLACE. BUT THERE ARE NO COLORS.

"I—I CAN'T. I CANNOT FIND THE—THE OTHER PART OF THE CHILD FROM HERE. I—" SHE LOOKS UP, ALMOST AS PALE THE WHITE TWINS BEHIND HER. "I'M SORRY—OH, PLEASE—I'M SO SORRY."

Twenty-three

"THEN I HAVE KILLED MY FATHER for nothing." Xerwin sat at the worktable in the Tarxin's study, documents and scrolls spread out in front of him. His glance at them was automatic, but Dhulyn was sure he did not see them.

"Hardly for nothing," Parno said. "You're now the Tarxin."

Xerwin looked up, little marks of white showing around his pinched nostrils.

Dhulyn looked at Parno, and when he shrugged, she spoke. "You likely would have had to kill him anyway," she said, in her most matter-of-fact voice. "He would have started a war with the Nomads and the Crayx, a war which would have cost Mortaxa a great deal, more perhaps than you know."

Xerwin looked at her, clearly wanting to ask whether this was something she'd Seen, and just as clearly unsure what courtesy required at this moment. "But Xendra was Found."

"She was." Dhulyn took a deep breath, trying to ignore her feeling of impatience. Since leaving the Sanctuary of the Marked, they'd been aware of the rising noises of the storm—wind, rain, and in the distance, thunder. She raised her voice to be heard over the noise of the wind rattling the balcony doors. The explanation given by the White Twins was the only one likely to make any sense to Xerwin. "This world, and the place of Visions are two different, separate places. Javen Finder cannot Find your sister from this world, and cannot Find your sister's body, nor the Storm Witch, from the place of Visions. Somehow the two must be brought together."

Xerwin squeezed his eyes shut and held both hands up in the air near his ears, as if to shut out any more information. Dhulyn fell silent, glancing quickly to where her Partner stood, arms folded across his chest.

Parno raised the index finger of his left hand. "May I? They want to try bringing the two worlds together. They succeeded in bringing Javen Finder into the Vision place with them, and they'd like to try the same with your sister's body."

"With the Storm Witch, you mean."

"Since she currently occupies the body, yes."

"And you need me for this."

"I don't think there is anyone else she will trust."

Xerwin was silent for so long that Dhulyn was beginning to wonder whether he had changed his mind yet again. And to consider, what, if anything, she could do about it if he had. One thing was certain, she thought. She would not be very happy if that lonely child in the thicket clutching her doll continued to appear in any of her future Visions.

And even if she didn't, how comfortable would Dhulyn be, knowing that the child was out there?

Apparently Xerwin came to the same conclusion.

"Where do I bring her?" he said at last.

"To the White Twins," she said.

Carcali leaned her eleven-year-old forehead against the trembling shutter on her bedroom window, her right hand to her mouth as she gnawed on her thumbnail. The wind had risen alarmingly, and the rain was much worse. There would be flooding by daybreak, she knew, at the very least. She switched to the other thumb. She just had to hope it would be no worse.

She let her hand fall into her lap, twisting her fingers together. She'd left it too long. A stupid apprentice's mistake—something she would never have done in a million years. She should have been watching more closely, and now it was too late.

"Except it isn't." There, she'd said it. The old Carcali, the confident, know-it-all Carcali, could fix this rain in a snap of her fingers. No problem. But not today, not this Carcali. Not the one who was afraid to release herself fully into the weatherspheres. Not her—oh, no.

A noise came from the outer room, and she jumped, banging her elbow painfully on the edge of the shutter. Who could be coming at this hour? *Someone who wants to speak to me about the weather.* And she could guess who. She smoothed back her hair and straightened her shoulders as she got to her feet.

As Carcali expected, Finexa, a robe thrown hastily over her sleeping gown, opened the bedroom door and stepped into the room. But it was a different Finexa from the one Carcali was expecting. There was not the carefully disguised triumph that a summons to the Tarxin usually brought, no smugness, no prim little smile. Instead Finexa was pale, licking her lips. Her attempt at an affectionate look when she caught Carcali's eye would have been funny, if it hadn't been so obviously born of fear.

"What is it?" Carcali said. "What's happened?"

"You are summoned to the Tarxin, Light of the Sun, Tara Xendra." The woman clung to the edge of the door. "The messenger says immediately, please. Do not stop for ceremony. It will be explained."

Carcali's first impulse was to refuse to go anywhere until she had the promised explanation. Finexa clearly knew something that had shaken her—though something that shook Finexa wasn't necessarily something Carcali needed to worry about. She let the woman wrap a robe around her and pin a veil on her hair—apparently that much ceremony was still required—and prepared to follow the three guards who'd been sent for her. She'd stepped into the hallway before she realized she was alone.

"Aren't you coming?" she asked her attendant, but Finexa was already shaking her head.

"The Tarxin, Light of the Sun, asked for you alone, Tara Xendra," she said.

Carcali felt a stab of fear. Was she being arrested? Surely that wasn't possible? She was the Tara Xendra, for the Art's sake. But it was possible, the more rational part of her mind said, even as her fear tried to choke her. Carcali had overheard her attendants talking, when they thought her so absorbed in her maps that she wasn't paying attention. They'd been talking about the first Tarxina, Xerwin's mother, and it was Xerwin's name that had caught Carcali's ear. A sudden illness, everyone had been told, and the whole country had gone into mourning. But that's not what had really happened, the ladies were saying. The Tarxina had displeased the Tarxin, displeased him *severely,* and not just by not having any more children—at least, not any more children by *him,* one of the older ladies had whispered while the others looked on, wide-eyed, frightened to be hearing such a thing, and yet avid for more, like children telling each other stories of demons. The Tarxin had sent for his wife, in the middle of the night, and she'd never been seen again. And even her attendants—some of them—hadn't been seen again either.

At the time, Carcali had dismissed the story as the kind of court gossip that ladies with nothing better to do titillated themselves with. Such things didn't really happen. Now, she was not so sure. The man had shown her that he could starve her to death if he chose to. Would it be so much harder for her to have an accident in the middle of the night?

She stopped in her tracks. Especially since she'd had one accident already. Is *that* what had happened? But what was it an eleven-year-old had done to anger the Tarxin?

"Tara?" the senior guard said. "We should not waste time."

"No, of course not." She resumed walking. She'd done what the Tarxin had asked for—well, not exactly, but he couldn't prove she hadn't. Was he going to upbraid her for the storm that could be heard even through the thick stone that surrounded the passage? Well, if he had any complaints, she knew what to say. "You rushed me," she would tell him. "I warned you there could be dire consequences and you only gave me two days."

Much sooner than she liked, Carcali found herself in front of the double doors that marked the Tarxin's section of the palace. From the chamber beyond these, doors on the right led to the public-use rooms, and on the left to the family's private rooms. Not that any of the ruler's rooms were really private. She took a deep breath and nodded to the leading guard. He opened the right-hand leaf of the doors and stood back to allow her to enter.

Carcali took three steps into the room and froze. There were more guards here, and most of them were wearing that same look of thinly covered pity that she'd seen on the faces of her escorts. One or two, she thought, eyed her speculatively.

"This way, if you please, Tara Xendra." A Steward stood at the set of doors in the left-hand wall. A private audience, then. But her thoughts were spinning so wildly Carcali couldn't work out whether that made disaster more or less likely. The Steward's face told her nothing, but then the man was trained not to react to anything.

Her hand lifted to her mouth, and she started on the nail of her index finger as she followed him through the door, across the anteroom within, and into the Tarxin's private study.

It seemed that every lamp in the room was lit, including those in the wall brackets by the door. All the Tarxin's rooms faced the sea, and the flames of the lamps flickered slightly in the wind that managed to get through the closed shutters of the three narrow windows. Carcali unclenched her hands and tried to stride forward with confidence, suddenly aware that she was the only person in the room wearing nightclothes.

As she drew closer to the table, the man looked up, and the face he showed Carcali was not that of the Tarxin at all. The man at the worktable was Xerwin. Suddenly, all she could hear was the pounding of her heart.

"Here, here, sit down." Someone with very warm hands was taking hold of her arms and easing her into a chair. Something soft, heavy, and warm was draped over her, and tucked around her feet.

"Thank you very much," she heard Xerwin say. "If you would leave us now? I will call when you are wanted. Thank you."

"What did they tell you? Why are you so frightened?" Xerwin had taken her hands and was rubbing them between his own. Carcali coughed, trying to get the muscles in her throat to loosen.

"The Tarxin sent for me," she croaked.

The rubbing stopped. "And you thought . . . ?" Xerwin

shut his eyes and took a deep breath. "Well, you would, wouldn't you?"

"Where is he?" Things couldn't be *too* bad if Xerwin was here, but there still had to be some kind of explanation. Now that it seemed she had less to be scared of, Carcali found she was starting to get angry.

"Through there." Xerwin sat back and nodded toward a door on the other side of the room. He glanced at the door she'd come in by and leaned forward again. Carcali edged to the front of her chair and put her head as close to his as she could manage.

"Carcali," he breathed. "He's dead. I killed him."

Carcali felt her mouth drop open. Was she dreaming? Had Xerwin somehow heard her thinking about it and killed the man? She blinked and swallowed. Time for all of that later. Xerwin was Tarxin now. That's what they'd meant when they'd said the Tarxin had sent for her. That's why they'd all looked at her that way, because her father was dead. The guards and soldiers were loyal to Xerwin, everyone knew that, but—

"Who else knows?"

Now Xerwin was blinking at her, his head tilted to one side. "Everyone," he said, his voice puzzled. Then a light seemed to dawn. "Oh," and with a flip of his hand he indicated how closely they were sitting. "No, this is just so that we can speak freely about *other* things."

"Should I start crying or something?" Carcali suddenly felt that tears would come easily, she was so relieved not to be frightened any more.

But Xerwin was shaking his head. "No one would believe it, I'm afraid. Look stricken, by all means when we leave the room, but shocked more than grieved is what people will expect."

Carcali nodded. "I can do that," she said. "So what happens now?"

"This is the tricky part," Xerwin said, lowering his voice. "You and I need to get to the Sanctuary of the Marked. Dhulyn Wolfshead is waiting for us there."

"Why?"

He blinked at her. Carcali felt a flash of impatience. "I'm not Xendra, remember?" She shook herself. She'd been more frightened than she liked to think about, but there was no need to take it out on Xerwin. "I don't know all the little rituals and ceremonies that come up when the Tarxin dies and there's a new one."

Now he was nodding. "Of course, of course. You are right, this is one of those rituals. You and I, because," he cleared his throat. "Because we are the only ones of the Tarxin's blood and must go to the Sanctuary and hold a vigil with the Marked. It is, uh, a tradition. Our wound is Healed, our hearts are Mended, and our serenity is Found." He smiled. "Oh, and the Seers give us a Vision for the new reign."

Carcali chewed on her fingernail. "They don't have to touch us, do they? I mean, this is just a formality, right?"

"Oh, yes, absolutely, just a formality. In fact, all the more so because," and he lowered his voice again, "you are not Xendra."

"And the Paledyn will be there?"

"Just in case there are any questions afterward," he said, tilting his head once more in the direction he'd said the old Tarxin's body lay. He stood up and began to draw her to her feet.

"Wait." She looked at the door and leaned toward him. "Wouldn't we get them to come here? The Marked?"

Xerwin sighed and sat down again. "I can see I'm going to need to explain more to you," he told her. "We're not going openly to the Sanctuary," he said when she was once more seated facing him. "Not yet. We're going to go now, privately, to prepare for the real ceremony, with the Paledyn there to vouch that everything is correct."

"But why the secrecy?"

He shut his eyes and sighed. "Because you're *not* Xendra. And the Marked know this. Because Dhulyn Wolfshead assures them that it is correct to do so, they are willing to perform the ceremony, but there are special preparations that must be done privately. Then, the public ceremony can take place in the usual fashion."

Carcali waved her hands in the air. "All right, yes, whatever you say." That was the problem with primitive societies, she thought. Empty rituals, ceremonies stripped of all meaning because there was no longer any Art to inform them. To say nothing of the silliness that politics was responsible for.

"Then, if you are ready, this way."

Xerwin could hardly believe that anyone, let alone a Storm Witch, would have fallen for the mass of confused nonsense that had just come out of his mouth. Though he had to admit, as he led Carcali through the hidden passage that was the Tarxin's private corridor to the Sanctuary, he liked that bit about Healing wounds, and Mending hearts. That was inspired. He should have taken more time to create a better story, but all had ended well. Carcali was a little arrogant, in her way—as all powerful people were, he realized. Otherwise she would have listened more carefully to him, questioned him more closely. He should take a lesson from this himself.

Even with the woolly shawl still wrapped around her, Carcali found the walk through the hidden passages chilly. She was glad to get out into the main hall of the Sanctuary, and gladder still to follow Xerwin into a more enclosed area, where small braziers warmed up the rooms. The room they finally reached was quite a large one, filled with the soft lights of candles and small shaded lamps. The Paledyn was there, as Xerwin had told her, with someone else, a larger, golden-haired man behind her. But Carcali's eyes were caught almost immediately by the two women on the far side of the room, standing close together, and holding hands. They peered at her as if they were standing at three times the distance.

They had the White Disease. Perfectly colorless, with pink eyes. Carcali had read about the affliction, but had never dreamed she would ever see such a thing.

"Look toward me, please." Carcali turned her head toward the rough silk sound of the Paledyn's voice, but her eyes remained fixed on the horrible twins. She felt cool fingers where her neck met her shoulder.

And then the world went black.

Dhulyn Wolfshead caught the slight form in her arms as the girl went down. She looked up at Javen Finder, who nodded.

"She's there," the Finder said. "The Storm Witch."

"Carcali," Xerwin said. "That's her name."

"Good," Dhulyn said. "That may help us."

"Dhulyn, Sister?" Amaia's voice trembled and was in a higher pitch than normal. She clung to Keria, and both pairs of blood-red eyes were round. It was easy for Dhulyn to forget, having Seen them so often in Vision, that the White Twins were children themselves.

"Parno," she said, as gently as she could. Her Partner immediately went to the two Seers, standing behind them and putting his arms around them. Amaia leaned into his chest, and Keria grabbed his forearm in both hands and clung to him.

"There now, my hearts, my own ones," he said in a voice that made Dhulyn's own heart skip a beat. "You're tired, I know, but this will soon be over, and then we can all rest."

"Tired now," Keria said, leaning her forehead against his shoulder. True, Dhulyn thought, they were all tired. The twins were tired as children were, more emotionally than physically. Still, the White Twins were *not* children, and they had an adult's ability to set aside the immediate needs of the body, to understand that there were reserves, and that they could draw upon them.

"Come, my sisters." Dhulyn put as much smile into her voice as she could. She laid the child's body down on the pallet they'd prepared for it, and signaled to the other Marked with her eyes. Ellis Healer took his position at the girl's dark head and bent low, his hands on her shoulders. Javen knelt to her left, centering the bowl carefully on the child's abdomen. Javen then took Ellis' left wrist in her right hand, and the child's left wrist in her own left hand. Rascon Mender mirrored Javen's position on the girl's other side.

"Come sing with me," Dhulyn said, holding her hands out to the White Twins. "One song before bed, please?"

Smiling now, Amaia and Keria let go of Parno and ran to Dhulyn's side, taking her hands and forming a tight circle around the kneeling Marked, and the child's body. *Too bad there aren't more of us,* Dhulyn thought. Even she, hardened Mercenary as she was, could feel a great weariness hanging over her. They'd done what they could to restore their own life energies with food and drink while waiting for Xerwin, but it was little enough in the face of what they had yet to do. It wasn't as though they had their pathway laid out for them, to run down swiftly. They would have to improvise as they went. That took time, and time took energy.

Energy. There was no ganje here, but there were other stimulants, other drugs.

"Ellis," she said. "Do you keep fresnoyn in the Sanctuary? Or any of the fressian drugs?"

"Here." Xerwin stepped forward, his hand already reaching into his pouch. From it he drew the tiny jeweled box that held his powdered fresa and held it out to her. Remm Shalyn was already pouring out a cup of the red currant juice on the nearby table. Dhulyn added the entire contents of the vial—not that it was much, and stirred it with her finger.

"Drink." Dhulyn held the cup out to Keria. "Just a mouthful, mind.

"You put your finger in it," the girl said, wrinkling up her nose.

"Ah, but I'm made of sugar," Dhulyn said. "Watch." She took a good-sized mouthful herself and swallowed. "Mmmm, that's good."

"Give it to me, I'll drink it," said Amaia. In the face of her sibling's readiness to obey, Keria took the cup and, still grimacing, swallowed a careful mouthful.

"Now me! My turn!" Amaia finished the liquid that was in the cup and smiled, licking her lips.

Dhulyn handed Remm Shalyn back the cup, nodding to him and to Xerwin. She looked at Parno.

"In Battle," she said, not caring who heard her.

Parno touched the fingers of his free hand to his forehead. "And in Death." He lifted the syrinx once more to his lips.

Dhulyn took hold of the girls' hands again, and this time they smiled at her. The room seemed very bright, the glowing light from the candles appearing almost to throb in time with the beating of her heart. When she moved her head, however slowly, colors and light trailed behind things, like paint smearing under a brush. The music, too, began to pull at her, and Dhulyn shifted her feet in time. Keria laughed, a deep-throated, woman's laugh, and began to sing. Dhulyn and Amaia joined in. As the music and the dance swept over them, Dhulyn looked down at the body of the child.

The child would want to dance with them. Would want to join them in their game.

THIS TIME THE VISION BEGINS WITHIN THE THICKET, WHERE THE CHILD STANDS ON HER FEET. IT APPEARS FROM THE POSITION OF HER HANDS AND FEET THAT SHE *HAS* BEEN DANCING, BUT SHE STOPS WHEN SHE SEES THEM APPEAR. SUDDENLY SHE CRIES OUT WITH DELIGHT AND RUNS FORWARD, BRUSHING AGAINST DHULYN'S THIGHS IN HER HASTE.

IT'S HER BODY, DHULYN REALIZES. XENDRA HAS SEEN HER OWN BODY WITHIN THE CIRCLE AND FAR FROM BEING FRIGHTENED BY IT, IS ANXIOUS TO RECLAIM IT. THE FINDER MOVES HER BOWL TO ONE SIDE AND, STILL PEERING INTO IT, TAKES THE STANDING CHILD BY THE WRIST. RASCON THE MENDER PLUNGES HER HANDS INTO THE CHEST AND INTO THE HEAD OF THE CHILD LYING AT HER FEET, AND STRUGGLES TO PULL THEM OUT AGAIN. SOMETHING RESISTS HER, BUT SHE GRITS HER TEETH AND PULLS. THE MUSCLES STAND OUT IN HER FOREARMS, AND THE VEINS IN HER NECK.

"SING LOUDER," KERIA SAYS. "SHE NEEDS ALL THE POWER WE CAN GIVE HER."

MAYBE WE SHOULD HAVE GIVEN THEM *THE FRESA*, DHULYN THINKS. EVEN AS SHE IS THINKING, SHE RAISES HER VOICE. SHE COULD NOT SAY WHAT WORDS SHE IS SINGING, BUT SHE KNOWS THEY ARE THE SAME WORDS KERIA AND AMAIA SING.

SUDDENLY, RASCON THE MENDER FALLS BACK FROM THE BODY. SHE MOVES HER HANDS TO ONE SIDE, AS IF SHE WERE THROWING SOMETHING DOWN, AND A YOUNG WOMAN APPEARS. THE CHILD XENDRA LEAPS FORWARD, AND DISAPPEARS INTO THE BODY. THE HEALER LEANS FORWARD, THE FINDER AND THE MENDER AS WELL, EACH ONE WITH THEIR EYES CLOSED, THEIR LIPS MOVING.

DHULYN CATCHES THE EYE OF THE NEWCOMER. SHE RECOGNIZES THE CLOSE-CROPPED HAIR, THE FINE-BONED FEATURES. BUT SOMETHING IS WRONG. THIS IS NOT THE MATURE WOMAN DHULYN HAS SEEN WORKING AT HER ART. THIS IS A YOUNG WOMAN WHO HAS SEEN HER BIRTH MOON NO MORE THAN NINETEEN, PERHAPS TWENTY TIMES.

"THIS ISN'T RIGHT," DHULYN SAYS. "SHE'S MUCH OLDER THAN THIS."

Twenty-four

THE CHILD'S BODY GASPED, arching this way and that, but the Marked kneeling and standing around her remained impassive and still. The Mender, Parno couldn't remember her name, perhaps *she* showed some agitation, her eyes moving under her closed lids, her lips pressed more firmly together.

The White Twins stood steady and firm, their skin so transparent that even in this light Parno thought he could see the movement of their blood under it. That same light gave Dhulyn color, made her pale skin a rich ivory, her blood-red hair almost ruby—though Parno couldn't be sure whether this seeming richness was the result of the contrast between Dhulyn and the White Twins, or of his own wonder at being able to see her at all. He still couldn't quite believe it. *Let me not be dreaming,* he prayed, though he couldn't have said which god he spoke to. *Or if I dream, let me never wake.*

The Marked sat back on their heels. The Healer reached up with his six-fingered hand to massage the bony ridge of his brow. The Mender was breathing fast, the Finder looking around her, blinking. The little girl curled over on to her side, the palm of her hand tucked under her cheek.

The Seers did not move.

#She needs help# The thought came from nowhere. #Your Brother, your Partner, she needs your strength#

How Even as he responded, Parno had lowered the

pipes and went striding over to where Dhulyn stood, eyes closed, holding the hands of the White Seers, ready to take her by the elbows and support her.

#No# #Urgency# #Keep playing# #Come with us# #Let your mind float# #Follow the music#

Parno set the syrinx to his lips once more, trying not to let his impatience get in the way of the music. How exactly was he supposed to let his mind float when Dhulyn was in danger? And how could she be in danger, for that matter, when she was standing right in front of him?

#Concentrate#

Parno squeezed his eyes shut, and made a better effort, letting the demands of the music control his breathing, letting the words of his personal triggering *Shora* run through his head. He felt himself relaxing, the muscles of his shoulder and neck loosening. He began to hear another tune, not competing with, but running counterpoint to the one he was playing. He began to play *to* that tune, answering it and following it with his own music, until he felt that the new tune carried him, and his music, away with it.

The new tune was the sound of the wind playing in the same vast meadow that he'd sensed before, the vast garden of souls where those who had gone to the Crayx at the death of their bodies could be found. The new tune was the tinkling fall of an unseen fountain, the songs of the birds, and the humming of the minds that lived there.

#Come further in# #This way, look here#

Parno found himself in a cool blue grotto, an enormous limestone cavern with an underwater passage to the sea.

#This is *our* place of refuge# came the thought. #For your Partner a forest, for the child Xendra a sunny beach, for us, this cavern# #Come# A head broke the surface and Parno looked into the deep, round eyes of a Crayx. It was a pale green, with a copper iridescence to its scales. Parno touched his fingertips to the his scaled cuirass; it was from this Crayx, he realized, that his armor had come. The Crayx extended its long, narrow head, and Parno knew immediately what was wanted, and climbed onto its back. Its neck was only slightly larger than the body of a horse, and he was able to take a firm grip with his knees, and brace his hands on the ridged scales.

#The link to your Partner is very strong now, and her Vision prevails, aided by her White Sisters# #It is there we must go# #Now#

#Fear not# the Crayx told him, and then it dove into the water.

❧

Normal, she felt normal. Carcali ran her hands over her face, hair, body, stunned with what she was feeling, almost frantic with delight. This was her real body, her own body. She seemed to be inside a hedgerow, but there was light, somehow, enough to see by in any case. There were people on their knees on the floor, and three others, standing to one side.

"This isn't right." She heard someone say. "She's much older than this."

And then she feels a sharp displacement of air.

❧

KERIA AND AMAIA ARE STILL HOLDING HER HANDS, EVEN THOUGH THEY ARE NOT CHILDREN HERE, AND THEY ARE NOT FRIGHTENED.

"DOES SHE LOOK YOUNGER TO HERSELF HERE?" DHULYN ASKS THEM. "IS THIS HER MENTAL IMAGE OF HERSELF?"

"THIS IS HER TRUE SELF," KERIA SAYS.

"JUST AS YOU ARE YOUR TRUE SELF," AMAIA ADDS.

"AND WE ARE OUR TRUE SELVES."

"I HAVE ALWAYS SEEN HER OLDER. A MATURE WOMAN AT WORK IN HER LABORATORY." *WHAT DOES THIS MEAN?* DHULYN WONDERS. WHAT FUTURE, OR WHAT PAST, HAD SHE SEEN, IF THIS YOUNG WOMAN IS THE TRUE SELF OF THE STORM WITCH?

THE MARKED ARE MOVING, THE CHILD IS SITTING UP, YAWNING. ALL FOUR TURN TOWARD DHULYN AND THE OTHER SEERS. ELLIS HEALER RUBS AT HIS FACE, EXHAUSTION WRITTEN IN EVERY LINE. RASCON MENDER HAS A HAND ON HER SIDE, BREATHING AS THOUGH SHE'S BEEN RUNNING. JAVEN FINDER LOOKS AS THOUGH SHE MIGHT START CRYING.

THEY WINK OUT OF EXISTENCE.

THE STORM WITCH LOOKS AT THE PLACE WHERE THEY WERE, HER MOUTH OPEN, HER BROWS DRAWN TOGETHER. SHE LOOKS UP AT THEM.

DHULYN ISN'T SURE WHAT TO DO, BUT THE TWINS ARE TURNING AWAY, TOWARD THE THINNER PART OF THE THICKET THAT

WILL LET THEM OUT INTO THE PATH OUTSIDE, AND SHE TURNS TO GO WITH THEM. SHE SEES THAT XENDRA'S PLAYTHINGS ARE NOW GONE. THERE IS ONLY A WATERSKIN, A PILE OF INGLERA SKINS, A SMALL PACK OF FOOD. THE SPACE IS BECOMING ONCE AGAIN THE PLACE WHERE DHULYN HID AS A CHILD.

"WAIT, WHERE ARE YOU GOING?" THE STORM WITCH IS ON HER FEET. SHE'S WEARING LIGHT BLUE TROUSERS, A PALE YELLOW TOP WITH SHORT SLEEVES. THERE ARE SMALL GOLD STUDS IN HER EARS, AND HER FEET ARE BARE. HER CROPPED HAIR IS DISHEVELED, SHORT SPIKES STICKING UP IN ALL DIRECTIONS. HER GRAY-GREEN EYES ARE ROUND, THE PUPILS TINY POINTS.

"WE GO BACK TO OUR OWN PLACES NOW," KERIA SAYS. "YOU SHOULD DO THE SAME, STORM WITCH. YOUR RULE OVER THE CHILD'S BODY HAS ENDED, YOU MAY RETURN TO YOUR OWN PLACE."

"YOU CAN'T DO THIS TO ME!" SHE TAKES A STEP TOWARD THEM, HER HAND LIFTED. SHE LOOKS AT DHULYN, AS IF TRULY SEEING HER FOR THE FIRST TIME. "PALEDYN! YOU CAN'T LEAVE ME. I HAVE NOWHERE TO GO." HER HANDS REACH OUT. "I WON'T GO BACK TO THE WEATHERSPHERES, I WON'T. YOU DON'T UNDERSTAND, I'LL GO MAD!"

DHULYN WONDERS IF THE GIRL ISN'T ALREADY MAD. "CAN SHE REMAIN HERE?" BUT THE TWINS ARE ALREADY SHAKING THEIR HEADS.

"THIS IS A REAL PLACE, A VISION PLACE, BUT IT IS TEMPORARY, A BUBBLE," KERIA SAYS.

"IT IS YOUR VISION, DHULYN, AND WITHOUT YOU, IT WILL NO LONGER EXIST," AMAIA SAYS.

"ONCE WE LEAVE HERE, THE BUBBLE WILL COLLAPSE." KERIA TURNS TO THE WITCH. "WE ARE SORRY," SHE SAID. "BUT YOU MUST RETURN TO YOUR OWN PLACE."

"BUT THE WEATHERSPHERES ISN'T MY PLACE, I DON'T BELONG THERE." SHE TURNS ONCE MORE TO DHULYN. "YOU KNOW THAT. YOU KNOW WHAT I REALLY AM. MY WORLD—MY *PLACE*— DOESN'T EXIST ANYMORE. YOU *KNOW* THAT." HER FACE HARDENED. "YOU HAVE TO HELP ME. IF YOU DON'T—IF I GO BACK TO THE SPHERES, I SWEAR TO YOU I'LL—I'LL BRING ON AN ICE AGE AND YOU'LL ALL DIE. I'LL DESTROY YOU ALL. THE WHOLE WORLD. I'VE DONE IT ONCE ALREADY."

DHULYN FEELS A SINKING IN HER STOMACH. THE GIRL *IS* MAD. THAT'S CLEAR.

"YOU DESTROYED THE WORLD?" SHE SAYS, STRIVING TO KEEP

HER VOICE REASONABLE AND CALM. "*YOU?* IN WHAT FASHION? THE WORLD STILL EXISTS."

"NOT *MY* WORLD," THE WITCH SAYS. "*MY* WORLD'S GONE. THE PEOPLE, THE BUILDINGS, THE KNOWLEDGE." HER VOICE HITCHES, AND HER EYES STARE. "EVERYTHING. GONE. LITTLE FRAGMENTS, SCRAPS OF STONE, BITS OF METAL. THAT'S ALL THAT'S LEFT."

"AND *YOU* DID THIS? BUT TIME ALONE WOULD DO IT, YOU DID NOTHING." DHULYN LIFTS HER HEAD. THERE IS A SOUND FROM OUTSIDE THE THICKET, A SOUND SHE KNOWS VERY WELL. "A HORSEMAN COMES."

The motion of the Crayx under him began to change from a smooth gliding through the water to short, rhythmic movements, like the prancing of a particularly well-schooled horse. Then he saw that it was, in fact, a horse he was riding, a coppery-shaded roan, with an oddly pale mane. They were riding down a hunting trail in a rough forest, thick with underbrush. It was winter here, and he could see old snow drifted up here and there. The horse followed the trail steadily, heading directly for a thicket of pines growing so closely together that their branches formed a kind of wall. The horse shouldered its way into the thicket, and Parno raised his arm to keep the branches out of his face.

The final branches parted, and he saw Dhulyn with the White Twins, and a young, fair-haired woman.

"YOU ARE JUST IN TIME, MY SOUL." DHULYN'S HEART SWELLS WITH THE SIGHT OF HER PARTNER. SHE REALIZES THAT BEING PARTED FROM HIM, SHE HAD BEEN AFRAID THAT SHE WOULD NOT FIND HER WAY BACK. THAT SOMEHOW THE NECESSITY TO KEEP THE STORM WITCH FROM THE CHILD WOULD KEEP HER FROM RETURNING. NOW THAT PARNO IS HERE, SHE STANDS STRAIGHTER. WHATEVER COMES, THEY WILL FACE IT TOGETHER.

"THE WITCH IS TELLING US THAT WE SHOULD FEAR HER, BE-CAUSE SHE'S DESTROYED THE WORLD."

"MY NAME'S CARCALI, FOR THE ART'S SAKE, NOT 'THE WITCH.'" FROM THE HARDNESS OF HER FACE, DHULYN KNOWS THAT THE WOMAN IS AFRAID, AND THAT HER FEAR IS TAKING THE FORM OF ANGER.

"YOU'LL HAVE TO EXPLAIN YOURSELF A LITTLE BETTER, CAR-CALI," PARNO SAYS, AS HE DISMOUNTS. DHULYN WONDERS WHERE THE HORSE CAME FROM, AND WHY IT IS SUCH AN UNUSUAL COLOR. IT TURNS ITS DARK, VERY ROUND EYES ON HER AND SHE SUDDENLY SEES THE TRUTH. THE HORSE IS A CRAYX, AND THAT IS HOW PARNO IS HERE. AT LEAST . . . SHE SQUEEZES HER EYES SHUT, BLINKS. SHE STILL DOESN'T SEE QUITE HOW.

"THE SUN WAS TOO HOT, AND EVERYTHING WAS GOING TO BURN AND DIE. CARCALI SAYS. "ALL THE PLANS AND SOLUTIONS THAT PEOPLE WERE COMING UP WITH WERE JUST WAYS TO BUY US MORE TIME. NONE OF THEM WOULD HAVE SAVED THE WORLD. I FOUND A WAY—I THOUGHT I'D FOUND A WAY TO COOL THE SUN, TO REVERSE THE PROCESS THAT WAS MAKING IT HEAT. BUT THEY DIDN'T AGREE, THEY TOLD ME I WASN'T READY, THAT THEY WOULDN'T HELP. AND WHEN I TRIED TO DO IT MYSELF, I . . . I LOST—" SHE SQUEEZES HER EYES SHUT, ARMS WRAPPED AROUND HER BODY, AND DHULYN GLANCES AT PARNO. HE MOVES HIS SHOULDERS IN THE SMALLEST OF SHRUGS.

"WHAT DID YOU LOSE, CARCALI?" HE ASKS.

"THIS," SHE SAYS. "MY SELF. MY BODY. I THOUGHT I DIDN'T NEED AN ANCHOR, BUT I DID. AND WHEN I REALIZED THAT I COULDN'T GET BACK, I PANICKED. THE WEATHERSPHERES—" CARCALI CLUTCHES HER HEAD IN HER HANDS, HER FINGERS DIGGING THROUGH THE TUFTS OF HER PALE HAIR. "IT WAS LIKE I COULDN'T FEEL THEM ANYMORE EITHER, BUT THEY COULD FEEL ME." HER VOICE DROPS TO A WHISPER. "DON'T YOU SEE? MY CONFUSION, MY PANIC MUST HAVE ENTERED INTO THE SPHERES, AND EVERY-THING WAS CHAOS AND POWER AND MY CIVILIZATION WAS DE-STROYED."

CARCALI, THE STORM WITCH, SINKS TO HER KNEES, STILL HOLDING HER HEAD IN HER HANDS. KERIA AND AMAIA GO TO HER, KNEELING BESIDE HER, AND PUT THEIR ARMS AROUND HER. AMAIA STROKES CARCALI'S HAIR, AND KERIA MAKES SOOTHING NOISES. DHULYN LOOKS AT PARNO OVER THE TOPS OF THEIR HEADS. SHE CAN SEE ON HIS FACE WHAT HE'S THINKING. THE CIV-ILIZATION OF THE CAIDS *HAD* BEEN DESTROYED, BUT NOT BY CAT-ACLYSMIC WEATHER CHANGE. PARNO LIFTS HIS RIGHT EYEBROW, AND DHULYN GIVES HIM AN IMPERCEPTIBLE NOD. EVEN AS SHE OPENS HER MOUTH, ANOTHER SPEAKS BEFORE HER.

#We know the time of which she speaks# #The time of the cooling of the sun#

DHULYN LOOKS UP, WONDERING WHERE THE VOICE COMES

FROM, WHEN SHE REALIZES THAT IT COMES FROM EVERYWHERE, AND NOWHERE.

"WHAT IS THAT? WHO . . . ?" CARCALI JERKS HER HEAD FROM SIDE TO SIDE, LOOKING FOR THE SOURCE OF THE VOICE. THE WHITE TWINS TRY TO CALM HER, BUT SHE SHIES AWAY FROM THEIR HANDS.

"IT'S THE CRAYX," PARNO SAYS. "CAN YOU ALL HEAR THEM?"

#We use you, Lionsmane, and your link with your Partner, and her link with her fellow Seers#

"AND CARCALI?" DHULYN ASKS.

THE COPPER HORSE TOSSES ITS HEAD. *IT MAKES A BEAUTIFUL HORSE,* DHULYN THINKS.

#She is just consciousness now, and she occupies this space for the moment# #As do we all# #So long as the music plays#

NOW THAT IT IS MENTIONED, DHULYN CAN JUST HEAR A FAINT TUNE PLAYING A LONG WAY OFF. IT SOUNDS AS THOUGH IT MIGHT BE JUST THE WIND BLOWING THROUGH THE TENT ROPES IN THE FAR OFF CAMP OF THE RED HORSEMEN. SHE LOOKS AT THE YOUNG WOMAN IN THE CROOK OF KERIA'S ARM. CARCALI HAS BOTH HANDS OVER HER MOUTH, HER EYES WIDE OPEN ABOVE THEM.

"WE KNOW," KERIA SAYS.

"YOU THOUGHT THEY WERE JUST FISH," AMAIA ADDS.

"MOST PEOPLE DO," KERIA SAYS. SHE PATS CARCALI'S SHOULDER.

DHULYN TURNS TO THE HORSE. SHE FINDS IT EASIER TO ACT AS IF THE VOICE COMES FROM IT. "YOU KNOW OF THIS TIME, YOU SAY?"

#It was before we made ourselves known to the Caids# #The changes in the sun would have brought about the destruction of the world in two generations of humans# #But the sun was cooled, and the world saved#

"NO, THAT'S NOT RIGHT." CARCALI HAS GATHERED HER STRENGTH. "WHAT HAPPENED TO MY WORLD, THEN? TO MY CIVILIZATION? TIME ALONE CAN'T DO WHAT I'VE SEEN."

#The Green Shadow came# #Oh, some time after the cooling of the sun# #After the Pod-sensed joined us# #After our treaties with your people# #A long while after, as humans measure time#

AND CARCALI HAS BEEN WANDERING ALONE IN THE WEATHERSPHERES ALL THAT TIME. DHULYN SHUDDERS. SHE HAS THE

FEELING IT WAS ONLY A FEW MOONS AGO, IN THE CRAYX'S WAY OF
MEASURING. CAN SHE HOPE THAT THE DISEMBODIED STORM
WITCH FEELS THE SAME WAY?

Parno looked with interest at the fair-haired young woman
kneeling between Keria and Amaia. So this was the Storm
Witch in her real shape. She didn't seem all that formidable.
She would be about the age of the younger of his two sisters.
At the moment she had her hands over her mouth again, her
eyes tightly shut, and tears leaking out of them.

Dhulyn stood to one side, her lips pressed together, drumming the fingers of her right hand on her sword hilt. Parno
almost laughed aloud. Those were clear signs his Partner was
impatient and uncomfortable—and she'd stay that way until
Carcali stopped crying.

Finally, the young woman heaved a great, broken sigh,
and accepted the offer of a scrap of cloth from Amaia to wipe
off her face and blow her nose.

"I didn't kill them." There was a note of wonder in her
voice, but she was still very close to tears. However good the
news, it was almost more than Carcali could take in. She had
clearly been living a long time with the pain and guilt of what
she'd done. It would take time still for her to truly believe she
was innocent.

"But you can't make me go back to the weatherspheres,
please." She looked from face to face, and her own hardened
when she did not see what she hoped for.

#Would you come to live with us# the Crayx suggested.
#Join our consciousness# #You are not Pod sensed, but per-
haps from here, with the links . . .#

"No, please, I couldn't." Carcali clung to the arms of the
White Twins, who looked at Parno and Dhulyn over her bent
head with pity in their red eyes. "I couldn't live like that. Not
like an animal."

#Amusement# #You would not be alone# #Compassion#
Carcali looked away. "I couldn't."

"Sun, Moon, and Stars girl, what can you do, then?" Dhulyn's voice cut through the air like her own well-sharpened
sword. "You can't have someone else's body, you can't stay
here, you don't want to go back to the weatherspheres, and
now you don't want to join the Crayx. What do you want?"

"I want to go home." Burst into tears.

Dhulyn threw her hands into the air and stalked off, as far as she could in this small thicket. Parno was torn between laughing at her inability to cope with so much emotion, and his very real sympathy with her feelings of frustration.

#Why should she not go home#

Dhulyn turned and looked at the horse, who was quite calmly flicking its ears back and forth. Keria and Amaia looked at each other, at Dhulyn, at Parno, and at the horse. Carcali once again searched one face after another watched to see where the next blow would fall.

"How can she go home?" *Dhulyn said in her rough silk voice.* "Her home is gone. It's in the past, hundreds — no, thousands of years."

"We See the past," *Amaia said, as her sister nodded.* "In the Vision place there is no time."

"Like the Crayx," *Parno whispered. Everyone looked at him.* "The Crayx," *he repeated.* "They don't experience time the same way we do. There's no past for them, there's only now."

"So Carcali's home . . ."

"Is just another place to them, another bubble like this one."

#But it is her bubble, as this one is yours# #We can take her, if she wishes to go#

Carcali was backing away from them. "It's a trick. You'll hand me over to these animals and they'll wait until you've gone and then they'll drown me."

"Oh, for the Moon's sake." *Dhulyn threw her hands into the air.* "You stupid little fool."

"Dhulyn." *Parno took his Partner by the arm and led her to one side.* "Think how alone she's been," *he said to her in the nightwatch voice.* "I know I went a little mad when I lost you. I could have killed some of the Nomads, just because I didn't care enough to be watchful. She's lost everyone, everything. Can we expect clear thinking from her?"

"Oh, I know." *Only Dhulyn could sound sullen using the nightwatch voice. The corner of her mouth twitched.* "I'm not saying I'd really kill her, just that I feel like it." *She glanced back at the others.* "But she doesn't trust us, so what are we to do?"

"I'll go with her."

The grip Dhulyn took on his forearm was painful. "No. I won't lose you again. No."

"Quietly, my heart. And I'd like the use of this arm again, if you don't mind." Her hand relaxed, but she did not release him. *"I trust the Crayx. If they say they can do it, they can. Even if they lose Carcali, they would never lose me. Can you think of another solution?"* Dhulyn shook her head. *"And you and I will never be separated, not really. We know that now."*

She nodded. *"I've Seen her older. In her own laboratory, but older than she is here. This must be what that Vision was showing me."*

"So we succeed. In Battle," he said.

"And in Death," she answered.

Parno turned back to the others, Dhulyn at his elbow. "I'll go with you," he said to Carcali. *"That way you can be sure there is no trickery."*

"You'll go? You'd do this for me?"

"If the Crayx can take us both."

#We can# #And bring you back again, Lionsmane# #But it must be quickly, while the links remain, and the music still plays#

Was he still playing? Parno wondered. How much time was passing in that world?

#Let the Seers sing# #Mount again, both of you#

Parno swung himself on to the horse and put out his hand for Carcali. Dhulyn stood ready to give the girl a leg up. She looked from one to the other, licking her lips.

"He'll keep you safe," Dhulyn said. *"You'll see. He'll take you right to your own door, like the son of a Noble House that he is. And you'll go to work on cooling that sun, now that you know it was done."*

"But they said no, they said it wouldn't work."

Dhulyn shook her head. "You really are an idiot, youngster. You did it, don't you see? You must have done it, before you were lost in the weatherspheres. Your people, they didn't say it couldn't be done, just that you couldn't do it alone. So get some help, you blooded fool."

❦

Javen Finder was on her knees, lower lip between her teeth, concentrating on her bowl. But she shook her head.

"Nothing," she said to the others. "No colors will come. I'm sorry, Light of the Sun, I can't Find them."

Xerwin hugged Xendra tighter in the circle of his arms. She muttered but did not awaken, only tightened her arms around his neck. "But they could still be in this Vision place, where you *cannot* Find them, could they not? Where Xendra was?"

"Yes, Light of the Sun, they could be."

The White Twins and Dhulyn Wolfshead still stood, motionless now, holding hands. The new Paledyn still played, but more softly now, barely audible, as if his mouth was drying.

"Shall we stop him playing?" Xerwin asked.

❧

They rode through the forest again, Carcali clinging to him, arms wrapped tightly around his waist. The forest turned denser, hotter, thicker, a real jungle, and suddenly they were in the sea, but that turned into a rainstorm, and either way, they didn't get wet. A village became a town became a city. There were strange smells, bitter, though they made Carcali laugh, and when he looked up, Parno saw the night sky was unfamiliar. All at once they were walking on the smoothest pavement Parno had ever seen, and Carcali ran ahead of him to a door painted the bright blue of a clear summer sky. She threw the door open and a wind rose up, blowing her into a small, tidy room with two beds, one against each wall. Carcali grunted as she landed on the bed to the right of the entry. She sat up right away, looking around her, tears falling down her cheeks, though she didn't bother to wipe them away.

"Paledyn," she said, looking around her through her tears. "Are you still here? Thank you, thank Dhulyn Wolfshead for me. Thank the Crayx." Before she can say anything more, she began to sob, and Parno heard the sound of hooves in the distance, and the sound of the sea. And music was playing, the Sleeping God's tune. Dhulyn was singing. She had a good enough voice, but not one people would pay money to hear.

"Oh, thank you very much," she said, cuffing him on the shoulder. She took the pipes from his cramping fingers. "I'll just stick to killing people from now on, shall I?"

Twenty-five

THE WIND WAS STRONG but steady, making the banners and flags that flew from mastheads, stays, and balconies flap and rattle.

"I never thought I'd see this day," said Remm Shalyn.

"The new Tarxin means to show his people what the new future is," Dhulyn said. "This is a strong beginning, but a good one."

The *Wavetreader* was at anchor in the deep harbor off the cliff face of Ketxan City. A vast floating platform, the size of a city square, had been erected between the ship and the permanent wharfs and piers, and in the center of it stood Xerwin, the Tarxin of Mortaxa, his sister, the Tara Xendra, and as many representatives of the High Noble Houses as could crowd themselves on. The balconies and windows of the City were packed with citizenry, all here to witness the historic betrothal of their Tara Xendra with Tar Malfin Cor of the Long Ocean Nomads.

"You think they realize their Tara is being wed to a mere sea captain?" Parno said out of the corner of his mouth.

"Some do, but those are the very ones who look to profit most from the connection, so they're unlikely to quibble." Dhulyn could hear the amusement in Remm Shalyn's voice.

The High Priest of the Slain God, who was officiating, caught Dhulyn's eye and motioned her forward with a frown. Dhulyn and Parno both stepped into their places at the priest's side.

"We call here to witness this solemn binding the Paledyn

Dhulyn Wolfshead, and the Paledyn Parno Lionsmane, Hands of the Slain God, come to us from the far side of the Long Ocean."

They had already witnessed the written documents of the marriage, carried at the moment by Scholars from the Library of Ketxan City who were standing to one side of the bride and groom. Much of the last few weeks had been taken up with the creation of the contracts of the marriage, and at that Dhulyn had been given the clear message that the whole process had been scandalously rushed.

"This marriage to be the symbol of the joining of our two peoples, the first of many such marriages . . ." the priest was saying. And it would be so, Dhulyn knew. That fact that all the marriages would be with Pod-sensed Mortaxans might not be immediately obvious, but eventually, with the royal family leading the way, the whole idea of the Crayx would be taken for granted by the landsters.

"To remain with her family until the age of fifteen . . ."

Malfin Cor was fourteen years older than Xendra, but such an age difference was not significant when it came to political alliances. The Nomads knew Xerwin, and the Crayx trusted in Xendra's confidence in him; all were content. On his side, Xerwin had wanted to establish an alliance between his people and the Nomads as quickly as possible. Malfin was the nearest Nomad of significant rank, something more important at this juncture than his age. As Dhulyn already knew, the relationships between Pod-sensed people were such that physical age really had no significance.

"To spend half of each year with her people . . ."

Malfin Cor and the Tara Xendra both caught her gaze at the same moment, as both rolled their eyes in identical expressions of amusement. Dhulyn stifled her own laughter with difficulty, but managed to look sober enough when the priest shot her a suspicious glance. Through her Pod sense, Xendra could be with the *Wavetreader* Pod whenever she wished to be, and one of the things the young Tara had made clear since her return was that she definitely wished to be—she had started, Parno had said, to privately call the Crayx "seahorses."

"Free access to the Sanctuary of the Marked . . ."

In fact, the Marked were now free to come out of their Sanctuary, if they chose to. Medolyn Mender and her friend

Coria Finder had already booked passage to Boravia, bartering their skills for the trip, and a young Healer Dhulyn had never met was going with them. Parno had provided letters of introduction to his noble cousin, Dal-eLad Tenebro, so the youngsters would have somewhere to go when they reached Imrion.

"Two ships to be built and manned with mixed crews . . ."

Dhulyn inclined her head. Not as mixed as people might think. *Wavetreader, Windtreader* and *Dawntreader* Pods would all provide crew members out of those who liked the idea of starting a new ship, but the Mortaxan element would be made up of newly discovered Pod-sensed.

After what seemed like hours of bowing and nodding at the right moments, the detailing of the contract was finally over. Malfin Cor gave his betrothed her own garwon, a rope of pearls as long as she was tall, and a small Crayx leather cuirass, in the same bright blue with golden tones as his own, which she seemed to value more than the jewels. She gave him a jeweled sword, a cloak in the same bright blue as the cuirass, and a miniature orange tree growing in its own tub, and already bearing fruit.

Finally, the two parties prepared to separate.

"Lionsmane," Darlara Cor said aloud. "Tide at the end of the third watch, don't be late."

Parno waved a hand in acknowledgment before following Dhulyn back into the City. There was no shortcut to the palace, not even for the Tarxin, and they took up their position for the procession behind the priests of the Slain God.

"That was for my benefit, I suppose, since Darlara does not need to speak aloud to you," Dhulyn said when Parno caught up to her.

"She's putting what distance she can between us, that's true."

"Would you rather we waited for the next ship?" Dhulyn watched her Partner's face carefully.

"What? Another moon at least?" He shook his head. "If we stay here any longer, Xerwin will find a way to keep us—him or the White Twins."

Dhulyn smiled. "I asked them if they wanted to come with us."

Parno hesitated between one step and the next. "Did they understand you?"

"Oh, yes, I asked them in a Vision."

"And?"

"And they would not live to make the journey."

"They know this?"

"We Saw it."

Ahead of them, the old priest was taking leave of his new Tarxin, and Xerwin signaled for the Mercenaries to join him as he turned to ascend the final staircase leading to the palace. Tara Xendra's face appeared, wide eyes blinking, peering around her brother and Parno burst out laughing. Dhulyn nudged him with her elbow.

"It's Xendra," he said. "She wants me to find out who made your trousers. She's determined to start living like a Nomad as quickly as she can."

Dhulyn looked over her shoulder to where Remm Shalyn walked with the Tarxin's guards. "Maybe I should pass Remm Shalyn's service to her. He could start teaching her weapons."

"*He* doesn't want to come with us?"

Dhulyn shrugged. "He's needed here, he says, until the slavery question is dealt with." Parno raised his left eyebrow and Dhulyn twitched her own in agreement. The Mortaxa would be a generation, at least, dealing with the slavery question, and that would be if they were very lucky indeed.

"Who knows, we may yet see him again, if the Nomads are going to start a passenger service. He'd make not a bad Mercenary Brother, if he lived through the Schooling."

They passed through the doorway into the Tarxin's private sitting room and found Xerwin struggling out of his ceremonial breastplate. He was entirely alone, his pikemen standing at their posts on the outside of the door, and his servants already dismissed.

"I'd forgotten how difficult this thing is to get out of," he said, as Parno gave him a hand with a tie that had knotted.

"You dismissed your attendants too quickly, Light of the Sun," Dhulyn said, careful not to smile too widely.

Now that his armor was off, Xerwin twisted his arm up behind him to scratch vigorously under his shoulder blade. "I'm not used to it yet," he admitted. "Even when I was Tar, I found it cumbersome to be constantly surrounded by so many servants."

"You're in a position to change that now, if you'd like,"

Parno pointed out. "My advice would be to keep a good personal guard, people you can trust, and know personally. Use them for your body servants, on the occasions you need any. Everything else is your Steward of Keys' problem, not yours."

"As we do in the Battle Wings. Yes, I like that notion." He looked from one to the other. "Are you sure I can't persuade you to stay? As you see, even the smallest advice from you is helpful."

Dhulyn shook her head. They'd been over this already. "You know we have unfinished business of our own, with our own House. Your instincts are good, Xerwin, follow them. Not every one on your father's Council can be a fool, listen to them until you know. Consult the Scholars of history for precedents. And don't forget that Xendra is now linked to a vast network of minds, many of which know far more about ruling than my Partner and I ever will."

Xerwin rubbed at his eyes with the heels of his hands. "Can they help me with the slavery problem? You've told me Mortaxa will collapse if we continue the practice, Dhulyn Wolfshead, and I believe you. So what do I do?"

Dhulyn shrugged. She knew what she would do, but then, she didn't have the welfare of a whole nation to consider. "Start small. Tax them. Tax the owners for every slave they own. Tax them heavily. Use the revenue to help the slaves who are turned loose."

"Dhulyn," Parno's voice had that listening-to-the-Crayx tone. "The tide turns. The *Wavetreader* is ready for us."

A little over a moon later, the Long Ocean ship *Wavetreader* arrived in the harbor of Lesonika, accompanied by a small Crayx who kept out of sight.

"I don't see *Catseye* anywhere," Dhulyn said when Parno joined her on the dock, with the last of their packs.

Parno took a quick glance around. "I didn't expect it, did you? Huelra might be anywhere along his usual route just now."

"And our horses? And the rest of our baggage?" He could tell that Dhulyn was disappointed. "At least the sun's shining. And here come the captains."

They had taken the last few days in the Midland Sea to say their good-byes to the crew, but the captains were doing them the honor of actually leaving the ship to say farewell in private—or in as much privacy as Nomads ever had.

#As much as they wish# #Amusement#

Parno grinned. Dar had no difficulty yet with the gangway, though she came down it with a hand to her belly. To Parno's eye, there was nothing yet there to see of the twins she was carrying, though both Dar and Dhulyn had sworn that he was blind.

Good wind, fair current came the Nomads' voices in his head, as they exchanged embraces.

Fair current, good wind he answered.

"Be near the sea in seven moons' time," Dar said aloud, so as to include Dhulyn. "You can be present when your girls are born."

"I will be," Parno said. "Expect me."

Dar suddenly stepped forward and hugged Dhulyn, who did her best not to shy away.

"Would have liked to keep you both," she said.

Dhulyn patted Dar's shoulder, knowing that the sentiment was sincere. But she had never again managed a Vision in which she could link with the Crayx, not even using her ancient vera tiles to help her concentrate. Without the White Twins, her Mark simply wasn't strong enough.

They shouldered their packs and, Dhulyn in the lead, headed back down the street toward the Mercenary House.

"We've missed the summer," Dhulyn said, pulling the throat of her red cloak closed. "But at least the sun's shining today."

"It's good to be back," Parno said.

"Let's see how good it is once we've been to Mercenary House."

Parno took her by the elbow. "What kind of problems can they give us? What could be worse than what we've been through already?

Dhulyn shrugged one shoulder. "You're probably right."

PATH OF
THE SUN

Acknowledgments

My first and fullest thanks go as always to my editor and publisher, Sheila Gilbert, and my agent, Joshua Bilmes. My thanks also go to my good friend Vaso Angelis, who suggested the location for *Path of the Sun*. "Why don't you write about my home?" she said, so the isle of Crete it is. I hope she likes what I've done. A belated thanks to my friend David Ingham. Way back when I was writing *The Soldier King*, David helped me out with a bit of theater business and I somehow forgot to acknowledge him then, so I'd like to do that here. To my friend Barb Wilson-Orange, who helps me with my proofs. And to Chris Szego, whose name I spelled wrong last time, even though she said it was okay. To mystery writer, friend and psychologist Barbara Fradkin, for recommending reading on psychopaths. And to add to the cast of old friends, I'd like to thank a new one, Dr. Kari Maund, who reminded me of how much I love, and how much I owe to that other mercenary brotherhood, especially to Athos, Porthos, Aramis, and D'Artagnan.

The right to have a character named after her was purchased at silent auction for Winter Ashley-Maie Lucas by her mother Teresa Lucas. Your mother said you chose a bad guy, and I tried to make her all bad—but it just didn't work out that way.

Prologue

EPION AKARION WAITED until moonrise to travel the last portion of his journey back to the palace in Uraklios. This part of the road was open and easy, even at night, and if it did pass rather closely to two or three wooded areas on its way through the hills, well, he had guards with him.

Still, he was surprised when one of the forward riders came back with news that there was someone on the road near the Path of the Sun. It was not unusual to find the curious exploring around the Caid ruins, which included the entrance to the Path of the Sun itself. But those who came at night generally came in pairs, carrying something to lie down upon while they watched the stars, and they were generally younger than this man. This was a man of Epion's own years, dressed for the road and leading two horses, one saddled and one, smaller, burdened with several packs.

A man smelling of blood.

The smile on the stranger's face was warm enough and charming enough that Epion Akarion found himself on the verge of smiling back—despite the blood that spattered the front of the man's tunic, decorated the edge of his cloak, and streaked his hands.

"Check his back trail, Jo," Epion said to the guard who had stayed with the stranger. He waited until Jo-Leggett and his brother Gabe-Leggett rode off before returning his attention to the blood-spattered man.

"I am Epion Akarion," he said. "Of the Royal House of

Menoin. Is that your own blood, sir?" Though his experience on the battlefield told him it was unlikely. "Are you injured?"

"Blood?" The stranger looked down at his hands, and for a moment Epion thought a look of surprise flickered over the man's face. Perhaps he thought it too dark for the blood to be seen. But the moon was brighter than the stranger realized, and Epion and his guard had greater experience of wounds and the patterns of blood spray than ordinary men.

"Well, I've had a rather difficult experience," the man said finally. "Very difficult, really. Trying in fact."

"My lord." The call came from several spans along the road, where a copse of pine trees formed a deeper darkness. The tone in Jo-Leggett's voice sent icy fingers dancing up Epion's spine. He signaled to his aide Callos to remain watching the stranger and went to join the guard.

Jo-Leggett led him to where his brother waited in a clearing Epion vaguely remembered. It was not many paces from the road, and full of moonlight. What Epion saw there tightened the muscles of his own throat and made him clench his teeth against the rising of his stomach.

"Fetch torches," he said. Once they were lit and set into the ground and the guards instructed to step away—which they were only too glad to do—Epion paced his way methodically around the thing on the ground. Now that he was over the initial shock, he saw several points that intrigued him. First, he was certain this was no man of Menoin, not with that hair the color of old blood. And not from what he could see of the beading on the man's clothes—what was left of them. Epion was also sure the limbs had been arranged—again, he'd seen enough soldiers fall in battle to know that bodies did not land like this naturally. And the cuts. They were precise. Some of them symmetrical.

This had the look of ritual. Epion drummed his fingers on the hilt of his belt knife. Nothing happened by accident. He could make good use of this.

"Bring him."

The stranger came escorted between Callos and Essio, but though his arms were held, there was something in the way the man carried himself—an air of calm and of ready helpfulness—that made it seem he was bringing them, rather than the other way around.

"Did you do this?" Epion gestured toward the corpse.

Again, a momentary expression, this time of confusion, flitted across the man's face and then cleared away. The stranger blinked and leaned back. "Of course not! Would I have been standing about on the road waiting for someone to find me if I had?"

Epion glanced at the Leggett brothers. They were the ones who had first encountered the stranger, the ones who could say. Jo-Leggett shrugged. Evidently the man *could* have been waiting on the road.

"You are covered with blood," Epion pointed out.

"By the gods, man! I was trying to help him. Of course I'm covered in blood. Look at your guard; he has blood on him, and I'll wager he hasn't even touched the body." Gabe-Leggett suddenly scrubbed his hand against the thigh of his trousers and managed to look green even in the torchlight.

It *was* possible. Possible that the fellow had stumbled on the body, tried to help what he took for an injured man, and become covered in blood in the process. The stranger's very calmness *might* be nothing more or less than a state of mental fugue, stemming from the shock of such a discovery. Epion looked at the man more closely. His cloak was of good quality, and he had rings on his hands, gold rings in each ear; a staff was thrust into the straps of his packhorse, but Epion saw no other weapons. Not a soldier, not a guard of any kind.

Still, the body was so carefully positioned. The cuts so precisely made. The man's story was not very likely.

"And you did not see the condition of the body?" Epion gestured toward it with an open hand.

The man's eyes followed the movement of Epion's hand. He grimaced, but he did not look away. "Not until the moon came up, no, I could not." The man rubbed his mouth with the back of his hand, then frowned. "As soon as I did, I . . ." he shrugged and looked away.

"You took his horse," Callos said.

"To save him wandering off while I went for help."

"You were heading in the wrong direction for help," Epion's aide pointed out.

"I'm a stranger here."

Epion held up his hand, and Callos fell silent. That was something else that did not ring true. However much a stranger the man was, how could he be on the road for Uraklios and not know that a city the size of the capital was just on the other side of the hills? You could smell the sea from here—or could if there weren't so much blood on the ground.

"My lord." A different tone in Jo-Leggett's voice this time. More triumph and considerably less nausea. He and Gabe-Leggett had been checking the stranger's packs, and the guard now held up a roll of soft leather. The kind commonly used to hold a set of knives. The torchlight flickered, but it was clear enough to show bloodstains as Leggett exposed three knives in their leather pockets.

"A strange way to help someone, or did you merely pick these up to keep them safe along with the horse?"

"What would be the point of my saying that? You'd only wonder why they had been left behind and who had wiped them off." Still the stranger was calm, in no way looking like a guilty man who had been caught out in a lie, but rather rueful, as if he were going to admit to something about which he was merely a little embarrassed. "I was benighted along the road there," he said, pointing to the direction in which he was heading when they came upon him. "I saw this man's fire and stopped to share it with him. When he learned I was a trader, he asked to see some of my wares. But when I took out some of my knives to show him, he went mad and attacked me. I did nothing more than defend myself, my lord."

"Not judging by what was done here. In self-defense you might have stuck the man, even slashed him a little, but what then? Why didn't you stop?"

"You can see I'm not a soldier, my lord. That staff's my real weapon. I sell knives, but I don't know their use—not in this way, not to fight with them. I panicked is the truth of it, sir. Panicked and struck out in a way I don't like to think of."

Epion might have believed him, so convincing was he, if it were not for the details he had already noticed: the positioning of the body and the style and nature of the cuts. And then there was something in the way the man hung his head . . . Epion was suddenly reminded of a troupe of players who had visited the Tarkin's court the year before.

"You'll have to do better than that, man," Epion said. "I'll have the real story, and we won't be leaving here until I've heard it."

Epion saw decision come into the man's face. A firmness that had up until now been lacking. He stood a little straighter, and his face became less like that of a servant and more like that of a man of means.

"It *was* self-defense," he said finally. "But not in any way that can be readily understood by the common person. I'll tell you, my lord, but not these." He indicated the guards with a tilt of his head. "What I have to tell you may be of great use to you."

"My lord," Callos began.

"Tush, man, I'm only asking that you go out of earshot. His lordship's in no danger from me. He's armed, for one thing, and for another, he has no darkness in him. That's a lucky thing, a very lucky thing. The same cannot be said for all your men, I'm afraid," the stranger said, turning back to Epion after he had waved his guards away. "That tall one—Callos? *He* has secrets."

"And the dead man, did he have secrets?"

"He did indeed." The man's eyes wandered back to the body. He stood, shoulders relaxed, with his hands clasped in front of him. A wrinkle formed between his eyebrows. "I followed him here, to see what the secret might be, and once I knew it, I could release the darkness," he said. "Let it out into the light of day before it killed him." Still facing the body, the stranger moved his eyes back to Epion. "And now you will arrest me. Put me to death." He tilted his head to one side. "Or will you?"

Epion Akarion smiled. "You have told me the truth, and you were right to do so." Epion waited, but the man did not move, except for the widening of his smile. The flickering torchlight gave movement to his eyes. "I cannot use a man who stops to help people," Epion continued. "Nor a man who defends himself so clumsily. But I *can* use a man who knows what to do about people with dark secrets. I can help such a man, and he can help me."

The stranger turned finally to look Epion fully in the face. "Know some people with dark secrets, do you?"

"I think so," Epion said. "And I'm sure you will agree with me."

One

THE BRIGHT AUTUMN sunshine made Parno Lionsmane blink at the view from the rooftop terrace of
the Mercenary House in Lesonika. The normally
dark, pine-covered hills to the north looked a brilliant
green, and the whitewashed walls of the town itself were
almost blinding. A young page ran across the courtyard below, drawing Parno's eyes from the view, but he had to
squint to make out any detail in the deep shadows.

From this vantage point it was obvious that Lesonika's
Mercenary House had once been a private home. The building fronted west on a small square, with its northern wall
running along a side street and the courtyard making up the
east end of the structure. Its southern wall was shared with
the building next door, the residence and workplace of Lesonika's foremost Mender.

Of course, once the Mercenaries had taken it over, the
building's defenses had been strengthened. The front door
was sealed with stone from the inside, as were the ground-
floor windows; the upper windows were barred, even those
on the third floor, and the staircase leading to the rooftop
terrace had been removed and replaced with a ladder—
easier to kick over should the need arise. The courtyard,
with its iron-reinforced gate, had been restructured into the
House's only entrance.

Everything planned. Everything familiar. Parno grinned.
That was one of the pleasurable things about the Merce-

nary Brotherhood. The Common Rule was the same everywhere you went.

"There," his Partner's rough silk voice murmured from behind him. Still smiling, Parno turned around.

Dhulyn Wolfshead lifted her hand from the vera tile she had just lined up on the small wooden table to the right of the trapdoor. Meant to hold arrows and spare crossbow bolts in time of trouble, it doubled nicely as a gaming table in time of quiet.

"Blood," said Dhulyn's opponent from the other side of the table. "You have the Caids' own luck." Kari Artagan pulled from her belt a pair of fine leather gloves, dyed a dark red with an intricate pattern of silver embroidery on the gauntlets, and dropped them on the array of tiles.

"Considering the Caids have long been dust, I think my luck is slightly better," Dhulyn said, drawing the left glove onto her own hand.

"These are brand new. I've only worn them once."

"I'll take the greatest care of them, my Brother." Dhulyn smiled. "You may wish to win them back."

"Oh, yes, when the sun rises in the east." Kari stood and stretched, moving her shoulders back and forth. She was much more finely dressed than either Parno or Dhulyn, in blood-red linen trousers and a bright white silk shirt with a silver-embroidered vest over it. An elaborately plumed hat sat on the floor next to her feet. "It's today, isn't it?" she said. "Your, ah, your meeting with the Senior Brother."

"No need to be so delicate," Parno said. "We're just waiting to be called in."

Kari Artagan shook her head. Her red and gold Mercenary badge, identical to Parno's, flashed in the sun. "And this one cool enough to beat me at Soldier's Sixes." She indicated Dhulyn with her thumb as she leaned over, scooped up her hat, and set it at an angle on her brow. Straightening, she rested her hand on the hilt of her sword. "I'm off to find some food," she announced. "Losing always makes me hungry." She touched her fingers to her forehead.

"You should lose more often, then," Dhulyn called out, as Kari lifted the trapdoor and let it fall with a bang. "Soon you'll be too scrawny to pull back your bow, let alone lift that sword."

Kari grinned. "In Battle," she said.

"Or in Death," both Parno and Dhulyn responded as their Brother stepped into the opening and dropped from view.

"You could have won some money, don't you think?" Parno said, taking Kari's empty seat across from Dhulyn. "Not that the gloves don't look well on you."

"Nervous, are you?"

"And you're not?"

Dhulyn frowned down at the tiles while she pulled off the glove she'd tried on and tucked it and its partner into the sash at her waist. She pursed her lips in a tuneless whistle, drumming her fingers on the edge of the table, as if she saw a pattern she did not like in the spread of the tiles. Finally she blew out a breath and swept the vera tiles back into their box.

"What do you think is taking them so long?" she asked, as she closed the box, latched it, and set it to one side.

Parno folded his arms across his chest. "Think of it this way," he said. "They've had months to go over the documents we left them. I'm certain the Senior Brother's decision is already made. We may as well relax, since there's nothing we can do about it now but wait to be told."

Dhulyn stared at him, her blood-red brows raised high over her stone-gray eyes. "I'm the Outlander," she said, the ghost of a smile on her scarred lips. "I'm the one who is popularly supposed to be naturally phlegmatic. What makes you so cool?" The corner of her mouth crimped, and Parno laughed out loud.

"There," he said, slapping his thighs. "I knew you weren't as calm as you looked." He leaned forward, elbows on the table, and extended his right hand toward her, waiting until Dhulyn took it in her own before speaking. "What's the worst that can happen?" he said, lowering his voice.

This was something they'd tossed back and forth many times during the weeks it had taken them to cross the Long Ocean and return to Lesonika, where they knew this hearing would be waiting for them. Dhulyn smiled her wolf's smile and gave the only answer either of them had.

"They can't separate us," she said. "Whatever they decide, that's beyond them." Still holding his hand, she leaned back in her chair. Mercenary Brothers Partnered for life, and not even the Brotherhood itself could dissolve the bond once it was formed.

"Since the worst can't happen," Dhulyn continued, "anything else they decide will be tolerable. Exile, for example, either to the lands across the Long Ocean—"

"Which would be manageable," Parno cut in.

"Or to the court of the Great King in the West, which would not."

"Caids take it, we've done nothing wrong." Parno exhaled sharply and released Dhulyn's hand.

"Then we have nothing to worry about."

They rose to their feet as light footsteps sounded in the hall below, and Jay Starfound stuck his head above the landing. Unlike Kari Artagan, Jay was a resident Brother in Lesonika, a dark-haired, oval-faced man with a sharp-pointed beard covering a scar at the corner of his mouth. The colors of the Mercenary badge tattooed on his temples and over his ears flashed a startling green and red in the sunlight.

"Brothers," he said, touching his fingertips to his forehead. "You're wanted." Nothing, neither his tone, his choice of address, nor his impassive face told them anything they wanted to know. Dhulyn tucked the box of vera tiles under her left arm and gestured to Parno to precede her.

Dhulyn Wolfshead had expected Jay Starfound to escort them to the ground floor hall, the largest room in the House, unaltered from its previous existence and still used for meals. Instead, he led them only as far down as the second floor, where they entered what had once been a private salon. The tiled floor was a warm golden color, and the walls still bore the murals of a forest scene, faded but rich in detail. A worktable had been set up between the two barred windows, and behind it, in a tall wooden chair with padded arms and back, sat the oldest Mercenary Brother Dhulyn had ever seen. His head had been shaved smooth, and his eyebrows were still dark and wiry, but the hair on his arms and the backs of his hands was gray. Those hands were gnarled, the knuckles swollen, and his face was heavily wrinkled, especially around the place where his right eye was missing.

Dhulyn blinked when she took in the faded blue and red of his Mercenary badge. She had never seen those colors before. The Senior Brother of Hellik raised his head as they entered and fixed them with his one pale blue eye.

"I am Gustof Ironhand, called the Boxer." Gustof's voice was unexpectedly light and musical. "I was Schooled by Jerzon Horsetooth." Which explained the old colors of his badge, Dhulyn thought, *and* why she'd never seen them before. "I have fought at Ishkanbar, at Beliza, and at Tolnek." As was customary, he cited only his last three battles. "I have come from Pyrusa to review your case, as I am the Senior Brother in Hellik."

And so he would be, Dhulyn thought, if he'd been Schooled by Jerzon. Jerzon Horsetooth had been dead for decades, his School dissolved. Gustof Ironhand could very well be the oldest Mercenary still alive. It was his age, Dhulyn imagined, and not his injury, that had led him to settle into a Mercenary House.

"For the record," Gustof gestured at Jay Starfound sitting to one side, pen and parchment at the ready. "Would you also formally identify yourselves?"

"I am Dhulyn Wolfshead." She was pleased that her voice sounded cool and relaxed. "Called the Scholar. I was Schooled by Dorian of the River, the Black Traveler, and have fought at the sea battle of Sadron, at Arcosa in Imrion, and for the Great King in the West at Bhexyllia. I fight with my Brother, Parno Lionsmane."

"I am Parno Lionsmane," her Partner said. His voice was deeper and firmer than that of Gustof Ironhand, but equally musical. "I'm called the Chanter. Schooled by Nerysa Warhammer of Tourin. I have fought with my Brother, Dhulyn Wolfshead, at Arcosa, Bhexyllia, and Limona—if that's to be judged a proper battle."

Gustof Ironhand's smile did nothing to settle Dhulyn's stomach. "That will be one of the things we rule on today."

Jay looked up. "You should note, my Brothers, that the ship of Dorian the Black Traveler is in harbor at the moment," he said.

"I doubt I will need to refer to him," Gustof said. "I have here the documents of your case. Some I understand you provided yourselves before you were . . . diverted by the Long Ocean Nomads. We had testimony at that time from

Captain Huelra of the *Catseye*, and the Nomads themselves have since provided witness—" here Gustof Ironhand tapped a rolled scroll to his left—"which supports your own explanation for the delay in these proceedings." He laced his fingers together and laid his clasped hands on the table before continuing. "To deal with the lesser business first, I rule that the delay was unavoidable and that the actions you took to save the lives of the *Catseye*'s crew were such as maintain the reputation of the Brotherhood."

Gustof turned a page over. "I note also that relations have been established with both the Nomad traders and the Mortaxa across the Long Ocean, who have asked that Mercenary Brothers be sent to them, as counselors." Gustof looked first at Parno, then at Dhulyn. "A return to the old ways, it seems."

"Yes, my Brother," Dhulyn said, as the Senior Brother seemed to be waiting for a response.

"Their request has been recorded and will be sent to all Mercenary Houses." Gustof paused, picking out a paper from among the ones laying flat in front of him, while Jay Starfound finished writing.

"As for the more important matter, we have here the request for outlawry from the then Queen of Tegrian, accusing you of the kidnap and murder of her son and heir, Lord Prince Edmir."

Dhulyn shifted her weight from one foot to the other, but didn't speak.

"This was followed by a document from the present Queen of Tegrian, withdrawing her mother's request." Gustof looked up. "You supplied this document yourselves, I understand?"

"Yes, my Brother," Dhulyn said. "You see it is written in her own hand and was sealed with the royal seal."

"Fortunate for you that the present Queen of Tegrian can write." The Senior Brother's tone was as dry as a sand lizard. "It appears that the late Queen was ill, and she was misinformed when she accused you," he continued. When Dhulyn and Parno remained silent, Gustof Ironhand's lips twitched. "The present Queen also assures us—for the ears of the Brotherhood only—that her brother is well and alive." Gustof leaned back in his chair, bringing his hands together, fingertip to fingertip. "That is something we would have had to check for ourselves, since, though she claims him to be well and alive, it is she and not her older brother sitting on the throne of Tegrian.

"Fortunately, while you were . . . *diverted* by the Nomads, a small caravan of traveling players arrived in Lesonika and gave further witness, and further proofs, to support the Queen of Tegrian's assertions." Now Gustof smiled outright and sat forward again, his elbows on the table. "In other words, the delay in presenting your case has helped to clarify it considerably."

Dhulyn glanced again at Parno, but his eyes were focused on the faded olive trees painted on the wall above Gustof Ironhand's head.

The older man spread his hands out on the table and looked at them, turning his head to get them both within the scope of his single eye. "I have reviewed your case," he said, his tone returning to strict formality, "and I accept the documents I have been given. I rule that there has been no breach of the Common Rule, nor does anyone outside of the Mercenary Brotherhood have legitimate grievance against you."

Dhulyn let out a sigh as muscles she hadn't known were tense, relaxed. Parno's shoulders dropped an almost imperceptible amount as he touched the fingers of his right hand to his forehead. Dhulyn repeated his gesture with her own right hand. Still, the old man had said "no one *outside* the Brotherhood."

"We thank you for your time and your attention to our dilemma, Gustof Ironhand," she said, her voice almost a whisper. "We are in your debt."

The old man returned their salute and leaned back once more in his chair, this time signaling them to sit as well. He waited until they had drawn up the backless chairs suited to Lesonika's warm climate and Jay Starfound had departed with his scrolls before speaking.

"My time and attention are indeed valuable," Gustof said. "I am gratified to hear you acknowledge as much. I have had to come twice from Pyrusa to attend to what you call your 'dilemma'—no direct fault of your own, I grant you," he added, lifting his palm toward them. "Nevertheless, this House and the Mercenary House in Pyrusa have undertaken actions on your behalf, and Brothers other than myself have been called upon as well. There is a manner in which you can repay these . . . favors if you will, to our Houses and to the Mercenary Brotherhood as a whole."

Long-winded type, Dhulyn thought. Substitute the word "fine" for "repayment," and you'd have it just about exactly right. Why not just out with it? As if she or Parno would refuse any request from a Mercenary Brother. This would only be some boring contract no one else wanted—private wall guards, perhaps, or a frontier outpost facing an amiable neighboring kingdom. The type of job, lasting only a few moons, that usually only junior Brothers who had yet to prove themselves in a real battle would take.

"We are Brothers," she said, as a way to acquiesce as well as a reminder. "And there would also be the matter of the stabling of our horses."

"You do well to remind me." Again, the faintest of smiles floated across Gustof's lips. "As you may have heard, the Princess of Arderon is to wed the Tarkin of Menoin. She has traveled with her own people as far as Lesonika, and as a neutral body we have been asked to provide her an escort by sea to the court of her betrothed. If you will undertake this task for us, we shall consider our expenditure of time repaid and the accounts balanced."

"Is it a large party?" Dhulyn did her best not to make a face. Menoin was an island, and they would have to travel by boat. After crossing the Long Ocean twice in the last three moons, she had been looking forward to getting back onto a horse.

Gustof shook his head. "The Arderons are notoriously plain in their style of living. The Princess has a kinswoman as her immediate attendant and witness, and two body servants. They take also four mares in foal from the royal stables as a wedding gift."

Dhulyn smiled back at him, careful not to let her small scar curl her lip back in a snarl. "Plain in their living style" indeed. An understatement if she had ever heard one. The Arderons considered themselves to be descendants of and kin to the Horse Nomads of the Blasonar Plain, and they affected the purity of living and conduct of their kinsfolk. Even the members of their Royal House were expected at the least to be instructed in arms and in the cleaning and care of their own horses.

"They are woman-ruled, are they not?" Dhulyn said. "I'm surprised they are willing to send a daughter away."

"This is a cousin of the present Tarkina, who has four female children of her own. There is little chance that Princess Cleona could inherit." The three Mercenary Brothers exchanged identical smiles; they all knew how easily a small chance became a certainty.

"Surely there are royal ladies of more note closer to Menoin than Arderon?" Parno asked. Though he rarely spoke of it, he had come from a High Noble House himself, and such speculation was in his blood.

"Certainly," Gustof said. "But there are ancient ties between the two, ties that the Tarkinate of Menoin seems most interested in reestablishing." He leaned forward. "There is something more regarding the lady of Arderon. Rumor has it that some years ago an application was made on her behalf, and later withdrawn, to Dorian the Black Traveler."

Parno cleared his throat. "The Princess wanted to become a Mercenary Brother and then changed her mind?"

"According to what Dorian tells me, she was turned away." Gustof looked aside, the fingers of his left hand tapping the arm of his chair. Dhulyn glanced at Parno, but he only lifted one shoulder.

What the older man said was likely. The histories told that at one time the Brotherhood was more numerous than it was now, but it took a particular kind of person to become a Mercenary Brother, and more than half of the applicants to the three existing Mercenary Schools were turned down. And since fewer than half of those who were accepted survived their Schooling, the numbers of the Brotherhood remained small. She studied Gustof's lined face. Was he old enough to have seen the numbers dwindling, even in his own lifetime?

As if he felt her speculative gaze on him, Gustof drew in a deep breath and sat straighter.

"A small party," he repeated. "And as the *Black Traveler* is in port, and it does not matter to Dorian what route he takes while he is Schooling, we have decided to allow the Arderons to use his ship for the Princess' journey to Menoin."

"And Dorian has agreed?" The words were out before

Dhulyn could stop them, her tone of frank disbelief bordering on discourtesy.

Evidently Gustof Ironhand thought so as well, for he only smiled again—his thin, old man's smile. "Perhaps you would do better to ask him yourself." *His* tone was so unmistakable that Dhulyn found herself on her feet, with Parno already turning toward the door.

"One question, Senior Brother, if I may," Dhulyn said.

"Certainly."

"The players, did they perform *The Soldier King*?" Dhulyn asked.

"They did indeed. In Battle, my Brothers," the old man said.

"Or in Death," they replied.

The Mercenary House was not large enough to have its own stable, but Dhulyn found that the public stable nearby had taken good care of their horses while they were on the other side of the Long Ocean.

"How old do you think Gustof Ironhand is?" Parno asked as he threw his saddle across Warhammer's back. The big gray gelding had pretended not to know him when they had first arrived, but a pretense it had clearly been, and the horse now nudged him companionably, snorting into his face.

"Sun and Moon only know," Dhulyn said. "I'd wager my second-best sword he's been a Mercenary Brother longer even than *you've* been alive." She tested Bloodbone's girth and turned to her saddlebags. "In fact, I'd wager he's been Senior Brother here in Hellik longer than that."

"Think he could still hold his own?"

Dhulyn stopped what she was doing and considered Parno's question seriously. "His hands moved well, though his knuckles are so swollen. He's had years to learn to compensate for the single eye. As for strength," she shrugged. "Technique beats strength almost every time. If his enemy was close enough, I'd say Gustof could still kill."

❧

DHULYN IS STANDING BEFORE A GRANITE WALL, THE BLOCKS FITTED SO CLOSELY THAT SHE HAS TO TOUCH THEM TO FEEL THE SEAMS. THE STONE IS SMOOTH AND COLD, CREATED BY THE HAND OF SOME MASTER CRAFTSMAN

OF THE CAIDS. HER FINGERTIPS PASS OVER SOME IRREGULARITY, AND DHU-
LYN STANDS TO ONE SIDE, ALLOWING SHADOWS TO FALL WHERE HER FINGERS
HAVE BEEN. A FACE STARES BACK AT HER FROM THE WALL, WIDE-BROWED,
POINTED OF CHIN, THE NOSE VERY LONG AND STRAIGHT, THE LIPS FULL
CURVES. THE EYES HAVE BEEN FINISHED WITH TINY CHIPS OF BLACK STONE,
SO THAT THE FACE DOES INDEED APPEAR TO BE STARING . . .

A THIN MAN WEARING A GOLD RING IN EACH EAR IS BENT OVER A CIRCLE
OF STONES, USING A SPARKER TO SET DRIED GRASS AND TWIGS ALIGHT. A
PILE OF BROKEN BRANCHES SITS TO ONE SIDE READY TO BE PLACED IN THE
FIRE. HIS LARGE HANDS HAVE LONG FLAT FINGERS. HIS STRAW-COLORED
HAIR IS COARSE AND THICK, CROPPED SHORT. DHULYN'S SHADOW FALLS
ACROSS HIM, AND HE LOOKS UP. "HERE," HE SAYS, STRAIGHTENING TO HIS
FEET AND REACHING TOWARD HER. "LET ME HELP YOU WITH THAT . . . "

A SHORT YOUNG WOMAN, ROUNDED AND WELL-DRESSED, LOCKS OF
DARK, CURLY HAIR ESCAPING FROM A SEVERE HEADDRESS, HANDS DEMURELY
CLASPED AT HER WAIST, LOOKS AROUND THE KITCHEN OF WHAT LOOKS LIKE
A MINOR HOUSE. THE WORKPLACE IS WELL-APPOINTED, WITH BOTH OPEN
HEARTH AND TILED OVENS, POTS, CROCKS, AND A WORKTABLE LARGE
ENOUGH TO ACCOMMODATE FOUR PEOPLE.

THE YOUNG WOMAN WALKS THROUGH THE ROOM, TOUCHING, ALMOST
CARESSING OBJECTS AS SHE PASSES THEM. SHE MAY BE SEEING THIS FOR THE
LAST TIME, DHULYN THINKS, OR ELSE SHE'S BUT NEWLY COME HERE AND IS
MARKING HER NEWLY ACQUIRED TERRITORY WITH THE TOUCH OF HER
HANDS. BUT THEN DHULYN SEES THAT THE BOWL THE WOMAN TOUCHES IS
CRACKED NOW, THE WOODEN LADLE SPLIT, THE CROCKS BREAKING AND
LEAKING THEIR CONTENTS ONTO THE FLOOR. FINALLY THE YOUNG WOMAN
COMES TO THE TABLE AND, SMILING, STANDS READY TO LOWER HER HANDS
TO ITS SURFACE . . .

A TALL, THIN MAN WITH CLOSE-CROPPED HAIR THE COLOR OF WHEAT
STRAW, EYES THE BLUE OF OLD ICE, DEEP ICE, SITS READING A BOUND BOOK
LARGER THAN ANY SHE HAS EVER SEEN. HIS CHEEKBONES SEEM CHISELED
FROM GRANITE, YET THERE IS HUMOR IN THE SET OF HIS LIPS AND LAUGHTER
IN THE FAINT LINES AROUND HIS EYES. DHULYN KNOWS SHE WOULD LIKE THE
MAN IF SHE MET HIM AND THAT THIS IS A VISION OF THE PAST, BOTH HER PAST
AND HIS, AND SHE WONDERS WHY SHE SEES IT AGAIN NOW.

THE MAN TRACES A LINE ON THE PAGE WITH THIS FINGER, HIS LIPS MOV-
ING AS HE CONFIRMS THE WORDS. HE NODS AND, STANDING, TAKES UP A
HIGHLY POLISHED TWO-HANDED SWORD. DHULYN OWNS ONE LIKE IT,
THOUGH SHE DOES NOT USE IT OFTEN. IT IS NOT THE SWORD OF A HORSE-
MAN. SHE CAN SEE NOW THAT HIS CLOTHES ARE BRIGHTLY COLORED AND FIT
HIM CLOSELY EXCEPT FOR THE SLEEVES, WHICH FALL FROM HIS SHOULDERS LIKE
INVERTED LILIES.

HE TURNS TOWARD A CIRCULAR MIRROR, AS TALL AS HE IS HIMSELF; IT DOES NOT REFLECT THE ROOM BUT SHOWS A NIGHT SKY FULL OF STARS. HIS LIPS MOVE, AND DHULYN KNOWS HE IS SAYING THE WORDS FROM THE BOOK. HE MAKES A MOVE LIKE ONE OF THE CRANE *SHORA* AND SLASHES DOWNWARD THROUGH THE MIRROR, AS IF SPLITTING IT IN HALF. BUT IT IS A WINDOW, NOT A MIRROR, AND IT IS THE SKY ITSELF AND NOT A REFLECTION THAT THE MAN SPLITS WITH HIS CHARMED SWORD; AND THROUGH THE OPENING COMES SPILLING LIKE FOG A GREEN-TINTED SHADOW, SHIVERING AND JERKY, AS THOUGH IT IS AFRAID . . .

ANOTHER FAIR-HAIRED MAN, THIS ONE YOUNGER, SHORTER, AND SQUARER THROUGH THE BODY. GUNDARON OF VALDOMAR SITS WHERE DHULYN HAS OFTEN SEEN HIM BEFORE, AT A TABLE, LOOKING DOWN INTO A FINDER'S BOWL. DHULYN KNOWS SHE'S SMILING NOW, HOPES THAT THIS IS NOT ALSO A VISION OF THE PAST. SHE WOULD LIKE TO SEE THE SCHOLAR AGAIN.

Parno watched Dhulyn out of the corner of his eye as they sat at breakfast on the aft deck the next morning. She'd experienced Visions during the night, but apart from one involving the Green Shadow, which they knew came from the past, not the future, there was nothing that required prompt sharing or action. Her Sight was more regular now, and if she could not always control what Vision came, and though they still came unbidden, they were not quite the unpredictable and useless things they had once been.

In fact, just lately, they had occasionally been greatly helpful, something neither he nor his Partner had ever hoped to see.

Dhulyn caught him looking at her and moved her head ever so slightly from side to side, though she smiled the faintest of smiles while she did it. With a nod just as minute, Parno did his best to put thoughts of Visions from his mind. They'd little enough time for speculation this morning. Their assignment had begun when the Arderon nobles came aboard the evening before, and now they were only waiting for the rowing tugs to come and pull the *Black Traveler* out of harbor. With the Princess of Arderon paying passage, Dorian of the River, Mercenary Schooler and called, like his ship, the Black Traveler, had no need to wait for the tide.

They both sat at the captain's table, Parno across from Dorian and Dhulyn on his right. Parno turned sideways in his seat with his back toward his Partner. His job was to keep his eye on the Princess Cleona, sitting three paces away with her cousin, being served breakfast by the two attendants they'd brought with them. Princess Cleona had declared her preference that her guards not stand over her while she ate, and since this was, after all, Dorian's ship, and there was no one on board that the Mercenary Schooler did not vouch for, Dhulyn had decided to let the Princess have her own way. This time.

Still, throughout the meal, as he was handed bread, cheese, figs, and cups of ganje, Parno kept one hand always free and close to a weapon, while his eyes were constantly shifting, checking the area immediately around the princess for anything that shouldn't be there—the wrong attendant, one of Dorian's sailors, even a seabird flying oddly. Dhulyn, he knew, was studying the larger field of danger, watching who was coming up the ladder from the main deck, who—if anyone—was in the rigging over their heads, and how close their duties brought them to the Princesses. Even here, where Dhulyn herself had been Schooled, they would take few chances.

The Princess of Arderon and her young cousin were dressed in a combination of traveling leathers and quilted silks, densely embroidered, and their short half boots were thick with beading. They both wore trousers, as befitted their Horse Nomad heritage. Their blouses had high collars and narrow sleeves, and their vests, worn open in the morning sun, would fasten with large buttons carved from oyster shell, a luxury and mark of wealth on the inland plains. Princess Cleona was the older and shorter of the two women, but both had the same golden hair and creamy skin, and their strong features marked them as close kin.

They were neither of them beautiful, Parno thought, but it would be hard to mistake them for anyone else, or to forget them, once seen.

"So why *did* you turn down the princess' application? She looks fierce enough to me." Parno kept his voice politely low. Without turning, he accepted with his right hand the refilled cup of ganje Dorian the Black gave him, and he leaned his elbow on the table.

Dorian laughed, handing a matching cup to Dhulyn. The Mercenary Schooler was a tall man, well over Parno's height, with skin so dark it seemed to have blue highlights. Though he had already been a Schooler for some years when he had rescued and begun training the eleven-year-old Dhulyn, Dorian seemed ageless, his face unlined and his straight black hair thick and showing no signs of gray. "Ferocity has very little to do with it, as you well know, my Lion. Nor was it, as some have suggested, her royal status. We have had many successful applicants from among Royal Houses over the years. No." His eyes grew more serious, though his mouth maintained its grin. "Cleona wished to join the Brotherhood because she was unhappy with her life, and that is insufficient reason to be accepted among us. We know that there are those who have a need to flee from their lives, but they must also be, in some fashion, running toward ours."

"Surely that old connection can't be all that lies behind this willingness to offer her escort to Menoin? With us to guard her, she could have taken any ship in port," Dhulyn said, her voice like rough silk.

"Ah, but the captain of any ship in port could not tell you what Gustof Ironhand, Senior Mercenary Brother of Hellik, needs you to know."

"Something he could not tell us himself, evidently."

"Something no one else knows—yet. Something that we hope no one else will ever need to know." They had all been speaking quietly out of courtesy for the nearness of the noble passengers, but Dorian now fell into the nightwatch voice, so quiet that very likely even the apprentices serving them would not hear a word.

Parno resisted the urge to turn and look at Dorian again. He would have given much to see the expression in the older man's eyes.

"Can you tell us now?" Dhulyn said. "We'll have to take turns sleeping during the day, if we're both to be on watch tonight."

Dorian took the last swig from his own cup and signaled to the apprentice hovering nearby, eyes round as coins. It was rare for youngsters like these to see, let alone to serve, seasoned Brothers like the Wolfshead and the Lionsmane. The youngster nodded and touched his forehead in response to Dorian's signal before scooping up the now empty jug of ganje and turning to go down the ladder to the main deck. Dorian leaned in.

"A little over a year ago the old Tarkin of Menoin sent to the Mercenary House in Pyrusa for two bodyguards."

Dhulyn Wolfshead leaned forward, putting her cup carefully down on the table. Parno sat up straighter, though he still did not take his eyes from the Arderon Princess. It was not unusual for a ruler, or even a High Noble House, to use Mercenary Brothers as personal guards if they could afford it. There were some who even preferred it, since the question of trust would never arise. Still, it seemed an ominous way for Dorian to begin.

"You say 'the old Tarkin,'" was all Dhulyn said aloud.

Dorian nodded. "The one who originally contracted for the marriage to our Princess."

"She seems a little older than the usual wife-to-be." Dhulyn glanced at her Partner.

Dorian smiled. "Indeed. But she is the Tarkina of Arderon's closest female kin—other than her own daughters—unmarried and of childbearing years. The two countries, Menoin and Arderon, were once most closely related, and this alliance is vital—some tricky point of political tradition depends upon it. Of course the alliance is still possible, still desirable, perhaps even more so, now that the old Tarkin is dead."

"Dead?" Dhulyn had no need to say anything more than that one word. Both her Partner and her Schooler understood what she was really asking. How did the old Tarkin die, when he had two Mercenary Brothers as bodyguards?

Dorian nodded, accepting a jug refilled with steaming hot ganje before motioning the youngster away. "A sudden illness—though definitely not poison. A Healer was sent for, but one could not arrive in time."

Again, nothing unusual there. Of all the Marked, Menders were most common, then Finders, and only Seers were rarer than Healers. Many Healers still followed the old custom of traveling a route prescribed by their Guild in order to provide the most service, though there were always rumors of Healers in Royal Houses, and Dhulyn knew from her own experience that the Great King in the West had one of his own.

"Word was sent to us that on being released from their contract by the death of the Tarkin, our Brothers had left Menoin, had in fact taken ship for Ishkanbar." Dorian poured fresh ganje into all their cups before continuing. "I know what you are thinking. Though I'd wager the two of you rarely send word to the nearest Mercenary House of your comings and goings."

"Not as often as we did when we were newly badged," Dhulyn said. "If we're near one of our own Houses, we'll stop, of course, even go a half day's ride or so out of our way. But send word? No, not usually. Still, as you suggest, it is not uncommon in newly badged Brothers."

"As one at least of these was." Dorian took a swallow of hot ganje and grimaced. "Kesman Firehawk, Schooled by Yoruk Silverheels, way to the west. But the other you may know, Delvik Bloodeye, called the Bull, Schooled by Nerysa Warhammer."

Parno shrugged without turning. "After my time, though I think I've heard the name."

"So, with an experienced Brother there, no alarm would have arisen—ordinarily—no special notice given to the fact that they have not been heard from since."

"Ordinarily?"

"Gustof Ironhand was the Senior Brother who sent these two to Menoin. He, now that the old Tarkin is gone, is the only one who knew that the contract had asked for two Brothers as bodyguards not for the old Tarkin but for the heir, the young man who is *now* Tarkin."

"With a specified term set?"

"No term."

"So their contract did not expire on the old man's death." The tone of Parno's voice, even nightwatch quiet, set chill fingers dancing up Dhulyn's spine. "They should still be in Menoin."

"And I'll wager my second-best sword that you've sent to Ishkanbar, and these Brothers never called into the Mercenary House there to announce their arrival," Dhulyn said. "Otherwise, we would not be having this conversation now."

"It is always a joy to find that one's students are still as sharp as two daggers, even all these years after leaving their School."

"So we're not being given a minor punishment by being sent to Menoin as the bodyguards of the Arderon Princess," Parno said. "That's merely our excuse for arriving there unasked for."

Dhulyn was nodding, her eyes fixed on Dorian's still smiling face. "We are being sent to find our missing Brothers."

Two

"WILL NO ONE but me say the word Pasillon out loud?" Parno said. It was the beginning of the early night watch, the first chance they'd had to speak alone since Dorian had told them of their real assignment.

"If our Brothers in Menoin have been somehow turned upon, as they were at Pasillon, then we will avenge them." Dhulyn's rough silk voice spoke for his ears only, though there was no one close enough to them to overhear.

Parno nodded, slowly, keeping his eyes on the shadowy movement of the waves. "The Visions you had last night, did they touch upon this?"

He felt Dhulyn shrug. "How can I be sure? A sandy-haired man offered help. A carving in a stone wall—oh, and I saw Gundaron of Valdomar, using the Finder's bowl. All of which could mean anything."

"Or nothing," Parno agreed. "I find myself in two minds about this assignment."

"Is that possible? I'd have said you had brains enough for one mind only—" Grinning, Dhulyn ducked the blow Parno aimed at her head. As she crouched under his swinging arm Parno reached out with his other hand and filched the knife Dhulyn always carried inside the back of her vest—only to find that she'd helped herself to his belt dagger as she went down. Silently laughing, he handed Dhulyn back her knife and accepted his dagger in return. Parno felt the soft pressure of her cool hand around his upper arm. He waited until they were once again leaning with their elbows braced against the port rail of the main deck, a few paces away from the door of the Princess' cabin, before continuing his thought.

"On the one hand, I would never knowingly wish for Pasillon to be repeated. For any Brother to be in such a position that revenge is the best we can hope for. But . . ." Parno shrugged. "If the alternative is to guard a woman on the way to her wedding . . ."

"Here I was thinking that after what we have been through in the last few moons, a quiet assignment would be very welcome," Dhulyn said.

Parno looked at his Partner, glad that the darkness covered the frown he felt forming between his eyebrows. This was the part of her that only he ever saw. The part that would just as soon lie under a shady tree with a book and a wineskin as ride into a battle. Not that she didn't do the latter very well indeed.

"We've just had a quiet sea voyage across the Long Ocean—that wasn't rest enough for you?"

Dhulyn was silent a long moment. "So much happened on the far side of the ocean." She laid her fingers on his wrist, as if she needed to touch him to speak of it. "I'm not sure that the few weeks we spent with the Nomads and the Crayx returning to Boravia has given us enough time to fully digest it."

Parno stroked the back of her hand with his own fingertips. "You haven't been worrying at this, have you? We were tested," he acknowledged. "Our Partnership, even our Brotherhood. We have come out of it stronger, as steel leaves the forge."

"And we have learned things about ourselves we did not previously know," Dhulyn said. "What does your Pod sense tell you? Can you feel any of the Crayx nearby?"

Parno closed his eyes and reached out with his inner sense in the way he'd been taught.

#Greeting# #Enjoyment#

He smiled. "They're just going through the Straits, planning to stop at Navra to pick up some jeresh."

"Not for Dar, I hope. She shouldn't be drinking until the babes come."

"No," Parno said, letting the link fade. "Just for trade."

"Still, in some things, we're left with more questions than answers," Dhulyn said.

"There's one answer we can always count on," he said, touching his fingers to his forehead. "In Battle."

"And in Death," she said, a smile in her voice.

Parno pushed himself upright. "Toss you for the post by the door," he said. "Maybe you used up all your luck winning Kari's gloves."

Dhulyn began her patrol on the starboard side of the deck, her bare feet soundless, one hand out for balance and the fingers of the other resting lightly on her sword hilt. As her eyes scanned for movements in the shadows, her mind returned to worry at the possibility that in Menoin they would find another Pasillon. This was not the first time she and Parno had brushed up against the legend. It was not uncommon, even now when their numbers were relatively few, for Mercenary Brothers to fight on opposite sides of a battle. In fact, to be killed by a Brother was widely considered the best way to die. More than thirty Mercenaries had been killed at the ancient battle of Pasillon when the victorious, maddened by their triumph, forgot that their contracts required them to spare any Mercenaries who had fought on the losing side. When they had seen what was happening, the Brothers from both sides united, holding off much greater numbers until, at nightfall, they could cover the escape of three of their own.

Those three had carried the word, and after that night, the leaders of the victorious army had learned exactly how costly their victory had been. Since that day, "Pasillon" had been a rallying cry for Mercenary Brothers everywhere and a reminder that the Brotherhood protected its own.

Dhulyn was on her third pass around the deck when the soft cry of a night bird made her pause and crouch into a patch of darkness formed by a sail locker. It didn't take her more than a breath or two to see the dark shadow where it paced along the port rail, slowing every now and again to edge around here a barrel of pitch, there a rack of boarding axes. Dhulyn leaned her head back, brought her hand up to her mouth, and returned the night bird's cry. The ship had changed not at all since her own Schooling, and Dhulyn already knew exactly where every crew member or apprentice aboard the *Black Traveler* should be, who had what assignment on this watch, what they looked and smelled like. This was someone else. According to Parno's signal, one of the Princesses, but which one?

Dhulyn took a deep breath, released it slowly and, sinking into the Stalking Cat *Shora*, began to follow. The hunting *Shora* heightened her senses, making her aware of the slightest noise, the smallest movements, including even the beating of her heart and the flow of her own blood through her muscles. Dhulyn's feet were noiseless on the smooth boards of the deck—and unlike her quarry, Dhulyn did not need to feel her way along, her eyes having long grown accustomed to the available light. When she was no more than an arm's length away, Dhulyn knew it was the younger woman, the Princess Alaria, that she followed. The woman's scent, a moderately-priced oil of morning lilies, was unmistakable; the Princess Cleona wore the much more expensive oil of orange blossom.

In a moment Dhulyn had matched her breathing and the beat of her heart to those of the younger woman. The young princess seemed agitated, but she did not head toward the rail, so she needed neither fresher air nor a place from which to vomit. Three more paces and it was clear that she was heading for the temporary enclosure amidships that housed the horses. For a moment Dhulyn wondered what could bring the young woman out to this place in the middle of the night, what girlish secret could be hidden in the packs and equipment stored with the horses in their stalls. Then she remembered that the Arderons were horse breeders, and she realized that Princess Alaria was likely taking it upon herself to check on what was, after all, the greater part of Princess Cleona's bride gift.

Alaria stumbled as she rounded the corner to the horse enclosure, and Dhulyn almost put out a hand to catch her by the elbow. Only the knowledge that finding someone so close to her would make the princess jump and squeal—something that was sure to frighten the horses—made Dhulyn hold back her hand. Instead, she waited until the younger woman had righted herself, entered the stabling enclosure, and shut the door behind her before following her into the warm, horse-scented darkness, this time making as much noise she could with the latches of the door.

Even so, Princess Alaria gasped and spun round to face her, dropping the unlit lamp she'd taken from its niche to the right of the door, and causing the nearest horse to toss its head and shy backward.

"So now, shhhhah shhhah," Dhulyn crooned, stepping around the princess to hold the horse's bridle, and stroke her hand down its long nose. The enclosure was a flimsy structure, meant as a temporary measure, and it wouldn't take much for these high-bred horses to kick it to pieces if they became excited enough.

"She should not let you touch her." The girl's tone was mixed, showing both her own awareness of their danger and surprised annoyance that Dhulyn was *not* being bitten or kicked to death.

"Horses like me," Dhulyn said. She released the animal with a final caress and stooped to retrieve the oil lamp. It was, as she'd expected, full of paste rather than oil and so had not spilled. She pulled her own sparker out of her belt and lit the wick.

"I do not require your assistance," Princess Alaria said, blinking in the light. "You may leave." Her voice was now tight with anger. She had been frightened, true, and that was enough to anger anyone of spirit, but Dhulyn wondered whether there was more to the younger woman's present emotion than that.

"Setting aside the fact that my own horses are stabled here and that therefore I have as much right to enter as yourself, I am a Mercenary Brother and your bodyguard, and you cannot tell me where I may go. Quite the contrary."

"You are not *my* bodyguard."

The relative darkness allowed Dhulyn to raise her eyebrows unnoticed. Was that the way the wind was blowing? Did the younger princess resent the older one's wedding? Had she hoped for something other, something better, than being another woman's companion?

"Our contract is to protect and deliver safely both yourself and your cousin." Dhulyn set the lamp into its niche. "For myself and my Partner Parno Lionsmane, there is no distinction between you."

"You are Dhulyn then, Dhulyn Wolfshead?" Some of the tightness had disappeared from Alaria's voice. It seemed curiosity was stronger than anger.

"I am, and it is pronounced 'Dillin.'"

"You are a Red Horseman." Blinking in the flickering light, Alaria gestured toward Dhulyn's hair, the color of old blood.

"I am a Mercenary Brother, Schooled on this very ship, as it happens. What I was before that is immaterial."

"But your family, your . . . your property."

Dhulyn shrugged, stepping past the princess to where her own horse, Bloodbone, was watching with interest. Dhulyn laid her forehead against the mare's neck for a moment before answering. "The Brotherhood is my family. We own no property in the sense you mean it."

Alaria had turned to the second of the four white horses that had come aboard with the Arderon party and placed her hand on its nose. "So then. No horse herds, no fields, no pastures. But you must own something."

The girl's back was rigid. Dhulyn hoped she wasn't conveying her emotional state to the horse. It would be a great shame if any of the mares miscarried.

"My weapons. My horse. My clothing. And of course, the most important item there is." Dhulyn waited until Princess Alaria turned toward her, eyes wide in question. "Myself."

"Yourself." Dhulyn had heard that tone before—envy. "You are free."

"Free to look for work every day, free to starve if I do not find it, free to be killed when my skill is no longer enough to keep me alive."

A rough gesture as Alaria turned back to the horses, combing imaginary tangles from a snow white mane with her fingers. "Oh, I know. I'm not a child, I know what being alone in the world would mean. But—" she twisted her head to face Dhulyn, careful to keep her hands steady in their stroking of the horse. "*You* would not give up that freedom to starve—not for land, nor wealth, nor children. Not even for your own horse herd."

"No," Dhulyn said, blinking at the younger woman's vehemence, and her own slight hesitation. "You are right, I would not. Nor would any of my Brothers. But the Brotherhood is not a life for everyone."

"No, I suppose not."

What, another Arderon princess running from home? Dhulyn looked the girl up and down, studying what she could make out in the flickering light of the small lamp. Younger than she first appeared, perhaps eighteen or nineteen, Alaria was almost as tall as Dhulyn herself, long-limbed and healthy, as befitted a member of a Royal House, no matter how minor. Her hair was a dark gold, though not as dark as Parno's, and was closely braided around her head like a helmet. There was not sufficient light for Dhulyn to see the color of Alaria's eyes, but they seemed light. She carried a long dagger sheathed at her belt as well as the more common knife, and she wore an archer's arm guard on her right wrist. *Left-handed*, Dhulyn noted automatically.

"Why are you here?" she said aloud. "Not here in the stable," she added. "Here on this boat?"

"I could not let Cleona come alone."

Dhulyn lifted her brows. That had the ring of simple truth. She followed her cousin from love . . . or was there more to it than that? Dhulyn reflected. The two women had shown themselves friends in the way they sat together, talked, even laughing more than once. Was there more? "I know it's unusual for a royal bride to bring an almost equally royal attendant with her," was all Dhulyn said aloud. "You must have chosen to come. Leaving your family, your property."

"*You* left *your* people, Horse people the same as mine."

Dhulyn clenched her teeth, inhaling slowly and silently through her nose. This is what her curiosity brought. "The Tribes of the Red Horsemen were broken," she said finally. "There is nothing left of them except myself."

For a moment the girl stood staring at her, shock making her face hard; then the lines of Alaria's mouth softened, and she took a deep breath.

"I've an older sister," she said. "And for all that we're cousins to the Tarkina, our House is a small one." She grimaced, glancing at Dhulyn from under her brows. "Do you know what is meant by a 'good marriage'?"

Dhulyn smiled her wolf's smile. She knew what such a thing would mean in woman-ruled Arderon. "Your marriage to some man who would bring wealth or property with him. Some rich woman's son." Dhulyn considered what she'd seen of Alaria's discontent. "And denied marriage to someone else? Someone poorer, but preferred?" That might be reason enough for the girl to follow her cousin to Menoin.

"Oh, no, *I'm* not in love with someone else. It was just—" Alaria stopped short, as if she suddenly realized what she had let slip. If *she* was not in love with another, *someone* clearly was. And who else was there but Cleona? Alaria had moved to the horse in the next stall. "Cleona is bringing these horses as her bride gift, each in foal to a different stallion, to reestablish herds on Menoin." Alaria looked up, her face suddenly animated. "Did you know our horses came from there, originally, in the time of the Caids? There may still be remnants of those ancient herds in the mountain valleys. Think of it—to rebuild the lost stables of Menoin. *That's* why I chose to come with Cleona."

"A decision all could accept." Dhulyn nodded. "And a worthy ambition." So the young woman was running *to* something, as well as running away. There was still an undercurrent of bitterness in Alaria's voice when the girl spoke of her mother and sister, but her tone had warmed when her subject was her cousin or the horses. The young princess had made the right choice, even if a part of her still looked back over her shoulder to her mother's House.

"That is quite a good mare you have," Alaria said finally. "May I ask where you got her?" A reasonable change of subject and a sign, as if Dhulyn needed one, that the time of confidences was over.

"Far to the west of here, in the lands of the Great King. She is somewhat larger than mares are here in Boravia, as you can see."

"You wear much armor?"

"Not much, no," Dhulyn admitted. "But enough that my mount must be strong enough to carry me. And she's battle-trained, you see, and must be prepared to fight as long as I do."

"She's not your first horse."

"And with luck, won't be my last."

"The other has been gelded. I suppose that was the man's idea?"

At this absurdity Dhulyn laughed outright, and she had the satisfaction of seeing another look of annoyance flash across the younger woman's face. "Believe me, Princess Alaria. It's no man's first notion to geld anything—rather the opposite, in fact." Now the look of annoyance deepened. "Stallions unwanted for breeding are frequently gelded, as you know, and especially if they are to be used as warhorses. And you may think what you like about most men, but only a fool undervalues my Partner."

Alaria shrugged, jerked her head in a parody of a nod, and walked out with only a muttered good night as farewell.

"Well," Dhulyn said to Bloodbone, "*that* could have gone easier." Still it was a typical reaction: first the confidence, then the embarrassment. Alaria would likely avoid her for the rest of the trip. Dhulyn doused the lamp, making sure it was out by spitting on her fingers and touching them to the wick, and set the little pot of oil paste back on its shelf beside the door. She crooned a good night to the horses and let herself out, keeping pace with Alaria, though well back, until the younger woman let herself into the cabin she shared with Princess Cleona. Dhulyn found Parno, standing relaxed in the shadowed corner made by the wall of the fore cabins and the portside ladder—the best spot for watching the fore-cabin door and all approaches to it—and touched his arm. He touched her shoulder and shifted to one side as Dhulyn settled in next to him, feeling the wood still warm where he had been.

"I found out what she's been so stiff about. Not much wanted or valued at home, it seems, and has come to be with the only person who *does* want or value her." *Sensible*, Dhulyn thought. And brave of the girl to face reality so squarely and act on it. But still. Hard to know that it was so easy for some to let her go.

"She told you?"

Dhulyn shook her head, relating the princess' story in a few words. "You'd have got more out of her, I know. She professes not to think much of men—what Arderon woman does? But she's of a High Noble House, practically royal, and that gives *you* more in common with her than I, whatever the Princess Alaria might think."

Dhulyn smiled her wolf's smile, her lip curling back from the scar that marred it. She had been a Mercenary Brother since Dorian had rescued her from the hold of a slaver's ship. House manners and pretty speeches did not come easily to her.

"I'm still surprised you asked her anything at all. It's not like you to be curious about a young woman's private life."

"The last time we let one of our charges keep something private, we were taken captive and almost killed." Even Dhulyn could hear the dryness in her tone. "I'll admit it's hard to see how these princesses could be involved in the disappearance of our two Brothers, but this marriage *was* contracted for before they vanished," Dhulyn said. "We cannot rule them out entirely, not just yet." She looked up at her Partner. "What of the other one? It seems she may be in need of sympathy and comfort, considering the role she's about to take on, especially if, as the young cousin implied, she leaves love behind her."

"What makes you suggest I was thinking of comforting her?"

Dhulyn looked at her Partner sideways, trying not to smile. "You're always thinking of comforting *someone*."

"That's because *you* never need any." Parno pressed his shoulder against hers, and Dhulyn answered his pressure with her own.

"You're all right then, being back here in your old School? I wonder how I would feel, to be back in the mountains with Nerysa." The tone was light, but Dhulyn felt the reality of Parno's concern under it.

"This was my home for many years, after I thought I would never have a home again," she said, knowing that Parno would understand. "But watching these youngsters, here where I used to be one," she shrugged. "It only makes me feel old."

"Old? You?" Parno spoke almost loudly enough for the man at the wheel to hear. "You'll never be old, my heart. Now me, I was *born* ancient."

⁓

"If it were not for the cover it gives you to enter Menoin without questions, I would tell the Princess Cleona to find another ship."

Parno took his eyes away from the apprentices practicing signals—some close together, others as far apart as the narrow-beamed ship would allow—and eyed Dorian with interest. The irritation present in the man's words was not noticeable in either tone or facial expression. At least, not that Parno could see. Dhulyn, of course, knew her Schooler much better, which was not to say that the man had no secrets. From what Dhulyn had told him, the first time Dorian had spoken to her, in the hold of the slave ship he'd rescued her from, it had been in her own language, the tongue of the Espadryni, known to the rest of the world as the Red Horsemen. Dorian had used that language only once more, on the day Dhulyn had passed from being a youngster apprentice to a Mercenary Brother. She had never asked her Schooler how he knew the language of a dead Tribe, and Dorian had never explained.

"Princess causing trouble, is she?" Parno said now. "Well, isn't 'passenger' another word for 'trouble'?"

"She is holding herself very stiff, very aloof, showing smiles only to the young cousin. Did I tell you Princess Cleona pretended at first not to know me?" Dorian said. He grinned at Parno, who couldn't help shaking his own head and smiling back. Who could possibly see Dorian the Black Traveler and not know him again? "But when she saw that I was content to let that be, in no hurry to claim an acquaintance, she deigned to recognize me and introduce me to her young cousin." He flicked his eyes toward where the two women were approaching with Dhulyn in close attendance behind them. "Watch how she calls me 'Captain' to make it less obvious that she is distancing herself from me in my capacity as Mercenary Schooler."

Parno hid his grin and came to his feet as the princesses approached.

"Captain, seeing all your pupils thus occupied puts me in mind that neither my cousin nor myself have had weapons practice in some days. May we have partners from among your students?"

Parno was not surprised when Dorian's smile stiffened. The man was a Mercenary Schooler, first and foremost. To carry passengers as a cover for a secret mission was one thing—to have them spar with his youngsters was another. Parno had counted eleven apprentices when he and Dhulyn had come aboard the day before. Three were young women—two obviously sisters—one a man almost Parno's own age, and of the seven younger men remaining, only two were not yet old enough to shave. The day before he had seen them drilling as a group—the Drunken Soldier *Shora*. From what Parno had seen, all eleven were more or less at the same stage of their Schooling—and therefore using white blades, not the dull, blackened practice swords.

"As your bodyguard, Princess Cleona, I must suggest that you do not spar with any of the apprentices."

The princess lifted her eyebrows and blinked. "I saw them yesterday when we came aboard. They appear skilled enough to me," she said in a tone that seemed to decide the matter. Her voice was rich and full, but Parno had yet to hear her speak with any real emotion. Was what Dhulyn suspected true? Had she left a love behind her, and did she show only her duty face to the world?

"They *are* just skilled enough to kill you," agreed Dorian. "But not quite skilled enough to avoid killing you. To be sure there are no accidents, you must have opponents much more experienced than these."

"And if we use staffs or wooden blades?"

"Princess, if you think you cannot be killed with a quarterstaff or a practice blade, then you are definitely not sparring with any of my apprentices."

"What about one of you bodyguards? Surely *you* must be sufficiently skilled." There. *There* was some emotion. Princess Alaria had the same rich voice as her cousin, but it was spoiled by an undertone of impatience.

Dhulyn caught Parno's eye over their heads. Parno was careful to keep his own face from registering anything. She raised her right eyebrow and shrugged. *Shall I do it?* she was asking. Parno blinked twice. *Go ahead.*

"I will spar at staffs with Princess Cleona," Dhulyn said.

"Excellent," the princess said. "And Alaria can fight the winner."

But the younger woman was shaking her head. "Anyone who can best you at the staff, Cousin, will have no difficulty besting me. Make mine an archery contest, and I'll agree." Now Parno thought he detected a little eagerness in Alaria's voice.

Dhulyn was already dressed for combat in her loose linen trousers and vest quilted with patches of brightly colored cloth, bits of fur, lace, and ribbons, but Princess Cleona had some preparation to make. She began by lifting off the headdress she wore against the sun, revealing her golden hair tightly braided and clubbed to the back of her neck. Next came the waist harness bearing her knife and belt pouch, then her jewelry, and finally the princess toed off her bright green half boots. In the absence of boat shoes, bare feet would give her the best purchase on the deck.

"Is there any part of the body you do not want bruised?" Dhulyn hefted the staff Dorian tossed to her and took her grip, right hand in the center, left hand halfway between that and the end of the staff.

For the first time Princess Cleona looked uncertain. If there had not been so many people already gathering to watch, Parno would have wagered the princess would have made some excuse to back out. But give the woman her due, she narrowed her eyes and took up her stance.

"Face, hands, shoulders," she said, with only the slightest tremor in her voice. "Everything else will be covered by the wedding garments."

Cleona knew her way around a quarterstaff, that much was obvious. It was a common enough weapon for nobles to be taught, even where it was not the custom for women to become soldiers. That was not the case in Arderon, if Parno remembered his tutor's lessons correctly. Two or three generations back there had been an uprising of the then predominantly male army, put down only with great difficulty—and help from the Mercenary Brotherhood—by the then Tarkina. None of that ruler's successors had made such a simple mistake again. Now more than half of all the soldiery in Arderon, including guard troops, was female.

Dhulyn and the Princess Cleona circled each other, looking for openings. The *Black Traveler* was moving smoothly, at least compared to what she and Parno had experienced on the Long Ocean, but it was obvious from the way Princess Cleona swayed and shifted her feet that she didn't have her sea legs quite yet.

Parno was beginning to regret that he hadn't opted to do this himself. There were two paths for Dhulyn to choose between. Deal with the princess quickly and cleanly—much harder to do when the object was to leave her uninjured and alive—or draw out the match to make the woman feel as though she was considered a worthy opponent. The latter was certainly the diplomatic pathway—but when it came to her Mercenary skills, Dhulyn was rarely diplomatic.

The princess struck first, a feint to the knee followed by a blow aimed at the head, which Dhulyn neatly parried with as small a movement as the staffs allowed. His Partner showed no excessive speed or knowledge, Parno noted as the bout progressed, matching herself carefully to the princess' abilities. Parno began to breathe more easily; it seemed Dhulyn would after all remember that she was a body-guard—and whose body she was guarding.

Another exchange of blows, much faster this time, and Princess Cleona's lips began to curve into a smile. Out of the corner of his eye Parno saw Dorian purse his lips and give his head a tiny shake, and he almost smiled himself, thoroughly understanding. The princess had forgotten where she was, and who she was fighting. That kind of confidence would lose her the match.

Dhulyn blocked a sudden jab to her ribs with the shod end of the staff and tapped the princess on the left side of her leg, just above the knee. Parno glanced at Dorian, but from the sparkle in the Schooler's eye, he'd caught it, all right. Had Dhulyn struck the knee itself with that much force, she would have broken it. As it was, she had badly bruised the muscle of the princess' thigh, and at any moment—there, the leg almost gave under her. Dhulyn stepped back, holding her staff across her body.

"I think you have pulled a muscle, Princess," she said, speaking slowly and with great clarity. "Further exercise may cause more serious damage."

Eyes wide, Princess Cleona looked from Dhulyn's staff to where her own hand had gone instinctively to her leg. She gave Dhulyn the minutest of nods. "Yes, you are right, thank you," she said. She handed her staff to one of her own servants and accepted Parno's hand to guide her to the nearest seat, a small bench that ran along under the ship's port rail.

"Will you rest, Dhulyn Wolfshead, or shall Alaria fetch her bow?"

"I can rest *while* the Princess Alaria fetches her bow and my Partner fetches mine."

"We shall have a simple target, first," Dorian suggested when Alaria returned carrying with her one of the shorter southern bows, useful for shooting from the back of a horse. The one Parno had fetched out of Dhulyn's large pack was much the same type, only made to be broken down into pieces for storage and traveling. Dhulyn nodded in satisfaction when she saw it.

"Perfect, my soul. The longbow would not have been an even match."

"There is no better bow than the horse bow of Arderon," Princess Alaria said.

"For mounted shooting, certainly," Dorian said. "But the longbow has its place as well. Mercenary Brothers are Schooled in five types of bow."

"Five? I know of only three types," Princess Cleona said from her seat by the rail.

"Nor will you learn of any others from me," Dorian said, softening his words with a bow.

"I am not counting crossbows," the princess said.

"Nor am I." Dorian smiled and turned to Dhulyn and the younger princess. "You know the target, my Brother," he said to Dhulyn. "Will you explain?"

Dhulyn looked up from the last metal fastening of her bow and stood. "Do you see where the forward mast has been painted white," she said to Princess Alaria and waited for the girl's nod. "We'll each have three shots at that. If we make all three," Dhulyn glanced sideways at Dorian, "things will become more interesting."

A tossed coin landed Ships and decided that Alaria would shoot first. Parno watched the girl carefully and saw that, like her older cousin, she had been well-trained. She knew enough to allow for windage, and she had evidently shot from horseback enough to accommodate herself to the swaying motion of the ship. She held the first shot too long—Parno thought at any moment to see her wrist tremble—but the arrow went smoothly into the white. Now that she had the range, the second and third shots went more quickly. All three were well-centered, and all struck within the space that could be covered by a large man's hand.

Alaria smiled as she stepped back, the first relaxed smile Parno had seen from her.

Dhulyn, face carefully impassive, stepped into position, slipped two arrows into the back of her belt and held the third in her right hand as she rolled her shoulders. At Dorian's nod she lifted her bow and took her first shot, reached behind her and took the second, reached once more and took the third. Her arrows appeared above Alaria's, in a precise vertical line, each three finger widths apart from the others.

Alaria looked from the target to Dhulyn and back again. "You did not say what grouping you wanted," she said. Parno wasn't sure he could hear a tremor in her voice, but she had stopped smiling.

"Yours are well grouped," Dhulyn said. "I think, Dorian, that there is no point in our using the single ring, since the princess can space her arrows so well. Let us go directly to the three rings."

Dorian signaled, and three of the apprentices who had gathered to watch, the older man and the two sisters, scrambled to obey. Between them they removed the used arrows and attached a short wand to the mast. From this wand they suspended three rings on braided thongs in such a way that they would line up behind each other. Each ring was about the size of the supper plates one would be given in an inn, perhaps as wide as a man could spread his fingers.

"We will have to shoot through them all and hit the mast," Dhulyn said to the princess.

Her eyes narrowed, Alaria studied the rings before nodding. Parno could almost read her thoughts. The rings were wider than the spacing of Alaria's three arrows; she felt she'd have no trouble with them.

"Are you ready?" Dorian asked. When he had collected nods from both Dhulyn and Alaria, he turned back to his waiting apprentices. "Start them swinging."

Alaria stood, openmouthed, looking from the swinging rings to Dorian and back again. Finally she closed her mouth, lips in a thin line. "It can't be done," she said. "It's not possible." She turned to Dhulyn. "You can't mean . . ." Princess Alaria fell silent at a gesture from her cousin.

The rings had already started to slow down, and Dhulyn signaled to the apprentices to start them up again. She stood apparently relaxed, the slightest of smiles on her face, but Parno knew she was chanting to herself, a meditating *Shora*. She would concentrate on the rings, not the mast. If the rings lined up, she would have the mast. Her face relaxed, nothing existed for her now but the ship, the rings, the wind. Parno closed his hands into fists. A murmur of a

voice from among the watching crew. A gesture from
Dorian and the crew member slunk away, shamefaced and
silent. Dhulyn showed no sign of having noticed it. She released the breath she was holding and let fly.

THUNK!

The rings no longer swung.

Three

ONCE AGAIN DORIAN of the River hired rowing boats, this time to tow the *Black Traveler* into the harbor at Uraklios, the capital of Menoin. The first boat that had come out to meet them, oars flashing in the late afternoon sun, had returned immediately to the pier, where even from the deck Parno could see that a runner had been sent scurrying through the crowds, carrying the news of the arrival of the Tarkin's bride. The runner must have been very fast, Parno thought. By the time they were close enough to distinguish the clothing and faces of the people on the docks, quite a crowd had gathered. Here in Menoin, five days' sail farther north than Lesonika, it was still summer, and the crowd showed it. There were bare arms, uncovered heads, and even some bare legs among the people waiting. Bells were ringing, and carefully timed clouds of black and white smoke were shooting into the air from somewhere on the palace grounds high on the escarpment.

Dhulyn had gone with the younger princess to see about the horses, while Parno waited outside the tiny cabin for Princess Cleona to put in an appearance. The older woman came out wearing a light cloak, pale blue, with the royal horse emblem prominently displayed, that flapped gaily in the wind that blew—warm but sharp—across the water.

"Is the Tarkin there to meet me?" she asked, joining Parno at the rail just as Dhulyn and Alaria came out of the horse enclosure.

"I see no purple banner," Parno said, squinting into the wind.

"There," Dhulyn pointed. "That looks like an honor guard, in black with purple sleeves." Dhulyn caught Parno's eye, and he blinked twice. "Those in blue, keeping back the crowd, they must be the city watch. And those to the left are Jaldeans," Dhulyn continued, "in the brown cloaks."

"Priests?" Princess Cleona raised her hand to shield her eyes against the angle of the sun.

"Of the Sleeping God," Parno said. "There'll be others, I imagine—look, there, in the green, priests of the horse gods. That would be the primary sect in Menoin."

"As it is in Arderon," the princess said, touching the horse crest on her cloak.

Parno glanced at Dhulyn, but she was still searching the pier with narrowed eyes. The horse gods would be the same ones that Dhulyn herself swore by, Sun, Moon, and Stars. With the lesser gods of Wind, Water, Earth, and Fire.

Cleona turned from the rail with an air of decision. "You and Parno Lionsmane will attend to the horses. Alaria and I will be escorted by our own attendants."

"Your pardon, Princess Cleona," Dhulyn said. "As bodyguards, Parno Lionsmane and I will attend you and the Princess Alaria. Your servants will bring your horses. Dorian," Dhulyn greeted the captain as he joined them. "You will have your people bring Warhammer and Bloodbone ashore after the royal horses have been disembarked?"

"Of course." The older man turned to the princesses. "It has been a great pleasure to have you aboard, Princess Cleona, Princess Alaria." He inclined his head to each in turn, touching his fingertips to his forehead. "May you have fair winds and warm days."

Cleona gave him a shallow bow in return but continued to look around her with a slight frown.

Dhulyn smiled her wolf's smile. "Lady, if you feel the Menoins will be expecting a larger party, I'm sure Captain Dorian will lend you some of his apprentices, but you can have no more impressive entourage than Mercenary Brothers."

For a moment it looked as if Princess Cleona might smile in return. "In Arderon we consider the horses of the royal lineage to be all the entourage we require," she said. "As for the size of my party, I am here to play my part in returning the Menoins to the traditions and practices they have allowed to fall away. They will come to understand my plain ways soon enough, Dhulyn Wolfshead. I will begin as I mean to go on."

Dhulyn caught Parno's eye. This must have been what Dorian had been speaking of, when he told them of the marriage. Old traditions reestablished. There seemed to be a spiritual as well as a political need for this marriage.

The harbor at Uraklios was deep enough that the *Black Traveler* could be towed directly to her docking place. The Royal Guard in their black tunics and purple sleeves kept the crowds well back, as Dorian's crew ran their widest gangplank down to the pier. To the left was a smaller group of four guards in green with only the left sleeve purple. They stood in a square around a litter chair swathed in curtains and veils. *I hope that's not for Cleona*, Parno thought. She wasn't the type to allow herself to be carried around in a chair. She'd sooner ride, even if the horses she'd brought *were* all pregnant. He signaled his readiness to his Partner.

Dhulyn Wolfshead went down the gangway first, her right arm swinging loose and her left wrist resting as if by accident on the hilt of her sword. She scanned the people around the open space, looking for any sign of trouble; no one in the crowd seemed anything but curious and excited. Buildings overlooking the area were set well back, she noted, nor were there any archers silhouetted atop their roofs. Even Mercenary Brothers would be hard pressed to make a successful arrow shot from any of them. Children were poking their heads around the legs of the City Guards, but even they seemed well under control. Several adults in the crowd had lifted children to their shoulders, so the youngsters could have a better view. Should Cleona turn out to be a popular consort, people would be boasting of their presence here today for years to come.

Dhulyn reached the end of the gangway and stood to one side, the signal that the princesses could disembark. Cleona had pushed her cloak back so that it hung in swinging folds from her shoulders. Under it she wore a deceptively simple dress, a straight gown of deep blue, split for riding, over gold trousers and knee boots. The overgown's sleeves were also slit from shoulder to wristband, revealing the rich gold and silver bracelets wound around Cleona's bare wrists and upper arms. Her hair had been pulled back and braided into a thick knot at the nape of her neck; shorter wisps were kept off her face with a jeweled headband very much like a crown. Alaria followed behind her in a similar, but more subdued, costume, her hair in a simple braid and her arms covered. Both women wore waist belts carrying long knives and daggers.

As Cleona stepped off the gangplank, at the very moment that her foot touched the ground, an enormous purple banner unfurled, snapping in the wind. It was the royal banner, Dhulyn realized, flown only in the presence of the Tarkin or his immediate family. The flag bearers had waited until Cleona was standing on Menoin soil before unfurling it.

Suddenly there were people kneeling in the crowds, some pulling down their neighbors who had remained standing. Voices called out to her from the crowd. "Stars bless you!" "Sun warm you, my Lady." Children began to cheer, and soon the adults had joined them.

Cleona looked around her, cheeks blushing, lower lip trembling, finally touching her hand to her lips and inclining her head to acknowledge her people's welcome.

One of the guards in green reached his hand into the litter chair, and out of the shadows beneath the canopy came a very old, very tiny woman. Grasping the guard's wrist, she pulled herself upright and accepted a black walking stick inlaid with silver filigree. She advanced, step by slow step, until she was close enough to Cleona to speak without raising her voice.

"I salute you, Princess of Arderon," she said, barely above a whisper. "I am Tahlia, House Listra, head and chief of the Council of Noble Houses. I am also the oldest female relative of the Tarkin Falcos Akarion, and in his name I welcome you to Menoin."

Very sharp, Parno thought as he watched the exchange of formalities between the two women. Very smart this Tarkin Falcos. Rather than coming himself, to send his ranking female relative, a House head in her own right, and chief of the council, to greet the royal daughter of a country where women had the exclusive rule—that was good thinking on his part or on the part of those who advised him.

Parno eyed the Royal Guard standing nearest to them.

Unlike the others, he wore a light metal helmet shaped to his head, with a short nose guard. When he noticed Parno watching him, his eyes widened, and he lifted his chin in acknowledgment. Parno gave the slightest of nods and shifted his attention back to the old woman.

"Mercenary Brothers," House Listra was saying. "If your contract is to bring the Ladies of Arderon to Menoin, you may consider your task completed. Here are guards enough of the Tarkin's own choosing." Those standing nearest wore a crest of black, blue, and purple sewn on the left shoulder. Those would be the elite of the Tarkin's personal Guard. *Some one of them knows what happened to our Brothers*, he thought.

"With respect, House Listra," Dhulyn said. "We must deliver our charges to the Tarkin himself."

"As you will," the old woman said. "The Mercenary Brotherhood is always welcome in Menoin."

Are we, Parno thought as he touched his forehead in acknowledgment of the old lady's welcome. *Then where are our missing Brothers?*

By the time they were mounted, Parno and Dhulyn on their own warhorses and the princesses on two beautiful bays provided for them by the Tarkin, more of the Palace Guard had arrived, along with additional squads of the City Watch, to control the increasing crowd. These guards formed an avenue that allowed passage to where the palace, a spread of ancient buildings in golden brown stone, stood high above the town on its rocky hill.

Parno looked around him with interest. Unlike his Partner, he was always happy to be in a new town. Uraklios, capital and principle city of the ancient island Tarkinate of Menoin was a prosperous trading center, visited by both coastal merchants of the Midland Sea and Long Ocean Traders, though the harbor was notably empty at the moment. To Parno's eye it presented a familiar aspect, white-washed buildings with tiled roofs, some with signs denoting shops and here and there a tavern. Houses, sometimes with balconies on the street, clearly built around central courtyards, cobbled and flagstone streets and alleyways narrow to make as much shade as possible, and growing steadily steeper as the Arderon party rode away from the water and up the hill to the palace.

There were Stewards and pages in plenty once they reached the main courtyard of the Tarkin's palace, but Cleona waited for Tahlia Listra to join them in the entrance doors. Waiting for them there was a woman of middle years, wearing the royal crest of black, blue, and purple on the left shoulder of her tunic and bearing at her waist a large ring of keys.

"My lady Princess," she said. "I am Berena Attin, your Steward of Keys. The Tarkin invites you to take refreshments informally with him prior to tomorrow's formal ceremony of welcome."

Cleona held out her hand, and Parno smiled. She had learned something about the customs of her new land, it seemed. Berena Attin blinked and took the offered hand.

"Is it the custom here, as I have read of, that the Steward of Keys cannot leave the House building of which she is Steward? So that you cannot even walk across the courtyard?"

"It is, my lady Princess," the Steward said, somewhat taken aback.

"And it pleases you?"

"It does." Berena Attin smiled, and after a few moments Cleona returned it.

"Very well," she said. "If my servants can be shown to the stables prepared for my horses, I would be pleased to attend the Tarkin now."

Tahlia Listra snorted. "Tell Falcos to be patient," she said. "I'm sure the princesses would rather see their rooms, rest, and unpack before seeing the Tarkin. This evening is soon enough."

"We rested well on the ship, thank you, Mother's Sister," Cleona said, using the formal term in Arderon for a ranking female relative. "And such a short ride cannot exhaust us. Until our chests arrive from the ship, we cannot unpack, and so we will meet with the Tarkin in the meantime."

"In that case, my dears, I will take myself away and leave you young people to it. I am an old woman now, and all this riding about in the heat of the day is quite enough for me." She smiled, revealing remarkably good teeth for the old woman she claimed to be. "Welcome to both of you," she reiterated, kissing first Cleona and then Alaria on the cheek. "Sun, Moon, and Stars bless you." And with that she was stumping away, leaning heavily on her cane and leaving her guards to catch up.

Parno glanced at Dhulyn and saw that she, too, was stifling a smile. Cleona *was* surely beginning as she meant to go on. Dhulyn signaled him with her left hand, and he edged closer to her.

"Interesting he wants to see her so soon. Is he anxious to be rid of us?" she said, barely parting her lips.

"Who's being paranoid?"

The right corner of her lips lifted in a smile, but Parno knew what she was thinking. Better cautious than cursing.

Berena Attin dispatched a page with a quick gesture before turning back to them. "You Mercenary Brothers will of course leave your weapons here at the gate."

Princess Alaria spoke up before either Dhulyn or Parno had a chance to reply.

"At the moment these Brothers form the Princess Cleona's personal guard. You would not ask your Tarkina's personal guard to disarm."

Parno saw Dhulyn shoot the younger princess a sharp look out of the corner of her eye, and he relaxed, knowing that neither of them need say anything.

Though her lips were pressed tight, the Steward of Keys gave a bow of acknowledgment, and she led them through the grand entrance hall. Dhulyn stepped quickly to take up position behind her, in front of the princesses, and Parno fell in behind them, neither surprised nor alarmed when six of the Tarkin's own Guard formed a guard square around all of them. They could have passed as escorts, to someone less experienced, but Parno knew precautionary measures when he saw them. They might be allowed to carry weapons into the presence of the Tarkin, but they wouldn't go unguarded, and unwatched. The Steward of Walls, though he had made no personal appearance as yet, had trained his men well to take no foolish chances.

The room they were led to was clearly the Tarkin of Menoin's private audience chamber. The floor was a pleasing pattern of russet tiles offset with small squares of brilliant blue and purple, and the walls were covered with mosaics depicting vines and flowering shrubs growing around and out of sharply rendered urns and stylized lattice. A man, his back very erect, his dark hair curling over the collar of his tunic, stood with his back to the room, looking out of the left-hand window. Between him and the door was a grouping of four chairs of time-darkened wood, very likely from the pine trees that covered the hills surrounding Uraklios. They were simple in design, unadorned and backless; three were distinguished by their cushioned seats. The chairs were spaced evenly around a low table whose tiled top was obscured with plates of food, gold-rimmed cups, and two fine-necked pitchers of liquid.

A younger man, who had seen his birth moon perhaps twenty-three times, was straightening up from the table as they entered. He seemed to have been arranging the plates of food, but he was clearly not a servant. He had the same dark, almost black hair as the older man who was now turning from the window, the same warm olive skin, but his eyes were a startling blue in a face so beautiful he might have been the joy of any acting troupe—if there had been any emotion showing.

"My lord," the Steward of Keys said. "Here are the ladies of Arderon."

Cleona looked from one man to the other, and Dhulyn held her breath, wondering if it was part of her job to prevent the princess from making a social mistake. But she need not have worried. Alaria touched her cousin on the elbow and passed some signal Dhulyn could not see. The older princess focused her attention on the younger man. Her upper lip stiffened for just a moment before her diplomatic mask reformed.

Dhulyn almost laughed. She'd seen exactly that look on the faces of noblemen in the country of the Great King, where women were valued only for their beauty—and their fertility. Was it possible that in Arderon handsome men were thought to be as shallow and frivolous as the beauties in the Great King's court?

And was it possible that Princess Cleona was now re-evaluating her upcoming marriage with that thought in mind?

"Tarkin Falcos Akarion," she said, with a slight inclination of her head. "I am the Princess Cleona of Arderon, and this is my cousin, the Princess Alaria."

"You are most welcome, Lady," he said, giving her a bow the exact measure of her own. "Allow me to present my father's brother, Epion Akarion." He glanced at Dhulyn and Parno, looked back at Cleona, and waited, his perfect features a sculpted mask.

Dhulyn smiled her wolf's smile. The uncle stepped up closer, narrowing his eyes. Epion Akarion was not as much older than his nephew as Dhulyn had thought. The family resemblance was clear, but there was something agreeably plain about the uncle's face.

"Falcos Tarkin," Dhulyn said. "I am Dhulyn Wolfshead, the Scholar, Schooled by Dorian of the River. This is my Partner, Parno Lionsmane, called the Chanter, Schooled by Nerysa Warhammer."

Rather to her surprise, the young Tarkin smiled back at her, and his chill beauty warmed. "I have heard of you," he said. His smile faded abruptly. "That is, your Brothers who were here before spoke of you. You are well known in your Brotherhood, it seems."

"Those of us who live long enough do gather a certain measure of fame to ourselves, this is true," Dhulyn said. "We come here as guards to the Princesses of Arderon," she continued. "They are in our charge until they reach your hands."

"And as they have now reached the Tarkin's hands?" This was the uncle, his voice a rounder, deeper baritone than that of his nephew.

Dhulyn turned to Princess Cleona and bowed. "Lady, our contract is fulfilled. We consider ourselves discharged."

"Is any payment required?" The uncle again. Dhulyn was beginning not to like the man. She glanced at Parno and saw that her Partner was stifling a smile.

"Our contract is with the Mercenary House in Lesonika," she said, directing her words to the Tarkin. "We are content."

Princess Cleona pulled off one of her gold and silver armlets. "Thank you for your company on this part of our journey, Dhulyn Wolfshead, and for the lesson in the staff."

"We come to serve, Princess." Dhulyn accepted the bracelet, tucking it into a fold in her sword sash.

"And I also thank you for your service to the Tarkina of Menoin," the Tarkin said. He put his hand to the dagger in his belt, and Dhulyn was afraid she would be forced to accept some jeweled monstrosity; but the weapon he handed her, except for a small horse inlaid in gold on the hilt, was plain and serviceable. And excellently balanced, she noted as she took it into her hand.

"If you would care to partake of refreshment before you depart, the Steward of Walls is ready to entertain you in the guard's hall."

"Thank you, Lord Tarkin." Dhulyn and Parno both touched their foreheads.

"And that sends us on our way with bells ringing," Parno muttered in the nightwatch voice as they exited.

They were just passing between the guards at the door when they heard voices coming from the antechamber.

"I understood there are Mercenary Brothers meeting with the Tarkin."

"That's not quite right, Scholar, they—"

Dhulyn walked faster, stepping through the door before the guard had it fully open. She knew that voice, the words clipped but the tone not unpleasant. Did this explain her Vision?

"Wolfshead." The young man moving toward her with his arms outstretched was thinner than she remembered him, but his blue Scholar's tunic and brown leggings were crisp and freshly laundered. Something in her face must have warned him, for Gundaron glanced at Parno as he let his arms fall. Parno, laughing, advanced on the youngster, clapping him on the shoulders.

"Gun. By the Caids, man, what's a Scholar from Valdomar doing here in Menoin?"

"And the little Dove, is she with you?" Dhulyn approached closer, keeping an eye on the guards who were watching them.

"The Library of Valdomar sent us. We have rooms at the Horse and Rider, off the main square." He looked from one to the other with a grin wide enough to split his face. "I heard there were Mercenary Brothers with the Arderons, but I never dreamed it would be you."

Dhulyn, smiling herself, turned to the guard nearest them. "Thank the Steward of Walls for his offer of hospitality, but as you can see, we have found friends of our own."

"We will accompany you to the gate," the man said.

"Of course." She turned back to Parno and Gun. "We're not keeping you from business here in the palace?"

"No, I came expressly to speak with you." Gun's grin faltered a moment. "Well, the Mercenary Brothers anyway." Dhulyn touched him on the shoulder to show she understood. Whatever had brought Gun looking for Mercenary Brothers, he had no wish to share it with the Tarkin's Guard.

It was not until they had retrieved their horses and were leading them through the relative privacy of the streets outside the palace that Dhulyn felt they could speak more freely.

"Is it your Mark we're not to speak of?"

Gun waved this away. "It's not that I'm hiding it, not anymore. It's just that I'm here as a Scholar, and I've learned since we were last together that if people know I'm a Finder, I don't get any Scholar's work done. The Library at Valdomar gives me many freedoms and privileges—thanks in part to you two—but they still expect me to produce work for them."

Dhulyn nodded. That made sense. Prejudice against the Marked had been on the rise a few years before, but the failure and eventual dying out of the New Believers—a sect of the Jaldeans—had put an end to that. People were unlikely to take against those who could Mend, or Find, or Heal, and if there were no longer many Seers to be found, well, people were well used to that.

Not that there weren't always a few, Dhulyn knew, who were afraid of the uncanny and even the uncommon. Still, Gundaron was right. If people knew he was a Finder, they'd be coming to him for service all the time. In fact, now that she knew he was here, she felt more confident of finding their missing Brothers.

"But you knew you would Find Mercenary Brothers at the Palace?" she asked. "You merely did not know who it would be."

Gun turned down a steeper street, little more than an alley, that led seaward, toward the main market square. "If I'd thought to try Finding *you*, I might have known. But it was just Brothers I was looking for, the nearest ones."

They turned the corner into a slightly wider street, and Gun led them under an arched gateway into what was clearly the stable yard of an inn. Dhulyn looked around; the cobbles were even, with clean straw spread to prevent shod hooves from slipping. The water in the troughs looked fresh, and the young boy currying a fat pony off to one side clearly knew what he was about. He looked up at the noise they made entering, and he laid his brushes down neatly where the pony could not get at them before running forward to accept Bloodbone's reins from Dhulyn's hand.

"We'll want rooms as well," Parno said.

"I'll speak to my father," the boy said, apparently unable to tear his eyes away from their Mercenary badges until Parno's horse Warhammer nudged him in the back. Then the boy bobbed his head, took up both sets of reins, and led the horses away.

"Back door's faster for our rooms," Gun said over his shoulder as he gestured them forward. "Unless you want to speak to the innkeeper first."

"The boy will speak to his father, and I assume if you can afford to stay here, so can we." Dhulyn tapped the armlet she'd tucked into her sash.

The door from the stable yard opened into a short hallway, with stairs leading upward on the right, three doors on the left—one of which Dhulyn's nose told her was the kitchen—and an opening at the far end that led directly to the common room at the front of the inn. Dhulyn caught Parno's eye as they prepared to follow Gun up the stairs. When she'd first met him, Gun had been Scholar in a High Noble House in Imrion for some months and had grown plump and out of shape with good feeding and little exercise. Now, from the way he ran without effort up the stairs, it appeared that he had returned to the good practices of his Scholars' Library.

"Hold back a bit, my heart," Parno said from behind her. "Give him a chance to tell Mar we're coming."

"And Mar a chance to pick up their dirty clothes off the floor?" Dhulyn stopped to let Parno catch up.

"Or draw up the bedcovers," he agreed.

They didn't need to see which room Gun had gone into; by the time they had reached the head of the stairs, Mar was out and running toward them. There were no strangers present, but Dhulyn still hesitated before opening her arms and accepting the younger woman's hug.

"There now, my Dove," she said, patting Mar's shaking shoulders. "You'd think we were returning from the dead." She caught Parno's eye over Mar's head and winked.

"You can't fool me, Wolfshead," the younger woman said as she stepped back. "You're just as glad to see me as I am to see you. Both of you," she added as she turned to receive Parno's kiss. "I know that Mercenary Brothers aren't supposed to have family outside of the Brotherhood, but I still think of you both as my kin."

Mar-eMar Tenebro alluded to the fact that they were actually kin, she and Parno. But more significantly, Parno thought, Mar, Dhulyn, and Gun shared something that Parno did not. All three were Marked. Though come to think of it, of the three, only Gun's Mark worked well and reliably. Without the assistance of other Seers, Dhulyn's Sight was erratic and almost impossible to direct, while Mar's Mark was gone now, burned from her by the awakening of the Sleeping God.

"Where now?" he asked. "This seems a public spot for a reunion. Your rooms or the common room downstairs?"

"The common room can wait, I think," Gun said. "For the moment I'd rather have the privacy of our own rooms."

The Scholar hadn't misspoken; he and Mar actually had rooms, a miniature suite comprised of a sitting room with a single window on the stable yard and a tiny bedroom, with just the bed, hooks for clothing, and a narrow cupboard.

"There was only the one table when we came," Mar was saying, as she pulled the room's two chairs around for her guests. "But the innkeeper helped us throw together this worktable when we told him what we needed." Two sawhorses had been set up along the wall under the window, and what was obviously an old door had been placed on it as a tabletop. Stacked neatly and clearly arranged in some order were bound books, scrolls, pens, drawing chalks and charcoal, inks in three colors, and clean, unused parchments and sheets of paper.

"We might be more private in a public room," Dhulyn pointed out, her hand on the back of the chair Mar had offered her, "where we can easily see who is close to us."

Gun raised his eyebrows. "Are you trying to tell me you couldn't tell whether there was someone close enough to hear us, even through these walls? It may be a long time since we last met, but not so long that I'd forget what Mercenaries can do." He looked from one to the other. "Well?

Is there anyone in the rooms around us? Anyone in the stable yard close enough to hear?"

Dhulyn signaled to him, and Parno shut his eyes, the better to concentrate on the Hunter's *Shora*. No one in the hallway on this side of the stairs, no one in the room next to them. He went into the bedroom, where, he noticed, the bed was tidy. No one in the room on the far side. He came back into the sitting room and went to the window. The innkeeper's son had finished brushing his pony and was nowhere to be seen.

"It would be fairly simple to climb up this wall," Parno remarked.

"Oh, certainly," Gun agreed. "For a Mercenary Brother. I don't think we need to worry about anyone else."

"Come now." Dhulyn sat down. "What is it you have to tell us that we must be so careful no one overhears? Evidently not merely what brings you to Uraklios?"

The two looked at each other, and when some signal had passed, Mar spoke.

"No, though I will have to tell you something of that, to explain how we learned what . . . what's troubling us now." She placed her hands on the edge of the makeshift table and hoisted herself up. Gun leaned on the table next to her, and she put her hand on his shoulder.

Parno looked at Dhulyn and lifted his right eyebrow. She blinked twice. There was no one outside of the Brotherhood itself—no land-based people in any case, he amended, that he and Dhulyn would trust more than Gundaron of Valdomar and Mar-eMar Tenebro. And he would have thought that they felt the same. What, then, was making them so hesitant to speak?

"We first came almost seven moons ago," Mar began. Perhaps, after all, she had only been ordering her thoughts. "There's no Library here in Menoin," she said, referring to the strongholds of the Scholars. "But there are Scholars, and one of them came across a reference in one of the ancient books belonging to the Tarkinate that seemed to indicate that the Caid ruins just north of Uraklios, on the other side of those hills," she gestured out the window, "were once a major city. Valdomar petitioned for the right to investigate and, if possible, excavate the site."

"The elders at Valdomar have been sending me on this

type of investigation," Gun said. "Ever since I revealed my Mark, they've found it useful." He grimaced. "No pun intended."

"So I take it you Found this Caid city?" Dhulyn said.

"Here, let me show you." Gun unrolled a map and laid it out on the table, which it covered like a cloth. "Here, you see? That's the pass through the hills. Here's the site of the old city." He looked up. "At one time it was probably the main city, and the ancient equivalent of Uraklios was merely its harbor."

"What's this," Parno said, laying his finger on an odd design on the map. "It looks like a maze."

Gun nodded. "A part of one, certainly, though we can't tell what it was supposed to defend. It's just to the west of the Caid ruins and may even overlap them somewhat, it's hard to say." He fell into silent contemplation of the map.

"Gun." Dhulyn's rough silk voice was gentle. "Just tell us."

He looked at her, lips pressed together, the corners of his mouth turned down. "It was here," he said, laying his ink-stained finger on a spot very close to the design he'd labeled the labyrinth. "It was here that we found the body."

Dhulyn frowned, her blood-red brows drawn into a vee. "A shepherd?" she suggested.

Gun and Mar both shook their heads. "How much have you heard about the death of the old Tarkin, Falcos' father?"

"The old Tarkin? It was *his* body you found?" Parno gave a silent whistle. "We'd been told a sudden illness, nothing out of the ordinary."

"Well, I've never heard of the kind of sudden illness that can cut a man into pieces and leave strange marks carved into his skin."

"You sure it was the Tarkin?" Dhulyn said.

"They pretended it wasn't, and we pretended to believe them," Mar said. "What else could we do? But it's not as though we didn't recognize the body. We'd seen Tarkin Petrion several times by that point. And besides . . ." Mar swallowed.

"Besides," Gun said, "we could recognize what was left of the clothing. It was later that day the Tarkin's illness was announced, and two days later his death."

Dhulyn leaned back in her chair. She braided the fingers

of her right hand in the sign against ill luck. She looked from Gun to Mar and back again before glancing at Parno. He shrugged one shoulder.

"There's more," she said. "Isn't there? Even if the Tarkin was murdered—however gruesomely—and his people covered it up, that in itself would not send you looking for Mercenary Brothers." Parno could hear the unspoken question that tightened his Partner's voice. Where were the Brothers *they* had come looking for?

"Tell us," Dhulyn said.

"This was not the first." Gun cleared his throat and said it again. "This was not the first body found mutilated. If even half of what I have heard is true, there have been at least seven."

Four

CLEONA OF ARDERON sat sideways in the wide window seat of the salon. *Her* salon. Large, and overly furnished for Cleona's taste with prettily embroidered stools and tiny tables, it was the public room of the Tarkina of Menoin's apartments. There was a smaller, more intimate sitting room within, where Cleona could expect to begin her day privately, with only her maids and attendants.

And perhaps her husband.

"Well, he's certainly pretty enough," she said aloud.

Alaria appeared at the door of one of the inner rooms. "Ah, but has he been trained in the arts to please a woman?" Her solemn face dissolved into a grin, and Cleona felt herself relax.

"I thank the gods for whatever impulse possessed you to come with me," she said to the younger woman. "I just had a sudden image of what I would be feeling right now if it were Lavanis standing in that doorway instead of you."

Alaria immediately raised her brows, made her eyes as round as possible, and hitched up her shoulders. She minced her way between the furniture in such as way that Cleona was already laughing by the time Alaria reached her.

"That is so perfectly Lavanis," she said, hand against her side. "Except that all the while you should have been lecturing me on politics and chiding me for not having studied the histories of Menoin since the time of the Caids."

"And all the while implying," Alaria said in a nasal voice, "that *she* would have made a better choice than you."

Cleona felt her smile freeze and was sorry, as the light suddenly left Alaria's face. They both knew that Cleona had tried very hard to arrange that it *should* be someone else who came. But the Tarkina's own daughters were not of an age for the marriage as it was originally planned, with the late Tarkin of Menoin, Falcos Akarion's father. And when the circumstances changed, well, they had changed too late to make any difference to Cleona. Alaria was one of the few who had known that Cleona had been about to ask their Tarkina for permission to marry when the representatives of Menoin had arrived, asking for their ancient rights and throwing all her hopes and plans into the wind.

"Alaria, why did *you* come?" Cleona waited patiently as her cousin came the rest of the way across the room and lowered herself onto the closest of the backless stools scattered through the room.

"What was there for me at home?" Alaria said at last. Her tone was matter-of-fact and practical, but Cleona remembered the child she'd found weeping in the Tarkina's garden not so many years before. "I'm the younger daughter of a small House, after all," she pointed out. "Not quite close enough to the Royal House for any real advantage and too close to allow me to enter the Guard or choose some other profession. The best I could hope for was marriage into a daughterless family, and even there, my mother and the Tarkina would have had the last say, not me." Alaria shook her head. "You know perfectly well I could have ended up an unpaid assistant in my mother's—and then my sister's—stables. Tolerated by my nieces and nephews. The landless aunt."

"A frightening prospect indeed." She smiled as she said it, but Cleona was very aware of how accurate Alaria's words were. "And so you preferred exile here in Menoin?"

"Yes." Alaria spoke simply, with her usual directness. "Though hardly exile, from my point of view. When I was little, when we did come to court, you were the only one of the cousins who became my friend, who didn't laugh at my country clothes or—worse—look right through me as someone of no importance, unworthy of notice." She was leaning forward, her elbows on her knees, staring into the middle of the room

"You? Small chance, my dear." Cleona spoke brusquely,

though again, she knew what Alaria said was true. She might easily have been in Alaria's stirrups herself, had she not been an only child and therefore the one to inherit. "You had only to get near a horse to prove your worth to anyone. Your mother was a fool to let the order of birth constrain her."

"Luckily, as it turned out, since it's meant I could come with you." Alaria looked at Cleona with her head tilted to one side. "After all, I'll be in charge of the new line of horses here. And seriously, I had only to imagine what my life would have been like without you at court to begin packing for the journey to Menoin."

Cleona fell silent, turning the unfamiliar rings on her fingers.

"So tell me," Alaria said now, "what do you *really* think of Falcos Akarion?"

Cleona smiled again. "We can hope that he's been given training as a Tarkin," she said. "And that he's as useful as he is ornamental. Though that might be hard to accomplish."

"Well, there's always the uncle."

"The uncle does not rule," Cleona pointed out. "He's the late Tarkin's younger half brother, from a second wife. Though I imagine he makes an excellent first adviser. He is too plain to succeed with his looks alone."

"Uncle to the Tarkin would be a good match, I imagine," Alaria said, her chin in her hand, though Cleona knew the girl well enough to know when she was jesting. "Even if he *is* quite plain."

"Shall I ask my uncle-to-be if he is wed? Perhaps you should have him?" Alaria answered Cleona's grin, but their smiles faded sooner than their light words suggested.

Cleona made up her mind, now was the time. "Alaria. There are things I must tell you, things I was charged to keep to myself until we arrived here." Cleona bit the inside of her lip. "About why this marriage is so important."

"I knew there had to be something to make you change your . . ." Alaria had begun in triumph, but her voice faltered as she neared the delicate subject of the plans Cleona had changed. "To make you decide as you did," she amended.

"How much do you know of the history between our two peoples?"

Alaria frowned. "Now *you're* sounding like Lavanis," she said, her brows drawn down in a vee. "I know our horse herds are said to have come from Menoin, from here, but long ago, perhaps in the time of the Caids."

"Not quite so far back as that, I think. The histories tell us that here in Menoin there was once a dispute about the crown between a brother and sister, twins."

"Even so, as I understand it, the one who was born first would inherit." Alaria got to her feet, poured out two glasses of watered wine from a pitcher on a nearby table, and returned, handing one to Cleona.

Cleona took a sip, cleared her throat and continued. "True. But there were those among the High Noble Houses who supported the old ways and insisted that, as it had been the mother who was Tarkina, the daughter should inherit."

Alaria paused with her glass halfway to her lips. "And naturally the Houses lined up, each behind their chosen candidate. I can see where this will end," she said, looking sideways at Cleona. "But how did they avoid civil war?"

"There is an ancient ritual of the Caids, called Walking the Path of the Sun, that usually settles such matters for the Menoins. In this case, however, both brother and sister passed the test." Cleona leaned on the arm of her chair as she considered the thought that had just struck her. "It was as if Mother Sun were telling them to resolve the issue themselves."

"What did they do?"

"Well, silly as it sounds, they finally decided to lay the problem in another god's lap. They drew lots, the winner to stay and become ruler of Menoin, the loser to go and establish a separate Tarkinate in lands Menoin owned to the south."

"And the sister drew Ships." Alaria was looking out into the middle distance, as if she were seeing the toss of the coin, the sunlight flashing on it as it fell, spinning.

"I don't know if they tossed a coin," Cleona said, "but you are right, the sister lost. You have heard of her, if not of this part of her story. She was Ardera, our first Tarkina, the mother of our country. Half the Royal Stables she took with her, and many of the Houses that had supported her went with her also, or at least their younger daughters and sons."

Alaria shrugged. "And so? We've prospered, have we not, each in our own way?"

"At first, yes. Despite the dispute, there was love between the siblings, and each swore they would send a child to the other, to marry the heir, and that there would be an exchange in every generation, so their lines would mingle and rule in both lands."

Now Alaria was nodding, her tongue tapping her upper lip. "When was the oath broken?"

"Before your time and mine," Cleona said, pleased that her cousin was so quick to understand. "During the reign of Auselios Tarkin, more than seven generations ago. The details are lost, so whether it was that Auselios had only the one child, or there was no one else close enough to the royal line to send, or whether he had another match in mind I cannot say, but Arderon sent a princess for his son and received no one in return."

"So they broke their oaths?"

"They did, and at first all seemed well. Then their horse herds began to dwindle, until there are, as you know, only a few left with perhaps some wild ones in the hills to the north. The harvests have been worsening for generations." She paused to give weight to her next words. "Last year a blight affected the olive groves."

"And Menoin is famous for its olive oil," Alaria said. "It's shipped everywhere, even across the Long Ocean."

"You may not have realized it, but there were no ships of the Long Ocean Traders in port today, nor have there been this season."

"Sun, Moon, and Stars! *That's* why you are here! And why you agreed to come. Why it had to be *you* and no other. You are the Tarkina's only unmarried first cousin." Alaria sobered. "And is that also why the people here in Uraklios were so happy to see you arrive?"

"I've always known you were quick," Cleona said, patting her younger cousin on the knee. "The late Tarkin, Falcos Akarion's father, went himself to petition the Seer's Shrine in Delmar, and it was the Seer who told him that he was cursed, he and his land, for breaking the ancient vow. And so this marriage was arranged." Cleona got up and refilled her glass. She held up the pitcher of wine, but Alaria shook her head.

"But why did we agree? We didn't break the oath, we've prospered all along."

"Ah, but if we now refuse, we would be the oath breakers. We had to agree. What?"

Alaria was shaking her head. "But in order for the oath to be kept, it would have had to be your child who inherited the throne, not Falcos."

"Correct," Cleona said. "Falcos would have been sent to Arderon, as consort for Moranna, the Tarkina's firstborn. Now my first child with Falcos will inherit, and we will send the next available son to Arderon."

"And if you don't conceive fast enough? Moranna is already eight."

"Then we will send Epion Akarion. He is the closest kin to Falcos, barring Tahlia House Listra." Cleona shrugged. "He will be old for her, but it is his blood that is important, not his companionship."

Alaria scrubbed at her face. "Well, better you than me, that is all I can say. To bring Menoin back to the old ways, to attract again the favor of the gods," she shook her head. "It goes without saying that I will help you in any way I can, and not just in the stables." Alaria reached out her hand.

Cleona took her cousin's offered hand, leaned forward and kissed her on the forehead. She drained her glass and stood, pressing her hands into the small of her back. "Ah, I am stiff with so much sitting." She went to the window. "Our little ride from the harbor has given me the taste for exercise, and the moon will rise early tonight."

"When does Falcos Tarkin expect you?"

Cleona turned back into the room. "Oh, we're excused for this evening," she said, "since he's greeted us already. It will make a better show, according to the Lord Epion, if we meet tomorrow in public as if for the first time."

"And you're going out riding? How would that show?" But Alaria was smiling and already on her feet.

"It was he who put me in the mind for it," Cleona said. "He spoke of the good riding country just there, in those hills we can see—can you imagine, when I said I might go, he actually suggested that it would be best for me to wait until he or the Tarkin could accompany me."

Alaria laughed. "He doesn't know you, does he? Very well, let's begin as you mean us to go on. Let them know what you expect in terms of your personal freedoms. Where shall we ride?"

Cleona hesitated. She knew that Alaria had to be at least as eager as she was herself to get on the back of a horse, but somehow, that did not match with the her own ideas. This would be her first ride here, and she'd seen herself alone, with nothing between her and her new land.

"Would you mind *very* much if I go alone?"

Alaria laughed, shaking her head and putting up her hands palms out. "Since you aren't yet Tarkina, I can tell you that I am just as tired of looking at your face as you must be of looking at mine."

Cleona smiled, relieved.

"Besides." Alaria stood up and straightened her chair. "I'm sure you won't be alone. I'll wager one of those guards stationed at the door will feel it necessary to go with you."

Cleona drew down her brows as she also stood. "No wager. That is an irritation I will have to learn to put up with." She met her cousin's eye. "I've agreed to be Tarkina here," she said. "And always having an escort is the price for that."

Alaria came suddenly closer and put her arms gently around Cleona. "Not the only price, cousin."

Cleona slipped her arms around Alaria for a moment and patted her cousin on the back.

Cleona was pleased to see that they knew enough to give her the same horse that had carried her up from the ship. It was a sturdy animal, and it showed signs of being as intelligent as it was beautiful. Alaria should learn who'd had the breeding of it. Cleona had expected interference or questions, but no one, neither the guard Essio, who rode a respectful half a horse length behind her nor the staff in the stables, had seemed to think it at all unusual for their Tarkina-to-be to ask for a horse just as the sun was setting. In fact, one of the stable girls had even asked the guard if a basket was coming from the kitchen. Moonlight rides were apparently commonplace here.

Cleona was as content with that thought as she was with the ready service of the Tarkin's household. Someone had a good hand on it, whether it was the pretty boy himself, or his uncle, or—as seemed more likely—the female Steward of Keys.

It took only minutes for them to pass through the small double gate of the stable precincts and directly out of the palace grounds. Though the temperature was warmer than she was used to for this time of year, it really was late summer, and the moon would rise, fat and red and clear, while the sun was still in the sky. She could ride as long as she liked and still have moonlight for her return journey.

With discreet indications, mere polite gestures of his hand, Essio the guard soon had them on a smooth wide road, much of it natural stone and the rest hard packed by the passage of many feet. Not a main road, Cleona thought, but clearly a well-traveled one. They skirted the city, the outer wall of Uraklios to their left, and were soon out in the open country, passing through olive groves. Cleona touched her heels to her mount and smiled when the horse trotted up with no signs of reluctance or discomfort. After half a span or so, however, she let the horse slow down and pick its own pace, mindful that, however smooth the road might appear, it was new to her, and the lighting was not the best for a gallop.

The guard stayed a respectful half-length behind her, close enough to give her ready aid but far enough away that she could feel herself private. Cleona had often seen her cousin the Tarkina of Arderon escorted thus, and it struck her, as if for the first time, that she, too, would be Tarkina. This, all that she saw around her, would be her country now, her responsibility.

"Where does this road lead, Essio?" She might as well begin learning as much as she could.

"Ah, well, it's hunting ground this way, mostly, my lady, once we've passed the olives." Essio narrowed the gap between them but still kept back of Cleona's elbow. "Deer, boar, and the like. Though there're goat herds as well, in season."

"This fine roadway for hunting alone?" A much richer land than Arderon, failed harvests or no.

"Well now, well, no, my lady, not as such." Essio put his hand to his mouth and coughed. *New to noble service*, Cleona thought. No harm in that. "The ruins lie this way, my lady. And the Path of the Sun. Caids' ruins the Scholars say."

"An old place of the Caids?" A piece of roadway said to be an artifact of the Caids ran straight through Arderon, and Cleona had heard of other, larger remnants of the Ancients, but to have one so close . . . "A holy place?"

"That's what's said, my lady. And they say too that there's Scholars looking there now for artifacts. All I know for certain is the Tarkina—beg pardon, I meant the late Tarkina, Falcos Tarkin's mother, had a favorite spot where she liked to come and sit in the afternoon with her ladies, and the road was kept up for her pleasure."

"And now mine," Cleona said.

The road took several more leisurely turns, and Cleona could well see what a nice ride it would make for the Menoin version of court ladies. They had not gone much farther when Essio sat up even straighter in his saddle and, with a muttered "your pardon," rode ahead of her toward what appeared to be a small fire burning just a few paces off to the left of the road. Cleona spurred her own horse forward until she was half a length behind Essio, in effect reversing their previous positions. Let the man know that an Arderon princess did not hide behind, any more than his Tarkin would.

The man at the fire could not fail to both see and hear them coming, and he stood as they approached, putting himself just on the far side of the fire, where the light from the flames would strike his features. Paradoxically, as they walked their horses nearer the fire, the night seemed for the first time to be growing truly dark, as if the flames stole their light from what little remained in the sky.

"Well met, well met," the man was calling out. "Are you benighted? Can I offer you any assistance?" His accent was strange—at least, stranger than the Menoin accents Cleona had been listening to all day.

"You can explain your presence here so close to the road," Essio responded. But though his words were stern, Cleona noted that Essio's tone was relaxed, and indeed, the set of his shoulders, so martial a moment before, had rounded again.

The man gave a warm chuckle, as if he knew why Essio was taking these precautions and was already looking ahead to the moment when they would all laugh about it. "I'm a trader, sir—and lady—as you can see from my packs." True, there were two well-stuffed packs sitting back away from the fire, where Cleona had not noticed them at first. "Unarmed," the man continued, "except for the knife you see at my belt. But with provisions enough to offer you both supper if you are hungry and a cup of fine Imrion wine, if you thirst."

Cleona relaxed even further. This was like the beginning of one of those tales of adventure that her cousin the Tarkina was so fond of. A moonlit ride, a chance-met stranger who would unfold a secret of mystery and honor that would set the heroine on her path.

"I would love a cup of wine," she said.

"The hour is already late, my lady, and you have much to do tomorrow." Essio spoke as one who gave necessary information, not as someone who had the right to tell her what to do. But somehow, though she knew the guard was right and she should even now be heading back, there was something in the smile of the trader that made Cleona swing her leg over her mount's back and step down, in the Arderon fashion, to the ground.

"My lady?" the trader was saying. "Tomorrow? But you are not—you can't be—" The man looked more closely at Cleona's clothing and then to Essio as if to read on the guard's face the answer to his unspoken question.

"The Lady of Arderon?" He had been faintly smiling all along, but the smile that now passed over the trader's face was at once humbler and yet more proud than it had been a moment before. And somehow genuine, as if before he had only been going through the motions of courtesy required of all honest folk on the road, but now those feelings of hospitality and friendship were real, and came from the heart.

"I would be honored beyond measure if the Lady of Arderon—the Tarkina of Menoin I should say—would take a cup of my wine. What a story for my wife! For our children!" As the man scurried over to the farther of his two packs, Cleona caught Essio's eye. The guard grinned, shrugged, and dismounted, joining her on the ground.

"We won't be long," she promised him. "A cup of wine for the man to tell his children of, and then we'll be on our way."

Alaria went early down to the Tarkin's stables. The sun was not yet up, and the night's chill clung to the air, but even so people were there before her. It was strange to see so many women and girls among the lower servants, but, she supposed, there were just as many men and boys. It was one thing to be told that here in Menoin she would find the division of labor more equally distributed between the sexes; it was quite another to see it with her own eyes. She could only hope she'd get used to it.

"You'd be the lady companion to the new Tarkina?"

It was the sharpness of the voice that startled her, but Alaria managed not to jump. This was the tone and, when she turned to view the man, the stance of authority. A man in charge of the horse stables. Something else she would need to get used to. Alaria cleared her throat and drew herself up; as Cleona would say, she might as well begin as she meant to go on and make her position clear right from the start.

"Only in a manner of speaking," she said. "I'm Alaria of Arderon. The Princess Cleona is my first cousin, once removed, and I am here to have the care of the horses she has brought as her bride gift. To see to their breeding and to manage the new herd."

"Then you're welcome, lass—I mean, my lady, very welcome." Alaria drew back a little, blinking, as the man grasped her hand and moved it up and down as though it were the handle of a pump. "I'm Delos Egoyin. If I spoke a bit sharp, it was only that I wondered where your grooms were. I looked after your four beauties myself this morning, but I wouldn't have time every day, you see."

"There are no grooms," Alaria began. She hesitated when she realized she was explaining herself to what was essentially a servant—and a male servant at that—but then she remembered what her mother had always told her. Courtesy costs nothing and purchases goodwill. "Only myself, and the queens were fine when I looked in on them before sleeping."

"Queens? Is that what you call your mares in Arderon? Well, I'm not surprised. Here they are." Alaria followed the man through a door much wider than she was used to into the stable building proper. The first section of the interior was brighter than she expected, with oil-paste lamps standing before well-placed rounds of highly polished metal. Beyond this lighted area, however, the barns were dark and empty, large enough that their voices echoed. *Of course*, Alaria thought with a shiver. Cleona had said the royal herd was dying out.

"You'll see I've moved them into the large front stall, as they'll be wanted this afternoon for the ceremony."

The sides of the stall were higher than Alaria was used to, but there was a step that enabled her to look over the top. Four long white faces turned to look at her. The stall was clean, each mare had been brushed already, and fresh hay and water had been placed in the feeders.

"They are beautiful," Delos said. "I've only ever once seen their match, and that was when I went with a caravan to the west as a lad. It's a pleasure even to touch them."

Alaria smiled, unable to resist the warmth in the man's voice. "This is Star Blaze," she said, stroking the first long nose that presented itself. She pointed to the others in turn. "Moonlight, Sea Foam, and Sunflower. They represent the best of our Tarkina's stable." She looked at Delos Egoyin out of the corner of her eye. "I thought you might be afraid I was here to displace you."

"Not a bit of it," he said, almost laughing. "There've been Egoyins in the Tarkin's stables, parent and child, seven generations. It was my aunt before me, and it'll be my son after me, since my daughter's gone into the Tarkin's Guard."

"Parent and child," he'd said. Not "mother and daughter," as they would have said in Arderon, nor "father and son," as she had expected. Very curious. But he was still speaking.

"No, the way I see it, my lady, is that you're in charge of the new blood, the management of the new line of Menoin horses—that's your plan, isn't it? To restore the line?"

Alaria found herself warming to what was so obviously a kindred spirit. "Exactly," she said. "My grandmother used to tell me that horses from Menoin were once the most valuable in Boravia, and even in the west, in the lands of the Great King. But it was generations ago . . ."

"Not quite in the times of the Caids, but some people think it's that far back, indeed." Delos scrubbed at his hands, dislodging a bit of straw.

"And are there still wild horses in the hinterlands that might be descendants of those ancient lines?"

Delos rubbed his chin. "That's your thinking, is it? There

are some wild herds out there, that's certain. But whether they'd be of any use—well, there's no time for that now, more's the pity. You've things to do today to get ready for the ceremony. Come down here when it's time, and I'll have the queens ready." He grinned and winked at her. "And I'll pick out a couple of likely assistants for you to have a look at in the next few days. You'll have your hands full trying to do everything yourself, especially once the foals come."

But having her hands full was exactly what Alaria wanted, she thought as she walked back across the stable yard to the doorway that would lead her back to the central portion of the palace. She didn't come to Menoin just to stand behind her cousin at court events. Alaria nodded at the pleasant-faced young guard who fell into step behind her. The young woman wore the Tarkin's crest of black, blue, and purple on her shoulder and had been waiting outside Alaria's door this morning. She wondered . . .

"Are you Delos Egoyin's daughter, by any chance," she asked.

The woman grinned, revealing a gap between her front teeth. "I am," she said. "Julen's my name. I traded another guard all my desserts for two moons to get your assignment, Lady. When we heard there were horses coming, I knew my dad would want me looking after you."

Alaria smiled, noting the sidelong glances of the servants and pages they were passing. She strode forward with confidence until she suddenly found herself in an unfamiliar hall. Alaria looked around, momentarily disoriented. She'd never thought of Arderon as a small country, but there seemed to be more corridors and turnings in Falcos' palace alone than there were streets and alleyways in the whole of Arderon's capital.

"If you wanted to return to your rooms, Lady Alaria, you should have turned left at the last corridor." Julen stepped to one side and gestured in the direction they'd just come.

"Yes, thank you." A little flustered, Alaria retraced her steps, recognized the staircase she'd been looking for, and ran up to the second landing. Julen, she was pleased to note, had no trouble keeping up with her. The young guard rejoined her counterpart as Alaria threw open the doors to the large suite of rooms that were the Tarkina's and crossed to the door of the private sitting room. She frowned when she saw that Cleona's bedroom door was still closed. Alaria had not heard Cleona return from her ride, but given the thickness of the walls, she hadn't expected to. Just how late had her cousin been? Surely Cleona wouldn't pick this day of all days to start lying in.

Grinning, Alaria flung open her cousin's door, but the derisive comment she had been ready to make died on her lips. The bedchamber was empty, the bed made. Alaria crossed to the door of the dressing room. The elaborate dress that Cleona was to wear for this afternoon's ceremony was hanging on a long pole against the wall farthest from the door. And there, arranged in the order in which it would be put on, was Cleona's wedding jewelry, her hair combs, and the high-soled sandals with their delicate gold-painted straps. The wedding dress itself was still in its box, though the box was open.

"Don't be silly," Alaria told herself, trying to ignore the pounding of her heart. "Cleona's here, she's just in the privy or . . ." Telling herself to stay calm, Alaria searched through every corner of the suite, finally startling two girls who were bringing hot water into the bathing room. Alaria hesitated. She'd look like a fool if Cleona was only out admiring the gardens. She swallowed. Better to look like a fool than to let some danger pass by unremarked.

"Have you seen the Princess Cleona?" she asked the two maids.

"No, Lady." The girl set down her container of water and looked at her companion, who shook her head without speaking.

Alaria ran for the main door. Julen spun around, her hand going to her weapon when she saw Alaria's face.

"The Princess Cleona," she said. "I can't find her, she's not in the rooms."

Julen turned to her fellow guard. The man raised his eyebrows. "Who did you relieve?" she asked him.

"No one," he said. "I didn't expect to, the rota wasn't changed until this morning."

But Julen was shaking her head. "Essio should have been with the princess. I'm sure I heard him say he had the duty."

Alaria looked from one stiff face to the other. "Take me to the Tarkin," she said. "Now."

Alaria paced up and down in the Tarkin's morning room, twisting her hands, not seeing the ganje and pastries that sat on their silver plates on the table near the window. She was an idiot. She should have asked for the guard commander—the Steward of Walls as the position was called here—not the Tarkin himself. Precious time was being lost.

The outer door opened, and a slim man with a dark beard walked in.

"Princess Alaria," he said, holding out his hand to be shaken. "I am Dav-Ingahm, your Steward of Walls."

She shivered as she took his hand and shook it. Nothing to worry about. Just because the Steward was a man, it didn't make him any less competent. She was in Menoin now. Men had been ruling here since the time of the Caids, and things functioned.

"I've started a search of the palace grounds," Dav-Ingahm said. "If we have no luck we'll widen into the city."

"How . . . ?"

"Julen Egoyin sent me word as soon as she delivered you here," he said. "Even if it turns out the Tarkina is only in the garden or gone for a walk on the hillside, her guard should have reported it."

That's right, Alaria thought. They'd had guards at their heels since they'd arrived, though they wore so many different colors she'd found it bewildering. The Steward of Walls, for one, dressed like any noble but had the black, blue, and purple Tarkin's crest on his shoulder. Julen and the other fellow, the male guard, wore the same crest but on black jerkins with purple sleeves, colors she *thought* were those of the Palace Guard—and she thought she had also seen blue tunics with purple sleeves. Julen and the man had been outside in the hallway when Alaria went out this morning. And they thought that Cleona must have had a guard with her as well. Perhaps there was nothing to worry about after all.

Except the Steward of Walls looked worried. Before she could ask him anything further, the inner door opened and Epion Akarion came into the room, followed by two pages. He was handing a scroll to one of them as he crossed the threshold. He came directly to Alaria and put out his hands. Before she knew what she was doing, Alaria had put her hands in his.

"The palace is being searched now," he said, glancing quickly at Dav-Ingahm and getting a nod before proceeding. "We will find her. I'm sure she's well." But there was an opaqueness in his eyes, in the way he looked at her, that told Alaria the man was far from sure.

"Is she," Epion pressed his tongue against his upper lip. "Forgive me," he said. "But of course I really know neither of you well, do I? Is Princess Cleona likely to—" he waved one hand in a circular motion. "Wander about on her own?"

"I cannot say no, Lord Epion, not exactly. But you must be aware that our customs are not yours. What might be commonplace for our high noble ladies may be much otherwise for yours." And *that* was putting it gently, Alaria thought. "Lord, could I, that is, would you . . ." Alaria hesitated. What she was about to ask might be considered an affront.

"You must actually ask the question before I can say yes or no." A gleam of humor shone in Epion's eyes.

"May I have the Mercenary Brothers sent for?" Alaria asked. "As you said, you don't know us. And I know no one here except Cleona. No insult is intended to the Tarkin or to his guards, but the Mercenaries are the only people in Menoin who are not strangers to me."

Epion searched her face, a small frown causing a line to form between his brows. He nodded. "Of course, I'll have them sent for. I'm sure Falcos would agree."

And where *was* Falcos, if it came to that? Alaria wondered what the Tarkin found more important than his missing bride.

While they were speaking, a junior guard had come into the room to whisper to the Steward of Walls. Now the older man came nearer to them.

"My lord? News from the stables. The Tarkina took out a horse last night and had an escort with her."

"Last night? It's true the moon was full, but—" Epion turned to Alaria. "What about midnight rides? Is that something Cleona would do?"

Alaria shook her head, but slowly. "But it was long before midnight—the sun had hardly set. She thought—" Alaria hesitated, everyone seemed to be staring at her. "It was something you had said, Lord Epion, that put the notion into her head. It would be a way to relax," she said. "Cleona wanted to be sure to sleep well."

"We spoke of riding, that's true," Epion began, his brow furrowing. "But I advised against it, and she seemed likely to heed my advice."

"But she returned?" Now it was Dav-Ingahm's turn. "You waited for her?"

"The Princess Alaria is not a servant," Epion said before Alaria could speak in her own defense. "There would be no reason for her to await her cousin's return. The safety and security of the Tarkina is the concern of the Tarkin's guards."

Perhaps so, but Epion's words did nothing to dispel Alaria's guilt. How had she fallen asleep so quickly? She'd been tired, but why hadn't she waited for Cleona? Better, why hadn't she insisted on going with her? Regardless of what Cleona may have said about wanting to be alone, Alaria should have gone.

But Epion was still speaking to the Steward of Walls. "Send out searchers along the riding paths, and send to find the Mercenary Brothers. Ask them to come as quickly as they can."

"The Mercenaries, my lord?"

There was something in the Steward's voice that gave Alaria a chill. The man sounded almost as though he were trying to warn Lord Epion of something without speaking aloud.

"You heard me, Walls. If nothing else, they are likely to be exceptional trackers."

"Immediately, Lord Epion."

"I tell you I *did* look for the other Mercenaries, the Brothers who were already here," Gundaron said. "Of course I did, as soon as I knew I needed help."

At a gesture from Parno, Dhulyn Wolfshead passed the plate of cheese pies they'd ordered, along with a jug of hot cider and one of ganje, for their breakfast. Long talk the day before had taken them through the evening meal, until they had been the only people still in the taproom and had finally taken pity on the inn's staff and moved off to their beds.

Gun's speculations about the murders were intriguing, and under other circumstances she would have been interested in offering their expertise in tracking down the criminals. But they already had an assignment, and their focus had to be on their missing Brothers. Dhulyn had gone to sleep congratulating herself that meeting Gun and Mar had made their task just that much easier. What better than a friendly Finder, when you've been sent to locate missing Brothers?

Breakfast had scattered her ideas. It seemed their task would not be easy after all.

Parno leaned forward abruptly, stabbing at Gun with the half-eaten pastry in his hand. "The Brothers *were* seen after your find in the ruins?" he asked.

"Parno," Dhulyn said. He looked at her and rolled his eyes.

"I haven't taken leave of my senses," he told her. "If the assignment given to our Brothers was the assassination of the old Tarkin, Dorian would have told us so. I meant merely to ask whether they might have suffered the same fate?"

"The Mercenary Brotherhood performs assassinations?" Mar-eMar said, her hands arrested in the motion of pouring olive oil on a piece of toasted bread.

"Never mind that just now, my Dove," Dhulyn said, patting the girl on the shoulder. "Our questions first if you don't mind." She turned back to Gundaron.

The young Scholar had his lower lip between his teeth, his mug of ganje cooling in his left hand. "They were still here when the announcement was made that the old Tarkin had died of a sudden fever. That's when we started to wonder whether something was amiss." Gun blinked and turned to Mar. "Were the Mercenaries here when the old Tarkin was buried?"

Mar was nodding as she chewed. "But after that I certainly never saw them again. When Gun couldn't Find them, we asked Dav-Ingahm, the Steward of Walls, and he told us they'd left and gone to Ishkanbar."

Dhulyn drummed on the table with the first two fingers of her left hand. "Gun couldn't Find them? No trace? That makes no sense. Gun, where is Bet-oTeb," she asked.

Gun shut his eyes. "In her bedroom," he said, still with his eyes shut. "Asleep, I think."

"If you can Find the Tarkina of Imrion, you should be able to Find our missing Brothers."

"Unless they are dead," Parno said.

Dhulyn's face felt stiff as she nodded. "Which merely changes the nature of our mission. Instead of finding them, we would find their killers."

"Could it be the same person who killed the late Tarkin?" Parno said. "Did you try to Find him?"

Gun shrugged. "I had nothing to focus on. At least with the Mercenary Brothers, I'd met them."

"But you've Found much more abstract things than a man you've never met," Parno pointed out. "After all, you've Found people's souls."

"Yes, but I knew those people, I'd met them. I've never met this person."

"So far as you know." Dhulyn sipped at her cider.

Mar and Gun, both with eyes wide and brows raised, looked first at her, then at Parno. "You already know a few killers," her Partner said, his voice warm. "Some of them at this very table. It wouldn't be beyond the realms of belief that you'd met others."

"But . . ."

"You don't think of us as killers," Dhulyn said, smiling her wolf's smile. "But don't you see? You might not think of the person who did this as a killer either."

Movement at the door of the inn drew their attention. Parno Lionsmane drew in his feet, ready to stand up, and was amused to see that both Gun and Mar had shifted so that they were out of the way. Apparently lessons learned long ago were still fresh in their minds. The intruder was a young female guard in the palace colors, her face flushed with the speed of her arrival.

"Mercenary Brothers," she said. "If you would please come with me. Alaria of Arderon requests your immediate presence."

Dhulyn was already getting to her feet. "Will we want our horses?"

"The Tarkin said 'as quickly as possible,'" the guard said. Dhulyn was two strides away from the table before she turned back to Gun and Mar. "Follow us as quickly as you can," she said. "And Gun? Bring your bowl."

Dhulyn Wolfshead had seldom seen anyone as frightened as the Princess Alaria was at this moment—though the girl was doing a good job of hiding it. The assured, even arrogant, young woman who had spoken to Dhulyn in the horse enclosure on Dorian's ship was gone, replaced by a girl with round eyes and a clamped jaw. When they had come into the room Alaria had actually rushed toward them, hands held out. Dhulyn had hung back, letting Parno take the girl's arm and lead her back to her seat on a bench near the Tarkin's chair.

"Wolfshead, Lionsmane, I thank you for coming so promptly." Dhulyn noted that the Tarkin, like all High Nobles, had been taught the proper forms of address and knew better than to call Mercenary Brothers by their given names. "What have you been told of our dilemma?"

"Nothing," Dhulyn said. "We thought it best to hear the problem from the source." She looked at Alaria. "Though evidently it concerns the Princess Cleona."

The Tarkin made a face, his blue eyes momentarily flashing icy cold. He gestured at the Steward of Walls.

Dav-Ingahm cleared his throat. "Last evening, while we were preparing for the late meal, the Princess Cleona expressed the wish to go riding," he said. "There would have been no reason to deny her," he added, speaking more quickly. "She is not a prisoner here. And we know that the Arderons are excessively fond of riding—even the Princess Alaria admits that her cousin has been known to ride at night—"

"I am not interested in who is dodging the blame for this," Dhulyn said. If she didn't stem the flow of words, they might be here until the moon rose again. "Am I to understand that Princess Cleona has not returned?"

"She is nowhere in the palace," the Tarkin said. "Nor is the guard who accompanied her."

"That is Essio," Epion Akarion cut in. "I vouch for him."

"*You* vouch for him? Whose man is he?"

"There are two sets of guards within the walls, Mercenary. The Palace Guard watch the buildings and grounds. The Tarkin's Guard watch over his person and his family."

Epion gestured to draw her attention. "I have a small group of the latter assigned to me personally," he said. "They do not rotate in the duty with the others. It simplifies things since I travel so much for Falcos. Until a few months ago Essio was one of these, but," Epion shrugged, "there's little room for advancement in my little cadre, and Essio asked to transfer."

Everyone seemed to accept this, though Dhulyn would have had something to say about it if she had been asked to review the palace security. She judged that the Tarkin was looking unusually pale for a man with his coloring. Paler, certainly, than he had looked the afternoon before. And there was a muscle jerking in the Steward of Walls' cheek that spoke of tightly clenched jaws. She looked at Parno; he blinked twice.

"Do you think the princess may have been taken by a sudden illness?"

If she had thought the Tarkin pale before, it was nothing compared to how he looked at those words. *Ah, a hit*, she thought with an inward smile. *He is guilty of something*. His blue eyes actually looked dark, and his eyebrows were like smudges of ink against his skin.

"What do you know?" he said.

"I know I have a Finder waiting in the outer chamber, and we waste time." She turned toward the door, but the guard there was already opening it and gesturing. Gun and Mar came into the room hand-in-hand, both in formal Scholar's dress with the crest of the Library of Valdomar on the left breast of their tunics. Mar's tunic had the crest of her Noble House sewn on the right side.

Falcos cut off their salutations with an abrupt gesture of his hand.

"We'll dispense with the formalities for the moment, Gun," he said. "Can you Find the Princess Cleona for us?"

"I've never met the princess," Gun began.

"Princess Alaria's her cousin," Parno said. "Will that help?"

"There's a room full of her things, if it comes to that," Alaria said. Dhulyn was glad to see the girl was becoming more animated. She was regaining some of her color, and her voice did not sound quite as tight.

Gun looked around and headed for the Tarkin's worktable. Knowing what was needed, Dhulyn joined him in clearing away the dishes and cups that were still sitting there, untouched, the food gone cold and ice melted to slivers in the drinks. When the end of the table was clear, Mar stepped forward, unslinging her shoulder bag and placing it on the surface. From inside the thick folds of leather she took out a silk-wrapped bundle and a small glass flask, tightly stoppered and sealed with green wax.

"Gift from my House," Mar said, when she saw Dhulyn was looking at it. Glass of that quality had to come from Tenezia and would normally be beyond the reach of Library Scholars such as Gundaron and Mar.

"Your House?" Alaria said.

"I am Mar-eMar Tenebro," Mar said, making a half-embarrassed face at claiming her noble status. "A High Noble House of Imrion. That and a copper piece will get me a decent room at an inn," she added with a smile.

As they were talking, Gun had been folding back the layers of quilted silk to expose a shallow bowl, perhaps as wide as two narrow hands. The outside was thickly patterned and glazed, the colors glowing in the sunlight from the window. The inside was a pure bottomless white. Gun placed the bowl close to the edge of the table and held out his hand to Mar.

"And what is the liquor in the flask?" the Tarkin asked as Gundaron poured a small amount into the bowl.

"Water from a pure spring, passed three times through undyed silk," Mar said. "That's what the writings tell you to use, though sometimes I think ordinary water works just as well."

Gundaron placed the tips of his fingers lightly on the edge of the bowl and leaned in until he could look straight down.

This is what I saw in my Vision, Dhulyn thought, catching Parno's eye.

Everyone fell silent, watching, though there was nothing to see. At first Gun's eyes moved as though he were reading, and then they grew still and focused. Dhulyn glanced at Mar and raised her eyebrows. The younger woman smiled and shook her head very slightly. Parno was completely still, his thumbs hooked in his sword belt, his eyes resting comfortably on Gun, his smile showing a tolerant affection. As if he felt Dhulyn's eyes on him Parno shifted his gaze without moving his head, and his smile warmed. Dhulyn winked and turned her attention back to the others.

Falcos Tarkin stood as though at parade rest, his hands clasped in front of him, his eyes focused on the middle distance, a frown pulling at his perfect lips. Alaria was also very still, her fingers twisted tightly together. Only her eyes switched from face to face, as if she were trying to decipher what they were all thinking.

"Snail scum." Gundaron slapped the tabletop with the palm of his hand, and Alaria jumped. "All I can Find is that blooded maze. The Path of the Sun," he said, turning to face the others in room. "That's all I've been Finding for the last moon. It's like playing a harp with only one string."

"Gun, what you've Found, what your Mark is showing you, is it anywhere near where you came upon—" Dhulyn checked as the Tarkin made a slight movement with his hands. "Where you came upon the body," she said.

"It was in that area, yes," the Scholar said. Out of the corner of her eye Dhulyn saw Alaria raise her clasped hands to her lips.

Dhulyn turned to the Tarkin. "Is it at all likely that the Princess Cleona would have ridden that way?"

"It is a popular trail, yes," the Tarkin said. "It only leads to the ruins and the Path, but the road is maintained. My mother used to take me that way when I was a child; she had a favorite grove she liked to visit. And, of course, the Scholars have been using it."

"Then that is where we start."

Five

HAH! This was luck. The rain was heavy enough to flatten the grass and to keep any aspiring shaman who was watching the Door of the Sun close to his own shelter—and far from noticing him. He checked the ties on the packs and gathered up the leads again, turning them once round his wrist for security. Horses never seemed to notice the peculiarities of the Path, too stupid, he supposed. He'd never tried to take any other animals through, but he was fairly certain that dogs wouldn't be able to stand it. Cats now, they might. Always landing on their feet. But there were no cats in these plains, and he wasn't about to bring one just to experiment. Catch him wasting his time.

He set off south and a little west, taking it slow. Riding would have been faster, but he just didn't like the smell of wet horse.

He'd never freed two at once, and he almost wished he'd had the time to try it now. Though the guard would have been a waste, really. Too simple to need his help. The woman, now she had really needed someone. Her life had been about to change very drastically, and while she'd been all calm and smiling on the outside, she wasn't happy. There was a real sorrow in her, and on the inside she was nothing but resignation, and determination, and under those real fear, almost terror. He'd been happy to help her with that. She was much calmer now and genuinely happy. It was a pity that the treatment—properly done—took so long.

And it was taxing for him—that's what no one realized.

He had to put so much of himself, his talent, into the treatment. It was hard work, and if he did gain by it in the end, well that was only fair, wasn't it? Considering the risks he ran to give people the help they needed so badly.

He'd left her sleeping, peaceful and quiet. She'd be awake now, maybe, and heading back for her wedding. If only—

"It's wet to be out walking, isn't it, trader?"

He was genuinely startled, and for an instant a flash of rage burned hotly through him, but he contained the anger, and exaggerated his jump of surprise. Let the boy think well of his abilities, his stealth, it would be useful later.

"I figured I wasn't getting any wetter," he told the boy. "And at least it isn't cold."

"A moment."

Parno Lionsmane caught the reins Dhulyn threw to him as she swung her leg over Bloodbone's rump and dropped lightly to the ground next to her horse. Bloodbone rolled her eyes at Parno as if to tell him she didn't need him holding her reins. Parno shrugged, as if to answer that he, like the mare herself, only did as he was told.

Dhulyn squatted down on her heels, forearms resting on her bent knees. Her eyes were squinted almost shut as she scrutinized the trail in front of them. After a moment she shifted to the left and sighted along the same stretch of ground from that angle.

"Two riders definitely came this way," Dhulyn said, without raising her head.

"I don't think even our best trackers could know such things, not for certain," Epion Akarion said. His tone was so neutral that Parno could easily guess what the man was too courteous to say.

"Nor many Mercenary Brothers either," he agreed. "But you'll have noticed my Partner is also an Outlander. They say the nomads of the Blasonar Plains can track a Racha bird in flight. Never underestimate what an Outlander with Mercenary Schooling can do."

"The horses are both geldings." Dhulyn straightened and rested her hands on her hips. "This one—" She pointed at something not even Parno could see. "This one is either favoring his left hind, or his shoe has been attached at a slight angle. His rider is light, perhaps eleven ten-weights, not very much more. The other is carrying a larger person, fifteen or sixteen ten-weights at least." She twisted her head around until she was looking at Epion. "The smaller person matches the size of the Princess of Arderon. What do we know of the guard who accompanied her?"

"Essio would be about that size," Epion said, nodding.

"He carried weapons but wore no armor." Dhulyn was studying the ground again. "Is he left-handed?"

"Yes," Epion said through gritted teeth.

Parno, his face as solemn as he could make it, exchanged glances with Mar and Gun. When he winked, Gun looked away suddenly, and Mar covered her mouth with her hand. It was by such little tricks as these that the Mercenary Brotherhood kept its reputation. At least in part.

Dhulyn stood and looked back along the trail, her brows drawn down. In a moment Parno heard it too, the sound of hoofbeats.

"A page boy comes, Lord Epion," he said, just as the youngster came into view. Not wanting to waste any time, the Steward of Walls had sent messengers to the other city gates; this page would be bringing Epion those reports.

"My lord," the boy was shouting even before he drew rein. "No one left the city by any wall gate last night, nor has the princess and her escort returned by one since the sun rose."

Parno, Dhulyn, and Epion exchanged looks. This confirmed that the princess had not ridden through the city but had left from the palace precinct.

"More likely, then, that this is our quarry. No one else has used this path since these two riders, and they have not returned along it," Dhulyn said. "If this is indeed the princess and her guard, they are still ahead of us." She swung herself onto Bloodbone's back and set off again, this time much more slowly, leaning off to one side with her eyes focused on the ground ahead.

Parno hung back this time, letting Alaria and Epion Akarion follow after Dhulyn. His reins slack, Parno drummed his thumbs on the tops of his thighs. He was not looking forward to the end of this trail. If the news was good, one or the other of the riders they looked for would have been back already. If injury had come to them, it had come to them both. He wished Alaria had stayed behind, as the Tarkin had clearly wanted her to. But she came of Horse Nomad stock. Alaria of Arderon would no more shy away from unpleasantness than Dhulyn herself would.

When the trail widened, Mar and Gun came up beside him.

"I see you haven't forgotten how to ride, Mar-eMar," Parno said.

She smiled, her dark blue eyes sparkling in the morning sunlight. "Do you remember how you hoisted me up onto your packhorse in Navra? I swear the animal gave me such a look." She shook her head, smiling. "It isn't that long ago, now that I think about it, for so much to have happened since that day."

"You mean besides your learning how to ride?"

"I don't know how you can joke about it," Gundaron said from Parno's other side. "What happened in Imrion . . ." The young Scholar lowered his eyes and his voice trailed away.

"We're still alive, Gun," Parno pointed out. "You're back where you should be, doing what you should be, which is more than you were before."

"And with me beside you, which is more than you had before," Mar added.

Gun rubbed at his square face with the fingers of his free hand. Parno snagged him by the elbow and tugged him straighter in the saddle. The youngster was no horseman, he thought, and never would be if after all this time he still couldn't keep his seat without concentrating.

"You'd best get the Wolfshead to give *you* some lessons," Parno said. "Or at least let her show you how to fall off without hurting yourself."

The entire party halted as Dhulyn dismounted once more. Parno edged Warhammer to the front. This time his Partner had wrapped Bloodbone's reins around the leather wrist guard on her forearm and was proceeding on foot, still examining the ground as she went. Finally, she stopped and stood still, her arms crossed, her head sunk forward until her chin rested on her chest.

Movement in the sky drew Parno's eye upward. "Dhulyn," he said.

She must have heard the warning note in his voice, for she looked immediately out and upward, for the danger his tone said was coming. Then she too saw the carrion birds circling high in the sky a little to the west of where the trail went winding before them, and she froze.

"Parno, my soul," she said in the nightwatch voice, so quiet that the others, waiting a few paces away, could not hear her. "Keep them away."

Parno turned at once, catching Epion's attention before glancing quickly at the others. "Wait here," he said. "Best if the Wolfshead and I go ahead alone."

"Mercenary," Epion began.

"We'll send if there is anything you can do." This time the noble caught Parno's meaning and nodded. Mar took Gun's hand, but Alaria kneed her horse forward. At a signal from Parno, Warhammer put himself between Alaria's smaller mount and the forward part of the trail.

"Wolfshead," Alaria called out. "I must be with you."

"You will see what you must," Dhulyn assured her. "Just let us see it first." The younger woman looked as if she would argue further, but finally she swallowed and nodded.

Dhulyn Wolfshead remounted and with a jerk of her head summoned Parno to ride alongside her.

"Whatever came upon them," she said, more quietly than she had spoken to Alaria. "It did not come from behind." She pointed to a telltale scuff on the trail in front of them. "There, you see? Still only the two riders, and the same two at that."

"What do you think we'll find?"

Dhulyn shot a sideways glance at her Partner. "Nothing good, as you very well know. The sun's been up what, four hours? And for the carrion birds to be already circling, the bodies must have been there much longer."

"Perhaps it's only the horses."

"And perhaps we've met Cleona and her escort walking back to the city." Dhulyn refrained from shaking her head. It was habit, she knew, rather than any actual optimism, which led Parno to make that kind of observation. He'd often expressed what he wished were true rather that what he believed.

The road continued some way flat and level. There were signs that once upon a time boulders had been moved, rocks broken and carried away, to make the trail wider in certain spots, but still it twisted and wound around larger outcroppings of rock and small clumps of trees. Around one such bend, Dhulyn could see the grove of wild quince trees the Tarkin had spoken of, where a creek formed a small bathing pool in the shade of the trees. The trail itself swung away to the right, toward what looked like a long mound of earth—not unlike the earthworks thrown up around a temporary military camp, but much overgrown. It was nearer that mound, Dhulyn saw, that the birds were swaying overhead. She slowed, looking over the ground more carefully, knowing that Parno was doing the same on the other side of the trail.

"They went into that grove," she said, and touched her heels to Bloodbone's sides. There was something in the shadows, there under the trees, something she had seen many times before. Her sword was hanging down her back, out of the way; she drew it now and dropped out of the saddle next to the body in the Tarkin's colors. Even though the guard's neck was at an awkward angle, Dhulyn pushed her fingers under his jaw. The skin was cold, the flesh hardening.

"Broken neck," Parno said from behind her.

"Masterly observation," she said, and then shrugged an apology for her tone. Parno would know she did not mean it. "I don't think that's what killed him, though," she added. "At least not just that. He's much stiffer than he should be, given the hour at which we know he was alive." Parno edged up for a closer look. They had seen many corpses in their time in the Brotherhood.

"Poisoned first, and then the broken neck for certainty?" Parno suggested.

"That would be my guess also." Dhulyn stood up and looked around what had obviously been a campsite only hours before. "One person, likely a man, on foot, though he has a horse." She pointed out the signs as she spoke.

"Princess Cleona sat here," Parno said. "This is her footprint, certainly. He must have poisoned them both."

"Poisoned and killed the guard, poisoned and kidnapped the princess?"

"Wouldn't be the strangest thing to have happened."

Dhulyn glanced at her Partner and found him looking

steadily back at her. She knew what was in his mind. It was in her own as well. "Strange when a kidnapping is the best you can hope for."

"It would mean she is still alive."

Dhulyn nodded. Neither of them mentioned the carrion birds, though she knew they were both thinking of them. "That way," she pointed. "One person on foot, three horses, two bearing burdens."

"Anything?" she said.

"If there were, would I fail to mention it?"

Dhulyn smiled her wolf's smile, letting the small scar pull her upper lip back in a snarl. She shook herself, earning an annoyed toss of the head from Bloodbone. She felt the tightness in her neck and shoulders—unexpected, given that she felt she knew what they were going to see. Something was making the small hairs on her arms and the back of her neck stand up, and it wasn't the knowledge that there was death in front of them.

Parno exclaimed under his breath, and Dhulyn looked over to him. He was not examining the tracks—tracks that still led clearly and cleanly ahead along the trail—but was gazing off toward the south, away from the trail and the strange mound. There the vegetation thinned even further, and the rocks that appeared out of the growth were too regular to be natural.

"The Caid ruins," Dhulyn said.

"So that," he said, pointing to the focus of the carrion birds' attention, "should be just about where Gun said they came across the old Tarkin's body."

"Mutilated."

"As you say."

Dhulyn took a deep breath and urged Bloodbone forward, doing her best to relax into the horse's easy movement. Whatever it was that both she and Parno evidently felt, it did not transfer to the horses, for which she found herself grateful.

They were still several tens of paces away when the smell hit them. Not of decomposition, not greatly, not yet, out here in the open. The sun had still to reach the middle sky. It was not *that* smell that brought the carrion birds. To Dhulyn it was unmistakable, almost as familiar as the smell of her own skin, of the horse under her. The smell of the battlefield, fear sweat, excrement, and above all, blood.

The smell could not prepare them for what they saw.

"Demons and perverts." Parno's voice came out in a tight whisper.

Dhulyn clenched her teeth and pulled back her lips as much as she could. "Smile," she said through her teeth. "You'll be less likely to vomit." From the corner of her eye, she saw Parno shake his head, then put his hand suddenly to his mouth. When he lowered it, his lips were pulled back in a wretched parody of a smile.

What was spread on the ground before them resembled a human being—that much could be said for it. It had to be Cleona, but how to be sure? The body was staked on the ground, spread-eagled on its back, though even that was not obvious at first glance. All of the skin on the exposed part of the body had been flayed, spread, and held open with sticks sharpened and skewered into the ground underneath. The way the skin was spread made it seem as though it were being held open by the staked hands, the way a woman might hold open her robe for her lover.

And it was a woman, Dhulyn could see from the internal organs set to one side. Cleona then.

"Caids keep us," Parno said. "Do you see the blood?"

"It's hard not to," she said.

"She must have been alive a long time to have bled so much."

Dhulyn nodded. "Hours. There's great skill involved here, that's certain." Other organs besides the purely female ones had been removed from their usual places, some completely, and cleanly, evidently after death, and some still partially attached, to keep the victim alive as along as possible. The eyes—

Dhulyn turned away and coughed, trying to force her diaphragm to loosen, to let her take deep breaths. If she was not looking at the body, she could even pretend the very air did not stink of blood. When she knew her stomach was under control, breathing carefully through her mouth to cut the worst of the smell, Dhulyn crouched down once more to what was left of the princess.

Almost at once, she saw something odd. Like the rest of the body, the skin of the arms had been flayed open but not detached. The effect was not unlike the slit sleeves of an overgown. But unlike the rest of the body, the skin of the hands, and the hands themselves for that matter, were clean and intact. She waved Parno closer.

"What do you make of this?" she said when she could take a breath without shuddering.

He crouched down beside her. Dhulyn turned and rested her forehead against his shoulder, breathing in his clean smell of sweat, the scent of almonds from the oil he'd used to shave that morning, the smell of ganje, and the wonderful, clean, living, human smell that was Parno.

"It's definitely Cleona," he said. "I recognize the shape of her fingers." He pointed without touching. "And that's her ring."

"Good," Dhulyn said. "If we can recognize so much, then Alaria will be able to as well. We will not have to show her anything else."

"Wait." Parno frowned. "Did Cleona have this scar? Here."

Dhulyn leaned in to peer more closely, finally using the point of the dagger Falcos had given her to turn the hand. The scar Parno had pointed out extended from the ball of the thumb, around the wrist and disappeared into the skin that had been flayed from the lower arm. Dhulyn shifted to the other side of the body. There was a similar scar on the other hand.

"Cleona had no such marks on her hands and arms," she said.

"Are you saying this is not Cleona, after all?"

Dhulyn shook her head slowly, eyes still focused on the hand. "As you said, these are the very shapes of her fingers and nail beds. This scar on her palm, that she had before. And this is her jewelry. Look." Dhulyn pointed out a ring that matched the gold and silver armlet she now wore above her left elbow. "This is Cleona," she said. "But these," she indicated the scars with the point of the dagger. "These are old, as if she was cut months ago and the wounds healed."

"But we know that can't be true," Parno said. He rubbed at his upper lip, making Dhulyn think of Gundaron. "The alternative is, well, a Healer."

"Can you imagine a Healer doing this?" Dhulyn stood gesturing at the remains. "Can there be a mad Healer?"

"I sincerely pray not, my heart." Parno straightened to his feet and rested his hand on Dhulyn's shoulder. "I'll get our cloaks and saddle rolls to take up the body in."

But Dhulyn raised her hand to stop him and stayed where she was, as she considered the remains once more.

"You must get Gundaron," she said. "The Scholar must see this before we move anything."

"I can't bring the lad here," Parno protested.

"He must tell us whether the Tarkin's body was also like this," she said. She shook herself. "And there is something familiar—"

"Don't tell me you've ever seen anything like this," Parno said.

"Not seen, no," Dhulyn agreed. "But still there's something . . ." she shot another glance at the thing on the ground. "It looks carefully planned, like a ritual of some kind. The way the skin is only partly flayed, the hands and—" she shot a quick look. "And the feet intact and what is more, clean even of blood. Gundaron has read far more widely than I; perhaps he has read of something like this."

"I almost hope he has not," Parno said as he lifted himself stiffly onto Warhammer's back. "The idea that such a thing has happened before, often enough to be written down . . ." he shook his head.

"It has happened here several times already, if Gundaron is not mistaken. Bring him, but make the others stay back at the campsite. Alaria must not see this until it can be restored to something more closely resembling—" the words stuck in Dhulyn's throat.

"A human being?"

She nodded.

⸻

"I don't understand," Gun said. He rubbed at his mouth with the long fingers of his left hand, looked at the fingers, and dropped his hand back on the dining table in the Tarkin's private sitting room. "Why didn't I Find her body? Why could I only see the Path of the Sun?" The Scholar had regained some color, but Parno was betting the boy was happy he'd had little for breakfast.

"There must be an explanation," Dhulyn said. She looked down on Gundaron from where she stood, leaning her right hip against the edge of the dining table. "Perhaps, after all, having her cousin with you was not enough to Find her." Dhulyn caught Parno's eye and tapped her sword hilt with the fingers of her left hand.

"What if it wasn't Cleona?" Parno did not realize he had spoken aloud until Alaria looked up from the other side of the table. The look of startled hope that flashed into her face faded in an instant.

"Those were her hands you showed me," she said, her voice heavy with unshed tears. Mar, sitting beside the Arderon princess, caught Parno's attention and shook her head with the tiniest of movements. She put her hand lightly on the princess' shoulder.

Once Gundaron had seen the body, Dhulyn and Parno had pulled out the stakes and skewers, folded the stiffened skin as best they could and rolled the remains into their cloaks and saddle blankets, leaving out only the intact hands, with their distinctive jewelry, for Alaria to see.

"That was her silver thumb ring in the shape of a saddle, that our Tarkina gave her," Alaria continued. "And the gold and silver bands on her middle fingers. And the scar, on her palm, where she cut herself once in sword practice. I remember her showing that to me when I was young, to teach me not to be afraid of the blades." Alaria clamped her teeth down on her lower lip and looked upward, blinking. Mar handed her one of the napkins that lay in a basket on the table.

Dhulyn was rubbing the skin between her eyebrows with her own scarred fingers. She looked up at Parno and shifted her shoulder in a manner that was not quite a shrug. *You got this started,* the gesture meant, *you end it.*

"I did not mean it wasn't Cleona's body," Parno said. "I meant that what we saw there is no longer Cleona. Her spirit, her real self, which is what Gundaron would have looked for, is elsewhere." He turned to the Scholar. "Remember when Dhulyn set you to Find the Tarkin of Imrion? You didn't Find his body, but his spirit."

"And if Cleona's spirit is gone . . ." Dhulyn said.

"Exactly," Parno said. "Gundaron would not have Found it." He saw that Dhulyn was following him. The moons that they had spent in the company of the Crayx, the mind-sharing creatures of the Long Ocean, had taught them a great deal about the nature of the spirit.

Alaria let her head fall forward into her hands. Mar picked up another of the napkins and with a lift of her chin signaled that they should move farther away. Alaria had shown remarkable courage, Parno thought, as he and Dhulyn, followed by Gundaron, moved to the far end of the table, nearer the open window. A princess, even such a minor princess of a realm as small as Arderon, could not have seen much in the way of butchery and bloodshed, and what they had seen near the Path of the Sun had been enough to sicken even him, experienced Mercenary Brother though he was.

Gundaron rubbed at his mouth again.

"Was it like anything you have read about?" Dhulyn said to him.

Gundaron nodded. "There's something like it in the *Book of Rhonis*." He turned to Dhulyn. "Do you remember? The book that tells of the origins of your people, the Espadryni. It goes back to the times of chaos, after the first coming of the Green Shadow."

Dhulyn smiled her wolf's smile, but Gundaron only blinked, having seen it many times before. "You know better than that, my little Scholar. My people are the Mercenary Brotherhood. But what does the book tell us? Why were such things done?"

Gundaron shook his head, lower lip between his teeth. "There is a portion of the Book that seems to describe rituals of obscure Tribes and cults. What we saw . . ." he swallowed. "There are similarities to a particular ritual, but whether it was meant to appease the Green Shadow or to draw the help of the Sleeping God . . ." Here Gun blushed and looked between Parno and his Partner, gauging their reactions. Dhulyn only smiled gently, patting him on the shoulder.

"It's all right, my own. Relax. I know as well as you that no such actions would bring the God. Do you think it possible it was done by those touched by the madness of the Green Shadow?" She turned to Parno. "Could it be some twisted way of unmaking?"

Parno leaned against the wall, his arms folded across his chest. "Whatever may have been the motivations of those ancients, the Green Shadow is gone, never to trouble us again, so why would such an ancient rite be reappearing now?"

"Could someone, having read the *Rhonis*, been driven mad, driven to duplicate what he'd read there?" Gun said.

"Interesting you think it is a man," Dhulyn said. "But as you're the only one here who admits to having read it, that's a theory I would be quiet about if I were you."

Gun blinked, then his brow furrowed. Clearly that thought had not occurred to him. "Something magical then? Some Mage's ritual?" He leaned forward. "The earliest bodies I learned of were found after the solstices, but then they became more frequent."

"Last night was a full moon," Parno said.

Dhulyn stopped them from continuing with a raised finger. "The body you saw before," she said, careful not to say the word "Tarkin" where it could be overheard and raise questions. "Did it look the same? Did you take any notes at the time?"

Gun shook his head. "I didn't need to," he said. "Not that it wasn't important." He looked up at her, anxious as usual that she understood him. "If necessary I can write down exactly what I saw before, and what I saw this morning as well. I will never forget it," Gundaron said. "Not one detail of it. Will you?" He turned suddenly, fixing his pale eyes on hers.

"No," she said. "No, I will not." Scholars and Mercenaries both received very similar training to perfect their memories, but Dhulyn doubted that special training would have been needed for any of them to remember what they had seen. On the contrary, the trick would be to forget it. It was for that reason she and Parno had prevented Alaria from seeing too much.

"But it was the same?" Parno asked.

Dhulyn thought she knew what her Partner was looking for. If Gun had seen corpses in this condition before, his reaction this morning was excessive. Most Mercenaries and soldiers knew that constant or repetitive exposure could cause even the worst horrors to become commonplace, at least to a degree.

Gundaron was rubbing at his lip again. "It was not . . . not as extensive," he said finally. "As if it had only begun."

"Or had been interrupted?" Parno said.

"Perhaps."

"And do you mean to tell me you *knew* about this?"

Alaria's voice made them all turn around. Evidently, Dhulyn thought, they had not been speaking quietly enough. "You *knew* this might happen and you did nothing to warn us?" Alaria was on her feet and shook off Mar's grip as if the smaller woman were just a child.

Gundaron had his mouth open, but he remained silent when Dhulyn clamped a hand on his arm. She turned toward the door and touched her forehead with her fingertips.

"It is not the Scholar's fault." The Tarkin of Menoin stood in the doorway with his uncle looking over his shoulder. "If it is anyone's, it is mine."

Alaria was already halfway around the table, heading for the young Tarkin with her hands in fists when Dhulyn spoke up.

"What do you know of this then, Falcos Tarkin?"

"You address the Tarkin of Menoin, Mercenary. Do you not think you should moderate your tone?" Epion loomed up behind the younger man, his square, dark features even darker with anger.

Parno unfolded his arms and straightened, letting his hand fall to his sword belt. It was all he could do not to laugh out loud. Uncle and heir to a Tarkin he might be, but Epion would soon learn he'd met his match in Dhulyn Wolfshead.

Sure enough, Dhulyn merely looked the man up and down as if he was a raw apprentice who'd dropped a weapon overboard. "My tone is the least of your difficulties. You have two Mercenary Brothers missing. Your Tarkin was murdered." Dhulyn nodded at Falcos in acknowledgment that she spoke of his father. "And now your new Tarkina has been killed in the same way. Whatever it is you have been doing to deal with these events, *you* may wish to 'moderate' your strategy."

"Listen here—" Epion began.

"Enough." Falcos had his hand raised. "Dhulyn Wolfshead is correct. We should have sent for help and advice before this. Caids grant it is not already too late."

"Then I suggest, Lord Tarkin, that we all sit down, and you tell us what you know," Parno said.

Falcos Tarkin hesitated only a moment before he took the chair at the head of the table. Epion immediately went to the chair on the left, but only to hold it for Alaria. Parno let him take the chair to Falcos' right before he nodded Gun and Mar into seats on the same side of the table as Alaria and sat down himself next to Epion. Dhulyn stayed where she was, leaning with her right hip against the table's edge.

"You speak of your missing Brothers. It was I who sent them to track the killers of my father." Falcos spoke quietly, his gaze focused over their heads, as if he were reading words from the far wall. "They never returned, or at least they have not returned as yet." He brought his focus down to glance between Parno and Dhulyn. "I do not give up, I have heard the Mercenary Brotherhood is very hard to kill. Had I known—I did not believe there was any further danger."

Parno glanced at his Partner. She lifted her eyebrow in acknowledgment. Since their Brothers had been here to guard Falcos, they would only have gone looking for the killer if they had believed the young man also in danger.

Falcos' gaze had shifted to Alaria. She glanced at him, her hands in fists, eyes glistening.

"I'm afraid your father's wasn't the only death, Lord Tarkin. There may be as many as seven more, if we go back two years." They all turned their eyes to Gundaron. He swallowed, and cleared his throat.

"Preposterous." Epion half-turned in his seat, as if physically rejecting Gun's words.

"Perhaps we shouldn't be so quick to argue with Scholars, Epion," the Tarkin said. He turned to Gun. "Are you certain of this?"

"It's not possible to be absolutely certain," Gun said, spreading his hands palm down on the table top. "I've had to put together my conclusions from bits of information that come from many sources, but that's the nature of scholarship. From what I've found out, the other remains were much disturbed by animals and carrion eaters before they were found."

"And why is that? Why were the victims not found more quickly?" Parno said.

"Because no one missed them," Gun said. In his tone was the simple awareness that there were many common folk whose disappearances, or deaths, caused not a ripple. "Unlike the Tarkin, or Princess Cleona, I believe these others may have been travelers, and no one knew to look for them, except perhaps long after they were dead."

"Lord Tarkin." Dhulyn's rough silk voice held the same cool scholarly note as Gun's. "Why did you say your father had died of an illness? If you had announced the murder, would you not have received more help in finding the killer?"

Falcos and his uncle exchanged an unreadable look. Finally the Tarkin licked his lips and spoke.

"Do you know that my father consulted the Seer of Delmar?" Dhulyn started, but Alaria nodded. "He and I disagreed . . ." Falcos' voice faltered and he cleared his throat. "We disagreed on how to follow her instructions. I thought I should go at once to Arderon, in exchange for one of their princesses. That Arderon blood should inherit the throne of Menoin, as laid out in the original vow. But my father said it was enough that we should have an Arderon Tarkina. That I should still inherit as the son of his first Tarkina."

"As Falcos' father inherited himself," Epion pointed out. "The son of *our* father's first wife."

And that, Dhulyn thought, explained why Epion was not himself the Tarkin.

"I thought my father was cheating," Falcos continued as if Epion had not spoken. "That he was not acting honorably by the Lady of Arderon." Falcos dipped his head in Alaria's direction. "When he was killed I thought . . . I thought if the people knew how he had died, so close to the Path of the Sun, they might think that the gods still turned their faces from us. That we were still cursed because of what he had planned."

Epion was shaking his head. "You make too much of this disagreement, Nephew. You and your father would have come to an understanding, given time."

"Time we did not have," Falcos said, his expression withdrawn, his gaze looking inward.

Of course, it might well weigh on him, Dhulyn thought, that he had been arguing with his father—perhaps they were not even speaking—when the old man died.

"If I might ask," she said. "Since you were pretending there was no killer, who, then, did you send my Brothers to find?"

Falcos shivered, as if the ice in her voice had transferred to his veins. "They did not agree. They said there was a human hand in the killings. I hoped . . ."

"You hoped they were right, and you wrong." Alaria had been silent for so long the sudden rasp of her voice startled everyone at the table, and even Dhulyn and Parno turned their heads to look at her. "Well, I don't know what killed your father, Falcos, but no curse of Sun, Moon, and Stars killed Cleona. Even if she were not here as an instrument of the gods—which she was—you Menoins should know better than anyone that horse gods' curses take time, even generations."

She slammed the table with her open hands. "Idiots. All this talk of what you thought and did and did not do—my cousin's killer is out there somewhere, *now*." Her eyes moved to study each of the faces around her. Falcos was the only one who lowered his eyes. "Something must be done."

"The trail is clear enough." Dhulyn pushed herself upright. "One man leading a burdened horse came out of the labyrinth. Three horses went back in. One was the same burdened animal that had come out, the other two were the ones we followed from your stables. One of those had a rider. If this is the same killer, and our Scholar seems to believe it is." She paused and waited for Gun's nod of agreement. "Then it's likely our Brothers found a similar trail." She looked around the table. "My Partner and I will walk the Path of the Sun."

Six

TARKIN FALCOS AKARION took a firm grip on the tree branch and leaned out over the edge of the cliff. He moved the curl of dark hair out of his blue eyes with a practiced flick of his head.

"There," he said, pointing with his free hand toward an irregular arch of stone and earth that was the entrance to the Path of the Sun. "From here you can just see the first section of the Path, the two false turnings, and the first true turning. That is the farthest that can be seen from the outside." He pulled himself upright once more. "I used to spy on it from here when I was a little boy, wondering if I would ever be called upon to walk it."

Dhulyn took the young man's place at the rock's edge and eyed the tree branch, her mouth twisted to one side. Grinning, Parno took hold of her sword belt and braced himself as she leaned out into space, imitating the Tarkin's position as closely as possible. Dhulyn was lighter than Falcos, and the tree branch would have held her easily—but why should she use a tree when her Partner was there?

"And once past that point?" she asked. She tapped Parno twice on the arm, and he pulled her upright.

"Well, it is a maze," Falcos Tarkin said, as he gathered his gleaming black hair back into its leather thong.

"I know the meaning of the word 'labyrinth.'" Dhulyn's tone was as dry as the sun-baked earth they stood on. She looked to Parno. "If it does not rain, we should be able to follow the tracks."

But the Tarkin was shaking his head. "From the entrance, there are no marks to be seen. Either the ground is too hard or it is some magic of the place itself."

Dhulyn pursed her lips in a silent whistle. "'From the entrance'? Has no one ventured? Is there no record of the key?"

Falcos chewed on his upper lip, drumming the fingers of his right hand on the elaborate gold and silver buckle of his sword belt. "There *was* a key." He looked from Dhulyn to Parno and back again. "I believe so, at any rate. Long ago, in the days we wish to regain, every Tarkin had to walk the Path upon assuming the throne," he said.

"Long ago?" Dhulyn glanced at Parno. "Part of the rituals you Tarkins stopped observing?" After their discussion of the day before, Dhulyn and Parno had spent some time with Alaria, familiarizing themselves with the details of the marriage treaty as Cleona had explained it to the younger woman.

"Let me guess." Parno resisted the urge to squeeze his eyes shut. "The key was passed from parent to child, and when it was lost, that particular ritual was dropped from the requirements."

Falcos dropped his eyes with the suggestion of a shrug. Parno resisted the urge to reach out and pat the young man on the shoulder. After all, none of this was Falcos' fault; the errors of judgment were generations old at this point.

"And the key was never written down? There are no drawings, no maps, among the palace books and scrolls?" Dhulyn stared down at the entrance to the Path, a frown line between her blood-red brows.

"None that I have found." And from his tone, Parno imagined that Falcos Tarkin had looked carefully.

Dhulyn stepped to one side, looking past Parno to where Gundaron waited by the horses. "Gun?" she called.

He was already nodding. "I can try," he said. "It probably isn't . . ." his voice faded away as his eyes lost focus. Suddenly they sharpened again, but it was clear that Gun was not looking at any of them. His eyes flicked from side to side as though he were reading. Dhulyn walked over and eased his horse's reins out of his hand.

Finally he blinked and cleared his throat. "I didn't Find anything," he said. "At least — " but he shook his head. "Perhaps with the bowl."

Dhulyn squeezed the young Scholar's shoulder, giving him back his reins as her eyes turned to her Partner. "The trail's getting cold as we debate it," she said. "Do we follow it, or have guards posted to catch the man when he comes to strike again?"

"*If* he comes to strike again," Parno pointed out. It was a sensible suggestion, but one that stuck in his throat. "And guards to be posted for how long? Told to look for what?" He shook his head. "I know we were discharged, but Cleona of Arderon was in our care five days, and it could be seen as a black mark on us and perhaps on our Brotherhood if we do not track down her killer."

Dhulyn's eyes danced, but only Parno knew her well enough to know that inside she was smiling. "Alaria won't like the idea of leaving guards, that's certain," she said. "And if, as we think, our own Brothers came to this same conclusion and have already walked this Path, key or no, so must we."

"Mercenaries," the Tarkin began.

Dhulyn turned back to him. "Have people entered the Path of the Sun and returned successfully? Even without a key?"

"There are stories of such feats, yes. But, Wolfshead, these same stories tell us that you must at least wait for tomorrow's dawn. 'In with sunrise, out with sunset,' is what they say."

"That makes sense," Gundaron said. "After all, it must have been given its name for some reason. What better time to start the Path of the Sun than at dawn?"

"Gun says the Path itself must be a Caid artifact," Dhulyn said as they prepared for bed in the rooms they'd been given in the palace. Falcos Tarkin had wanted to give them every comfort, and Alaria in particular had wanted them close. "He's seen drawings of mazes in the documents left from their days. From what he says, they were used for gardens, not as defensive works. Can you imagine?" She looked at him over her shoulder. "It would be like building a wall so that vines could climb up it."

"An artifact of the Caids," Parno said under his breath. "How lovely. I wonder what *this* one is supposed to do?"

Dhulyn smiled her wolf's smile. "You never know, my soul. The odds say *one* of their artifacts must prove to be of beneficial use some day. . . ."

"Well, you're the gambler, but somehow I don't think this is the day." Parno grunted as he shifted to give her more room.

Dhulyn paused just as she was lifting her legs onto the mattress. "What? Is the bed too soft?"

"My back hurts," he said.

"'Don't buy that red saddle,' I said." Dhulyn rolled over until she could press her back up against him. "'But it'll look so pretty on my horse,' he said. 'Don't do it,' I said, 'It'll hurt your back,' I said. 'How could it hurt my back, he said . . .'"

Parno put his hand over Dhulyn's mouth.

GUNDARON OF VALDOMAR IS ON HIS HANDS AND KNEES, RETCHING. MAR IS ON HIS FAR SIDE, WHITE-FACED, AND HER DARK BLUE EYES ARE ROUNDER THAN DHULYN HAS EVER SEEN THEM. GUN SITS BACK ON HIS HEELS, WIPING AT HIS MOUTH WITH HIS SLEEVE. THEY ARE IN THEIR SCHOLARS' DRESS, BROWN LEGGINGS, BLUE TUNICS, SO DHULYN JUDGES THIS SCENE IS LIKELY TO BE IN THE FUTURE. SHE LOOKS AROUND, BUT ALL SHE CAN SEE IS A SEA OF WILD GRASS, HEAVY WITH SEED. . . .

IT IS A GRANITE WALL, WEATHERED AND IN PLACES CRACKED BY THE PASSAGE OF TIME. BUT IT IS WORKED, HUMAN-MADE, AND OBVIOUSLY CREATED BY THE HAND OF SOME MASTER STONE MASON AMONG THE CAIDS. THE SHADOWS ARE SUCH THAT IT TAKES A MOMENT FOR DHULYN TO SEE THE ROCK HAS BEEN CARVED. A FACE STARES BACK AT HER FROM THE WALL, WIDE-BROWED, POINTED OF CHIN, THE NOSE VERY LONG AND STRAIGHT, THE LIPS FULL CURVES. THE EYES ARE EMPTY. . . .

A SMALL BOY IS SQUATTING ON HIS HEELS IN THE GRASS, DANGLING A PIECE OF WILLOW OSIER FOR AN ORANGE KITTEN. AS THE KITTEN LEAPS AND JUMPS, THE BOY TOUCHES IT, AND THE KITTEN FALLS, PANTING, ITS EYES GROWING MILKY AND DARK. HE TOUCHES IT AGAIN, AND IT LEAPS UP, BLINKING, AND THRASHING ITS LONG TAIL. THE BOY DANGLES THE OSIER AGAIN, AND ONCE MORE THE KITTEN POUNCES, AND ONCE MORE, SMILING, THE BOY REACHES OUT TO TOUCH IT. . . .

THE TALL THIN MAN STANDS BEFORE HIS MIRROR THAT IS NOT A MIRROR. THIS TIME IT SHOWS HIS REFLECTION. HIS WHEAT-COLORED HAIR IS LONG AND UNKEMPT. IT APPEARS HE HAS NOT SHAVED IN MANY DAYS, NOR EATEN. HIS EYES ARE NO LONGER THE COLOR OF OLD ICE BUT THE COOL GREEN OF

JADESTONE. HE HAS THE SAME LONG SWORD IN HIS HANDS, AND HE CUTS DOWNWARD, SLASHING AT HIS IMAGE IN THE MIRROR FRAME. IT IS AS IF HE LOOKS AT HIS REFLECTION IN A POOL OF WATER. THE SWORD PASSES THROUGH IT AND LEAVES IT RIPPLING AND DANCING UNTIL IT SETTLES AGAIN. DHULYN WONDERS AGAIN WHY THIS OLD VISION SHOULD BE COMING TO TROUBLE HER NOW. A MESSAGE, BUT WHAT? AND FOR WHOM? . . .

A CIRCLE OF WOMEN, EACH WITH HAIR THE COLOR OF OLD BLOOD, DANCE FIRST ONE WAY, THEN THE OTHER. THEIR MOUTHS MOVE IN THE CHANT, BUT DHULYN CANNOT HEAR THEIR VOICES. DHULYN HAS SEEN THIS VISION MANY TIMES; THESE ARE THE WOMEN OF HER TRIBE, BEFORE THE BREAKING. BUT WHERE IS HER MOTHER? . . .

GUNDARON FALLS TO HIS KNEES IN THE LONG GRASS AND VOMITS . . .

THE STONE FACE SMILES AT HER, ITS PUPILS INLAID IN GREEN STONE . . .

PEOPLE WORK IN A FIELD OF HAY. RAGGED PEOPLE, FACES DRAWN WITH EXHAUSTION. MOUNTED GUARDS PATROL THE PERIMETER OF THE FIELD, THEIR FACES MARKED WITH THE SAME FATIGUE. ONLY THE FACT THAT THEY ARE FACING OUTWARD TELLS DHULYN THAT THEY ARE GUARDING THE REAPERS FROM EXTERNAL DANGER, NOT FROM ESCAPE. IN THE DISTANCE THERE IS A SMALL FORTRESS, WITH A WALL MUCH TOO LARGE FOR IT . . .

A THIN MAN WEARING A GOLD RING IN EACH EAR IS BENT OVER A CIRCLE OF STONES, USING A SPARKER TO SET DRIED GRASS AND TWIGS ALIGHT. A PILE OF BROKEN BRANCHES SITS TO ONE SIDE READY TO BE PLACED IN THE FIRE. HIS LARGE HANDS HAVE PRONOUNCED KNUCKLES, LONG FLAT FINGERS. HIS STRAW-COLORED HAIR IS COARSE AND THICK, CROPPED SHORT. DHULYN'S SHADOW FALLS ACROSS HIM, AND HE LOOKS UP. "HERE," HE SAYS, STRAIGHTENING TO HIS FEET AND REACHING TOWARD HER. "LET ME HELP YOU WITH THAT." . . .

AN OLD MAN, HIS HAIR STILL SHOWING STREAKS OF RED THE COLOR OF OLD BLOOD, PEERS AT HER. SHE CAN SEE THE LINES FANNING OUT FROM BESIDE HIS EYES, AND THERE IS WHITE IN HIS EYELASHES. FROWNING, HE RAISES A HAND WHOSE FINGERS ARE TWISTED, JOINTS SWOLLEN, AND TRACES A SYMBOL ON HER FOREHEAD.

"What did you See?"

Obviously she hadn't been quiet enough. Or, perhaps Parno's Pod sense had made him more sensitive to her Visions.

Dhulyn described the stone face again. "I think it must be a piece of the Path of the Sun. We will have to watch out for it."

"And an old bit of carving made you jump in your sleep?"

She made a face, knowing that he couldn't see her in the dark. "I saw a most unpleasant child, some people harvesting in time of war. The Green Shadow again, and you know that repetition is significant." She paused, breathing deeply. "I Saw a Red Horseman."

"Avylos?"

Dhulyn shook her head. "And not my father either. At least, I don't think so." She settled herself against him more snugly. "Oh, and I should warn Gun to be careful of what he eats."

⁓

The sky to the west was a dull pewter, barely lighter than the vault above them, where no stars showed through the thick cloud cover. The moon had set hours before, but Dhulyn and Parno had not had any difficulty finding their way to the entrance of the Path of the Sun. Parno had dismounted to retie a thong that had come loose on his saddlebag and now swung himself once again into his saddle. He'd gone back to the old one, Dhulyn noticed with a smile.

From on the ground in front of it, the entrance to the Path of the Sun looked like no more than a pair of wide boulders surrounded by thick hedges, taller than a person on horseback and far enough apart to allow two such persons to pass between them. But a closer look showed Dhulyn that the "boulders" were far too even and regular to have occurred naturally, and that there was even the suggestion of a long-ago fallen arch in the way the top of the left one seemed to reach out toward the one on the right. Caids' work, for certain.

"We might have lost the trail anyway," Parno said, looking up. "From the look of those clouds, there'll be rain before long."

"Not before the sun rises," Dhulyn said. She turned to look behind them. The others were waiting where the trail divided, one fork leading to where they stood, the other fading away into the Caid ruins. Overcast or not, the slowly growing light of dawn showed her Falcos Tarkin and the Princess Alaria, booted and cloaked against the morning's chill, and between them Epion Akarion on a tall black gelding.

Dhulyn touched the spot on her quilted vest where she had sewn the pearls Alaria had given her. The jewels, effectively priceless to those from a landlocked country, were Alaria's personal property, and their use as payment made it clear who had hired the Mercenaries. Falcos Tarkin may have put all his resources at their disposal, but it would be to Alaria that they would report when they returned.

Behind the nobles, and off to one side where their view could not be obscured, Gundaron and Mar-eMar stood with their ponies. Or rather, Gun stood. Dhulyn grinned. No wonder his riding didn't improve—the boy took every chance he could to get down off his mount. She hadn't teased him about it this morning, however. He'd had no luck Finding a key to the Path, not even using Mar's scrying bowl, and he was feeling incompetent enough.

"Well?" Parno said.

Dhulyn looked over at him and smiled. "Well enough." She turned back to those waiting and touched her forehead with her fingertips. Mar and Gun returned the salute, and the others nodded in acknowledgment. Dhulyn turned Bloodbone's nose toward the entrance, waited until Parno drew up beside her.

"Half a length behind me," she reminded him.

"Teach your grandmother," he said, and followed her in. "In Battle," he said as she passed through the stones.

"And in Death," she answered.

It was unreasonable, Mar-eMar knew, this feeling that they should wait exactly where they were until Dhulyn Wolfshead and Parno Lionsmane reappeared—that somehow, if she and Gun waited here, it would help the Mercenaries in some unknown way. But Wolfshead and Lionsmane would not return before sunset—and probably not today's sunset at that. It could be days before they came out again. Or weeks.

"They *will* come back," she said.

"What was that?" Gun still had to use all his concentration to get up into the saddle, otherwise the hill ponies they'd bought for their expedition to the Caid ruins were likely to play some trick on him. Mar repeated herself.

"Of course they will." Gun tried to stand in his stirrups to get a better angle on the entrance to the Path, but his pony shifted and he sat down again.

"Their not coming back wouldn't be the worst of it," Mar said. "After all, they expect to die some day. The worst would be not knowing what happened to them."

"Well, they wouldn't know what happened to us, either."

Mar reached over and patted Gun on his knee. "That's right, stay logical." But she knew that logical or not, Gun was just as worried about Wolfshead and Lionsmane as she was herself. She thought of them as her own kin, and she knew that Gun felt much the same. Parno Lionsmane actually was a distant cousin of hers—though because of the Common Rule they didn't speak of it much to others.

"Mar." The quiet warning note in Gun's voice drew Mar's attention to the approach of the Tarkin's party. With plenty of warning, Gun could get his pony off the path and out of the way of the nobles without too much trouble. The last thing Mar wanted was to draw the attention of Epion Akarion. They had started off badly with him when they'd first come to get the Tarkinate's final approval on their researches. They'd arrived after a voyage almost the full length of the Midland Sea to find that Lord Epion had already prepared a schedule for them, outlining exactly how they should proceed to examine the ruins and containing a list of artifacts he wanted them to find, in order of importance. All this despite the fact that all these details, and more, had been firmly agreed upon already.

Mar had had to be very clear about the rights and duties of themselves as Scholars and of Valdomar as their Library. Epion had changed his tune, turning warm and helpful, welcoming them, showing how deep his interest, how sincere his concern that they have all they needed to accomplish the work. But Mar couldn't forget that he'd first tried to intimidate them. After all, the man was half brother—and legitimate at that—to one Tarkin and uncle and first counselor to another. How could it possibly matter to him what a couple of traveling Scholars thought?

A fine thing, she thought now, *when experience taught you to be wary of friendliness*. Still, she couldn't shake the feeling that Menoin had really dodged the arrow—to use an old Mercenary expression—when the birth of Falcos Akarion had bumped his father's half brother into a lower spot in the line of succession.

"Well, Scholars." It was typical of Epion Akarion that he

would address them both together, though Gundaron had the senior rank. Mar felt that courtesy required her to smile back at him. She wished she could make her lip curl up as Dhulyn Wolfshead's did. "Back to your researches now, is it?" the man continued.

There might be some people, Mar thought, who would see his courteous enquiry as genuine interest, the mark of a man who took thought even for those people who stood only on the periphery of a crisis. But it made Mar uneasy; it seemed too studied to be real.

Falcos Akarion's behavior was more natural, she thought. He had ridden past them with only a nod, preoccupied with his own serious concerns, giving them only what courtesy required. Only when Alaria of Arderon drew rein next to Epion did Falcos stop as well and look back.

Princess Alaria studied them for a moment, her gold-blonde brows drawn down. "You are their friends, are you not? The Mercenary Brothers? It was with you that Wolfshead and Lionsmane went, to share your meal rather than eat with the soldiers in the palace."

"We count them as our kin," Mar said.

"But the Mercenary Brotherhood have no kin," Epion said with a smile.

It was all Mar could do not to roll her eyes and heave a great sigh. From the way Alaria's mouth twitched, Mar thought the princess might feel the same way.

"We have the kinship of blood between us," Gun said. "Though not blood kinship, if you follow me."

"I think you are quite clear," Alaria said. "Will you come with me? Stay with me at the palace?" Epion began to speak, but Alaria turned to Falcos Tarkin. "I may do this? Please?" He was nodding, his eyebrows raised, but Alaria had already turned back to Mar. "I have no one with me but Cleona's two servants. No sisters or cousins. No one who is . . ." Here Mar thought Alaria was about to say "on my side," but the princess must have realized what that would sound like. "No one who is my friend," was what she finally said, her lips pulled back in a strained smile. "We have the friendship of the Mercenaries in common; perhaps you would extend me your friendship as well?"

It almost seemed that Epion Akarion was about to answer before the Tarkin could, though Mar noticed that his warmly encouraging smile did not quite reach his eyes, but the Tarkin was already speaking.

"An excellent idea," the younger Akarion said. "There is certainly plenty of room in the Tarkina's wing."

"This is very kind," Mar said, more because she was aware that an immediate answer was required than because she knew what she wanted that answer to be. She glanced at Gundaron and saw that he had the index finger of his left hand extended. "Of course, we would be delighted to accept your hospitality, Princess of Arderon." Mar hoped she'd done right. In wording her acceptance so carefully, she was making herself and Gundaron part of Alaria's official party—and putting themselves under whatever protection that afforded them.

In response she received three smiles, each different and each telling in its own way. Alaria's was genuine and showed some degree of relief, as if she hadn't been quite sure what Mar's answer would be. That relief, however, did not in any way disturb the marks of sorrow—yes, and of anger and fear that still remained on the princess' face. Falcos Tarkin seemed pleased enough, his handsome face easy, as at a minor problem solved. As for Epion Akarion, Mar was certain his smile had faltered a little before reestablishing itself, broader and warmer than ever, though his eyes seemed to have narrowed even further.

"If we may, we'll fetch our things from the inn," Mar said to Alaria, "and join you later in the day."

Mar waited until the royal party had proceeded a span or so down the trail toward the city before she turned to Gundaron.

"Whatever your plan is," she said, "I hope you realize we've just put ourselves plainly into the Arderon camp. Whatever happens to Alaria can happen to us as well."

"What could be worse than what happened to her cousin?" Gun's voice was quiet, though steady. "And that's not likely to happen to any of us." He looked back along the trail to where they could just make out the Path of the Sun. "Not now that we know it can."

Mar pressed her lips together and frowned. "I suppose you're right. Still, you must have had something in mind when you signaled me."

Gun rode along in silence for several minutes, twitching

at his reins unnecessarily. "Can you see us, a day or two from now, going to the palace and requesting an audience with Falcos Tarkin in order to ask him what news has come about Dhulyn Wolfshead and Parno Lionsmane? I don't think we'd get very far past the Deputy Steward of Keys, do you?"

"If that far," Mar said, beginning to see where Gun was going. "But if we are right in the palace . . ."

"Attending upon the very person who has the most right to ask questions and have them answered," Gun continued, "then our questions are answered as well."

"This is why I love you," Mar said.

About three horse lengths in, just as Dhulyn had seen from the vantage point on the cliff, the Path of the Sun divided sharply to the right and left. Falcos had said the path to the left was known to be a false one, so Dhulyn and Parno turned right. The walls of the labyrinth closed out all sound from without, as if they had entered a tightly closed room and shut the door behind them. Dhulyn dropped immediately into the basic Hunter's *Shora*, but that only made her more aware of the breathing of the horses and of the sound of her own heart, beating in time with Parno's.

"The sun is shining."

Dhulyn glanced behind her, but Parno was still only half a horse length behind. For a moment, he had sounded much farther away.

"I'm thinking you should ride beside me after all, my soul," she said to him. "I do not like the way these walls flatten the sound of our voices." She waited until he had come abreast of her, still looking upward at a morning sky as blue as a child's eye.

"No blooded chance the sky cleared that quickly," he said.

Dhulyn shot a quick glance upward before lowering her eyes to continue her careful examination of the route in front of them. "I think it's warmer as well."

"That might be nerves."

Dhulyn smiled her wolf's smile, still looking ahead.

The path turned again, and now the walls appeared older, the stones worn and covered in places with lichen and moss. Somewhere, Dhulyn could hear water dripping. Just past that spot, another path, this one walled in thick hedges of black walnut, met theirs on the right.

"Odds," Parno called, holding up his fist.

Dhulyn held up hers as well. "One, two, three." She held out two fingers, Parno four. "Your turn next," she said, dismounting and pulling out her sword.

"Don't go more than twenty paces," Parno said. "If it's not a dead end, come back for me."

Dhulyn answered with a grin and a rude gesture. She was no more than three paces into the new path when it turned right. Raising her sword, she placed herself against the inside corner, crouched, and sent out her senses. Nothing. She could sense no breathing, no heartbeats, nothing. Nevertheless, she shot only a quick glance around the corner from her crouch, and only when she was satisfied that there was nothing to see did she proceed.

When it looked as though the path would turn right again Dhulyn stopped, frowning. This was not possible. Given the length of the sections of pathway, the direction in which she had been turning, if she turned right again, she should find herself back on the path behind—

Parno was in front of her. He had been leaning into the pathway she had taken, but as soon as she stepped out behind him, he spun to face her, sword up. Even the horses had turned to look at her.

"How—"

"Don't ask." She waved at the entrance she had just come out of. "There was no entrance here when we passed a moment ago, as you very well know."

"But—"

"Parno." At her warning Parno whirled back to face the direction they'd been heading in. The entrance he was standing next to, the one she'd followed away from the path they were standing on, was gone.

Her Partner grinned at her. "What do you say? Shall we both go this time?" He pointed at the new entrance.

"And end up behind ourselves?" Dhulyn looked ahead to where the entrance had been. "Or ahead of ourselves?"

"Carry on, then?"

"What else." Dhulyn swung herself back into her saddle. Perhaps twelve horse lengths farther along they came to a place where the path divided, and they must decide to go right or left. Dhulyn leaned out of the saddle and tapped with her fingertips at the wall closest to her. The stone was cold, as if the sun had only just now moved to shine on it.

"It's the Path of the Sun, my soul, is it not?" she said.

"That's what they keep telling us." Parno's tone was not as sour as his words. Warhammer tossed his head, and Parno leaned forward to stroke the horse's neck. Bloodbone did no more than flick an ear at her fellow; she had always been the more phlegmatic of the two horses.

"The sun rises in the west and travels eastward until it sets." Dhulyn pointed to the right-hand path. "That way leads almost precisely east."

"According to the Scholars I had as a child," Parno said, "the sun does not move; it is the earth that revolves, turning its face always away from and then toward the sun."

Dhulyn turned to her Partner, her left fist propped on her thigh. "And that helps us how?"

Parno shrugged, but there was a ghost of a grin hovering around his mouth. "If this labyrinth was built by the Caids, as Gun suggests, they would certainly have known the true movements of the sun and earth."

Dhulyn nodded. "Still, knowledge that does not help us can be put aside, I think. This is not literally the path of the sun, but we know that successful attempts to walk must start at sunrise. Perhaps as a working theory we can extend the metaphor so far as to take the paths that lead in the more easterly direction."

Parno looked down the left-hand path, frowned, and looked down the right-hand one before nodding. "As a working theory then."

Dhulyn's theory worked long enough for them to become hungry and pull roasted chicken, hunks of bread baked that morning by the Tarkin's cooks, and fruit out of their saddlebags. They had travel bread, and hard-cured strips of fish and meat in their packs; time enough to eat that when the fresh food ran out. Dhulyn was just taking a swig from her water flask when they approached another turning in the path. The stone and rock walls had gradually given way to dense cedar shrubbery, in places rough and straggly, in others trimmed as though by gardeners. Here the hedges looked as though they had been cut with a knife.

"Listen," Dhulyn said, in the nightwatch whisper.

"Voices," Parno agreed, in the same quiet tone. "On the other side of this hedge."

"No, ahead of us."

Parno slipped down out of the saddle to peer around the corner. Dhulyn joined him, sword in hand.

"Nothing," he said, straightening. "Empty as all the others have been." He squinted at her. "Some trick of the walls, sound bouncing?"

"Our own voices echoing back to us, you mean?"

Parno frowned. "Not very likely when you put it like that."

Dhulyn turned until they were almost back to back. "There's nothing likely about this place. It's the very definition of *unlikely*."

They turned back for the horses and remounted without saying anything more. Had the voices sounded familiar? Dhulyn was no longer sure she'd even heard them.

"We are now heading east, with possibly a finger's worth of south—"

"And if we take this corner, we'll be heading north, yes, my soul, I had realized that." Dhulyn drummed her free hand on her right thigh.

"We could turn back to the last dividing of the path, take the other direction."

"Which would turn us away from the east in any case," Dhulyn pointed out. "So far, our working theory has led us well; at least, we have not run into any dead ends."

"I suggest we continue, and if we don't find another path that will take us east within, say twenty horse lengths, we reconsider."

"Agreed."

Dhulyn took three deep breaths, letting each one out slowly, and once more triggered the Hunter's *Shora*. A tightening of her knees signaled Bloodbone to move forward slowly. There was no wind and none of the usual sounds of birds Dhulyn would expect from beyond the walls of the Path. The temperature was not uncomfortable, or even unseasonable for Menoin, but she did not think it had varied in all the hours they had been here.

Suddenly she coughed, blinking, and gagged slightly as

her stomach twisted, and she felt as though she were about to fall. "Parno?"

"Yes, I feel it as well. Just as though—" Parno's words trailed off as the feeling of nausea and disorientation died as abruptly as it had appeared. "Dhulyn?"

She nodded. "We're facing east again," she said. She looked back along the Path.

"Don't bother," Parno said. "The path hasn't curved, nor have we turned a corner. We haven't even gone the twenty horse lengths we were planning on—you can still see the corner we came around."

And so she could. "Onward, then, Hunter's *Shora*."

"I've spoken to you before about teaching your grand-mother."

They passed several more turnoffs, including one that led into a rock garden, but as the path they were on still led them east, they did not take any of the other ways. Some minutes after the last branching to the south, Dhulyn shut her eyes.

"Now we're going downhill," she said. She opened her eyes again. The path ahead of them looked as level and as smooth as a dance floor. And yet her senses were not deceiving her. There was a slight difference in the way Bloodbone's haunches tensed that told her unmistakably that they were walking down an incline.

And the ground fell out from beneath her.

Seven

PARNO TWISTED, thrusting out with his legs to distance himself from the flying hooves and crushing weight of his horse. Warhammer, trained for the accidents of the battlefield, would also be struggling to land well and safely. Parno's ears popped as air pressure changed, and for an instant he felt as though he were falling upward. He barely had time to think that Dhulyn would be safe—her Bloodbone was steadier, less inclined to panic than was Warhammer—when he hit the ground hard enough to bruise. He stayed where he was, only bringing up his arms to shield his head. To roll in any direction was possibly to roll under a falling horse.

A sharp whinny, and a curse, came from his left where Dhulyn, on her hands and knees, was already moving toward him. He held up his hand.

"A moment." He took a careful breath but found no pain in his rib cage. His arms and legs were likewise sound. He rolled until he could prop himself up on his elbow and winced, his hands pushing against thick turf where there had been dry stone a moment before. He looked around.

They were still in the Path of the Sun. "Demons and perverts," he cursed. "What *was* that?"

"Whatever it was," Dhulyn said as she got to her feet, "it is part of the labyrinth. Blooded Caids." She staggered and fell again to her knees. Parno saw that on the other side of his Partner Bloodbone was only just struggling to stand. He looked around. Warhammer was over against the wall, lying half on his side. But his head was up, his eyes alert, and as Parno watched, the gray gelding hitched at himself a couple of times and wobbled to his feet.

"Whatever this sickness is, it is passing from the animals more quickly," Dhulyn said. She was sitting back on her heels, her forehead in her hands as the world spun. Parno tried to sit up and winced, his hands going to his own head. He swallowed as his stomach twisted, and the grass beneath him seemed to want to exchange places with the stone walls of the Path. He hoped that his Partner was right, that this illness would indeed pass.

Dhulyn crawled over to him and held out her hand. Using her grip on him as leverage, she pulled herself upright until she was sitting cross-legged and could help him to do the same. Parno sucked in his breath; he was going to have quite a bruise where his sword hilt had dug into his side. Lucky it wasn't worse. When Dhulyn grabbed his other hand, he realized what she was doing and sat up as straight as he could. The twenty-seven basic *Shoras* that all Mercenaries learned included a meditation *Shora*, intended to increase relaxation and, by strength of focus, to make the other *Shoras* easier to learn and use. Partners often performed their meditation together, and that was what Dhulyn was doing now.

He took a deep breath, consciously making sure that they were breathing together. Almost immediately he felt his heart rate—their heart rates—slow and their breathing come easier. In a moment his head stopped spinning, as if the concentration of the *Shora* was all that was needed to clear the fog from his brain. The ground they sat on made a final wobble and steadied. Everything felt normal. Parno opened his eyes.

Dhulyn's eyes were still closed, a frown creating a tiny wrinkle between her blood-red brows. The scar that made her upper lip turn back when she smiled in a certain way was just visible, slightly paler than her own pale skin. Her eyes blinked open.

"Better?" he asked, and waited for her nod. "Do you know what it was?"

"It was like being at sea, after the typhoon hit," she said. "After a long while in the water, I couldn't tell what direction the waves were carrying me—even which way the surface was, at times." She shrugged.

"We'd lost our sense of direction," he remembered. For a Mercenary Brother, that was serious indeed. They could not afford to be turned around in the heat of battle, for example, and people with poor senses of direction rarely made it through their Schooling. The Schooling itself, to say nothing of many of the *Shoras*, further enhanced whatever natural talent a Brother might have.

Dhulyn squeezed his hands and released them, hopping to her feet in one motion, her dizziness plainly gone. She went immediately to Bloodbone, stroking the mare's side and rubbing her face and nose. The warhorse snorted and bumped her head against Dhulyn's shoulder, like a large cat. Parno approached Warhammer with caution, crooning the soothing noises Dhulyn had taught him, and it was a mark of how nervous the horse was that he responded to Parno with the same ready affection that Bloodbone had shown his Partner. Anything familiar was welcome, it seemed.

"My soul." Parno looked over to where Dhulyn still stroked absently at Bloodbone's nose. She was looking not at him but at a knob of rock that protruded from the gray granite wall not far from where she stood. "What time would you say it is?"

Parno's stomach rumbled, but he didn't think that "time to eat something" was the answer Dhulyn was looking for. "Perhaps the middle of the afternoon watch," he said. "Why?"

"Because if so, then these blooded shadows are pointing the wrong way."

"It must be the time of day that has somehow changed," Dhulyn said, as she recapped the water flask.

"It's one thing to know that your Visions show you both past and future, and that to the Crayx all of our recorded time is 'now.'" Parno took the flask from her and hefted it before replacing it among his gear. "It's another thing entirely to experience that in a matter of moments we've lost half a day."

"Can you think of another explanation?" Dhulyn said. "Somehow, in passing through that spot where we seemed to fall, we have reached a place where, as these shadows tell us, it is still morning."

"*Blooded* demons," Parno cursed. "Will it take us that much longer to find the end of the Path, then?"

"I'm glad to hear you so optimistic," Dhulyn said. "I don't feel so sure we'll find the end at all."

Parno grinned at her. "We've been in worse spots."

"Happy you think so."

Food and water repacked, every tie, strap and girth double-checked, they set out once again, still side by side but leading their horses now, as Dhulyn felt it would be safer if the ground should once again decide to throw them down. They had not gone far down the turfed path when what looked like a marking caught Parno's eye.

"This is something we haven't seen before." Parno pointed at the rock wall on his side, just above his own height. Someone using great patience and skill had chiseled a shape into the rough granite wall. It was the first human-made thing they'd seen since entering the Path of the Sun — always supposing that the Path itself was not a human-made thing.

Dhulyn reached up and brushed at the carving with her dagger before stepping to one side to view it from a different angle. "It is the face," she said. "See here the chin? And here the nose and brows. I Saw this in my Vision the other night, when I Saw the Red Horseman."

Parno squinted his eyes and stepped to one side, squinting. Yes, he could see it now, the shape of the lips, the little hollows that were the pupils of the eyes. A face without doubt.

"Who could have put it there?" he wondered. "Someone taller than I am, for certain."

"Or someone on horseback, perhaps."

"Is it a warning? Or a guide?"

But Dhulyn was already shaking her head. "I've Seen it twice, I think. Once when it was very clean and fresh, as if newly done, and once again, like this, the eyes empty. But that was all, nothing else, just the face."

Parno touched his fingers to his forehead. "It does no harm to be polite," he said when he caught Dhulyn looking at him with a smile.

"I'll leave the courtesies to you," she said, dipping her head in a shallow bow, but to him, not to the carving on the wall.

They set off once again, leaving the carved face behind them, still carefully choosing every path and turning that would take them east. They had gone perhaps ten spans when Parno looked up to his left . . . and stopped.

"Maybe it's a different one," he said. But even he could hear the disbelief in his voice. It was identical, the pointed chin, the scrubbed line of the nose, the hollows of the eyes. Even the slight scratch where Dhulyn's dagger had scraped away a piece of lichen. She came to stand next to him, her shoulder brushing his.

"It seems you were right to be courteous." Dhulyn's voice twanged with anger, and Parno knew she was frightened. "We haven't circled back," she said. "We would have felt the change of direction."

Parno cast about for something, anything, to say to her. He narrowed his eyes. "We based our choice of direction on the way the shadows fell," he said. Dhulyn shot him a venomous look out of the corner of her eye. "No, listen, my heart. What if the shadows were *not* wrong?" Dhulyn turned, but she was listening now, though with a frown drawing down her blood-red brows. "What if they tell us truly?" he asked.

Dhulyn looked skeptical. "Shadows are neither right nor wrong in themselves," she said. "They *are*."

"Yes, exactly." Now it was becoming clearer to him. "If the shadows just are, then somehow we've interpreted them wrongly. We took the position of the sun from the angles of the shadows," he said, gesturing with his hands at an angle to show her what he meant. "We decided that the angles told us the time of day had changed after we passed through that . . . that falling place. What if we were wrong?"

Dhulyn chewed on her lower lip, turning slowly to look over the ground and rock around them. "So. If it is *not* the time of day that has changed, and this *is* the late afternoon . . ." This was Dhulyn's Scholar's voice, and Parno relaxed.

"Then it is the direction of the sun's path that has changed," they said in unison.

"East is west, and west is east," Dhulyn said.

"Here, wherever 'here' is, the sun rises in the east and sets in the west."

"And we have been traveling in the wrong direction." Dhulyn nodded, looped Bloodbone's reins more closely around her wrist, and set off again, this time with the carved face to their right. They had gone only a few paces, perhaps a quarter of a span, when they found the turf under their feet had been cut.

Parno squatted to examine the phenomenon more closely, alert to any clue it might give them. It looked as though someone had taken a dagger and cut a design into the turf. He glanced to one side. Yes, there were the pieces which had been removed, tidily placed at the bottom of the wall.

"Well?" Dhulyn said from where she stood guard to one side.

"A moment, my heart." The design looked familiar, rounded edges, perhaps a loop . . . Parno felt his face heat as he recognized the shape. Grunting, he straightened to his feet. "It's a badge," he said. "The shape of a Mercenary badge cut into the grass."

"It took you that long to recognize something you look at every day?" Her tone was lighter than the words would have suggested.

"Something I *see*, not something I look at," he said. "And besides, without the colors, and cut so large, the pattern is not so very easy to descry."

"But it means our Brothers have been before us, and we are on the right path."

And that was why, Parno thought, Dhulyn's tone was so light.

From there it was as if the badge brought them luck, and the Path was working with them. They turned only two corners, both to the right, and suddenly they were standing in a grass plain. Parno looked back and forth, stepped to one side and looked back in the direction they had come.

"My heart," he said. "There's no archway here, no marking of the Path."

"Riders approach from the north," Dhulyn said.

Alaria had no trouble finding her way down to the stable yard. Even if she had not remembered the route through Falcos Tarkin's royal palace, she now had two guards with her to show her the way—though she knew very well that was not their primary function. Again Dav-Ingahm, the Steward of Walls, had shown enough sense to assign her female guards, and she had been pleased to recognize one of them as Julen Egoyin, the stable master's daughter. Other faces were already becoming familiar to her, she realized, as she returned bows and curtsies with a smile and an inclination of her head.

The normal morning bustle of the stable yard was as familiar to her as her own home. She felt the tension ease from her shoulders. Two grooms were unwrapping a bandage from the right fore hock of a tall chestnut horse while a third stood back and watched, hands on hips. Younger boys and girls were striding back and forth with buckets of water and handbarrows loaded with pots of steaming mash. It took her a moment to realize there was about the same amount of noise and work as there would have been in her own mother's stables—perhaps less. Nothing like the bustle and commotion she'd seen in the Tarkina of Arderon's House. Alaria was reminded of the empty stalls she had seen a few days ago. Still, there were stalls occupied here, and they were already being cleaned, so Alaria picked up her pace. It had been three days since she'd last been down to check on her queens, but surely Delos Egoyin would have understood, would have known that this was the first chance she'd had. With Cleona gone—Alaria cleared her throat and squared her shoulders.

Alaria knew something was different the moment she entered the block of buildings that made up the stables themselves. She had not expected to find her queens still in the special front stall, where they had been made ready for a ceremony that had not taken place—and now never would. But a quick glance was enough to tell her that none of her horses were even in this part of the stables at all. Her heart thumping, Alaria relaxed the hands that had formed into fists and turned to her guards.

"Where might I find your father at this hour?" she asked Julen.

The guard frowned, sending short, sharp glances around the enclosure and out into the yard. "His rooms are in that wing, at the end of the yard," she said finally.

They were making their way back through the yard when the figure of Delos Egoyin appeared out of the middle of the stable block, wiping his hands clean on a scrap of cloth.

"Ah, there you are, Princess." The older man bobbed his head in the sketch of a bow. "I was wondering why I hadn't seen you before, though of course we know of your loss—our loss, I suppose I should say, if it comes to that, though I only laid eyes on your cousin the once, when I picked out her mount for her. And now they're both gone, cousin and mounts, and Essio as well."

Alaria almost smiled. It seemed that for Delos the loss of the horses was almost as important as the loss of the people. She understood his feelings and sympathized. But she had other horses on her mind.

"Where are my queens, Delos Egoyin?" she said. "Who has moved them without my knowledge?"

The older man rubbed at his upper lip with a rough finger. "I wouldn't have moved them, you understand, Princess. And it was against my advice it was done. Not that they're so close to their time, but with so much at stake—I wouldn't have moved them."

Which meant someone else had, someone with greater authority here even than the stable master. Her hands formed into fists again, and this time she let them. Time for everyone to learn that there was only one person in Menoin with authority over Arderon horses, and that was the remaining Princess of Arderon.

"Who requested the transfer?"

"Notice came down with the Tarkin's mark on it," Delos said.

Alaria crossed her arms and took a deep breath, letting it out through her nose. "Where is the Tarkin now?" she asked Julen.

Her eyes round, Julen Egoyin glanced at her father before answering. "It's time for the morning audience, Lady of Arderon, for common folk and foreigners."

"Well, Caids know, I'm foreign enough. Lead me."

The waiting room of the Tarkin of Menoin's morning audience chamber was larger than Alaria expected. There were seats, pitchers of ganje kept warm over small pots of oil paste, with watered wine and glazed clay cups on the small tables that were scattered around the room. The floor was tiled in large squares of black and white, the walls were patterned in green, red, and white tiles to about shoulder height, and painted above with scenes of what looked like ceremonial games: javelin throwing, archery, and the like. The coffered ceiling showed signs that a master carver had been employed to work on it. All this Alaria saw in a quick glance, as the dozen or so people waiting all got to their feet when she came through the open doorway.

"Please," she said, making a sitting motion with her hands. Her fury was subsiding, and she began to realize that she was intruding on the legitimate business of the people of Menoin. As she hesitated, however, the senior page attending on the inner door beckoned her forward.

"I will wait my turn," she said, approaching him, but the scandalized look he gave her—mirrored on the faces of the people waiting nearest the door—showed her that she had better go in, and quickly. Gesturing her acknowledgment of the inevitable and murmuring her thanks to the others in the outer room, Alaria allowed the door page to escort her into the audience chamber.

Falcos Akarion was just grasping hands—shaking hands they called it here—with a petitioner in a beautifully embroidered robe as she came in. The room steward stepped forward to lead the man out, and he announced Alaria at the same time.

The face Falcos turned to her was paler than she remembered it. She had not seen the Tarkin since the Mercenary Brothers had entered the Path of the Sun, and though his eyes were bright, and his thick black hair still hung in perfect waves over his shoulders, he seemed tired. Somehow, his beauty struck her as less inhuman than she had felt it to be.

This room was smaller than the waiting room, but it had two windows in the right-hand side that gave on a courtyard full of flowers and sculpted trees. Between the windows was a desk where two men were seated, one writing. Clerks, Alaria thought, who would be recording the Tarkin's judgments.

Falcos stepped down off the shallow dais to greet her as an equal, extending his hand. Alaria was so taken aback by this that she was shaking hands with him before she quite realized what she was doing.

"Lady of Arderon," he said, leading her to take the seat next to the throne-like one on the dais. "How can I help you?"

"My horses," she said. She didn't want to sit down, but she knew enough about courts and courtesy to know they would get down to business faster if she did. "They have been moved from their place in the royal stables, moved from the care of Delos Egoyin. Why has this been done? Why was I not informed?"

"I know nothing of this," Falcos said, his blue eyes narrowing.

"It was my doing, Falcos." As soon as he spoke Alaria realized that the man she'd taken for the second clerk was in fact Epion Akarion. She hoped her surprise and confusion was not evident. A male clerk, that was only to be expected, but what was the Tarkin's own uncle and first counselor doing sitting down at the same table? He had risen and now came out from behind the worktable, inclining his head to her as he came, a rueful look on his pleasantly craggy face. "They are not needed at present for any ceremony, and I was not happy with them there in the outer stables, accessible to all the curiosity seekers, especially now that they are so close to foaling."

It was a reasonable explanation. In fact, that had been Alaria's own purpose in going down to the stables this morning. But somehow Epion's very reasonableness rubbed at her.

"And why was I not informed?"

Epion's eyes grew round and he looked from Alaria to Falcos and back again. The look on his face reminded her of the expression her tutors had when she hadn't grasped some point of logic, and Alaria stifled the urge to apologize.

"But, my dear Princess," Epion was saying. "Why should you be troubled with the disposal of the Tarkin's horses, any more than you should be troubled with the news that his clothing had been sent to the laundry?"

Alaria gripped the arms of her chair and raised her chin to look Epion straight in the eye. The very reasonableness of his tone was grating. "Because unlike his clothing, those horses are not the Tarkin's property," she said, in as measured a voice as she could muster. "They were a bride gift for a marriage that has not taken place, and as such, they still belong to Arderon. To me, in fact," she added, "as the only representative of Arderon in this court." She turned to Falcos. The Tarkin was watching them, his face carefully neutral, but Alaria swore his eyes were twinkling. She straightened her spine.

"I require the return of my property," she said.

"Really, Falcos, I had no idea—"

The Tarkin cut his uncle off short with a raised hand. "Kalyn?" he said. The older man, the real clerk, rose from his place at the worktable and came forward.

"It is as the Princess of Arderon says," he said. He had his hands folded in front of him, but he looked each of them in the eye as he spoke, and his tone was not a servile one. "The horses were not a personal gift from the Tarkina of Arderon—one ruler to another—but rather they were a bride gift accompanying the Princess Cleona, which would pass to the crown of Menoin only if the marriage took place. Seeing as that is not the case," the man cleared his throat, the corners of his mouth turned down. "The mares and their foals remain the property of Alaria, Princess of Arderon, as her cousin's heir."

Alaria turned immediately to Epion. "Where are my horses?"

"I but moved them to the inner courtyard, where they might be more secure," he said, with a slight bow. There was nothing but concern on his face. "And if I have anticipated the event, I'm sure I beg your pardon and indulgence." Here he bowed more deeply.

"What event?" Falcos had the question out before Alaria could ask it herself.

"Why, your marriage to the Princess Alaria, of course." Epion looked between them, brow furrowed in a frown. He seemed genuinely worried, genuinely concerned—was it possible? Then the import of his words penetrated.

"Marriage?" she stammered out. "Marriage to *me*?"

"Why yes." The older man looked once more between them. Alaria thought she saw her own shock mirrored on Falcos Tarkin's face. "Surely you realized? Naturally the treaties and agreements between our two nations are still of vital importance—perhaps even more so now," Epion said. "Of course, nothing has been said in the wake of this terrible tragedy, but I assumed—that is, it seemed to me logical that after the passage of a suitable, and short, mourning period, a marriage must take place between the two of you."

"The Princesses of Arderon are not interchangeable game pieces," Falcos said.

Alaria felt her ears grow hot. Of course not. She was not as close to the throne of Arderon as her cousin Cleona, though the Caids knew there could very well be no one closer. She shivered as an unpleasant thought occurred to her. Was this the real reason she had been allowed to come? In case something unforeseen had happened to one of them, there would still be an Arderon princess to offer to the Tarkin of Menoin? The more Alaria thought about it, the more the idea made sense. It had not occurred to her before because Cleona had at least been a first daughter, and Alaria was used to thinking of herself as a younger child, a nobody at court. She realized through the buzzing in her ears that the Tarkin was speaking to her.

"I merely meant—" Falcos appeared to be blushing. "I merely meant that you had not come here with that purpose, that you might prefer to return to your own land, to your family."

For a moment Alaria saw her home again, the hills behind her mother's fortress, the fog burning off the valley floor as the sun rose. The color of the grass with the year's first frost on it. Then she saw the harbor here in Uraklios, empty of trading ships, and the stables empty of horses. The small signs of age and neglect even on the walls of this room, and the outer one, that she had not really taken in when she'd first seen them. The joy and relief on the faces of the people who had come to the ship to greet them. The cheering with which they greeted a Tarkina who had come to save them.

"I know my duty," she said the gooseflesh forming on her arms. "I will stay."

~

They were in the saddle, swords loosened in their scabbards and throwing knives to hand, while the approaching riders were still only a sound through the earth.

"Sure we shouldn't run for it?" Parno asked.

"Run where?" Dhulyn answered, knowing full well Parno didn't need to be told. What would be the point of fleeing, when they did not even know who approached? They knew nothing of the surrounding land and would be easily run down and caught by those who did. And once caught, they would have to explain why they ran. There really was nothing for them to do but wait, politely, and hope to be given a hearing. Of course, if there were a great many with bows among the approaching riders, she might not live long enough to regret her decision.

"Think they might shoot first and ask questions after?" Dhulyn shivered at Parno's eerie echo of her thoughts. She was beginning to wish they'd never chosen to walk the Path of the Sun. But that reminded her of the Common Rule.

"The path of the Mercenary is the sword," she said aloud.

"The path of the sword is death," Parno completed the chant.

She grinned at him. "In Battle," she said.

"*And* in Death," he answered.

The riders were close enough now to see that there were nine of them, riding practically elbow to elbow in a compact group, and that they rode closely, and straight, as though they followed some trail in the grassland that Dhulyn could not see. But there was something else.

"Parno," she said.

"I see it."

Though it was late in the day here, the sun still shone, and it showed clearly the colors of the clothing of the riders coming toward them. And, unmistakably, the blood-red color of their hair, identical to her own. Not possible. Her mouth formed the words, but no sound escaped her lips.

"Red Horsemen," Parno said.

Eight

DHULYN AND PARNO had done many hard things since they'd left their Schooling, but sitting still and watching as the Red Horsemen rode closer and closer was perhaps the hardest. Finally, Parno twisted in his saddle until he could push up the flap on his left saddlebag; he reached in and took out four crossbow bolts.

Dhulyn shook her head, patting the air between them with her left hand. "Let's not appear more hostile than necessary. It may be they are merely riding in this direction. Perhaps the Path signals them somehow when it has been used."

Parno shrugged, but he slid the crossbow bolts into the tops of his boots, as if he were unwilling to put them away now he had them out. "That will be useful for us, if they know who has come through and when."

They knew the moment the Red Horsemen sighted them. With no break in stride or speed, four of the approaching riders split off from the main group, two to each side, spreading out in what was clearly a flanking maneuver. When the central group had advanced perhaps a span, one of the riders raised what looked at this distance like a spear and the Horsemen came on faster.

"Demons," Parno said. "They're not slowing. So much for not showing any overt hostility." He snatched up his crossbow from its hook on his saddle and cocked it, forcing the string back by hand until it hooked over the trigger, pulled out the two bolts he'd slid into his left boot.

"Centaur *Shora*," Dhulyn said. "No blood. Some one of these may know something about our missing Brothers."

"Blessed Caids, woman." Parno lowered the crossbow, but he didn't uncock it. "Are you trying to kill us? *They* have bows."

"And spears too, and they haven't used them yet," Dhulyn pointed out. "Nor are they likely to. There is no honor in killing us at a distance."

"Blooded Outlanders," Parno said, though his tone was lighter than his words. "We'd have no such scruples, were the situation reversed."

"Ah, but we're Mercenary Brothers, not blooded Outlanders." Dhulyn smiled her wolf's smile. "What? There are only eight of them." She pulled her best sword out of its scabbard across her back and her second-best sword from where it was strapped along her saddle under her right knee. As she was testing her grip, Parno suddenly twisted, turning Warhammer partly around, and cut an arrow out of the air, the broken shaft falling practically under Warhammer's hooves.

"I thought you said they wouldn't shoot," he growled, as two more arrows fell short.

"They'll avoid hitting the horses."

"I'm not worried about the horses," he said, but he was grinning as he said it, and Dhulyn found herself grinning back. Fighting was always easier than waiting.

There was a whisper of displaced air, and Dhulyn knocked aside two more arrows. Only the riders who had split off from the rest were shooting, having ridden far enough that they would miss their own men. The five central Horsemen came straight on, four in front, one behind, swords swinging over their heads, hooves thundering an accompaniment to high-pitched cries. Dhulyn felt her heartbeat slow and readied her blades, holding them in the opening position of the Centaur *Shora*. Bloodbone and Warhammer did not spook, though a volley of arrows fell close to their hooves.

"Ah, I see," Parno said. "They are only meant to distract while the others come upon us."

As the Horsemen closed with them, Parno held tight with his knees and shot Warhammer forward, forcing the two riders trying to flank him to pull up sharply lest they crash into one another. Warhammer knew what to do without prompting and whirled immediately to ride down the left-hand horse, using his greater weight and iron shoes to advantage. The rider spilled to the ground and rolled away. Meanwhile Parno leaned backward, still clinging tightly with his knees and, remembering to use the flat of the blade, gave the second Horseman a calculated blow to the side of his head. Already off-balance from his fight to keep from crashing into his fellow rider, the man fell out of his saddle, flailing his arms like a man trying to fly.

As Dhulyn parried the blows of the second pair of riders, she saw out of the periphery of her vision that one at least of Parno's opponents was already down. Her own attackers were using the agility of their smaller mounts against her, sweeping nimbly back and forth, slicing at her as they passed. But Bloodbone was an old hand at this kind of fighting and dodged and kicked of her own accord, with scarcely more than an occasional shouted command. The riders were good, but they executed their sweeps a little too regularly, and by careful timing Dhulyn was able to kick out and unseat the one to her left. Mindful that these were nomads, she kicked him in the head—a civilized rider might have been unhorsed with a good shove to the chest, but no Horse Nomad could be unbalanced that way. The second man, missing his mate, was just turning to engage her head-on when the four flanking riders came pounding up. A high-pitched whinny, a heavy thud, and Dhulyn realized that Parno was down. She kicked her feet free of the stirrups, vaulted to stand on Bloodbone's back. One of the new riders turned his spear toward her. She tossed her left-hand sword into the face of another man, grabbed the spear just under the collar of hawk's feathers that decorated the shaft near the head and used it to swing herself, kicking and striking out with her remaining sword, into the circle of Horsemen that threatened her Partner.

She pulled her dagger out of the top of her boot and braced herself, weight evenly distributed and knees slightly bent.

"Hold." An old voice, but Dhulyn did not turn toward it. The man who spoke was one of the recent arrivals, the one whose spear she had made use of. From the note of command in his voice, he was likely the leader and therefore unlikely to be the source of the next blow. He was holding his spear in the air over his head, parallel to the ground.

"You did not run," he said. "You endanger yourself to help your comrade. It is the act of an honorable person."

Dhulyn's heart leaped. She could not have been sure with only the one word, but now that the man had spoken more, she recognized the old tongue, the language of her childhood. These did not merely *look* like Espadryni, they *were* Espadryni. She relaxed slightly but did not lower her weapons. Some remnant of her old Tribe they might be, but at the moment they were also an unknown quantity and therefore to be watched with care. Of the other riders, only two let their weapons rest; the others, especially those who had been knocked down and were only now getting back in the saddle, seemed to want to keep their weapons to hand.

Parno rolled to his knees and then his feet. He'd been winded, that was clear, and he was favoring his side where he'd landed on his sword hilt on the Path, but he seemed otherwise unhurt. She grinned. He had even managed to keep his swords in his hands when he'd been knocked from Warhammer's saddle.

The man who had stopped the attack dismounted from his horse. He moved easily, though, with a catch to her breath, Dhulyn saw there was a great deal of white streaking his blood-red hair. This was the man of her Vision, clearly a chief or shaman, since only such could have stopped the others with a word. Would they meet with the thin man as well, then? The one who was going to help them?

"He is my Partner," she said finally, answering the old man in the Espadryni tongue. "His life is mine, and mine his. Do you speak the common tongue?" she asked, switching to that language.

"I do, and I greet you, young one," he replied, his words accented but clear. "You and your Partner." Like the others, this man was dressed in loose trousers tucked into boots that came almost to the knees, topped with vests of various colors. This old man wore the only leather vest, and it was closely embroidered with symbols and shapes, some sewn over the others in disregard for any pattern or decoration. A shaman, then, for certain.

"We greet you, old man," Dhulyn said, half bowing.

"May I touch your markings?" He lifted his hand to his own temple, to show that he meant her Mercenary's badge.

"Dhulyn," Parno murmured at her back.

Dhulyn acknowledged his warning with a lifted finger and lowered her weapons slowly, not moving forward, but allowing the shaman to approach her. This might be what she had Seen in her Vision, when the old man had appeared to draw on her forehead. She felt the cool, dry touch of his fingertips on the skin where her Mercenary badge was tattooed.

"This is shaman's work, very clean, very powerful," the old man said. "It is not what binds you to your Partner, however, but merely the symbol of the binding. From what Tribe do you come, my child?" Out of the corners of her eyes Dhulyn saw the other riders had not relaxed, though they had heard the shaman address her formally as a kinswoman. Instead there was more shifting of eyes, and exchanging of frowns and glances.

"I am of no Tribe, Grandfather," she said, addressing him in the same style. "I am Dhulyn Wolfshead, called the Scholar. A Mercenary Brother. I was Schooled by Dorian of the River, the Black Traveler. I have fought with my Brothers at the sea battle of Sadron, on the plains of Arcosa in Imrion, and at Bhexillia, with the Great King in the West. I fight with my Partner, Parno Lionsmane." She indicated him with a gesture, but Parno only inclined his rough gold head without speaking.

"I am Singer of the Wind, Cloud Shaman to the Long Trees People. I do not know these places you speak of." He reached out again for her badge, and this time touched Parno's as well. Dhulyn felt a jolt run through her, familiar and yet . . . "As I do not know this magic of yours, though I would like to. You are not the shaman who created these marks, young man?"

"I am not," Parno said.

Singer of the Wind nodded, as if he had known the answer, and was asking out of some intricate courtesy. "As any eye can see, you are of our blood, Dhulyn Wolfshead. Which *was* your Tribe, if you no longer ride with them?"

"The Tribe of which you ask was called the Darklin Plain Clan," she replied. "Though once we pass our Schooling, Mercenaries have no ties other than to the Brotherhood. In that sense, we have no pasts." Though that was easily said, as Dhulyn had come to know. Mercenary Brothers might let go of their pasts, but those pasts didn't always let go of them.

"That Clan, too, is unknown to me." His eyes narrowed once more. "This is the season for the People of the Long Trees to attend the Doorway of the Sun," Singer said. "This place is currently in our charge. You must tell me where you come from, my children. What do you want here so close to Mother Sun's Door?"

So the Horsemen *did* know about the labyrinth. Dhulyn's shoulders loosened at this confirmation that there would be a way home. But then they stiffened again. Could the killer they sought be among these Horsemen?

"We have come through the Doorway, my Partner and I, though among our people it is called the Path of the Sun." Dhulyn fell silent as there was another exchange of glances between the Horsemen. One who rode a spotted horse muttered something under his breath. Nothing good, she thought. Singer of the Wind's attitude did not change, but those few who had laid down their weapons picked them up once again.

"It has been long since we have met with others who came through the Door. In the times long ago, they were kings and leaders among their people who came." He hesitated for a moment, looking from Dhulyn to Parno and back again. "Though there were others also, put to the trial, to see if their lives were forfeit to the Mother of us all."

Tarkins who didn't come back, Dhulyn thought. Or did the old man mean something else?

"You will understand," the shaman continued, "that we must satisfy ourselves as to *your* natures and purpose. You do not have the look of kings or leaders. You, Dhulyn Wolfshead, are obviously a woman of our people, but you do not hold Parno Lionsmane at your mercy, as some of us believed. You risked your life to save him, you neither ran when you had the opportunity, nor did you seek to trade his life for you own."

Dhulyn shook her head, but no clarity presented itself. "I don't understand, Grandfather."

"Nor do I, my child, and as I have said, I would like to."

The man on the spotted pony muttered something under his breath again.

"Sun Dog," Singer of the Wind said. "You are not a child. Speak if you have something to say before men."

The man shrugged. "I do not think I have ever seen a woman armed."

"Sun Dog's frightened," another young man said.

"I saw her knock you out of your saddle, Rock Snake, so perhaps I'm right to fear her, if only for your sake."

The others laughed.

"Do you doubt my magic, Sun Dog." The smile on Singer of the Wind's face was cold. "Do any of you?" he looked around, carefully meeting the eyes of each of the other Horsemen. Each, in turn, shook his head. Several lowered their eyes in the face of the old man's fierce gaze.

"No, I imagine you do not," the shaman said. "I have said that this young woman is whole and safe. I do not know how it is possible, but I hope to learn." He turned back to them. "I am right, am I not, my child? You are Marked with the Sight?"

"I am."

"And the other women of your Tribe? Are they like you?"

"I believe so, Grandfather. But in our land, the Tribes of the Espadryni were broken when I had seen my birth moon only six times. I remember very little, though I have Seen more."

"And your women lived freely?" Dhulyn lifted her shoulders in the face of the man's persistence. "Though they were Seers? They went armed? They married? Did they love their children?"

Dhulyn blinked, thinking of the tall, red-haired woman whom she had Seen so often in her Visions. "My mother loved me," she said. "She hid me from the Bascani, those who broke the Tribes. I cannot say what the other women felt for their children. I have only Seen them in Visions, and then usually dancing."

"And they did not bring about the breaking of your Tribes?" There was a shuffling among the other Horsemen at these words.

"That I cannot know," Dhulyn admitted.

"If they did so," Parno interrupted, his tone dry. "They brought about their own destruction as well. So far as we know, Dhulyn Wolfshead is the only living Espadryni in our land."

Singer of the Wind looked around him at the other Horsemen, as if to draw his followers' attention to Parno's words. Several of them nodded their acknowledgment.

"Tell me, then," the shaman said. "What *is* your purpose here? What has brought you to this side of Mother Sun's Door?"

"There have been killings, on," Dhulyn hesitated. "On our side of the Door. Almost six moons ago two of our Brotherhood set out to track the killer, and they disappeared, never to be seen again, though now we have reason to think they may have come this way. Three nights ago, during the full of the moon, there was another killing, and the killer's trail led us into the Path of the Sun. So we seek this killer, but we also seek our missing Brothers."

The shaman was nodding. "So your purpose is one of honor and mercy. To find this killer and to stop him taking any more life. To give aid and rescue to your Brothers." Once again Singer looked around at his companions. This time they all nodded. He turned back to Dhulyn and Parno. "There is more we need to speak of. Will you come to our camp?"

Parno was not at all surprised that the Espadryni allowed them to mount, especially when he and Dhulyn were casually maneuvered into the center of a loose grouping of riders. The old man, Singer of the Wind, rode between them, Dhulyn on his right and Parno on his left.

"Grandfather," Dhulyn said when they had been riding in silence for half a span. "How did you know to come when you did? Can you sense when the Door is open?"

Singer of the Wind smiled. "Only if I wish to pass through myself," he said. Parno pricked up his ears. So the shaman, at least, could use the Path. "Still, I do not doubt our Mother the Sun has some hand in the chance of our meeting. We came to escort this young one." He indicated a younger version of himself, riding to Parno's left.

The boy, as if knowing himself spoken of, looked over and met Parno's eye. This was the fifth rider, Parno realized, the one who had ridden behind the central four.

"We come to make him acquainted with the place of his ordeal. Soon, after the proper rituals and meditation, he will try to pass through the Door."

Dhulyn leaned forward just enough to glance at Parno,

making sure he too had heard this. Parno lifted his right eyebrow, showing he understood. It was not only the old shaman, then, who could pass through the Door.

"We didn't interrupt his attempt?" Parno asked.

"No, Ice Hawk has not yet camped here alone for a full cycle of Father Moon, asking his blessing. He is some days away yet from his ordeal."

Parno had already concluded that the Espadryni's camp was only a short ride away. It was clearly no more than a temporary stopping place where the Horsemen had taken advantage of a large dip in the surrounding plain, where the winds had exposed a few large boulders. Here they had set up two shelters formed with spears and skins—one, from the look of the amulets and talismans suspended from it with strings woven from hair the color of old blood— belonging to the cloud shaman, Singer of the Wind. A fire ring had been made with stones, and there were packs and blankets neatly disposed around it, along with six riderless horses pegged out along the eastern edge of the hollow.

From the western edge of the camp, Parno scanned the area more carefully, looking for what he knew must be there—and found it. Concealed in the shadow of one of the boulders, his clothing almost an exact match for the rock, dirt, and scrub grass, was another Horseman, clearly left to guard the camp and the spare horses. When he saw that Parno had spotted him, the man stood up and came nearer to the shaman, keeping his eyes locked on Dhulyn and his face as expressionless as a spear head.

"Singer of the Wind," he said. "All is well?"

"Do not look so round-eyed, Moon Watcher, these travelers will think you have no manners. This is Dhulyn Wolfshead and Parno Lionsmane, visitors from the far side of the Sun's Door."

The man dipped his head to them without lowering his eyes, which he kept on Dhulyn, watching as she got down from her horse. He showed the same kind of watchfulness that the other men had earlier. Taking his cue from his Partner, Parno ignored him and dismounted. This was by no means the first time they had encountered Horse Nomads— though never before Espadryni—and courtesy dictated that no one ride within the perimeter of another's camp, no matter how temporary. Parno noticed the man's eyes get rounder still and his brows rise as he watched Dhulyn walk Bloodbone over to the horse line. Moon Watcher didn't ask the Cloud Shaman, nor any of the other men, any questions, however. Unlike the others, he seemed to trust implicitly that Singer of the Wind knew what he was doing.

The old man took his seat cross-legged on a pile of what looked like inglera skins with the fleece left on, though they were an unusual rusty color. He signaled Parno and Dhulyn to sit next to him, one on each side.

After they had seen to their horses, the others sat down in a circle around the fire pit, and the boy, Ice Hawk, fetched skins of water and small rounds of travel bread to distribute among the men. Parno accepted his with a nod, waiting as Dhulyn did until the others began to eat before breaking open his own round, to find some sort of dried meat baked into the center.

Singer of the Wind pulled a knife from his belt and thrust it into the ground in front of him. After some fidgeting from a man to Parno's right, the Horsemen fell silent.

"As I have said, Dhulyn Wolfshead, it has been long since warriors or kings have come through Mother Sun's Door. There are tales of others. Mages who have come to test themselves against the path, as our young men do, or criminals, set the path as task or punishment. Though, as I say, it has been long since we have seen, or even been given warning, of any such. Before my own birth moon, or the birth moon of any of my acquaintance. You say you have come seeking a killer. Are you the arm of justice, then, in your own land, that you would brave the ordeal of Mother Sun's Door?"

Dhulyn shot him a quick look, her lips parted. This would be the first time, Parno thought, that they had ever had to explain to anyone what the Mercenary Brotherhood was. Even the Mortaxa, on the other side of the Long Ocean, knew of the Brotherhood.

"We are a warrior brotherhood," she said finally. "As our name implies. But we follow very strictly our Common Rule, and all in our land know the Brotherhood and know that we cannot be paid to go against our training, or our words, or our Rule. This same Rule bids us, for example, never to leave abandoned any of our Brothers who may be in peril or need of rescue, and it seems that, as I have said, two of our Brothers have walked this Path before us. We would brave more than the Path of the Sun to find them, and to avenge them if it is needed." She paused, licking her lips, and looked to Parno, clearly unsure how to continue. It was typical of her to speak at this juncture of their missing Brothers and forget to mention the killer they were also looking for. Parno took up the explanation.

"It's not uncommon," he said, "in places where the rule of law is scarce or distant, for a Mercenary Brother to be asked to sit in judgment or to enforce the law of the land. We've done it, more than once, in our time. But this case," he shook his head. "This is a little more complicated. Though we come with the knowledge and approval of the law of Menoin—" he broke off, as there was a muttering among the seated Horsemen. Singer of the Wind gestured the men silent once again, and Parno continued. "So we've come with their approval," he repeated. "But primarily because the last victim of this killer had until recently been in our charge, and we feel, well, we felt . . ."

"We felt the killing had been done in despite of us," Dhulyn said. "And that we cannot allow. It is this killer we look for. The one whose tracks we followed into the Path of the Sun was in our land three nights ago—"

"The full moon," one of the Horsemen raised his hand. *Well that simplifies things*, Parno thought. Even if the sun moved in the wrong direction here, at least the moon went through its phases at the same time. The weather here seemed to agree that it was late summer. Perhaps there would other similarities.

The man who spoke was Sun Dog, the one who rode the spotted horse. Not a shaman, Parno thought, but perhaps someone in line to be chief. The young man had that kind of assurance. Singer of the Wind frowned at him, and the younger man merely dipped his head, as if in apology for the interruption. The shaman turned his attention back to Dhulyn, signaling her to continue.

"As for the killer." Dhulyn swallowed and took a breath. Parno wished he were sitting close enough to her to touch her. "As for the killer," she repeated and stopped again. "Tell me, Singer of the Wind, have you seen anything of this kind, here?"

Dhulyn began to describe the mutilated corpse they had

seen in Menoin. At first her voice was calm, detached, as though she were doing no more than giving a routine report to a Senior Brother. As she continued, however, even though she gave only the necessary, telling details that would trigger recognition or memory among those listening, her voice thickened, her words slowed, and she began to falter and hesitate. Finally Parno signaled her with a wave of his index finger and finished the description for her, giving the last details of the untouched hands and feet.

When he stopped talking, several of the men were looking away. The young boy, Ice Hawk, had his hands over his mouth, and stared straight ahead. The long silence was broken only by that same man, who shifted again in his seat. Parno was beginning to think the man was sitting on an anthill and that some protocol prevented him from changing his place.

Singer of the Wind patted Dhulyn on her knee. "My child, take heart," he said. "We must all see things in our lives that we would wish not to have seen." He looked around him, gathering the attention of all the men. "But *we* have seen something here and can now bear witness to it. You can all of you swear of your own experience to what I know by the force of my powers. This woman is whole, her spirit intact, and she feels as anyone would feel." He turned back to Dhulyn and patted her again. "Some might have said you have learned to act a part, my child, that anyone can study the correct words to use and the manner of using them. To make the voice sound heavy with sorrow or warm with interest. But no one can change the color of their skin at will. No one can turn pale, as you have done, without genuinely feeling the weight of what they say."

Sun Dog, sitting on Dhulyn's other side, also reached out and patted her on the knee. There were smiles on several faces.

Dhulyn's face was impassive, but Parno could tell she was thinking furiously. Clearly what the old man was saying had great importance, but why? What was the meaning of all this talk of feelings and safety and wholeness? If they were in their own land, Parno thought, Dhulyn would not hesitate to simply ask, but here, she obviously felt she must be more circumspect. She had somehow gained the Espadryni's trust, and she needed to keep it.

"Thank you, Grandfather," she said. "Do I think correctly? You have not seen here a killing such as my Partner and I have described?"

There were general head shakes—but one man frowned, his eyes narrowing as he looked inward.

"Sky Tree, do you know something of this?" the Cloud shaman said.

"No! Grandfather, no! Not in that way, at least." The man turned so white his eyebrows looked like stains on his face.

"Then tell us."

"It was not I but Jorn-Thornis, of the Cold Lake People, who told me of it at the last Gathering of the Tribes. A hunting band reported having found the spoor of a demon." The man swallowed. "What he told me sounded much like what we have heard today."

"How did they know the spoor was left by demons?" Parno said.

"What else but a demon would do such a thing?"

Clearly Dhulyn was not inclined to argue. Nevertheless she spoke. "Our demon left footprints, and rode horses," she said.

"Perhaps a man in your world and a demon in ours," Sky Tree said.

"Certainly there has been nothing of such moment here." Singer of the Wind glanced behind him at where Ice Hawk stood and waited until the young man shook his head before turning back into the circle of seated Horsemen. "There cannot be many such tales, or we would have heard more. Perhaps among the men of the fields and towns—and why can you not sit still, Gray Cloud?"

The old man's words snapped out, and everyone turned to look at the man who had been fidgeting and shifting since they began talking.

"If I am not mistaken, he has dislocated his shoulder," Dhulyn said.

"Possibly the wing bone is broken," Parno added. "Do you have a Healer among your Tribe, or is there one nearby?"

"A Healer? What do you mean, my child? Are there Healers also in your land?"

"And Menders and Finders," Dhulyn said.

"Whole? Safe?" This was Sun Dog.

Dhulyn looked at Parno, the question in her eyes. He nodded. "You've used that phrase many times," she said. "I confess I do not know what you mean by it."

"My child, here *all* the Marked are broken and dangerous, not like other people. They are put to death as soon as they are discovered."

"This is why we Espadryni became nomads," Sun Dog added. "Our women are Marked, and broken in the way of all Marked. But without them we would have no magic, the Tribes would be broken, and we would cease to be. Who then would guard Mother's Sun's Door?"

"In the old days, when we saw what the men of field and town would do, we withdrew, we became nomads," Singer of the Wind said. "To keep our women, to keep the Seers safe."

"Demons and perverts," Parno said.

Nine

"THERE, that takes care of most of it." Gundaron looked around the rooms they'd been given near the Princess Alaria's apartments and sighed. "How could we have accumulated so much baggage? We haven't even been here a year."

Mar understood Gun well enough to know that it wasn't accumulated baggage that was bothering him. They were both Scholars, Library-trained, though technically she had still to pass her final examinations. And though she was, again, technically, part of a High Noble House in Imrion, she had been brought up as a foster child in a family of weavers, and Gun's family had been farmers. Which was to say, neither of them found the frugal, simple life of Scholarship to be much of a challenge.

"I know we didn't bring much with us," she said now. "But most of that was clothing wrong for this weather." Of course, they'd known it was hotter in Menoin than they were used to, since Imrion was farther south. They just hadn't realized how much hotter. "Our heavier clothing doesn't pack very small," she pointed out. "And it's not as though we can afford to get rid of it. When we go home, we'll need it again."

She refrained from pointing out how much of the "accumulation" was made up of the books they'd borrowed from local Scholars and the Tarkin's Library. Those alone had necessitated the use of a middle-sized cart, complete with donkey, to move their things to the palace.

Mar sank down into one of the cushioned chairs with a sigh and looked around the room. Most of their gear had been shoved in loosely organized heaps in the second bed-chamber, and their clothes had been thrust hastily into chests and presses in the first. The only truly neat spots in their three rooms were the two worktables in the sitting room, with their tidy rows of books and scrolls, pens, inks, and blank parchments. At least the discoveries Mar and Gundaron had made in the Caids' ruins, painstakingly un-covered and cataloged, had already been sent here to the Tarkin's palace for storage.

Gundaron fidgeted around his worktable, picking up and putting down the parchment on which he'd been making notes at the dig on the day they'd learned of Dhulyn Wolf-shead's and Parno Lionsmane's arrival. They'd been follow-ing standard practice, dividing the area of the ruins into sections and squares and examining each one carefully be-fore moving on. When he put the parchment down for the third time, Mar spoke up.

"Can't concentrate?" She shoved a chair toward him with her foot.

He rubbed at his upper lip and sat down. "I know I should settle to some work, but there are just so many more urgent things to think about. After all, any artifacts in those ruins have been there since the days of the Caids. They can easily wait a few more days."

"Or weeks for that matter."

"Exactly." Gun stopped himself just in time from leaning back. Like much of the furniture in these warmer countries, the chairs were backless, little more than wide stools with arms. "Whatever's happening to Wolfshead and Lionsmane, *that's* happening right now."

"And we've got to be ready for when they return with news of the killer," Mar said. What would Alaria need from them, she thought.

"Or when they don't return." Gun swallowed, rubbing again at his upper lip with the fingers of his left hand.

Mar gritted her teeth. She'd been avoiding saying the words aloud—but just the same, she'd been thinking them, too. What would Alaria of Arderon do if the Mercenaries did not return? What would any of them do?

"We should be finding a way to help them," she said.

"They don't need our help." Gun's lips formed a shallow smile, and Mar grinned back at him. It was hard to imagine that either Lionsmane or Wolfshead would ever need anyone's help. But still . . .

"We *have* helped them before. You know we have. Surely there must be some way to help them now."

"If I could only Find the blooded key to the Path of the Sun. It's *got* to exist! A map, a drawing of the labyrinth — *something*."

Mar thought she understood the source of Gun's frustration. For years he'd hidden the fact that he was a Finder, thinking he wouldn't be allowed to become a Scholar if it was known he was Marked. Now his Mark was out in the open, and he'd even spent three months in a Guild House learning from other Finders, and he *still* couldn't Find something he knew had to exist.

"It's like a logic puzzle," Mar said. She got up and fetched them each a plum from the bowl of fruit on the table. "The Tarkins must have had a key at one point. How else could they be able to walk the Path themselves and return? Therefore, there must be a key."

"That's not logic," Gun said, with just a hint of irritation in his voice. "That's just arguing in circles."

Mar looked away so Gun couldn't see her grin. He was well on his way to getting over his frustration if he had the energy to quibble over her wording.

"I've looked for a map and Found nothing," he said. "And before you say anything else, there are no drawings, paintings, or patterns in brick, tile, or stonework that provide a key."

Mar sucked plum juice off her fingers. "What other things have patterns?" she asked. "Weaving? Music? Songs? Poetry?"

"Poetry." Gun had been leaning forward, his elbows on his knees. Now he straightened up so quickly that Mar was surprised his spine didn't crackle. "I'm an idiot."

"Only sometimes." Mar smiled.

"I wasn't looking for the key," he said, looking up at her. "I mean, not *a* key in general. I was looking for a map, or a drawing. I've been warned about making my searches too specific. What if it isn't a map but a description? A set of instructions? What if I was being too specific to Find?"

Mar ran into their bedroom, tossing clothing aside until she found the pack that held her scryer's bowl.

Gun meanwhile had cleared a space on the sitting room table and fetched the pitcher of water that stood with its net cover on the sideboard.

"I don't have a piece of clean silk to pour the water through," she said.

"Doesn't matter." Gun placed the bowl near the edge of the table and poured in the water. "I've never thought that part of the ritual was so important."

Without bothering to move a chair closer, Gundaron placed his fingertips along the edge of the bowl and took several deep breaths to calm himself. The light coming in the window slanted across the surface of the water, flashing little highlights as the liquid settled. A bit like letters meticulously copied onto a page of parchment or paper, as if he were hypnotizing himself by staring at the ink and page. The water—

❧

It's not water. It's a bright page of paper, and suddenly he's in a library. Not one that really exists—at least he's never tried to Find it anywhere but here—but one he knows all the same. Here he should be able to find the text he's looking for. He glances around, lip between his teeth, looking for the marker, the clue, that will lead him through the acres of bookshelves to the place he needs.

There's a shaft of sunlight on the floor, though there isn't any window to let it in.

Of course. He's being thick again. He's looking for the Path of the Sun, what else should show him the place but sunlight? He walks quickly now, down the main aisle, shelves and scroll holders branching out to left and right. He follows the sunbeam until, for a moment, the shelving seems to shimmer, and then Gundaron is walking between high stone walls, splotched with moss and stained with smoke, which abruptly become grass, damp with dew, and tall enough to brush against his thighs as he walks through it. The sunbeam still leads forward, however, and as Gun follows it the grass disappears once more, and, superimposed on the shelving and books of his mental library there is a wide, tree-lined avenue. The ghosts of people, dressed in every style and in many colors, walk around him, talking, though he hears nothing. The sunbeam leads him toward a broad flight of marble stairs, each step inlaid with a pattern of moons and stars in contrasting stone. And then he is in a library again, this time a small room whose windowless walls are completely covered with books. There are many colors in the spines of the books, but only one seems to have a gold spine. He pulls the book off the shelf; it has a sunburst on the cover.

Gun stepped back away from the table and blinked. Mar was smiling at him.

"I know where it is," he said. "I know exactly where it is."

Alaria leaned on her folded arms and looked over the side of the stall. Delos Egoyin had sent his head page for her just as the sun was rising, saying that one of her queens looked to be starting to foal. Alaria had come as quickly as she could, making her guard trot to keep up with her. As she'd thought, it was Star Blaze who was foaling. All the mares had foaled before, and there was very little for either her or Delos to do but stand ready to assist if assistance was needed.

Now Alaria entered the stall and took hold of Star Blaze by a handful of mane, stroking the mare's nose with a practiced hand.

"Look now, Sister," she said to the horse. "You've given us a little stallion, the first of our new herd." As she spoke, the tiny animal staggered to its feet, its legs thin and wobbling beneath it.

Alaria freed Star Blaze's head as the mare turned to nose at her foal, licking at it so fiercely she almost knocked the tiny thing from its feet. Alaria stood up, pushing her hands into her lower back and stretching out muscles stiff with tension. "There," she said. "That's the first. Goddess grant the others go as smoothly."

"It's easy to see you're a practiced hand at this, Lady of Arderon," Delos Egoyin said. The man seemed to be grinning all over as he beamed down at the little white horse with its black mane and tail.

"Egoyin! What are you thinking of? What is the Princess of Arderon doing in that stall while you stand by?"

It wasn't until she heard Falcos Tarkin's voice that Alaria even remembered the messenger who had come for her—and been sent away—more than an hour before, just at the most interesting moment. Alaria met Delos Egoyin's eyes, and the stableman moved his head a shade to the left and back again. Such was the authority in the Tarkin's voice that even the mare took her attention away from her foal long enough to shake her head at the man. Alaria rose slowly to her feet.

"In Arderon we do not show respect to people by expecting them to stand idly to one side while there is work to be done," Alaria said, taking her time to approach the opening where Falcos stood. "And to serve horses is an honor to all people. Even our Tarkina attends the births of royal horses."

Well, officially at least, that's true, Alaria thought. Whether the ruler of Arderon actually got down on her hands and knees and dealt with the afterbirth was something she would have wagered against.

Falcos Tarkin stood quite still, the muscle in the corner of his perfect jaw jumping, when suddenly he took a deep breath, came into the stall, and plumped himself down on the small bench placed there earlier for Alaria.

"I knew that," Falcos said, sounding tired. He leaned back against the boards and shut his eyes for a moment before straightening and looking down at his clasped hands. "I'm sorry. I spoke without thinking. Of course I studied your customs carefully when negotiations for the marriage began—I'm sure you did the same." His voice was softer now, and the mare and foal paid him no mind.

"Cleona did," Alaria said.

A few minutes passed with only the sounds of the foal suckling and the mare shifting her feet as she looked from her son to the Tarkin of Menoin and back. *The mare accepts him*, Alaria thought. Not everyone could come into the stall with a breeding queen.

"Do you want to go home?"

Alaria sucked in her breath, turning sharply to look at Falcos Tarkin, her teeth clamped down on her lower lip. "I've already said that I know my duty," she said finally.

"And I thank you for that. But set aside your duty just while we sit here, and tell me what you wish for."

Alaria lowered her eyes and scrubbed at her dirty hands with the cloth she had hanging from her belt, but she kept silent. After all, talk would change nothing.

"Come, there is only old Delos here, who put me on my first pony." Falcos turned to smile at the old stableman, before turning back to smile at her, the first genuine smile she'd seen on his face, Alaria realized. It transformed him completely, his cold marble beauty warm now, and human. "And the horses certainly won't be shocked if we ignore protocol a little and just speak like ordinary people."

Alaria involuntarily smiled at the mare with her new foal. "I don't want to go home," she heard herself say. "There's nothing for me there but to be the younger sister." She looked Falcos in the eye. "To find a rich woman's son to marry so as not to be a drain upon my older sister and my family's stables."

To her surprise Falcos' smile widened. "Well, I'm probably rich enough to qualify," he said.

Alaria found herself smiling back. "I didn't come here to be married," she reminded him. "I came so that my cousin, my friend, wouldn't be alone." She glanced at Star Blaze and back at Falcos. "And I came for the . . . the adventure of the new herd. The importance of that work."

Was it her imagination, or did his smile grow a little smaller before it widened again? "We'll have to check the precedents. This is not Arderon, and we may find ourselves having to explain why the Tarkina is in the barns with the horses. I must ask Kalyn, he's sure to know." Falcos suddenly stroked his chin in so exact an imitation of the clerk's movement that Alaria laughed. *I'm giddy*, she thought. *It's the foal.* Though it was good, very good, to speak to someone as a friend.

"It would be pleasant," Falcos continued in the same bantering tone, "if you chose to stay for more than your duty and the horses."

Alaria felt her face grow hot. These were the words, if not precisely the tone, of flirtation. And yet there was nothing in his face of the conceit she would have expected to find in so handsome a man. He did not seem to feel that his beauty alone was enough to entice her. And he was kind enough, gentle enough—or at least so it seemed—to make all this feel like a courtship and not a political agreement. A friendly gesture, in its way, and Alaria felt again how badly she needed a friend.

So much had happened, and so suddenly, that she hadn't felt alone, really alone, until now. She glanced at Falcos again, but he had let his gaze drift, so that he seemed to be studying Star Blaze and the foal. There was a stiffness in his bearing, however, that hadn't been there a few moments before. Was it possible, Alaria thought, that Falcos Akarion, Tarkin of Menoin, was shy at having spoken to her? Was he as badly in need of a friend as she was herself?

"I have said that I would just as soon stay," she said, trying to keep her own voice light. "Even if, for the moment, it is only for the sake of the horses."

Did she imagine it, or did Falcos relax?

"Then it appears that, for the sake of the horses, we will marry." He put out his hand to her, and she took it. It was warm, and the palm surprising rough for a man's. *He has held a sword*, she realized. She would have to stop thinking in this old way. She would share the rule of Menoin now.

"I will return after the midday meal, Delos Egoyin," she said, turning to the old stableman. Her hand was still in the Tarkin's. "Let me know immediately should any of the others show signs that the foals come."

"Of course, Lady." The old stableman was unexpectedly gruff, but Alaria saw there was a twinkle in his eye.

So talk *could* change things, Alaria thought, as she walked out of the stable hand-in-hand with the Tarkin of Menoin. Or, at least, it could change the way you felt about things.

"We are neither of us Knives," Parno said. "But we have seen and treated many injuries over the years, Dhulyn Wolfshead more than I." He looked from Singer of the Wind to Sun Dog. These two held the authority between them, that much was clear.

Dhulyn was squatting on her heels, speaking directly to the injured Horseman. "I can understand if you would rather I did not touch you." She shrugged. "If you are afraid that I am insane . . ."

"No," the man ground out between his clenched teeth. "Not afraid."

Parno caught Sun Dog looking at him and answered the man's sparkling eyes with a broad grin of his own.

"It was ever so with Gray Cloud," Sun Dog said. "He is vain of his courage."

"Many men are," Parno said.

With delicate touches, using only the tips of her fingers, Dhulyn prodded at the injured man's arm, his shoulder, and the upper part of his back before patting him on his good shoulder and straightening to her feet. "There is too much swelling," she said, as she joined them. "Even if the bone were not broken—and I can feel it move—there is too much swelling to put the shoulder back together. If he had said something right away . . ." She shook her head and shrugged. "I do not have the skill to set the bone," she said finally. "I have seen it done, I understand the theory, and I would attempt it were it not for the swelling, but as it is, I think I would do more harm than good. I fear even a skilled Knife cannot now make him completely as he was before." She fell silent and looked away, toward the horse line.

"You have thought of something, however," Parno said.

"If they know how to use the Path from this side, we could take Gray Cloud through. There are Healers in Menoin."

"It shows your good heart, Dhulyn Wolfshead, and the quality of your honor that you think of delaying your own task to help Gray Cloud." Singer of the Wind had come to join them.

"And what of yourself, Singer of the Wind?" Parno said. "You've passed through the Sun's Door, haven't you?" Dhulyn turned toward him, eyebrows raised, and Parno laughed. "Well? Don't looked so astonished. We've been told that they use the Path as a test for their young men. It stands to reason, of the people here right now, he's the most likely to have done it."

"Of course," Dhulyn nodded slowly. "A test for shamans." She eyed Sun Dog. "And perhaps for chiefs."

But Sun Dog was shaking his head. "Any who wish to may make the attempt," he said. "But few, and those usually among the most powerful of our mages, can pass through the Door of the Sun at will."

"And then only alone," Singer added. "I might pass through myself, but I can bring no one with me. That the two of you managed tells us much of the bond between you." He patted Dhulyn on the shoulder. "Do not be concerned for Gray Cloud. We may have no Healers here, but at least among the Espadryni, there *are* Mages." He turned away. "Star Watcher, Moon Watcher, come," he called. "You have heard the nature of the problem. Exercise your talents on your cousin Gray Cloud."

The young man who had been left to guard the camp was joined by another, so like him in appearance that it was obvious they were brothers.

"But, Grandfather, you said I could try the next curing." Ice Hawk appeared at Singer of the Wind's side, lips pressed in a thin line. Something in the boy's tone told Parno that the title was here no courtesy, that he really was the old man's grandson.

"Sun, Moon, and Stars are not aligning for you today, Ice Hawk. You are not ready for so complex a cure as Gray Cloud must have. Go and help the Watchers, learn."

The Watcher brothers, with Ice Hawk tagging along, eased the injured Gray Cloud to his feet and led him toward one of the skin shelters on the far side of the fire pit.

"Am I correct in thinking that a guard is not kept on the Sun's Door?" Dhulyn said, as they all settled once more into their seats.

Both Sun Dog and Singer of the Wind turned to look at her.

"You've said that not all among the Espadryni can pass through it," she pointed out. "But we are seeking at least one man who has done so repeatedly."

"Perhaps it's easier from our side," Parno said. "After all, we have passed through ourselves, and likely our Brothers as well."

"Ah, but you knew of the Door and that there was a Path. This knowledge is held here only by the Espadryni. The Door has been our charge since the time of the Green Shadow, and knowledge of it has disappeared from the men of the fields and cities."

But Dhulyn was shaking her head in tiny arcs, her brows furrowed. "Since the time of the Green Shadow—it has been here as well?"

"Of course. Why else did the Caids create the Marked, except to defeat the Shadow?"

"And it was defeated?"

"Oh, long ago. But we believe that it found some way even then to strike out at us, even as it was dying. It was after its defeat we discovered that the Marked were broken." There were murmurs and nods of agreement among the listening Horsemen.

Dhulyn and Parno exchanged looks. Their own experience with the Green Shadow was not so very far behind them. Clearly there was more different between the two worlds than the survival of the Espadryni.

"Might one of the other Tribes . . ." Dhulyn, once more cross-legged, rubbed her palms on her knees. "Would they harbor such a killer? Or, without your knowledge, would they travel the Path of the Sun?"

The Tribesmen fell silent.

"I do not know how things are on the far side of Mother Sun's Door," the shaman finally said. "But here the Tribes of the Espadryni live in a spirit of trust with one another."

Dhulyn drew her eyebrows down in a vee. "I believe you, Grandfather. But in our land, other nomads, other Horsemen, go through periods of hostility with each other."

Singer of the Wind shrugged, showing his understanding of such things. "We have, perhaps, better reasons to prevent us, than these others can know of. If we fight among ourselves, what would become of the Seers? We must stand united, of necessity, against those who might break our Tribes." He held up his hand. "But let me speak of these things with the others, so that you may be reassured. Stay with the Mercenary Brothers, Sun Dog, give them any aid they require while I am occupied." He gave Dhulyn and Parno each a sharp nod before going off, not to where the Watcher brothers were helping Gray Cloud but to the far side of the vale, where he began the easy climb out of the camp.

"Where does he go?" Dhulyn asked as she and Parno rose to their feet out of respect. "To whom will he speak?"

Sun Dog smiled at them as he dusted off his leggings. "You are news of importance, Dhulyn Wolfshead, you and your Partner. And also, you have asked him a question, so Singer of the Wind will tell all the Tribes about you, and ask about both your killer and your missing Brothers."

"And he can do this? Speak to other Mages mind-to-mind?" Parno hoped his eager interest would be mistaken for simple curiosity. Dhulyn would know better, of course. But she would also understand and sympathize with his interest in anything that smacked of talking mind-to-mind, especially after their long months with the Crayx of the Long Ocean. But to these Horsemen, who knew nothing of their pasts, any excessive interest might appear intrusive, and anything intrusive had the potential for danger.

"He will read the clouds," Sun Dog said. "It is a thing the best of our shamans can do."

Parno glanced up, but the sky was remarkably clear, even with the sun beginning to lower toward the western edge of the world.

"No, no," Sun Dog said, laughter in his voice. "He will call the clouds to him, using them to write his message in the sky. Those who can will see it and read what he has written."

"That is great magic indeed," Dhulyn said. "Beyond what Mages can do in our world."

"We cannot work such magics with all things," Sun Dog said. "The farther removed something is from its natural state, the less power we have over it."

"I know that all Mages and shamans must have a source for their power," Dhulyn said. "Which is true even of the Marked, in their way."

"Ah," Sun Dog nodded. "It is the natural world itself from which we draw our power, everything beneath the Sun, Moon, and Stars. We belong to it, all of the Espadryni, and our magics are such that can affect it and are affected by it."

They had been walking as they talked, away from the tent where the Watcher brothers tended to the injured Gray Cloud, but now footfalls sounded from that direction, making Parno turn to find Ice Hawk coming after them.

"It is done," he said. "Gray Cloud sleeps. And my grandfather?"

"With the clouds," Sun Dog said.

"If I may," Dhulyn said. "As it now seems likely that we will remain here until at least tomorrow, I should attend to our horses."

"Ice Hawk will assist you," Sun Dog said.

"With pleasure," the boy said. "I would enjoy a closer look at your horses."

Dhulyn touched her fingers to her forehead and made a fist of her hand, fingers toward Parno. *In Battle.* Parno returned her salute and held up his open hand, palm toward her. *And in Death.*

As courtesy required, Dhulyn allowed Ice Hawk to lead the way to the horse line, even though she could see Bloodbone and Warhammer from where they had been sitting. Both horses were still bridled, and still wearing saddles. When she and Parno had arrived in the Espadryni camp, they had done no more than set the heavier packs on the ground, things they could afford to lose if they had to leave quickly. If, as it seemed, they were to spend the night, she could make the horses more comfortable. And besides, she thought as she slung her saddlebags over her shoulder and untied the bag that held Parno's pipes, there were things they would prefer to have with them.

"You have been here almost a full moon, Singer of the Wind said." Dhulyn looked over Bloodbone's back to find Ice Hawk's eyes fixed on her face. He immediately dropped his gaze to her hands.

"One of the things I do remember from my childhood among the Espadryni of my land is that it is discourteous to stare."

The boy blushed and shifted his feet. "Your pardon, Dhulyn Wolfshead. I was looking for what my grandfather saw in you."

Dhulyn pulled Bloodbone's saddle off and laid it on the ground next to the packs. "And can you see it?"

Given this tacit permission to look, Ice Hawk resumed his scrutiny of her face. "I believe so. There is something in your face that is not in the faces of our Seers. There is a depth to your eyes when you look at me." He gestured to his own face, blushed again, and dropped his hand. "This is my horse, Dusty," he said, putting his open palm on the nose of the horse tied next in the line to Bloodbone. "Will you touch him for me?"

Puzzled but willing to play along, Dhulyn stepped around Bloodbone and laid her hand on the sand-colored horse's shoulder. Dusty turned his head to stare at her, a black blaze above his eyes giving him a comically serious look. When she did not move, he stretched his nose out toward her, as if he would snuffle her face with his reaching lips.

"You see?" Ice Hawk said. "He is not nervous with you, shying away from your hands. It is not your own horses only, but ours as well, who trust you."

"Why should they not? I am good with horses." Dhulyn gave Dusty a final pat and walked back to where Warhammer was snorting at her impatiently. He was used to waiting for Bloodbone to be seen to first, but he seemed annoyed at the idea that any other horse should take his place.

"But our horses have been magicked against the Seers." Ice Hawk followed her and, after receiving her nod, began to remove Warhammer's bridle.

Dhulyn paused, her hands on the tie that kept giving Parno trouble. "Magicked how?"

Ice Hawk turned from her and drew a symbol in the air. Dhulyn could just persuade herself that she could see the flash of color that followed the movement of his forefinger. A smaller glow, of the same nameless color, flashed from the forehead of each of the Espadryni horses. "They will not allow a Seer to mount them or to lead them anywhere."

There was a time Dhulyn would have said she wasn't Seer enough to qualify, but she had a better understanding of her powers now. "You will be like your grandfather one day, then. A powerful shaman."

Ice Hawk blushed again, reminding Dhulyn of just how young he was. "Singer of the Wind says I have great potential. My connection with the natural world is strong."

"Your Seers are like the other Marked, I assume?" Dhulyn finally worked the knot out of the tie and pulled the lacing loose. "They renew their life force from rest and food or from dance and music?"

"Are all Marked the same in this then?"

Dhulyn smiled. Like a true Mage, Ice Hawk valued information. "And obviously they cooperate to produce children?"

This time the expected blush did not come. "I'm not sure what you mean." He took Warhammer's saddle from her hands and set it on the ground next to Bloodbone's.

Dhulyn frowned. She should have realized that with so little experience of the Marked in general, the boy might know even less than she did herself. "The Sight rises out of the same life force that builds a child," she said. "A Seer cannot bear a living child unless there are others who will take her Visions for her as the child grows within."

"I see." Ice Hawk grew still, his lips pursed in a silent whistle. Evidently she had given him something to think about. "Then they must cooperate, as you say. It must be part of the Pact they have with the Tribes. They bear children, as you can see, and we boys live with our mothers until we have seen our birth moons seven times, when we come to live with our fathers. The girl children stay with the Seers."

"Singer of the Wind asked me if the women of my Tribe cared for their children," Dhulyn said. She cleared her throat, remembering the touch of her mother's hand on her face, the feel of her mother's lips on her forehead. They were finished with the horses, but Ice Hawk showed no inclination to move. "He seemed to say that your Seers did not love their children."

"They do not." It was clear from Ice Hawk's voice that he merely made an observation. "They cannot. It is what makes them broken. But they will care for our health. It is part of the Pact."

"And your shamans, your Mages, they cannot cure the Seers?" Dhulyn watched Ice Hawk carefully. She did not want to think ill of these people, who might be all there was under Sun, Moon, and Stars of her own Tribe, but she wondered why they didn't fix the women? Was having the Visions so important to them?

"It has been tried. Ever since the first, and many times since then. Many believe it will never be done, but my mother—" Ice Hawk broke off to look at Dhulyn, and he licked his lips before continuing in a rush. "I heard my mother say that one would come with knowledge of how to help them."

Dhulyn pressed her tongue to her upper lip, blinking. "Did she tell you anything more?"

The boy shook his head. "She would not even admit a second time to as much as I had overheard," he said.

"He is looking at her like a man dying of thirst who sees a spring before him. Is he safe with her?"

Parno grinned. "As safe as he would be with his own mother."

"I hope safer than that," Sun Dog said. He smiled, but stiffly.

Parno studied the other man's face, but his expression remained the same. "She will not seduce him, if that's what worries you. He's too young for her, for one thing, and for another she finds that kind of adoration uncomfortable."

Nodding, Sun Dog turned away from where Dhulyn still talked with Ice Hawk. "You said the killer you seek struck three days ago, when the moon was newly full?"

"That's right."

"We were not here then. And we have seen no one of the fields and cities for a moon at least."

"And why does this seem to disappoint you?"

"In part because if we had met with your killer, your task would be simple, and you would return quickly to your own place on the other side of Mother Sun's Door. But also because, since Dhulyn Wolfshead told us what happened, I have hoped it was not someone from our world."

Parno could understand that, he thought. That such a thing could happen at all was horrible. To believe that it was one of your own people—what would the man's family think?

If he has family. Parno's blood suddenly ran cold. Your family knew you best. How likely was it the killer's family was still alive?

"Other than what Sky Tree tells us of these demons, there are no tales of such killings as your Partner described to us," Sun Dog was saying. "Not in any of the histories of our people, and our histories go back to the time of the Caids." He looked sideways at Parno. "I could not say for certain about the people of the fields and towns," he said. "But I think even we must have heard if such a thing as this had happened there."

"If it had been discovered. Could the killer be a Marked one?" Parno asked.

Sun Dog pressed his lips together in thought. "They are tested for Marks and put to death as children. Except for the Seers."

"How sure are you? Yours may not be the only people who are hiding Marked ones."

Sun Dog was nodding, considering Parno's point. "Under the Sun, Moon, and Stars everything is possible," he conceded. "But it is unlikely. We do not live among other people. We do not hide only our Seers; we hide ourselves, the whole of our people, every Tribe and clan. If we did otherwise, our women would be exposed. How do you hide a Marked one from your neighbors and friends? Particularly when those same neighbors and friends are always looking out? How can you hide that children were born to you? Even if you move to another city or village, you must produce the proof that your child has been tested and been found whole and safe. And except for the Espadryni, who would hide a Marked one, even of their own blood, knowing what they are?"

Parno searched Sun Dog's face but saw no awareness of irony there. At that, he supposed there might be a difference between wanting to save your children and wanting to save your whole race. Without the Seers, there would be no Espadryni.

"You say it is unlikely that other Marks are being hidden. But we in the Mercenary Brotherhood don't deal with likelihood, we deal with possibility. We plan for what *can* happen, and worry less about how likely it is."

Dhulyn laughed, and both men turned to watch where she still stood with Ice Hawk.

"With what I have said in mind, how safe is it for my Partner to travel among your people?"

"Safe enough now that Singer of the Wind has read the clouds to the other Tribes."

"And if we must look beyond the lands of the Espadryni? If we must travel to the people of fields and towns?"

"Singer of the Wind has said you are honorable people, both of you. So you will not tell the world what you know of us; our secret is safe with you."

This was not phrased as a question, but Parno nodded his agreement all the same.

"If it becomes known that our women are Marked," Sun Dog continued, "there would be war between us and the people of the fields and towns."

Parno raised his hand. "Say no more. We're well used to holding our tongues. Even in our world, for example, where the Marked are respected, we don't make a show of my

Partner's Sight." *And if no one knows of the Espadryni women, then Dhulyn is in no danger either*, he thought. Well, not more than usual.

Dhulyn and Ice Hawk joined them, both smiling. "Can Singer of the Wind tell when he is being lied to?" she said.

Sun Dog shrugged. "If a man knows how to tell the truth carefully, he may lie to anyone."

Dhulyn took in a deep lungful of air and exhaled slowly. That much was true. Even drugs such as fresnoyn could be circumvented by someone who had been Schooled in the drug *Shoras*. She would have to rely on her own instincts when she questioned the Seers. She turned as the others fell silent. Singer of the Wind reappeared from behind the small hill where he had gone to read the clouds.

"I have shared the news of the Mercenary Brothers, Dhulyn Wolfshead and Parno Lionsmane," he said. "It is now safe for you to go among our people as you will. But I have news also to give to you. Did you not say that in addition to this killer, you seek two Brothers of your own, Mercenaries like yourselves?" He gestured with a sweep of his hand to their Mercenary badges.

"They have been seen?"

"The Salt Desert People found them, four days' ride to the south and west of here. One of them dead and the other injured in the leg. I have told the shaman of the Salt Desert People that they may expect you. So much the clouds told me and nothing more."

These last words were so obviously ritual that neither Dhulyn nor Parno asked anything further. They would have to wait until they met with their Brother to find out how he had been injured and the other man killed.

"You are right, Grandfather. We will go first to our Brother and give him what aid we can." And learn from him, Dhulyn said to herself, what, if anything, he knew of the killer.

"Now," Singer of the Wind said, "it is late. Tonight we rest, and tomorrow, when Our Mother is once again with us, we will set you on your way."

Ten

PARNO LET THE last note of the Lament for the Sun die away, releasing the pressure on the air bag of his pipes slowly until chanter and drones fell silent. The Horsemen drummed the ground with the palms of their hands, making a sound, the Mercenary thought with an inner grin, not unlike the thunder of distant hooves.

"Come, Lionsmane, another tune!" There was general approval for this request, but Parno held up his hands, palms out. "Another time, perhaps," he said, smiling. "We have had a long, tiring day, my Partner and I, and with your goodwill," he nodded to Singer in the Wind, "we will take our rest."

There were nods and good nights, and even a few touches on the shoulder, as Parno carried his pipes to where a separate fire had been made up for them at the edge of the camp farthest from the horse line. Parno suspected that had he been alone, the men of the Espadryni would have been happy to share their fire with him all night. But even though Dhulyn had been passed as "whole" and "safe" by their Cloud Shaman, and the men were clearly fascinated by her, they would not have been comfortable with her sleeping among them.

Dhulyn had water heating in a small pot and had laid out a pattern of vera tiles in the light cast by the fire. She looked up and gave him the smile she saved only for him. Parno took a deep breath, exhaling slowly and feeling the muscles of his neck and shoulders relax.

"Charmed them as usual, did you? They'll all sleep the better for your music."

"Are you saying my playing puts people to sleep?"

She frowned, her head on one side. "Yes. Yes, I suppose I am."

Parno grinned and sat down beside her, starting to take his instrument apart. "Careful now, wouldn't want the warmth of your affection to burn me, my heart." He looked back at the larger fire and the men still seated around it. "I must say, though, that I find our present circumstances somewhat ironic."

"How so?" Dhulyn turned a vera tile so that the symbol on it was upside down.

"These are your people, and I sit with them at their fire, and you sit here alone. I confess that when I saw the riders coming toward us were Espadryni, I understood—*truly* understood—your past worries about my possible return to my own people."

Dhulyn shifted until she was sitting cross-legged. "And why should you have this sudden knowledge now?"

"It was never a danger before, not in this way," Parno said. "You remember when we were last in Imrion, you worried that I might want to leave the Brotherhood, return to my own family—"

"But this is not the first time we have met with Espadryni," Dhulyn said.

"True," he said, mindful that his Partner must be upset to have interrupted him. "There was Avylos of Tegrian. You did startle me when you called out to him in your own tongue, and I realized he was a Red Horseman. I felt a stabbing coldness, here." Parno indicated the center of his body, under the ribs. "And I wondered, I have to admit. But Avylos was still only one man. One man could not replace your whole family, your whole Tribe."

Without raising her eyes from the pot heating on the fire, Dhulyn reached out and touched him on the chest, in the spot where he'd said he'd felt cold. "Don't be so certain."

Parno smiled, but he shook his head. "I'm part of the Brotherhood, we both are. In Battle."

"And in Death. So Avylos worried you, but not for long and not greatly. And now?"

"Now I realize I never had the same worry you did, that I might lose you to your family. You've never had any family to return to, until now."

Dhulyn took a deep breath and let it out noisily. "Forgive me, my soul. Are you worried, then, or not?"

Parno shook his head. He wasn't sure he could explain it. Dhulyn, Outlander as she was, and for all her reticence and reserve, was better read than he was and was more comfortable with words. "I'm saying that a year ago I might have been, but after all we've been through in the last few moons . . ."

"When I thought you were dead," Dhulyn said, her rough silk voice very quiet.

"When each of us thought the other was dead." Parno put his hand on her thigh and squeezed. "After that," he said, "we'll never doubt each other again."

"Oh, we might, we're human. But we won't doubt for long." She covered his hand with her own.

Parno nodded. "What if we can't get back? What if we need to make a life for ourselves here?"

"Somehow I don't think there will be much welcome for me here, not among the Tribes anyway. Not unless . . ." Dhulyn's voice died away, but Parno waited. *No point in rushing her.*

"Ice Hawk says someone will come with the answer to the problem of the Marked. That he overheard the Seers speaking of it when he was a child."

"You think *we* might be this 'someone'?"

"Do you have such an answer?"

Parno shook his head, but slowly. What about his Pod sense? "Not unless there are Crayx in the oceans here, and they know it."

"Nor I, though that is a good thought. But if we must remain here, we are still a Brotherhood. Ourselves and the third man the Salt Desert People have."

"You could start your School. What? Don't tell me that's not your plan. It would only mean you started a little early, that's all."

"It's too early to be discussing these things, that much I *do* know," Dhulyn said, her eyes flicking over his shoulder. "Company."

Leaning back on his hands, Parno looked over his shoulder. Sun Dog was approaching their fire with the boy Ice Hawk in tow.

"The boy's curiosity is greater than his courtesy," the young man said. "I come with him to be sure it is not *too* great."

"You may join us," Dhulyn said. "Is guarding the candidate of the Sun's Door somehow part of your apprenticeship?"

"I am no one's apprentice, Mercenary." The tone was wary.

"Are you not? You seem to work in partnership with the Cloud Mage. I thought you might be his pupil."

Sun Dog laughed, his face clearing. "Singer of the Wind is Cloud Shaman, true enough," he said. "But in our Tribes the most powerful shaman is always partnered with the least powerful, lest he become too narrow in his vision. Thus, I am Horse Shaman—at least of this group."

"And one day of the whole Tribe," Ice Hawk put it.

"It doesn't trouble you, to be the least powerful?" Parno glanced up from wrapping his pipes in their silk bags. The Espadryni had settled themselves cross-legged, one to each side of the small fire. Parno was a little surprised that it was Sun Dog who sat next to Dhulyn, but perhaps Ice Hawk had realized that by sitting next to Parno, he might gaze at Dhulyn to his heart's content.

"Why should it? I have the opportunity to become a chief, as I would have also if I were the most powerful shaman. Did you not have two chiefs then, in your Tribe, Dhulyn Wolfshead?"

"I do not know how my Tribe was governed," Dhulyn said. "I was too young. But what you say strikes me as very reasonable. I know that all Mages do not have the same level of power—any more than all Marks have the same level of skill—and your method of dividing the chief's position would ensure that all would feel equally represented."

Sun Dog nodded, but his lips had compressed into a tight line at Dhulyn's mention of the Marked.

Parno glanced at Ice Hawk as Dhulyn threw a handful of dried chamomile flowers into the water she'd been heating.

The younger Horseman had shifted until he was sitting with his feet flat in front of him, knees bent, forearms resting on them, right hand clasping the fingers of the left. A defensive position, Parno noted, apparently casual, but with arms and legs creating a barrier. But then again, not a good position from which to actually defend yourself. By the time you could get your arms and legs out of the way and pick up a weapon, you'd be food for worms.

"We have a saying in the Mercenary Brotherhood," Dhulyn said, just as if there was no silence to break. "That knowledge is a good tool." She had set out two round clay cups and now hesitated. She smiled her wolf's smile, shrugged, and poured some tea into each cup, handed one to Ice Hawk, one to Sun Dog, and kept the small metal pot for herself and Parno to share.

"What knowledge can we give you?" Sun Dog said, accepting his cup and inhaling the fumes of the herb. "We cannot help you find the killer you seek."

"That knowledge would be a knife in the hand, for certain," Dhulyn said. "But spoons are good tools also, and cups and bowls. Tell us something of the Tribes of the Espadryni and of the Door of the Sun."

Sun Dog tilted his head back, and his eyes sparkled. "I should make the boy recite his lessons. But, in reality, as the Horse Shaman of this group, this task falls to me." He took a sip of tea. "There are three Tribes, the Long Trees, the Salt Desert, and Cold Lake, and we take it in turn to send our most promising young men to the Sun's Door," he began. "If they make it through and come back, they might one day rise to become Cloud Shaman, if not . . ." He shrugged. "Some go in and are never seen again. Some never gain entrance. Some, like myself, decide not to try."

"And knowledge of the key is not shared?" The metal pot had finally cooled enough, and Dhulyn raised it to her lips before passing it to Parno.

Sun Dog was shaking his head. "Not among Horsemen, no," he said. "Each candidate must discover it for himself. But the old tales say that it *is* shared with one who might come through the Door."

"Who might that be?"

"By ancient right and treaty, with the Tarkin of Menoin," Ice Hawk said, and then lowered his eyes as they all turned to look at him.

So, Parno thought, the key to the labyrinth might well

involve not how to pass through to this side, but how to get back.

"That *is* what the old tales say," Sun Dog agreed. "But as Singer of the Wind has told you, it has been generations since such a visit has occurred."

"And how is access to the Door arranged?" Parno asked. "Do the Tribes mix freely?"

"We have our own territories, our own areas for hunting and grazing our herds, and unless it is a year for the Great Sight—a gathering of all the Tribes—we do not mix a great deal." He flashed Parno a grin. "But at the Great Sights, there is music and drinking, dance and horseplay. And business, as well. We set the schedule of access to the Door, the Seers unite to share their Visions, and we men trade horses, and goods and make marriages with other Tribes."

"You trade the women then?" Dhulyn asked. Her voice was so carefully neutral that Parno knew what she was feeling only from his own knowledge of her past. Dhulyn had been a slave once—that had been where she'd got the scars on her back and the one on her lip that could turn her smile into a wolf's snarl. Mercenaries had a living to make, but he and Dhulyn would happily kill slavers for free.

But Sun Dog was shaking his head, clearly shocked. "Mother Sun and Father Moon would curse us if we did such things, we would lose all their favor. The women are broken, but they are after all human people, not horses or cattle. It is Mother Sun herself who told us that it should be the men who changed Tribes in marriage, not the women."

"Is there love between you, then?" Parno asked.

Ice Hawk's lips pressed tight as he glanced quickly at each of them, and the look that fleeted over Sun Dog's face—though gone in an instant and replaced with his usual expression of friendly interest—suggested that the man hid some dark sorrow. "We can love them," he said, his voice grown very quiet. "They are our mothers, our daughters, our sisters." His lips stretched back, but his expression could only by courtesy be called a smile. "Our wives and the mothers of our children." His grin faltered. "But they, the Seers, they do not love their husbands, they cannot, nor their little ones either." He shot them each a quick glance, and Parno thought that, somehow, the man spoke from his own experience. "It's in this way that they're broken, you see, as if they haven't any hearts. As if they were born missing a hand or a foot."

He stopped long enough that Parno thought Sun Dog had said everything he was going to say when he spoke again. "Singer of the Wind knew you were not broken in that way, Dhulyn Wolfshead. There's love between you, is there not? He could see that. And anyone could tell that you felt something when you described that killing." Now he did fall quiet.

"The Lionsmane and I are Partners," Dhulyn said in her rough silk voice. "This is sometimes more than love and sometimes less. We are a sword with two edges," she added, quoting the Common Rule.

Sun Dog nodded. As if her words had somehow confirmed something for him, he seemed to have recovered his equilibrium. "That is the very type of connection that we cannot have with the Seers, or any Marked person." His voice was stronger now.

"Ice Hawk spoke of a Pact," Dhulyn said.

"The women are intelligent—one can appeal to their logic, even their common sense. They will act in their own interest, if they are convinced it *is* in their own interest. They'll lie with their husbands—and other men of their choosing—because it's pleasurable for them."

Here Ice Hawk flushed red to the roots of his hair, and Sun Dog grinned at him, then shrugged. "And they do not hesitate to tell you if you have not pleased them, since they do not care if they hurt your feelings. They join in the work and in caring for the children because if they do not they are punished." He glanced at both of them again. "They have two chances to ignore their duties and suffer only minor penalties," he said. "The third time they are constrained." He indicated the hamstring behind his knee with a slashing motion of his hand.

Parno felt suddenly cold, and he looked to his Partner. Dhulyn was whiter than usual under the layer of today's dirt. Then she nodded. "Of course, if they cannot be made to see that cooperation is in their own interest, they are a danger to the whole camp."

Both the Horsemen regarded her with some dismay, and Parno laughed aloud, though it sounded cold to his own ears.

"Careful, my heart. It might be difficult, at that, to tell the difference between heartlessness and plain practicality."

Dhulyn shrugged and put down the empty pot. "And their Visions?"

"It is part of the Pact, but oddly, we never need to ask them to See. They are quite content to do so." Sun Dog tossed back the last of his tea, letting the hand that held the cup fall slack. "And so far as our shamans can tell, and our experience can show us, they speak truly. They've the same three chances to be caught lying before they pay the penalty."

A spark flew up from the fire, and Parno picked up a stick to poke into the flames. He had wondered where the Red Horsemen found wood for their fires, but from the smell of this one, wood wasn't what they used. "And the women don't run away?" he asked.

"Where would they run? If the Tribes didn't hide them, shelter them, they'd be put to death like all the other Marked as soon as they were identified. Seers or no. If they don't keep the Healers, Caids know they wouldn't keep Seers."

Parno exchanged a look with Dhulyn. Their own experience had taught them there were those who valued Seers above all other Marked, but there was no reason to argue Sun Dog out of his ideas.

"Besides, the horses have been magicked not to carry a woman without at least three men with her."

"So that one of them cannot trick a man into running away with her?" Parno guessed.

"Exactly."

Dhulyn looked at him, and Parno knew what she was thinking. They knew that the Espadryni shamans could not magic the women directly, that much their experience with Avylos had taught them.

"And they could not get very far on foot," Sun Dog was saying. "Especially if they have been constrained."

Sun Dog fell silent, and finally he rose to his feet, wishing them a good sleep and collecting Ice Hawk with a flick of his hand. It seemed the visit was over. As Parno stood, Dhulyn turned once more to her vera tiles. There had been something in the pattern she'd made earlier that had reminded her . . . .

THREE MEN WITH HAIR THE COLOR OF OLD BLOOD SIT ON HORSEBACK LOOKING OUT OVER A SEA OF GRASS THAT STRETCHES OUT TO THE RIM OF THE WORLD. THE GRASS IS DISCOLORED IN PATCHES, AS IF A FARMER HAD SOWN DIFFERENT STRAINS OF WHEAT OR GRAIN IN THE SAME FIELD. THE MEN ARE HEAVILY ARMED; EACH CARRIES A BOW, SEVERAL SPEARS, AND TWO SWORDS. . . .

THE HOUSE IS IN DARKNESS, AND ALL ARE ASLEEP. A THREAD OF RUBY LIGHT LEADS FROM A SECOND STORY WINDOW. A LIMBER YOUNG MAN LETS HIMSELF IN AND FOLLOWS THE LIGHT DIRECTLY TO A SPOT IN THE CARVED PANELING OF THE DINING ROOM. HE OPENS THE HIDDEN DOOR AND RE-MOVES AN OLD GOLD ARMBAND AND A SMALL SACK OF COINS . . .

THE CAID MAGE AGAIN, WITH HIS CLOSE-CROPPED HAIR THE COLOR OF WHEAT STRAW, EYES THE BLUE OF OLD ICE, ONCE AGAIN READING HIS BOOK, ONCE AGAIN TRACING A LINE ON THE PAGE WITH HIS FINGER, HIS LIPS MOVING. DHULYN STEPS CLOSER TO THE TABLE, THINKING THAT THIS TIME—SINCE THERE IS NO TIME HERE AFTER ALL—SHE MIGHT SPEAK TO HIM. BUT HE DOES NOT SEE HER. STANDING, HE TAKES UP A HIGHLY POL-ISHED TWO-HANDED SWORD, AND HIS LILY-SHAPED SLEEVES FALL BACK FROM HIS WRISTS.

AGAIN HE TURNS TOWARD THE MIRROR, REFLECTING A NIGHT SKY FULL OF STARS. AGAIN HIS LIPS MOVE, AND DHULYN KNOWS HE SPEAKS THE WORDS FROM THE BOOK. ******* HE SAYS, AND ********. AGAIN THE SWEEPING MOVE FROM THE CRANE *SHORA* AND THE SLASH DOWNWARD THROUGH THE MIRROR, THROUGH THE SKY, SPLITTING IT, AND THE GREEN-TINTED SHADOW COMES SPILLING INTO THE ROOM LIKE FOG THROUGH A CASEMENT . . . .

A RED-FACED BOY IS FURIOUSLY STRIKING OUT AS HIS MOTHER DRAGS HIM BY THE UPPER ARM INTO WHAT IS OBVIOUSLY THE KITCHEN OF THEIR HOME. THE MOTHER SITS ON A KITCHEN STOOL AND STRUGGLES TO DRAW THE BOY INTO HER LAP, SAYING, "LOOK AT ME, DARLING, PLEASE, JUST LOOK AT ME." SUDDENLY THE STOOL FALLS TO PIECES, SENDING THE WOMAN HEAVILY TO THE STONE FLOOR. THE WOODEN SHUTTERS ON THE WINDOW EXPLODE INTO SAWDUST, THE DISHES AND PLATES ON THE SIDEBOARD SHATTER, AND THE MOTHER BEGINS TO VOMIT BLOOD ON THE FLOOR. . . . THE BOY STAMPS HIS FOOT, SCREAMING, "YOU COW, DON'T TOUCH ME". . . .

GUNDARON IS KNEELING ON A PATCH OF DARK GREEN GRASS IN FRONT OF A CLIPPED WALL HEDGE. EVEN THOUGH THERE IS NOT ENOUGH DETAIL FOR DHULYN TO RECOGNIZE THE SPOT, SHE KNOWS THAT GUN ISN'T IN ANY GARDEN BUT ON THE PATH OF THE SUN. "GUNDARON," SHE SAYS, BUT HE DOESN'T LOOK UP. SHE FOLLOWS THE ANGLE OF HIS EYES AND SEES A TWISTED

CORD OF LIGHT, BLACK, BLUE, AND GREEN. GUN GETS TO HIS FEET AND FOLLOWS THE LIGHT. . . .

A FINELY DRESSED WOMAN, DARK BLONDE HAIR PILED IN ELABORATE CURLS AND TWISTS ON THE TOP OF HER HEAD, STANDS WITH HER HAND TUCKED INTO THE ELBOW OF A LARGE MAN DRESSED IN BATTLE LEATHERS, HOLDING A LONG SWORD IN HIS HAND. THERE ARE FOUR OTHER SIMILARLY DRESSED MEN BEHIND THEM IN THE SHADOWS CAST BY TWO FLICKERING LAMPS. A MAN OF ABOUT THE SAME AGE AS THE FINELY DRESSED WOMAN AND HER ESCORT, DRESSED ONLY IN HIS SHIRT AND LEGGINGS, STANDS WITH HIS ARMS CROSSED ON HIS CHEST, LIPS PRESSED TOGETHER, SHAKING HIS HEAD.

THE WOMAN LAUGHS AND POINTS TO A SPOT ON THE FLOOR. THE MEN PULL UP THE FLOORBOARDS AND HAUL OUT A WOMAN, AN OLD MAN, AND THREE CHILDREN.

DHULYN SHIVERS AS SHE WATCHES. *THIS MUST BE THE PAST.* . . .

THE THIN, SANDY-HAIRED MAN IS STILL WEARING THE GOLD RINGS IN HIS EARS, BUT HIS FACE IS LINED NOW, AND HIS FOREHEAD HIGHER. HE IS SITTING AT A SQUARE TABLE, ITS TOP INLAID WITH LIGHTER WOODS, READING BY THE LIGHT OF TWO LAMPS. A PLATE TO HIS LEFT CONTAINS THE REMNANTS OF A MEAL—CHICKEN OR SOME OTHER FOWL, JUDGING BY THE BONES. HE LOOKS TOWARD THE ROOM'S SINGLE WINDOW AND RISES TO PEER OUT. IT IS DARK, AND IT MUST ALSO BE CLOUDY AS DHULYN CAN SEE NOTHING OUTSIDE THE WINDOW. THE MAN TURNS TOWARD THE TABLE AGAIN AND, SMILING, SAYS, "HOW CAN I HELP?"

❧

"I thought at first all my Visions of the Green Shadow had something to do with the killer, but since Singer of the Wind told us the Green Shadow was here also, I think it's obvious why I have been Seeing it and the Caid Mage who called it." Parno and Dhulyn were approaching the encampment of the Salt Desert People carefully, from upwind to ensure that the scouts—and their horses—who were undoubtedly stationed around the camp would smell their approach long before they could be seen.

"Do you think the Shadow has anything to do with the other Visions? Where the people seem to be unmaking?" For their camp the Horsemen had chosen a spot where the land rose slightly, giving them a view in all directions. There was a wide creek curling around the rise on the west side, which no doubt provided fish as well as fresh water.

Dhulyn pulled back on the reins, bringing Bloodbone to

a halt. She lifted her blood-red brows, and her gaze turned inward. "I had not thought of that," she said. "It might follow that those possessed by the Shadow would act differently in this world from the manner in which they acted in ours. But that does not explain why I should be Seeing such Visions of the past." She turned to look at him as she urged her horse forward once again. "We haven't met the man who is going to help us," she said. "Perhaps he has these answers."

By this time they were within sight of the distant tents, and three scouts were riding out to meet them.

"Greetings," one of these called out as soon as they were close enough for voices to be heard over the hooves. "You are the Mercenaries Singer of the Wind told the clouds about?" He looked at Dhulyn with narrowed dark blue eyes, flicked his glance to Parno and back. He could have been anywhere between twenty and thirty, and his voice had the fullness of youth. A scar divided his left eyebrow, and a ghost eye had been drawn on his left cheek.

His face cleared. "It is as the old man said. When you know what to look for, it is clear. You are whole. Can you do as much for our Seers, woman of the Sun's Door?"

"I regret that I cannot, man of the Salt Desert."

He nodded, matter-of-fact. He'd clearly had no expectations, so he wasn't disappointed. But it would have been stupid not to ask. "I am Star-Wind," he said. "I am one of those who reads the clouds for the Salt Desert people. I may be the next Cloud Shaman, who knows? But I have hopes." He grinned, and his blue eyes sparkled. Parno revised his estimate of the man's age downward.

There was much about the Salt Desert camp that was familiar to anyone who had spent time on campaign. Even with the cool evening breeze blowing, Parno noted the aroma of stews slowly simmering, the sharp, not-unpleasant smell of the horse line, and the merest whiff of the latrine. He noticed Dhulyn looking around her even more carefully than she normally would, her eyes taking in not just the presence and position of weapons—short swords, spears, and bows—but even the details of the cook fires, the babies sitting on the hips of fathers or mothers, all with ghost eyes marked on their foreheads to make them easier to find. Older children, marked like Star-Wind on the left cheek, were either looking shyly out from behind a parent or stood boldly in the forefront, staring at the newcomers. Though many were barefoot, most were dressed identically to their elders in short boots, baggy trousers, and sleeveless jerkins. There did seem to be fewer females, both adults and children, and those he saw stood back, behind the men and older children, but watched intently, some with smiles, some with furrowed brows.

It was then that he noticed something—a kind of attitude he had seen without noting in the smaller Long Trees group, but that was far more obvious now. It was not until they had dismounted to lead their horses through the camp to the horse line that Parno began to understand what it was. He had been in many camps, of soldiers, of Mercenary Schools, and even of other Horse Nomads, on their own side of the Path of the Sun. And this camp was quieter than even the legendary reserve of the Outlander could account for. There seemed to be a shadow on these people—no, on their spirits, that was it. It was as if he and Dhulyn had arrived on a day of mourning. Or rather, as if these people were always in mourning. And perhaps, in a way, they were. There was about them a quality of sadness he could not remember noticing in any other group.

Perhaps this awareness is a legacy of the Crayx, he thought. *Perhaps it is my Pod sense that allows me to feel this*. It was possible that his recently discovered ability made him more sensitive to people, even when he couldn't share their thoughts.

Once the horses were unsaddled and had food and water, Parno and his Partner were returned to the center of the camp where an old man, older even than Singer of the Wind, awaited them, standing straight as the spear shaft he held, in front of the large central tent. This would be, Dhulyn thought, the home of the Tribe's two chiefs, the Cloud Shaman, and the Horse Shaman. She wondered if, in their own world, before the breaking of the Tribes, there would have been another chief, a Seer. Obviously, that could not be the case here.

"Father," Star-Wind said. His tone was gentle, but formal, which told Dhulyn the younger man was indeed the Cloud Shaman's apprentice, as he had implied. "Here are the guests sent to us by Singer of the Wind, the Long Trees Tribe. The Mercenary Brothers Dhulyn Wolfshead and

Parno Lionsmane. Mercenaries," Star-Wind turned to face them. "These are Singer of the Grass-Moon, Senior Cloud Shaman, and Spring-Flood, Horse Shaman to the Salt Desert People."

The strongest and the weakest Mages, Dhulyn thought. The Cloud Shaman was shorter than the men around him, though it may have been from age. His eyes were faded to the palest of blues, and his hair was entirely white. The Horse Shaman was a vigorous man of middle years, well-muscled and with the greenest eyes Dhulyn had ever seen.

The old man beckoned her forward with a gnarled hand and looked Dhulyn in the eyes, considering her with his head on a slant. "From beyond the Door of the Sun?" he said. His voice had a hollow whistle to it, as if lungs or throat had been punctured.

"Yes, Grandfather," she said. Good thing that patience was part of the Common Rule, Schooled into all Mercenaries, otherwise this constant questioning on the same topic would very soon grow annoying.

He reached out to touch her face, brushing away the few stray hairs that had escaped from her braiding and fallen over her cheek. Dhulyn held still, blinking slowly. She felt Parno's tension to her right.

"I had thought my old friend, Singer of the Wind, must be deceived, perhaps even magicked in some way, but I see that I was mistaken. You are welcome, my child. Very welcome." Having said this, however, the old man turned back into his tent, leaving them standing.

Spring-Flood turned away from the tent opening and held both hands high above his head in a command for attention. "Listen, everyone," he called out. Though he hadn't raised his voice very much, many had come closer as the old man was examining Dhulyn, and everyone now gave the Horse Shaman their attention. One or two of the women, tending to their own concerns, were nudged by their neighbors until they either stood or turned to watch.

"These are the Mercenary Brothers we were told of, Parno Lionsmane and Dhulyn Wolfshead. It is as we have been told, the Wolfshead is whole and safe. She may be treated as a woman of fields and cities, though you will see she is dressed as a warrior and belongs to the same Brotherhood as our other guest, Delvik Bloodeye."

Eyes turned toward her, some narrowing in calculation, others with simple curiosity.

Parno cleared his throat, and Dhulyn signaled him with a lift of her left eyebrow. For all that the Horsemen appeared to be willing to follow the guidance of their chiefs and accept her, they would still probably feel more comfortable dealing with a man.

"If we might see our Brother now," Parno said to the Shaman.

"Of course. Star-Wind will escort you. Consider him your guide as you stay among us."

Or our guard, Dhulyn thought. Judging from the blandness of his expression, Star-Wind had already known what his assignment was to be. Doubtless why he had been one of the scouts sent to meet them.

The Mercenary Brother Delvik Bloodeye had been given a small round tent not far from the central fires. No one stood guard, Dhulyn noticed, and the tent flap was tied back. A lamp, smelling oddly of inglera fat, had already been lit inside. There was another smell, a familiar one that made Dhulyn grit her teeth. She nodded her thanks to Star-Wind, ducked her head, and entered the tent. Parno stopped in the doorway and turned so that he could watch both outside and in.

Crammed into the round space were two pallets with a low stool between them, the collapsible kind made with three thick sticks of wood, a piece of hide and some thongs. The pallets were no more than layers of bedding and skins spread over piles of cut grass. The bed to the left held a man whose skin was sallow under his tan. Even lying down it was obvious he was a huge man, easily a full head taller than Parno and almost twice as big around. At the moment, however, what drew Dhulyn's notice was the sweat on his skin and the way his mouth twisted from side to side.

The young man on the stool leaped to his feet as they entered, his blood-red hair tied back with a scrap of thong. He stared at Dhulyn round-eyed, warily taking in her Mercenary badge before looking beyond her to Parno and Star-Wind.

"He is comfortable," the young man said. "We have dealt with most of his pain, but the fever we cannot keep away; always it returns."

Dhulyn placed the back of her fingers against her Brother's damp brow. He was fevered, no doubt of it. "You are Delvik Bloodeye," she said, recalling the information Dorian of the River had given them back on the Black Traveler. "Called the Bull, and Schooled by Yoruk Silverheels. I am Dhulyn Wolfshead, called the Scholar, Schooled by Dorian the Black Traveler. I've fought at Sadron, Arcosa, and Bhexyllia. With me is my Partner, Parno Lionsmane, called the Chanter, Schooled by Nerysa Warhammer."

"You're Senior," Delvik said, his voice like a thread.

"I am. What happened?" she asked, not that she needed more than the smell to tell her the worst of it.

"We were heading north—well, south in this place—"

"We understand," Parno said from the doorway. "And we know why you are here. Take your time, my Brother."

Delvik Bloodeye shut his eyes, took two deep breaths and released them slowly. When he opened his eyes, he was visibly calmer, his eyes clearer. "As you know, my Brothers, there is no mark of any trail when you have completed the Path of the Sun, but our Brother Kesman Firehawk saw prey birds to the south and reasoned there might be water, so we went that way." Delvik continued, telling how they had found water, but nowhere the marks of the killer they sought. How they had finally met with a trader who had directed them to the camp of the Salt Desert Horsemen.

"It was while we were on our way here that we crossed another trail, one that we finally recognized, though it was faint. So far as we could tell, it headed back toward the Path of the Sun, or at least where we had been when we came out of the Path. It was as we followed this trail that the ground opened beneath us, and we fell into a pit filled with stakes of wood, sharpened."

"It is an orobeast trap," Star-Wind said. "A fierce cat that during bad seasons will come down out of the western hills to follow our herds. We leave them uncovered and unstaked, and therefore safe, unless there is news of such a beast. We do not know who armed this one, or why."

"Someone who realized he was being followed, perhaps," Dhulyn said.

"It worked well enough," Delvik said. "Kesman was killed instantly, a stake passing through his body. I watched him die and was resigning myself to the same fate, since I was under my horse and could not free my leg from the stake that held me, when I heard the sounds of hoofbeats, and the Red Horsemen found me."

Dhulyn drew back the covering and hissed when she saw Delvik Bloodeye's leg. "What has been done?" she asked.

"Singer of the Grass-Moon saw to him, and at first it seemed that all was well," Star-Wind said. "And then these lines began to draw themselves upon his skin, and his toes began to darken."

"And the Mages can do nothing more for him?" As the young man's face changed, Dhulyn added, "I mean no disrespect. I ask out of ignorance of your abilities."

"They've tried, my Brother, I swear they have." Delvik's voice shook and his breath was momentarily shallow. He'd seen his birth moon perhaps thirty-five times, Dhulyn estimated, and had probably never been seriously ill a day in his life. He must have gone late into his Schooling to be junior to both her and Parno. He was looking better now than when they had first come into the tent, but Dhulyn knew that this was only from relief, now that he knew he wasn't going to die alone, away from home and with no Brothers around him.

"They knit the bone," Star-Wind was saying. "But this poison of the blood—" he shook his head. "We cannot cure that."

"I know this to be true," Delvik added. "It almost killed the old man when he tried. And as old as he is, he's still the best Mage they have."

"I am second to Grass-Moon," Star-Wind said, "And lucky to be half the Mage he is, when it comes my time to Sing."

"We must get him back through the Path of the Sun," Dhulyn said. "Somehow, we must get him back." She looked at Parno over the young Brother's head. "Without a Healer, he will die."

"We won't get him back in time, Dhulyn my heart, you know that." Parno spoke softly, but firmly.

"Then we must take the leg."

Eleven

IT WAS A lucky thing, Gundaron thought, that he had taken the most sedate of their three ponies and that the trail to the Caid ruins was so familiar. Otherwise he might find that riding and having to make conversation with Epion Akarion at the same time was too much to handle. As it was, he considered himself lucky not to have fallen off somewhere along the way. He had expected Mar to come with him as usual, but she had reasoned that one of them had to stay with Alaria. He would never have chosen Lord Epion as his companion, but once the Tarkin's uncle had discovered where Gun was going—and why—there had been no way to refuse his offer to come along.

"This concerns the Tarkinate," was the argument the man had put forward. "And my family in particular. Falcos cannot possibly spare the time to go, but I can and will."

Gun had agreed as graciously as he could and had taken some secret amusement in making the older man, and the two guards he brought with him, keep their horses to the pony's pace. The guards, Gun couldn't help but notice, were dressed in what he'd come to think of as Epion Akarion's colors. Instead of the black tunic with purple sleeves that identified the Palace Guard, these men wore blue tunics, with only one purple sleeve. He should change that, Gun thought. These men could so easily be mistaken for the City Watch, in their solid blue uniforms.

The pony suddenly shied to the left, and Gun clamped

his knees together as he felt himself slipping and then had to grab the pony's mane as she shot forward.

"You will find," Epion said, his voice gentle and his tone warm, "that the animal has been trained to increase speed when you press on its sides with your knees."

Gun stifled a curse. He'd left his father's farm to go into a Scholars' Library and had foolishly thought he'd be leaving all beasts behind him at the same time. "I thought it better not to fall off," he said to Epion. "Of course, it would help if the stupid animal didn't jump at dry leaves blowing across the path."

"She is testing you," Epion said, still with the same gentle humor. "And I'm very much afraid she's finding you wanting."

Gun laughed. He knew that Mar didn't like Epion, but Gun didn't think the man was so bad. An amateur's enthusiasm was sometimes hard for a Scholar to take, but enthusiasm was all it was, he was sure. "I wouldn't be much of a Scholar if I could be thrown off my path by someone's looking down on me," he said. "Not even the most superior of ponies—" or of nobles, he thought inwardly "—can compare with the upper Scholars and teachers of a Library when it comes to snubbing and finding people wanting. Any student who can't take being made to feel inferior soon goes home."

Finally Gun reached the spot where he and Mar usually tied up their ponies, and the beast would go no farther. There was soft grass here, and once upon a time someone had moved rocks around to turn a trickle of water into a tiny pond. Gun heaved a leg over the pony's back and thumped to the ground.

"Did you bring your scryer's bowl?" Epion asked. He looked with interest at Gun's pack.

"Now that I know *what* to look for, I don't need the bowl," Gun explained. "Any more than I would need it to Find Menoin, or this pony, or any other known object, for that matter." He removed the pony's saddle and set it on a convenient rock. The beast bumped him companionably with her nose, and Gun, careful of the creature's teeth, obliged her by taking off the bridle. It was only then that he remembered Mar was not with him to put it back on. Perhaps one of Epion's guards would do it for him. The taller one, the one with the crossbow, stayed on his horse, but the shorter one with the dark beard dismounted to accompany them.

"I realize that you now know what to look for." Epion had dismounted from his own horse and tossed the reins to the taller guard, without doing anything else to make the horse more comfortable. Obviously he didn't expect this to take very long. "But how does that tell you where it is?"

Gun looked a little upward, and a little to his left, at the thin gold line no one but he—or perhaps another Finder— could see. Not unlike the golden sunbeam that had guided him through the Library in his mind, the line would lead unerringly toward the book he was looking for, until he either found it or stopped looking. Really experienced Finders, those who made it their full-time occupation, didn't need this kind of clue, but Gun didn't feel he was at that stage yet.

"There's a line," he said to Epion. "As though it were painted on the air, that I can follow." He hoisted his small pack, waited politely for Epion to say or do something further and then set off down the path, following the golden line as it led to the edge of the ruins. Here he turned north and east, heading down a wide flat area with obvious—to the trained eye—smooth patches.

"Mar-eMar and I think this was one of the main boulevards of the Caid city," he told Epion as they walked. "These large flat areas are the remnants of paving. There are better examples than these, of course; some of the ones on the Blasonar Plains are almost intact under the grass."

"And these little flags?" Epion pointed to the left.

"They mark the grids of our search squares," Gun said. "Each one is attached to a metal rod that has been driven into the ground, blue for areas we've finished with, red for those we have still to investigate and catalog." Gun thought Epion's interest was genuine. After all, the man had tried to direct their research when they'd first arrived, and while he hadn't come to the site very often, Gun thought that was likely because Mar had made it plain he wasn't welcome— or as plain as you can make such a thing to the Tarkin's uncle. Not that Mar was in the wrong, Gun quickly brought his thoughts back into loyal lines. The last thing any Scholar needed was interference from someone who wasn't even technically their patron. Gun shivered. He'd had enough previous and unlucky experience with people who wanted to guide his researches to last him a lifetime. Just as well Epion had learned to keep his distance. Until now at least.

"I see a green flag." Now Epion was pointing off to the right.

"There are a few," Gun said. "That shows where I Found something worth digging for, still buried under the surface. Once we've finished our preliminary survey, if enough underground artifacts are discovered, a full expedition will be mounted."

"And will more Scholars come then from Valdomar?" Epion's tone was neutral, but Gundaron had dealt with enough politically charged situations to know what the man was really asking.

"Oh, no," he replied. "A site like this is far too important to be left to one particular Library. Bids for participation will be asked for from as many as might want to apply, and a final mix will be chosen from the total group of applications. By Valdomar Library in partnership with the court of Menoin," he added. It was true, but it was also what Epion wanted to hear.

Even though he didn't really need it, Gun checked the position of the golden line that led him along. He had recognized that inlaid pattern of moon and stars the moment he had seen it in the bowl, and now that he was here, he could have headed straight for the right spot, relying on his memory of the site alone.

"This way," he said, leading Epion off the main road across what might very well have been a public square, toward where a green flag fluttered in the morning breeze. They walked over a section of stone pavement from which the dirt and grass had been partially removed, revealing the worn and broken remains of a large medallion set into the original paving materials, a medallion that incorporated the shapes of a blazing sun and the crescent moon. On the far side of this remnant, perhaps half a span farther away, was the green flag.

"Look," Gun said, walking faster and pointing ahead. "Do you see that bush there? It's been pulled out since Mar and I were here last." What had been the beginning of a wide staircase—the one he had seen in the bowl—had been partly uncovered by him and Mar about a month earlier.

Gun, looking for Caid artifacts in general, had Found something below the dirt, and so the square had been marked accordingly. But someone had been here since and had dug farther than he and Mar had gone, pulling aside even more of the growth and exposing a jumble of rocks that were too even to be anything but broken chunks of ancient paving.

"They built to last," he said, tracing the layers of material with his fingertips. "You have to give them that."

"What now?" Epion said.

"My line leads me right inside," Gun said. "Obviously, whoever moved the bushes and shoved that flagstone over has hidden what we're looking for in some underground vault of the Caids."

"Let me," Epion said, starting down the steps.

"Better not," Gun said. "We don't know what there is underground, and I may be the only one who can Find it."

"Of course." But Epion did not retreat back to the level of the old square. "But is it safe? Jo-Leggett," he called to the guard who had accompanied them. "Come and stand here at the top of these steps. Keep a clear line-of-sight to your brother." Epion pushed at a leaning bit of rock with both hands.

"Safe enough for whoever has been here before us," Gun pointed out. "Where underground rooms have been found before, they've usually been quite stable. As I said, the Caids built to last, and whatever has not been exposed to the raw elements—" *and other things I won't go into*, Gun thought with a shiver—"generally remains intact." He looked back at Epion. "I don't know how much room there will be underneath," he said. And that was true enough. What the bowl had shown him—a small room lined with shelves full of books and scrolled documents—would not necessarily be exactly what was under their feet right now.

"Fine then, in you go." Smiling, Epion dusted off his hands on his trousers, heedless of the embroidered linen. Of course, Gun thought as he shrugged off his pack and placed it carefully on the ground, it's not as if the man had to launder his clothes himself.

Epion helped him shove one of the smaller pieces of paving to one side until a pointed opening was cleared, made by two stones leaning against each other. Crouching down, Gun duck walked under. The steps were gritty under

his boots, and he had to pull his head down almost to the
point of pain to fit into the opening. Only the gold line, now
quite obvious and necessary in the darkened space, told him
he could continue forward.

Eleven steps farther down, the grit was gone, and Gun
was able to straighten out bit by bit, until he was almost
upright. He still kept one hand over his head, in case of
unseen obstacles. Finally there were no more steps, and the
sound of his own footfalls echoed differently, and he realized he must be in the room he had seen in the bowl. He
fumbled open the pouch attached to his belt, carefully pulling out his sparker and the stub of candle that he was never
without.

He sparked, once, twice, and the oiled wick caught. Gun
waited, eyes shut against the glare, until he could safely
open them. There, laid out in front of him, was the room he
had seen in the library. Here and now it was covered with
dust, much of it, unfortunately, what was left of the books
and scrolls that had slowly been disintegrating since the
time of the Caids. Gun turned, careful not to disturb the
dust any further. This room would have to be very carefully
excavated if any of the ancient parchments were to be preserved.

"Can you see it?" Epion's voice was startlingly close.

"Not yet. Someone's been here, though. You can see
where the dust's been disturbed."

"Can you tell who?"

"Maybe if I were a Mercenary Brother."

Gun edged forward, pulling the neck of his tunic up over
his nose to serve as a filter against the dust he couldn't help
raising. There. Exactly where he had seen it, only now, instead of standing on end, spine out, tucked in the middle of
the row between other books, it was lying on its side, alone
on a thick layer of dust. There was the gold spine, and the
sunburst on the cover, glittering in the light.

"I see it." Gun stepped forward, still taking care not to
send up clouds of dust. He was reaching out for the book
when a crunching, squealing sound came from the direction
of the stairs, and a shift in the air almost blew out the candle. Gun turned, ignoring the dust, and raced back to the
steps, bumping his head as he crawled back up the way he
had come. It was not until he was actually touching the rock

that his heart was convinced of what his brain had already told him.

The stones had moved. The exit was blocked.

~⬧~

The wind had picked up with the setting of the sun, making the horsehair tent ropes creak and the edges of both tents and ground sheets flutter. The tall grass in the distance, uneaten by the herds of horses or inglera, rustled, sounding like far-off rain. As Dhulyn lit the lamp, Parno glanced out the narrow tent opening and saw Star-Wind with the younger Horseman, both sitting on their heels, five or six paces away. Close enough to be of service, they were far enough off to show that they made no attempt to listen. *He's a Mage, though*, Parno thought. There was no telling what he could and couldn't hear.

"We'll need a saw," Dhulyn said under her breath. "Preferably one with very small teeth."

"No." Delvik's hoarse whisper almost startled them; they had thought from his breathing he was asleep. They turned to find him with his eyes open. Parno crouched down on his heels, bringing himself eye-to-eye with the injured man.

"My Brother," he said, "Dhulyn and I are not Knives, but we know how to remove a limb without loss of life."

"No," Delvik repeated. He licked his lips, and Dhulyn fetched a waterskin from the other pallet and held it for him to drink. Once he had wet his mouth, he spoke again.

"Do not take the leg." His voice was stronger now. "Give me the Final Sword."

Dhulyn kneeled down next to Parno, where Delvik could see her and hear her without having to move his head. "It is dangerous, what I plan, but it can be done. I can cut just above the knee," she told him. "Any lower and I risk missing the path the poison has already taken."

Delvik shook his head, and raised a hand that trembled. "If it were a hand," he said, turning his over as of showing her what he meant. "I would accept your offered skill. A one-handed Brother can still serve. But a leg gone? A Mercenary Brother who cannot walk unaided? Who cannot ride?" He shook his head again. "It must be the Final Sword."

"You could serve the Brotherhood in a House." Dhulyn

shifted her glance to Parno, who managed to meet her eyes steadily. His Partner's face was neutral as always, pale skin showing a smudge of dirt on the left cheek, but he could see, from the little fold in the corner of her mouth and the darkening of her gray eyes, what Dhulyn was thinking. There were not many cripples in the Mercenary Brotherhood, and the few there were all served somewhere in a Mercenary House.

Delvik sketched a waving motion before his hand fell, limp, back to his side. "How could I serve? I cannot read," he said. "I would not even be able to carry trays."

"Perhaps a School—"

"No!" Somehow Delvik found the strength to grasp Dhulyn's wrist. She let him. "Give me the Final Sword. It is my right." His hand fell away again, his strength exhausted.

Dhulyn sat back on her heels, mouth set in a thin line. Parno watched her face. To someone else it might seem impassive, a typical Outlander's face, but he knew how to read the tracks left by her emotions. Anger, Denial. Resignation. She was trapped by the Common Rule—he knew it, and she knew it. She had given Delvik every option, and three times he had asked for the Final Sword. As Senior Brother present, Dhulyn must abide by his choice. She rose to her feet and turned away, massaging the spot between her eyebrows with her left thumb.

"The Rule is common to us all, Delvik," she said without turning around. "It shall be as you wish." Dhulyn began to rummage in her belt pouch. "I have iocain leaves here, my Brother. They will make you more comfortable. Rest. I must speak with the elders of the Salt Desert People."

Parno followed her out of the tent to where Star-Wind rose to meet them.

"Our Brother has the blood sickness," Dhulyn told the Espadryni Shaman. "He will not let me take the leg, and without a Healer he will die."

Star-Wind, lips pressed tightly together, looked away to survey the camp, then turned back to them. "In three days we move on; our herds need fresh grazing. We will leave you what supplies we can spare and the tent, but with respect, Mercenaries, we cannot carry your Brother with us."

Parno looked to Dhulyn, but her eyes were focused in

the middle distance, the small scar on her upper lip standing out white against her ivory skin.

"Thank you for your courtesy," he said, when it became obvious Dhulyn could not speak. "But it doesn't arise. Our Brother has asked for the Final Sword. Three times he asked, and so we must give it."

The Horseman was already nodding. "Of course," he said finally. "Can we assist in any way? Is there a ceremony?"

Parno thought that the Horsemen must have their own methods of dealing with whatever wounds and illnesses their Mages could not cure. The extremes of age, illness, weakness—these were things a mobile people could not tolerate for long. Still, he shook his head. "Thank you, but this is a matter for our Brotherhood. Dhulyn Wolfshead is Senior Brother and—"

"But it will not be she who kills him?" Star-Wind's voice had hardened. He looked from Parno to Dhulyn and back again.

"She is Senior," Parno repeated. "It is our Common Rule."

But Star-Wind was shaking his head in short sharp movements. "To have a Marked woman kill . . ." He looked up and caught both their gazes. "Do you see? We have said that she is whole, and safe, and now she wishes to kill someone."

Dhulyn cut through the air with her right hand. "Can you cure him? Can any of your Mages? He has asked for the Final Sword. I must give it to him. It is the oath that binds all of us."

"Cannot Parno Lionsmane do it?"

"He is Senior to Delvik, but he is not the most Senior Brother present. I cannot even order him to do it. I must do it myself."

"It is an act of mercy," Parno said. "Surely, it would be more cold-blooded in her, more unfeeling, if she left him to die, to slowly rot away . . ."

Star-Wind was plucking at his lower lip with the thumb and first finger of his right hand, but he was nodding. Slowly, but nodding. "What you say is true. If it were one of the Seers, she might cut his throat without a qualm, but not for

mercy. His pain and suffering would be as nothing to her—
unless it was noise she wished to stop. But even then she
would not kill him if there were cost to herself. She would
as soon walk away."

"Will your Elders, your people, see this the same way
you do?" Dhulyn asked.

Star-Wind once more looked over his shoulder at where
the rest of the camp were preparing for sleep. "We must
hope that they do." He turned back to them. "Do nothing
now. This cannot be done with stealth, or in the night. This
must be seen by Mother Sun."

"It's a while since you've had to do this," Parno said. Dhulyn looked up from the small quantity of iocain she had left in
her pouch. Delvik Bloodeye was asleep and breathing more
easily now that the drug had taken away some of the pain.

Dhulyn nodded, folding away the leaves once more into
her belt pouch. "Not since the time there was the Dedilos
sickness in the camp outside Bhexyllia."

Parno grimaced but said nothing, knowing Dhulyn did
not like to speak of it. The illness was rare but frightening.
With luck it would kill you quickly; without it, it would only
take your wits and leave you with a wandering mind. That
time there was no Healer in the camp, and by the time one
could have arrived, it would have been too late. There were
not enough Healers, Parno thought, not for the first time.
There was no rarer Mark, except the Sight. "Bad enough
when there're not many Healers," is what he said aloud. "I
never imagined a place where there were none at all."

Dhulyn nodded. "Delvik will sleep now until sunrise,"
she said, standing up. "I don't want to wake him."

"Why would we?"

"Neither of us knows him," she said. "Who will tell his
story?"

Parno looked down at their Brother. "We know his
story," he said. "It is the same as ours. In Battle."

"Or in Death," Dhulyn answered.

They had been offered another tent alongside the horse
line, as far from the area of the Espadryni women as it
could be and still be considered within the camp. They had
refused it, preferring to take over caring for Delvik.

"It would be much better if you did not have to do this

thing." Dhulyn stretched out on the other cot, and Parno perched on its edge. They had not slept apart since they had left the Mortaxa, across the Long Ocean. Parno thought it would be as long again or longer before either of them was ready to bed with another.

"Much better if he had died before we arrived, I agree." Dhulyn turned over on her back.

"If the younger one—Kesman?—had lived, could Delvik have ordered *him* to give him the Final Sword?" Parno reached behind him without looking and felt Dhulyn's cool, calloused fingers slip into his hand.

"It's an interesting question, isn't it? There are limits to what a Senior Brother can require of a Junior. Is this one of them?"

Parno squeezed her hand. "Well, don't think you can ever order me to do it. To you I mean."

"Not even if I were in dire pain?"

"No," he said flatly. "I would keep you alive until we found a Healer, no matter how much pain you were in."

"I'd kill you, if the situations were reversed," she said. He could hear a smile—and the approach of sleep—in her voice.

"Charming. *Now* how am I supposed to sleep?"

"You'll take first watch," she said. "I have to kill someone in the morning."

"Just another day in the Brotherhood."

Dhulyn drifted off to sleep, hoping she would not dream . . . .

<hr>

IT IS A COLD, DARK HILLSIDE, AND THE MOON SHINES BRIGHTLY OVERHEAD, THE EYE OF THE FATHER IN THE SKY. THE AIR IS CRISP, CRINKLING THE HAIRS IN HER NOSTRILS, AND SMELLS LIKE SNOW BEFORE MORNING. WHAT DHULYN NOTICES FIRST IS THE SILENCE. EVEN IN THIS COLD, SHE WOULD EXPECT TO HEAR SOMETHING—MICE UNDER THE SNOW, THE HOOTING OF AN OWL ON THE HUNT.

BUT THEN DHULYN HEARS THE FOOTSTEPS, AND WHEN SHE TURNS, SHE SEES A MAN OF MEDIUM HEIGHT, CLOAKED AND BOOTED AGAINST THE COLD, STRIDING AWAY FROM HER. HE LOOKS LIKE A DARKER STAIN AGAINST THE TREES, A PURPOSEFUL SHADOW IN THE MOONLIGHT. SHE SEES HIS FOOTPRINTS DARK AGAINST THE GROUND AND KNOWS THEY WILL BE GONE BY MORNING, COVERED BY THE COMING SNOW.

SO HOW CAN SHE SEE THEM NOW? AGAINST THE DARK GROUND?

SHE CROUCHES DOWN AND TOUCHES THE TIP OF ONE FINGER TO THE MAN'S FOOTPRINT, AND IT COMES AWAY DARKENED. THERE IS NOT ENOUGH LIGHT TO SHOW HER THE COLOR OF THE STAIN, BUT DHULYN DOESN'T NEED IT. SHE KNOWS THE SMELL OF BLOOD, NO MATTER HOW DARK OR COLD IT MIGHT BE. SHE LOOKS DOWN THE PATH TOWARD THE MAN, BUT HE'S GONE. SHE LOOKS BACK IN THE DIRECTION THE MAN HAS COME FROM AND HOPES SHE WILL NOT SEE ANYMORE. . . .

SHE HAS SEEN THIS ROOM MANY TIMES, AND THE MAN IN IT. HERE IS THE MAGE WITH HIS PALE CLOSE-CROPPED HAIR. WHEN HIS EYES ARE THE BLUE OF OLD ICE, HE CAN READ THE BOOK AND CUT THE MIRROR. WHEN, AS NOW, HIS EYES ARE A BEAUTIFUL JADE GREEN, HE CANNOT. WITHOUT CUTTING THE MIRROR, HE CANNOT OPEN THE GATE. HE FALLS TO HIS KNEES AND BOWS HIS HEAD, HIS HANDS COVERING HIS FACE. DHULYN IS NOT ONLY DHULYN HERE, SHE IS SOMETHING MORE, NOT UNLIKE THE MAN ON HIS KNEES. BUT HERE THE VISION CHANGES, AND DHULYN TAKES A STEP AWAY AS THE GREEN OF THE MAN'S EYES SPREADS THROUGH HIS BODY, UNTIL THERE IS A JADE STATUE KNEELING IN FRONT OF HER, A STATUE THAT EXPLODES SOUNDLESSLY INTO DUST AND VAPOR.

NO, SHE SAYS, THAT IS NOT WHAT HAPPENS. THE DHULYN OF THE VISION LOOKS UP AT HER, AND SHE KNOWS THEY BOTH WEAR THE SAME CONFUSED LOOK . . .

A DIFFERENT DARKNESS, WARM, HUMID ENOUGH TO MAKE THE SWEAT POOL ON THE SKIN AND THE CLOTHES CLING TO THE BACK. SHE IS STANDING IN THE GARDEN OF A GREAT PALACE, AND EVEN IN THE DARK SHE CAN SEE THAT IT IS WEEDY, UNTENDED, THE BOWL OF A FOUNTAIN DRY AND CRACKED. BUT THERE IS NOISE AND LIGHTS WITHIN. A YELP OF PAIN BRINGS HER CLOSER TO THE WINDOW. SHE SEES CHILDREN TORTURING A SMALL DOG WHILE THEIR ELDERS LOOK ON AND GIVE ADVICE. A WOMAN TURNS TOWARD THE WINDOW AND LOOKS AT HER.

HAIR THE COLOR OF OLD BLOOD AND A FACE DHULYN KNOWS. IT IS NOT HER OWN FACE, BUT ONE ENOUGH LIKE IT TO MARK THE WOMAN AS KIN. CLOSE KIN. BUT DHULYN NEVER WANTS TO SEE THIS WOMAN'S EXPRESSION ON THE FACE OF ANYONE NEAR OR DEAR TO HER. THIS IS NO PAST SHE HAS EVER SEEN BEFORE.

Gundaron sat stiff, knees drawn tight to his chest, hands pressed over his lips. He wasn't afraid of the dark, he told himself. Nor even of small, enclosed spaces. The chamber was large, and there was plenty of air—fresh air at that. He wouldn't suffocate in the time they would take to find him.

Epion—or one of the guards, that was more likely—was probably halfway back to town by now to fetch workmen to dig Gun out. It would only be a matter of hours. He wouldn't even have time to get hungry, not really.

Epion or the other guard, the one with the dark beard, would wait by the entrance, Gun thought. So they would have no trouble finding the exact spot again. Gun brushed away that thought with a brisk mental wave of the hand. Mar knew where he was—or at least where he'd intended to go. If the upper area was relatively undamaged, she should be able to direct the digging from the portion of their notes where the sun-and-moon marked steps were described.

Did Mar know that Epion had gone with him? Did anyone? *The stable boys*, he thought. They'd know, even if no one else did, that horses had been taken out and, for that matter, that Gun and his pony had not returned.

And of course, there were other Finders in the city. One of them would surely be available to Find him.

If the guard wasn't thrown by his horse while riding back to Menoin for help. If Epion and Dark Beard weren't also buried somewhere in the cave-in.

Strangely, instead of frightening him further, this thought made Gun uncurl, drop his hands, and sit up straight.

"You can't plan for what *might* happen," he said aloud, paraphrasing something Dhulyn Wolfshead had said to him once. "You plan for what *can* happen." You couldn't know how likely something was, the Wolfshead had said. But you could know whether or not it was possible.

It was possible that it would take hours or days for anyone to come looking for him. Possible that even if they came quickly, it might take hours or days for them to dig him out. There was something he could try first.

He rolled his shoulders to loosen the tight muscles of his neck and stretched out his hands. He didn't have the bowl, but before he met Mar, he used to Find with books. And he *did* have a book.

He steadied the Caid volume on his knees and opened it to somewhere in the middle, grinned when he saw the language—at least in this section—was unfamiliar. That should actually be of help. He began trying to read the words backward, just letting his eyes drift over them, letting the letters calm him, letting his mind float.

I need a way out, he thought. *Where is the way out?*

At first he thought nothing was going to happen—after all, no one could Find what wasn't there. But then a blue line appeared in the air in front of his eyes. He closed the book, tucked it under his arm, and got to his feet. At that moment the candle guttered and went out.

But the blue line was still there, glowing softly in the darkness, the same midnight blue as Mar's eyes. Warm and soft like velvet. It even seemed to shed a bit of light. Not as much as a candle or lantern, of course, but enough, Gun thought, to help him keep more or less oriented. He stepped forward with confidence—and tripped over a chunk of fallen masonry.

He landed on the book, coughing at the dust raised by his fall. He sneezed, and pulled the collar of his tunic over his nose, trying not to breath in more dust. Blinking, Gun found he could still see the blue line. He put out his hand as if to touch it, as if it were an actual, palpable line made of rope, and walked forward more cautiously, the Caid book once more under his arm.

At first Gun expected at any moment to feel the wall of the book chamber with the fingers of his outstretched hand. After all, the room hadn't seemed particularly large when the candle was lit. But he must have got turned around at some point, he decided, and was now walking down the length of the room. Even so, surely the room hadn't been *this* long? He hadn't thought to count paces when he began following the blue line, and it was too late to start now. Mar would be disappointed in him, he thought. Even after all they'd been through, when he was focused on something—especially a book—it was easy for him to forget more practical matters. Just as he had that thought, Gun's reaching fingers stubbed against the hardness of the wall.

The blue line lead directly into it.

He put the book down between his feet and ran his hands over the cold stone until he realized they were trembling too much to do him any good. He took several deep breaths, exhaling slowly, and willed himself to be calm. This time, he could feel texture under his fingertips, as if the wall were made of bricks about the size of his hand, very smooth, with hardly any mortar between them. No, not bricks, *tiles*.

Gun rubbed at his upper lip. The line was still in front of

him, still leading into the wall. Clearly this was the way out.
But how? If he could step back, if there were more light,
would he be able to see the outline of a door? He hadn't
seen one when he'd entered the chamber, but then he hadn't
been looking for one, had he? He'd been focusing on the
golden line that led him to the book.

He reached out again to touch the blue line. His hand
passed through it.

"You're not really there." His voice did not echo, nor did
it sound particularly nervous, he thought. "You're in my
head, not out here in the world at all. You're just the pointer
my own mind is using to help me Find."

He touched the point on the wall where the blue line
seemed to disappear. Was this tile a little rougher than the
rest? He pushed against it with the tips of his fingers. Did it
move? Give just a little under the pressure? Or was it hope
that made him think so?

Gun rubbed his hands together and blew on them. The
tiles were cold. He set his feet, braced himself, and pushed
at the tile again, this time with his thumbs. There was a
grinding noise, and the floor opened beneath him.

⌐⌐⌐

"There. That should do it, my lord." Jo-Leggett pushed the
final rock into place, tossing the loose bush to one side. In
another day or so it would be dry enough that no one would
notice it again.

Epion walked around to view the section of ruin from
another angle. With the green flag gone, there was nothing
to distinguish this spot from any other. He nodded his satisfaction. "Can you get the pony back without being seen?"

"Nothing easier," Jo-Leggett said with a grin. "I walk
him into the stable yard complaining loud and long how the
young Scholar ran off leaving me to manage both beasts,
and no one will notice they didn't see him with me."

"If you can do it naturally, suggest that the boy ran off to
see Falcos."

Gabe-Leggett had brought his horse down to him, and
as Epion swung himself up into the saddle he saw Gabe was
still staring at the pile of broken stone that marked the
Scholar's grave.

"Do you hear something," he asked.

Gabe looked up. "Won't we want it then? The book?"

"I do not believe so." Epion smiled. "Have any of the men we sent through the Path ever returned?"

"No, my lord." Gabe stood patient.

"Then I don't think the book has been of any real use to us, has it?" Epion glanced down at the entrance again. "Until now, at any rate."

Twelve

BEKLUTH ALLAIN LIKED this time of year best. The sweltering temperatures of summer were over, leaving cooler, crisper days ideal for walking or riding. True, the nights were also cooler, but they weren't yet so cold that a fire was needed for more than cooking, so he was relieved of the constant search for fuel—or from having to use dried horse dung, the smell of which, in Bekluth's opinion, you never entirely got out of your clothing. The only drawback to this time of year, he thought, was that in about a moon or so he'd have to stop trading entirely for the season and decide what small town should be his winter base this time. Even the Red Horsemen would start moving farther south soon.

At least Bekluth had money enough to pick and choose, thanks to the foreign horses. He'd been clever about them, quite clever really, though he said so himself. He did not get horses every time of course, that would have been too much to expect. So far he'd taken two to the trading center in the Gray Hills, claiming to have obtained them from the Red Horsemen, and both had fetched good prices, which he'd taken part in coin and part in the type of provisions—salt, sugar, and dried fruit—that the Horsemen would trade for or he could use himself. These last two were better horses, as befitted beasts from the stables of a Royal House, and would have brought much better prices at Gray Hills had he been foolish enough to make such an amateur's mistake as having more horses to trade again so soon. One of them he'd traded to the Cold Lake People—telling them it came from Gray Hills—for the sky stones found in creek and stream beds in the dry season. The other he'd keep for now, stashed away in the place only he knew of.

He smiled broadly. It was years now since he'd left his mother's people to go trading on his own; he could say anything, tell any tale he liked, and no one the wiser. Everyone he traded with thought he was based with someone else, and he was the only one the Red Horsemen would trade with at all. Why he could—

He stopped so suddenly that the three ponies he had with him kept moving for several paces until their lead ropes pulled taut. His smile faded away. His mother had taught him many valuable lessons before her death, the most valuable being not to draw attention to himself. He'd been careful to follow her lessons, and they had kept him safe so far.

And new wealth might bring him that kind of attention. It would bring him better quarters, surely, a more comfortable inn with a better cook than usual. But if he showed too prosperous, the Guilds would take an interest in his trading route, and that he couldn't have. So he couldn't, he absolutely *could not*, splash money about, no matter what tale he had to tell. He shook himself.

"What if I paid them their cut," he said aloud. They'd leave him be then. Or would they?

No. That was dangerous thinking, the kind his mother had punished him for. He couldn't show his new wealth. It was as simple as that. He was tolerated as a small, independent trader, his route ignored by the Guilds, considered too risky for too small a return. If he showed up at a Guild with enough money or goods to pay them their fees, some rival would decide his route was worth taking. And then how could he help anyone?

It took a nudge from one of the ponies, strong enough to make him take a step forward, to get Bekluth's thoughts to stop chasing themselves in circles. He set off again, a tune coming to his lips. He was worrying for nothing. Soon none of this would matter. Very soon now he would pass through the Sun's Door for the final time. Where people understood him and appreciated his skills. That was what he'd been promised.

He turned west and began to angle his way toward the territories of the Salt Desert People. It took him the rest of the day and most of the next to find the spot he was looking for. He'd cut the angle too sharply and ended by having to cast back and forth a bit before he was able to follow the smell of burned flesh directly to the pit. He left the ponies well back and approached the orobeast trap on foot. The Red Horsemen had been here, that much was obvious. The ground around the edge had been trampled. They had not been able to lift the bodies out of the pit and, unable to expose them cleanly to the Sun, Moon, and Stars, had burned them where they lay. This was even better than he'd hoped; the Horsemen would avoid a death fire for at least a moon or more.

He squatted on the edge of the pit and looked down. With the sun almost overhead, there was only one corner in shadow, and even there he could make out shapes clearly. The Horsemen had come unprepared, and without extra fuel the fire had not burned hot enough to reduce the bodies completely. If you knew what to look for, it was easy enough to understand the traces. There were the remains of one horse, and there the second. Between the two you could make out the shape of one of the men, and the second was—

Bekluth leaped to his feet and ran around the other side of the pit. The other body was there. It had to be. They had both gone into the pit, horses and all. He squatted again, but no amount of squinting could make another body appear.

Somehow the second man had escaped. Or no, not escaped. If the fall had not killed him, perhaps the Salt Desert People had found and taken him when they made the death pyre.

Bekluth stepped back from the pit and held his hands to his head. He forced himself to take deep breaths, deep and slow. He would go to the Salt Desert People and see what the man had told them. The man was a stranger to them, Bekluth was their friend. They would believe what Bekluth told them. He could take care of this. It was simple.

Dhulyn knew she'd only been a short time asleep when she felt Parno's hand on her shoulder. He did not shake, or squeeze, so while she came instantly awake and clear-headed, she did not reach immediately for a weapon.

"The Espadryni wish to speak with us, my heart." Parno spoke in the nightwatch voice.

"Now?" She answered the same way. Soft voices could not awaken Delvik, but Parno evidently saw no reason to share their thoughts with their hosts, and she had ample reason to trust his judgment.

"They have been sitting in council," he said. "I suppose they wouldn't wake us if they didn't think it of some importance." He shrugged, and she felt the movement through his arm. "Star-Wind doesn't meet my eye."

"Not a good sign." Dhulyn threw off the light cover Parno must have laid over her and rolled upright, stretching out first her shoulders, then her arms, back, and legs. She tightened the laces on her vest, made sure her hair was well tied out of her face. A glance told her Parno was armed, though his weapons were sheathed, and she picked up her own sword from where she'd placed it ready to her hand and slipped it through her sash.

"And Delvik?" she asked.

A shadow in the doorway answered her. "I will sit with him, if you will allow it." It was the same younger Horseman who had been sitting in the tent when they arrived.

"I have given him iocain for the pain," she told him now. "He should not awaken before sunrise."

The camp was quiet, with very few even of the night sounds common to any large encampment of men. There were lights burning in three of the tents in the women's area, Dhulyn saw, but otherwise the camp slept. A light rain was falling, little more than a mist, but enough to keep people inside. Dhulyn glanced up, but there was too much cloud to see the stars, shining backward in the sky. There would be more rain before dawn.

The tent of the chiefs held perhaps twenty-five men, sitting at their ease around the central fire. All the men, Dhulyn estimated, who had passed their naming day and would be counted as adult members of the community. Those present now would represent all the adult men who were not out on sentry duty, gone hunting, or with the herds. A space had been left empty next to where the two chiefs, Singer of the Grass-Moon and Spring-Flood, sat next to each other at the far side of the tent from the entry. Everyone in the tent turned to look at them as they entered, though Dhulyn noticed that many seemed reluctant to meet her eyes.

"Will you sit, Mercenaries?" Spring-Flood said indicating the space to his left.

Dhulyn touched her forehead and picked her way through the seated men. It didn't make the least difference where they sat. They were badly enough outnumbered to make it a question whether they could fight their way out should the need arise. If these were town men—even soldiers—she might have given good odds that she and Parno could deal with all of them. But nomads, that weighted the wager in a different way.

The men moved their feet out of her way, some still without actually looking at her, though there seemed to be no reluctance in allowing them to pass. It was apparent that whatever the council had brought them to hear, all were in agreement with it.

"We regret, Mercenaries, that we were unable to heal your Brother." It was Singer of the Grass-Moon who offered this apology, Dhulyn noted. As the most powerful of the shamans, such magic would have been his responsibility, even if he had not undertaken it himself.

"We accept that there is a limit to all things," Dhulyn said. A more profound silence fell at her words. Someone in the shadows coughed.

"It is distracting for us to hear a woman's voice in this tent, Dhulyn Wolfshead. We do not wish to offend, but we would take it as a great favor, if Parno Lionsmane could speak for you both."

"I am the Senior Mercenary Brother present," Dhulyn said. She was more than a little surprised to find that she *was* offended. She was familiar with this attitude of male superiority—what woman who traveled wasn't?—but she realized that she had taken it for granted that she would be treated as an equal by the Espadryni, regardless of their attitude toward their own "broken" women. *Pretend you are in the Great King's Court*, she told herself. But it was hard to do when she looked around her and saw what might have been her own people.

"But you are bonded, are you not? The two of you are as one person. It should not matter to you which of you speaks, yet it matters a great deal to us. You would do us much honor if you agreed."

Dhulyn drew in a deep breath. On the one hand, that they were Partnered did not change the fact that she had been a Mercenary Brother longer than Parno. On the other hand, they *were* Partners, and the fact that he did not normally speak for the two of them did not mean that this would be the first time. *Remember the Great King's Court*, she told herself again.

She signaled Parno with a flick of her left thumb.

"As we are guests in your home," Parno said, smoothly picking up on his cue. "We will agree."

The older man leaned back against the saddle that had been placed behind him as a rest. Spring-Flood cleared his throat. "It is as our honored guests that we wish to speak with you," he began. "We have talked long on the subject of your Brother, Delvik Bloodeye. We understand the need for a warrior to end his life when he sees his usefulness to his Brothers is over, and we would not stand in the way of such an intent."

Here it comes, Dhulyn thought, fighting to keep her face from showing her irritation. *There's a "however" coming, clear as clear*.

"However," Spring-Flood continued, "we ask that Parno Lionsmane's be the hand that releases your Brother to the Sun, Moon, and Stars."

Dhulyn didn't even bother to signal Parno; he knew what her answer would be.

"Dhulyn Wolfshead is Senior Brother," Parno said, just as she expected. "Senior to Delvik Bloodeye, as well as to me. Our Common Rule requires this of her, not of me."

"With respect to your Common Rule, it would still be seen as a killing done by a woman of the Espadryni." This time a murmur of sound and movement followed the Horse Shaman's words. This time he had not referred to the women as "Seers," Dhulyn noticed. "Dhulyn Wolfshead might be seen as no longer whole. We cannot allow it."

This time Parno looked at her, waiting for her sign before speaking. She drummed her fingers on her knee.

"We will wait here until you have gone on. We'll manage," he added.

"Your determination to abide by your oath, and give your Brother Delvik Bloodeye the Final Sword, despite ill consequences to yourself, actually weighs in your favor, young one." Singer of the Grass-Moon reached across Spring-Flood and touched Dhulyn on the back of her right hand, so there could be no doubt whom he addressed. His voice was raspy with overuse. "But it is not consequences to *you* that concerns us here, but consequences to ourselves, to our Seers. You may ride away, even pass once more through the Door of the Sun, and this land, and our concerns, will be behind you. But our women will know that you killed a man and were not punished for it. It will make them restless, make them test the boundaries and constraints of the Pact, and we will be forced to punish them because of your example."

Dhulyn inhaled sharply, opened her mouth . . . and closed it again, before the flash of anger made her speak. It was unthinkable that they could do this, that they could take her duty from her. She looked at Parno. His eyes flicked to the gold and silver armlet Dhulyn wore on her right arm, and she pressed her lips together in frustration. Finding and aiding their Brothers was only part of their mission here, if the most important part. They had still to find the killer of the Princess Cleona, which the help and goodwill of the Espadryni would make easier.

And even if she might be willing to throw such aid away, was she willing to be responsible for the maiming, perhaps even the deaths, of Espadryni women? Dhulyn took a deep breath. She could hold to the exact letter of the Common Rule, risk failure in their mission, and endanger innocent people. Or, she could let Parno act for her in this, reasoning that it was much the same as his speaking for both of them. Was that an argument that would hold before a Senior Brother such as Gustof Ironhand?

Of course that would only matter if they were able to pass back through the Door of the Sun. *Today's troubles today*, she thought.

She rested her left hand on her knee, small finger extended to the side. *I agree, but I don't like it.*

*   *   *

When Mother Sun was well up, Dhulyn helped Delvik Bloodeye, sweating and with teeth clenched against the pain, out of the tent into the watery sunshine. An area had been cleared in the center of the camp, in front of the main tent of the chiefs. The women's section touched one side of this area, but there were only a few sufficiently interested to gather closely enough to watch, and these seemed to be watching Dhulyn rather than anyone else. Once again most of the men of the Salt Desert had gathered to watch the ceremony, leaving the underage boys to mind the herds and flocks. Dhulyn frowned. She would have much preferred that Parno give Delvik his Final Sword in private—this was something between Brothers, after all—but she could understand that the Espadryni felt very differently.

Dhulyn blinked against the light, her eyelids feeling gritty. Parno's pipes were an unfamiliar weight on her left shoulder. They had all three washed themselves as clean as possible, put on their best clothes—which in Delvik's case meant borrowing Parno's cleanest trousers and a cloak of Dhulyn's that she only used in the worst cold. The sword at his side, however, was his own.

When she had their Brother positioned properly, Dhulyn caught Star-Wind's eye and nodded. At his signal, everyone except the Mercenaries sat down on the ground.

"I would have been proud to give you my death, Dhulyn my Brother," Delvik said almost in her ear.

Dhulyn cleared her throat. She had judged the dose of iocain correctly. "I would have been honored to receive it." She nodded to Parno, who drew his sword. "Parno is my Partner; you know that we are the two edges of one sword."

Delvik nodded. "Find that cursed murderer, my Brothers. Give him an extra blow for me and for Kesman." He looked around them, at the faces of the Horsemen, some curious, some frowning. "Things would be so much better if we Brothers ran the world."

"There would be fewer people." Dhulyn was rewarded by Delvik's crooked smile. "Are you ready, Delvik my Brother?"

"I am. But . . . may I stand alone?"

Dhulyn released him slowly, giving him time to find his

own balance. Delvik had to put his weight on his left foot, he could not even touch his right to the ground.

Delvik drew his sword with his right hand, and smiled. Then he saluted Parno with his sword, the motion as crisp as if they were putting on a demonstration. Parno extended his own blade and gave that of Delvik a sharp rap, making the steel ring.

Don't play. Dhulyn closed the words in behind her teeth. *End it quickly.*

"I give you my death, Parno Lionsmane," Delvik said, pointing his sword to the sky and touching his trembling fingertips to his forehead.

Parno returned the salute. "Delvik Bloodeye, I receive it. In Battle." He plunged his sword into Delvik's heart.

Dhulyn took one step forward, but Delvik only fell to his knees, Parno moving so that the blade did not pull free. Delvik put his left hand on top of Parno's blade, his right hand still held his own. "Or in Death," he whispered, finishing the salute.

His eyes closed, and his hand opened. Dhulyn caught his sword before it touched the ground.

Parno pulled his blade free.

The Espadryni got to their feet, and Star-Wind approached them. "The doorway has been prepared for your Brother," he said. "Will you need help to move him?"

Dhulyn cleared her throat, but Parno answered for her. "No, we thank you. We will carry him ourselves."

Parno wiped his blade clean and sheathed it before taking his pipes from Dhulyn and slinging them over his own shoulder. They laid Delvik's body out straight on the blanket they'd brought from his bed. Dhulyn tucked his hands into his belt so they wouldn't fall loose. She smoothed back his hair and straightened the cloak she had given him. Since Parno had waited to draw out the blade, the wound showed very little blood.

"Show us the place," she said when she straightened to her feet, moving to stand at Delvik's feet.

"If you will follow me." Parno lifted his end of the blanket, and Dhulyn followed suit. The mass of men watching parted for them as Star-Wind led them east of the camp—toward where, in this world, the sun would rise. Here the Espadryni had constructed a narrow platform made of crisscrossed poles and lathes, perhaps shoulder height on a tall man.

Among the other things that had been decided the evening before, Dhulyn had agreed to have Delvik's body disposed of in the manner normally used by the Espadryni. Delvik had expressed no preference for burial or burning, and it was within the dictates of the Common Rule that the bodies of Mercenary Brothers could be treated according to the practices of the land in which they died. Delvik's body would be exposed to Mother Sun and Father Moon, Stars, Cloud, Wind, Rain, and Snow, until there was nothing left of it.

Dhulyn and Parno lifted their dead Brother up onto the framework, and Parno stood back two paces. Dhulyn took hold of the pole nearest her and looked up, as if to speak to Delvik.

"I did not know our Brother well, Delvik Bloodeye, called the Bull, Schooled by Yoruk Silverheels. I met him for the first time in the lands beyond the Path of the Sun. He sought a killer of men, to do justice and to keep to his oaths. Delvik Bloodeye, called the Bull, died in the best fashion. On his feet, his sword in his hand, killed by the blade of his own Brother." Dhulyn's voice was strong, but she felt the sting of salt in her eyes.

"So may it pass with all of us. In Battle or in Death," Dhulyn added, and Parno echoed her. She stepped back, leaving Parno closest to the body. He adjusted his pipes, and began to play, using drones as well as chanter, which drew the admiration of the Horsemen who had followed them to the site.

"We would have left weapons with him," Star-Wind said, approaching her quietly from her left side.

"Better they should go on and serve other Brothers." Dhulyn looked sideways at the young Espadryni. "Delvik takes with him the weapons no Mercenary is without."

"May he rest with the Stars now," Star-Wind said. "And with Mother Sun and Father Moon."

Dhulyn nodded without speaking and let the music of Parno's pipes wash over her.

Thirteen

"THIS IS GOOD," Gun said to the carter. "I can walk from here."

"You sure, boy? I can easy take you as far as the main square."

Gun didn't take offense. The man was more than old enough to call *anyone* "boy." He'd rarely seen anyone as old who was not a Healer. The amazing thing was that the man was spry enough to manage his cart.

"I'm certain, sir. I've kept you from your business long enough." And there was no way Gun wanted the old man to take him as far as the palace. Too many explanations, including why he thought that a Scholar, dirty, wet, and with scratches on his face, would be allowed in at this time of night. Gun had met the old man on the west road, not far from the sea where the tunnel out of the old Caid ruins had ended in a rocky grotto, half full of cold seawater. The old man was coming in early for the morning's market, planning to spend a few hours in the home of his granddaughter and meet his new great-grandchild and namesake. Gun couldn't believe his luck; not only did he have a ride to save him the long walk back to the city, but the old man was so interested in his own news he had no curiosity left over to question Gundaron's appearance in the middle of a lonely road.

Tired as he was, the thought of a hot fire and dry clothes helped Gun make good time up through the narrow streets to the palace. He avoided the main gate and entered with the scantiest of explanations through the gates to the stable yards, anxious to get to Mar and relieve her worries as quickly as possible. Again luck was with him; many of the junior guards knew him and Mar from their frequent visits to the palace, and everyone senior enough to question him more closely was asleep.

The guard at the entrance to the royal wing was another matter.

"Scholar, you look as though the cat swallowed you and vomited you up into a mud puddle." The man's face was familiar, but Gun had never heard his name. What was clear from his dry tone and his narrowed eyes was that no one was either looking for Gun or worried about his absence. So Epion had raised no alarm.

Gun hesitated, knowing that the longer he took to answer, the more suspicious he would look. And yet this was not the time or place to make accusations against the Tarkin's uncle. *Blooded nobles*, he said to himself. When was he going to learn? His hands formed into fists. He thought he'd been cured of trusting people just because they came from a High Noble House—but evidently not. He hadn't wanted to believe it, but the cave-in had been no accident.

"Her husband came home unexpectedly," he finally said. It was the one excuse he could think of that would account for his bedraggled appearance and the lateness of his arrival—and his hesitation.

The guard's lip pulled back. "I'm sure your own wife will be pleased to hear that," he said, disgust heavy in his voice.

Gun ducked his head and sidled past, his ears burning. The guard's low opinion was just something he'd have to live with. Fortunately he reached the door to his and Mar's rooms without meeting anyone else he had to lie to. As he would have expected, the thin line of light along the bottom edge of the door showed that Mar was still up. Gun lifted the latch with fingers suddenly stiff with cold and entered the sitting room.

"Mar, I—"

Suddenly there were soft lips pressed tight against his mouth and Mar's warm body wrapped around his. As he returned her kisses, he felt his eyes stinging and a trembling begin in his knees.

Then Mar stopped kissing him as suddenly as she'd begun. "You're wet to the skin," she said, pulling him toward the brazier glowing in the center of the room. "Caids, where have you been? How did you get wet? Did you Find it? Where's the book?"

Her soft musical voice was low and controlled, but all the time she was speaking, Mar was touching him, hugging his arm, cupping his face in her hand, and from that Gundaron knew how frightened she had been. So happy was he to see her—to be in their rooms—that it took him a long moment to realize the odd noise he heard was his teeth chattering.

"Out of those wet clothes, quickly." Mar turned away and ran into the bedroom, where the open door let him see her rummaging through their packs.

"I don't f-feel cold," he said, as he pulled his wet tunic off over his head and tossed it on a nearby stool.

"I'm not surprised." Mar handed him a soft towel as big as the bed sheets in cheaper inns and took his wet garments as he peeled them off. "It's a wonder you can feel anything at all."

Gun scrubbed at his face and his goose-pimpled arms. The heat from the brazier was just beginning to make itself felt. "Why wasn't there someone looking for me? The guards at the gate didn't even seem to know I was missing."

The corners of Mar's mouth turned down. "I'm so sorry. I spent most of the day with Alaria, helping her prepare for the wedding, and I didn't even start getting worried until it was almost sunset." She held her lower lip in her teeth before continuing. "I went down to the stable, and your pony was there, but no one seemed to remember when it came in. I was on my way to ask the Steward of Walls' help when I ran into Lord Epion, and he said he would take care of it."

Gun stuck his head through the neck of his tunic, pulled it straight, and sat down to pull on his leggings. "He did, did he? Well he'd just about taken care of me already." As he finished dressing, Gun told Mar what had happened at the ruins. He spoke as coolly as he could manage, but she was still white-faced at the end of his narration, her deep blue eyes like stains on ivory. Without saying anything, she went into the bedroom and fetched a blanket, wrapping it neatly around his legs before she sat down in the other chair, but still close enough to be able to reach out and touch him.

"Epion said he'd send someone to look for you," she said, eyes narrow and focused on the memory. She glanced up at Gun. "Though he didn't tell me he'd gone with you in the first place." Her lips pressed into a thin line. Gun knew that look and was grateful it wasn't meant for him. Mar looked away again, tapping the arm of the chair with the palm of her hand. "What about the book?" she said finally. "Did you Find it?"

"I had to leave it, I didn't know what damage the water might do. There was a ledge, just a bit downstream from the trapdoor, and I left it there. Caids grant the tide doesn't raise the water level so far inland." He stuck a hand out of the blanket and rubbed at his upper lip. "I can Find it again if I have to."

Mar gave a brisk nod that was at odds with the abstracted look on her face and went to the fireplace, where she had a kettle simmering on the hearth. She poured the warmed water into one of the beautifully glazed cups that matched a jug on the mantelpiece and was bringing it to Gun when a light knock, barely a brush against the door panels, made them both look to the door.

The thick pine, paneled and painted in hunting scenes, eased silently open. Mar froze, still holding the cup in both hands at breast level. When Gun saw who it was, he struggled with the folds of the blanket, wanting to be on his feet.

"Gundaron! The guards have just told me you came in." Epion strode forward, hands outstretched, all the angles of his craggy face turned down in misery. "Thank the Caids you got back safely."

"No thanks to you, I understand, Lord Epion." Normally Gun would have been more polite—or at least more circumspect—but he found he was tired of being polite to nobles who were trying to get him killed. From the look on Mar's face as she set down the cup of warmed water, she felt exactly the same way.

"I came as soon as I heard—" Epion thrust both hands through his hair. "Caids, what you must be thinking." He looked from Mar to Gun and back again, his eyes dark and staring in a white face.

"I think you started a rockfall that trapped me in the underground chamber." Gun was pleased to hear how steady his voice was. He didn't want Epion to know just how close he was to collapsing on the floor.

"And even if that was an accident," Mar said, taking up the attack just as though she realized how little energy Gun had left, "you certainly left him there to die. When I went to you for help, you did nothing. Worse than that, you pretended to know nothing of it." Epion squeezed his eyes shut. Mar waited. "Well, Lord Epion?" she said finally. "Is *this* what you expected us to think?" It was at moments like these, Gun thought, that Mar's awareness of her own High Noble status came to the fore. Gun would never have spoken to Epion in *that* tone.

Epion put his left hand down on the back of the chair Gun had vacated and scrubbed at his face with his right. Finally, he lowered himself into the chair. If Gun had known the man better, he would have said he was trying hard not to cry. Gun looked over at Mar, and from the look on her face, she was as confused as he.

"You had better tell us what you are about," she said. She waved Gun forward into the chair she'd been sitting in and remained standing, leaning her hip against the table. "If what we think isn't correct—or isn't the whole story—now is the time to tell us."

Epion raised his head. "I can't—" he scrubbed at his face again, then shook himself all over like a dog just out of a lake. "I have to tell someone. I wish the Mercenary Brothers were still here." He pressed his lips together, took a deep breath in through his nose and let it out again, relaxing his shoulders as he did so. Gun shot a look at Mar and saw she was watching Epion with a neutral face. Whatever was coming, it seemed she was prepared to meet it with an open mind. Gun wasn't sure he could say the same. But sometimes a willingness to listen, genuine or not, obtained more information than the most careful interrogation.

"Did you cause the rockfall?" he asked the nobleman.

Epion started nodding before he looked up. "Yes, I think so," he said. He sat up straighter and squared his shoulders as if he had made up his mind to something. "But it was an accident, I swear it. I tripped over a loose bit of pavement, and when I put my hand out to steady myself, the rocks moved and crashed down. I called out, I kept calling for you, but I heard nothing. Then I thought I should waste no more time but get back here for help. I even left one of my guards there, with instructions to keep calling your name until I returned."

"What changed your mind?" Mar's voice was now quiet and warm, as if she were interviewing a shy child.

"I didn't change my mind." Epion's voice hardened. "I had it changed for me." He glanced at them both in turn before continuing. "I needed the Palace Guard, not just my few men, and for that I needed Falcos. I went straight to him in his private chamber and told him what had happened." Here Epion swallowed and Mar handed him the cup of cooling water she'd placed on the table. He nodded his thanks and tossed back half the contents of the cup before returning his gaze to the floor between them. "He told me, Falcos told me, to let it be," he said without raising his head. "He said with you gone there was one less complication."

Gun blinked heavy lids and pulled his blanket tighter around him. Despite the brazier, he couldn't seem to get warm. And his brain seemed just as cold and sluggish. *Falcos* had said this? The same Falcos who, when his father was still alive, had sat up with them after his duties were done, drinking wine until the early hours and talking about the Caids? *That* Falcos?

I really have to stop trusting nobles. "Did he send you along to kill me, or at least to make sure I wasn't coming back?" he said.

"Not exactly." Epion looked up. "I was to watch you. To see if you found the book and to take it from you if you did."

"But why?" Gun shook his head, then wished he hadn't when the room spun a bit before settling down again. "It was for his sake I was Finding it."

Epion's glance flicked between them. "Was it? *Someone* hid the book in the ruins. We have only his word that Falcos does not already have the key. Why did he send the first Mercenary Brothers away? Why did he let Alaria send *your* good friends after them? He has some plan, but I cannot see what it could be."

Gun rubbed at his upper lip. Did Falcos know about the underground chamber? Had all the interest he had shown in their work been with an ulterior purpose?

Mar was shaking her head. "You didn't tell me any of this when I was looking for the Steward of Walls."

"How could I? Falcos is my family, the only family I have left. And even if he wasn't, he's my Tarkin."

"So why are you telling us now?" Gun asked.

"When I heard you were back—when I saw you—I couldn't let you think . . ." He hung his head again. "I didn't know it would be so hard."

"It's hard to know that you've killed someone dishonorably," Mar allowed. "But you're right, it *is* harder when others know about it."

"This is not the worst," Epion said. He sat leaning forward in his chair, his square-fingered hands clasped together and hanging between his knees. He looked dejected, as well he might, Gun thought. In telling them this, the man had taken the first step against his nephew and Tarkin.

"Not the worst? Leaving someone to die is not the worst?" Mar's gentle voice was beginning to harden. "What could be worse?"

Epion was nodding, as if she'd said something he could agree with. "I keep thinking how angry he was with his father. He says now it was because he wanted to go to Arderon, but that was not the impression I had at the time." He pressed his lips tight. Gun glanced at Mar, but there was no doubt Epion was speaking of Falcos. "And then I think about how my brother's body looked—you saw it, you know— not as bad as what happened to Cleona, you said—"

"As if the killer had been interrupted," Gun said, remembering.

"Or as if it were a different killer," Mar put in. "Someone who had only *heard* of the mutilations."

"You think it was Falcos." Gun said. "You think Falcos used the other murders to make it look as though his father's death was just one of a series of killings?" The way Epion's face crumpled was answer enough. He had wanted it said without being able to say it himself.

"But what about Princess Cleona?"

"From what you and the Mercenaries have said, that must have been the work of the real killer, if I may call him so." He rubbed at his face with his hands. "Falcos could not be so evil, I cannot believe it. We are still under a curse from the gods."

Mar's lips were pursed in thought as she looked down on Epion's bent head. "Forgive me, Lord Epion, but are *you* not the next heir to the throne?"

He glanced up without straightening. "Why do you think I have been gathering my own guard? People loyal to me? I do not want to believe any of this, but when I remember how angry Falcos was—" He sat up and sighed. "What do we do now?"

Gun blinked. His mind was a complete fog.

"We sleep on it," Mar advised, straightening to her feet. "Gun is exhausted past the point of planning. So far as Falcos knows, we're still in ignorance, and let's leave it there for now. There's nothing we can do in the middle of the night," Mar pointed out. Gun had the feeling she was the only one operating with her whole brain. He himself was so tired he could barely keep his eyes open, let alone concentrate on the issues at hand. And the shock and confusion Epion was suffering from was clear on the man's face.

"For the moment we're safe, aren't we, Lord Epion?" Mar was saying. "The Tarkin doesn't suspect you, or us for that matter? Go, get some rest, and we'll meet again in the morning."

"What do you think?" Gun said as soon as the door had closed behind the older man. He rubbed at his eyes with hands that felt made of lead. "Do we believe him?"

"He looked genuinely upset," Mar said. "But then Falcos . . ." She shook her head. "We've seen actors on the stage look just as distressed."

Gun pushed himself to his feet, accepting Mar's arm around his waist both for her warmth, and for help to keep him standing. "One of them is acting a part," he said. "But which one?"

"Maybe both."

Epion waited until the door was well shut behind him before he raised his bowed head and straightened his shoulders. He barely noticed the Leggett brothers fall into step behind him as he strode off down the corridor to his own rooms.

"You were clever to bring me the news straight away, Gabe," he told the dark-bearded guard.

"Yes, my lord."

"I've just turned a possible disaster into a definite advantage."

"Yes, my lord."

He'd made the Scholars his allies, and when the time came, they would speak for him to Alaria.

⟡

The walk back from the exposed corpse took them past the horse line, where Bloodbone and Warhammer were causing a great deal of interest among the younger men and boys. The Espadryni were being respectful, Dhulyn was happy to see. After what had passed that morning, she was in no mood to tolerate anything less.

"It seems they have no proper horses then, in the lands beyond Mother Sun's Door." This was a particular youth whom Dhulyn had noticed the others called Scar-Face, no doubt from the mark which dragged down the left corner of his lip. He was one of the ones who were always watching her, but always turning their eyes away if she looked back at them. Even now he addressed his remarks to Parno.

"I'm not surprised you don't recognize proper horses when you see them, having had so few opportunities," Parno cut in before Dhulyn could open her mouth. *Just as well*, she thought. The mood she was in, she was just as likely to give Scar-Face's friends another nickname for him as she was to give the man a civil answer. "*These* are quite puny specimens." Her Partner walked a few paces up the horse line, his hands clasped behind his back. When he had gone a few paces more he stopped and turned back to look at Scar-Face. "I suppose you keep them for food?"

There was a shocked intake of breath from among the younger ones in the group, but also hastily covered smiles on older faces. Dhulyn said nothing, merely showed them all her wolf's smile. This exchange of insults was no more than the normal bandying between two newly met groups who had in mind to test each other's mettle. She wondered if these young men were here with or without the approval of their elders.

"Oh, no. No, ours are not for *racing*," Parno was saying with a superior smile in response to a sally Dhulyn did not hear. "Come now, you say you're a horseman, and you can't tell that much just from looking at them? I'm not saying they can't keep up a good pace over time if needed." Parno laid his hand on Warhammer's flank. "Look at the chest he has, and the strength in his back. But these are battle mounts, not toys. Specially trained and large enough to carry riders bearing weapons and body armor." He tapped himself on the chest to show them what kind of armor he meant.

"You do not have any armor with you now," pointed out one of the other young men.

"If we had brought our packhorse through the Path of the Sun," Dhulyn said, "we could have shown you all of our weapons. As it is, we have only what seemed reasonable to bring with us." She refrained from telling them that what seemed reasonable to a Mercenary Brother might seem excessive to a Horseman.

"Of what does this special training consist?" Star-Wind stepped forward, but not, Dhulyn noted, until it seemed there were to be no blows. He had reached out to stroke Bloodbone's shoulder but had held back his hand when the mare turned to look at him. Dhulyn smiled again, this time careful to keep the scar from pulling her lip back.

"Well, now, I have the same Schooling as any Mercenary Brother, but each of us has his or her own special talent, and that of my Partner, Dhulyn Wolfshead, is horses." Parno looked around him with a smile. "Something that should cause you no surprise." He got some smiles in return, but there were also some uneasy sideways glances aimed her way. "I've practiced horse tricks many times, but if it's a demonstration you'd like, it's my Partner you should be asking."

In a moment all eyes were on her.

"With or without saddle?" she asked.

"My heart," Parno cut in. "In battle a saddle is always used." He was giving her an out, a chance to show them the easier techniques. Dhulyn all but rolled her eyes.

"Of course, but I thought our friends would be interested in a more difficult demonstration." Dhulyn scratched her left ear with her right hand and Parno raised his right eyebrow in acknowledgment.

"Well, then, without saddle by all means," Star-Wind said.

Parno held up his hand for silence as his Partner stroked Bloodbone's nose and, catching the mare's head between her hands, rested her forehead against the horse's face. *I hope you know what you're doing, my heart.* He'd seen and recognized the signs of Dhulyn's impatience and frustration growing in her since the night before. Very rarely did her temper get the better of her, but when it did, Parno had learned to watch out. He knew of no one more skilled on horseback than his Partner, but any Mercenary knew that anger made you stupid and that stupidity led to mistakes.

Dhulyn was breathing deeply now, and Parno had hopes that she was using a *Shora* to help her concentrate—or even to keep an even temper.

"Women have no magic over horses," the one called Scar-Face said, the sneer in his voice just below the surface.

"Where there is love and trust, there is no need of magic," Parno answered. Star-Wind made a sign, and Scar-Face fell silent, but his tightly pressed lips showed his disapproval.

Dhulyn took a final deep breath and stroked her hand down Bloodbone's nose. The mare tossed her head and breathed into her mistress' face. Smiling, Dhulyn swung herself onto Bloodbone's back.

"I'll begin with the easy steps," she said. Her voice was quiet and tranquil, and it was hard to be sure she spoke to the men and not the horse. "Is there a short piece of rope to hand?" When one had been found and tossed to her, Dhulyn wrapped an end around each hand and held her arms up over her head.

"What does she do?" Star-Wind asked.

"She shows you that she is not directing the horse with any action of her hands," Parno said. "The point is that in battle, you may need both hands for your weapons." He turned to the young shaman. "I'm certain you are all skilled at guiding your horses with just your knees."

"To be sure, there is nothing new in that," Star-Wind agreed.

"Then watch."

For Dhulyn the easy steps consisted in showing her fine control over Bloodbone's motion and her own excellent balance. She stood on the mare's back as Bloodbone trotted, then galloped, back and forth, turning first one way then the other. She lay prone on the mare's back, then hid herself from their view by hanging down Bloodbone's side. At one point she stopped, looking around her, and had Bloodbone kneel. Suddenly, they both disappeared from view.

"What is this? Who has done this?" Star-Wind looked around him outraged, clearly expecting some trick on the part of one of the better shamans among the other Horsemen.

"Wait," Parno said. He pulled his chanter out of his belt and gave three long whistles. Immediately Dhulyn and Bloodbone popped up from behind the crest of grass, which had been hiding them in a shallow depression, and were thundering down toward the gathered men, Dhulyn whooping out a war cry and swinging the piece of rope around her head like a battle-ax. Suddenly, without lowering her hands, she stopped short, and Bloodbone spun first one way and then the other, as if dodging unseen foes. Then Dhulyn had Bloodbone move forward with a peculiar hopping gait, hooves kicking out before her.

"If there were men on the ground, they would fall beneath those hooves," Star-Wind said. "And Dhulyn Wolfshead could be striking out at those farther away. I begin to understand."

"Wait, there's more."

At the unseen signal, Bloodbone leaped straight up into the air like a cat and struck out sideways with all four metal-shod hooves. She spun and did it again, and again.

Parno shrugged apologetically. "Doesn't look like much here, it's a little more impressive in the field of battle."

Star-Wind gave a whoop and slapped Parno on the shoulder. "You are a very funny man, Parno Lionsmane, very funny. Not look like much? Mercenary, it is impressive enough, believe me. Can you train our horses to do such things?"

"It takes a long time," Dhulyn said, walking Bloodbone nearer. "And the rider must be trained as closely as the horse. Yours aren't shod," she added, sliding off Bloodbone's back and tossing the reins to one of the boys now jostling each other to catch them. "That makes a deal of difference to the damage that can be done. But you must ask yourself, Star-Wind, whether the nature of your enemies and the battles that you fight justify such an expenditure of time."

Star-Wind nodded, tongue tapping his upper lip. "It is pretty, though, isn't it?"

"As pretty as killing people ever is."

Fourteen

"GUN." Mar touched her sleeping husband softly on the cheek, waited until he'd blinked his eyes open and focused on her face before she stood up and went to open the shutters on the day. Half the morning had gone, and she'd waited as long as she could, expecting at any moment that Epion would appear at their door, but evidently the Tarkin's uncle had duties that kept him occupied this morning. If only he'd had such duties the day before — though according to what he'd said, in a manner of speaking, he had.

Mar resisted the urge to go back and help Gun out of bed, to touch him again. They'd spent the whole night wrapped together, and it still hadn't quite managed to dispel the dread she'd felt the day before when hour after hour had passed and Gun still hadn't returned. They'd not been apart since they'd met, not since Imrion, not even in the Library at Valdomar, since Scholars recognized marriage as well as other forms of partnering.

"This tunic's shrunk," Gun said from inside the folds of blue linen.

"That's because it's mine." Gently Mar helped Gun get his head out of her spare tunic and handed him his own. One of the things she greatly enjoyed about being a Scholar was that their dress was decided for them, blue tunic with their Library crest on the shoulder, brown leggings, a brown hood when the weather called for it, and a black cap for formal occasions. It didn't hurt that blue was a good color for her. Though a cousin of a High Noble House, Mar had been fostered with a family of weavers, and while she had a respect for and a knowledge of good cloth, she had little understanding of and less interest in the nobility's preoccupation with fashion.

"There," she said, giving Gun's tunic a last pull to straighten it into place. "We've fruit, ganje, and biscuits in the sitting room."

"A person could get used to this," Gun said. He started to stand up, groaned, and sat back down on the edge of the bed.

"Muscles sore?" Mar said with sympathy.

"I don't think I'll need a Healer." His voice was so solemn Mar couldn't be sure he wasn't joking.

She'd let Gun sleep, knowing that both body and mind needed rest after his ordeal the day before, but she'd had a couple of hours with nothing to do but think over their position in the face of what Epion had told them, and she kept herself from fidgeting while Gun ate his breakfast by force of will alone.

He glanced up from spooning fig preserves onto his third biscuit and must have seen something of what she was feeling on her face.

"Do we believe him or not?" he asked around the bite of food in his mouth.

"Gun, did you tell Epion it was a book you were looking for?"

Gun's jaws froze in the action of chewing, but his head was slowly shaking from side to side. "I don't think so," he said after swallowing. "We told Alaria, though. Might she have told him?"

Mar frowned. She'd been hoping for a more definite answer. "What about all the details of the mutilation, the differences between the bodies? Were Epion and Falcos even in the room when we were talking about that?"

Gun was rubbing his upper lip again, a sure sign of distress. "I'm sorry, I can't remember. I can see why you ask. If we knew he *hadn't* been told about the book, or the mutilations, it would mean he has guilty knowledge, the kind he could only have if he were somehow involved in the killings. As it is . . ."

Mar sighed. "As it is, we're no closer to that answer than

we were last night." She leaned toward him, shoving the plate of fruit closer to him. "But I think I know what we should do first."

"And from the look on your face, it isn't finding Epion."

Mar leaned back in her chair, nodding. "We still have to tread carefully, but maybe not as carefully as Epion implied. Think about this: We have our own standing here, through our Scholars' Library, and our permission to dig in the ruins comes directly from the Tarkinate. If Falcos wanted to get rid of us, all he'd have to do is rescind that permission, and we'd have no choice but to return to Valdomar. There's no need to kill us."

"So if we are in danger," Gun said, "it isn't because of who or what *we* are."

That was the great thing about Scholars, the path of logic wasn't a strange journey for them. "We're only *here*, in the palace I mean, because of Princess Alaria, so whatever this is, it touches her more than it does us."

"So we go to Alaria." Gun wiped his mouth and hands on the napkin provided and started to stand, winced, and pushed himself upright with his hands on the edge of the table. "I only hope there's no riding today," he said. "I don't think my muscles could take it."

Fortunately, it was only a step from their rooms to the Tarkina's apartments, or the abuse Gun's muscles had taken the day before might have been tested further.

There were two guards outside the door to the Tarkina's suite instead of the one Mar expected. Still, one of them was Julen, wearing the crest that marked her as one of the Tarkin's personal guard, and the other—an unfamiliar older man in an unadorned Palace Guard tunic—merely raised his eyebrows when Julen nodded to them and led them through into the anteroom of the Tarkina's chambers. She opened the inner door.

"The Scholars of Valdomar, my lords," Julen said.

Lords?

They were clear of the doorway and into the room before the word really registered and Mar understood why there had been two guards at the hall door.

"Lord Tarkin," she said as soon as she'd gathered her wits. "Lady."

The strange thing was that Falcos and Alaria each had

much the same look on their faces. Not the besotted, "I'm not thinking straight" look of new lovers, nor yet the strained, "I'm just here because my position requires it" look of people who are making the best of what their duty demanded. Rather this was the look of people who had been interrupted while discussing something apart from themselves, something serious.

Something that worried them.

"I am pleased to see you looking so well, Gundaron of Valdomar," Falcos said. There was a slight smile on his beautiful mouth and a twinkle in his eye. "From what the Lady of Arderon has been telling me, it was not so sure a thing. When did you return, and what delayed you?"

Mar bit at her lower lip. Of course she'd been unable to hide her fears from Alaria the day before, and the princess had no reason not to share the story with the Tarkin. *Relax*, she told herself. Even if everything Epion had told them about Falcos was the truth, it appeared that Falcos still meant to play his part.

"You should have come to me yourself, Mar-eMar, and not left things to chance. I know you may not be accustomed to palace life, either of you, but, please, next time take a guard or at least a page with you when you leave the city. Though the Caids know, there was no safety in numbers for the Princess Cleona. What was it that took you out alone, Scholar?"

So, the Tarkin was pretending not to know that Epion had gone with Gun to the ruins. Mar pressed her lips together. Who to trust, who to believe? Falcos looked open and honest enough, and Alaria—who had not struck Mar as a fool—certainly seemed to trust him. Dhulyn Wolfshead had not liked Epion, she remembered. Was that enough to guide her?

"Mar, what is it?" Alaria rose and approached her, touching her on the arm.

She knew what Dhulyn Wolfshead would do in this spot, Mar thought. The Mercenary Brother would simply say what she thought. She'd say that more trouble and confusion was caused by people hiding their thoughts and being afraid to find things out than by any other thing.

"It's Epion," she said, watching Falcos closely. His face changed. She saw resignation, and a touch of what she thought might be despair. She did not see fear of discovery, annoyance at having his plans upset, or even calculation.

Mar made up her mind. "You said Gun shouldn't have gone alone," she said. "He didn't. Epion went with him." In as few words as possible, she and Gun between them explained what had happened to Gun the day before at the Caid ruins and what had happened afterward, when Mar had gone to Epion for help. As they spoke, Mar watched Falcos' handsome face get whiter and whiter, until even his lips seemed to be leached of color—and she felt her breathing come easier.

Even the best actor cannot make the blood drain from his face. She didn't remember who had told her that, but watching Falcos now, Mar understood it.

When they finished, Falcos sat with his hands pressed palm to palm, the tips of his index fingers resting on his lips. Not like someone who was calm and in control of himself, but like someone who wanted to give you the impression he was.

"Let me guess." Alaria's voice was dry in the extreme. "Epion thought he should have been Tarkin."

"His mother, my father's stepmother, certainly thought so. And why not? Such a thing doesn't make a man a villain. Until I was born, as his younger brother, Epion was my father's heir. And I came very late, certainly after my father had given up hope of a child." He looked around then, licking his lips. His color was beginning to return. "If he was disappointed—and he must have been, who would not be?—he never hated me for it. On the contrary, since Father was so much older . . ." Falcos shook his head. "It was always Epion who—he would never . . ." Falcos' mouth formed a thin line, but his eyes had nowhere near as firm an expression.

Mar's stomach dropped. "Falcos, you said you quarreled with your father because he wasn't sending you to Arderon, while Epion told us you didn't want to go. When did your father tell you what he'd decided?"

Falcos shook his head. "No, it was that my father had changed his mind. I was to go, and then, suddenly . . ." he stopped with his mouth open.

"Epion told you your father had changed his mind," Gun said. "And why wouldn't you believe him, your good uncle who had always been your friend."

"The one who started the quarrel he's now carefully reminding people of," Mar said.

"But I spoke to my father," Falcos said.

Alaria put her hand on Falcos' arm. "Spoke to him? Enquired politely what his plans were? Or confronted him and demanded explanations?"

"You don't understand. I thought he was throwing away our chance to set everything right again, to put ourselves right with the gods. I was so angry, and he didn't listen—"

"I wonder what Epion told *him*," Mar said.

They were looking at each other in silence when the door opened once more to admit the guard Julen. She was ashen under her tan, and her eyes seemed very round.

"My lady," she said. "I am here to escort you, and the Scholars of Valdomar, from this room, if it please you to leave it."

"Julen! Whatever are you talking about?" Alaria turned in her chair to face the guard completely. "What has happened?"

"Escort them where?" Falcos was on his feet. "What are they accused of?"

Julen's gaze flicked from face to face. "Not them, my Lord Tarkin." She swallowed. "I am here to escort them to safety. You are to remain here, under arrest. A full squad of the Palace Guard is outside."

Mar felt as though the air had been sucked from her body. She saw rather than felt Gun's grip on her forearm. Alaria's hand closed on the hilt of the dagger at her belt.

"What is this? Come, surely you are allowed to tell me?"

Julen cleared her throat and began again. "Lord Epion Akarion has called an emergency meeting of the council. He has accused you of your father's death," she said. "He has convinced enough of the council to have them ask for your arrest until a full investigation is made."

"Convinced them with what?" Gun was on his feet.

Julen frowned, flicked her eyes to Falcos and back to Gun.

"With this story of the quarrel." Falcos sat down. "I killed my father so I would not have to go to Arderon. And what of the Princess Cleona? Am I accused of her death as well?"

Julen glanced at Alaria before she lowered her eyes again.

"Perhaps he's saying you liked the younger princess better," Gun said.

Falcos began slapping the tabletop with his open right hand, at first softly and then harder and harder, until Alaria put her hand on his shoulder and he stopped, looking up at her. "Epion has told them I killed my father," he said. "And because we told no one about these other killings, it may look as though he tells the truth."

"But it was your father's decision to do so," Mar said.

"On Epion's advice." Falcos had his eyes shut.

"And now we know why." Alaria's voice was cold. "How soon do you think he planned to use these killings in this way? Right from the start? Long before the Tarkin's death, that I'm certain of."

Falcos took in a deep breath. "Go, all of you. You'll be safer away from me, and you can work to help me from outside." He looked at Alaria. "If, that is, you believe me."

Mar was astonished to see Alaria smile. "Of course I believe you," she said. "The queens like you, and the horses of Arderon are excellent judges of character."

"All very well," Gun added. "But as soon as we leave you alone, what's to stop Epion from sending someone in to put a rope around your neck and claiming you killed yourself?" He looked toward the doors. "Can't we bar the doors? There must be someone who will come to help us."

Julen gave a sharp nod, her lips tight, and turned toward the doors to the anteroom. Mar hadn't noticed, but the decorative wooden pillars that flanked the doorway were in fact bars that slipped into the iron fittings that had been holding back the hangings. Julen signaled to Gun, and between them they fitted the first bar into place.

"An excellent idea," Falcos said, stepping up to help steady the second wooden beam. "But perhaps we have no need to remain in this room waiting. There is another way out, a secret passage from my mother's bedroom." He gestured toward the inner bedroom.

"The guard knows nothing of this," Julen protested.

Falcos' grin was a ghost of its former self. "That is because it is a *secret* passage."

"And don't be so sure about that," Alaria said. "There was a secret passage in the palace at Arderon and all us young cousins knew of it."

Mar glanced at Gun and caught his eye. He lifted his left eyebrow. They had both heard that the Mercenary Brotherhood had maps and drawings, some of them unbelievably old, floor plans of palaces and fortifications, including secret passages and tunnels. If Wolfshead and Lionsmane were here, would they have known of this one?

"Did you tell anyone else about them," Falcos was saying to Alaria.

"Well, no, it was supposed to be for family only, but surely . . ."

"Exactly. It may be that Epion knows," he added, turning to Julen. "But if you were sent here to get the princess out and leave me behind, my guess would be none of the guard outside these doors know of the passage."

"Which would mean Epion believes *you* don't know," Gun said. "All the easier for him to send someone in through the passage to dispose of you without being seen."

"Then we need to be quick, and go while they are still waiting for Julen to bring us out." Alaria was already on her feet.

Gun hung back, indecisive, as Falcos stood and waved them after him into the large bedroom of the suite. Not that he didn't agree with Alaria, it was just that he and Mar had left their rooms empty-handed—something they should have known better than to do. He wasn't worried about weapons so much—he and Mar carried hardly anything of that kind—but what about the bowl? That was worth more than weaponry, for him at least, and perhaps for all of them. He had to hope that nothing would happen to make him do more than regret not having it.

"More than once, when I was a child playing in the sitting room, my mother or one of her senior lady pages came out of *this* room, her bedroom, without having gone in," Falcos was saying as Gun reached the doorway of the bedroom. "I asked her about it, and I finally got her to admit that there was a secret passage."

"While you open it, I'll fetch packs." Mar moved as if to join her but Alaria waved her back. "Julen will help me, we won't be a minute," she said, dashing past Gun into the outer room with the guard on her heels and disappearing into the other bedroom.

"Where's the entrance," Mar asked.

Gun looked around the bedroom, eyes narrowed. A lamp was burning brightly enough to cast sharp shadows from every piece of furniture. Unlike the sitting room, the Tarkina's bedchamber had no large windows, nor balcony doors. Instead, narrow, arched eyebrow windows near the ceiling let light in through the room's only exterior wall, and carefully placed mirrors directed that light around the room itself. To dim the room during the day—something that would definitely be needed in the heat of the summer—one would only need to turn the mirrors out of alignment.

Ingenious, but it also meant that no one could come or go from the room using a window.

"Not through the outside wall, obviously," Mar had seen it as well. "You can tell from the angle of the light they're no thicker here than they are in the outer room, and those aren't thick enough for a passage."

Alaria and Julen came rushing back in, the guard dragging two backpacks, and Alaria with a strung bow over her shoulder, plus two swords hanging from her belt. "What, why isn't it open?" She turned to Falcos. "I thought you knew where this passage was."

"I do know, that is, my mother told me, but I have never actually . . ." Falcos looked around the room, still frowning. Beside the dressing table with its silvered mirror and matching stool, there was only a settee, another small table with a chest holding jewelry placed centrally on it, and two armchairs padded with leather dyed in soft colors.

Falcos was rubbing at his forehead as though he had the grandmother of all headaches. "Why am I so stupid?" he said through clenched teeth. "I do not know how to walk the Path of the Sun. I do not know how to open the secret door in my own mother's room." His eyes were squeezed shut and he was pressing his fingertips into his eyes.

"Gun?" Mar's voice was crisp.

"Behind the headboard." He'd answered automatically, he realized with a grin spreading across his face. Without focus or trance. He was getting better at this.

The headboard was a massive structure of pale wood stained a pleasing shade of red. It reached the ceiling, was thick with carving and must be, the practical side of him thought, a nightmare to dust. There were two matching red tables, one on each side of the bed, and a narrow bench along the foot. There were no posts or rails to hold up bed curtains, from which Gun deduced that the weather here was never cold enough to require them.

Aware that they were now all looking at him, Gun rubbed at his upper lip. He looked at the floor, square cream-colored tiles offset with smaller red accent tiles. No other coverings. There were hangings on the walls, however, above the bedside tables. He walked over to examine them more closely. Each was held up by its own wrought iron bar and was hung about a hand's width out from the wall. He shook his head. Nothing was standing out as the trigger for the hidden mechanism.

The sudden sound of pounding made them all look toward the outer room.

"No need for worry." Falcos sounded as though he were trying to convince himself, though his steady smile seemed genuine enough. "That's just knocking. It will take them a while to bring up something heavy enough to break the door."

Gun doubted very much that a ram could be used in the outside corridor, but then again, breaking down doors wasn't his primary field of study, so he couldn't—

"Gun, please try to focus." Mar placed her hand on his forearm and squeezed.

Alaria signaled to Julen to set the packs down and squinted up at the wall, frustration, and perhaps a little fear, making her wrinkle her nose. "Your mother used this door?"

"She said she did, to visit my father." Falcos shrugged at their questioning looks. "It was a game they played."

"So it's not like the Path of the Sun, there's no trick or magic to the key? I mean," Alaria added when everyone turned to look at her, "there's no magic to the taming of horses, at least, none past the natural touch for the animals that someone like Dhulyn Wolfshead has. You don't break a horse, you gentle her. Study, observation, that's the Arderon way. 'Five minutes of thinking is worth thirty minutes of tugging the rein,' my granna used to say."

All very well, Gun knew, and good advice most of the time. But they didn't have any time, the increased noise from the other room reminded him, and now that he was trying, the answer didn't seem to want to pop into his head. Mar pinched his arm hard enough to make him yelp.

"The mechanism's in the headboard as well," he said.

"Of course," Alaria agreed. "The mechanism has to be easy enough for a woman to do it herself. Even an old woman. Maybe especially an old woman." She came to stand next to Gun, examining the headboard as carefully as he was himself.

"And it wouldn't be so high that it would be difficult to reach in a hurry," Mar said, also coming forward. "Nor so low that old joints would make it impossible."

Gun stepped up on the bed just as the rhythm of the pounding changed. It was slower now, and much heavier. An ax? He rubbed at his upper lip. There had to be some clue, some guide that would show him . . . From this angle the carvings on the headboard took on different shapes, even the shadows seeming to fall differently, though the lamp had not been moved. What had appeared to be a pattern of stylized roses, now looked like simpler flowers, poppies perhaps, with their stems woven into a series of braids. Gun shifted, trying to place himself exactly in the center of the bed. The pattern was soothing, flowing smoothly . . . now the flowers looked as though they might be faces, peeping out from behind foliage and petals. The faces of animals, cats, hunting dogs, hawks, and horses. No, not horses. *A* horse. There was only one.

"Here," he said. He centered both thumbs on the horse head and pushed. With a soft click, the central panel in the headboard popped out, releasing a smell of stone and a cold draft of air.

The sound of the ax blade was lighter now, as if it was almost through the door.

"Grab the packs," Falcos said as he leaped onto the bed beside Gun. "Follow me."

It had been a few days since they'd had a good practice, so when the Seven Brothers *Shora* was complete, Parno was not surprised to find himself a little short of breath—Dhulyn perhaps more so, as she lacked his training for the pipes. Still, he'd have wagered that no one else could have known they were in the least winded. The smells from cooking fires wafted over them, and Parno's stomach rumbled.

"I've been thinking."

"Really? You mean that wasn't your stomach growling?"

Parno smiled, then swung, but as he expected, Dhulyn danced away in time, laughing. The laughter faded out of her face, however, and Parno glanced over his shoulder to see what had caused the change. Of course. The young man called Scar-Face, with three of his fellow Espadryni, had apparently been watching the *Shora*, and now approached.

"For a moment we thought we must come to your rescue, Parno Lionsmane. It looked as if your Partner might kill you."

Parno forced himself to smile, keeping his temper with some effort. If he was getting tired of this constant suspicion, he could only imagine how Dhulyn was feeling. Then a sense of fairness made him consider that this might be nothing more than the heavy banter that so often signaled friendship among males in certain societies.

"That was a *Shora*," he said. "It's the way we practice. Over and over, patterns within patterns, until there is not a blow or a strike that we have not learned to counter instinctively, without wasting time in thought." He glanced at each of the Horsemen in turn. "That's why we're so hard to kill—barring accident or illness—and why we're so highly valued by those going to war."

Scar-Face frowned as though he wanted to find something in Parno's words to argue about, but it was one of the others behind him who spoke up next.

"Some people are saying you are no Seer, Dhulyn Wolfshead," the younger Horseman said. "That in your world our women were not Marked."

Dhulyn left off pretending to straighten her swords and daggers and moved to stand a little closer to Parno.

"I *am* a Seer," she said. "The Marked in our land are *all* what you call whole and safe, and that is the reason *I* am whole and safe. Not, as you might think, because I am not Marked."

"You've met many Marked then?" This was Scar-Face, his curiosity finally outweighing whatever wariness he might feel.

Parno signaled Dhulyn with a flick of his fingers, and they began to walk, bringing the young Horsemen with them, toward their own tent.

"The Marked aren't particularly numerous in our land," Dhulyn said. "But we've met many in our travels. Finders and Menders are comparatively common, and we have met a handful of Healers as well. Though the only other Seers we have ever met are across the Long Ocean, in the land of the Mortaxa."

"And all of the Marked we've met are exactly like other people, barring their talent," Parno added. "They have families and children and are happy or sad or whatever the occasion calls for. Some are greedy and some are generous, some suspicious and others fair-minded." He looked at Dhulyn pointedly, and when he was sure all the young men were looking at him, he added, in an exaggerated whisper, as if speaking to them privately, "Some have good tempers and some bad."

Dhulyn stuck her tongue out at him, and the younger of the Horsemen laughed. Even Scar-Face smiled.

"It is time for the midday meal. Will you join us at the young men's fire?" he asked. "We would hear more of the land beyond Mother Sun's Door."

"We would be pleased." Dhulyn slowed and Parno followed her lead. This was a good sign and an improvement over their experience in the Long Trees camp, where the men had not wanted to share their fire with Dhulyn. The Horsemen were becoming used to them, and the demonstration yesterday seemed to have won them some friends, and Dhulyn more admirers, but as she would say herself, better cautious than cursing. When he saw that heads were turning away from his Partner, Parno took a step away and turned to look for himself. He relaxed slightly when he saw it was the approach of the Horse Shaman, Spring-Flood, that had drawn attention.

"Dhulyn Wolfshead, if you will. The Seers of the Salt Desert Tribe would have speech with you."

"May it wait, Horse Shaman? We have asked the Mercenary Brothers to share our meal," Scar-face said. "Or do the Seers wish to offer hospitality?"

There was something flat in the way Scar-face said those words, and some of the others turned their heads away to hide smiles, but Parno was sure the Horse Shaman was not fooled.

"After the meal will be soon enough," he conceded, nodding to the Mercenaries before he went his way.

*   *   *

It was later in the afternoon that they approached the Seers' area. The handful who were currently sharing tents with one of the men—usually those with children—were in their own quarters, but the bulk of the women stayed more or less in the portion of the camp assigned to them.

"Look," Parno said, angling his eyes toward a woman leading a child by the hand. "If we stay, could you have a child here?" Dhulyn glanced at his face. Apparently it was one thing to know that there were sufficient Seers here among the Espadryni to allow them to bear children; it was another to see it with his own eyes. "Would it be safe?" he said. "What happens if the other women don't take the Visions for you?"

"A good question," Dhulyn said. She watched as the one leading the child disappeared into a tent. "I expect the life force would then be taken from the child, and I would miscarry."

"But *you* would not be in any danger?"

"No more than I usually am." They were drawing closer to the Seers' area, and a few of the women were gathering. "They look like other women, don't they?" Dhulyn said. "Except for their coloring, we could be in any camp of nomads."

"I have been twice in the south, and I have spoken with other women, whole women. These may look like other women, but they are not." Star-Wind had come up beside them. "I see you are watching the children, Dhulyn Wolfshead. Is it in your mind to join us for a time in order to bear a child? You tell us that Seers are rare on your side of the Door, and there are no Espadryni left. When you have found your killer, you are welcome to stay with us."

Dhulyn stood very still, the blood suddenly pounding in her ears. "What if she is Marked," she said.

"You think the child may be Marked in the way of our world, soulless and broken, and not in the way of your own world?"

"We can't know," Dhulyn said. "What controls the flaw? The parentage, or the place of birth?"

"Caids no," Parno said. "I hadn't thought of that."

"The Caids? Sun burn them, Moon freeze them cold, the stupid beggars." Parno and Dhulyn spun around to find that one of the Espadryni women had come up behind them—

closer than she should have been able to come. She was substantially older than the other women they had glimpsed, her blood-red hair marbled with veins of white, but her skin was remarkably smooth and youthful, as if she rarely moved her face.

"What have you got against the Caids?" Dhulyn asked.

"It was they who made us wrong, wasn't it? And then died and left us to our fate, curse them. Made us well enough to defeat the Green Shadow and then tossed us aside like chipped hammers. And now we are as we are, and treated as we are, and why? Through no fault of our own, but because they made us wrong. And then they die off anyway, lucky cowards that they were, leaving us to bear the consequences of their haste and carelessness."

Her words were bitter, but her tone was matter-of-fact, as if she merely stated what all knew to be true.

"That's enough, Snow-Moon."

The older woman shrugged her left shoulder. "There's wind and rain coming, young Singer, and plenty of it. But the trader comes first." She turned to Dhulyn. "So our business will wait, whole woman, as it always must, until the outsider is gone. And we can thank the Caids for that as well." She turned away.

"There's something in what she says," Dhulyn said. "If the Marked here were created, as our Marked were, to deal with the Green Shadow, it's obvious that the Caids are somehow to blame."

Parno watched the old Seer hobble away, a chill running up his spine. Sometime in her life the old woman had broken the Pact seriously enough to be punished for it. Is this what might await a daughter of theirs?

"What would you have us do, Dhulyn Wolfshead? Kill all the Seers, as the others do their Marked? Break the Tribes? Die out ourselves? Who then would guard the Path of the Sun?"

"One of the Long Trees People told us there is a belief that someone would come with a cure. Do you wait for that?"

"We have heard this as well, it is a Vision the Seers have had in every generation. Does it encourage us to keep the Seers alive?" Star-wind shrugged. "Perhaps. We cannot disprove the belief, and many are hopeful."

Sounds coming from the southern edge of the encampment drew their attention, and several people began to move in that direction. Even some of the women, though they did not head that way, stopped what they were doing and looked up.

"And there's the trader," Star-Wind said. "They could have given us a bit more notice."

So some outsiders did visit the Tribes, Parno thought. Though from what the old woman had said, it was clear they did not know about the Seers.

"I must go to the Singer with this weather news, but you may wish to speak to the trader of what he has seen," Star-Wind said. The man's face was a little unhappy, and Parno suspected the conversation about children had done them no good in his eyes.

"The trader seems a popular man," Dhulyn remarked under her breath as they joined the crowd of men and young children who had dropped what they were doing and were making for the lanky fair-haired man leading the short train of burdened horses. They were small beasts, Dhulyn noted, much the same size as those ridden by the Espadryni.

"Or else it's his goods that are popular," Parno said. Dhulyn gave him the tiniest push with her closed right fist.

"I believe *I* am the cynical one," she said. But she was not exactly smiling, Parno noted.

The trader was not as tall as the average Espadryni male—closer to Dhulyn's height, Parno thought—but his thinness gave him the appearance of height. His hands were large, the knuckles pronounced, but not with disease. It was rather as though he was still growing, and his body hadn't quite caught up with his hands and feet. His straw-colored hair was coarse and thick, cropped short as if for a helm, though the trader bore no arms other than the knife at his belt.

He was wearing a gold ring in each ear. Parno caught Dhulyn's eye and she gave a small nod. *Yes.* This *was* the man of her Visions, the one who had offered his aid. Perhaps some solid luck was finally coming their way.

Dhulyn and Parno hung back, keeping to the fringes of the small crowd surrounding the trader, watching as he greeted children by name, asked after the absent, and dodged queries about ordered merchandise.

"Now, Horsemen, patience please," he said, patting at the air with his palms held outward. "Everything in its time, and I've yet to pay my respects to your Shamans." The crowd began to disperse, leaving him a wide space that would lead him to the central tents. His packhorses he left in the charge of some of the older boys—old enough to be trusted to see to his horses without examining their packs too closely. Parno and Dhulyn held their ground as the trader passed close to them, and stopped.

"Mercenary Brothers?" he said, eyeing their badges. "Will there be more of you then? I must increase my stock of weapons and harness if so," he added with a grin. Parno found himself inclined to grin back. The man's good humor was infectious.

"You met with our Brothers, then?" Dhulyn asked.

The trader started to answer her, gave her a closer look and hesitated.

"No fear, Bekluth," Star-Wind said, coming up to join them. "You dishonor no one by speaking to Dhulyn Wolfshead. The Espadryni do not sequester their women on the far side of Mother Sun's Door."

"Is that right?" It seemed for a moment the sunniness of the trader's face was clouded over. But then Bekluth smiled again, and the moment passed. "Well, then I'm very glad to meet you. I did *not* meet with your Brothers, as it happened, but I have heard of them from the Cold Lake People, who met them as they emerged from the Door."

"Trader Bekluth Allain, of the City of Norwash." There was a tone in Star-Wind's voice Parno could not quite place. It was as if he were giving a warning, but at whom was it aimed? "These are Dhulyn Wolfshead and Parno Lionsmane," the Horseman added. "Once you have spoken with Singer of the Grass-Moon, they have questions for you."

"I await them with pleasure, particularly if I may ask a few of my own."

The rains began just as people were sitting down to the evening meal, but with the warning they'd received, everyone—except those assigned to watches—was already inside the inglera and horsehair tents or under other shelter. It was only a short time afterward that Bekluth Allain came to where Dhulyn and Parno had set out their evening meal of skillet bread, curds, and thin beer on the blanket they were using as a table.

"I won't join you," the trader said. His soft voice made the unfamiliar accent almost pleasant. "The Singer was good enough to feed me in exchange for news, and they've also told me something about your mission here and that you may have questions for me." He spoke to Parno, but he was looking with frank interest at Dhulyn. "You'll forgive me staring," he said, when Dhulyn raised her eyebrow at him. "To see an Espadryni woman so closely—you can imagine how fascinating it is for me."

"You do not normally meet with them?" Dhulyn said.

Bekluth Allain shrugged. "Never. At first I thought it was the custom of the Salt Desert People only, but I learned that all the Red Horsemen keep their women apart from other men." He lowered his voice. "Do I have my suspicions as to the reasons for this?" He nodded, top lip sucked in. "I have my notions. Have I asked in so many words? No, I haven't. And why not? Because they wouldn't tell me, and they'd stop trading with me. Or, they might decide they needed to stop me from sharing my notions with others. If I don't ask, things continue as they are, and to tell you the truth, I like my own company better than I like being a younger cousin in the largest trading family in Gelbrado." He shrugged again.

"It's true what we've been told? There are no Marked anywhere?" Parno asked the question he knew Dhulyn was hesitating to ask.

"So far as I know—and my family trades extensively—there are no adult Marked anywhere." The trader let his voice return to normal volume. "But tell me of your problem; I'm sure you did not brave the Sun's Doorway to question me about the Espadryni."

Trying to give only the necessary details, Parno outlined what had happened in Menoin and what their mission here was in consequence. "There was torture," he said finally, "before the death came. From the condition of the body it seems likely the torture was as important as the death, perhaps more. Nor can we be sure whether this was part of some ceremony or ritual—there are Mages also to consider, on both sides of the Path of the Sun. We followed the trail of the killer into the Path, but when we emerged on this side, the trail was gone. Have you seen or heard of anything in your travels that might help us?" But Bekluth Allain was already shaking his head.

"Have you, yourself, been near the Path of the Sun at any time in the last ten days?" Dhulyn asked.

"I have not," he said readily. "Though I'm cursed if I can know how to prove it to you. But wait, there is often someone of the Espadryni keeping vigil or awaiting the opening of the Door—it is a ceremony common to the whole of the Tribes," he added, "which so far as I know has never involved any ritual sacrifices. Perhaps that person can speak for me."

"There was a young man there when we came out of the Path," Parno said. "And it is true that he did not report seeing anyone else."

"And yet the man that we followed must have been there," Dhulyn said. "Unless, of course, there is more than one way out of the Path."

Bekluth sat back, slapping his hands on his knees.

"You are very open, do you know that? Both of you." He smiled at the look of polite interest on Dhulyn's face. "You see? Others might take that look of polite interest for courtesy only, but I can tell—you *are* interested." He put up his hands. "If only to the extent that politeness allows. But it's unusual to meet people who are hiding nothing, not even from each other."

"And how is it you have this talent?" This time Dhulyn smiled her wolf's smile, her lip curing back from her teeth. Bekluth blinked, but his smile faded only a little.

"I'm a trader," he said, tapping himself on the chest. "From a long family of traders. Generations. If I couldn't tell what people's hidden desires are, how could I know what to sell them?"

"And what are our hidden desires?" Dhulyn asked.

"That's just it." Bekluth was triumphant. "You haven't any."

Fifteen

"I THINK WE WERE on shipboard with the Long Ocean Traders the last time we checked our weapons for damp." Parno squinted along the metal shaft of a collapsible crossbow before wiping it with an oiled linen cloth and returning it to its bag. The rain had stopped before sunrise, but it had been heavy enough that, though the sun was well up—and shining brilliantly, as if the weather here matched that of Menoin—the dampness had them undoing their packs to inspect their weapons for wet spots, damp, and rust. Espadryni passed them, most politely averting their eyes from the rows of weapons neatly laid out between the two Mercenaries, but many began to pass again and again, the bolder ones slowing to stare their fill—clearly curiosity was overcoming politeness.

"Do you miss the Crayx?" Dhulyn asked. They were sitting on two thick fleeces Parno had exchanged for playing his pipes the evening before, cross-legged and facing each other, so each had a clear view of the camp over the shoulder of the other.

Parno narrowed his eyes, though he continued scanning the area over her left shoulder. "It's not so much that I miss them for themselves, if you understand me. It's as though there is an absence, an emptiness where none was before." He looked at her and smiled. "Which is odd, when you think about it, since I was never aware of my Pod sense before."

"Well, they do say that you can't miss something unless you've known it," Dhulyn pointed out. She wound her extra bowstrings around her right hand and put them back into their pouch.

"I do sometimes find myself listening for the sounds or voices of the Crayx in my mind," Parno admitted. "But less so now."

"I wonder if there are Crayx in the oceans here," Dhulyn said.

"I wonder if there are oceans." Parno refastened the tie on the crossbow kit and reached for his roll of knives. He did not open it, however, but sat silent for a few minutes. "What was making you so quiet last night while I was playing? I'll wager it wasn't thinking about the Crayx." He had dropped his tone into the nightwatch voice, though none of the curious were close enough to overhear.

Dhulyn shook her head. "When we implied that we did not approve of the way the Seers are handled, Star-Wind asked us what we'd have him do, break the Tribes? Let their race die out? But isn't that exactly what my own people did? How else can we account for the fact that a race of Seers did not foresee the coming of the Bascani? Or did nothing to prevent the massacre? Hasn't that been our question since we knew of Avylos the Blue Mage? Why didn't my mother and her sister Seers stop the breaking of the Tribes?"

"They allowed it to happen, that's what you're saying."

"That's what I'm saying."

"But why?"

"That's what we still don't know."

A shadow fell across them, and they fell silent. Parno looked up and sideways. Dhulyn untied her last pack and pulled out the silk bag that held her vera tiles. She examined the olive-wood box with care, turning it over in her hands, holding it up to the light, before opening the plain clasps and checking over the tiles themselves.

"What, no maces? No pikes?" Bekluth Allain, cloak tied as if for traveling, with what was clearly a mock frown on his face, surveyed their equipment with his fists on his hips.

"We wouldn't mind, but the horses would object," Parno said. "We thought it best to bring with us only these few weapons that we could carry ourselves."

Dhulyn let their voices pass over her head as she smoothed out a place in front of her to lay down the bag her tiles were normally stored in. Absently, she began to lay out the old-fashioned Tailor's Hand, one of the simplest patterns and one of the first games vera tile players were taught. Each player chose nine tiles to begin, and the object was to take turns pairing up matching tiles, until you had matched all the tiles in your hand. The first to do so was the winner. Dhulyn frowned at the pattern the tiles had made and scooped them up again, turning them facedown preparatory to shuffling them and laying them out once more.

"You are formidable warriors indeed if you consider the array I see here as 'few.'" Bekluth sounded more serious now. "There might be much work for you here."

"Only if there were more of us, and we take a long time to School."

Dhulyn made a face. If possible, the new hand was even worse than the previous one: not a single pair visible out of all the exposed tiles. Perhaps these ancient tiles, made as a tool to focus the Sight, resented being laid out for gambling.

"Vera tiles—are these your own? A follower of the gods of chance, are you?"

"We're Mercenary Brothers, Bekluth Allain. Our lives are nothing *but* chance."

Bekluth squatted down next to her. "Still, you've given me an idea. Would you sell me these?" He gestured toward the tiles with his smooth hand.

Dhulyn turned her head to eye him sideways. "No," she said.

Bekluth froze, his hand still extended. "They are very beautiful—and old, too, if I'm any judge of bone." Bekluth reached to pick up the tile nearest him, sucking in his breath when Dhulyn shot out her hand and had him by the wrist.

"I apologize for startling you," she said. "But you would have touched it by the time I had spoken to stop you."

"And *I* apologize," he said. "I should have asked permission. It's bad in a trader to show so much interest in anything," he added with an easy smile. "My mother would be ashamed of me." A shadow flitted across his face as he spoke. Perhaps his mother had died recently, Dhulyn thought, and he still felt her loss keenly.

"There would be a market for such things as these, if I can find someone to make them. Are there many games that can be played with them?"

"I know seventy-two variations," Dhulyn said. "All of which can be used for gambling, or not, as the players desire. Some are even suitable for children." She began to gather up the tiles, setting them facedown into their box. She refrained from mentioning their usefulness as a Seeing tool. Or perhaps they would have little use here, where the presence of so many Seers was in itself an aid to focus the Sight. Bekluth Allain either did not know the Espadryni women were Seers, or he pretended not to know, for the sake of his trade. *Either way*, Dhulyn thought, *it's not for me to enlighten him.*

Bekluth had remained silent long enough that Dhulyn looked up. His smile was now a sad one. "I have said you are so open, you and your Partner. It seems a pity to force you to lie to me. As I've said, better I ask no questions and see nothing out of the ordinary." He looked over his left shoulder, smiled and acknowledged a passing Horseman with the lift of his hand.

"May I borrow these?" he said, looking back to them. "The tiles? If you will not sell them, may I have copies made from this set? I believe we can negotiate a fee for use that you would find reasonable."

Dhulyn looked up and met her Partner's eyes. There was something about this request that struck her as wrong, though she did not know why. It was more, somehow, than not wanting to let these particular tiles, used for focusing the Sight, out of her hands.

"I'm afraid we don't know how long we'll be here or where our mission may take us," she said. "We cannot lend you the tiles."

"Perhaps it's just as well. I don't have the contacts among the people of fields and cities that I once had."

Dhulyn noticed that he used the Espadryni's phrase to refer to his own people. "How is it you came to trade among the Espadryni?" she asked. She would keep him talking, she thought. Somehow the way in which he was to help them would manifest itself. "Even in our world the Tribes were known to shun outsiders."

Bekluth looked up and away, and for a moment Dhulyn thought he might not answer, that rather than put her off with lies, he might say nothing at all. Then, still looking into the distance, he began to speak.

"I mentioned to you yesterday that I come from a large trading family, one that goes back many generations. It was my family, in fact, that founded the Guild in Norwash, the city of my birth." He glanced at them, then turned his eyes away once more. "My mother married against the wishes of her brothers and was left widowed very early—but not so early that she had not broken with them. It was only when I became old enough to take my place in the family, to join my cousins and uncles in the business, that my mother renewed her contact with them, though she never agreed to live again in the family compound, preferring to remain in the house my father had made for her."

He paused, but it was evident he merely looked for the right words to use, Dhulyn thought. She had the impression he had not spoken to anyone about these things for a very long time.

"My mother asked that I not be sent on caravan, that I be given a post close to her, though it meant a smaller share, since I was her only child and she depended upon me. Her brothers persuaded her otherwise, assuring her that she was as much their responsibility as she was mine. They did not modify the training for me, and so I was sent to apprentice in a smaller trading house. At first all went well, and my mother's fears were allayed; but while I was gone on my first caravan, my mother's house was entered by robbers, and she was killed."

He fell silent again, this time blinking. With quiet movements Dhulyn shook out the worn silk bag, brushing off any dirt that it might have picked up from the ground. She slipped the box of tiles back into the bag and pulled the braided ties shut.

"It was months before I was home again," Bekluth said. "Months. It was all over by then, everyone had put her death behind them. They had even sold the house. My house. No one cared anymore. My grief annoyed and embarrassed them." He hung his head.

Dhulyn glanced at Parno and found her Partner studying the trader with a look of concentration on his face.

"She died without me." Bekluth's voice was quiet. "I found I could not forgive them. They were so callous. They said it could have happened at any time, whether I'd been there or not." He shrugged. "They just didn't care. Ah, well."

He scrubbed at his face with his hands, then turned to them with a faint smile. "I left them. I trade on my own now." He straightened to his feet. "And if I cannot convince you to let me buy or borrow your tiles, I must be on my way. My trading here is finished, and the Red Horsemen do not like me to tarry. Sun shine on you, Mercenary Brothers, until we meet again."

"Good trading, Bekluth Allain."

"That's been weighing on him some time," Parno said. "I hope telling us will be of some benefit to him."

"Was there something in his story that might help *us*, do you think?"

Parno was silent a moment, looking at her out of the corner of his eye. "Again," he said dryly, "it is occasionally hard to tell pragmatism from heartlessness."

Dhulyn gave him the smile she saved only for him. "I am lucky that at least *you* can tell the difference, my soul. But listen, do you think his mother might have been the victim of our killer?"

Parno drew down his brows. "He didn't mention any mutilations."

"Would anyone have been cruel enough to tell him such a thing?"

"How ironic. They may have seemed more callous and uncaring than they actually were, in an effort to shield him from the full story."

Now it was Dhulyn's turn to look sideways at her Partner. "You are always seeing irony. We do not even know if there is any substance to our speculations."

They fell silent as another set of footsteps approached. They stood as Star-Wind neared them, escorting the old Cloud Shaman, Singer of the Grass-Moon.

"The Seers are asking for you again, Dhulyn Wolfshead, Parno Lionsmane. Will you come?"

The inside of the secret passage was narrow, so narrow that in places Falcos, with his broad shoulders, had to turn slightly sideways to get through. It wasn't the space that complicated things so much, Gun thought, as it was the need to be as quiet as possible as they crept away from the entrance that led to the Tarkina's bedroom. They only had the light from the lamp Julen had grabbed up at the last moment, at least until Gun had a chance to find the candle stub in the kit he went nowhere without. Mar would likely have hers as well. They reached the first turning without hearing any noise behind them and stopped around the corner, where the passage widened. *We are in the outside wall.* Or at least he thought they were. He was a little turned around, and he wasn't going to be given the chance to stop here long enough to Find his directions again. He supposed it was easier for the Mercenaries, since their sense of direction was constant and natural. He must remember to ask them. He started, blinking, as Mar elbowed him in the ribs.

Alaria was handing Falcos her extra sword, shrugging out of her bow, and the Tarkin was whispering some instructions when Julen spoke up.

"My lord, I should be in front." Gun and Mar squeezed themselves against the rough wall to make room for the guard to get around them.

"I'll stay in front, Julen, since I know which way to go." It was hard to be sure, since their voices seemed hollow and muffled in this narrow space, but Falcos sounded more confident than he had in the bedroom.

"And how is it you know the way," Mar asked, "when you weren't sure how to open the entrance?"

Falcos grinned, teeth flashing in the light of the lamp. "Because I know the marks." He tapped on the wall a little above the height of his own eyes. Gun squinted. From this angle, and his own much shorter height, he could barely make out the symbols drawn on the stone. They were painted, he thought, but the paint was old, and it reminded him of the drawing chalks Mar kept in her kit.

"Can they be wiped away?" he asked. An important question. Not that Gun had any doubt he could Find his way out of here, but what of the rest should they be separated?

Falcos frowned and reached up to rub at the bottom edge of the right-hand mark. The paint was unchanged. "As you see," he said. "This green crown," he tapped the symbol he'd tested. "That leads to the Tarkina's suite." He pointed the way they had come. "Which we know. And you see here, on the other angle of the wall are two signs, a blue crown, which should lead to the Tarkin's suite, and a horse head, which should lead to the stables."

"There's a secret passage in the stables?" Julen's tone was ample evidence that she was disgusted at not knowing this already.

"Again, I remind you, *secret*," Falcos said. "My mother made me swear I would never tell anyone I knew of the passages, not even my father. I don't think even she was supposed to know." He rubbed his eyes. "So, we will stay in the order we have. Alaria you follow after me—that's a good short bow for these close quarters—then the Scholars, who if I am correct, are not armed, though one of you should take the lamp. Julen, you will take rear guard, if you please."

And if she doesn't please, she'll do it just the same, Gun thought. Though, to be fair, either in the front or in the rear was the best place for the guard to be. Gun hefted one of the packs Alaria had brought from her bedroom, handing the other to Mar. Gun had heard that the Arderons maintained the habits of their nomad cousins, and that included always having a travel pack at the ready. From the weight and size of these packs, he'd heard correctly. Julen waited until Mar had slipped her arms through the straps before passing along the lamp.

The stones of the passage walls continued rough and undressed, showing signs of plaster finishing only where the passage branched or met another. They had already learned, even in the short distance they had come, to walk carefully if they didn't want to raise too much dust.

Gun hitched the pack a little higher on his shoulder, wishing he'd thought to put both arms through the straps when he'd had a chance. He touched the wall with his free hand. "This is like the underground tunnels in Gotterang," he said to Mar. He was using the quiet tones Scholars assumed in the study halls, but he knew she could hear him. "Except those were bigger." Mar nodded without turning around. He refrained from saying that then he'd also been with a full squad of Mercenary Brothers, though oddly enough, he didn't feel as frightened today as he'd been then. He smiled. *I must be getting tougher.*

At the next turning a new symbol appeared, what Gun was sure was meant for a cauldron. *The way to the kitchens?*

he thought. The stables, the kitchens, both places where extra comings and goings wouldn't draw too much attention. Unless you were the Tarkin, of course, then you couldn't help but draw—

He stopped short. "Um, Lord Tarkin? Where exactly *are* we going?"

Falcos stopped and looked back. The look on his handsome features told its own story.

"Perhaps we'd better decide *before* we go any farther," Gun said.

Falcos leaned his shoulders against the wall and wiped his forehead with his sleeve. It wasn't particularly warm here inside the stone walls, but heat wasn't the only thing that could make you sweat.

"It's all right." Alaria put her hand on Falcos' shoulder. "We're safe, and that's thanks to you." She sent a glance at Gun, but the Scholar wasn't offended. He'd only been able to Find the secret passage because Falcos had thought to look for it.

"You can't think of everything," Alaria was still talking. "We have some time now, so take a deep breath."

Falcos had been through a great deal already this morning, Gun thought. It was no wonder he was a bit shaken. Once they were in the passage and safe, the man's instinct had been to keep moving, and activity had felt right. But now *was* the time to think about what they were doing, and where they were going.

"Do you know where, besides the suites, the stables and the kitchens, these passages might lead?" Gun asked.

Falcos looked up at the symbols painted on the bit of plastered wall above his head. "My mother did tell me . . ." His eyes closed and his mouth twisted to one side. He seemed to be counting something over in his head. "The crowns are the suites, he said aloud. "The horse head, the cauldron." He opened his eyes. "If we see a chair symbol, that way leads to the throne room, and a sun symbol leads right outside the palace, to the hillside, I think, on the way to the Path of the Sun."

"That's the way to go then," Mar said, glancing first at Gun and then back to Falcos, where he stood close to Alaria.

"I agree," Alaria said. "Let's get right out of here."

"I cannot." Falcos was shaking his head. "If I run, it will seem as though what Epion is saying is true, that I am guilty. No, I need to—"

Alaria, her hand still on Falcos' shoulder, suddenly looked up and to her right. Julen must have heard something as well. She pushed past Gun, murmuring, "Douse the light," as she edged around Mar, who asked no questions but twisted the wick until it was out.

Gun was beginning to think they'd heard nothing after all, when he made out a faint glow of light from farther down the corridor. *Caids*, he thought. *Alaria has good ears*.

Falcos motioned them back around the corner they'd just turned, but Alaria shook her head, holding up her bow. Gun could make them out clearly, silhouetted against the light that was coming toward them. When Falcos in turn shook *his* head, Alaria pointed at the approaching glow, then at Falcos, then made an unmistakable throat-slitting gesture with her hand. Falcos blinked at her and looked around at them. Gun nodded vigorously, hoping that Falcos could see his agreement from where he stood.

This is exactly what he'd warned Falcos about. Stay alone in the room, he'd said, and Epion will send someone through the passage to kill you. Gun frowned. It was always nice to be proved right, but this also removed any doubt that Epion *did* know about the passage.

Alaria remained where she had been standing; she pulled an arrow out of the quiver that had been hanging down the center of her back and fitted it to the string. Gun opened his mouth to warn her when he realized that the person carrying the approaching light couldn't possibly see her yet, whereas the light itself made for a perfect target.

Slowly, smoothly, Alaria drew the bow up and let fly, the only sound the faint thrumming of the string. She had a second arrow fitted and ready, but the distant light had fallen.

This time Falcos allowed Julen to set him to one side with a sweep of her arm. The guard advanced with caution, her crouching form clearly outlined in the light of the other lamp, but she was soon motioning them forward.

"Have you the Sight as well as Finding, Gundaron of Valdomar?" Julen said when they caught up with her. She was on her knees next to a man with an arrow in his chest.

Good shooting, Gun thought, licking his lips. He didn't think even the Mercenaries could have done better. The dead man's eyes were staring, and his blood had already stopped flowing from the wound. Gun pulled his gaze away from the man to look where Julen was pointing. Lying still coiled where it must have fallen from the dead man's shoulder was a thin green rope, twisted with golden threads.

Alaria, her bow still in her hand, crouched down to touch it with her free hand. "This looks like one of the ties from the hangings in the sitting room," she said. She also looked up at Gun. "So he *was* coming to kill Falcos, and it *would* have looked like suicide." She turned to face the Tarkin. "We were right not to leave you."

Bekluth Allain found himself whistling the tune the Mercenary had been playing the night before. He grinned, but he made himself stop whistling. It was hard not to be pleased, however. Pleased at his luck, and pleased with his cleverness in taking advantage of that luck. He was usually more circumspect when speaking of his own past, but there was enough truth in what he'd told the Mercenaries to engage their interest and their sympathy. They'd both lost family, that was easy to see, and now they'd be predisposed to think well of him, to take his side.

And he was usually a great deal more circumspect when he headed for his special hiding place. He never took the same route twice and even avoided using the same beasts to get there, since the Espadryni were such great trackers.

"When they know they have something to track, that is," he said aloud. The horse he rode flicked its ears at him, but the other two were more used to his ways and just kept walking. Since he was in a hurry this time, however, Bekluth was taking the most direct route.

He laughed, and his horse shied just a little. The fact was he'd always been cautious out of habit, not because it was really necessary. The Espadryni were too used to him to suspect him of anything at all—so much so that the boy Ice Hawk hadn't even bothered to mention having seen him near the Door of the Sun. How was *that* for luck?

"Luck favors those who favor themselves." It was a

reminder his mother had frequently given him, and one he had cause to believe. He chuckled, remembering the look on his mother's face the last time he had seen her. How surprised she'd been, since he was supposed to be already gone with his caravan.

He reached the place where grass grew sparsely at midmorning, and as he expected, the horse had to be beaten to encourage it to continue. This spot was forbidden to the Espadryni; the land was poisoned, they believed, cursed by the gods, and they wouldn't even graze their horses or ingleras nearby. It was true that there were strange glassy patches where nothing grew. But if you persisted, if you were lucky and followed your luck, you found that in the center of this damaged place there was an old Caid ruin, very well preserved, with a spring of water that rose up out of the ground and formed a pool before sinking away again, where good grass grew around small sections of smooth paving.

What could be handier? What could be luckier for him than a place everyone else was afraid of going? A well-hidden place where Bekluth could leave his stock and his extra horses, from which he could travel, not on foot as the Espadryni always saw him, but on horseback. And much faster than anyone knew or suspected.

The horses began to walk faster, as if they could smell the water and good grass that was close in front of them. Once they'd reached the spot where Bekluth usually left them, he unloaded as quickly as he could, hobbling the two horses he was going to leave—he thought he had time for that much caution at least—and, mounting the third horse, he headed out in the direction of the Door.

He'd almost answered with the truth when the Mercenary woman asked him about being near the Door. Even now he could feel it, as if light shone from within her. To be so open, to have nothing—*nothing*—hidden. It was amazing.

"Of course, she has no reason to hide." Where she came from, no one was going to kill her just for being born. She was safe even here, where even the foolish Mages of the Espadryni could see that she was full of light. He leaned over the horse's shoulders and squeezed with his knees. He wouldn't ever have to kill her. Unlike with his own mother, there was nothing in Dhulyn Wolfshead that screamed to be let out. There probably never would be.

Still, she was bound somehow to her Partner, and *he* was a different matter. There was something in him, all right, something he was hiding. Some darkness that needed to be released. Bekluth almost sat up straight in the saddle, confusing the stupid horse, who thought he meant it to slow down. If he opened the man, let the darkness out, freed him, wouldn't that free her as well? Wasn't she in the same danger from the darkness that the man was?

But he'd need to find just the right time. It might be best to wait until the Mercenaries had given up and were on their way back. Then no one would be looking for him, and he could free them in safety. No one else would be looking for him.

Once he'd taken care of the boy.

🙟

The woman called Snow-Moon didn't even look up from the pot she was stirring. "There's some wish to speak with you. Younger ones." She waved vaguely toward the group of women hovering behind her.

"Over here, you silly old woman." The woman who stood up on the far side of the cook fire was tall and had Dhulyn's gray eyes, though her nose was much longer. Standing there, her left hand propped on her hip, her lips twisted in a sideways smile, it was hard to tell there was anything wrong with her; she seemed merely annoyed. "Though there's more than we who'd like a change from minding the children and looking out for bad weather," she said when the old woman looked narrowly at her. She smiled at Dhulyn. "You're the Seer then, are you? Dhulyn Wolfshead? I'm Winter-Ash."

The older woman, Snow-Moon, still looked at Winter-Ash with narrowed, calculating eyes. Would she forbid it, Parno wondered. Did the women observe a type of hierarchy among themselves? Finally Snow-Moon shrugged.

"You'll need at least two others," she said, as she turned and limped away.

"I have them right here, as you very well know," Winter-

Ash called after the elder. Two other young women stood up, grinning, to join her.

Parno glanced at Dhulyn and was not surprised to see her face an ivory mask. How could the trader Bekluth Allain say that there was nothing hidden about her? About either of them. He could only hope that his own face was as impassive as his Partner's, that the emotions raised in him by the halting, dragging gait of the Seer Snow-Moon remained hidden.

"Will you do this then, whole woman? Help us?" Winter-Ash asked when the other two women reached her.

"What is this, Winter-Ash? What would you have from Dhulyn Wolfshead?" The creaking voice of Singer of the Grass-Moon forestalled whatever answer Dhulyn had been about to make.

"Seer's business, old man. I needn't give you any explanation, and that's part of the Pact, so don't glower at me."

Singer of the Grass-Moon turned to Dhulyn. "I will advise against it, that *is* allowed under the Pact."

Winter-Ash made a face and waved this suggestion away, tossing her long hair over her shoulders and away from her face. "The oldsters are always against us." There was laughter in her voice and charm in her smile. "She needs help, doesn't she, her and her man? Well, we need her help also. Haven't we Seen her, again and again?"

"Snow-Moon does not seem to agree," the Singer said.

Winter-Ash shrugged, and Dhulyn almost expected her to roll her eyes. "And do you all agree? Always? All you men? Go on. Mind your business and we'll mind ours." She turned back to Dhulyn. "Come, do you agree?"

"You have Seen me, you say?"

"Many times, have none of them told you? Come, all will be revealed."

Dhulyn's eyebrows twitched, but she agreed with a short bow. Parno found himself doing something he hadn't consciously done in more than a moon, reaching out with his Pod sense. He sometimes thought he could sense *something* in other people, especially with Dhulyn, but now he felt nothing at all from the Espadryni women.

The three Seers led them through the women's area, to a clear space on the north side of the encampment, where the grazing of the camp horses had clipped the grass short.

"This will do," Winter-Ash said. "This is sufficient space, far enough away from prying eyes. Here we may be calm and call the Visions to us."

"How do we do this?" Dhulyn asked. "Are we enough? In my own Visions of the lost Tribes in our land, there are many more in the circle."

The three women exchanged glances, but Parno could not tell what they were thinking.

"Music will help," one of the other women said. "Can your man play for us?"

"I'll get my pipes," Parno said.

"Just your chanter," Dhulyn called after him. The skin crawled up Parno's neck as he went. Even three Espadryni women could be no match for his Partner, but he found he didn't like leaving her alone with them.

Dhulyn looked at the three women and found them all looking back with steady gazes, clear eyes, and encouraging smiles. The only hint that all was not perfectly normal, in fact, was that their smiles were a little too much alike. It was clear from the variation in eye shape, breadth of cheekbone, and form of mouth that these three were not closely related, and yet their smiles had this eerie similarity.

"You don't seem any different to me," Winter-Ash said. She was scrutinizing Dhulyn's face, almost squinting. "How are you fooling them?"

Dhulyn knew immediately what was meant. "I'm not. I am as they believe me to be."

"Well, we'll have the secret soon enough. That's why we're here, after all." This was the shorter, huskier of the two other women. Her face was open and sincere.

"There is nothing I can tell you," Dhulyn said.

"Your man, does he rule you?" Winter-Ash asked. "Or can you come and go as you please, even without him?"

"Parno Lionsmane is my Partner," Dhulyn answered. "As for coming and going, I am the Senior Mercenary Brother, and in things of the Brotherhood, all decisions are finally mine to make."

"And the things not of the Brotherhood?" asked the huskier woman.

"There are no things not of the Brotherhood."

The three women laughed, and though their laughter was warm, and intimate, Dhulyn shivered. Wit had not been her intention; what she had said was no more or less than the Common Rule. These women thought her Seniority gave her power over Parno, while all it did was bind them closer together.

"Quiet, then, here he comes now."

Parno trotted up on Dhulyn's left, brandishing his chanter. "What now?"

"Do you stand there and play," Winter-Ash said. "While we Seers clasp hands."

Dhulyn unsheathed her sword, placed it next to Parno, and took position between Winter-Ash and the shorter woman. Their hands were as rough as her own, but the calluses were in different places. *I don't cook*, Dhulyn thought. *I don't weave or spin or sew.* Since the Seers were not allowed to bear weapons of any kind, not even to defend themselves, the Espadryni women were oddly limited in the tasks that traditionally left their marks on a person's hands or body.

The three Seers began to hum a tune and shuffle their feet, and Dhulyn felt a moment of displacement, not unlike what they had felt while walking the Path, until she realized the tune they were humming was not the familiar one she associated with using her Mark, but something totally unknown to her.

Parno took up the melody quickly, but it took several repetitions for Dhulyn to take it in and begin to hum it herself. She took a step and a half to the right. Back to the left, with her right foot crossing in front of her left. Back and forth.

GUNDARON THE SCHOLAR WALKS DOWN A LONG LINE OF SHELVES, SPAN AFTER SPAN OF THEM, WOOD, FOLLOWED BY METAL AND THEN BY STONE BEFORE BECOMING WOOD AGAIN. DHULYN CAN HEAR THE HEELS OF HIS BOOTS CRACKING AGAINST THE FLOOR. GUN'S EYES FLICK BACK AND FORTH, SCANNING THE MARKS AND TITLES ON THE BOOKS AND SCROLLS THAT SURROUND HIM. THE AIR IS HEAVY WITH THE SMELL OF PARCHMENT, PAPER, AND THE PECULIAR SCENT OF OLD LEATHR BINDINGS. *GUN'S FINDING SOMETHING*, DHULYN THINKS, A SENSE OF WONDER WELLING UP INSIDE HER. THIS IS THE LIBRARY HE'S OFTEN SPOKEN OF, WHERE HE GOES FOR CLUES, WHERE HE FINDS. AS SHE WATCHES, HE STOPS AT A BLUE-GREEN VOLUME AND PULLS IT OFF THE SHELF. HE GLANCES TOWARD HER, AND AS THEIR EYES MEET, HIS WIDEN AND "DHULYN," HE SAYS . . .

SHE TURNS AWAY AND LOOKS OUT OVER THE PLAIN THAT STRETCHES OUT BEFORE THEM. IT IS CLOSE TO SUNSET, AND THE ANGLE OF THE LIGHT GIVES EVERYTHING A LONG SHADOW WITH SOFT EDGES. IT IS A TIME OF DAY FOR THE LAST STROLL OF THE EVENING. BUT NO ONE STROLLS BELOW. DHULYN KNOWS AT ONCE THAT WHAT SHE SEES WAS ONCE CULTIVATED FIELDS. CORN, SHE THINKS. BUT THE FIELDS ARE BURNED NOW, BY A FIRE THAT SPREAD FROM THE WEST, LEAVING STALKS BLACKENED AND ONLY JUST DARKER THAN THEIR OWN SHADOWS. THE FIRE MUST HAVE BEEN FOLLOWED QUICKLY BY A FREEZE, WHICH PREVENTED THE GROWTH OF THOSE PLANTS THAT NORMALLY SPRING UP AFTER THE PASSAGE OF FLAME. NO PLOUGH HAS TOUCHED THE LAND SINCE.

"DO YOU KNOW THIS PLACE?" SHE ASKS THE WOMEN WITH HER.

WINTER-ASH SHAKES HER HEAD, LOWER LIP BETWEEN HER TEETH. "WE DO NOT KNOW THE LANDS OF FIELDS AND TOWNS," SHE SAYS. "THEY WOULD KILL US THERE. COME, HERE IS A PATH." . . .

THIS PATH LEADS THEM DOWN AND AROUND AN OUTCROPPING OF BOULDERS AND THROUGH ANOTHER FIELD, WITH THE SUN SHINING OVERHEAD. THIS IS HAY, WITH ITS CLEAN GRASS SMELL, BUT IT IS FOUR OR MORE SEASONS OLD, GROWN WEEDY, WITH SMALL TREES ALREADY THRUSTING UP TALLER THAN THE GRASS. SOMETHING WHITE CATCHES DHULYN'S EYE, AND SHE STOPS, CROUCHING ON HER HEELS TO EXAMINE IT MORE CLOSELY.

"BONES," WINTER-ASH SAYS FROM ABOVE HER. "WHAT MAKES THEM SO WHITE?"

"HUMAN BONES," DHULYN AGREES. "THE SUN AND TIME HAVE BLEACHED THEM. THEY'VE LAIN HERE MORE THAN ONE SEASON, THAT'S CERTAIN."

"LOOK." THE SHORTER WOMAN HOLDS UP WHAT LOOKS LIKE A STRAND OF SILK, THE COLOR OF OLD BLOOD. DHULYN HOLDS OUT HER HAND FOR IT AND SEES THAT IT IS A LONG TRESS OF UNBRAIDED HAIR.

"IT MIGHT ALMOST BE FROM ONE OF US," WINTER-ASH SAYS, AND THERE IS A NOTE IN HER VOICE THAT DHULYN DOES NOT EXPECT. "IS THERE ANYTHING OTHER THAN EMPTINESS AND ABANDONMENT FOR US TO SEE IN THIS WORLD THAT IS TO COME?" . . .

THE THIN, SANDY-HAIRED MAN IS STILL WEARING THE GOLD RINGS IN HIS EARS, BUT HIS FACE IS LINED NOW, AND HIS FOREHEAD HIGHER. HE IS SITTING AT A SQUARE TABLE, ITS TOP INLAID WITH LIGHTER WOODS, READING BY THE LIGHT OF TWO LAMPS. A PLATE TO HIS LEFT CONTAINS THE REMNANTS OF A MEAL—CHICKEN OR SOME OTHER FOWL, JUDGING BY THE BONES. HE LOOKS TOWARD THE ROOM'S SINGLE WINDOW AND RISES TO LOOK OUT. HE MUST HAVE STEPPED IN SOMETHING WET FOR HIS FEET, CLAD IN THE EMBROIDERED FELT OF HOUSE SLIPPERS, LEAVE DARK MARKS ON THE FLOOR. IT IS DARK OUTSIDE, AND THERE MUST BE NO MOON, FOR DHULYN CAN SEE NOTHING

OUTSIDE THE WINDOW. THE MAN TURNS TOWARD THE TABLE AGAIN AND, SMILING, SAYS "HOW CAN I HELP?" . . .

GUNDARON AND MAR ARE SITTING ON THE GROUND, LEANING ON ONE ANOTHER. MAR HAS HER ARM AROUND GUN, AND SHE IS WHISPERING TO HIM, THOUGH EVEN WITH THE HEIGHTENED EXPERIENCE OF BEING HERE WITH OTHER SEERS, DHULYN CANNOT MAKE OUT THE WORDS. WHAT IS WRONG WITH GUN? WHY DOES MAR LOOK SO WORRIED? DHULYN TAKES A STEP CLOSER AND SITS DOWN ON HER HEELS TO GET A BETTER ANGLE ON GUN'S FACE. HE TURNS TOWARD HER, BUT HE DOESN'T SEE HER. NOT ONLY BECAUSE HE IS NOT HIMSELF USING HIS MARK AT THIS MOMENT, BUT BECAUSE HIS EYES ARE COVERED WITH A STRIP OF CLOTH. DHULYN REACHES OUT A HAND BUT STOPS WELL SHORT OF TOUCHING HIM—EVEN IF SHE COULD. DOES A BLIND FINDER STILL HAVE HIS MARK?

"WHO ARE THESE PEOPLE?" WINTER-ASH ASKS.

"FRIENDS OF MINE."

"YOU HAVE FRIENDS?"

THIS TIME DHULYN RECOGNIZES THE NOTE OF LONGING IN THE OTHER WOMAN'S VOICE, AND SHE TURNS TO LOOK AT THEM MORE CLOSELY.

"THESE VISIONS ARE FOR YOU, TO HELP YOU FIND YOUR KILLER. DO THEY TELL YOU ANYTHING USEFUL?"

"YOU ARE SURE IT IS THE FUTURE WE SEE?" DHULYN TURNS, AND SHE IS STANDING ON A ROCKY OUTCROP, THE THREE ESPADRYNI WOMAN ARRANGED AROUND HER. SHE FEELS HER HEART LIFT, AND SHE LOOKS AROUND, SMILING. THIS IS WHAT SHE HAS SEEN AND FELT BEFORE, WHEN SHE WAS WITH THE WHITE SISTERS OF MORTAXA. COLORS ARE SHARPER, SCENTS CRISPER, AND SHE CAN FEEL THE COOLNESS OF THE AIR ON HER SKIN, AS IF SHE EXPERIENCES THEM HERSELF, NOT MERELY AS A WATCHER. AS IF THE VISION HAS NOW A REALITY IT CANNOT HAVE WHEN SHE SEES ALONE.

SHE LOOKS OVER AND SEES THE ESPADRYNI WOMEN DIRECTLY, STANDING BEHIND HER, ARMS AROUND EACH OTHER'S WAISTS IN THE FIRST FREELY AFFECTIONATE GESTURE SHE HAS EVER SEEN FROM THEM. SHE LOOKS INTO THEIR FACES. AT FIRST SHE ISN'T SURE, BUT THEN SHE SEES THEIR SMILES ARE DIFFERENT, AND THERE IS LIGHT, WARMTH, HUMOR, AND EVEN HOPE IN THEIR EYES. DHULYN SWALLOWS AND BLINKS BACK THE MOISTURE THAT FORMS IN HER OWN EYES. THIS IS THE SAME PHENOMENON THAT HAD GOVERNED THE VISIONS OF THE WHITE SISTERS OF THE MORTAXA. THOSE WOMEN, SUFFERERS FROM THE WHITE DISEASE AND WITH THE MINDS OF CHILDREN, HAD BEEN THEIR ADULT SELVES WHILE IN THE WORLD OF VISIONS. HERE THE ESPADRYNI WOMEN, ALSO, ARE WHOLE AND UNBROKEN.

"SO, YOU SEE HOW IT IS FOR US. THOUGH THE WORLD OF VISIONS IS NO REFUGE," WINTER-ASH SAYS. "WE CANNOT STAY HERE, WHERE THERE IS NEITHER FOOD NOR DRINK. THE OTHERS WOULD NOT FEED OUR BODIES."

"Anymore than we would feed theirs, were our positions reversed," says the shorter woman. Winter-Ash hugs her.

"Here are Night-Sky," she says. "And Feather-Flight. Our hearts are full to meet you finally, Dhulyn Wolfshead."

"What happened to you? To all the Marked," Dhulyn asks. "Have you ever Seen?"

"Look, we will show you." Winter-Ash gestures, and Dhulyn follows the sweep of the young woman's hand until she is standing once more in the room she has Seen so many times. Here is the Mage with his pale, close-cropped hair. He is on his knees; he bows his head, his hands covering his face with their jade green eyes. Dhulyn, except it isn't Dhulyn here, it is someone else in the part she usually plays. This someone else lifts his sword high and strikes. As the blade enters the Mage's flesh, the flesh turns to stone and shatters, exploding into a pale green dust that blanks the Vision out . . .

"There, you see? That is what we are shown, over and over, when we ask to See what has happened to us. Always the room, the mirror, and our Champion defeating the Green Shadow. The fine dust that obscures all and prevents us from seeing why, how, we Marked became what we became."

Dhulyn shakes her head. "That is not what happened in our world."

"You Saw it? How was it different?"

"I did See it, yes, but I was also there, at the end."

"How can that be? The Green Shadow is what caused the fall of the Caids, and you are not so old as that, surely." The three women smile at her, shaking their heads.

"In my world the Green Shadow was not defeated quickly, but appeared and reappeared. When it was finally defeated," she waves her hand at where the Vision replays around them, "this is not what happened."

"In what manner was it different?"

"Have you seen the Mage when his eyes are the blue of old ice?" They nod. "That is the real Mage, the one who can read the book—"

"What book?"

Dhulyn looks around, but at that moment the Green dust has exploded, and there is nothing of the room to be seen. "There is a spell book on the Mage's table," she says. "It is how the Shadow was called. And the Mage can read the book, and . . ." Dhulyn's voice dies away. The Vision is repeating once more and she can See the

DESK, BUT IT IS BARE, THERE IS NO BOOK UPON IT. ONCE AGAIN THE SWORD FALLS, AND THE GREEN SHADOW SHATTERS INTO DUST.

"WHERE DOES THE DUST GO?" SHE ASKS.

WINTER-ASH BRUSHES AT HERSELF AND THEN AT THE AIR, BUT THE DUST DOES NOT DISPERSE. SHE CANNOT TOUCH IT; IT IS AS IF THEY WERE NOT THERE. "WE CANNOT SEE BEYOND THIS MOMENT."

"HAVE YOU EVER ASKED HOW YOU MAY BE MADE WHOLE AGAIN?" DHULYN SEES FROM THEIR PATIENT LOOKS THAT OF COURSE THEY HAVE. "AND WHAT WERE YOU SHOWN THEN?"

"YOU."

"PARDON?" DHULYN WANTS TO SHAKE HER HEAD, SHAKE AWAY THE IDEA THAT CREEPS ITS WAY INTO HER BRAIN.

"WE SEE YOU, DHULYN WOLFSHEAD. THAT IS WHY WE ARE HERE. SOMEHOW, YOU WILL HELP US FIND WHAT WE SEEK."

I WISH WE HAD A FINDER WITH US, DHULYN THINKS. *I NEED GUN.* "PERHAPS YOU ARE NOT ASKING THE RIGHT QUESTIONS," DHULYN SAYS. SHE TAPS HER TEETH WITH THE TIP OF HER TONGUE. "IN OUR WORLD, THE GREEN SHADOW WAS SHATTERED OVER AND OVER AGAIN, AND ITS PIECES CAUSED MUCH MISCHIEF BEFORE THE END FINALLY CAME." SHE WAVES HER HAND AT THE ROOM AROUND THEM. "YOU ASK HOW YOU CAME TO BE BROKEN, AND YOU ARE SHOWN THIS VISION. IN MY WORLD THE GREEN SHADOW WAS A NOTHINGNESS, AN UNPLACE, A FORMLESS NOWHERE THAT UNMADE." DHULYN TAKES WINTER-ASH'S LEFT HAND IN HER RIGHT AND HOLDS OUT HER LEFT FOR NIGHT-SKY. THE WOMEN QUICKLY UNDERSTAND AND FORM A CIRCLE. "WHERE IS THIS DUST NOW?" DHULYN ASKS.

THE VISION BEGINS TO CHANGE, THE ROOM FADING AWAY, AS IF IN ANSWER TO HER QUESTION. SHAPES BEGIN TO FORM, BUT THEY FADE AGAIN. "WHERE IS THE DUST?" DHULYN ASKS AGAIN, AND THIS TIME THE SHADOWS AROUND THEM ALMOST CLEAR. DHULYN THINKS SHE SEES HORSES WALKING IN THE FOG, TWO WITH RIDERS. THEN THAT IMAGE FADES ALSO, THE SHADOWS DISAPPEAR, AND NOW THERE ARE TWO WOMEN BEFORE THEM, TWO WOMEN WITH WHITE SKIN, BONE-PALE HAIR, RED EYES. "SISTER," THE ONE ON THE LEFT SAYS, THE ONE WITH THE GOLD FLECK IN HER EYE. "SISTER, WAKE UP. YOU HAVE BEEN TOO LONG IN VISION PLACE. YOU MUST RETURN."

"NO," CRIES WINTER-ASH. "WE ARE SO CLOSE, WE ALMOST SAW, WE MUST NOT STOP NOW."

"SISTER, DHULYN," SAYS THE SECOND WHITE TWIN. "YOU MUST GO BACK NOW. THE TIME TO DESTROY THE SHADOW IS NOT YET."

"WHAT DOES SHE MEAN," NIGHT-SKY SAYS. "THE SHADOW WAS DEFEATED LONG AGO."

"DHULYN KNOWS. SHE HAS THE ANSWER, BUT YOU MUST RETURN NOW."

"NO," WINTER-ASH IS CRYING. "WE ARE SO CLOSE, WE MAY NOT WANT

TO TRY AGAIN, ONCE WE RETURN TO OUR WORLDLY SELVES. THEY ONLY DID THIS OUT OF CURIOSITY, AND NOW THEY WILL NOT CARE. WE CANNOT GO BACK NOW." SHE CATCHES UP DHULYN'S LEFT HAND IN HER RIGHT AND GESTURES AT FEATHER-FLIGHT AND NIGHT-SKY, WHO QUICKLY JOIN HER IN CREATING THE CIRCLE.

DHULYN LOOKS TO THE WHITE TWINS, BUT THEY ARE GONE.

Sixteen

EPION PULLED AT his lower lip. The corridor outside
the Tarkina's apartments was not wide enough to allow for a ram—had in fact been designed that way—
but neither was the door designed to withstand two men
with battle axes for more than a short period. Only enough
time as would be needed, in fact, to access the secret
passage—that is, if anyone but Epion still knew about the
things. He sighed and dropped his hand. He knew he should
have insisted on sending in one of his own people, Julen was
known to be fiercely loyal to Falcos. But preventing the
guard from performing what was, after all, her actual duty
in protecting the princess would have raised too many questions.

It was a simple plan, and a good one. It was a shame,
really, that it had not played out. The first steps had gone
beautifully. The guards he had spoken to had been shocked,
but in the face of all that had happened in the last two years,
and the rumors about Falcos he'd had circulating since the
old Tarkin's death, they were ready at least to listen and to
follow his orders. After all, he wasn't asking them to do anything more than hold Falcos safe. And if he had anticipated
events slightly, if he had not actually consulted the council
as yet, well, no one knew it but him.

If Alaria and those blooded Scholars had only come out
of the rooms, this would all be over now and the council
faced with the fact of Falcos' apparent suicide. Epion
straightened up. He could only hope that when the assassin

realized the rooms were still occupied he would go back to the library entrance.

With luck, this was only a small hitch in the plan. Once they were through the door Falcos could still be isolated—perhaps in his own rooms—and the assassin could pay him a visit then. Let Alaria and the Scholars think whatever they liked for the moment. Falcos' "suicide" would answer all questions.

"My lord." Gabe-Leggett was signaling to him. They had breached the door, finally, and the guard with the ax was reaching through, trying to get leverage on the bars to lift them away.

Epion gestured him aside and stooped to peer through the opening. The room within was empty, doors to the balcony open, curtains blowing in. Epion stifled a smile. Not even Falcos was stupid enough to try that route of escape. The tide was out, and there was nothing outside that balcony now but rocks. No, they would be hiding in one of the other rooms, that was all.

He stepped back from the opening. "Continue," he directed. "But take care, there were weapons in the princess' baggage, and the Tarkin may have forced her to supply them. Do your best not to hurt anyone, especially the princess and the Scholars, but do not put yourselves at risk either. I have called for the Healer, but he has not yet arrived."

Another lie that would not matter if all else went well. A lie, moreover, that should convince them he was on the side of the Caids. Concerned for their safety, worried about the precious princess, but reluctantly doing the right thing when it came to his poor mad nephew. And if they thought he'd called for the Healer to help Falcos, well, so much the better.

It would not take much longer to open the door, Epion decided. He signaled to the Leggett brothers.

"With luck he will fight," he told them in low tones. "Try to make it so. Engage with him yourselves."

"Finish with him?" Jo-Leggett said in the same quiet voice. His brother, Gabe-Leggett, remained impassive, his eyes steady on Epion's face.

"Not if you can avoid it. Knocking him senseless would be preferable at the moment." The two men nodded.

"My lord."

This time the door was open, and at Epion's signal the men went through, the Leggetts in front. In a moment, Gabe-Leggett was back, his mouth set in a grim line.

"The rooms are empty, my lord."

Epion's hands closed into fists. He had been certain, *certain* that only he knew of the existence of the secret passages. His brother, the old Tarkin, had not told Falcos—he had only admitted their existence when Epion had asked about them, refusing to give any more details and demanding to know how Epion had learned of them. Epion had passed off his knowledge as a story he'd heard in childhood, but in truth he had found the map of the passages in the same old book in which he'd found the key to the Path.

Though thus far only the diagram to the passages had been of any use, and that somewhat limited. The locations of the exits and entrances had been indicated, but not always how they had been hidden, and Epion had only had time to find how the library entrance worked. With help, he would have found more, but anyone who helped him had to be fed to the man from the Path.

Still, the passages were complicated, and there was time to use what he *did* know. He signaled to his own men.

"Jo-Leggett, send men you can trust to the Tarkin's rooms, the throne room, and the stables." Those seemed the three likeliest places for Falcos to go. "Also the library and the kitchens." The latter was so public it was probably safe, but he could take no chances. "Send half a squad at least to each place. And then come to me in the stables." There *was* one more exit, the most likely one, now that he thought of it. Best the Leggett boys go themselves. "The same instructions apply, mind you," he said. "Detain him only."

Only long enough for me to arrange his suicide. The suicide that would be all the proof anyone would need that Epion's accusations were true.

Jo-Leggett nodded and went.

⊂⊃

Ice Hawk heard the horse approaching long before it came into view, just as he would have expected to. Town people, he'd heard, thought the grass plains were perfectly flat, like a wooden table he had seen once in a city shop, when his grandfather had taken him, as a small child, to visit the people of fields and cities. But all Espadryni knew the plains rippled like a cloth laid on the ground, with crests and valleys—not all deep enough to hide or camp in, but many were.

Partly through his own evolving magics, and partly through the study of wind and air that told any man, Mage or not, much about the world around him that would be handy to know, Ice Hawk also knew who it was that approached, though it was rare that Bekluth Allain had only the one horse with him.

When Bekluth the trader finally came into sight, he was on foot, leading a sand-colored mare with two white feet. The horse didn't seem much laden with merchandise, but it was possible that Bekluth, not knowing who would be at the camp just now, had left the major part of his goods—along with his other horses—on the other side of a nearby rise. After all, not all the Espadryni were as trustworthy as the Long Trees People, nor as welcoming as Ice Hawk.

"Ah, Ice Hawk," Bekluth said when they were close enough to speak. Why city men thought they had to repeat your name when they saw you was more than Ice Hawk yet understood. At least the trader did not wave his arms and shout while still at a distance as the young Mage had seen others do.

Though, now that he thought about it, perhaps those particular travelers had been lost.

"Still here at Mother Sun's Door, I see," Bekluth said. At Ice Hawk's signal the man squatted down next to the fire spot, though the ashes were cold now, courteously retaining the lead of his horse in his hands until he was invited to do more than merely sit. He looked around him at the marks on the ground.

"I see others of your people have been here," the older man said. "Checking on you, were they? Making sure you hadn't gone through and not come back?"

Ice Hawk was careful to keep his smile friendly. The trader had to be a good man to travel so much alone, but he was neither Espadryni nor Mage.

"If the information will be of use to you, you might trade me something for it," he suggested with a smile. Ice Hawk knew that information could be just as valuable a commodity as knives and other artifacts.

Bekluth laughed. "Oh, very good, very sharp! Are you sure you don't want to come trading with me? Learn the business?"

Ice Hawk knew that the offer was meant as a compliment and refrained from showing his disgust at the idea that an Espadryni could ever become a man of field and city. Refrained with some success apparently, as the trader was still smiling at him.

"Nah, lad, I was curious only. You show me respect, however, by your willingness to trade. And it's only right I show you the same." Bekluth looped the leading rein around his arm to leave his hands free and began to pat his belt pouches. "Let's see. A man can't have too many knives. What do you think of this one?"

Ice Hawk sat up straighter. This was the first time anyone had called him a man. No one in the Tribes would call him that until he'd faced the Door of the Sun. Whether Mother Sun granted him access to the Door or not, he would leave here a man. Either a superior Mage ready to follow the path of his grandfather, Singer of the Wind, or simply a man among his people.

"It is a skinning knife," Bekluth said, holding it out. "From Cisneros. You see how the blade is very slightly curved, and the patterning hammered into the upper edge."

Ice Hawk nodded as if he saw Cisnerean blades every day. "For this knife I will answer your question."

"For this knife you will answer my question and . . . five more."

Shaking his head, Ice Hawk tried to look disinterested. "Two."

"Three."

"Done."

Ice Hawk had the hilt of the knife in his hands almost before he finished speaking. Bekluth unwrapped the leading rein from his arm and tossed it to one side. Now that trading had taken place, a tacit invitation to do more than sit had been offered and accepted. Ice Hawk sheathed his new knife and set it to one side. This would be the first time he would play host in a camp, but he knew what was expected.

"Your first question concerned the presence of my people," he said. "They came to bring me supplies, the kind I cannot hunt for myself if I am to complete my meditation."

Bekluth nodded and tapped his lips with his index finger, as though he sorted through questions in his mind. "How long did they stay?"

"Longer than they had planned, I am sure, as two Mercenary Brothers came through the Path of the Sun." Ice Hawk felt his face heat, remembering the touch of Dhulyn Wolfshead's hand on his arm.

Bekluth grinned and shifted his seat until he was sitting cross-legged. "You've been in the sun too long, Ice Hawk. The Mercenaries came through moons ago."

Stung, Ice Hawk was quick to defend his knowledge. "No, Bekluth Allain. These are different ones, new. One is a woman—like our women, but not like . . ." Ice Hawk let his voice die away, his stomach cold, his ears buzzing.

The trader's brows crawled high and his eyes were almost round. "What do you mean?"

Ice Hawk scrambled to find a way out of his mistake. It was widely thought among the Long Trees People that Bekluth Allain knew the truth about the Espadryni women, but the Mages said that so long as it was never spoken of openly, Bekluth Allain could never reveal their secret. "Apparently, there were once Espadryni on the other side of Mother Sun's Door, though their women were not sequestered as ours are. Then the Tribes were broken. This Mercenary is the last of her kind, she says."

Now the trader swung his head from side to side "She is tricking you, Ice Hawk."

Ice Hawk shrugged. Bekluth Allain was asking without asking, and Ice Hawk had to find a way to answer. "Me they might have tricked," he admitted. "I was only lately a cub. But my grandfather, Singer of the Wind, was here also, and he cannot be tricked. Not in such things."

At these words the trader fell silent. A breeze gusted, stirring the ashes in the fire spot and bringing with it a faint smell of Ice Hawk's latrine pit.

"A great marvel," Bekluth said, suddenly coming to life as he absorbed Ice Hawk's words. "The last of her kind. So they went off, then, with Singer of the Wind?"

"Question three." Ice Hawk felt the tension ease from

his back and shoulders. "You need not look so cunning, Bekluth, they are warriors, and not likely to need anything from you."

"Oh, no? And you had no need for your new knife?"

Ice Hawk grinned and shrugged. "I am young and need many things. These two, they did not look to be short of knives. I think they will want to talk to you, though, so it may be that *you* have information *they* will trade for."

Without answering Bekluth stood and began to free his horse from its saddle, pulling loose a tie here and opening a buckle there. First he detached a pack from the back of the saddle and set it down at his place on the ground, then he lifted off the saddle itself, taking pad and all into his hands. Ice Hawk did not offer to help, not even to take the leading rein and stake it to the ground. It would have seemed as though he wished to pry into the trader's goods.

"What could I know that people from the other side of Mother Sun's Door would trade me for?" The horse led a short distance away to where the horse line would normally be, Bekluth sat down once more across from Ice Hawk, opened his saddle pack, and began looking through it.

"You have no more questions left," Ice Hawk said, grinning.

"Let's see, what might I have that would be worth such knowledge?" Bekluth raised his eyebrows and looked at Ice Hawk sideways. "Especially considering that all I have to do is wait to meet them and they will tell me themselves for free."

Ice Hawk shrugged again, unashamed. *Who doesn't try gets nothing.* Even the young cubs knew that.

"They're looking for someone, a killer, who has passed to their side of the Door of the Sun, and killed some of their people. Not just killed, but tortured and mutilated in a way unknown to us." Ice Hawk blinked, the image of what the woman Dhulyn Wolfshead had told them momentarily before his eyes. "We thought to help them, but they told us when the last killing had been done, and we had seen no such killer."

"When was that?" Bekluth finally straightened from his pack with two cups and a round flask in his hands.

Ice Hawk thought for a moment, counting back the days since the Mercenaries had left for the camp of the Salt Desert People. And they had said the killing had happened three nights before that. "Five or six nights ago," he said.

"At the full moon? But you were here, Ice Hawk, did they not suspect you?"

Ice Hawk blinked, but the trader was already laughing. "Ah, forgive me, a bad jest I admit, but Caids, man, you should see your face." His own face grew suddenly serious. "Were *we* in any danger then, do you think? Was that not the time I met with you on my way to the Cold Lake camp? You told them this, of course." The trader poured out two glasses of clear liquid that had a most exquisite smell.

Ice Hawk felt the heat rising to his ears. "No," he admitted. "I forgot." He wrinkled up his nose. Was this why the Mother Sun had not yet shown him the key to her Door? Because he was still unseasoned and forgetful? "You were here such a short time and naturally I thought them to mean some stranger to us. Still, I must tell them," he decided. He would have to admit his error to Dhulyn Wolfshead, but then, it would give him an excuse to speak with her.

"I will tell them myself," Bekluth said. "I travel much, and possibly I have seen something that they alone will find significant. And if, as you say, they come from beyond the Door, I admit I will be curious to meet them." He held out one of the cups. "In the meantime, taste this orange brandy for me, and tell me whether you think your people will trade for it."

Ice Hawk considered reminding Bekluth the Trader that strong drink was only for those who had become men and that he had not, in fact, reached that status yet. But even as he was thinking so, he was reaching out for the cup. After all, he would not be the first to enjoy some of the privileges of manhood in advance of the ceremony, nor the last.

Bekluth raised his cup, and Ice Hawk imitated him, wondering whether he was required to make the salute, and wracking his brain for one he had heard the men use.

"Your health," Bekluth said.

"Confusion to our enemies," Ice Hawk responded, and he set his lips to the edge of the cup. The liquid was fiery, much more so than he expected, and Ice Hawk fought not to choke or sneeze. It tasted something like the honeyed orange peel they sometimes traded for but—

It felt as though a hand had closed around his throat, large and hard as sword steel. Ice Hawk waved his right hand at Bekluth, signaling for help, but the man merely sat there, looking at Ice Hawk with narrowed eyes, as if watching an ant crawl across a leaf. Sun and Moon curse him. Ice Hawk's lungs continued to heave, trying for air, but he ignored them, ignored the black edges to his vision, and how they crowded in. Concentrating on, focusing on, the handle of his dagger, and how to reach it, to recognize the familiar feel of the thong-wrapped hilt, forcing his hand to pull it out, even though it made the black edges thicker. He lurched to his knees, putting out his empty hand to steady himself, and reached—

The trader stopped smiling and hastily scrabbled back and away.

At least I made him afraid. The black closed in, and Ice Hawk followed the thought down into it. *Confusion to . . .*

Bekluth Allain waited for a count of one hundred, to make sure the boy was unconscious. He should not have been able to move so much; either he was very determined, and very strong, or the poison in the orange brandy was losing its potency. Bekluth shrugged. He'd poured out all he had, the chief's share into the boy's cup, leaving barely enough in his own to stain the lips. Barely enough to do the job, it seemed.

When he was sure, Bekluth stood up and nudged the dagger away from the boy's hand with his toe. Can't be too careful, he told himself with a smile. Look what happened to people who weren't.

"She might have tricked you, eh, boy? Well, I've tricked you and your grandfather both, what do you think of that?" Bekluth rolled the boy over and put the dagger back into its sheath. He wouldn't need it, and the boy couldn't use it. At the same time, he took back the skinning knife he'd traded for information. The Horsemen were excellent trackers, but there was no point in leaving them such a clear sign he'd been here after them. These people knew each other's belongings as well as they knew each other's horses. Not that there was any chance he'd ever let *this* knife go.

He looked down at where the boy lay half on his back, half on his side, face relaxing from its determined expression, the blue eyes still wide open and aware. Yet there was something hidden there—or was he wrong? Bekluth squatted down on his heels, elbows resting on his knees.

No, he was not wrong. The boy did have a darkness hidden within him, a secret. Bekluth inhaled sharply and forced himself to exhale slowly, very slowly. He reached out with the hand that still held the knife and brushed the boy's hair away from his face.

"Don't worry," he said. "I'm going to help you. I can free what's hidden inside you, and you'll be open, full of light. No need to fear anymore. You'll see. Be patient."

When he was finished, the waning moon had risen, and Bekluth knelt beside the fire, invigorated as usual despite the length of the ordeal. But the boy would be well now, open and free of the darkness that had lived inside him, the secret. Bekluth had taken it from him, freeing it, taking it into himself where he could destroy it. Saving the boy. He felt again that wondrous sense of completion, of satisfaction, that he felt only when he'd helped someone.

He took a deep breath and straightened, setting his shoulders back, and clapped his hands on his thighs before standing and resaddling his horse. That done, and the nervous animal steadied, Bekluth looked around for the tinder pile Ice Hawk would have had nearby. He checked the direction of the prevailing wind, gathered up the dry grass and twisted it into a loose wick, laying one end in the fire pit and making sure the other end would reach to the grass—equally dry—surrounding the small campsite. The fire had been laid against a cool night, and all Bekluth had to do before getting on his horse was set the construction of dry grass and sticks alight with his own sparker.

He looked back three times as he rode away and was rewarded the third time with the sight of dark smoke blowing away from him. He stopped at the next rise to watch the direction of the smoke and to see, finally, the bright shiver of the fire itself. It was moving away from him, according to plan. As he was riding, the wind grew colder, and Bekluth shivered. He pulled his cloak free of his saddle pack, and as he swung it around his shoulders, he examined the sky in the direction of the wind.

"Rain," he said, pulling up the horse. "Rain before morning." He looked back over his shoulder to where the fire was spreading behind him. He took his upper lip in his teeth. He needed to get back to the Mercenaries.

But perhaps he should wait. The Mercenaries should give him no more trouble than the rest of these simple people did.

He would wait. The rain might wake the boy up.

It was seldom Parno played his chanter without the air bag and drones of his pipes attached. And while he was used to keeping the air bag filled, of course, the chanter was held differently in the lips, and he'd been playing for so long now, while Dhulyn Saw, that a muscle in his lower lip was beginning to cramp. He saw Dhulyn flinch, wrinkling up her nose, and only long force of habit kept him from interrupting his playing, since to do so might interrupt the Vision Dhulyn was sharing with the other Seers. Though they were not perfectly still, they had stopped dancing as soon as the full trance was upon them, and they still clasped hands. Parno was familiar with the effects of Seeing. The Visions were sometimes disturbing, and when they came during sleep, Dhulyn often twitched, moaned, or even spoke aloud. As he watched this time, however, he saw something he had never seen before. Dhulyn's face became at first masklike, and she looked as she did when practicing a *Shora*, calm, determined, concentrating. Then Parno noticed a tremor in her left eyelid, so slight he wasn't sure at first that he'd seen anything. Almost as though she merely *thought* of opening her eyes. The same tremor seemed to possess the other muscles of her face, her neck and shoulders, and even her arms. The other women too were showing the same signs, the same look of fierce concentration, the tiny movements of their muscles, their eyes moving under their closed lids. Parno realized that his own muscles were beginning to vibrate in time to theirs.

As though I were struggling to move against tight bonds, he thought. As though *they* were struggling. Their breathing, which had sounded for a moment as if they were running, had gradually quieted. Dhulyn's body jerked once, twice, as if she were struggling to step away, but then she steadied again. All four were breathing more quietly. Still more quietly. Until they did not appear to breathe at all.

They were not breathing at all.

Parno felt a familiar tightening in his own chest, and the notes of his pipe faltered.

"Demons and perverts." Parno thrust his chanter into his belt and backhanded the woman on Dhulyn's right, sending her sprawling and breaking the link of their hands. He took his Partner by the upper arm and pulled her, unresisting, away from the other Seers. Putting her behind him, he drew his long dagger out from his boot and, holding it in one hand, faced toward the other women. Winter-Ash was still lying on the ground, her hands to her face, and the other two had fallen to their hands and knees. Using his free hand, he took Dhulyn by the nape of the neck and shook her until she coughed, heaved in a great breath of air, another, and then another.

Parno straightened, his arm around Dhulyn's waist, until he was sure she had recovered her wind completely and could stand without help. Something—perhaps the abrupt cessation of the music—had attracted the attention of the nearest Espadryni, and three men were heading toward them. The Seers were sitting up now, and Winter-Ash was touching her face and frowning at him, clearly incredulous.

"I'm going to have a bruise," she said. From the movement of her tongue she was checking for loose teeth.

"A bruise may be the least of your worries, Winter-Ash." Star-Wind held up his hand to the other men who had come running with him and placed himself between Parno and the Seers. "What happened here?"

"We could not return—the shadow—" Dhulyn cleared her throat and spit to one side.

"They were preventing her from awakening, from the look of it," Parno said.

"No." Dhulyn shook her head and winced. "That is not the way of it."

Star-Wind looked the women over. "Well?"

"He struck me," Winter-Ash said. "That's contrary to the Pact."

Star-Wind turned more fully toward her, studying her face as if he could read there the truth he looked for. Winter-Ash's look of righteous indignation faltered, to be replaced by impatience.

"Seers have been known not to return, to die while

Seeing," Star-Wind said finally. "Perhaps now we know why." He turned to the men with him. "Take and bind them. The elders must meet."

"You can't." Winter-Ash was on her feet. "You can't punish us because of something these people have said. They're liars—we were only trying to help them. She asked us to. And *she* was going to help *us,* but she didn't."

"The shamans will decide." Star-Wind nodded to Parno and turned away, ushering the women before him.

"They weren't trying to hurt me," Dhulyn said, turning her face into Parno's shoulder. There was a tremor in her, as if she shivered against the cold, though the sun was warm overhead. He folded her into his arms. "Parno, my soul, they are *whole*. Like the White Twins, they are healthy and whole while in Vision."

"Blooded demons." Parno swallowed. "Why weren't we told? The men must know." What a horror. No wonder Dhulyn was so shocked.

"Can we be sure anyone knows? In the Visions they look for the answer to their breaking. They have Seen that I am somehow involved in it, and Winter-Ash wanted to keep looking for the answer now." Dhulyn coughed again, and licked her lips. "She said it was possible that once they left the Vision, their waking selves would not care enough to pursue the answer again."

"Not care enough?" Parno found that difficult to fathom.

Dhulyn's eyes were squeezed shut. "You should have heard her. In the Vision they were desperate to find out what had happened to them. They wanted to stay until we could find out." Dhulyn blinked, looking at him. "Even after the White Twins joined us, telling us we had stayed for too long, they were willing to risk staying. And now? You heard her, she didn't care that the opportunity had been lost. Only that she would not be blamed for hurting me."

"The White Twins were there?" Parno shook his head. "I don't suppose you learned anything useful."

Dhulyn took a step away, the left corner of her lip lifting in a smile. "That depends on what you mean by useful. A very dark future is coming to this place, though I am still unable to see how or why. And the trader, Bekluth Allain, we are right to think he will help us in some way. I Saw his older self, still alive, still offering aid. There is something the matter with Gun; he is definitely sick, though again, I do not know how or why." She stopped smiling. "I think we did See how the present came about. I saw the Mage's room again. But this time the book was missing, and the Green Shadow exploded into dust and faded away."

"Exploded into dust?" Parno shook his head. That was not what happened in their own world.

"I had an idea about that, and we wanted to go on searching for the answer, but that was when the White Twins came and warned us that it was time to leave the Vision. And though we tried, we could not. We kept Seeing the Green Shadow over and over."

"But the Green Shadow did not rise again in this world, as it did in ours."

"They say not, but . . ." she shrugged. "There *is* something wrong, here. That much is evident." She looked toward the area of the camp where the Espadryni women lived. "And for a moment, while in the Vision, I Saw the answer, I know I did, but now it's gone."

Parno frowned, but he held his tongue. He could tell from the look on Dhulyn's face that she would be asking to share Visions with the Espadryni women again. He could not blame her, but he hoped it would not be soon.

"Mercenaries, will you come? The shamans would examine the Seers who harmed Dhulyn Wolfshead." Scar-Face approached them moments later as they were walking back to their own tent, and they followed him at once to where the Salt Desert People had assembled in the small clearing in front of the chief shaman's tent. This time, along with every adult man in the camp, five of the older women had been included, led by Snow-Moon and sitting cross-legged, off to one side. The Cloud Shaman and Horse Shaman sat facing the assembled Tribe, and Dhulyn and Parno were shown to seats on their left. Star-Wind and another young Horseman sat to the right, closer to the grouped Seers. Only the three accused women were standing, their hands bound in front of them.

Winter-Ash, hair pulled back off her face, was shrugging. "We helped her, showing her what would come in her quest," the woman said. "We showed her our own past, the Vision that comes when we ask what was done to us. But it meant no more to her then to us. She would not stay to help us further, though she must know the answer, seeing that she is 'whole' and 'safe.'"

Winter-Ash's tone was very close to a sneer, and Dhulyn shut her eyes. This was not the attitude that the young woman had shown in the Vision. There she had trusted Dhulyn and believed her—believed also that the damage done to her waking self was real. The difference between the real, whole person and this broken one made Dhulyn feel like weeping.

The Horse Shaman Spring-Flood glanced at Singer of the Grass-Moon, but the old man gestured to him to speak. "Did you force her to help you? Did you deliberately keep her too long in the Vision? She is a guest in our camp," the younger man said, "sent to us by Sun, Moon, and Stars. You are not to harm anyone, not yourselves, not each other, nor any other. That is our Pact."

Winter-Ash shrugged again, lips pursed. "You do not understand the world of Visions. If there was any danger, and I do not say that there was, we were as much affected by it as she. And you see us all, here in front of you, healthy. No harm was done."

"It is an unusual circumstance." Singer of the Grass-Moon's voice was frail, but firm. "We men do not usually interfere in the Seeing of Visions. We would not do so now, except that you, our guests, are touched by it." He looked first toward Parno and Dhulyn, his mouth twisted to one side, and then turned back to face his own people. "We all know that it is not rare for Seers to stay in the world of Visions, to fade and die while there. What are we to think now but that those deaths were deliberate, and that you tried to kill Dhulyn Wolfshead in the way that others have been killed?" There was great bitterness in his face, but under it was a layer of resignation. Winter-Ash looked around her, defiance mixed with indignation on her face.

Dhulyn held up her hand. "I would speak in their defense, if I may." A murmur ran through the men watching, a ripple of movement as they nodded and exchanged looks. There was even some drumming of palms on the ground among the younger men seated toward the back of those assembled. Dhulyn looked at the three accused Seers. Winter-Ash merely shrugged one shoulder, her lips twisted in a confident smile. Night-Sky's eyes were turned downward, as if she studied something on the ground. Feather-Flight was the only one who looked back at Dhulyn, fearful, and apparently wishing to speak.

She might well have died, Dhulyn thought, and these women with her. If it had not been for Parno, and the unique bond they shared as Partners, they might not have come back from the Vision—Dhulyn because she did not know how and the Espadryni women because they could not let go of their hope. And now there was no consciousness of what had passed, what they had lost, in the behavior of the three women. They knew they were to be punished for what had happened, and their reactions were only varying degrees of fear, resentment, and defiance. It did not even occur to them that they should tell the men what really happened when they Saw.

"I am a Mercenary Brother, and many people have tried to kill me," Dhulyn began. "I am not offended, nor frightened, by it. And I assure you these women made no such attempt."

"But in their carelessness—"

It was true, then. The men could not know. Not if they believed the women had no more caring in the Visions than they did in the real world. "They are not careless in the Visions," she said, raising her voice to half-battlefield tones so that all would hear. "They are whole. In the Visions your women are whole."

Spring-Flood looked to his fellow chief, Singer of the Grass-Moon. It seemed to Dhulyn that some unspoken communication, some private consultation, took place between them, reminding her that though Spring-Flood was the least shaman of the Tribe, he was still a Mage. Parno leaned forward, his brow furrowed. *Can he hear them*, she wondered. Was his Pod sense somehow alerted?

"That is why they sometimes don't return," Dhulyn said, as she watched belief slowly replace the shock of denial on the faces around her. "Because when they are whole, they don't want to become broken again; sometimes they cannot face it."

"But why would they not tell us this?" Spring-Flood said.

"Ask them." Dhulyn turned to where the three Seers still stood, awaiting their judgment. "Winter-Ash, why have you women not told the men that you are whole and safe while in your Visions?"

The young woman looked quickly away and back again, as if she sought for the answer that would please. "What is 'whole' and 'safe'? This is only words. We're not such fools. What would that gain us? We are always the same, always what the Caids made us."

Dhulyn turned back to the shaman. "You see? When they are here, they don't feel the difference. They don't feel."

Seventeen

"WE SHOULD BE passing under the courtyard now," Falcos said. They'd come down two sets of narrow stairs, the second little more than steps created by blocks of stone identical to those making up the walls around them, to a passage that was wider but not as tall as those they had already seen. Parno might have had to stoop here, Mar thought, though none of them was tall enough to bother. They passed by an opening to a separate, narrower passage, marked only with the horse head symbol, and kept going.

It had taken them a few minutes of arguing, when they were still standing over the body of the assassin, but they had finally persuaded Falcos that using the throne room, or any other exit within the palace itself, was a bad idea.

"Look," Alaria had finally said. She'd been pointing to the crest sewn on the man's blue tunic. The crest that was identical to the one Julen had on her own tunic. "Even if we knew which rooms are safe from assassins, you won't know which of your own guards can be trusted. We must get you away from the palace entirely. You say the sunburst symbol will lead us out?"

Falcos was shaking his head. "What's to prevent Epion from having guards there to apprehend us?"

"What's to prevent him from having guards anywhere?" Mar had said. "That argument applies to any exit."

"Maybe." Gun had been rubbing at his upper lip, a sure sign of thought. "Epion must know by now that we are not in the Tarkina's suite. If these passages are not flooded with guards loyal to him in the next few minutes, we can be sure that either Epion does not know the mechanisms for all the entrances or that he would prefer to keep the passages . . . well, secret. The conditions we've seen, the dust for example, support that idea. He's sent this one man in, not a squad."

"Then we will have a chance," Alaria had said. "And a better one, as I've said, if we try for this outer exit."

"If you're outside, and safe," Julen had argued. "I can go to House Listra. Once I take this uniform off, no one would be looking for me."

"And if House Listra cannot be trusted?" Falcos had said. But he spoke more in the spirit of someone who wanted to go on arguing than as someone who really meant what he said.

"The worst that will happen," Julen had pointed out, as if she was taking Falcos' question seriously, "is that I will be captured. You will still be free and able to rally your own support. But Listra is the most important House next to the Tarkinate itself. She is chief of the council and has her own allies and connections. She, if anyone, can call for a full investigation and examination of the truth. It is a chance worth taking."

So they had gone on, still with Falcos in the lead, but now heading for the exit outside the walls of palace and town.

"How far outside of Uraklios will we be?" Mar asked. As far as she could tell, this passage was running straight, and it was the longest they'd been in so far.

"My mother never told me."

"And you never tried to find out?" Mar wouldn't have been able to stop herself from trying to explore the secret passages, once she knew they were there.

Falcos glanced back over his shoulder. "Do not think I never looked. You saw for yourself that it took Gundaron to Find the mechanism in my mother's bedroom. I do not think the triggers are such things as can be found by accident."

"And a Tarkin-to-be's time is kept quite full," Alaria said. "He is watched more carefully than you might think and is hardly ever left alone."

Interesting, Mar thought. Not what Alaria said but that she felt motivated to say it. *Clear enough whose side* she's *on.*

Mar had made up her mind that they would likely have quite a walk ahead of them, so it was a pleasant surprise when Falcos stopped at another set of steps, these leading upward. The young Tarkin, holding his upper lip in his teeth, looked up and around them, back the way they had come, and up the stairs.

"Unless I'm completely turned around, I think we're under the olive grove to the west of the palace," he said. "Gundaron, where is the Path of the Sun?"

"There." Gun pointed up, and to the right.

Falcos nodded. "As I thought. There's a small shrine to Mother Sun in the center of the grove, and I'd wager we are under it now. Gundaron?"

"Third stone up from the top step, left-hand side." Falcos started up the steps. "But if I might make a suggestion?"

Halfway up, Falcos stopped and turned back.

"The Mercenaries say that you plan for what can happen, not for what might happen. The possible, not the probable." Gun jerked his head toward the exit. "Remember what we said. It's possible Epion knows there's an exit here and that someone is waiting above."

Falcos sat down on the steps, rubbing at his forehead with his fingers. "So there is no escape for us this way, after all," he said finally.

Mar's heart felt like lead in her chest. This didn't seem like the kind of answer Gun's Mark could Find for them.

"Not necessarily." They all turned to look at Julen. "Epion has guards who are willing to detain you based on the suspicions he has created, but he cannot have many. As you pointed out, he sent in only the one assassin—though he may have had good reason for that. We have here three swords and a formidable bow. Even the Scholars have daggers, and I'd wager that the friends of Mercenary Brothers have learned a trick or two. Luck has been with us so far."

Falcos stood up again. "Any more suggestions, Scholar?"

Gun's eyes swiveled sideways until he was looking at Mar. She knew as much about strategy as he. "We're prepared to fight, and we should also prepare for capture," she said. "If Gun and I were soldiers, I'd say that Alaria and the

Tarkin should go back down the passage, far enough to be outside the circle of light, while the three of us went ahead. As it is, we're the least use in a fight, so we should be the ones to hang back. If things go well, we rejoin you—"

"And if they don't go well, you are still free and the most likely to find your way out to help," Julen finished for her. The guard turned back to Falcos. "I agree, my lord. This is a good plan."

It was hard to sit quietly in the dark, ears straining to pick up any noise that might tell them the fate of their friends. It was easy to imagine noises that weren't there. If they'd had Mercenary training . . .

"I wish we knew one of the Hunting *Shoras*," Gun said, almost echoing Mar's thoughts.

"If we did, we'd be up there with swords in our hands, not back here in the dark," she said. She got to her feet, unable to stay sitting down, no matter how much more sensible it was to rest. "What's taking so long?"

Gun stood also and, feeling for her in the dark, put his arm around her. "It always feels longer when you are the one waiting," he reminded her. "Julen's cautious; she'll be making sure Falcos and Alaria are safely hidden before she comes back for us."

Mar nodded, but her heart wasn't in it. "I have a bad feeling about this," she whispered.

Moments later footsteps in the dark seemed, at first, to deny her fears, but then Mar realized that the footsteps came unaccompanied by any light. Gun squeezed her to him and then stepped away. Mar licked her lips and, as silently as she could, drew the dagger she had at her waist, using the space Gun had given her. She felt cautiously for the wall and oriented herself next to it. They might not be soldiers, but they could at least try to defend themselves. She might even remember one or two of the moves Dhulyn Wolfshead had once shown her.

"Scholars?" came the whisper in the dark, and Mar relaxed. Finally, Julen had come for them. "Scholars?"

"Here." There was no point in moving from where they were; they would only bump into the guard in the dark.

"Have you a light?"

Mar heard scraping, and then had to shut her eyes

against the sudden glare of Gun's candle. What she saw brought her hand to her mouth.

Julen was bleeding from a cut on her sword arm, and her left arm hung limp from her shoulder.

"It's only dislocated, I think." Julen bared her teeth in a parody of a smile. They showed bloody. "There was almost a squad waiting." She spat to one side, grimacing. "So much for all our logic. Falcos managed to shut the opening, and as he does not know the trigger from the outside, they cannot come in after us."

Gun had handed Mar the candle and was now supporting the guard with his own shoulder under her good one. "Epion knows at least one other entrance," he reminded them.

"Which is why we'll have to get out as quick as we can, Scholar."

"No," Mar said. "Give these people time to get back and Epion time to call off his other guards. Now that he has Falcos and Alaria, he doesn't really care about us. He might leave one or two people to watch, but no squads as he had here. That will give us a better chance." They'd been wrong once already, but surely logic couldn't *always* be wrong?

"But Mar, Julen's hurt."

"The stables," Julen said, jaws clenched. "I know the place like my tongue knows my teeth. There're only so many places the entrance can be, and the sensible place to put watchers . . ." she shut her eyes as if she were trying to visualize the area she was describing. "We would have good odds, I think. And my father will be there to help us."

"To help *you*," Gun said. Julen twisted her head to look at him. "Think about it," he said. "We'll get you there and get the door open, but I think there's a better place for Mar and me to go." Even as he was talking, he had gestured to Mar to lead the way back to where the side passage led to the stables. Mar picked up Gun's pack and set off, holding her pace to what Julen could manage.

"You're to go to House Listra, according to the Tarkin's instructions; she'll at least be able to put a stop to any further assassination attempts. But I'm afraid the only people we can absolutely trust to help us have gone where neither you nor the House can find them," Gun said. "And by the time they get back with the real killer, it may be too late for us."

Mar nodded without turning around. She saw where Gun was going. "We need the Mercenaries."

"I agree," Julen said. "Judgment given by Mercenaries would be acceptable to most if not all of the council. But they have gone through the Path of the Sun, where we cannot follow."

"Ordinarily, I'd agree, but I think I could Find Dhulyn Wolfshead," he said. "No matter what was between us, I think I could Find her."

Mar's lips spread in a wide smile, and she had to catch herself from walking faster.

Dhulyn sat cross-legged on a pile of fleeces facing the Cloud Shaman, Singer of the Grass-Moon. Spring-Flood, the Horse Shaman, sat to the old man's right. Star-Wind and Scar-Face sat close behind the Shamans. Grass-Moon reached out toward her, and Dhulyn placed her hands in his. It was the first time, she realized, that any of the Salt Desert People had offered to touch her.

"My daughter," Grass-Moon said, "the news that you give us of our Seers—there is no manner in which I can convey our gratitude. It has been many years, since I was a young man, that the Seers have spoken regularly of the one who would come to make them whole. We had long given up hope that those old Visions would ever come to pass."

"There is no way to know if I am that person," Dhulyn protested. "We Saw nothing just now that gave us such an answer."

The old man inclined his head, gripping her hands more tightly. "I have spoken with Winter-Ash, Night-Sky, and Feather-Flight, and they agree that the Seers who appeared to you stated that you have the answer. It seems clear to me that it will be only a matter of time until it becomes apparent."

The White Twins *had* told her she had the answer, Dhulyn thought. So there was something she had already Seen that would provide a clue, if only she could think what it was.

Grass-Moon leaned forward and kissed the back of her left hand, his lips cool and papery against her skin. "Only telling us that the Seers are whole while in Visions gives us so much hope, that we could live upon it for years, if that should prove necessary."

"If I could experience Visions with them again," Dhulyn said. "Perhaps, now that I know the answer is there, I could revisit the Sight with fresh eyes."

"I have asked, of course I have." The crease of his forehead showed Dhulyn what answer he'd received. "They say no, their interest and curiosity in this matter have passed, and we would not force them, even if we could." He gave her hands a final squeeze and released her. "But as I said, you have given us so much to hope for, and I will remain optimistic. In the meantime, you have your own mission here; do you pursue it, and perhaps our Seers will change their minds, or, and this seems to me very likely, the Seers of one of the other Tribes will be inclined to join with you."

Dhulyn leaned back, letting her wrists fall to rest on her knees. It would almost be a relief, she thought, to return to something as relatively uncomplicated as finding a killer.

"What can we do to help you with your mission?" Spring-Flood asked.

Dhulyn exchanged glances with Parno. This was the first time the Salt Desert Tribe had offered active help. Until now, they had merely been given the freedom to go where they would.

"The person we look for is someone who can pass through the Sun's Door," Parno said, "but whose comings and goings are not watched over."

"It is most unlikely to be a man of the Espadryni," The old Singer said. Again, Dhulyn and Parno exchanged looks. They had been reluctant to make such a suggestion themselves, it was a relief to have it so calmly addressed for them.

"Not so many of us know the clue of passing through the Door," Spring-Flood said. "And it is clear to those who can who their brethren are—the ability cannot be hidden. And except for someone who is performing the vigil and meditation for the attempt, no Espadryni is alone."

"Your pardon," Parno said. "We have been told that one does not have to be a shaman to pass the Door and that the clue is sometimes shared."

The two men exchanged smiles. "Truly, anyone who knows the clue may use the Door, though they do not always return," Grass-Moon said in his thin voice. "But in order to discover the clue, one must have the true magic."

"Then a shaman is *somehow* involved," Dhulyn said. "Do the people of fields and towns have any Mages among them?"

"Not that we have ever heard," the Horse Shaman said. "I believe we would have, but in truth our connection with them is limited." He paused, frowning slightly. "What of the trader, Bekluth Allain? He travels widely, and his schedule is not so regular that we would greatly question when he comes and goes."

"The Visions show that he's to be of some help to us," Dhulyn added.

"Nothing makes greater sense," Grass-Moon said. "He is not a Mage, that I can assure you, but he may have seen or heard something the significance of which has not yet struck him."

"The Long Trees boy, Ice Hawk," Parno said. "He was doing his vigil at the time of the last killing, and he never mentioned seeing the trader, or anyone else. It seems far more likely that the killer was able to avoid the boy's notice."

"Making it more likely that he is a Mage of some sort."

"Well, we have dealt with Mages before," Dhulyn said. "We will deal with this one."

Singer of the Grass-Moon made a signal, and Star-Wind came forward to help him to his feet. "Do you consider what your next action will be, my daughter. In the meantime, I cannot delay longer sharing the knowledge and hope we now have with the other Tribes."

Delos Egoyin felt once more around the pastern of the black horse's off hind hoof. His fingers moved as of their own accord, while his eyes, seemingly squinched up in concentration, allowed him to watch the guard standing in the courtyard without attracting any notice. He lowered the hoof to the ground and straightened with his hands to his lower back before patting the horse's rump. He nodded to the groom Melos, who held the black's head, and stood watching as the horse was led away.

Five guards, half a squad, had appeared just after the

midday meal, spread themselves out through the stable precincts and tried to look as though they were doing nothing
but lounge in the sun. Delos had known better. He'd already heard the rumors that were flying—ridiculous stories
that Falcos was mad, that the old Tarkin's line was cursed,
that Falcos had been the one who killed the Princess Cleona, and even that the boy had killed his own father.

Delos snorted. As if anyone who knew the boy would
believe such a thing. You had only to see him around the
horses and other animals to know Falcos was not mad—or
cursed either for that matter. Humans could be fooled,
some very easily, but animals? That was something altogether different. By the Caids, even the barn cats liked him,
and they cared for no one.

Delos began to rub his hands clean on the piece of old
cloth he carried for that purpose, hanging from his belt.

Eventually another guard, this one in what everyone
now considered Epion Akarion's colors, had come and sent
the other guards away and stayed here himself.

Where was Dav-Ingahm, Delos wondered. Surely it was
the job of the Steward of Walls to station the guard, not
Epion Akarion. Something was definitely going on. Something more than met the eye. Which undoubtedly meant
something wrong. Delos tucked the cloth away again and
followed after Melos and the black horse, but only far
enough to stand in the shadow of the open stable door.

There. The guard was moving again now he thought no
one was looking. Going to pass through the circuit he'd
done twice already. Into the main stable block, where young
Thea had seen him go right back to the farthest corner, past
where the Arderon queens were still settled, awaiting the
birth of the last foal. He'd hovered there a while, seeming to
check the stonework, before coming out again into the
courtyard and then to the old hound kennels, empty now
that the dogs had been moved to a section closer to the
outer wall. Out from the old kennels and into the mews,
where he must have moved quietly enough not to disturb
the hunting birds.

The guard's movements resembled nothing so much as a
patrol, but what could he be watching for in these older
parts of the stable buildings? Nothing good, Delos would
wager. There was no longer a large staff working under him,

but every youngster was handpicked, and Delos had several of them strategically placed through the buildings, hidden in spots that would allow them to watch the guard's movements. As the man passed this time, Delos eased out of the shadow of the door to follow.

As expected, the man went down the main aisle between the larger horse boxes, with Delos drifting like a shadow in his wake, taking the shortcut behind the empty stalls and coming around a stack of hay that only appeared to go back to the walls. There was Melos, crouching under the very belly of the black horse. He nodded as Delos caught his eye and pointed to the rear of the building. There was Thea, hidden in the shadow of the great water trough, the one that caught the rain from off the roof. She touched her left eye and held her hand, palm down, in front of her face.

In answer to her instruction, Delos turned and rounded the stalls that held the Arderon queens on the left side, the feeding side rather than the wider, more obvious passage on the right, where the stall openings allowed for the movement of the horses themselves. He followed the sounds as the guard moved all the way through the building, past row after row of unused stalls. Delos had opened the roof vents, both for light and air, and to give the guard no reason to light a torch.

Finally the sounds of walking ceased, and Delos slowed, creeping forward as quietly as he was able to where he could just make out the guard. As Thea had said, the man appeared to be scanning the stonework, as if looking for something that had been attached to the wall. Delos squinted. He knew this part of the building as well as anyone. He could remember, when he had first come to be his aunt's assistant, that there had still been a few horses kept down here, old horses who would have been upset if they had been moved. Everything was empty now, swept clean and tidy, but left ready, as if the horses were expected back any day. The feed and water troughs were maintained in good condition, and even the old oaken bars for temporary gates, were left resting in their places.

And there was the guard, Gabe-Leggett, Delos thought his name was, standing at the wall, hands on hips, looking up and around just as Thea had described him. Delos was weighing the likelihood of getting some questions answered by simply walking out and surprising the man when he was startled himself by a noise like trying to sharpen a rock on a grindstone. He was lucky the guard was facing in the other direction, Delos thought, or he'd have given himself away.

But the guard didn't seem startled at all, the old stable man noted. He just stepped back and drew his sword. Whatever was happening, it came as no surprise to him.

Delos edged himself around to the open end of the last stall, trusting that the sounds of grinding stone would cover any noises he made. Moving forward, closer to where the guard stood braced, his sword in his hand, Delos wrapped his fingers around one of the oak bars, longer than a man's arm and a good four fingers' thick, that would have been used, once upon a time, to close off the open end of the old stall. Slowly, conscious of how his knees protested so much squatting and crawling, Delos straightened and hefted the bar.

Standing, he could see what he had only been hearing to this point. A large stone at the base of the wall was moving slowly outward, as if being pushed from behind. Delos' eyebrows crept up, and the hairs on his arms stood on end. Finally the stone cleared the wall, and an opening was revealed behind it. The guard moved not a muscle, seeming not even to breathe, and for a moment long enough to make Delos' feel the tension in his arms and shoulders, there was no sound.

Then, as if the silence had been some kind of encouragement, a single hand appeared from behind the stone. It was grimy and had a long scratch across the knuckles. But Delos would know that hand anywhere. He had held it many times in his own when it was much smaller. He had put the first sword into it.

Without making any noise himself, he stepped forward and struck the guard a heavy blow on the back of the head.

⚓

"Do you need the bowl?"

Gun dropped his hand away from his forehead and turned toward where Mar made a darker shadow against the rock formation that was the entrance to the Path. "We don't have it?"

"Well, no."

"Then I guess it's a good thing I don't need it." He felt rather than saw her recoil. "Sorry, love. I'm just trying not to borrow things to worry about. We couldn't have known we'd need the bowl when we left our own rooms."

When they'd come out in the stable to find Julen's father, Delos Egoyin, standing over the unconscious body of one of Epion's guards, they'd decided not to use the passage to get outside after all. Delos, once he'd understood why they had to go, and where, and after enlisting the help of his staff, had been able to smuggle them out of the stable precincts with little difficulty, in the back of a wagon. But going back through the palace, particularly into the Tarkin's wing, had been out of the question.

"It's just that I remember Dhulyn Wolfshead telling me never to be without it," Mar said.

"I don't think I'd need the bowl to find the Wolfshead any more than I would to Find you. Not after we—" he gestured in the air. "Not after we were linked in Imrion. I don't think the . . . the *Mark* forgets that." He looked into the sky. "I wish there was more light." It was only just dark enough for the stars to be appearing. The moon would not rise for a few hours yet. Hours he somehow felt they did not have.

"Are you sure we shouldn't wait until morning?" Mar said in an eerie echo of his own thoughts.

"I'm sure," he said. "I don't know why I'm sure, but I am."

"Can I do *anything* that will help you?"

Gun rubbed at his upper lip. He usually had something like the bowl or a page of writing to help him achieve the trancelike state that would allow him to Find. There was nothing like that in the packs Alaria had left with them, even if there were light enough to see by.

"Can you sing?" he said. "You know, the 'Weeping Maid' song."

Without other answer, Mar cleared her throat and began to sing the children's song they both associated with their time in Imrion, the song that Dhulyn Wolfshead had proved was an ancient trigger for the Mark.

"Weeping maid, weeping maid,
Hold with all your might, win your heart's delight."

A part of Gun was aware that Mar continued singing, but the rest of him saw

❧

shadows forming around him, aisles stretching away from him, shelves looming above his head, filled with books and scrolls. The spines of the books and the ribbons of the scrolls are of all colors, but as he begins to walk through the library, this changes, until almost all the colors he sees are blue, and green, with a few clear lines of black, and others of the dark red of old blood. He knows that these colors are Dhulyn's, and he's relieved that his plan is working. These are the colors of her Mercenary badge, with the black lines that show she's Partnered and the blood-red of her hair. The aisle narrows as he walks faster and faster, and the colors grow more intense, the books cleaner, smelling of new leather. He squeezes around a final shelf of books, and she is there, perched with one hip on the edge of a table, her sword lying next to her, an open book in her left hand. She looks up at him and smiles.

"Dhulyn," he says.

❧

And then he was back, standing next to Mar, but the thread of colored light, blue and green, black and red, was still with him, stretched out in front of him, leading them into the Path.

"Is it there," Mar said, "The clue?"

Gun nodded and reached out for her hand. "We just have to follow it," he said. "Whatever happens, we just follow it.

❧

"You'll come to wish you'd taken Epion's offer to be rid of me." Falcos' voice rumbled in his chest. He sat in the armchair next to the open hearth in the center of the room, leaning forward with his elbows on his knees and his head hanging down. When Alaria had refused to leave him, they had not been returned to either the Tarkin's or the Tarkina's suites but were sent to one of the older guest suites in the northern end of the palace. At least Falcos was fairly sure no secret passage came into this room.

"No such fool, me," Alaria said from where she sat on the edge of the cold hearth. "And not that good an actress either. I don't see how Epion would believe I'd go with him happily, not after I tried to escape with you." Alaria wrinkled her nose. She was glad to hear her voice was steady, with none of the squeakiness of the fear she felt. "I don't trust him, and he can't trust me. No, I'm safer here with you, no matter how bleak things look at the moment."

He tilted his head, drawing his eyebrows down in a frown. "You really are *that* certain, then, that what Epion says of me is not true?" He continued to look at her, eyebrows raised. He needed more. They had been so rushed, events had moved so quickly, this was the first chance they'd had to think about what they'd done and the choices they'd made.

"I said it before, the horses like you," Alaria said finally. She raised one shoulder and let it drop. "I know that sounds simple. People say things like that about their dogs and cats all the time. But the queens really are sensitive to people, especially now, when they're foaling. They've been trained for generations to accompany the Tarkins of Arderon. More than once, when there were several candidates for the throne, the queens have been used to chose the most suitable. So for us, when our horses like you, it means something."

Falcos sat up and smiled, but looked away, rubbing at his eyes with his fingertips. Could he be crying?

"Do you think Epion might be the killer?" she asked, as much to change the subject as to give Falcos time to control himself.

"I know he isn't," he said.

Alaria frowned. "How can you know?"

"The same way he knows it isn't me." Falcos stood and walked over to the windows, as if to check, once again, that there was no escape that way. They opened onto the same gorge that Alaria's suite had faced, but with no balcony. "I was with him when your cousin was killed." He turned back to her. "But that doesn't mean he isn't using the killer somehow, as he's accused me of doing."

Alaria shook her head. "I don't believe this. *This* is why my mother stays away from court. She always said the closer you were to the throne, the less likely you were to know what was really important." Heat rushed over her face. "I beg your pardon, Falcos Tarkin. I spoke without thinking."

But he was laughing, and part of her rejoiced to see it. "Don't think your mother is so far wrong," he said. "My father would often say much the same thing. It's a terrible job, he used to say to me. Watch carefully those who think they want it."

"Like Epion?"

"Like Epion."

"I guess you weren't watching him closely enough."

"I'm not as good a Tarkin as my father was."

"I know what my mother would say to *that*."

"What?"

"Stop your whining."

The instant they stepped into the Path of the Sun, Gun saw that the phenomenon he'd experienced in the underground room held good here as well; the Finding clue that led him forward toward his goal glowed slightly in the dark, just enough that once his eyes became accustomed to it, it illuminated the surroundings so that—

Mar stepped on the back of his foot.

"Sorry." Her voice sounded hollow, as if they were in fact underground, whereas Gun knew very well . . . he looked up. There was nothing but blackness above them, no stars, no moon. He lifted the hand that wasn't holding Mar's, but if there was a ceiling up there it was too far away for him to reach.

"I forgot you can't see," he said, lowering his hand.

"And you can?"

"The clue sheds a kind of light," he said. "Just enough that I can place my feet and make out a bit of the wall."

Mar reached to one side, bending slightly until her fingers scraped the wall to their left. "It feels like dressed stone," she said. "And it's much cooler in here."

"Does it sound to you as though we were in a tunnel? Underground?"

"Wooooo." Mar's hoot echoed back to them. "Yes, it does."

"Wait, hold on, here's the first turning."

"It's much farther in than what you can see from outside."

Gun considered, thinking back to when they had all

been up on the cliffside, looking down on the Path. Had it been only three days ago?

"I don't think the inside of this has anything to do with what you can see from the outside." Gun drew Mar's arm into his. It would make them no less mobile than having Mar stumbling around in the dark, and what they would lose in mobility, they would more than gain in morale.

"At least with it so dark we won't be tempted by different turnings and pathways," Mar said. "We can't even see them."

"We couldn't go astray in any case," Gun said firmly. "We only have to follow the clue." *And not get separated*, he said to himself, knowing he didn't need to say it aloud.

The distance to the next turning was very much shorter, and for the next two hundred paces or so they wound around and around, sometimes to the right, sometimes to the left, until Gun felt sure he was getting dizzy. Finally the clue stretched out in front of him, a long line that seemed almost to disappear in the far distance.

"Looks like a long straight stretch coming up now," he told Mar.

"Good. Can we sit down for a minute? My left foot is starting to cramp."

Gun could just make out Mar as she took off the half boot and handed it to him. "Since you're the one who can see," she said. "Don't lose that."

"I'm sorry," he said. "I keep forgetting you can't see anything. This must be much harder on you than it is on me."

"I don't know," Mar said. "It's beginning to seem normal to me, as if we'd been in here for days—but we can't have been, can we? I mean, I'm not even hungry."

Gun rubbed at his upper lip. Surely they hadn't been walking the Path long enough for Mar's mind to begin to drift? Still, with nothing to concentrate her attention . . . "Recite me something," Gun said. "Keep your mind focused while I concentrate on Finding."

Every Scholar in every Library knew dozens of books and scrolls by heart, usually the basic ones of their own specialty. But each also memorized a book their Library had only one copy of, both as a precaution against the loss of that copy, and as an item of knowledge to trade at another

Library when traveling. As they continued following the blue-green clue, Gun wasn't surprised that Mar chose to recite from her own personal book, *Air and Fire*, which told the tales of three sisters who had left their home to seek their fortunes. In a way, that was what Mar had done when she'd left her foster home with the Weavers in Navra and set out to find her real family in Imrion.

Instead she'd found Gun, and the Scholar's life.

"What is it?" she said. "You're squeezing my arm."

"Nothing," he said, glad the dark covered his smile. "I was just thinking how happy I am to be here."

"I hope by 'here' you mean with me, and not stuck in this particular place." He could hear the warmth and laughter in her voice. He started to answer her in the same way.

"I think you know—" he fell to his knees, clutching his forehead between his hands.

"Gun. Gun, what is it?" Mar was on her knees beside him, feeling for his head and clutching at his sleeves. He had to steel himself not to push her away, to remind himself that she couldn't see, and that if she lost her sense of where he was, she might never find him again.

"I was dizzy," he said. "It was as if I were falling, as though I were suddenly going uphill, then down, and then the ground just fell out from under me."

"But the ground's level here," Mar said. "The floor's as smooth as a sanded tabletop."

Gun swallowed against the nausea in his throat, licked his lips, and forced his eyes open. The clue was still there, still leading away, blue and green, red and black.

"I'm all right," he said. "Just give me a minute." Clinging to her, Gun managed to get back on his feet. His head felt hollow and seemed to want to sway from side to side. Mar, evidently sensing something was wrong even though she couldn't see him, pulled his left arm over her shoulders and propped him up.

"You lead," she said. "I'll make sure you don't fall down again."

Leaning heavily on Mar, Gun reached out for the clue, wishing that it were solid. If he held his hand between it and himself, he could concentrate better, seeing his hand silhouetted against the colors of the clue. He closed one eye. That seemed to help. He could feel Mar murmuring, still reciting from the first book of *Air and Fire* under her breath as they went around yet another corner.

"Is the ground slanting downward?" he asked.

"Yes," Mar said.

A searing light stabbed through Gun's right eye, like a cold dagger into his brain. He hissed in his breath, gasping for air.

"Push your breath out," Mar said, holding him up in her arms. "The Wolfshead says you're stronger on the exhales."

"Curse the *blooded* Wolfshead." Nevertheless Gun struggled to push out his breath through his clenched teeth. "What's that blooded light?"

"The sun," Mar said. "We're here."

Gun blinked at the harshness of the sunlight. The world seemed still to be spinning, and his stomach turned over. He blinked again and squinted.

"The clue is gone," he said.

Eighteen

PARNO FOUND DHULYN fastening the ties on her bedroll. His own was already neatly tied and placed next to his open pack. They had waited until morning, to give the Seers a chance to change their minds, but no summons had come from them.

"You didn't pack my pipes," he said, seeing them still out on the pallet where Delvik Bloodeye had lain.

"You like to do that yourself." Dhulyn tightened the strap on her own pack and straightened, automatically checking the placement of sword, boot daggers, sleeve knives, and the small ax that hung between her shoulder blades. Parno watched her for a moment before turning to his pipes, detaching the drones and the chanter from the air bag and slipping each one into the padded sleeve designed for it in the roll of felted cloth.

"You are sure you would not like to wait longer, give them more time?" he said, without turning toward her.

"While we are giving them more time, we can look for our killer." She pushed her hands into the small of her back and stretched until the muscles cracked. "There are others who depend upon our help, besides the women of the Espadryni."

Parno pressed his lips together and finished closing the heavy silk bag that held his pipes. No point in talking about it any further just now. He knew that tone.

A shadow darkened the doorway to the tent. Parno was relieved to see Dhulyn turn immediately, her hand already reaching for a weapon, and turning the movement into a gesture of welcome when she saw Star-Wind. Whatever thoughts were distracting her, it did not interfere with her reflexes. She would be herself again.

"You *are* going then," the junior shaman said, as his glance through the tent took in their packing. His tone was wistful, as if he would like to ask them to stay if he could think of a reason. Finally, he cleared his throat. "I will ride a short way with you."

"We thank you for your courtesy," Parno said. He slung his pipes over his left shoulder and hefted his pack in his other hand. He expected Star-Wind's offer was more an excuse to stay close to Dhulyn than an act of courtesy to departing guests.

They walked together through the camp to the horse lines. There was no sign of any of the women, and very few even of the children were out of their tents. The men they passed all paused in their work to greet them civilly, and some showed an inclination to follow along until a gesture from Star-Wind returned them to their tasks. When they arrived at the horse line, a young boy, the ghost eye clear on his forehead, stood beside Star-Wind's horse. He waited while Dhulyn and Parno saddled their own horses, and even though it was clear they would need nothing further, he hovered until Star-Wind once more waved him away. Star-Wind grabbed a handful of mane and swung himself onto his horse's back without benefit of either saddle or bridle.

Touching her forehead to those who lifted a hand to them as they rode, Dhulyn chose the most direct route away from the camp.

"There are some who are asking that Winter-Ash be punished for endangering you," Star-Wind said after they had been riding a short time. It was clear that he was addressing Dhulyn, but Parno noticed that he looked away from her. So he did not notice immediately that she had stopped.

"We must go back," she said. "They did not endanger me; they would not, not while we are in Vision."

"No need," Star-Wind said. "Both Cloud and Horse Shamans have spoken against it."

"It is hard, when I see the old woman, Snow-Moon, crippled, not to be afraid that the same may come to Winter-Ash through my fault."

"It is used only rarely, but there are things we cannot let go unpunished. Snow-Moon would have allowed her child to starve from neglect, even after she had been warned three times."

Dhulyn nodded, but it was easy to see she was only partly convinced. Star-Wind sighed, and his voice hardened.

"What would you have us do? Confine the worst ones? In the cities, perhaps, that might be possible, but we cannot be so soft here. It is impossible. They know the meaning of the Pact, and they must all see that punishment comes swiftly." There was regret in his voice, but there was impatience also.

"Your pardon, Star-Wind of the Salt Desert, it is not my place to approve, or disapprove. Forgive me." Dhulyn inclined her head in a short bow. It was against the Mercenaries' own Common Rule for her to comment on the political or social structure of another society. The Brotherhood was always neutral.

Except when we're not, Parno thought, remembering a couple of slavers he and Dhulyn had once waylaid and killed.

Star-Wind accepted Dhulyn's apology with a shallow bow of his own. "Where do you begin your search for the killer, Dhulyn Wolfshead?"

"We'll follow your back trail to the place where you found our injured Brothers," Dhulyn said. "He said they had been following some trace of the killer when they fell into the orobeast trap. Perhaps there will still be something for us to see."

"There has been rain toward the Door, but perhaps not as far as the place you wish to go. That is the direction you want," Star-Wind said, indicating the northwest. "We were three days from here when our scouts found Delvik Bloodeye. But that was our whole camp, women, children, and all. You should make better time, only the two of you." He spun his horse around to face them. "We look forward to your return. Farewell, Dhulyn Wolfshead, Parno Lionsmane. Sun warm you, Moon and Stars light your way."

"And yours, Star-Wind of the Salt Desert."

*　　*　　*

"You are very quiet, my heart." They had ridden much of the day in a more or less comfortable silence, with Dhulyn answering whenever Parno had spoken to her but offering no conversation herself. Now she straightened in the saddle and seemed to give herself a shake.

"I am feeling low," she said, in a voice that matched her words.

Parno felt a jolt of alarm pass over his midsection. Except when she had an obvious injury, Dhulyn rarely admitted to feeling any kind of pain, still less an emotional one.

"Should we have rested longer after your ordeal with the Seers?"

Dhulyn shook her head, but the frown of abstraction didn't leave her face. "You did not meet them, the unbroken women; no one ever has. And they might have been punished—crippled—because of me."

The alarm rang louder. Dhulyn never felt sorry for herself. Parno inhaled deeply and prepared to go to work.

"I see," he said in a tone that suggested a challenge. "When I worry about killing people, you roll your eyes to Sun, Moon, and Stars, and my concerns are dismissed as unfortunate remnants of my overly refined upbringing in a Noble House. But when *you* are worried about women who are not even going to be punished because of you, then I'm supposed to be full of sympathy, hold your hand, wipe away your tears, and say, 'There, there, it's all right, my sweet one'?"

The dark look that Dhulyn shot at him gave Parno hope.

"You've never been in favor of needless killing," he pointed out, returning to his normal tone. "Or maiming."

"Luckily for you."

Parno smiled. *She's back*, he thought, but he said nothing else out loud. Dhulyn might speak more about it now, once she'd begun—or not. But she already seemed more her normal self, and she had stopped her unhealthy brooding over the difficult circumstances of the Espadryni.

They had ridden perhaps half a span farther, when Dhulyn took in a deep breath and shook her hair back from her face. It had grown long enough that the braids and tails she wove it into were brushing her shoulders. Soon she would be able to tie it back with some hope that it wouldn't escape.

"It is not," she said, "that I ever expected to return to my home." Parno waited, knowing there was more. "There was never any hope of that, and I have always known it. But I feel an echo of that loss when I look at these people, so like the people of my childhood and yet so unlike." Dhulyn turned to him, her blood-red brows raised in question, and Parno nodded his understanding and encouragement.

"They did not know that the women are whole while in Vision—and what could they have done differently, what *can* they do, now that they know? Star-Wind says they are doing the best they can. I wonder if my own people would have done the same. Did they face a similar dilemma—not the same one, obviously—and choose to allow the breaking of the Tribes rather than live on in some distorted version of themselves?"

"Their choice led to life for you and, eventually, freedom, safety—well," Parno amended when Dhulyn grinned. "As safe as a Mercenary's life can be." He shrugged. "I won't complain of a decision that led to the two of us riding together, as we are now. But that is easy for me to say—I lost nothing by it. And from what we've been told, the choice *these* Espadryni made must also have been a difficult one, if in a different way." Parno cast about for the words he needed to express his thoughts. "It's not as if the Marked gradually became broken and soulless, over generations. These people had to cope, not with a *change* in their circumstances, but with the very circumstances themselves."

Dhulyn nodded, but slowly, more as if she were acknowledging he'd spoken than as if she agreed with him. Parno edged Warhammer nearer to her until he could nudge her knee with his own. "If their choice was annihilation or sequestration, perhaps they really are doing their best."

Dhulyn raised her hand toward him, palm out. "I know that the Seers would not be alive at all if the men did not take these precautions, however harsh. I merely wondered if my own people would have chosen differently."

It was evident, Parno thought, that Dhulyn would have done so. But how much of that was the effect of Mercenary Schooling, where the Common Rule taught them not to fear death, but to accept it as something that would come to all.

They had stopped to eat and were sharing a travel cake

and a dried sausage when Parno returned to the subject from another angle.

"Do I imagine it, or did the Salt Lake People seem much less comfortable with us at first than those of the Long Trees?"

"The Long Trees had no women with them," Dhulyn pointed out. "Isolated, with nothing to compare me to, they reacted to *me*, to *who* I am, and not so much to *what* I am."

"Now, of course, it is both." Parno handed Dhulyn her half of the travel cake. "Your presence is now both a constant reminder of what their own women are not and a symbol of what they can become."

Dhulyn bit off a piece of cake, chewed and swallowed. "Perhaps. If I am indeed the one they wait for."

"You feel no closer to the answer?"

"Are the White Twins correct? Is there some detail I have already Seen but don't understand? And they seemed to say, too, that I had the answer to the question of the killer as well."

"Obviously the trader is part of the clue. What did you think of him?"

Dhulyn frowned. "A little too charming for my taste, too easily my friend."

Parno grinned. Dhulyn was notoriously reserved, even among the Brotherhood. "A trader who doesn't charm is a trader without custom."

They could not stretch out their meal any longer and were soon back on the road. Even after almost half a moon, they had no trouble following the back trail of the Salt Desert Tribe. The signs were still clear: the cropped grass, the hoof marks of horses both mounted and running free, the animal dung, even the marks of nightly cooking fires carefully dispersed. They were moving much faster than the Tribe had been able to, but still they held their horses to a fast walk, keeping a sharp eye out, Dhulyn looking on one side, Parno the other, for the signs of scouts returning to the main body of the Tribe with horses carrying extra weight.

Only when the angle of the setting sun made it useless to look for tracks did Dhulyn agree to stop for the night.

"We really didn't need to be so careful today," Parno said. He watched as Dhulyn cleaned and skinned a rabbit she'd shot as they rode. "Star-Wind said they were three days out at least when their outriders found our Brothers in the trap. We're at least a day's ride away ourselves." He handed her the skewer from their parcel of cooking implements.

"Better cautious than cursing," Dhulyn said.

The rabbit was a small one, and they made short work of it. Parno was wondering whether to break out his pipes for some music—perhaps he could even encourage Dhulyn to sing—when she broke the silence herself.

"I'd better take the first watch."

Parno tilted his head to look at her more closely by the flickering light of the fire. "It's my turn," he said.

"I don't feel like sleeping just yet," Dhulyn said. She hesitated, frowning, before adding, "I am a little afraid of having a Vision, to be honest." She blinked and looked away. "I fear meeting them again and seeing their real selves. It would break my heart." She sighed.

Parno rocked back a bit in surprise, then nodded. "I can see that," he said. "No pun intended. Come." He shifted until he was sitting leaning against his pack and saddle. "Put your head in my lap and sleep," he told her. "If you are Seeing and I think you're in a bad way, I'll wake you."

DHULYN NOW KNOWS THAT THE THIN, SANDY-HAIRED MAN IS BEKLUTH AL-LAIN. HE IS STILL WEARING THE GOLD RINGS IN HIS EARS, BUT HIS FACE IS LINED NOW, AND HIS FOREHEAD HIGHER. HE IS SITTING AT A SQUARE TABLE, ITS TOP INLAID WITH LIGHTER WOODS, READING BY THE LIGHT OF TWO LAMPS. A PLATE TO HIS LEFT CONTAINS THE REMNANTS OF A MEAL— CHICKEN OR SOME OTHER FOWL, JUDGING BY THE BONES. HE GLANCES TO-WARD THE ROOM'S SINGLE WINDOW AND RISES TO LOOK OUT. HE MUST HAVE STEPPED IN SOMETHING WET, FOR HIS FEET, CLAD IN THE EMBROIDERED FELT OF HOUSE SLIPPERS, LEAVE MARKS ON THE FLOOR. IT IS DARK OUTSIDE, FOR DHULYN CAN SEE NOTHING THROUGH THE ARCH OF THE WINDOW. THE MAN TURNS TOWARD THE TABLE AGAIN AND, SMILING, SAYS, "HOW CAN I HELP?" SHE WISHES SHE KNEW THE ANSWER . . .

PEOPLE WORK IN A FIELD OF HAY. RAGGED PEOPLE, FACES DRAWN WITH EXHAUSTION. MOUNTED GUARDS PATROL THE PERIMETER OF THE FIELD, THEIR FACES MARKED WITH THE SAME FATIGUE. THE GUARDS FACE OUTWARD, WHICH TELLS DHULYN THAT THEY ARE GUARDING THE REAPERS FROM EXTER-

NAL DANGER, NOT FROM ESCAPE. IN THE DISTANCE THERE IS A SMALL FOR-
TRESS, SURROUNDED BY A WALL MUCH TOO LARGE FOR IT . . .

DHULYN STANDS LOOKING OUT OVER A GROUP OF RED HORSEMEN
SEATED ON THE GROUND, SOME CROSS-LEGGED, SOME WITH THEIR FEET IN
FRONT OF THEM AND THEIR FOREARMS RESTING ON THEIR KNEES. SHE
KNOWS THIS PLACE; SHE RECOGNIZES SOME OF THE MEN IN THE GATHERING.
THERE IS SUN DOG, FROWNING, AND THERE ROCK SNAKE. THERE IS ALSO
A MAN SHE DOES NOT KNOW, WHO CARRIES A LONG KNIFE IN HIS HANDS. A
THIN, CURVING BLADE. A BUTCHER'S KNIFE. A FLENSING KNIFE PERHAPS. BUT
WHEN SHE TURNS TO LOOK WHERE EVERY MAN IN THE GROUP IS LOOKING,
IT IS NOT A BROKEN SEER WHO IS HELD BETWEEN TWO STRONG GUARDS. IT
IS GUNDARON OF VALDOMAR.

"GUN." DHULYN TAKES A STEP FORWARD, BUT HER VOICE MAKES NO
SOUND. . . .

THE THIN, SANDY-HAIRED MAN IS STILL WEARING THE GOLD RINGS IN
HIS EARS, BUT HIS FACE IS LINED NOW, AND HIS FOREHEAD HIGHER. HE IS
SITTING AT A SQUARE TABLE, ITS TOP INLAID WITH LIGHTER WOODS, WRIT-
ING IN A BOUND BOOK. THERE IS A TALL BLUE GLASS AT HIS RIGHT HAND
AND A MATCHING PITCHER JUST BEYOND IT, HALF-FULL OF LIQUID. DHULYN
CAN SEE THE WINDOW ON HIS FAR SIDE FROM WHERE SHE IS STANDING, AND
IT IS DAYLIGHT NOW, THE SUN SHINING. THE WINDOW LOOKS OUT ON
RUINS, WATCH TOWERS FALLEN, BRIDGES CRUMBLED INTO THE RIVER,
STREETS FULL OF RUBBLE. THE MAN LOOKS UP, SAYING, "HOW CAN I
HELP?" . . .

Parno woke, completely alert in an instant. It was almost
the change of watch. He folded aside his bedding, rolled to
his feet, and secured his sword and daggers before stepping
aside to the designated latrine and emptying his bladder.
He could make out where Dhulyn sat cross-legged, a dark
shape like a boulder in the light of the almost full moon. He
folded his own legs and sat down next to her, close enough
for their knees to touch. She turned and leaned her forehead into his shoulder, breathing deeply in through her
nose. Since they had been separated in the Long Ocean and
reunited in Mortaxa, there had been two Dhulyns. In front
of others she was still the typical Outlander, cool and
watchful, undemonstrative. But she was more likely to
touch him when they were alone—and he her, now that he
thought of it. In many ways, he was reminded of the days

when they were first Partnered, when the bond burned fiercer than it did now.

"When I was a child, before Dorian the Black took me from the slaver's ship, I would pray to the gods of Sun, Moon, and Stars, offering them anything, everything, if they would only restore my people to me." Dhulyn lifted her head from his shoulder, speaking in the whisper of the nightwatch voice. "Do you think what we have found here is the answer to that prayer?"

Parno knew her tones well, and under the cool sarcasm there was a faint splash of bitterness and something that was not quite anger, not quite fear. These were night thoughts, and her earlier Vision of their friend Gundaron alone and in danger at the hands of the Espadryni did not help. He shrugged. "Didn't you once tell me that the gods are remote, that they don't concern themselves with every little request? After all, they have the whole world to see to." He waved his arm at the night sky, where the stars burned in unfamiliar patterns. "And more than one world, it appears."

She nodded. "I would hate to think I somehow caused this place to come into being."

Parno began to laugh, tremors beginning in his belly and building until he laughed out loud. When Dhulyn shoved him, he controlled himself enough to speak. "I never thought *I'd* be the one to say this to *you*," he said. "But you aren't so very important, you know. The world doesn't revolve around you, not even this one. Go on, get to sleep, my heart."

"In Battle," she said, standing.

"And in Death," he answered, touching his fingers to his forehead.

It was well into the fourth watch of the next day, and Dhulyn was thinking they should be starting to look for a place to camp overnight when Parno pulled up on War-hammer's reins.

"Found," he called out to Dhulyn. "Here is a clear trail of three horses returned to the main column together, something no scouts would have done."

Dhulyn stopped a few paces off and leaned over herself,

the better to see what Parno was pointing at. "Your eye is getting better for tracking, my soul." She straightened up. "Somewhere there to the east, I mean the west, is the trap in which our Brothers were caught."

"Try not to kick up any of this ash," Mar said as she picked her way carefully through the burned grasses. It looked as though there had been a fire followed by a rainstorm. In the places where their feet disturbed the surface of the ash, the sodden layer on top gave way to the dry ashes underneath. There were even one or two spots where Mar was certain she felt heat through the soles of her boots.

"This isn't as easy as it looks." Gun's tone was much milder than his words suggested. He seemed to be holding up well, but Mar didn't like the grayness of his skin. He took two more steps forward and stood swaying. Recognizing the signs, Mar was at his side to hold him up out of the black ash as he bent over, retching. Nothing but a line of saliva came out of his mouth, not even bile. His stomach was as empty as it could be.

Gun stayed bent over for several minutes, getting his breath back, and waiting for the next convulsion. Finally he straightened, but his hands went immediately out to his sides to balance himself. Mar kept her grip firmly on his waist, her lower lip between her teeth.

"Gun," she said, trying to keep the desperation from her voice, "what can I do?"

He made the merest negative motion with his head and grimaced. "It doesn't stop spinning," he said.

Mar licked her lips and looked around. The sun was not nearly as bright as it had been in Menoin. It seemed more southerly, softer, and at the angle she would have expected of the Hunter's Moon.

"A blindfold," she said. "That's what you need. Sit, carefully." She helped him lower himself to the ground before she caught up the knife at her belt. Used for sharpening pens, it was more than sharp enough to cut the seam of her tunic and notch the edge of the material to tear off a wide strip. This she folded in half lengthwise and, gently pushing Gun's hands away from his face, tied it tightly around his eyes.

"Any better?" she asked. Give his brain less to work with—or against—and it should steady down.

Gun rubbed at his upper lip, and Mar spit on the loose corner of her tunic, leaned forward, and wiped off his mouth. Until they could find a source to refill the water flasks from Alaria's packs, that was the best she could offer him.

"Better," he said, panting.

"Try to take deep breaths," she said. "Deep and slow." She smiled as he obeyed her, struggling to take in one slow shuddering breath after another. The smile faded as she straightened and looked around. Was there unburned grass over there, toward the sun? Or was she just wishing?

"Less wobbly," Gun said.

Mar crouched down on her heels and put the back of her hand against Gun's face and forehead. No fever that she could detect. "Can you stand?" she said. "I think I see the end of the burned section over to the east."

"You can tell which way is east?"

Mar blinked, a spot of cold growing in her belly. "The sun's setting," she said. "That way's the east, isn't it?"

"I don't know." With uncanny accuracy he reached for her forearm and gripped it. "I can't tell. Everything's spinning." Gun pressed his lips together and swallowed, once, twice, and again.

The cold spread from Mar's belly up her arms. He'd said the clue had disappeared. Now he could not tell east from west.

"Your Mark?" Mar licked suddenly dry lips.

"It's gone."

Mar knew that Gun was doing his very best not to lean his whole weight on her, but the unburned section of prairie was farther away than it had appeared, and she was staggering by the time they reached it. She tried to lower him slowly to the ground, but her knees gave out in the last minute, and they both went down heavily onto the trampled grass. Joints and muscles screaming, Mar lay still, listening to Gun's ragged breathing.

Finally she pushed herself upright until she was resting on her knees, and she took hold of Gun's wrist with her grimy hand. They had fallen only once, but it had been headlong, and it had coated them both with a fine layer of gritty ash. Mar checked their water flask, took a careful sip to rinse out her mouth, and then swallowed it rather than spitting it out, wrinkling her nose at the taste of ashes.

"Here, Gun. Water." She nudged him until he rolled over onto his back, shoved her arm under his shoulder and lifted him upright enough to give him just a little more than the scant mouthful of liquid she'd allowed herself. Like her, Gun swallowed the gritty water, and Mar relaxed. If Gun was able to remember that bit of wisdom, perhaps he was starting to feel better.

She shifted so that Gun could lean against her, his head resting in the hollow of her shoulder. "I'm going to need some help," she said.

"Go. Leave me." His voice was a thread finer than the ash.

"We haven't reached that point yet." *And never will*, she thought. Mar scanned their surroundings, but she saw nothing but the unburned version of what she'd been looking at for what seemed like days. Knee high grass, stunted trees, and, a long way away, what looked like the horizon. "If I knew where we were, or where I could go for help, it might be a good idea for me to go on ahead without you," she allowed. "As it is, there isn't even a defensible place I can leave you. Not even a tree you could put your back against." She shook her head, even though he couldn't see her. "No. We'll wait. See if you don't feel better after some rest. It may be better for us to travel by night."

"The stars."

Mar smiled. "That's right, we can get directions from them, good thinking. So just lie down for a bit, and I'll see what I can do about setting up a camp."

When they had first met, Mar had spent most of a moon traveling with Dhulyn Wolfshead and Parno Lionsmane, and she'd learned one or two things about making a camp in the middle of nowhere, with just the supplies you had to hand. In their own pouches they each had sparkers, and their writing kits—and not much else in practical terms. The quick glance that was all they'd had time for until now had already told her that Alaria's two packs were identical. Now she had time for a more thorough check of supplies. Two water flasks, one empty, one almost so. Two rounded clay containers with closely fitted lids that, when opened, revealed themselves as paste lamps, along with two sparkers. Each pack also contained a head scarf, a set of nested copper bowls suitable for cooking, a quilted bedroll, and a folding knife. Mar examined this last with some curiosity. She'd seen them before but had never had one in her hands. They were too expensive for Scholars. She fingered the latch, slid it aside, and let the knife open. She closed it again and put it away.

There was also, she was relieved to see, a substantial packet of travel bread, along with some twists of dried meat and fruit wrapped in oiled cloth.

Mar repacked everything except the bedrolls. It was warm enough to do without a fire, but rest they had to have. Though quilted, the bedrolls were not very thick, and since she and Gun were not hardened Mercenary Brothers . . . Mar pulled her knife out of her belt, took a deep breath and stood up. "I'm going to cut grass for bedding," she said.

It took a few tries for Mar to learn the most efficient stroke to cut the tough grass with a knife, but she eventually had enough to lay out Gun's bedroll and help him crawl into it. She decided against cutting more since one of them would have to stay awake to keep watch, and besides, her arms already felt as though they were pulling out of her shoulders, and her palms were starting to crack and bleed. And her knife, when she tested it on the ball of her thumb, was now badly in need of sharpening.

"This is much easier in books." Mar pushed her hair out of her eyes with the back of her wrist, eyed the water flask leaning against their packs, and turned her eyes resolutely back to the horizon.

She blinked and looked more carefully, slowly getting to her feet. A single man on horseback. Mar looked around quickly, heart thumping, mouth drier than ever, but he appeared to be alone. *Manageable then*, she told herself, trying to calm down, and shifting her grip on her knife. On the other hand, this one man had been able to get this close to them without her noticing him. At this rate, there might be an enemy behind every blade of grass.

And she should have remembered that there was a killer here, and that this man could be him. Mar took a deep breath, squared her shoulders, and put herself between the horseman and Gun. Nevertheless, she found herself relaxing as the horse and its rider came close enough to see clearly.

A thin, fair-haired man. No armor, no helm, not even wearing gloves. Though he wore a short sword and had a crossbow hanging from his saddle, he didn't look like a soldier but more like a man of business. Mar automatically noted that his dull red tunic was a very fine weave of wool and that his leather trousers were equally finely tanned and dyed. He had a silver ring on his left index finger and wore round gold rings in his ears. His boots, ankle high like a town man's, were scuffed and dusty but again, were clearly of good quality.

The man lifted his sand-colored brows. "Greetings," he said, smiling. "I am Bekluth Allain of Norwash, trader by profession."

Mar felt somehow reassured by the man's smile. This was obviously no such maniac as had been responsible for the horror of Princess Cleona's death. Gun was sitting up now, his hair full of bits of grass and his blindfold askew. Mar, seeing the state of him through the stranger's eyes, brushed at herself. "We're Scholars from the Library of Valdomar," she said, reaching down to straighten Gun's blindfold. "I'm Mar, and this is my husband Gundaron."

Bekluth Allain frowned a little. "Valdomar? I'm not familiar with it." He shrugged. "But then, I don't know of every town. What ails him," he added, indicating Gun with a long-fingered hand. "Is he blind?"

"Dizziness," Mar said, helping Gun to sit up. "I was trying to limit the information reaching his senses, to see if that would help." She started to unwrap the bandage around his eyes, but Gun caught her hands in his own.

"I'll do it," he said.

He sounds better already, she told herself.

"That is a very clever idea. I have powdered fens bark for tea, which could be of use," Bekluth said. "Have you anything to trade for it?" He dismounted and began to untie the laces on his left-hand saddlebag.

Mar hesitated, a little taken aback. The last thing she would have expected to encounter on this side of the Path of the Sun was the oh-so-familiar perspective of the merchant mind. She would have to be careful. Gun needed help, but what little they had might have to last them a long time. "As

I said, we're Scholars. If you're a trader, is there something we can read or write for you?"

Again, that look of puzzlement crossed his face. "I'm sorry," he smiled. "I'm not familiar with the term—at least," he shrugged, "not as you are applying it to yourselves. You are past the age of leaving your tutors, I would have thought."

"He means they don't have Scholars here," Gun said. He had the piece of cloth off and was squinting at the light. "No Libraries."

"Oh," Mar looked back to the trader. "In that case, I'm not sure what we might have that we could trade you."

But the man was smiling again, shaking his head as if in admiration. "You thought I wouldn't catch that? I heard your man say 'here.' When were you going to tell me that you have come through the Door of the Sun?"

"You know of it then?" Mar was eager. "Do you know of others who've come through? We're looking for two Mercenary Brothers—though if you don't have Scholars here, perhaps you don't have the Brotherhood either."

"You are quite right, we do not. But I believe I know the two you are speaking of. One tall, golden man and one woman of the Espadryni people."

"There are Espadryni here?" Gun lifted his head and winced, bracing his hands against his forehead.

"Here, now, help me to build a fire, and let me get you that fens bark," Bekluth said. "I am sure that there will be something you can trade me for it, if not now, then later. Even if it is only tales of your own land and how you made your way through the Door." He turned back with a look of concentration to his saddlebag.

Mar turned anxiously back to Gun, lower lip between her teeth. His eyes were shut, but she could see them moving behind the lids. Did that mean—she caught at the hope before it flew away. Had his Mark returned? Even as she thought this, the corners of Gun's mouth turned down, and he paled enough to look green.

"There is something more than the headache, I believe."

Mar flinched and almost overbalanced. How had the man come so close to her?

"He's a Finder, and he can't Find," she said.

"Marked, is he?" the man's brow furrowed, and Mar for

an instant wondered if there was something wrong, if this man might be one of those rare individuals who were afraid of the Marked. But then his face cleared, and the smile played once more around his eyes.

"That's beyond my meager skills," he said, shaking his head in regret. "Bind up a cut, or a few sleeping powders for those who know how to use them. The fens bark." He shrugged. "You need one of the Mages, at the very least."

"The Espadryni," Gun said. He sounded as though he were parceling out the words between slow breaths.

"That's right." The man looked from one to the other. "They are Mages on your side as well, then?"

Mar shrugged. Something in the man's tone told her that she should horde even this apparently useless bit of knowledge as it might turn out to be worth trading. She waited as Bekluth quickly built a fire, filled a metal pot about the size of an ale mug with water from a bag hanging on his saddle, and set it at the fire's edge. She licked her lips and settled herself comfortably next to Gun. Dhulyn Wolfshead was the shrewdest trader—in her way—that Mar had ever met, but right now Mar would have settled for her foster mother, Guillor Weaver.

"Can you take us?" she asked Bekluth Allain. "To the Red Horsemen?"

Bekluth had shifted the metal pot away from the fire with a small hooked rod evidently designed for the purpose. Into the cooling water he tapped a measure of powdered fens bark from a fold of paper. He looked back at her, shook his head with a smile of admiration on his lips as he handed her the pot.

"There now, I wish I had some brandy to give you both; it seems you could use it, but I'm fresh out." His brows furrowed, but then he smiled again. "As for acting as guide, I cannot. I've my trading route, you must see that. I'm answerable to my family and they to our guild if I'm late and cannot show profit to justify it."

Mar nodded. This argument she understood. All that time keeping accounts for the weavers in Navra had taught her a thing or two about profit and the justification for it.

"I would give you directions," the trader continued, "but I thought you said you had nothing to trade." He handed her the pot of tea.

Mar tested the water with the back of her knuckle before passing the cup along to Gun. "Perhaps I spoke hastily," she said. She ransacked her memory for what might be in her pouch or in Gun's. Or perhaps she could offer something that was duplicated in the packs?

"What of these copper bowls?" she said, pulling one set out of the nearest pack and setting them on the ground between them.

But Bekluth was already shaking his head. "Such kits are commonplace here. Have you nothing else?" he asked, and Mar almost believed that his regret was sincere. She looked to Gun. He was slowly sipping the cup of fens bark tea. Was he looking a little less green, or was she just hoping very hard? She glanced back at the trader and came to a decision.

"I will show you what I have," she said. "Tell me what you can give me for it."

A new smile, a different smile, flickered across Bekluth's face and was gone before Mar was sure she'd seen it. She hesitated, hand halfway into her belt pouch. Bekluth's expression had returned to its half-smile of serene interest, a look she was familiar with, having seen it often on the faces of traders everywhere. Nothing then, she'd seen nothing.

First, she pulled from her own belt pouch a fine scarf, teal patterned with black, edged thinly with a dark red, her House colors. Next she put out one of the folding knives.

"What is this?" Bekluth reached for the scarf, but did not pick it up until Mar nodded. "Seda?" he asked.

"We call it silk," Mar said. "But I've heard the term you're using as well."

Bekluth ran it through his fingers, closely examining it for a flaw Mar knew he would not find. He set it down and indicated the knife. "May I?"

Mar nodded again and watched his long fingers with their large knuckles prod at the knife until she took it from him, showed him how the latch worked, and handed it back to let him try it himself.

"This is ingenious," the trader said, and Mar could hear the sincerity in his voice. "Anyone can use it? It is not magicked in any way?"

"Anyone can use it," Mar said, holding out her hand.

Gingerly, Bekluth folded the knife shut again and

returned it. He sat back on his heels and tapped his chin with his fingers. "It would fetch a good price, but it might be years before I found the person who would pay it." He sat back, resting his long wrists on his knees, and contemplated her offerings. Finally he inhaled deeply, let it out, and nodded.

"For the knife and the seda scarf, I will fill your water bottles, and give you directions to the camp of the nearest Espadryni, who may be able to help your friend and direct you to the others you seek."

Mar shook her head and began to put away her things, starting with the scarf. The directions were the most important, but if she agreed too readily . . . Her hand hovered over the knife. "For what you offer, the knife alone is already more than enough. After all, directions are things you can trade over and over, and water you will replenish at no charge from the next source you know of." She shrugged. "It's not as though you're guiding us yourself."

Bekluth drummed his fingers on his knee before finally nodding. "Very well. What then will you take for the seda scarf?"

"The rest of your fens bark and five day's food."

"Three."

"For both of us. And a satchel to carry it in," she added hastily. It was all too easy to imagine Bekluth simply dumping the food out onto the ground.

"Done." Bekluth held out his fist to her, and Mar hesitantly tapped it with her own. He rose easily to his feet, scooping up the folding knife and her scarf as he went. Mar eyed the scarf with a pang. Her House, Dal-eLad Tenebro, had given it to her himself. But Dal was a practical man, she reminded herself. He wouldn't grudge that she'd traded the emblem of her House for food.

The trader returned with a thick linen bag, complete with drawstring and shoulder strap. From his right-hand saddlebag he sorted out a cheese about the size of a large melon, wrapped in waxed cloth and smelling delicious. To this he added two small loaves of travel cake, and a dozen each of dried figs and plums. Finally he put a small waterskin into the bag and handed it to her. Mar accepted it with a nod.

"If you follow my directions carefully, you will meet the

Cold Lake People. They have many great shamans, one of which is likely to be able to help you. Begin by heading due west, toward the setting sun —"

"East," Mar corrected automatically.

"I beg your pardon?"

"You said west," Mar said. "You meant east. The sun sets in the east."

"How interesting. For that you will get another travel cake." Bekluth rummaged in his bag. "So the sun sets in the east on the other side of the Door. Are the worlds mirrors then?" He waved his hand in the air. "No matter. This is not knowledge I can sell, since the town philosophers do not know of or believe in the Door of the Sun. It appears the directions are reversed, so listen carefully, and remember. Go west, toward the setting sun until you reach a great ravine. This should not take more than a day of walking. Follow the ravine north, that is, turn to your right. The Cold Lake People are in that direction, and you cannot fail to find them. I cannot tell you, however, exactly how many days away they will be. You should not run out of food, but I would eat sparingly in any case."

"Thank you for your advice," Mar said.

"Here is more." Bekluth frowned as though he were thinking something through. "I would not tell them immediately that you have been through the Door of the Sun. It is a holy place to them, and they may object to your use of it. But," he held up his finger, "be sure to tell them that your friend is a Finder." Bekluth leaned toward her to emphasize his words further. "They will need to know that to prepare the right magics for him."

"We will, and thank you."

The man gave a sharp nod, almost a bow and stood up again. "Then I will be on my way," he said. "Good trading to you."

"And to you," Mar said. Part of her wanted to ask him to stay, or to ask if they could travel with him. But he'd made it plain that he wasn't going their way. Part of her was a little surprised by his abrupt departure.

"Well, that was helpful." Mar kneeled once more beside Gun and touched the back of her hand to his forehead. "Is the fens bark helping?"

"A little, I think." Gun cleared his throat. "What he said,

about the directions being reversed, I wonder if that is what's making me so bad?"

"I suppose it could be."

"Did you think he smiled too much?" Gun accepted her offered arm and inched himself to his feet.

"He's a trader," Mar said, slinging the satchel over one shoulder and preparing to take Gun's arm with her free hand. "They all smile too much."

Nineteen

PARNO SQUATTED ON his heels, watching Dhulyn pick her way through the sharpened stakes at the bottom of the orobeast trap. There was the smell of old blood, and of bodily wastes, faint now, but unmistakable.

"What kind of animal did they say these were used for?" he asked.

"An orobeast they said." Dhulyn answered without looking up. "Some kind of prowling cat apparently, something fast and deadly but that didn't cover too much ground in its leaps."

Parno nodded. If the beast's paces when running were long, the odds were against this kind of trap, or any other for that matter, catching it.

Dhulyn crouched closer to a particular set of bones, laying the tips of her fingers along what they both recognized as a human thigh bone. "In Battle," she said.

"Or in Death," Parno responded.

Placing her feet delicately, like a dancer moving unusually slowly through the measure of a dance, Dhulyn made her way over to the side of the pit and held up her left arm. Parno took hold of her wrist, made sure she had a good grip on his and, bracing himself, lifted her out in one unbroken movement.

"It's already too dark to see details at the bottom," she said, dusting off her hands on her leather trousers. "Even if we suppose there is something worth our while to see."

Parno squinted against the setting sun. "Camp here, then, and start again in the morning?"

Dhulyn took another look around at the trampled ground before she nodded. "Eat first," she said. "Then we'll say a few words for Kesman Firehawk. Delvik couldn't have managed much in the state he was in. We'll divide the night into four watches," she added as they walked back to where they had left the horses. "Odds for me, evens for you."

Parno raised his eyes to look over her shoulder. "Someone's coming."

Dhulyn swung herself onto Bloodbone's back, to have better line of sight in the direction Parno had indicated.

"It's the trader, Bekluth Allain," she said, squinting against the lowering sun. "Off his normal route, I imagine."

It seemed that the trader recognized them almost in the same moment. His right arm swung up over his head, and the pace of the horse he was riding, and the two he led, increased until he was dismounting a few paces away.

"I should have known you would be interested in this spot," he said, coming forward to greet them with nods and smiles, pulling his sleeves straight as he came. "I confess I was curious myself."

"Would you mind moving your horses," Dhulyn said.

The trader glanced back over his shoulder. "My horses?"

The corners of Dhulyn's mouth pressed tight. "As I am making a study of the tracks, Bekluth Allain, I would be grateful if you defaced them as little as possible." She turned away without waiting for the trader to move, already looking for the best place for them to camp. Bekluth, Parno saw, kept his focus on Dhulyn, as if to memorize her shape.

"We wouldn't have expected to see you again so soon," Parno said.

The trader breathed in and turned to Parno, though his eyes still lingered on Dhulyn's back. "Ah, well, the Cold Lake People were not at Flat Water, where I expected them to be." Bekluth Allain shrugged. "Perhaps they travel more slowly than usual, or the weather was against them. It rained heavily two nights ago. It's not unusual, it sometimes happens thus. These are the risks of my kind of trading." He glanced past them at the deep shadow that was the trap. "Since I had time, I thought I might take a turn out of my way to satisfy my curiosity, as I said. I must say, I am not displeased at the occurrence, since it allows me to meet you once again. Something tells me there is as much profit to be found in your company as there might be among the Horsemen."

Parno found himself grinning. Bekluth Allain's interest in Dhulyn was not unusual—even on their own side of the Path, she was worth a second look, and a third if it came to that—and the man's very good humor was infectious. "We were about to make camp," Parno said, gesturing with a sweep of his hand to where Dhulyn, squatting on her heels, was brushing a smooth spot on the ground. "You're welcome to join us."

"No fire," Dhulyn said, when, his horses settled in the spot she'd marked out, Bekluth Allain joined her. The trader looked up in astonishment from where he was pulling grasses and small twigs together. "The body of one of our Brothers is lying in that hole." Dhulyn nodded in the direction of the dark pit. "And we're not sure yet how that came to be. This place is little more than a tabletop from which a fire could be seen from hundreds of spans away. Our Common Rule says we should not draw too much attention to ourselves in these circumstances."

"Does your Common Rule say we should freeze?" Bekluth's face was serious, but there was a perceptible shine in his eye.

"You're welcome to use the bottom of the pit, if you'd prefer it. No fire would show from there," Parno pointed out.

Bekluth swung his head from side to side, throwing up his hands as if in surrender and smiling widely enough that his teeth shone white. "What about eating? Does the Common Rule allow that?"

"Certainly," Parno said.

"Just not all at once," Dhulyn added. "You may do as you please, but only one of us can eat with you at a time, in case there is something wrong with the food."

The trader shook his head, lips parted. "And I used to think the rules and restrictions of the Trader's Guild were rigid." He stretched. "And then, which of us shall take the first watch?"

"My Partner and I will share the watches between us, Bekluth Allain," Dhulyn said. The man's face seemed to stiffen, and his eyes shuttered, but the impression was so fleeting, Parno couldn't be certain he'd seen anything.

"Nor is offense intended," he said. "It's merely another part of our Common Rule."

The moon was not going to rise high enough to give much light, but Bekluth wasn't going to let that worry him. The sky was clear, the stars bright, and all he was missing was color—and considering that there was nothing around him but drying grass, a couple of horses, and Dhulyn Wolfshead's patchwork vest, he wasn't missing much. Even the Wolfshead's hair was just dark now, not the telltale red of old blood that marked her so clearly for an Espadryni. Her skin was the soft pale of alabaster, so rich that your hand was always surprised by how cold it felt to the touch.

Not that Dhulyn Wolfshead's skin would feel cold. She wasn't a pretty woman, not by any means, not with that scarred lip she had and that way of smiling that was more than half snarl. But still . . . Bekluth pursed his lips and remembered just in time not to start whistling. She was asleep, but he thought not deeply. He could see the movement under her eyelids that showed she was dreaming, a slight shiver of her skin, as if, in her dream, her muscles tensed.

Is it true what they say? He wondered. Were all the Marked like her on the other side of the Sun's Door? Full of light, so open and without secrets to hide? He might not have believed it if only the man had said so, but those two youngsters, so innocently telling him that the boy was a Finder. He grinned. The boy wasn't as clear and open as Dhulyn Wolfshead, but what would it matter over there, so long as the Marked weren't "broken," so long as no one was hunting them down.

A loose tendril of hair blew across her face, and Bekluth reached out, but again caution stopped his hand. If only he'd known all this before. Surely he could cross through and stay there if he rode far enough from the Door. He could live there, openly. He smiled as he stepped quietly back to where his own bedroll had been tossed aside. Think of the number of people with dark secrets he could help then.

I wouldn't have to hide, he thought. His heart beat faster, and he tapped his upper lip with his tongue. He could come and go as he pleased, just as he liked. Be welcomed wherever he went. Respected.

"I would not have to hide," he said aloud.

"Are you talking in your sleep, Bekluth Allain?"

Caids. He twisted his neck and jumped just a little. He didn't have to pretend very much—he'd actually forgotten Parno Lionsmane was there. He smiled and shrugged one shoulder.

"Can't sleep at all," he said. "Can you believe that for a moment I forgot I was not alone?"

"If you're wakeful, let's move farther away from my Partner," the other man said. "There's only so much noise we can make before she'll wake—and if we wake her before her watch for no good reason, none of us will be happy."

Bekluth followed the Mercenary around to the far side of the pit, where he'd arranged their saddles into a place to sit, and from where there was a clear view of the camp, the dozing horses, and the prairie around them.

"You could see me moving from here." Bekluth made his tone shine with admiration, even as he thanked his own good luck that he hadn't been doing anything he needed to hide.

"It's a good spot to look out from," the Mercenary agreed. "What was it you wouldn't have to hide, Bekluth Allain?"

"Ah, you heard me as well?" Bekluth shrugged, making sure to show just a touch of embarrassment. "It'll seem like very small meat to someone who's traveled the paths you have taken." Flattery with a sprinkling of admiration was always good bait.

"Try me," the man said. "I haven't always been on these particular paths."

And thus the trap was sprung. Really, it was almost too easy. All he ever had to do was get someone to start listening to him. There was no one he couldn't persuade. He tucked his hands under his arms, as if against the night's chill, and chewed for a moment on his lower lip.

"Well," he began, as if still hesitating, "you might be surprised to hear this, Mercenary, but I'm not such a fine trader as I make myself out to be."

The other man chuckled. "Come now, Bekluth. You must

have fine skills indeed to trade alone among the Red Horsemen and to gain their trust in the way that you have."

Bekluth shrugged again, letting his hands fall to his lap, as if he were relaxing. "Oh, I have the skills, I suppose—though you might not think so if you heard the way my uncles talked about me. Back then, before my mother was killed, I'd already gone to them with the idea of trading with the Tribes. They said they were considering it, though the plan they suggested . . . You see," he leaned forward, drawing his brows together, "trading with the Tribes isn't like trading with anyone else, and my uncles didn't understand that. They didn't see the difficulties that—well, that are so clear to *you*, for example."

The man nodded, as Bekluth had known he would. "It's a problem that time might cure—either *their* impatience or *yours*."

Bekluth felt a flash of annoyance. *He* wasn't the one—except that he was playing the part of a young man misunderstood by his elders, and apparently with his usual easy success. But the man was still talking.

"But there's more, isn't there? Nothing you've told me so far is anything you would need to hide."

There, now he had the man hooked completely. He let his head bob up and down a few times as though he were weighing his options. "You're right," he said, exactly as if he'd made up his mind to confide in the man. "Impatience isn't the only thing that time will cure." He took in a deep breath and looked the Mercenary right in the eyes. "You know my story, what happened with my mother. A part of me is still angry, a part of me *never* wants to forgive them. But another part . . . another part wants to go back." He quirked his eyebrows, displaying, now that he'd committed himself, an endearing uncertainty . . . and then let his glance fall away.

"Why?" But there was no disbelief in the man's voice, only a sympathetic curiosity.

Bekluth looked sideways and managed his most sheepish look. "I'm successful here. I've quite a stockpile of goods and money. But I've nowhere to spend or show it where it matters. I was right about the trade, right about the Horsemen—you should see the sky stones I get from them, worth almost any effort—but no one knows it but me. I've been telling myself for years that I despise them, my uncles and aunts and all my dear cousins, who spend their days and their evenings and their nights counting profit and balancing the scales." He rubbed his face with his hands. "But they're the only ones who can understand and appreciate what I've achieved."

Bekluth waited, and when the other man chuckled, he joined in, just as if he were seeing the humor of his situation for the first time. He felt something like a real warmth for this man, this Mercenary, who was so ready to understand and feel for someone else. It was easy to see why there was so strong a bond between him and Dhulyn Wolfshead.

But though his outer self kept on chuckling, smiling, shrugging, and pouring hopes and dreams into the man's sympathetic ear, his inner self grew colder, and more aware.

Bonds are still bonds, he thought, as he accepted the man's advice and his pats on the shoulder. This Parno Lionsmane had a darkness hidden within him, a secret. Bekluth could see it, if no one else could. And he was never wrong about such things. Never. Not since he had seen the darkness in his mother for what it was, something that made her beat him, punish him, and bind him. Something that needed to come out, to be exposed to the light. He'd helped her with that, as he'd helped others after her. Including the young shaman he'd first followed through the Door.

Dhulyn Wolfshead, so clear, so open. How could she have such a strong bond with someone like Parno Lionsmane? As usual, the moment he posed the question, the answer flashed into his mind. The bond was obviously there to help the man, not the woman.

If I free him, I would free them both. If he could open the man, the bond would be unnecessary. They would both be free. Parno Lionsmane could go his way, fulfill his own destiny as he was meant to.

And Dhulyn Wolfshead can help me.

Parno Lionsmane was glancing up at the sky. "That's my watch over," he said, getting to his feet.

"I think I'll be able to sleep now," Bekluth said, following the other man back to where Dhulyn Wolfshead still lay on her back. "Thanks for letting me bend your ear," he added.

"Sometimes it's easier to tell things to strangers," the

Mercenary said. "They go their way, and there're no embarrassing questions."

He does understand, Bekluth thought. He wasn't a stupid man. He was reacting in exactly the right way—if any of what Bekluth had told him had been the truth. And he wouldn't have been easy to fool if Bekluth weren't so very good at it.

Maybe I don't need to wait. Maybe I can help him right now. He deserves it. No one should have to live with that secret hidden inside him.

Parno Lionsmane motioned Bekluth closer with a tilt of his head and squatted an arm's length away from Dhulyn Wolfshead. He tapped his cheek just under his right eye, and Bekluth put on his best look of concentration. What was the man up to?

As he watched, Lionsmane reached out very slowly with his right hand, moving it closer and closer to the sleeping woman's shoulder. Closer, slowly, closer—

Her left hand flashed out and grabbed Lionsmane's wrist, her right hand pointed a dagger at his throat.

Bekluth jumped back, genuinely startled this time. She had moved literally in the blink of an eye. One moment asleep, and the next alert and menacing.

"Do you all wake like that?" he asked, when the other two had finished chuckling at each other.

"Of course." Dhulyn Wolfshead was now on her feet, just as if she hadn't been asleep five breaths ago. "Otherwise, we might not wake up at all."

"More of your Common Rule, I suppose," Bekluth had said, shaking his head ruefully.

When he had wished them both a good night, and the woman had gone to the lookout place, and the man had rolled himself in their bedding and dropped off immediately to sleep, Bekluth lay in his own bedroll and thought. He'd need more of the drugged brandy, that was certain. No just waiting for either of them to fall asleep. And somehow he'd have to use it on both of them at the same time. He mentally waved this problem away. He'd solve it when the time came—he always did.

Now, where was his closest supply of brandy?

Alaria became aware she was dozing only when she came abruptly awake as the bed moved under her. Enough light came through the open door of the bedroom to show her a profile she recognized. "What are you doing?"

Falcos was sitting on the far edge of the bed, his blue eyes catching the light and his mouth twisted into a sideways grin. "You didn't expect me to sleep on the floor, did you? I thought you trusted me."

Alaria felt her face and neck grow hot—though with any luck her blush couldn't be seen in the scant light. She could hope so, at least. She cleared her throat.

"My mother said that men were never to be trusted," she said in as conversational a tone as she could manage. "Most especially never in any sexual situation. That they control themselves only with great difficulty, if at all."

Falcos nodded slowly, shifting until he was sitting with his back against the headboard—a far less elaborate one than the one in his mother's bedroom. "There's some truth to that, for certain men and, as you say, in certain situations." Alaria, blinking, sat up herself, and shoved her combs back into place. "But I'm not one of those men, and in case you hadn't noticed, this is not a sexual situation."

"You *are* in my bedroom," Alaria pointed out, keeping her voice as firm as she could. "About to lie down on my bed."

The corner of his mouth twitched. "This is not anyone's bedroom, and it's no one in particular's bed." His mouth drooped, and Alaria could see again how close to the edge of despair Falcos really was. "Alaria," he said, "if I do not rest soon, I'll go mad."

Alaria sat up straighter, pulling her feet up to sit cross-legged. At least she'd gone to sleep fully clothed. "Come," she said. "Stretch out. Shut your eyes."

He curled up on his side, facing her, one arm tucked under the pillow. He didn't look younger, as she'd been told all sleeping people did. And sleep couldn't make him more beautiful—but only because he was so beautiful to begin with. Even with the smudge of a bruise on his left cheek and dirt under his fingernails. She still found it surprising that Falcos was not the vain and featherheaded fool that his beauty had led her to expect.

Which was a good thing, all things considered, since

she'd thrown in her lot with his. Agreed to stay here, marry him, become the Tarkina of Menoin. And nothing that had happened since she'd sat hand-in-hand with Falcos in the stables, watching the new foal, had given her reason to change her mind. On the contrary. Her breath caught a little in her throat. She would rather be sitting here on the bed with Falcos, their futures uncertain, than on the throne of Menoin if it meant she sat with Epion.

"I want you to reconsider surrendering to Epion."

Alaria jumped; she'd been so sure that Falcos had fallen asleep. How strange that they'd both been thinking along the same lines, even if they hadn't reached the same conclusions.

"Hear me out," Falcos said when she didn't answer. He propped himself up on his right elbow. "You could say you have grown afraid of me, that you now think I tricked you in some way."

"Falcos, we've talked about this. He wouldn't believe me. Abandoning you won't make me safe."

"I think he'd *want* to believe you, and I believe you *would* be safe," he said. "You must think I'm not a very good judge of character if Epion could fool me for so long, but trust me, knowing the truth about him now just puts all I've observed over all these years into the right context, and I assure you, you'd be safe." He took a deep breath. "You are not the one who is standing between Epion and his throne. On the contrary, since we can change from one Arderon princess to another to answer the demands of the treaty, I should think we can change from one Menoin prince to another. Oh, no." He shook his head. "You are in no danger from Epion. And besides," he continued when Alaria opened her mouth to argue, "you have the horses to think about."

That made Alaria stop and think. The queens *were* her responsibility, though perhaps not her first priority.

"He'll never believe it," was all she could think of.

"I tell you he'll want to. That's your strength. You must use it. You cannot go down with me." His lips pressed tight and Alaria wondered what he'd stopped himself from saying.

"I don't want to leave you." She surprised herself, but only by saying it aloud.

"And I don't want you to have to deal with Epion alone." Falcos reached out and touched her cheek.

"As if I couldn't manage one man," she said.

But Falcos didn't return her smile. "That's the over-confidence that will lead you wrong," he said. "You have a poor opinion of men and you think that because you can manage the men in Arderon who don't have any real power, you won't have any trouble here. But you're not in Arderon now. Do not underestimate Epion, what he will do, how he will think and act."

Alaria was stung, but she bit back her angry retort. Part of her knew that what Falcos had said was true, and just. Her own upbringing might lead her astray, as it almost had with Falcos himself. Part of her simply didn't want what might be the last words they said to each other to be angry ones. "I'll think of him as a woman then, shall I? Someone close to the Tarkina and ambitious."

"You will be safer if you do." He was smiling, but his eyes were sad.

She put her hand gently on his bruised cheek, leaned forward, and kissed him on the lips. Somehow they were warmer than she'd expected.

"You'll be careful," he said. "Promise me." He was leaning his forehead against hers, his blue eyes shut. Something clutched at Alaria's heart.

"Promise me," he repeated, leaning away from her.

"I won't marry Epion." She held up her hand. "And if you tell me that Menoin needs a Tarkina from Arderon, very well, but Epion won't survive the marriage night. That I *can* promise you."

His blue eyes suddenly became much warmer. "Menoin will need an heir from the line of Akarion."

Alaria smiled.

❧

"Let me do the talking," Mar said. She slipped the satchel off her shoulder, letting it rest on the ground at her feet.

"Why not? I've been letting you do pretty well everything else." Gun's voice was flat, but Mar smiled nonetheless. The spirit of teasing was there, even if the strength to lift his tone was not.

Gun had rested fairly well the night before, but his nausea had returned with walking, and Mar had finally covered his eyes again, this time using the headscarf from his pack.

They had been walking the better part of the day, but with the slow pace and frequent rests Gun's condition required, they had not even reached the crevasse Bekluth Allain had told them about when noise and movement from what they now understood to be the north told them they were no longer alone. It was hard to be sure at first, but eventually Mar could tell there were five Espadryni approaching. Remembering something Parno Lionsmane had once told them, Mar and Gun had immediately put down their burdens and stood with their hands empty facing in the direction of the Horsemen. "Let them see you are no threat," the Lionsmane had said. "Unless of course you are, in which case you should let them see that."

"Stand steady," Mar said as the Horsemen rode toward them with no apparent intention of stopping. "I'll speak to them."

"You said that already." Mar glanced at Gun, but his momentary smile was wiped away with another grimace. He swallowed and licked his lips.

Mar turned back to face the approaching Horsemen and willed herself not to shut her eyes as all five horses came nearer and nearer without slowing down, until, in the last moment, they turned aside and rode in circles around them. The Horsemen passed so closely that her own headscarf fluttered in the breeze of their passage.

That's meant to intimidate, she thought. *So stay calm and unimpressed.* She glanced at each of the riders, looking for the one who would be in charge and wracking her brain for what little she knew about the Espadryni. Dhulyn Wolfshead was the only Red Horseman Mar had ever met—the only one in existence, for all anyone knew to the contrary—and while these five men all had the pale southern skin and the long, blood-red hair she associated with her Mercenary friend, they were armed strangers, and Mar had to treat them as dangerous.

And there was still, somewhere on this side of the Path, a killer, though Mar thought he was very unlikely to be one of this group. A man would need to be alone, she thought, to do what the killer had done.

All five men were dressed in leather dyed in a rainbow of colors, with their sleeveless jerkins decorated with patches of cloth and patterns of beading. Three carried spears, and two had short bows already strung and hanging easily to hand across the horns of their saddles. Except for the very long knives that each man had at his waist, Mar could see no swords. She blinked at the dust raised around her and cleared her throat as the men came to a halt. One came nearer and spoke to her, and while the words sounded familiar, they were in a language Mar did not know. Gun looked up and frowned, but when she touched his sleeve, he shook his head.

"Do you speak the common tongue?" she asked, forming her words slowly. She had hopes they would, since the trader had. "Are you Espadryni of the Cold Lake People?" she added.

"We are," the one who was clearly the leader answered. "I am Josh-Chevrie," he added. "We saw the burning and are come to investigate." It was plain from his tone that he expected a similar explanation of their presence.

Mar was suddenly at a loss. How to explain who and what they were, and why they were here, when the fact that they were Scholars would mean nothing to these people? Mar had never before realized how much Scholars could rely on their distinctive blue tunics and their Library connections to give them an introduction and gain them a welcome wherever they went.

She hesitated only a moment more, pushing the scarf back away from her face and squinting up at the man on horseback. Even without Bekluth's warning not to mention the Path of the Sun, Mar would have known to proceed carefully. Things left unsaid were not really lies, and she could always explain afterward, if the Espadryni seemed less superstitious than Bekluth had claimed. Better cautious than cursing, as the Wolfshead always said. There would be time to give the whole story, once she found Gun some help.

"I am Mar-eMar Tenebro and this is my husband, Gundaron of Valdomar," she said. "We are looking for friends we have been told are in this area, but more immediately we are seeking help for my husband's sudden illness. The trader Bekluth Allain told us that your shaman may be able to help us."

"The trader sent you?" Josh-Chevrie slid down from his horse and came closer. Mar stood her ground. The man's eyes were the same curious shade of stone gray that the Wolfshead's were.

"Is it an injury of the eye?" he asked, reaching out to touch Gun's bandage.

"Are you a shaman then? A Mage?" Mar asked. Though with so few Healers in the world, it made sense to send a Mage along with a scouting party.

"We are all Mages, we of the Espadryni," Josh-Chevrie said. "If I cannot help your man, there are those more powerful at our camp."

"It's not the eyes exactly," Mar said. She took Gun by the shoulder to steady him. "It's nausea and dizziness. Gundaron's a Finder you see and . . ." Mar's words dried in her throat. If she hadn't known Dhulyn Wolfshead so well, seen so often how very little of her moods and feelings showed on her face, Mar might have missed the way Josh-Chevrie's face froze for just a split instant before it returned to his previous expression.

She looked around, but the faces on the other riders told her nothing. Somehow, she felt a tension in the air that hadn't been there a moment before, as if they were all more watchful, though Mar wouldn't have believed that possible. She tapped out a code against Gun's shoulder, hoping he was not in so much misery that he missed it.

Josh-Chevrie let his hands drop and took a step back. "Marked is he?" the young Horseman said. "Are you Marked then yourself, girl?"

"No. That is, well, no." Mar looked from one man to another. They all had the same wary hardness in their faces now, which told her this was not the time to explain that she *had* been Marked, in a way, once upon a time. Gun's grip on her elbow warned her further.

"Step away from the Marked one, girl," Josh said, holding his hand out to her.

"What? No. I don't understand," Mar said. Her grip on Gun tightened as one of the riders set an arrow to his bowstring. The Red Horsemen couldn't possibly be prejudiced against the Marked, not when all their women were Seers. Unless that was not true here—in which case, why would Bekluth Allain make such a point of their telling the Espadryni Gun was a Finder?

Unless all were against the Marked here, which the trader would have known very well. An icy ball formed in Mar's stomach.

"You are safe now, come away," Josh said, beckoning her forward. "He cannot hurt you any more. Release her at once, Marked one, you cannot escape."

Go, Gun was signaling her, his fingers tapping rapidly on the back of the hand she had on his forearm. *Go,* he signaled again. "One of us must be free," he muttered under his breath. Mar took a scant step away.

"I don't want to escape," Gun said, louder, but in the gentle, reasonable tone he would use to the youngest apprentices in the Library, those who still thought of their homes with longing. "I'm ill, I'm no danger to anyone. As you can see, I can barely stand up."

For answer a rope came snaking out of nowhere, the loop falling over Gun's head and immediately tightening around his upper arms. Another, from a different rider, flicked out and settled around his throat. The bowman, Mar now saw, had raised his weapon only to cover the movement of the men with ropes. Mar tried to lift the loop of braided leather free from Gun's neck, but she was seized, firmly but gently, from behind and pulled away from Gun. He swayed only a little, the noose around his shoulders actually helping him to stay upright.

"All is well now, my girl," Josh said, his arm around her shoulders. "See, we have caught him, and you are safe."

She wrenched herself out of his grasp and ran to Gun. The noose around his throat had tightened, and his breathing was slow and painful.

"What are you doing," she said. She tried to get at the knot of the noose with fingers that wouldn't stop trembling. Finally she pulled the knife from her belt, only to find her wrist caught in a grip of steel.

"You do not wish to be free of him?" Josh's voice was as hard as his grip.

"Mar." Gun's voice was a rasp, but firm.

"I . . ." Mar looked from Gun's set face to the that of the Red Horseman. "Why are you doing this? Is it against the law to be Marked?"

One of the other riders gave a harsh laugh, and Josh-

Chevrie himself moved his lips in a way that held no humor. His knife was suddenly in his hand, and he took Mar by the hair, bent her head back and held it to her throat.

"The Marked are broken, unsafe for all they come near, and are to be killed, as you must very well know," he said. "And those who would help them are no better than they. Did you think that because you are so far from your streets and fields that we would not know this? Did you think us ignorant of the laws of the world?"

"She's not Marked, don't hurt her." Gun's voice was tight. "Mar, tell them."

"But—" Mar coughed. It was almost impossible to get her throat to work when her head was being held at this angle. "We're from the Path of the Sun," she managed to croak. "The other side."

"Of course you would say so now," Josh-Chevrie said, signaling to his comrades. "But the Marked lie as easily as the rain falls." The hand holding her hair shook her and Mar winced at the sharp pain. "I ask you again, do you wish to be free of him."

"Yes, yes, she does." A tug on the rope brought Gun to his knees.

One of them had to stay free. One of them had to find the Wolfshead and the Lionsmane. But she knew full well that neither one of the Mercenaries would save themselves at the other's expense. *Never?* A small voice inside her spoke up. Not even to save others, many others? Not even to fulfill their mission. If she gave Josh-Chevrie the answer that would keep her free, would it really be because Gun wanted her to?

Mar tasted cowardice in the back of her throat. "Yes," she said. "Free me." She almost staggered as the hand in her hair loosened, but the young Horseman caught her, holding her up with an arm around her waist.

"Josh." One of the others had been looking out from the circle. "Here are their tracks," he said. "They have indeed come from the direction of the Door of the Sun."

Mar's heart leaped. Here was proof, the Red Horsemen would believe them, and all would be well.

"They may well have," Josh agreed. "Did we not see the smoke?" He pointed with the knife still in his left hand to where Gun lay on the ground. "Doubtless this piece of inglera dung set the fire when he found he could not escape through Mother Sun's Door." He released Mar and squatted next to Gun.

"For that we will burn him ourselves."

"Josh." The pensive tone came from one of two men still on horseback, guiding their mounts with their knees to keep the ropes around Gun taut.

"What now, Tel-Banion?" Josh-Chevrie's tone was clearly impatient.

"Are we sure? He seems to care about the girl, to want her to save herself. A Marked one, a broken one, would not do such a thing."

Mar's heart lifted with hope.

"Unless he is trying to trick us," another of the Horsemen said.

"Gun would never hurt anyone," Mar said. "Never."

"If these *have* come through Mother Sun's Door, perhaps they are like the Mercenary woman we have been told of." Once again it was the Horseman called Tel-Banion.

"Wonderful." Josh-Chevrie threw his hands into the air. "Now all broken people will simply claim to be from the other side of the Door. I lead here," he said. "And I have decided."

"You lead here so long as we agree," Tel-Banion corrected. Something told Mar he'd had to make that distinction before. "Why not at least cloud speak? Get the assistance of those who have had to make this decision in the past."

Josh strode over to where Gun was kneeling on the ground and pushed off the headscarf, grabbing a fistful of his sandy hair. The Horseman looked at each of his companions, and he evidently did not care for what he read on their faces. For a moment Mar thought that Josh would simply cut Gun's throat, and she covered her mouth to keep from crying out.

Finally he lowered his knife hand, and thrust Gun away from him.

"Very well," he said.

The next morning, when the sun was creeping toward the middle sky, Dhulyn Wolfshead was a handful of spans away from the pit, examining the ground as she rode in ever widening circles.

"What is she doing?" Bekluth tapped his thigh with the fingers of his left hand. He could see even from this distance how the light shone right through her. *There's no darkness in her, not even a spot.*

"There's quite a mix of tracks here, immediately around the orobeast trap," Parno Lionsmane said. "My Partner is looking farther afield for the tracks of our two Brothers, to determine the direction they were coming from when they fell into the pit."

Bekluth's hands tightened into fists, and he forced them to relax and open again. He could still see the element in this man that turned away, that spoke to something other than the light. *I've got to get away*, he thought. He needed his cache of brandy if he was going to have a chance of helping these two.

"And what will their direction tell her?" he said aloud.

The Mercenary Brother tilted his head and looked at Bekluth from under his golden brows. The corner of his mouth quirked up. The tattoo on his temples flashed red and gold in the sun. "Traders usually show more patience."

Bekluth gave the man his brightest smile and touched him lightly on the shoulder with his closed fist. "Ah, but I've learned the value of information," he said. "So what is it the Wolfshead hopes to learn?"

"Their direction, the manner in which they rode, the speed. Other things. If, for example, they rode side by side, then they were traveling, not tracking. Or if at high speeds, they were chasing."

"So you are hoping they were either riding in single file, or quickly." He took his lower lip between his teeth and furrowed his brow, to show how deep his interest was.

"Exactly. We already know they were following tracks, so the direction they came from would tell us where we should look for the tracks they were following. And how close they felt they were to their quarry."

"And you mean to say she can tell all of this from their tracks? How fast they were riding and all the rest of it?"

"Most Mercenary Brothers could, yes," the man answered with a grin. "It's part of our Schooling, though my Partner is exceptionally skilled. Much of tracking is a question of applying experience to your interpretation of what the signs you find tell you."

"It's very complicated to be a Mercenary Brother, I must say. No wonder you're all so open—you haven't time to be devious," he added putting a carefully judicious expression on his face.

"It might be that," Parno Lionsmane agreed. "Myself, I think it's more likely that we kill the dishonest ones in Schooling."

Bekluth let his eyebrows rise in shock. "Kill them, you say?"

Parno shrugged. "We're a Brotherhood. We can't trust anyone else. We *have* to trust each other."

Bekluth tilted his head to one side and affected a studious expression. "Yes," he said finally. "I can understand that."

All the while they were talking, Parno Lionsmane was watching Dhulyn Wolfshead, not taking his eyes from her for more than a few seconds at a time. Bekluth had seen this look on the man's face before, in the faces of other men. He'd tried wearing that look himself, and with some success if he was any judge. Still, how could a man with hidden darkness truly Partner a woman who was made of light?

Unless, of course, someone helped to rid him of that darkness.

At that moment Dhulyn Wolfshead raised her arm, and her Partner nudged his horse forward with his knees.

"They came from that direction," she said, pointing to the southwest, "and were heading that way."

"Toward the Path of the Sun?"

"I know of nothing else in that direction," Dhulyn Wolfshead said. "They were side by side," she added. "Riding at a good pace and sure of the trail they followed."

"And are you sure?"

Bekluth looked from one of the Mercenaries to the other. Dhulyn Wolfshead regarded her Partner with her blood-red brows raised and her mouth twisted to one side. The look said, "I love you, but you make it difficult."

"Sorry," the man said, grinning. "I forgot who I was speaking to." His look said, "I love you, but you have no sense of humor." Bekluth stored away both expressions in his mind.

"Age will do that to a man," Dhulyn Wolfshead said, with the same kind of teasing expression on her face. "I have seen a mark that occurs with some regularity, at least five times, and not, before you ask, in conjunction with the tracks of our Brothers."

"So what now?" Bekluth asked.

"Now we ride round to the far side of the pit. With luck, we'll find these marks there, and we will be on the same trail our Brothers were on when the pit intervened."

"Well, I wish I could come with you," Bekluth said, squinting at the ground. "This is all so interesting. But," he straightened, "goods don't trade themselves, and I'm off." He gave the Lionsmane an expression of particular acknowledgment, lifting his eyebrows and pressing the center of his lips together. "It has been a pleasure passing time with you," he said. "Good luck in your hunting."

Whistling, he watched them ride out of sight. They'd be easy enough to find. After all, it wasn't as though Bekluth didn't know where the trail they were following led.

Twenty

"IT'S NO USE." Dhulyn got up from her knees, and dusted off her leggings with a few sharp slaps. "I can't be sure," she continued, still frowning at the ground. "They're as likely to be the wrong marks as the right ones." As she straightened, she rubbed the small of her back with her fists in a way that Parno found familiar.

"Is it your women's time?" he said.

Dhulyn looked at him with narrowed eyes. "How is it that *you* remember a sore back means my women's time is coming, and *I* always think it's just a sore back?"

"You're keeping count of the days," he pointed out. "Or at least you usually do. I have to keep track by other means." She shot him a look that was half annoyance and half amusement. That was familiar too. "I know you don't believe me when I say I hate to ask you this, but as your women's time *is* so near, do you want to try using the tiles? You may get a more useful Vision than you did the other night."

Her blood-red brows drew down into a vee. "You may be right," she admitted. Hands still at the small of her back, she bent, twisting first one way then the other. She shrugged and walked back to where Bloodbone waited for her, swinging herself into the saddle. "I could have a good, clear Vision with Winter-Ash and her friends, if they would only agree. As good a one as I ever had with the White Sisters."

"But even without help your Sight is improved, isn't it? Since the White Twins I mean. Or am I mistaken?"

She looked over at him, eyes still narrowed. "You are

not. It is. But perhaps it will take me a little time to think of it that way, after so many years of my Sight being more burden than help to us."

Dhulyn wouldn't say the word fear aloud again—fear of what might happen to her, fear of what she might See—not even to him. Of course, he was the only one she didn't need to say it to.

Still, Parno was not surprised, when they stopped for a meal several hours later, that Dhulyn brought out the silk bag in which she kept her box of vera tiles and set it down next to her as she ate. "The fear behind you eats your spine." That was the Common Rule. Only a fear you faced couldn't hurt you. He let her sit silent as he cut off rations of dried meat pressed with raisins and seeds and set them on large slices of the pan bread they'd been given by the Espadryni. When she was ready, Dhulyn would tell him.

Finally she took a last swallow from the water bag, took a little more to clean her hands, and, opening the ties of the bag, pulled out the plain olive-wood box that held her tiles. Parno got to his feet and fetched Dhulyn his bedroll, spreading the heavy cloth on the ground in front of her, to give her a kind of tabletop. She nodded her thanks without speaking, set aside the Lens tile in its tiny bag, and began searching through the loose tiles for a Seer, a Healer, a Mender, and a Finder. As she set the last one aside, she hesitated, finally looking up at him.

"Bekluth Allain wanted to buy these, or borrow them. He said he could make a good profit if he found someone to make them."

"What of it?"

"If they are unknown here, how did he know they are called vera tiles?"

Parno frowned. "*Did* he know, or did one of us use the term?"

Dhulyn shook her head, her lips twisted to one side. "I do not believe so, but . . ." She shrugged. "Whose tile shall I use this time?"

"Yours or mine, I should think," he told her. She was nodding even before he finished speaking, her long scarred fingers searching through the remaining tiles for a Mercenary of Swords, which would do, in a pinch, for either of them. She then returned all the loose tiles to the box, set the

Mercenary of Swords face up in the center of the cloth and, starting with the Marked tiles, began to lay out, facedown, the pattern she called the Seer's Cross, drawing tiles from the box as she needed them.

Then, one by one, in the prescribed order, she turned each tile over. A pattern began forming as she turned the final three tiles, colors shifting . . .

GUNDARON OF VALDOMAR IS ON HIS KNEES, A NOOSE AROUND HIS NECK. A YOUNG MAN WITH BLOOD-RED HAIR AND A GHOST EYE ON HIS LEFT CHEEK STANDS OVER HIM, A LONG KNIFE IN HIS HAND. . . .

SHE IS RUNNING DOWN A WIDE ALLEY, OPEN TO THE SKY. NO, SHE IS RIDING BLOODBONE, SHE CAN FEEL THE HORSE MOVING UNDER HER EVEN THOUGH SHE CANNOT LOOK DOWN. BLOODBONE'S HOOVES CLOP AS THOUGH THEY RIDE ON PAVEMENT. THERE IS A RED BRICK WALL ON HER RIGHT AND DENSE, THORNY HEDGES ON HER LEFT. THE AIR IS WARM AND SMELLS LIKE SUMMER, THOUGH THERE ARE SPRING FLOWERS ON THE BRIARS. THE ANGLE OF THE LIGHT, THE TWISTED QUEASINESS OF HER STOMACH, TELL HER THAT SHE IS ON THE PATH OF THE SUN. BUT SHE HAS NEVER SEEN THIS PART BEFORE. IS SHE LOST? . . .

BEKLUTH ALLAIN'S FACE IS LINED NOW, AND HIS FOREHEAD HIGHER. HE IS SITTING AT A SQUARE TABLE, ITS TOP INLAID WITH LIGHTER WOODS, WRITING IN A BOUND BOOK. THERE IS A TALL BLUE GLASS AT HIS RIGHT HAND AND A MATCHING PITCHER JUST BEYOND IT, HALF-FULL OF LIQUID. DHULYN CAN SEE THE WINDOW ON HIS FAR SIDE, ACROSS FROM WHERE SHE'S STANDING, AND IT IS DAYLIGHT NOW, THE SUN SHINING. THE WINDOW LOOKS OUT ON RUINS, WATCHTOWERS FALLEN, BRIDGES CRUMBLED INTO THE RIVER, STREETS FULL OF RUBBLE. THE MAN LOOKS UP, SAYING, "HOW CAN I HELP?" . . .

DHULYN STANDS AGAIN ON THE ROCKY OUTCROP, THE THREE ESPADRYNI WOMEN ARRANGED AROUND HER. THEY ALL STAND WITH THEIR ARMS AROUND EACH OTHER, SMILING, BUT WITH SADNESS IN THEIR EYES. . . .

"SISTER." DHULYN TURNS AND BEHIND HER, GESTURING HER FORWARD WITH BECKONING HANDS, ARE THE WHITE TWINS, THEIR COLORLESS HAIR AND SKIN, THEIR PINK EYES, IDENTICAL EXCEPT FOR A FLECK OF GOLD COLOR IN THE LEFT EYE OF THE WOMAN TO THE RIGHT. BEHIND THEM SHE CAN SEE THE FLOOR OF THEIR ROOM, SCATTERED WITH TOYS. "TAKE CARE," THEY SAY. "LOOK WELL AROUND YOU. YOU KNOW. YOU HAVE ALREADY SEEN THE ANSWERS." . . .

GUN IS RUNNING IN FRONT OF HER, LOOKING BACK OVER HIS SHOULDER TO BECKON HER ON WITH A GESTURE NOT UNLIKE THAT OF THE WHITE TWINS. THIS TIME SHE RECOGNIZES THE WALLS OF THE PATH OF THE SUN.

A FACE STARES BACK AT HER FROM THE WALL, WIDE-BROWED, POINTED OF CHIN, THE NOSE VERY LONG AND STRAIGHT, THE LIPS FULL CURVES. THE EYES HAVE BEEN FINISHED WITH TINY CHIPS OF BLACK STONE, SO THAT THE FACE DOES INDEED APPEAR TO BE STARING . . . .

"Nice of the White Twins to tell us to be careful, but I don't think that gives us as much help as they might have wished. And what answer is it that you've already Seen?"

"It strikes me that if I can connect with the White Twins while in Vision, my Seer's world has just become a much larger place." She might not need to be physically with other Seers, she thought. It might be enough to speak with them while within the Visions themselves. "That may be the answer for the Espadryni as well. Perhaps I could see them in a Vision, whether we are together or not."

"It's a big perhaps, and you are usually the one who says better cautious than cursing."

Dhulyn nodded, but slowly, finding herself unwilling to give up the possibility that she was not completely alone with her Mark. "If I See them again, I'll try to speak with them; perhaps that will give me proof, one way or another."

"And in the meantime, is there anything useful we can glean from what you Saw?"

"Bekluth Allain still offers us his help, even as an older man—do you think that means we shall still be here?" Dhulyn did not wait for Parno's answer. "Visions of the past have always had special importance for me, but seeing the Path as it must have been in the time of the Caids . . ." She shook her head. "How is that useful?" She looked up. "I Saw Gundaron again."

"On the Path or with the Red Horsemen?"

Dhulyn looked over to him sharply, but Parno was doing his automatic check of ties, buckles, and straps, preparatory to mounting Warhammer. So he hadn't realized what he'd just said.

"That *is* how I've Seen him," she acknowledged. "Both on the Path and with the Horsemen." She shoved her box of tiles into her top pack and tied it shut so fast she almost cut herself on the leather thong. She swung herself into the saddle. "Quickly," she said. "He's come through the Path, and the Espadryni have found him."

"And so?" But Parno was already in the saddle himself, already urging Warhammer to follow her at the horse's top speed.

"So he's a Finder," she shot over her shoulder, and was rewarded with a look of instant comprehension.

Alaria crept out of the bedroom with her clothes and boots in her arms, leaving Falcos sleeping. She let the door swing quietly shut behind her. She was sorry to leave him like this, but she wasn't certain she would be able to say good-bye again.

I wouldn't be saying good-bye at all, she thought, her nose wrinkling at the thought of dealing with Epion, *if it wasn't for the queens*. Quickly she pulled her tunic on over her head and tugged it straight before picking up her trousers. Her responsibility to the Arderon horses was a real one, weighty enough that she was not justified in putting her own safety first. Exactly the kind of responsibility she would have to the people of Menoin if she ever became their Tarkina.

When, she told herself. When *I become their Tarkina*. What Falcos had said was very likely true. No, was definitely true. She, herself, had nothing to fear from Epion. And who knew? Once out and free, she would find a way to free Falcos as well.

Like stick a knife in Epion. She smiled grimly as she pulled on her boots.

Heading for the door, she found her footsteps hesitating. What if they didn't let her out? She straightened her tunic again and pushed back her hair. Only one way to find out.

Alaria took a deep breath and crept up until she could bring her lips close to the edge of the outer door.

"Hello?" She winced as her voiced trembled and cracked. She only wished she were acting. She cleared her throat.

"Is there anybody out there?" she said. "Hello?"

Alaria sat back on a padded and cushioned settee while a Healer took her pulse. As she'd hoped, the guards Epion had left outside the door had been instructed to let her out if she'd asked them to, and one had escorted her to Epion's own sitting room, where the Healer had been quickly summoned.

Footsteps sounded in the anteroom, and the guards with her straightened more carefully to attention as Epion Akarion entered the room.

Alaria leaped to her feet, pulling her hand away from the Healer.

"My lord," she said, using the possessive for the first time. "Oh, my lord, can you forgive me? Oh! I have been so foolish!" She put one hand on Epion's arm and covered her face with the other. She had said she wasn't a good enough actress to fool anyone, but it was easier to put a catch in her voice and tears in her eyes than she would have expected. And, with luck, Falcos was right—Epion would *want* to be fooled.

"Lady of Arderon," he said, taking one of her hands in his own. His blue eyes were narrowed. "Thank the Caids you are safe." He looked at the Healer. "She is well?"

"Anxious, but otherwise bearing up soundly after her ordeal," the Healer said, a touch dryly Alaria thought.

"I'm so sorry," Alaria interrupted. She was horrified to find she was shaking, but hoped it made her more believable. "I believed him, that's what makes me so ashamed. He swore he was innocent, he . . ." Her voice drained away as her throat dried. What should she say Falcos had said or done? Why had they not planned this more carefully? She could not say that he'd admitted to the killing—Epion of all people knew that was not true and that Falcos would never say it was. Epion would suspect her immediately if she said such a thing.

"I thought he was so brave," she said finally. "To stand up for his rights, to fight. A hero out of the old tales." She screwed up her face. "But when I was worried about the horses, he raised his voice to me, he told me not to be so silly. He's nothing but a coward, a bully, and he . . . he was crying. Like a child. *Crying*." She shook her head and wrinkled up her nose, hoping she had not overdone it.

Epion patted the hand he still held. Apparently she'd given a convincing performance of a girl silly enough to endanger herself out of storybook illusions. "There, there, my dear." Epion's voice was smooth and warm, his eyes rounded now in concern. "We have all made mistakes with

Falcos—all been tricked by him into seeing something that is not there. Are you feeling better now?"

Alaria accepted a linen handkerchief from the Healer and used it to wipe her eyes and nose. "I just feel so foolish. My cousin would not be proud of my behavior. But I am better," she said, smiling what she hoped was a brave smile.

Epion made a gesture toward the door, and Berena Attin, the Steward of Keys, stepped into the room. The woman looked tired, Alaria thought, as if she had not been sleeping very well.

"Have you a suite ready for the Lady of Arderon?" He turned back to Alaria. "You may imagine that the Tarkina's rooms are not safe enough for you, my dear."

"The blue suite has been prepared, Lord Epion," the Steward of Keys said. She held her hand out toward the door, indicating that Alaria should precede her.

Alaria turned to Epion. "May I have a guard with me? Please?" she said, ignoring the guards who had already started to move to the door. "I know it is very foolish of me, but I fear to be left alone." There, that should help him believe her sincere. Since she was going to have guards anyway, she might as well make some use of it.

"You will not wish to go far? Not riding?"

Alaria put her hands to her mouth. "Moon and Stars, no. At least not until . . . but I will wish to go to the stables. To see that the queens are well. And ready for the marriage."

Did she imagine it, or did Epion just relax?

"Of course you may go to the stables, my dear. So long as you are safe." He kissed her hand and led her to the door. At the last moment, as she turned away, he gave her a look she could only think was one of admiration.

It was possible, Alaria thought as she allowed the Steward of Keys to lead her away, that she was not fooling Epion any more than he was fooling her. It was possible that Epion believed she merely wanted to be Tarkina and had calculated that Falcos was no longer her best chance.

It was possible that last look meant he was applauding what he saw as a valuable performance, one that supported his own.

Alaria shivered, remembering that Falcos had warned her not to be too confident. She would have to be even more careful than she'd thought.

It was after midnight when Bekluth Allain reached his cache in the Caid ruins. He led the wheezing and stumbling horse as far from where he camped as it was possible to go and yet still be inside the perimeters of the forbidden area. He'd Healed it twice to enable it to reach his camp, but it was useless now, too far gone to recover by itself. It had got him here in record time, and that was the important thing. Unfortunately, he couldn't just let the thing drop—at least not before getting the saddle and bridle off it and taking it far enough away from his campsite that its rotting corpse wouldn't attract the wrong kind of attention. Fortunately there was an old cellar hole—so deep that its bottom was dark even when the sun was directly overhead—not more than a couple of spans away that he'd used for this purpose before. There was a spot near one edge where it was easy to push a horse over, a horse that was barely able to stand, that is. Whistling, he retraced his steps to his own campsite and proceeded to unburden and hobble the packhorses. They hadn't been carrying as much weight as the horse he'd been riding himself. He'd give them until daylight to rest, judge then which of them had recovered enough to be useful. Still here, grazing on the plentiful grass, was the second horse he'd brought from the other side of the Door, but caution told Bekluth he should be saving that one . . .

Bekluth set about making camp, taking his usual care that the fire wouldn't be seen. The Mercenaries weren't the only ones who knew how to be careful. Still, he might as well make himself comfortable. He wouldn't be able to fetch out his cache of drugs until the sun came up.

"Tracks here," Parno said. "And Horsemen ahead."

"You astonish me." Dhulyn ducked just in time to avoid the blow Parno half-heartedly aimed at her head.

"You're the one who's always telling me not to argue ahead of my facts," he pointed out. "That could be a copse of trees ahead, and not Horsemen at all."

"Then why are you riding faster?" Dhulyn angled Bloodbone over until she was riding knee to knee with her Partner.

"I have a bad feeling," he said, all traces of humor gone from his voice.

As she rode, Dhulyn mentally reviewed what weapons she had to hand before pulling her short bow loose from the loops of hide that held it under her left knee and freeing the bowstring from the hidden pouch sewn into her quilted and beaded vest. She fitted the loop at the end of the bowstring onto one end of the bow and, bending the flexible yew around her shoulders, forced the other end of the bow into the corresponding loop. She immediately let go of the weapon and let it hang, perfectly positioned for quick use, across her back from shoulder to hip, leaving her right arm free for the sword if it was needed.

From the number of mounts, there were five Horsemen in the group they were approaching, and it was clear at what moment the group became aware of them, as three of the Horsemen swung up into their saddles and began to ride toward them. Dhulyn could now see that there were two people on the ground, sitting or kneeling, along with the two remaining Espadryni. Though she could not make out whether their tunics were blue, Dhulyn did not doubt they were Mar and Gundaron.

Parno drew off to the left, giving Dhulyn maneuvering room, without even troubling to signal to her. His simple action was enough to show her the plan as clearly as if they had discussed it for hours. He would take the three mounted men, she would go for the captives. The three advancing Horsemen spread out slightly, but they didn't seem inclined to split up completely. Dhulyn took aim between the two to her own right and drove Bloodbone between them. When they saw what they thought was her trajectory, the two drew a little closer together, as if to concentrate on her and leave Parno for their fellow.

Dhulyn looped her reins loosely around the pommel of her saddle and signaled Bloodbone with her knees. She drew her sword but didn't raise it, leaning forward along Bloodbone's neck. In the last possible moment, when the other two riders, their own short blades raised high overhead, were close enough that Dhulyn could see the ghost eyes on their foreheads, Bloodbone suddenly stopped dead in her tracks, hopped stiff-legged six paces to the right, and bolted. Dhulyn, laughing and crying out encouragement, sheathed her sword as she clung to the mare's mane.

She was close enough now to see that one of the two remaining Horsemen was holding the smaller, dark-haired Mar in his arms, while the other—a blade in his hand—held the kneeling Gun by the hair. Dhulyn swung her bow off her back, pulled two arrows free from the quiver tied to her saddle. The man holding the blade reached down with it, bringing it closer to Gun's throat. Mar struggled in the arms of her captor, almost succeeding in pulling herself free.

Dhulyn raised herself slightly until she was standing in the stirrups, legs flexed to minimize the effect of Bloodbone's gallop, and took aim. This shot was easier than clearing the rings on Dorian's ship, she reminded herself. Here, she was the only thing moving. She let out her breath, held, and shot. And shot again.

The first arrow passed through the forearm of the hand that held the knife, pinning it to the man's upper thigh. The second went into the man's left arm, just below the shoulder. He released Gun, and staggered back. By this time Dhulyn was in the camp, her sword pointed at the man who held a still struggling Mar in his arms.

"I think you should let go of her, don't you?"

The man holding Mar kept his hands on her and his eyes on Dhulyn's face long enough that Dhulyn thought he might hold to his pride and honor rather than admit defeat. She was just wondering if she could manage without actually killing him—or whether that in itself might be considered the greater insult—when he snatched his hands off Mar as though she were burning and stepped back two paces. As soon as the girl was free, she ran directly to Gun and began pulling off the nooses that encircled him.

Seeing her friends were taking care of themselves, Dhulyn drew sword and dagger, threw her leg over Bloodbone's shoulders and slipped to the ground. "Do I have your parole?" she said to the boy who had been holding Mar.

"You have," he said, backing away a further pace and looking around him. Both his horse and that of the other young man had stood their ground, well-trained beasts that they were, but he made no further move toward them, and Dhulyn turned her attention to the wounded man.

He looked away as she squatted next to him.

"What do you think now, Tel-Banion? Does she seem so whole and unbroken to you?"

"Hold still, you young fool. No need to make simple flesh wounds worse by squirming." Dhulyn looked at the other boy. "Tel-Banion, is it? Come here and help hold him."

"She's going to kill me, don't help her, Tel."

"If I were going to kill you, you'd be dead," Dhulyn observed. The wounds seemed as straightforward as she'd intended. "Will you give me your parole as well, or should I leave you skewered?" By the normal rules of her world, Dhulyn wasn't bound to help him unless he surrendered, and it seemed from the young man's hesitation that those rules might be different here. "By my oaths as a Mercenary Brother, if you surrender to me, I cannot hold you as slave or hostage, nor can I sell you for ransom. On the other hand, if you *don't* surrender, I *am* permitted to either kill you or leave you to die."

Still, it seemed that this young man also considered refusing her. "If *you* give me *your* parole now," he said, clearly serious, "I will stop my Tribesmen from killing you when they have dealt with your friend."

"Three against one are considered easy odds for Mercenary Brothers. We don't get worried until there's at least, oh, seven or eight against one of us. But I don't mind waiting."

"Josh!" Tel-Banion's voice held a warning. Dhulyn looked from one to the other. Their expressions were very much alike.

Finally Josh licked his lips. "You have my parole," he said.

"Here, brace his arm first," Dhulyn instructed Tel-Banion. As soon as the boy had wrapped his hands around the wounded boy's elbow, Dhulyn snapped off the fletching of the arrow and pulled the now clean shaft through the wound. This was the fleshy part of the upper arm, and there was very little bleeding. The wounded boy, she noted with approval, hadn't even flinched, though it must have been quite painful.

"Mar, the wound cloths are in my left saddle pack."

"I remember," the girl said, and with a last touch on Gun's hair went to Bloodbone. Both of her friends looked pale—understandable, Dhulyn thought—but there wasn't time yet to find out why they were here.

"This other arrow—hold still, I said—will be trickier," she

said to Tel-Banion. "Hold his arm tight to his thigh while I break off the fletching. Then you'll hold his leg and the arrow shaft while I pull his forearm free. Mar, stand ready to wrap a cloth around his forearm should there be any spray of blood, though, to be honest, I don't believe I hit an artery. Are we ready?" Both Mar and the boy nodded. "Now."

The fletching broken off, Dhulyn pulled Josh's forearm free, and as she suspected, there was very little bleeding. She was examining the wound to the thigh when the sound of hoofbeats made the two Espadryni boys look away. The light that was dawning in their eyes soon faded, however, and Dhulyn was careful not to smile at their disappointment.

"Took you long enough," she said to Parno, without looking around at him. A good show of confidence right now would make the young Espadryni easier to handle.

"If you were in a hurry, you should have let me kill them."

At that Dhulyn did look around. Parno was leading the three horses, saddles empty, while their riders walked behind.

"Did you get their parole?" Dhulyn asked.

Parno made an elaborate show of looking around him. "Is your grandmother here? Is she in need of lessons?"

Dhulyn grinned. "Have a look at Gun while I finish here." She estimated she had just time enough to finish removing the arrow from Josh's thigh before his fellow Tribesmen arrived.

"I will have to cut around the head of the arrow to free it," she told the boy. "It will hurt, but it is most important that you don't move. The artery is here," she indicated a line along his inner thigh. "But it's best to take no chances."

He swallowed, licked his lips, and nodded.

"Do you want bite down on this?" She held up a clean piece of arrow shaft.

"I won't need it."

Dhulyn shrugged. "Fine, they're your teeth. Brace his leg, Tel-Banion, and, Mar, make a pad of that wound cloth, and as soon as I have the arrow head out, press down on the wound as firmly as you can."

Luckily these were not war arrows, with their barbed heads, but razor-sharp hunting arrows. Dhulyn prodded delicately at the wound. The head had gone cleanly through Josh's forearm and imbedded itself perhaps two finger-widths into the meat of the young man's thigh. Dhulyn found she had to enlarge the wound only very slightly to allow room enough to withdraw the arrow head. However, she had to be very careful that the head, as sharp as it was, would not slip deeper into the thigh, causing more bleeding and endangering the artery.

She looked first at the young Espadryni, Tel-Banion, then at Mar. When she had their nods, she began to cut. Her dagger was as sharp as the arrow head itself and made the cut cleanly, though blood immediately welled up into the space she had created. The leg trembled under her hands. "Steady," she said, and the trembling stopped. She spread the cut wide with the hard edges of her fingertips and, gripping the arrow shaft with her left hand, yanked it free. Mar was already there with the pad of wound cloth, handing Dhulyn another piece with her free hand as she applied pressure.

"Lift the leg—keep the pressure on!" Dhulyn unrolled the wound cloth Mar had handed her and with a few deft turns had the wound wrapped and tied off.

Dhulyn stepped back, straightened to her feet, and found her arms full of Mar. She kissed the little Dove on the top of her head and moved her gently away, indicating Gun with a flick of her eyes. Dhulyn then looked around her, taking in the group of young men. The wounded Josh and the one who had helped her, Tel-Banion, looked to be the oldest in the group. Dhulyn frowned. Whether a scouting or hunting party, it was unusual to have so many young men without a seasoned oldster with them.

"Now, then, who is the leader of this band?" All eyes looked at the wounded boy. "And who wants to explain to us why you were trying to kill our friends?"

Twenty-one

"SO HERE ALL the Marked are—are *murderers*?" Gun still looked pale, Parno thought, but he seemed to have regained his appetite.

"Keep in mind that we have only met the women of the Espadryni, but so, in a manner of speaking, we have been told." Dhulyn spoke with the natural caution of the Brotherhood but in terms that the Scholar Gundaron would equally understand. In both their professions, facts weren't facts until they'd been tested and proved. As the Common Rule said, "It's neither sugar nor salt 'til it's tasted."

"And in your place, on the other side of Mother Sun's Door, the Marked are as normal people are?" This was the group's second-in-command, the young man called Tel-Banion. One of the others had used a magic of healing on Josh-Chevrie, who now slept to one side, rolled and padded with several blankets and horse pads. A fire had been built, water warmed, and tea made. Dhulyn had demonstrated once more her skill at shooting from horseback, and two prairie squirrels and a rabbit were roasting on the coals, next to a handful of flat cakes Mar had made from the flour and salt in Parno's pack.

"Aside from the Mark itself, yes," Dhulyn said. "They have the normal range of human emotions, love, hate, anger, pity, envy—"

"Stubbornness, vanity, conceit," Parno added with the most innocent look he could manage.

"And let's not forget patience, forbearance, tolerance, indulgence—" Dhulyn riposted sweetly.

"All of which mean the same thing," Parno pointed out, "which is why Dhulyn Wolfshead is called 'the Scholar.'"

"Rather because I need them in such a great supply."

The young Espadryni men looked sideways at each other until Parno and Mar started laughing, and even Dhulyn smiled. Then the Horsemen relaxed, several of them also smiling—which was the whole point of the banter, Parno thought, out of character as it was for Dhulyn to put on a show for people. Anything to underscore and remind these young men that both she and Gun were, by the definitions of the Espadryni, whole and sound. Dhulyn looked to be feeling pleased with herself in any case, her face and smile as relaxed as he'd ever seen them. But just as he had that thought, she caught his eye and, still smiling warmly, flicked her glance to where Gun lay with his head in Mar's lap.

Patience, she was saying, and Parno knew it was as much a reminder for herself as it was aimed at him. As anxious as they were to learn what had brought their young friends through the Path of the Sun, it was more important to first secure the goodwill of these Espadryni. He had never realized before how much the Brotherhood took for granted the acceptance and respect they generally encountered. They did not usually have to earn the trust of every casually met stranger; their Mercenary badges were like Tarkin's passes, allowing them entry practically everywhere they went.

"Perhaps after we have eaten, I can persuade my Partner to play his pipes for us." Dhulyn's words drew Parno's attention back to the present. "He loves to learn new songs and to share the ones he has."

They were eating, and both Gun and the now awake Josh-Chevrie had been given fens bark tea from Dhulyn's own supply when the Espadryni on watch, eating while mounted not far away, gave a whistle in three long notes, sounding not unlike a high-pitched wolf.

"The Long Trees People." Tel-Banion helped Josh-Chevrie to stand, and the other Espadryni immediately put down what food they might be holding—though one youngster simply stuffed his piece of flat cake whole into his mouth.

"You are not at war with them," Parno said, though he and Dhulyn had both stood when the Horsemen did and, feeling the tension in the air, were automatically checking their weapons.

"No." Josh-Chevrie cleared his throat. "But it is not our season to be in these lands. We must act as guests."

Parno caught Dhulyn's eye, and she nodded. She had picked up her sword from the ground when she stood, and now she hooked it to her belt, where it would be at hand without making her look actively aggressive. Mar was helping Gun to his feet, and when Dhulyn went to stand beside them, Parno took up a position on their other side, leaving space enough to swing his own sword if needed.

The scout, his horse barely trotting, entered the camp. "Only two," he said, turning his mount around so that he was facing in the direction from which he'd come. The rest stayed on their feet, Parno noticed, perhaps for the same reason that he and Dhulyn had sheathed their swords. It would take them only a moment to whistle up their horses and mount, but to do so before the others arrived would not be acting like the guests they were.

It seemed only a moment until they heard hoofbeats slowing to a trot, and the two Long Trees Tribesmen entered the camp.

"Greetings, Josh-Chevrie." The taller one had his head tilted to one side, and both were grinning. "Did you fall off your horse?"

"Had a small disagreement with these Mercenary Brothers," Josh said, gesturing behind him. "But we are sorted now."

"Parno Lionsmane, Dhulyn Wolfshead, it is good that you are here." It wasn't until the man greeted him that Parno realized the two Long Trees Tribesmen were Moon Watcher and his brother Star Watcher. It was clear from their faces, and the way they smiled at Dhulyn, that they had received the news. "Is it you who have brought the Cold Lake People?"

"We have no need of others to bring us," Josh-Chevrie said, a hint of steel coming into his voice.

Parno took a breath, but at the flick of Dhulyn's left thumb held his tongue.

"Our Singers sent us when they saw the fire's smoke in

the sky, to see for ourselves how bad the damage was and how far it might spread," Josh-Chevrie said. "We were on our way back to our own territory after the rain when we found these two," he gestured at Mar and Gun, then winced as his wound moved.

"Found them, left them, and found them again, if the trail we have been following tells us anything," Moon Watcher said.

The Cold Lake Tribesmen looked around at one another. Dhulyn's fingers moved in a flash of signals.

"If I may," Parno said, and waited until everyone was looking at him. "It's obvious there is much to discuss, news to exchange. Why should we not sit down and talk at more leisure?"

The suggestion was too sensible to ignore, and they were soon seated once more around the fire, the two Watcher brothers together, Parno seated next to Star Watcher, the silent one, with Josh-Chevrie next to Moon Watcher. Dhulyn sat on the far side, with Mar and Gun just behind her, Tel-Banion at her elbow, and the other Cold Lake Tribesmen scattered between. Introductions were made, and Moon Watcher began to nod as soon as Dhulyn explained who Gun and Mar were and where they had come from.

"That explains then, how it is that their track comes out of the area of burning." Moon turned to Josh. "But along their trail we found a place where they met a man riding a Cold Lake horse. This man sat with them a while, made a small fire, and then left them, heading east. Sun Dog and Grass Snake are following that trail now. Was it not one of you then?"

Josh shook his head. "We came upon them here, where you find us." He raised his head until he could direct his gaze across the banked fire and over Dhulyn's shoulder. "Who was it you met then," he asked Mar. The Espadryni might accept Gun because Dhulyn had said to, but Parno noticed they didn't speak directly to him if they could avoid it.

"The trader that we told you about, Bekluth Allain," Mar said.

"That's an odd coincidence," Parno began. "Ah, no, forgive me. If there is only one trader who moves among the Espadryni, of course it's not odd that when anyone meets a trader, it should be the same man." He shrugged. He didn't recall the trader saying he'd met anyone, but then again, why should he?

"Nor is it odd that you should have seen the marks of a Cold Lake horse," Tel-Banion said from his seat next to Dhulyn. "We traded horses with him some time ago."

The Watcher brothers looked at each other, and so strong was the sense that they were exchanging information between them that Parno actually reached out with his Pod sense to see if he could feel the exchange. But, of course, he felt nothing.

"We do not wish to give offense," Moon Watcher said finally, turning away from his brother to address Josh-Chevrie, "but we would like to examine the hoofprints of the mounts you have with you."

A heavy stillness fell over the Cold Lake Tribesmen, and Parno mentally located the four weapons he had closest to hand.

"I do not know in what way *we* have offended *you*," Josh said finally. "But it appears you believe us to be lying."

"May I ask a question?" Dhulyn's rough silk voice fell into the silence like a delicate shower of rain drops into a pool. "Moon Watcher." She was careful to address the brother who spoke. "A fire may happen accidentally, and in any case, the rains had apparently stopped this one long before great damage was done. Your people have gone to much trouble to follow the trail of my friends. Perhaps if you told us why?"

"You are right, Dhulyn Wolfshead." Moon Watcher looked in her direction, but Parno noticed the man lowered his eyes as if shy to stare at her directly. "If it were only the fire, we should not be here. It is what we found within the area of burning."

"And this was?" Parno took up the questioning, and Moon turned toward him with a look that was close to relief in his face.

"We found a body, partially burned," the man said. "Not killed by the fire, but before, and the fire set to conceal the crime."

"I swear by Sun, by Moon, and by Stars, this was not our doing, nor the doing of any Cold Lake man. Please, examine the tracks of our horses." Josh-Chevrie gestured toward the horse line.

Leaving Mar with instructions to wait with Gun by the banked fire, Dhulyn Wolfshead let the Espadryni lead the way to the horses, deliberately hanging back, giving them privacy and at the same time space for herself to think. If the Watcher brothers were here, and Sun Dog and Grass Snake accounted for . . .

"Moon Watcher." She increased her pace until she was at the man's elbow. "May I ask whose body you found?"

Moon Watcher's eyes flicked toward her, but he must have been reassured by something that he saw in her face, for he answered without looking away. "The boy, Ice Hawk."

Dhulyn froze between one step and the next. She thought of the boy as she had first seen him, his blue eyes watchful, but curious, as his grandfather and the others had brought her and Parno into their camp. And later, as he came to her, big-eyed with excitement, bringing information and ideas he believed might be of use to her. To think that he was gone, and in that way. She drew in a deep breath. Moon Watcher, finding her no longer beside him, hesitated, stopped, and waited, looking back at her.

"And Singer of the Wind, his grandfather, he knows of this?"

"It is why he is not here himself, why we are sent instead. He stayed with the body of his grandson. Gray Cloud and Sky Tree, who I know would wish to be remembered to you, stayed also, to be of help to the Singer in this."

"Of course." Dhulyn nodded. It would have been a great shock, and Singer of the Wind, though by no means as old as the Cloud Singer of the Salt Desert Tribe, was still an old man.

"And he was *not*, you say, killed in the fire?" They'd be looking for the killer then. There would be a blood price to pay, at the very least.

"Not killed by the fire; we wish it were so. The body—" Moon Watcher's voice faltered. "It was a body such as you know of, such as you described to us, Dhulyn Wolfshead."

The truth was there in his voice, in the starkness, in the pain. Dhulyn saw again the horror that had been the Princess Cleona, but her mind refused to show her the image of the boy Ice Hawk. For which she thanked Sun, Moon, and Stars.

Sounds from the horse line reminded her of their present

purpose, and Dhulyn imagined Moon Watcher was as happy as she to turn his attention to the horses of the Cold Lake Tribesmen. One was out with the man on watch, Dhulyn reflected, but the Watcher brothers would have seen those tracks as they followed the man into the camp in any case. The remaining four horses were led off a short way, so that their tracks could be seen more easily.

Both Moon Watcher and his brother Star Watcher inspected each set of tracks, separately and then together. Dhulyn, her professional interest aroused, inspected the tracks herself as each brother finished. The last one examined, Moon looked at his brother, brows raised, and waited for Star Watcher's nod before he spoke.

"None of these horses is the one that rode away from the young strangers."

Dhulyn was still examining the last set of tracks when she stopped again, frozen by what she could not believe was in front of her eyes.

"Parno!"

Her Partner was at her side in an instant, looking to where she was pointing.

"I see it," he said. "But how?"

"What do you see, Mercenaries?" Moon Watcher and Josh-Chevrie had approached them together.

"I know this track," Dhulyn told them. "This is the track of the horse ridden by Princess Cleona of Arderon, one of the tracks that we followed into the Path of the Sun." She turned around and quickly spotted the horse whose tracks these were. Unlike Bloodbone or Warhammer, it was only slightly larger than the other Espadryni horses, and there was nothing in its color or care that would distinguish it. "Where did this horse come from?"

"He is mine." Josh-Chevrie had been leaning heavily on Tel-Banion's shoulder, but now he came forward to his horse and slung one arm over the animal's flank. "I have not had him long; my father traded two horses for him."

"Traded with whom?" Dhulyn had an idea already what the answer would be. "Another Espadryni?"

"No, it was Bekluth Allain," Josh said.

And somehow I am not surprised, Dhulyn thought, remembering the vera tiles. "Did your father ask from where the horse had come?"

"From the fields and towns, of course; from where else would Bekluth Allain bring him? There is not a horse in the land of the Espadryni that we do not all know or recognize."

"But that's the man we met, the man who told us to come this way and find the Cold Lake Tribe." Mar had walked up behind them. Dhulyn went to her and took her hand.

"Are you sure it was the same man?" *Anyone can use a name,* Dhulyn thought. "Describe him."

Mar frowned, drawing her brows down over her dark blue eyes. "As tall as the Wolfshead, perhaps a touch taller, but he may only seem so because he is so thin." She gestured to her ears. "Gold rings in each ear. Straw-colored hair, coarse and thick. Wearing very well woven clothes, expensive cloth I'd judge . . ."

Dhulyn looked to Parno and found him looking back at her. He touched his right ear. *Go slowly.* She lifted her left eyebrow.

"That is the trader," Josh-Chevrie said. "And what else did he tell you?" He sounded almost angry. "Did he tell you to say that your man is a Finder?"

"Yes."

Moon Watcher was looking back and forth between them. "But that would be easily explained, surely. He would have wanted him to find one of the Tribes, so that he could be judged whole or broken. As apparently he was, though it was judged badly."

"You would have done no better," Josh said, stepping away from his horse, his face hard, his injuries forgotten. Moon Watcher looked him up and down, consulted his brother with one look, and put his hand on his sword. "I am no friend of the trader's," he said, the implication clear.

Dhulyn stepped deliberately between them. Normally she'd leave arguing hotheads with noble ideas to Parno—he was used to such people. But she knew that neither of the Espadryni would strike while she stood between them. Their own training—the very honor they were about to fight over—the respect in which all the Tribesmen now held her, would prevent any such actions.

"Sirs." She used her most moderate tone. "In the interest of solving the puzzle we have before us, can we not put honor aside long enough to allow for free discussion?"

"How can honor be set aside?" Star Watcher's voice was so like his brother's that for a moment no one realized it was the silent brother who had spoken.

"What of Ice Hawk's honor?" Dhulyn said, still in her quiet voice. "Since he cannot speak and act for himself, we all," she gestured to herself and around at them, "who are concerned with his death must speak and act for him. Should that not be the first action of honorable men?" Moon Watcher's stance became just a hair less militant, though his hand remained on his sword hilt. Josh-Chevrie showed he was listening by a narrowing of his eyes. Behind him Tel-Banion extended his hand as if to catch Josh by the sleeve. Dhulyn searched frantically through her mind for further, weightier, arguments.

"And what of the honor of your Tribes?" she said. "Are you not obligated to clear yourselves, even in your own minds, of any complicity, however accidental, in the death and the fire. Is that not an honorable task?"

"These are fair words, and true." Star Watcher spoke as if pronouncing from a seat of judgment.

"I agree." Moon Watcher said. His voice was just a little lighter, a little less rounded than his brother's, Dhulyn decided. "I withdraw my remark. It was ill-judged, and I apologize for having caused any offense."

Josh hesitated, and Dhulyn held her breath. Moon Watcher had apologized completely and thoroughly, but Josh-Chevrie had shown himself to be more than a little hotheaded. Finally the young man relaxed, taking a deep breath.

"I accept, I take no offense. Come, let us return to our seats, where we may have this 'free discussion.' "

Leaving the horse line behind them, they found that Gundaron had opened the banked fire and was heating more water, using the largest of the Cold Lake Tribesmen's pots. In it he had put the bones of the rabbit and prairie squirrel, along with some dried herbs Dhulyn recognized as having come from her own pack. Her lips compressed, and she drew in a breath through her nose. Gun's idea was a good one—she might even have suggested it herself—but she thought he knew better than to go into her packs.

When everyone had been served some of the broth, and Dhulyn had explained where to find and how to recognize the wild version of the saphron herb, it was Parno who had the first question.

"Are we sure this is the same killer? The one that my Partner and I have been looking for?"

"Singer of the Wind had no doubt, and I must say we all of us agreed with him. The body was opened and the parts . . . dispersed, in the way you have described to us, Dhulyn Wolfshead."

Dhulyn nodded, grateful that she did not have to describe yet again what she and Parno had seen, that she could push the image of the body—she coughed. "But can we therefore assume that the fire was set to delay or to confuse the discovery of the body? Is there no possibility that it started accidentally?"

Moon Watcher consulted his once more silent brother with raised brows. Star Watcher moved his head once to the left and back again. "We would say none," Moon said. He indicated the fire before them. "The stones of the fire spot had been moved aside, opening the circle. Ice Hawk was young, but even a child would not have prepared his fire in that careless fashion. No Tribesman's child in any case."

"So we can say the fire was deliberate." Josh was drinking his broth one-handed.

"Then the person we seek had both reason to kill Ice Hawk *and* reason to disguise that fact." Whether or not that killer turned out to be the trader, Bekluth Allain. The others seemed to have set aside his actions toward Mar and Gundaron for now, but Dhulyn knew they were still unexplained.

"But why would the killer *you* seek have reason to kill Ice Hawk?" Moon Watcher said. "The tales we have heard from Sky Tree concerning the demons—they have never touched the Espadryni before."

"You speak of the blood demons?" Tel-Banion cut in.

Moon nodded. "True, it was a man of your Tribe who told Sky Tree the tale, now I remember. You know of this then."

"We know." The Cold Lake Tribesmen exchanged glances. "But if it is a demon you seek . . ."

"As we have said, he leaves footprints and rides horses. If he is a demon, he at least wears the body of a man," Parno said.

"How can we know what such a man is thinking?"

"Gundaron of Valdomar has made a study of the killings in our land." Dhulyn turned to Gun.

"Usually a person kills for specific reason: for gain, in revenge, in defense, for love or hate, or for honor." Gun inclined his head in a short bow to their hosts. Gun's manners had become more polished since she and Parno had seen him last, Dhulyn thought. Now that he had recovered from the ordeal of the Path, he sounded like a Scholar of twice his age and experience.

Though Gun had experienced some things no other Scholar could.

"Even those whose minds have been touched by some illness, even they have reasons that make sense to them, however much it appears irrational to us. But this killer . . ." Gun shook his head. "This killer seems to have chosen people who were . . . available, for want of a better word. Lone travelers with little or no escort. Young people—or in one case a married person who had gone to meet a lover."

"Ice Hawk was no such stray person," Moon Watcher pointed out.

"And in no other case was there an attempt made to cover up the killing."

"As if," Parno suggested, "the killer needed Ice Hawk dead but could not stop himself from killing in his preferred fashion."

"And then tried to disguise the deed, so that we would not associate it with him," Moon Watcher said.

"I agree," Dhulyn said. "The setting of the fire shows that Ice Hawk was himself the intended victim, killed as himself and not because the killer came upon him unaware."

"Would the trader have particular reason to kill this Ice Hawk?" Mar's voice was quiet, but this was the first time she'd spoken since they'd returned to the camp from the horse lines. Trust the little Dove to keep her eye on the trader.

Moon Watcher shook his head. "I cannot believe this. We are seriously talking about Bekluth Allain, someone I've known almost the whole of my life, to commit such an act . . ."

Dhulyn saw the merest glimmer of an idea. "Which is precisely why Ice Hawk never mentioned him," she said. "We described the killing, we asked who had been near what you call the Doorway of the Sun at the times we knew about. Of course Ice Hawk never mentioned Bekluth Allain—a man you have known for many years, and certainly a man Ice Hawk had known his whole life. It would not occur to Ice Hawk that the atrocity I described could have anything to do with a man so well known to all. A fair man, an honest man, a charming man, accepted by all the Tribes."

The three young men of the Cold Lake Tribe looked stricken, but not, Dhulyn thought, as if they did not believe her. No, they seemed more to be wondering if they might themselves have made the same mistake that Ice Hawk had evidently made, given the same circumstances. The Watcher brothers looked at each other in their now familiar silent communion.

"We live with the Marked, with those soulless ones, and we have never seen or heard of such a thing as you described to us." Moon Watcher's voice was rough, as if the nature of his thoughts had somehow affected his throat.

"Perhaps they are not so broken, not so soulless as you have believed," Dhulyn said. "Perhaps, after all, there is something worse."

Parno cleared his throat. "May we return to the subject more directly at hand?" he said. "Do we agree that the trader Bekluth Allain may be the killer?" He looked at the faces around him, so similar in coloring, all marked somewhere with a ghost eye. "We know the day the killer passed through the Path of the Sun. We know that either he eluded Ice Hawk entirely or that he was someone so well known to him that the boy did not consider him a possibility. The trader certainly falls into that category."

Parno paused and waited for the slow signs of agreement.

"He drew attention to that himself," Dhulyn said, remembering. "When we first spoke with him, he asked who had been at the Door, pointing out that whoever was there would have seen and recognized him had he been there himself."

"But would that not show him innocent?" Tel-Banion was still trying to push the whole idea away from him.

Dhulyn found herself nodding. "It could be," she acknowledged. "But the fact that he was not being hunted will

have told him already that he had not been named. And—"
Dhulyn held up a finger, an idea just having occurred to her.
"He would not have needed to kill Ice Hawk when he first
came through the Door, since he would have no way of
knowing we were just behind him, ready to accuse." A sudden cold landed in Dhulyn's belly. "Once we told him, however, he would know that Ice Hawk could denounce him at
any time."

"You are saying that he went back and killed the boy
after we spoke to him. After *we* told him that the boy could
be a danger to him." Parno's voice showed the same sense
of cold despair that Dhulyn felt herself.

"He had a horse that came from your world, so at the
very least, he has had some contact with the killer," offered
Moon Watcher. "For that alone he should be found and
questioned."

"I think we can also say that he deliberately endangered
your friends by sending them to us and advising them to
confess the Mark." Josh-Chevrie was nodding now.

"But surely we have explained that? Surely we cannot
hold that against him?" Tel-Banion said.

"A moment." Dhulyn turned to Mar. "Did you tell him
you were looking for us?"

"Yes," Mar said. "Oh, we may not have mentioned you
by name, but we said Mercenary Brothers, and he certainly
knew who we were talking about."

Dhulyn looked around at the Tribesmen. "Bekluth Allain certainly knew we were not with the Cold Lake People,
and yet that is where he sent our friends."

Now even Tel-Banion was nodding. "Nor are we the
closest to the Door, not in this season."

"So Bekluth Allain deliberately misled them," Josh-
Chevrie agreed.

"At the very least, he has questions to answer." Moon
Watcher stood. "We will try a cloud reading, so the next
Espadryni who meets Bekluth Allain will hold him for us."

The others were getting to their feet as well. "I thought
only the Singers could do that," Dhulyn said to the Watcher
brother.

"It is true that only Singers can send complicated messages through the clouds, but my brother and I together can
send simple ones. 'Look for the trader,' 'hold him for us.' We

can manage that much, but it takes both my brother and me to do it."

While the Watcher brothers went to find a good spot for cloud speaking, the others kept on talking, turning over and over again their thoughts, ideas, and speculations as to why, if Bekluth Allain was not whole, no one had seen this, as if even now they had trouble believing it.

"How could our Singers not have seen something in him?" a Horseman would say. And the others would brighten.

"Is it because he is a man?" another would suggest, and then the light would fade as they turned to look at Gun.

"You say you saw him at the orobeast trap?" Josh asked Dhulyn, the first time, she noted, that he had addressed her directly.

"He said he was going to find your people—by the way, is your main camp in some unusual or unexpected spot? Have you moved recently?" The looks on their faces were all the answer she needed. "Another lie." She nodded. "We'll have to go back to the trap and track him from there."

"Um, I can do better than that." Gun had been quiet for so long that several of the Espadryni jumped a little on hearing his voice. Dhulyn found herself smiling her wolf's smile. The boy had color, his eyes were bright.

"I can Find him."

Twenty-two

LARIA PRESSED HER head against Sunflower's
shoulder and breathed in. The familiar scent of hay,
of the grain mash, the good, half-bitter smell of the
horse's sweat and the faint aroma of the dung underlying
all. Alaria closed her eyes against the sting of tears. Home.
The horse smelled like home.

Somehow it was only this morning that she had fully realized that she would never see her home again—that if she
didn't lay down her tiles very carefully, she might not even
see the next moon. Servants had come in to help her bathe,
to help her dress, and to serve her breakfast. All the things
that Cleona would have enjoyed so much. Alaria swallowed
the sob that threatened to leave her throat, straightened her
shoulders, and stroked the mare's neck where her forehead
had been.

Horses were sensitive, foaling queens even more so, and
she must not let her own emotions transfer themselves to
Sunflower.

Epion had asked her to dine with him the evening before,
but her nerve had failed her. She'd pleaded a headache—a
real one as it happened—and stayed in the rooms they had
given her. Her own things, her clothing and personal belongings, had been brought there by the lady pages. Epion had
sent her a flowery note by means of the Steward of Keys,
offering to send the Healer, but Alaria had thanked them
and said no.

Berena Attin, the Steward of Keys, had been stiff and

formal with her, not at all the warmly friendly person she'd seemed to be when Alaria had arrived with Cleona. Alaria had seen some of that same stiffness in others of the palace staff.

Alaria leaned against Sunflower's water trough and wrapped her arms around herself. She'd known almost immediately why Berena Attin no longer smiled. The woman must be loyal to Falcos and was probably thinking the less of Alaria for deserting him. And the horrible thing was, Alaria had to go on letting Berena think so. That had not occurred to her. When she and Falcos had talked this over, she'd been thinking in terms of tricking Epion; she'd forgotten that she wouldn't know who to trust, who she could confide in, any more than Falcos could. She hadn't realized how much it would hurt to have these people believe what she needed Epion to believe.

I'm not marrying Epion, she thought, forcing her breathing to slow, her shoulder and neck muscles to relax. No matter what happened, Falcos was still alive, and there was still much that could be done. Berena Attin couldn't be the only person here loyal to Falcos, though it was hard to think how a woman who could not leave the palace proper could be of any real use. But Dav-Ingahm, the Steward of Walls, where was he?

There was a part of Alaria that had wanted to stay in the blue suite. She felt safe there, even knowing that the guards were there to keep her in. But instead she'd sent a page to ask Epion for permission to visit the queens, showing him that she made no move without his knowledge and consent. If she was going to be any use to Falcos, she had to convince Epion at the very least that she *was* playing her part, that she could be trusted. And for now that meant leaving the suite, however much she might have preferred to lock the door again and stay behind it. She'd also known that if she gave in to her fear now, she might never be able to leave, and those rooms, instead of a refuge, would become a prison.

The two guards who had accompanied her to the stables this morning were different from the ones who had stayed with her overnight, but Alaria had noticed that while they wore the palace colors of black tunics with purple sleeves, none of them had the crest that marked them for the Tarkin's personal guard. She passed fewer people in the upper corridors of the wing of the palace that housed the Tarkin's actual residence than she'd remembered seeing before. Where were the servants bringing hot water, or ganje, or even breakfasts, to the rooms on the upper floors? Even the lower levels, the public audience and meeting rooms, the suites allotted to minor nobles, the rooms of upper servants—often the same people—the clerks' offices, the kitchens, and the dining hall itself where many of the servants slept as well as ate—all these seemed half-deserted.

And many of the people who had been attending to their duties had passed her with their eyes down, though a few had shown her sympathetic faces before bowing and letting her pass with her guards in tow. And once or twice she'd seen knots of pages and servants in the distance that broke up as soon as they saw her, with her guards, approaching. But there also seemed to be a few who were already saying things like "mad Falcos," and only occasionally "poor mad Falcos."

Alaria let herself out of the horse stall, latched the gate shut, and leaned her arms on the top of the low wall that formed the enclosure. After a flick of an ear in her direction, Sunflower went back to searching for overlooked oats in her feedbox. Who, who among all these, could be trusted?

Alaria sighed and looked toward the door. The guards were there, one outside and one in. She badly wanted to go out into the courtyard and see if she could make out which of the square stone towers that rose above this level housed the rooms Falcos was in. She took another deep breath, releasing it slowly. Best not to think of that right now. Best not to wonder if he was even still alive. She thought she knew enough about how Epion's mind worked to understand that Falcos might be found dead at any moment—in his prison suite, or even at the bottom of the tower, if Epion still wanted his death to look like a suicide.

I should have stayed with him, she thought, a wave of cold passing through her like a winter's wind. But would her presence really have made it harder to murder Falcos? Wouldn't her staying just have meant that she would be killed too? Wasn't that why Falcos had wanted her to leave? She rubbed her arms, trying to feel warmer. She could only hope the day wouldn't come that she wished she'd stayed.

Two young stable pages came chasing each other down the ladder from the haylofts, their whoops and laughter stopping abruptly when they saw her standing at Sunflower's stall. The guard was suddenly beside her, sword drawn.

"Pardon, my lady, oh, please, we didn't know you were here." Eyes round, looking from her to the guard's blade, they paled even further, stumbling over their apologies and edging away to get a clearer shot at the open door. Mindful that anyone, even children, might be a source of news and help, Alaria forced herself to laugh and hold out her hands to the two young pages. *And surely these were too young to be suspect.*

"Are you the ones who have been taking such good care of my queens?" And in response to their nods, Alaria added, hoping her smile didn't look as false as it felt, "Then I must send you a special pastry from the Tarkin's kitchen. Which kind do you like best?"

Careful negotiation established that it was already too late in the year for strawberries, and the two pages settled for plums.

"You may go back to your duties. I will see that the pastries are sent."

"One for each of us—what?" said the blue-eyed page when the other elbowed her in the ribs. "The princess *said*."

Alaria laughed. "Yes, one each, don't worry. Now, before you go, find me Delos Egoyin; tell him I wish to speak with him."

"I hope you're not leaving the princess alone, you two." Delos Egoyin arrived in minutes, drying his hands on an old bit of blanket. "Only the other day a guard was attacked, actually attacked, here in my stables. I ask you, with the Tarkin gone mad, poor boy, is there anything left for the gods to visit on us?" Delos shook his head.

"Come to see your queens, have you, my lady?" he continued. He was smiling now, but Alaria thought she could see a shadow behind his eyes just the same. His fondness for Falcos had seemed genuine, Alaria thought. Did he believe the rumors and accusations that Epion was busy circulating, or did Delos, like Alaria herself, merely play a part, hoping that circumstances would favor their side once more?

"Sunflower seems to be in fine shape," she said. The mare thrust her head over the gate and snuffled Alaria's hair, knowing, in the way that horses do, that she was being spoken of.

"The others are just as fine, and their foals as well. Perhaps you'd like to see?" He led her back through the barn to the inner section where mares with foals were kept. This time the guard, Alaria noticed, did not follow. He probably knew there was no escape through here. The three queens were set next to each other in separate stalls along the wall of undressed stone, which was actually the outer wall of the palace grounds, with nothing but air behind it. It was quieter here, and darker, though shutters had been left open on the roof to let in air and light.

"Tomorrow or the next day I'd like to move these ladies out of doors," Delos was saying. He and Alaria were leaning their elbows on the top of the enclosure. They were almost the same height, Delos stooped not from age but from the necessities of his work. "I was waiting for Sunflower to foal first, to keep them together, but it looks as though she might have other ideas."

"Where is the paddock you are thinking of?" Grateful for the distraction, Alaria was trying to remember where she had seen open-air paddocks for the royal horses.

"Ah, well now, I'll show you right now, if you wish. But I have another plan in mind. How would it be if you came this afternoon, after the midday meal, and I'll give you a complete tour of the whole yard, horse stables, barns, hawk mews, dog kennels, everything, so you'll be better able to make plans for the breeding of the new herd."

There was something in the way Delos' eyed her that told Alaria this invitation was important, more important than an inspection of what one day might—or might not—become her responsibility.

"I'd love it," Alaria said, her heart already lifting at the prospect of possible action. Then the memory of the part she was playing came back to her. "But let me ask leave of Lord Epion," she said. "There may be other duties that require my presence."

"Cara!" Delos called, and then jumped as the blue-eyed page appeared out of nowhere. "Caids, girl! Don't sneak up on a man like that!"

Cara grinned, shrugging up one shoulder. "It's my job to be ready, to jump when you call, and you've always told me to do my job well."

"At least let me know you're there, for the Caids' sake;

you've taken years off me, child, years. Now go to the Steward of Keys and find out what duties Princess Alaria has for this afternoon."

Alaria smiled, watching the child run off. She barely remembered her own father as a handsome face, a warm laugh, and gentle hands. He'd had the charge of running her mother's household, but he'd died when Alaria was a little girl, and her mother had hired a woman to be housekeeper and clerk. Alaria was brought back to the present by the sound of her own name.

"So far as the Steward of Keys knows, Princess Alaria has no official duties this afternoon," the page Cara said, panting slightly from her run. "Berena Attin says she'd be hard-pressed to know what official duties she *could* have before she becomes Tarkina." A silence fell. Alaria tried to keep her face from showing what she actually thought about that eventuality, at least as it involved Epion.

"Well, then, this would be the time then for our little tour, before the princess becomes distracted by other matters. It would take your mind off things, my lady." Delos turned to address her directly. "Set your mind at rest, is what I thought, as to what you'll have to deal with in the future, if you follow me."

Alaria's smiled stiffened. Delos had no gift for intrigue, she thought. The rats that were undoubtedly in this as in every other stable, no matter how well looked after, could probably follow him, understanding that there was something he wanted to show her and that this afternoon would be the perfect time.

"How can I resist," she said, giving the old man a genuine smile.

Alaria did not get away from the head table of the dining room quite as quickly as she would have liked. Epion had been there, carefully not sitting in the Tarkin's seat but in his own usual seat one chair to the right. They'd had Falcos' empty seat between them, and that was a convenient excuse not to exchange more than the necessary civilities. Epion enquired as to her health and how she had slept, and he scattered a few polite enquires as to whether she enjoyed certain of the dishes. Alaria asked for, and received, his gracious permission to tour the stables and barns, whereupon she was left to herself. She couldn't be sure, but there seemed to be more guards in blue wearing the single purple sleeve that marked them as Epion's than there had been before—and again, no one with the Tarkin's crest on their tunics. Many of Epion's guards found the need to consult with their lord during the meal.

Every time one of them approached the table, she tried to react naturally, and not as if she expected each and every one of them to suddenly point at her—or bring news she was afraid to hear.

She was finished long before everyone else at the table, pushing a piece of honeyed pastry back and forth on her plate and hoping that Epion wouldn't notice and offer to have the pages bring her something else. Alaria had always envied the head table for being served first, the few times she had been at court, but she now realized it meant you were also finished first, and that you couldn't leave without everyone in the room noticing it and wondering where you were going.

So she waited, smiling at those who caught her eye, until Epion stood. She waited for a count of three before standing herself, which earned her a dazzling smile. By letting him rise first, she'd treated him, Alaria realized with a sinking stomach, as though he were the Tarkin.

Let it not be an omen, she thought.

Alaria had no difficulty with the two guards who were now with her. These again were new, but she thought they must have been briefed by their brethren. It seemed that after not even two days of watching and following, the guards assigned to her were already getting bored. Epion had granted his leave for her to go on a tour of the stables and yards, and apparently these two men saw no reason to accompany her into every barn and shed, since Delos Egoyin himself would be with her.

They began in the cow barns, and, as she had expected, the old stableman led her, talking volubly all the way, through to the back where this building, like the horse stables, shared a wall with the palace.

"Would you like to see the lofts?" he asked, with his hand on the ladder. "I'm afraid there's only the ladder," he added, "no staircase."

"I wouldn't expect one." Delos stepped aside to allow

Alaria to go up the ladder first. Having some experience with barns and stables, she had changed from the gown laid out for her in the morning into her Arderon riding clothes. Though she'd been told the hay harvest had not been a good one in Menoin that year, the loft was nevertheless piled as high as Alaria could reach.

"Is every barn as full as this one?" she asked. Considering how few were the animals in the Tarkin's barns, perhaps some distribution could be made to the people.

"Ah, no, my lady, not exactly. It's just that we found it easier to consolidate what we had, if you see what I mean. Easier to keep track of, easier to distribute."

Barely hearing the man's words, Alaria nodded, examining the wall in front of her. Was this where the secret passage came out in the stables? Would she be able to access that network and somehow free Falcos? She heard Delos move behind her and started to turn.

A hand clamped down on her mouth, and a knife appeared at her throat.

❧

The three riders appeared out of nowhere and were upon him before Bekluth could change direction. He congratulated himself that his luck had held as usual, however, since he was the better part of a day's ride away from his hiding place. He could tell right away that he'd been seen, and to change direction now would only make it obvious that he was trying to avoid them. So he stopped and waited for them, waving greetings, just as he normally would. That had been one of the first things his mother had taught him. Do the things that people expect whenever they're looking, and they won't notice anything else.

When they came close enough for Bekluth to recognize their Salt Desert hair braiding, he relaxed even further. The Salt Deserts were the most numerous of the Espadryni Tribes, and he traded more with them than with the other two. They were all inclined to like and trust him, of course, he'd seen to that, but the Salt Deserts liked and trusted him more.

"Greetings, trader."

"I greet you. Fox-Bane, is it not?" Bekluth focused his most engaging smile on the leader of the small band. "How are those arrow heads I traded you last Harvest Moon?"

"I have lost one." As Bekluth expected, however, the other man smiled back.

"Then we are very well met, very well met indeed." Bekluth dismounted and, letting the reins of the horse fall to the ground, went to the pack on the smaller horse. In the end he'd had to use the remaining horse from the other side, the guard's horse, much as he would have preferred not to. But neither of the other two horses was capable of carrying him, though they were not quite as bad as the one he'd had to dispose of. He'd taken the better of the two, with a lightened pack.

As he expected, Fox-Bane also dismounted and joined him.

"This horse is almost done," the man said, passing his hand over the beast's neck and feeling down its right foreleg. "What have you been doing, trader, running races?" The other two Horsemen laughed.

"Is it not well then?" Bekluth asked innocently. "I just got him from the Cold Lake People a few days ago."

"It is not a Cold Lake mount," one of the other men said, edging his own horse closer and pointing. "Look there at its mark. That's a Long Trees horse."

All three men looked at him. Bekluth affected disgust, shaking his head with his lips pressed together.

"Well," he said, shrugging his shoulders, "it appears I am not as canny a trader as I thought." Just as he planned, the Horsemen laughed at him, and the tension disappeared.

"Perhaps I *will* trade you for new arrow heads, then," Fox-Bane said, "since your skill is so bad at the moment—though I warn you, I have no half-dead horse to offer you." They all laughed again, and Bekluth forced himself to join in.

"Fox-Bane, you forget we have a message," one of the other men, still on his horse, said.

"I forget nothing." Fox-Bane's tone was sharp. "And you would do well not to forget who bested you the last time you spoke out of turn."

For a moment it seemed the other man would challenge, but then he gave a slightly sardonic bow, and the moment passed. Just as well, Bekluth thought, these idiots were always fighting over nothing.

"There is a message for you, trader." His authority established, Fox-Bane turned back to Bekluth. "You are being looked for, sir. There has been a cloud message asking that any who find you should accompany you to where the Long Trees People await you."

Bekluth's mind worked furiously. The Long Trees People. In all the years that he had been dealing with the Espadryni, he had never been sent for. This could be bad, very bad.

"Happily," he said aloud. "Do you know why I am wanted?" Three of them, all armed, though none of them had anything in their hands at the moment. Bekluth closed his hand on one of the knives he had hidden in his trade pack. Could even he kill Fox-Bane fast enough to deal with the other two before they armed themselves, or, worse, rode off?

"The cloud message did not say," Fox-Bane said. "Only that you were needed." Bekluth released the blade and drew out his hand with the small pouch of steel arrow heads in it.

"Perhaps the Long Trees People have also been losing their good hunting points," suggested the man who had spoken before.

"Just so long as they have no more poor horses to trade me," Bekluth said, shaking his head with a rueful smile. "Come, I was just about to stop and have my meal in comfort. Will you not join me?"

"Only a man of fields and towns would need to sit on the ground to eat," Fox-Bane said. But the other two were already dismounting.

"May I ask one of you to build a fire?" Bekluth said. "I have a new five-spice tea I would like you to try, and I take so long to make a good fire . . ." As he'd suspected, the opportunity to show off was hard to resist, and while the three Horsemen argued about the best kindling materials, Bekluth returned not to his trader's pack but to the saddle-bags on his horse. His hand brushed his special knives, but he passed them by after only a moment's hesitation. Undoubtedly at least one of these men needed opening—there were very few people without enough darkness inside them that some needed to be let out. But he had no time. He could not take the chance that this summons meant him ill.

When the five-spice powder had had its effect, Bekluth transferred his pack to Fox-Bane's horse and rode away. He must get to the Door of the Sun, he thought. He regretted leaving Dhulyn Wolfshead. Regretted it more than he could say. But it was time for the trader Bekluth Allain to disappear.

⊂⊃

"Perhaps he is not Marked after all."

"Don't be silly, Tel, he'd know whether he was Marked or not. Wouldn't he?" Josh-Chevrie was scratching at the healed arrow wound in his forearm. Parno caught the young man's eye, tapped his own forearm and shook his head. Josh shrugged and grinned, but he stopped scratching.

Though Parno had overheard the exchange, the two Tribesmen had been speaking quietly enough that they had not disturbed the group gathered around Gundaron. Dhulyn, Mar, and Gun sat cross-legged on the ground, with the Watcher brothers seated just outside their small circle. Gun was shaking his head, rubbing at his eyes, and Mar put her hand on his arm. Parno moved closer and squatted beside Dhulyn.

"I can Find, I tell you, my Mark's back, I just can't Find *him*."

"Where's my second-best bowstring?" Dhulyn asked.

"That won't work," Mar pointed out. "We've both seen you pack often enough that *I* could probably tell you where it is."

"Where is the mate to this?" Moon Watcher took a silver ring banded with thin gold wire from his left ear and handed it to Gun. The Finder closed his hand on the earring, closed his eyes tight, and pressed his lips together.

"Your son is wearing it," Gun said without opening his eyes.

Dhulyn looked at Moon Watcher with raised eyebrows. The man nodded, his eyes fixed on Gun's hand. When the boy offered him back his earring, he hesitated before taking it.

The Cold Lake Tribesmen, who had gathered near to listen to the exchange, flicked glances at each other, and two of them moved casually farther away, as if they were afraid Gun would Find something in them without being asked. Parno would have laughed if the matter at hand were not so serious.

And if it wouldn't have led to a time-wasting challenge to satisfy someone's honor.

"That's easy," Gun was saying. "Even a untrained Finder

can find the mate to a pair of objects if he's got one in his hand. I'm trying to Find a person I don't know, someone I met just once."

"But it was not so long ago," Dhulyn pointed out in her mildest tone.

"I know, but I was sick then, and now I just can't seem to concentrate."

Mar scrubbed at her face with her hands. "It's the bowl," she said. "If we had the bowl here Gun could do it."

"It's not your fault, Mar," Gun started to say when Dhulyn raised her hand.

"Wait. The little Dove is nevertheless thinking in the right direction—I intend no pun. Before you had the use of Mar's scrying bowl, did you not use books as tools to concentrate your mind?"

Gun turned to Dhulyn, reaching out his hand. "You've got a book with you?" But at the look on her face Gun let his hand fall to his lap.

"I'm afraid I don't. But you have writing tools, do you not? And paper of some kind?"

Mar put her hand on her belt pouch but froze with the flap halfway open. "Gun, where is the other folding knife?"

Grinning, Gun shut his eyes once more. "In a leather satchel, in a . . ." he paused, and reached out with his hand as if to grab something that Parno could not see. "In some ruins, four or five hundred spans south, southwest of here."

Moon Watcher was nodding. "It is an evil place, and brings bad luck," he said. "There are areas of the plains that are hard and shiny like a glazed cup. If there are ruins there, we have never seen them. None of the Espadryni go there."

"Which makes it the perfect place for the trader to hide." Now it was Dhulyn who began to get up, and Dhulyn who was stopped, halfway to her feet, by Gun's raised hand.

"He's not there, though. The folding knife is, but not Bekluth Allain."

Dhulyn blew out a breath and sat back down. "Then show me your blank pages," she said to Mar. The little Dove quickly sorted out half a dozen pieces of parchment and a dozen more of paper, in various sizes. Dhulyn shuffled through them and picked out one piece of paper, handing the others back and accepting the thin leather-covered board that served as a portable writing surface.

"Parno, will you be my desk?"

First giving her his best bow, Parno knelt in front of Dhulyn, positioning himself so that she could use his back as a table. Mar handed Dhulyn a pen and knelt to one side, near Parno's head, with the ink pot.

"Careful with that," he warned her. "My badge needs no modification."

The girl smiled back, but it was the thinnest smile Parno had ever seen from her.

"Now," said Dhulyn, dipping the end of the pen neatly into the ink. "Start reciting your book."

"My book?"

"The book you have memorized, my Dove—you *have* a book memorized, don't you?"

"*Air and Fire*," she said, nodding. "In a small Holding," Mar paused to allow Dhulyn to write.

"No, my little Dove, just recite," Dhulyn said. "Regular reading speed."

Out of the corner of his eye Parno saw Mar's face clear as she nodded and began again. "In a small Holding to the north, whose name I do not recall . . ." The girl's frown faded as she continued, her lips even taking on the slight curve of a smile. Parno could just feel the motions of Dhulyn writing, conveyed through the pressure and minute shiftings of the board on his back.

"That should be enough," Dhulyn said, leaning away far enough that Parno could stand up.

"Here." Dhulyn handed the sheet of paper to Gun. "Do you need anyone to hold it for you? Act as a desk?"

Gun's face cleared as he saw what Dhulyn had handed him. "I couldn't understand what you were doing," he said. "This should work." He sat once more cross-legged, laying the paper down flat in front of him. He began reading, his eyes flicking back and forth across the page.

"What did you do?" Parno asked. He shifted to one side, trying to get a look at the paper without disturbing Gun.

"I wrote down Mar's recitation in the Scholar's code, the short form of writing that all Scholars are taught. Mar forgot that I know it also."

Parno felt a smile cross his face as he nodded. Dhulyn had spent a year in a Scholars' Library while she was deciding that it was to the Mercenary Brothers that she really belonged.

"That one sheet of paper is at least four regular pages," Dhulyn explained. "It should be enough to allow Gun to concentrate—shhh."

"Shush yourself," Parno said, under his breath. Gun had looked up from his reading.

"I know where he is."

Twenty-three

"IF YOU SCREAM, I'll cut your throat, and you'll be dead before your guard can get here. Do you understand?" It was just a whisper, from a voice Alaria could not recognize.

The whisperer's right hand held her mouth closed and pulled her head up and to the right, exposing her throat to the cold metal. Slowly, Alaria reached up and patted the whisperer's right forearm. She was afraid to nod, afraid to move her head at all. Anyone who had been trained with the sword knew that a blade *pressed* to the skin won't cut, but a blade *drawn* across skin . . .

"Gently, Dav. Julen says the lady's with the Tarkin, she's on our side."

The hand holding her mouth relaxed, but the left hand, the blade hand, stayed where it was. "Let her explain then, why she's out here, and our Tarkin's in the north tower."

Alaria licked her lips, her mouth too dry to swallow. Now she recognized the voice. This was Dav-Ingahm, the Steward of Walls, and this was why she had not seen him before, with Epion. He must have been in hiding all along.

"Falcos wanted me away from him," she said. "I would have stayed, I *wanted* to stay, but he thought I would be safer away from him."

"That sounds like Falcos," Delos Egoyin pointed out.

"Rather convenient for you, though, is it not?" But the blade eased away from her throat. Alaria took a deeper breath than she'd allowed herself before.

"Is it? Epion has no interest in killing me, whether I remained with Falcos or not." Alaria could do no better, she thought, than to marshal Falcos' own arguments to convince his followers. "Epion wants me alive, to keep the treaty with Arderon and to keep the favor of the people of Menoin. If he wants to, it will be easy enough to dispose of me once I've borne an heir." Alaria staggered forward as the Steward of Walls released her. Delos took her by the elbow and led her to a seat on a nearby stool. It was evident from the blankets in one corner, a pitcher of water, and the stool itself that this was Dav-Ingahm's hiding place. Which was the real explanation, she realized, for all the hay being gathered in one place.

"It would have been far more convenient for me," Alaria continued after accepting a swallow of water from Delos, "to have stayed with Falcos instead of having to ingratiate myself with Epion—and alienate Falcos' real friends." The two men exchanged a glance.

"Why, then, did you agree to leave him?"

Alaria hesitated, finding herself reluctant to tell the truth. Men were notoriously impractical and inclined to be squeamish and sentimental, even in the face of dire necessity. Still, Falcos had agreed with her. "He'd be careful who he lets near him, Epion, I mean," she said finally. "But he'll let me into his bed—if it comes to that, if Falcos is killed—I would have a better chance of killing Epion if it seems I came to him willingly."

The reaction of the two men was not what she expected. Far from being horrified, Delos was grinning, and Dav-Ingahm, nodding, sheathed his dagger and came to sit cross-legged at her feet, a look of approval on his face.

"'Keep your friends close and your enemies closer,'" he said. "It's an old saying, and a good one. I'd have tried the same myself—barring the bed part, he's not my type—except that Epion hasn't been able to stand the sight of me since I gave him a thrashing years ago for abusing a hunting dog." He clapped his hands together. "Good. Now that we know where you stand, we can concentrate on freeing Falcos."

Alaria leaned forward. "What's your plan?"

"I know which of the guard I can trust," Dav-Ingahm said, "and they will be on the alert, if not actually on watch, this evening. We have heard from Julen Egoyin that House Listra has been quietly contacting the other Noble Houses and the leaders among the council. She will come in the council's name at the supper hour and demand to see Falcos. She will bring her own guards with her, and, if my messages to the Steward of Uraklios have borne fruit, a complement of the City Guard as well. Whatever the outcome of Listra's representations, we will have enough force to take Falcos ourselves."

"I know Dav here doesn't trust all of the Palace Guard," Delos said. "But I think there are many who are just waiting to see where the arrows fall—not bad men, just unguided. Right now they see Epion in ascendance and fear they have no choice but to follow. If we give them a different option, they may take it."

The Steward of Walls shook his head, but he was smiling while he did it. "Ever the optimist, my friend."

"I merely point out that we may have more allies than we suppose," the stable master said. "I was right about the princess here, after all."

But there was something else in what had been said that interested Alaria. "You say Julen will bring House Listra. What of the Scholars? Mar and Gundaron of Valdomar? Are they with the House as well?"

Again the two men exchanged looks. "They took the Path," Dav-Ingahm finally said.

"What? The Path of the Sun? But why? How?"

"The Finder said he could bring back the Mercenaries," Delos said. "It seemed like an excellent suggestion at the time."

Dav-Ingahm suddenly lifted his hand. "The guard," he mouthed, getting silently to his feet and pulling out his dagger. "Go before he comes any closer. Be ready after supper."

They'd been too long, Alaria realized. They could have seen a barn three times this size in the time they'd left the guard standing at the entrance. Quickly she got to her feet and began to descend the ladder.

"And do you have a mechanism, then, to raise the hay up here?" she asked as loudly as she could, hoping to cover any noise Dav-Ingahm might be making. If they had to kill the guard, so be it, but it would throw off all their plans.

"We have something better," Delos said from where he held the top of the ladder for her. "The palace is on the crest of a hill, as you must have realized coming up here from the harbor. Because of the steepness of the incline, this section here, where the doors are—this section is also at ground level, albeit ground that is higher than where we entered. So then," he added, swinging himself onto the ladder with a practiced movement. "So then, we neither raise nor lower the hay, but drive it right in through those doors."

"Marvelous," Alaria said, carefully not looking around her at the approach of the guard. "A very clever use of existing terrain and circumstances. The original architect was a person of much thought, it seems. Yes? Is there a message?" The guard had by now come so close that she had to acknowledge him.

"My lady, if you will." The man looked from her to Delos Egoyin and back again. "The Lord Epion Akarion sends for you to come at once."

"Of course." She turned to Delos Egoyin. "We must complete our tour another day, stable master. If you will excuse me."

Alaria kept a smile on her face by sheer force of will. This was not an arrest. They could not have been overheard talking in the loft, or Delos Egoyin would have been asked to accompany her, and guards would even now be going into the barn to fetch out the Steward of Walls. But why then was Epion sending for her?

"I think I'd like to take a long rest after this, wouldn't you, my heart?" Parno was riding just to her left, and close enough that he could easily be heard, even over the noise of the horses.

Dhulyn shifted her seat a little so that Mar, riding behind her where the saddle packs would normally be, wouldn't be constantly slapped by the blade of her sword as they rode. Warhammer was the larger horse, which gave Parno and Gun a little more room for comfort, but the Scholar's eyes seemed to be shut tight, and his grip on Parno painful. The boy never could feel easy on a horse. They were moving along at the good, ground-covering pace, steady, that the horses could maintain for hours with only short periods for rest. The Espadryni had all offered to spell her by taking Mar onto one of their horses from time to time, but only the Watcher brothers had offered to take Gun.

Dhulyn glanced over, but Parno was looking ahead once more.

"Feeling your age, are you? What luck your Partner is so much younger and healthier."

Parno turned his head to face her, and lifted his right eyebrow. "What, a man can't get bored with racing back and forth rescuing people? A little variety, that's all I ask for. A few days lying in the sun—you could read a book—a few nights in a good tavern, playing my pipes, drinking wine—or you could read a book."

"Or I could be playing the tiles, winning us the money we'd need to pay for this little rest you seem so fixed on."

"You don't think the Tarkin of Menoin will pay us well for this job? Falcos seemed like a very reasonable young man to me."

"And his uncle seemed to have a very good grip on what things cost, so much will depend on which of them is the Tarkin of Menoin when we return." Dhulyn pursed her lips. Considering what Gun and the little Dove had told them of events in Menoin, should they, even now, be trying to get back through the Path to rescue Falcos? But without the real killer, what help could they give? Better to put their hands on Bekluth Allain and show everyone exactly who was lying, uncle or nephew.

"I'll believe in that money when I see it," she said finally. "Better not to plan on it."

Mar shifted, and Dhulyn automatically did the same to compensate. They didn't know what there was ahead, and Mar was ready to slip off when signaled. Dhulyn reviewed her mental checklist of the weapons she had to hand. Short sword at her left hip, longer sword in its special scabbard along the saddle pad under her right leg; unstrung bow back in its special sling, under her left leg, with arrows hanging just behind her right hip; a dagger in each boot top, a wrist knife under the bow guard on her right wrist; a moon razor under the guard on her left wrist; a small hatchet sewn to the inside of her vest and hanging between her shoulder blades. There were also the lockpicks and wires twisted and sewn into her hair and vest, but, though you could kill people with them, these did not count as weapons.

"But you think it's a good idea."

"Hmmm?"

"Quit taking an inventory of your weapons and pay attention. I'm talking about our having a rest." Parno wasn't teasing now.

"I do," she said. "An excellent idea. But I think that this comfortable tavern, as well as having music lovers and losing gamblers, should be near the coast, so you can practice your Pod sense, and we'll be handy when Darlara's children are born."

Parno, a broad grin on his face, saluted her, fingers to forehead. "You mean when *my* children are born."

"Well, that's what Dar said, but perhaps she was just being polite."

"What's this, what are you talking about? Parno has children?" The little Dove's voice was just behind and below Dhulyn's left shoulder.

"Last season we spent with the Long Ocean Nomads," Dhulyn said. Since Mar could rest her ear against Dhulyn's back, she spoke quietly. This was their private business, after all. "And the Mortaxa on the far side of the world. The Nomads are sworn companions to the Crayx, sea creatures as old as the Caids themselves. Turns out Parno has the Pod sense, the ability to communicate with the Crayx. It's rare, so the Nomads were happy to add his bloodline to theirs."

"But the children?"

"The Mercenary Brotherhood always fostered its children, the few we might have," Parno said, edging close enough that his knee was only a handspan from Dhulyn's. "This way, they are with their mother, and if I wish to visit with them, all I have to do is be close enough to a coast for my Pod sense to reach the nearest Crayx."

Dhulyn could tell that Mar wasn't perfectly satisfied with this explanation—the little Dove had stiffened against her back—but there was no time now for more details.

Not that the ways of the Mercenary Brotherhood were always understood by others, in any case. Add to that the complicated relationships of the Crayx and the Nomads, and they would be here forever explaining.

Moon Watcher signaled a rest break, and everyone got down to walk beside the horses for thirty spans. Those riding scout changed positions with two who had kept to the main group. Josh-Chevrie took Mar up behind him when they remounted, and Moon Watcher took Gun. The part of Dhulyn that thought about such things wondered if there was a book in any Scholars' Library that told about the Crayx. Gun might know. With luck they would have a chance to check.

They had ridden perhaps another sixty spans when Tel-Banion, the westerly scout, came pelting back. The Watcher brothers had identical frowns of disapproval on their faces. What was the point of resting horses, their looks seemed to say, if rest was to be followed by this kind of reckless riding? Their frowns changed when they heard what the younger man had to say.

"Tracks." Tel-Banion's smile was triumphant. He nodded toward where Gun clung on behind Moon Watcher. "Just as the Finder told us. A horse unknown to me."

"I'll wager my second-best sword it won't be unknown to us," Dhulyn said. If the Princess Cleona's horse was under Josh-Chevrie, then the only unknown horse here must be that of the Menoin guard, Essio, the man who had accompanied Cleona.

"I think you left your second-best sword back in Menoin," Parno said.

Alaria set her guards such a brisk pace they had almost to trot to keep up with her. Let them think she was happy to be summoned by Epion. And let her get them away from Dav-Ingahm's hiding place as quickly as possible. She paused only where the main corridor from the stable yard branched.

"Where *is* Lord Epion?" she asked. "The great hall?"

"In the small audience room, my lady," the taller guard said.

"Very well, then you must lead me," she said.

Alaria recognized where they were going as soon as she saw the anteroom with its comfortable chairs and small tables. This was where she had come to speak to Falcos when the Arderon horses had been moved without her permission. This was where she had learned that she was expected to marry him. And where she had agreed.

This time, however, the anteroom was empty, the tables bare; there were no petitioners waiting, sipping cups of watered wine or ganje. The attending pages opened the door for her, and she walked into the audience room, half expecting to see Epion seated in the raised chair.

Apparently he wasn't quite ready to do that, any more than he was prepared to sit in Falcos' seat at the high table in the dining hall. He had, however, had two more tables brought in, and several high-backed chairs with arms, so that the room resembled more the domain of the palace clerks than a Tarkin's audience room.

He put down the scroll he was reading on the table in front of him and turned toward her as she entered the room.

"My lord," Alaria said, smiling as she advanced toward him. "You sent for me."

"I would ask your advice," he said. "There is a school of thought that suggests dark deeds are best done by night. What would you say to that?" There was a sharpness to his eye, and she was suddenly reminded of one of the barn cats in her mother's stables, who could spend hours watching a hole, waiting for the mouse to show itself.

He's trying to frighten me. Either just to see if he could bully and intimidate her, or to see if she had something she was hiding from him. And since she did . . . Alaria walked across the room to one of the other chairs with a back, trying to put into her walk a little of the natural swagger she'd seen in the movements of the Mercenary Brothers. Epion *might* just be testing her, knowing that she played a part, to see which part it was. She sat down, leaned back, rested her elbows on the arms, and laced her fingers together.

"Who decides?" she said.

Epion blinked and Alaria kept her face still, her eyebrows ever-so-slightly raised. Good. She had managed to startle him.

"I meant," she continued without giving him a chance to speak, "who decides whether the deed is dark?"

Epion spread his hands wide. "Shall we say then, merely a deed one wishes to perform in secret, or which one wishes others to overlook. What do you think of this advice?"

Could she do this? Could she make Epion think she was

just as hard, or as shrewd as he? Would that make him more inclined to trust her? Or less? She flipped a coin in her mind. It came up horses.

"I counsel against it," Alaria said. "My mother once said to my sister that if one were caught climbing out of the boys' dormitory window in the middle of the night, there was only one interpretation to be put on one's actions. Whereas, if one were caught doing the same thing in the middle of the day, one could claim merely to have been peeing in the water jugs."

Epion laughed, and Alaria cringed inside. *I have to do this*, she reminded herself. She had to let him think she was on his side.

"In other words," he said when he had finished laughing. "Do what you must do openly, in daylight, as if it were something of no particular note."

"Or, at least, something of lesser importance. Waiting for the dark of night rather gives significance than removes it, wouldn't you say, my lord? People are more curious about things that seem to have been hidden away." Alaria swallowed, hoping that she hadn't gone too far by reminding him of things that might be hidden.

"I do, I must say, agree very strongly. What one gains by narrowing the field of witnesses one can lose by having those few raise unanswerable questions." Epion rested his chin in his hand as if he were thinking over what she had said.

Alaria was not fooled for an instant. She remembered Falcos' warnings about his uncle—and she'd just had a forceful reminder from Delos Egoyin and Dav-Ingahm that men were not fools and ditherers. Epion had made his decision about whatever action he was talking about before she had come into the room. He had meant to frighten her with his ruthlessness, not ask her opinion. She could only hope that she had thrown him off his stride, if only a little, by her own display of ruthlessness.

Epion stood up. "Well, then, seeing as we agree, let us go and dispose of Falcos now."

"Why not just kill me yourself?" Falcos' calm voice quieted the thoughts swirling in Alaria's head. She could barely remember the walk through the palace corridors, her hand on Epion's arm, trying to look at ease and unruffled. Her heart felt frozen in her chest. Epion alone she might have escaped from, but he'd brought with them the two guards he had always by his side. Brothers, she thought. Why hadn't she said something to make Epion delay? Why couldn't she think of something now? House Listra wasn't coming until later in the day, perhaps not until after supper. By that time it could well be too late.

"And put myself into the power of anyone who aids me? I think not." Epion smiled. "No, no, much better if you do it for me. Or, here's a thought. Perhaps I should let you walk the Path of the Sun. Without the key, the Path may very well kill you for me—and if by some action of the gods, you return?" Epion shrugged. "As you have already realized, every now and again a demon comes out of the Path. He looks and walks like a man, and he can be dealt and bargained with like a man, but he's a demon for all that."

Alaria felt her knees give way and stiffened them. She would not faint. She would not fall. Now she knew why Epion had left the two guards out in the hall. Certainly Falcos had suspected his uncle, but to hear Epion, so freely and so blithely confess that he was in league with the monster who had killed Cleona, and before her so many others—even the old Tarkin, Epion's own brother and Falcos' father. Alaria straightened her spine and gritted her teeth. Epion was still speaking.

"I don't know what else may be on the far side of the Path," he was saying. "I don't know if there are more ... men like him." For a moment Alaria saw the man Epion might have been if the gods had not made him heir to the throne of Menoin. A contemplative man, a Scholar perhaps. "Whatever is there, it seems to eat Mercenaries. Perhaps it would eat you as well."

"Epion." Alaria cleared her throat. She didn't know exactly what she meant to say, but she felt she had to do something to distract him.

"Ah, thank you for reminding me, my dear Alaria." Epion turned back to Falcos. "Here are your options then, Nephew. You will voluntarily leap from out that window onto the rocks below in guilt and horror at having killed your father."

"I cannot say that I like that option much. What are the

others?" Alaria could not believe how calm Falcos still seemed. He sat with his right ankle resting on his left knee, as if he was relaxing after some successfully concluded court business, and not discussing the details of his own murder. His wrinkled and dusty tunic and the tear in the knee of his trousers, along with his unshaven face and uncombed hair, illustrated how he had really spent the last two days. His glance shifted to her, and she could not help smiling. She only hoped that if Epion saw it, he would take it for a sneer.

Alaria gasped as Epion suddenly took her by the nape of the neck, his long fingers wrapped around until they almost met at her throat. She grabbed at his arm, twisting to kick out at him, but Epion shifted away, and squeezed until black spots appeared in front of her eyes. She released his wrist, and he loosened his grip. Falcos was on his feet, and Epion squeezed again. When Alaria held out her hand, Falcos froze, and Epion loosened his grip once again.

"You go willingly," Epion repeated. "Or Alaria dies, and you will go in any case, unconscious, or awake and screaming if need be. Yet another murder, this time followed by suicide. Or, I will call my guards, having failed to stop you from choking the princess to death, and we will avenge her. You will die in any case; you have merely to choose who goes with you."

"I don't think you will do anything of the kind, my dear nephew."

The whispery cool voice of House Listra made even Falcos jump, though he was facing the door which had swung silently open. Released, Alaria ran to Falcos, turning to look back toward the door. Behind the tiny body of Tahlia, House Listra, was the dark, bearded face of Dav-Ingahm, the Steward of Walls. He had not waited until the supper hour after all.

"If he's as much as ten spans ahead of us, I would be very much surprised," Josh-Chevrie said.

Dhulyn agreed, scanning the marks Tel-Banion had found. It seemed that tracking might be young Josh-Chevrie's strength. "No more rests," she said, and spurred Bloodbone forward.

They had gained perhaps a half span when the Espadryni all raised their heads. In a moment Dhulyn heard it too.

"Horsemen coming from the east," one of the Cold Lake boys said.

"Ours," Moon Watcher said. "Do not slacken, they will reach us."

In a moment there were five more horses galloping with them. Dhulyn recognized Singer of the Wind, Sun Dog, and Gray Cloud, though the others of the Long Trees People were strangers to her.

"The trader is heading for the Sun's Door," Moon Watcher called out to his leader as soon as the other group came near enough. Dhulyn saw the old man's lips press tightly together. His face seemed thinner, more aged. Ice Hawk's death had taken its toll.

They crested a gentle roll in the landscape, and suddenly Bekluth Allain was before them. He must have heard them at the same time. He seemed to be standing still, examining the ground, and they saw him turn and look around at them. Dhulyn expected him to immediately bolt—either to the Path of the Sun, since he must know the secret of finding it from this side, or simply in an attempt to get away. About to call out instructions to the others, she was struck dumb when the trader, instead of riding away, got down off his mount and began to walk it forward, head once more lowered, as though he were following some trail or pattern on the ground that could not be seen from where she watched. The wind shifted, bringing to them the smell of old burning.

Dhulyn smiled her wolf's smile, signaled to Parno and kneed Bloodbone into a gallop. The thunder of hooves told her she had not moved alone. But though Bekluth Allain must have heard them closing in, this time he did not even look up from his examination of the ground, did not re-mount his horse, but continued walking it, now in the direction in which he'd started, now to the right, then on a diagonal angle to the left, and even, for a few short paces, toward them.

Dhulyn leaned forward in the saddle and drew her sword.

"Stop!" It was Singer of the Wind. "Dhulyn Wolfshead, you must stop!"

Dhulyn drew back sharply on the reins, simultaneously

signaling Bloodbone, and without actually losing momentum the mare hopped sideways, as if to avoid stepping on something unpleasant on the ground. In a very few more sideways paces they had stopped completely, and Dhulyn whirled around to confront the old Espadryni shaman.

"I could have had him by now."

"No." The old man was as out of breath as if he had himself been running. "Bekluth has triggered the opening of Mother Sun's Door—I recognize the pattern he is making. It is the key to opening the Door. He is already walking a closed path, one you cannot see. You cannot enter the pattern from this angle, both you and your horse would be destroyed."

Dhulyn sheathed her sword and pulled her bow free, feeling in her vest pocket for the bowstring.

"Make the attempt if you must, but I assure you that the arrow can no more penetrate the pattern in this way than you could yourselves. If you would follow the trader, you must follow his path exactly, and you are neither of you shaman."

"Parno?" Dhulyn asked.

"Haven't taken my eyes off him. Ready when you are."

Dhulyn turned back to the Singer, smiling her wolf's smile. "We're better than shaman, Grandfather, we're Mercenary Brothers."

The old man peered at her, and suddenly Dhulyn

SEES THE LINES FANNING OUT FROM BESIDE HIS EYES AND THE WHITE IN HIS LASHES. HE RAISES A HAND WHOSE FINGERS ARE TWISTED, JOINTS SWOLLEN, AND TRACES A SYMBOL ON HER FOREHEAD.

"Wolfshead!" Mar slipped off Josh-Chevrie's horse and came running up to them.

Still feeling Singer of the Wind's cool touch on her forehead, Dhulyn called out, "Stay here, little Dove. Singer of the Wind, I leave my friends in your charge. If we do not return, do what you can to send them home."

The old man nodded. "It shall be done."

Dhulyn was already turning to follow Parno as she raised her fingers to her forehead.

*   *   *

Mar ran to where Gun was rubbing his elbow. Moon Watcher had dumped him rather hurriedly to the ground. Mar took Gun's arm and licked her lips, hoping to keep her fear and worry from her voice.

"Are you all right?"

"Sure. I've fallen off horses before." They ran back to where Singer of the Wind sat on his horse. The old man was arguing with the Cold Lake Tribesmen.

"With respect, sir, you are not my Cloud Shaman, nor even a member of our Tribe," Josh-Chevrie was saying. "If I choose to follow these Mercenaries you cannot stop me."

"But by your own admission you have not passed through the Door, young man. I would have to answer to your elders if something happened to you."

"If these Mercenaries can find the pathway, then so can I." Without saying anything further, the young man wheeled his horse around and took off after Dhulyn and Parno.

"Do not think to follow your friends," the old man said, looking down at where Mar and Gun were standing.

"No fear," Gun said. His hold on Mar's hand tightened. By this time the Wolfshead and the Lionsmane had apparently reached the spot where Bekluth Allain had first dismounted.

"That is the very spot," Singer of the Wind said. "How could they know it?"

"It'll be some part of their Schooling," Gun said. "Some *Shora*—like a meditation," he added at the man's enquiring glance. "It helps them concentrate."

The old man was nodding, his eyes narrowed as he watched the Mercenary Brothers copy exactly the pattern of movements they had just seen the trader perform. "It is meditation and long concentration that enables one to see and follow the entry pattern. Some are never able. The old tales say that the true Tarkins of Menoin can be shown the pattern, but it has never happened in my lifetime."

A sudden flash of light made Mar gasp and shield her eyes. For a moment afterward an image of a hedged maze superimposed over the plain before them, clear but translucent, like the curtains of light that were common in the night skies of the far south. Wolfshead and Lionsmane were clearly walking this maze and were about to reach a stone archway.

The image did not fade so much as it winked out between one instant and the next.

One of the riders to their right cried out, pointing. The plain was empty except for the two Mercenaries. Josh-Chevrie was nowhere to be seen.

At that moment the flash of light occurred again, the maze with its stone archway reappeared, and Mar watched, holding her breath, as their friends passed through it and the image faded once more.

The old man, Singer of the Wind, turned to them. "Your friends have entered the Door of the Sun. May the Mother watch over them."

"You young people are much mistaken." House Listra had commandeered the largest chair in the suite and, with Alaria standing beside her, had both Falcos and Epion lined up on their feet before her like delinquent apprentices. Alaria felt calm for the first time in days until she realized it was merely because there was a woman in charge, something that felt normal to her.

"You, Epion, are particularly mistaken if you believe that the decisions you have made and the actions you have undertaken in the last few days have permanence without the agreement of the Council of Houses. The Tarkinate has been in the Akarion line for many years, but not without our support."

"My dear aunt—" Epion began.

"I am not here as your aunt but as House Listra, chief among the Noble Houses, and let me remind you, *Nephew*, with almost as much Akarion blood in my veins as you have yourself, though mine is older." She looked both men over, her thin and wrinkled lips twisted to one side. "Each of you has presented your tale of events, and neither of you has more than your own words to give as proof—if I do not take into account the word of paid employees or friends of the heart." Here the old woman patted Alaria on the arm. "However, in the absence of true proof, which only the Mercenary Brothers can bring us, we must decide which of you is lying."

Epion again opened his mouth but subsided when House Listra raised her hand. *He's not going to learn any time soon*, Alaria thought. She could only hope Listra's solution was a good one.

"Fortunately, neither I nor the council need to decide which one of you we believe. There is an infallible test for such things. The Path of the Sun."

"But House Listra," Falcos said. Trust him not to make the same mistake of undervaluing the old woman that his uncle had, Alaria thought. "We do not have the key for the Path."

"That is what makes the test infallible." Listra struck the floor with her cane. "I told your father, Falcos, that he should walk the Path, and he did not. At the time, the Council of Houses voted with him." She pursed her lips. "We have seen what *that* decision has brought us. Well, the Council of Houses votes with me now." There was clear satisfaction in the old woman's voice.

"Will they both walk the Path?" Alaria asked.

"No, my dear. The Path tests only the Tarkin. And don't you look so smug, Epion. If Falcos does not return and you wish to be Tarkin after him, it will then be your turn. No more half measures. We return to the old ways completely. So say all the Nobles Houses." Listra turned and took Alaria's wrist in her cold hand. "You, my dear, can wait for the outcome. If neither Falcos nor Epion is chosen by the gods, there are still others, not so close but still of the blood, who can be tested."

Like me, Alaria thought. Not so close, but still of the blood. She had said she would not marry Epion. She had sworn it, if only to herself. Would she wait for the Path of the Sun to choose someone for her? She looked at Falcos. Perhaps someone else? She took a deep breath. No. She would make the choice herself.

"I will make my own choice," she said. "And trust in the horse gods and the Path of the Sun to prove me right. I will go with Falcos. I will walk the Path of the Sun with him. And when we return, we will give Menoin a new beginning."

Twenty-four

BEKLUTH ALLAIN YANKED on the reins, but that only made the stupid animal more stubborn, not less. For the hundredth time since he'd seen the riders silhouetted on the low ridge to the north of the Sun's Door, he thought about simply abandoning the stubborn beast. But he'd need the thing later, no matter how foolish and ill-behaved it was. Too bad it didn't have a broken leg—*that* he could have fixed; he could do nothing about a bad attitude. He finally climbed into the saddle despite the animal's dancing around to ûnbalance him. Once he was in the saddle, at least, the beast settled down and seemed likely to obey instructions.

A shimmer in the air warned him that someone else had entered the Sun's Door behind him. Bekluth almost turned around to look before better sense prevailed, and he touched his heels to the horse's side.

It had to be the Mercenaries, more specifically Dhulyn Wolfshead.

"I knew it," he said aloud. "I knew it." He'd known there was something special about her; no one could be so clear and open and not have other talents as well. What a pair they would make if he could only free her from her companion. Perhaps it wasn't too late.

He turned left, then right, into a section of the labyrinth where the footing was pressed earth and the walls solid rock, rugged yet smooth, like cliff faces after eons of being pounded by seawater. Here he *should* keep to the long path that stretched out in front of him, but they would see him as soon as they turned into the area themselves and catch up with him.

Instead Bekluth turned down the first archway on the left and dismounted. There was a crossbow hanging from his saddle. He cocked it, placed the bolt, and waited.

And waited.

Finally even he ran out of patience and, pressing himself flat against the stone, he peered around the edge.

The pathway beyond was empty. They had obviously turned down the wrong way. His luck was with him after all. Too bad, in a way. He was sorry to have missed his chance with the Mercenary woman. Such an opportunity.

Whistling, Bekluth put away the arrows, unstrung the bow, and got back on the horse.

"Don't stop, his scent goes this way." Dhulyn had first let Bloodbone fall into a trot and then a walk. Clearly, she did not want to lose the only trace they had of the trader, but she likewise did not want to fall into the type of obstacle they'd encountered on their way along the Path the first time.

"Did you see that?" Parno edged up beside her. "Through that last opening, between those cedar hedges?"

"What was it?"

"It looked like the hem and trailing sleeve of a court dress."

"What color?"

Despite their predicament—*were* Gun and Mar safe with the Espadryni?—Parno grinned. Typical of Dhulyn that she believed him utterly, even when he said something that made no sense. "Pink," he said.

"I didn't see her," Dhulyn said, "but I smelled vanilla oil." She shot him a glance, the whisper of a smile on her lips. "Not our trader's choice of perfume, I thought."

The path in front of them angled to the right, but as they turned the corner, they noted that tiny shift in their senses of direction that they had experienced before, this time without any of the disorientation.

"It appears that even here, practice makes perfect," Parno said.

"Perhaps, but I don't remember seeing this pathway before, do you?"

The ground stretching out in front of them resembled hard clay, like a road that had been pressed smooth and then baked in the sun. The walls to either side were solid rock, rugged yet smooth.

"Limestone?" Dhulyn suggested, and Parno thought she was right. Except that they were here, and not at the seaside, the rock surfaces resembled nothing more than cliff faces after untold years of being pounded by water.

#Joy# #Welcome# #Greeting# #Joy#

"Dhulyn!" Parno reined in, making Warhammer spin on his hind legs. The horse snorted his poor opinion of this kind of nonsense.

Now a pace or two ahead of him, Dhulyn stopped and looked over her shoulder, her pale face a mixture of concern and irritation. "I tell you we will lose the scent," she said.

"The Crayx, I heard them." Parno closed his eyes and concentrated, letting his Pod sense rise to the surface of his mind in the way he'd been taught. He shook his head. "They're gone."

Dhulyn licked her lips, uncertainty in her eyes, but once again she did not ask him if he was sure, once again she took him at his word. "Do you want to continuing trying?" she asked. "Or should we carry on?"

Parno hesitated for only a moment. "Carry on," he said. "It was only a touch; there's nothing there now."

Dhulyn nodded and set off, though she slowed again almost immediately. They were approaching an archway in the rock on the left, and just short of it Dhulyn held her left fist up at shoulder height, extended her thumb, then her two smallest fingers, then her thumb again.

The scent was stronger through the arch. Parno hung back, edging to the left as Dhulyn was edging to the right. The trader meant either to hide or to ambush them, knowing that he had left no telltale tracks on the Path itself. But he could not be aware of the heightened senses that the Stalking Cat *Shora* gave a Schooled Mercenary Brother. When so little time had passed, Dhulyn would have been able to follow him blindfolded.

With timing perfected through the thousands of repetitions in the *Shora*, Parno and Dhulyn spurred in unison around the corner, swords and daggers out and ready.

And came to a complete stop, frozen with their weapons still in the air.

It was not the trader, Bekluth Allain, who awaited them in the new pathway but an enormous snow cat, its black and white stripes giving it a strange camouflage against the rocky walls behind it. It was clear the animal had seen them, but, as close as they were, they could not smell it, nor, from their reactions, could the horses. The cat looked at them as if bored, blinked its huge yellow eyes and leaped in one clean motion to the top of the wall. There it sat and began to wash its hindquarters.

"I believe we've been dismissed," Parno said, lowering his sword.

"I believe you are right." Dhulyn clucked her tongue, and Bloodbone once again moved forward. "Ah." Dhulyn's tone was full of satisfaction. "The cat did not eat our prey, his scent continues on this pathway."

The cat they did not see again, but twice more, as they followed Bekluth Allain by his scent, they caught glimpses of other people along the pathways they did not take. Once Dhulyn saw what she thought was a man in black walking away from them, wide-brimmed hat worn on an angle, the edge of his cape held out by his sword. Once Parno saw a fair-haired person on a pale horse trot across the end of a pathway.

And once they heard something. They were in a section of the Path of a type they'd seen before: closely cropped grass underfoot and well-trimmed hedges to either side. Murmurings seemed to indicate that there were people speaking on the other side of the hedge.

"My soul, that is you?" Dhulyn used the nightwatch voice.

"Impossible."

"Do you think I could mistake another's voice for yours?"

Parno concentrated more carefully. His Partner was right, that was clearly *her* voice beyond the hedge, he could recognize the tone and heft of it, like music, even though he could not make out the words. If Dhulyn claimed the other voice was his, he was willing to believe her. She had dismounted, and was reaching into the hedge, beginning to part it with her hands, when he stopped her.

"Are you sure you want to try this?" he said. "It may mean we will lose the trader."

For a moment she looked at him, her eyes sparkling with curiosity, but then she withdrew her hands. "Quickly then, before I change my mind."

She swung back into the saddle and set off at a fast walk, but it seemed that the Path held no further surprises for them. The branch they followed crossed two others without incident, and suddenly they were through a huge squared opening and out of the Path of the Sun.

Parno saw movement out of the corner of his eye, ducked and signaled Warhammer in the way Dhulyn had made him practice over and over. As he ducked, Warhammer's right fore hoof flashed out, catching the advancing Bekluth Allain a glancing blow that staggered him, knocking him down. In a heartbeat Parno was on the ground, lashing the trader's ankles with a few quick turns of his reins. Warhammer, knowing perfectly well what was expected of him, backed off a pace, taking up the slack.

"You see." Dhulyn hopped down from Bloodbone and came to help him secure their gasping captive with a couple of spare ties. "I told you that trick with the horse was easy. You have to trust, and let Warhammer do his job."

Parno grinned without looking up. "Clearly I needed the right motivation."

His final knot finished, Parno glanced up and around for Warhammer, and his interest in horse tricks or even Bekluth Allain himself faded away. There were no rocky hills to be seen here, no pine trees, no Caid ruin in the near distance.

This was not Menoin.

Alaria had turned to ask Falcos a question when her ankle twisted under her and she went down. The ground here just inside the Path's entrance was not, apparently, as smooth as it seemed. Falcos exclaimed and was on his knees beside her in an instant. The sun, bright now that they were inside the Path, glinted off the gold-chased horse-head pin on the collar of his tunic. And there was something else, also shining.

"Falcos," she began.

"I'm right here," he said. "Are you hurt anywhere?"

"No," she said, waving her hand at him while maintaining her position. "Did you drop something? A ring or a pin from your tunic?" Using her fingers, Alaria parted the grass in front of her face with care, in case the thing she had seen moved and became lost.

"No, I don't think so. Why?"

"There's something here—oh!" Alaria sat up, sticking her barked knuckles into her mouth. She pushed the grass aside with her other hand. What she had mistaken for a jewel of some sort was a tiny horse head, inlaid into the stone wall just above the ground, and partially covered by the grass.

Falcos squatted beside her. He touched the emblem with the tips of his fingers. "It's clean," he said. "No dirt on it, no tarnishing or dulling of the surface."

"It's not painted, but it looks like the symbol in the secret passage," Alaria said.

Falcos looked at her with one raised eyebrow. "Do you think we'll find the crowns here as well? The cauldron? The throne?"

Alaria frowned. "This is a kind of secret passage, isn't it? If we do find other symbols, how do we know which one to follow?" She reached out and touched the horse head, but she drew her hand back quickly. "It's warm," she said. She looked up. "Do you think this might be the key?"

Now it was Falcos' turn to frown. "Surely it could not be that simple. There will be other symbols, you'll see. If we get out of here, we'll make a map."

"*When* we get out," she amended. Though she didn't need it, she let Falcos help her to her feet and hold her while she tested her ankle. She straightened her tunic and looked farther down the branch of the path they were in. The undressed stone walls continued straight until it ended at what appeared to be another branching of the Path. What she could see of that showed her a trimmed hedge.

"I have an idea," she said to Falcos. "I'm going to have a look around that corner, you wait here."

"I believe I see what you are thinking," Falcos said. He nodded slowly as he rose to his feet. "But do not, whatever you do, turn the corner. We should keep each other always in sight."

"Don't worry, I don't want to manage this alone."

Alaria took her time reaching the end of the stone wall,

walking exactly in the middle of the path. The air was still and warm, like a summer's day, but there were no sounds, not even the buzz of insects. It was hard to be certain without going on her hands and knees—though she was prepared to do just that if it became necessary—but she was reasonably sure there were no further marks along the straight walls between Falcos and herself. When she reached the turn, she went first to the right-hand wall, then to the left, and examined the stone close to the ground.

"There's another one here," she called out. "Here on the left-hand side. A wavy line." She felt around the corner, where another symbol should be. When she felt it, she stuck her head around and squinted. "A horse head around the corner."

"There's a wavy line here on the left as well," Falcos called back. He joined her. "Taking it from how we entered, we would turn left in order to leave," he said.

Alaria smiled at him. He actually did understand what she'd been trying to determine.

"If the wavy line takes us home," she said. "Where will the horse heads take us?"

He looked back in the direction they had come from. His dark brows were drawn down, and his lips pressed tight. There were marks on his wrists, Alaria saw, and around his mouth as well, showing where Epion had bound him.

"We must go forward," Falcos said finally. His hand went to the pin on his collar. "We know that much, in any case. We are horse people. Let us trust to the horses."

"You have no reason to kill me," Bekluth Allain said. Dhulyn could tell that the man was still winded. There was one great bruise on his torso, but faded and already yellowing. She could find no other damage from the horse's hoof—though experience told her there should have been some. After examining him, they had propped the trader up against the stone archway. Neither she nor Parno had said anything, but neither of them wanted to move very far away from it.

"Oh, we have *reason*," Parno said. "But we've been charged with finding you and bringing you back to Menoin."

"But not to kill me. You see? You haven't been charged with killing me. There's a reason for that." Bekluth Allain's voice was quiet and his demeanor calm. He was obviously not afraid, Dhulyn thought. Rather, he had the manner of someone who was just taking a few minutes to give directions to an enquirer—sure of himself and his explanations.

"Of course there's a reason," Parno was saying. "The Menoins want to kill you themselves. You've murdered their Tarkin, and now their new Tarkin's bride."

"The Lord Epion Akarion is not going to let anyone kill me." The trader shrugged. "For one thing, I can reveal much too much about him. So we need have no worries there." His smile made his eyes twinkle. "Besides, *did* I kill those people? I say no. I say I released them." He turned to Dhulyn. "You *do* understand?"

His manner was so warm that just for an instant, Dhulyn wanted to agree with him, to say that she did understand. A moment later, and she wondered where that urge had come from. "I am afraid not," she said.

"It's so simple. I had to find a way to protect myself. You know what the people here do to the Marked—even the Espadryni are not beyond the cruelty of maiming and crippling their Seers. It disgusted you, I could tell. Even at its best, the sequestration, the living always in hiding, constantly watched, monitored—the best any of us can hope for and only the Espadryni are willing to do it. I wouldn't even have had that if they had known that I was a Healer."

"They would have put you to death," Parno said. "Isn't that the penalty for all the Marked?"

Bekluth shut his eyes and shook his head, clearly frustrated with their inability to follow his reasoning. "The common penalty, yes. If the Mark is commonly known. Do you think there's no black market for the Marked? My people are traders—do you think for one moment they would not have tried to turn a profit out of me? That they wouldn't have sold me to be locked up in some High Noble House? I had to stay hidden, I had to stay secret. It was the only way I could be free."

"Fine then, a reason to go into hiding yourself and make your living among the Espadryni, far from other people, But why did you kill, if you are a Healer? Was Epion paying you?" A Healer could use his Mark to kill, Dhulyn knew, just as a Mender could break, or a Finder could hide. Cold fingers crept up her spine. *I've Seen the answer already*.

Bekluth shut his eyes and swallowed. *He's about to lie*, Dhulyn thought. She signaled Parno, caught his response. How could the man manage to be sarcastic with a hand signal?

"Some people have a darkness hidden inside them, something only I can see. Like a secret hidden from the rest of the world." Bekluth's glance at Parno was so swift Dhulyn almost missed it. Parno *did* have a secret, in a way. His Pod sense was hidden inside him, at least from those who were not Pod-sensed themselves.

"My mother showed me that," Bekluth was saying. "She was the first—this darkness inside people, like the darkness inside her, can spread, and kill them, destroying all their light, their essence. By releasing that darkness, I free the light."

"But in the ... process—" Dhulyn turned her mind away from the image of that process. "Those people die."

"Oh, no—well, but the darkness would have killed them anyway—the hidden thing, the secret, that would have killed them anyway. You see? Their light would have been wasted, eaten by the darkness. By my actions the light at least was saved, was freed."

His tone was so reasonable, so matter-of-fact, that Dhulyn almost found herself nodding. Almost. He wasn't just freeing the light. Not from what Dhulyn had Seen. The Healers she had known in Mortaxa had spoken of the life essence, of how and from where the power of the Marked came, and how it was limited by the strength of each individual's life force. And of how that life force was restored with rest, food, even certain forms of exercise. It seemed that Bekluth Allain had found another way.

"So the darkness, that is the illness, the thing that might kill them," Parno said. "That is what you see in people?"

"Of course."

"And you let that darkness out, so it will not hurt them anymore?"

"That's right, and then it can't hurt anyone else either, because you see, if it's the right kind of darkness—or the wrong kind I suppose we should say—it damages others as well."

Bekluth looked at them both, quite pleased with his own cleverness.

"Except you don't just let out the darkness and free the light," she said. "You take the light for yourself."

"Of course I do, weren't you listening?" For the first time, a hint of impatience marred the music of his voice. "It. Would. Have. Been. Wasted." He shrugged again, as if he would have spread his hands if they had not been bound.

"But why didn't you just . . . use the light to burn the darkness away. You know, *Heal* them?"

Dhulyn stifled her own grin. Trust Parno to always put his finger on the right point.

"But that would take *my* light, and wouldn't that have been just another kind of waste?" His equilibrium had returned, and Bekluth spoke like a tutor of slow children, asking a question to which they should already know the answer. "I need that light. I can put that light to much better use than the people I took it from. I am the best Healer in two worlds, the strongest, the most powerful, there's nothing I can't Heal, *nothing*. Take me back with you by all means, but don't waste my talents and my power." He looked from one to the other, held out his hands. "What's done is done, and I deeply regret letting Epion use me in that way. I've never been allowed to work as a Healer, surely you see that. Think of the Healing I could do, if I was only given the opportunity."

"Heal yourself," Parno said. Bekluth looked at him, lips parted, eyebrows beginning to pull together. "Heal yourself," Parno repeated. "Our Healers do it all the time, here and there, as they can. Many of them live very long lives."

"But I have no sickness," Bekluth said. Again, his tone was one of a master speaking to a slow apprentice. "There is nothing to Heal."

"Aren't you broken in the same way that the women of the Espadryni are broken?"

Bekluth blinked, and shook his head. "Of course not, that's nonsense. How do we know even what those women would be like if they were not kept sequestered and apart?" He shook his head again. "I'm nothing like them. Even the Horsemen themselves never thought so." A fleeting gleam passed through his eyes, and a shadow of a smile across his lips. If Dhulyn had not been paying such close attention, she would have missed it.

There was some truth in what Bekluth had said, Dhulyn

thought. The Seers were honest and straightforward in their dealings. Cold, unfeeling, and uncaring, but honest and straightforward. Bekluth Allain was nothing like that. He was nothing but a tissue of lies.

"Have you ever tried Healing one of them? The Seers?"

"But not even I could Heal them all, so what would that have achieved but my own betrayal?" He shook his head and then abruptly leaned forward. "But what about the Marked in your world? The Healers there? You claim concern for the women of the Espadryni, why don't you bring them Healers?" Bekluth's eyes widened, and his smile deepened. "That's it. Don't you see? You bring Healers from your world, and all the Marked can be helped. Not just the Seers of the Espadryni, but the others, as soon as they show signs of the Mark, Healers could help them. They could all be saved."

Parno turned to her, his eyebrows raised. Again, some of what the trader was saying seemed like the truth. Dhulyn lowered her eyes, buying herself time to think. Would it work? There were not so very many Healers, but surely, if it meant that they could save all the Marked here, stop the executions and allow the other children, the Finders and Mender and Healers, to live? Was that how she was supposed to help the Marked? That was a future she would like to See.

But she had not. Dhulyn felt herself grow still, and quiet, until the sound of her heartbeat was loud in her ears. She had never Seen *that* future. She had Seen only Visions

SHE SEES THAT THE BOWL THE ROUNDED, WELL-DRESSED YOUNG WOMAN TOUCHES IS CRACKED NOW, THE WOODEN LADLE SPLIT, THE CROCKS BREAKING AND LEAKING THEIR CONTENTS ONTO THE FLOOR. . . .

SHE SEES THAT THE KITTEN LEAPS AND JUMPS, THE BOY TOUCHES IT, AND THE KITTEN FALLS, PANTING, ITS EYES GROWING MILKY AND DARK. THE SMALL BOY TOUCHES IT AGAIN, AND IT LEAPS UP, BLINKING, AND THRASHING ITS LONG TAIL. HE DANGLES THE OSIER AGAIN, AND ONCE MORE THE KITTEN POUNCES, AND ONCE MORE, SMILING, THE BOY REACHES OUT TO TOUCH IT . . .

SHE SEES THAT IN THE DISTANCE THERE IS A SMALL FORTRESS, WITH A WALL MUCH TOO LARGE FOR IT . . .

SHE SEES THAT A RED-FACED BOY IS FURIOUSLY STRIKING OUT AS HIS

MOTHER DRAGS HIM BY THE UPPER ARM INTO WHAT IS OBVIOUSLY THE KITCHEN OF THEIR HOME. THE WOODEN SHUTTERS ON THE WINDOW EXPLODE INTO SAWDUST, THE DISHES AND PLATES ON THE SIDEBOARD SHATTER, AND HIS MOTHER BEGINS TO VOMIT BLOOD ON THE FLOOR. THE BOY STAMPS HIS FOOT, SCREAMING, "YOU COW, DON'T TOUCH ME" . . .

SHE SEES THE WOMAN LAUGHING AND POINTING TO A SPOT ON THE FLOOR. THE MEN PULL UP THE FLOOR BOARDS AND HAUL OUT A WOMAN, AN OLD MAN, AND THREE CHILDREN . . .

SHE SEES THE WINDOW BEYOND WHERE BEKLUTH ALLAIN IS SITTING, AND IT IS DAYLIGHT NOW, THE SUN SHINING. THE WINDOW LOOKS OUT ON RUINS, WATCHTOWERS FALLEN, BRIDGES CRUMBLED INTO THE RIVER, STREETS FULL OF RUBBLE. BEKLUTH LOOKS UP, HIS EYES CATCHING A GLINT OF GREEN FROM THE LIGHT, AND SAYS, "HOW CAN I HELP?" . . .

Horrors. Devastations. Armed camps. Mutilations of friends, despair of mothers and fathers. This. *This* was all along the help the trader had been offering. She had thought them Visions of the past, before the people of this land had taken steps to guard against the broken Marked. But they were not. They were the *result* of accepting the only kind of help Bekluth could give. What she had Seen, *that* would be the result, *that* would be the Espadryni's world, if she followed Bekluth's suggestion.

The White Sisters had told her she already had the answer.

What had the old Healer in Mortaxa said? Few if any Healers had enough life force to heal someone who was born deformed. Healing could not replace limbs cut off or eyes lost. If these Marked were born with their spirits deformed, with some vital part of themselves missing, then it followed that they could not be Healed.

And that flash, the glimmer of green in his eyes—eyes that had never at any other time shone green. She had seen that before. And *Seen* it too. That told her where the Green Shadow's dust had *really* gone and what it was that had broken the Marked.

That was the meaning of her Visions.

Dhulyn pulled the dagger from her belt and cut Bekluth Allain's throat.

Clinging to Falcos' arm, Alaria finally stumbled out of the Path and stood, swaying, looking out at what was clearly a field that had been recently burned. Though to be fair, she thought, it was hard to tell whether Falcos was holding her up or the other way around.

"I think I'm going to vomit again," Alaria said.

"Look." Falcos lifted his free arm just enough to indicate direction. "Horsemen."

"Then I'd better vomit before they get here." Alaria tightened her grip on Falcos' arm. They had come without arms, as House Listra had told them they must. They'd trusted to the horse heads to bring them through the Path of the Sun, and here they were, alive, on the other side.

They'd just have to go on trusting to the horses.

"Gun! Gun! Come quick. They're bringing someone from the Door." Mar was calling from the far side of the camp, where she had been talking to Singer of the Wind.

Gun leaped to his feet and started running. Wolfshead and Lionsmane—they'd done it again. How long had they been gone? He glanced at the position of the sun. A few hours?

But he slowed to a walk when he saw the party that approached, two people on foot. Two familiar people, but not the ones he'd been expecting. Not the Mercenaries. He began to walk faster.

"Gun!" Now Mar was running toward him, and he sped up to meet her. "Gun, it's Alaria. Alaria and Falcos Tarkin."

He almost didn't understand her. But he let her pull him forward, to where the Tarkin and the princess were being escorted to Singer of the Wind's own fire.

Though they had already been seated, both Alaria and Falcos rose to clasp them by the hands and kiss their cheeks, just as if they were kin. Gun found himself reddened, and he rubbed at his upper lip

"You've escaped from Epion Akarion," Mar said once they were again seated around the fire and water was being passed from hand to hand. "But what made you try the Path?"

"Escaped is not exactly what we did." By the time Falcos and Alaria between them had described the events which had led them here, and Gun and Mar had explained in their turn the whereabouts of the Mercenary Brothers and the killer, a meal of roasted rabbits and roots was already prepared and being served.

"If they don't have Bekluth Allain to take back with them, how will they be able to prove that Falcos is not the killer?" Gun asked as he waited for his rabbit to cool.

"Did you not hear what was said by the elder of the Tarkin Falcos Akarion's council? That is not what will furnish the needed proof," Singer of the Wind said. He turned to address Falcos. "Our peoples are linked, Falcos Tarkin, the Horsemen of the Espadryni and those of Menoin. Long ago, in the time of the Caids, we were friends and kinfolk, and your people chose to adventure beyond Mother Sun's Door."

"But we're not Red Horsemen, I mean Espadryni," Falcos said.

"Perhaps no longer, if you ever were. That is more than I can speak to. But the Tarkins of Menoin are the only ones to whom we are bound by ancient oaths to show the secret of the Path, and only the true Tarkins can learn it. The only ones who are not shamans, or, it seems Mercenary Brothers."

"But Bekluth Allain, he learned it," Gun pointed out.

"He has some magic of his own about him," one of the other Horsemen pointed out. "Else how is it we did not see him for one of the Marked?"

"How many Marked have you actually seen?" Gun asked. "You couldn't tell that I'm Marked."

"Well, but you are not broken," the man replied. Mar caught Gun's eye, and he subsided without further argument. Mar was probably right, this was not the time. Whatever else the Horsemen knew, they couldn't know all there was about the Marked.

"But you will show Falcos the clue?" Alaria said. "And we can go home. And that will prove to everyone that he's in the right."

Singer of the Wind smiled at her. "If he can see pattern that is the clue, then he has the proof. And if they have further need of witness, we can do that for them. We have here three who can pass through the Door of the Sun and who will speak to the trader's guilt."

And from the look on the old man's face, Gun thought, he'd enjoy that very much.

"What if they don't, uh, if they don't believe you?"

"I am Singer of the Wind, of the Long Trees Tribe of the Espadryni. Who will not take my word must meet my sword."

"That should work," Mar said, grinning.

Gun found himself smiling as well. "Or you could always challenge them to walk the Path of the Sun."

"You'll come back with us?" Alaria said. "Even if you can't see the pattern, you can Find the way?"

Gun looked at Mar. "We'll wait for Dhulyn and Parno," she said.

"And if they do not return?" Singer of the Wind's voice was very soft.

"I'll Find them," Gun said.

"That's it then." Parno put his hands on his hips and looked with disgust at the square stone opening. "It doesn't matter if we go through on horseback or on foot, at night, at dawn, or at sunset. Whatever it is that turns this blooded thing back into a doorway, we don't have the key." He turned to Dhulyn. "What now?"

"Didn't you say you wanted some time to rest?"

"I believe I mentioned taverns? Wine?"

"Well, you'll have to settle for hunting and the clean out-of-doors."

Parno groaned. "For how long?"

"Until Gun comes to Find us, of course."

Barbara Ashford

Spells at the Crossroads

A brand new omnibus edition of *Spellcast* and *Spellcrossed*, together in one volume for the first time!

"[A] novel about the transformative power of the theater...a woman with an unsettled past...and the intersecting coincidences that move her toward the future. Maggie is relatable and her journey compelling. Four stars."

—*RT Book Reviews*

"*Spellcast* had me spellbound, and *Spellcrossed* was no different. [It] moved me to tears more than a few times, and was equally heartwarming and heartbreaking.... Magic and the magic of musical theatre intertwine seamlessly to create a read worth savoring. I can't recommend this series highly enough!"

—My Bookish Ways

ISBN: 978-0-7564-1021-6

To Order Call: 1-800-788-6262
www.dawbooks.com

DAW 204

Julie E. Czerneda

A TURN OF LIGHT

"An enchanting and gentle fable, rich with detail and characters you will love." —Charles de Lint

"A gorgeous creation. Julie Czerneda's world and characters are richly layered and wonderful—full of mystery, hope and, most of all, heart." —Anne Bishop

"I was captivated.... Many fantasy novels out there are *about* magic. Few, like Julie's, embody it."

—Kristen Britain

"*A Turn of Light* is deft, beautiful storytelling. Marrowdell is real, and full of 'the country folks' so often overlooked in favor of princes and knights in armor. This book shines, and I want sequels. Many sequels. One can never have too many classics." —Ed Greenwood

978-0-7564-0952-4

To Order Call: 1-800-788-6262
www.dawbooks.com

S.L. Farrell

The Nessantico Cycle

"[Farrell's] best yet, a delicious melange of politics, war,
sorcery, and religion in a richly imagined world."
—George R. R. Martin,
#1 *New York Times* bestselling author

"Readers who appreciate intricate world building,
intrigue, and action will immerse themselves effortlessly
in this rich and complex story."
—*Publishers Weekly*

A MAGIC OF TWILIGHT
978-0-7564-0536-6

A MAGIC OF NIGHTFALL
978-0-7564-0599-1

A MAGIC OF DAWN
978-0-7564-0646-2

To Order Call: 1-800-788-6262
www.dawbooks.com

Tanya Huff

The Enchantment Emporium
978-0-7564-0605-9

The Wild Ways
978-0-7564-0763-6

and now...

The Future Falls
978-0-7564-0753-7

To Order Call: 1-800-788-6262
www.dawbooks.com

Seanan McGuire
The October Daye Novels

"...will surely appeal to readers who enjoy my books, or those of Patricia Briggs." —*Charlaine Harris*

"I am so invested in the world building and the characters now.... Of all the 'Faerie' urban fantasy series out there, I enjoy this one the most."—*Felicia Day*

To Order Call: 1-800-788-6262
www.dawbooks.com